READER'S DIGEST
CONDENSED BOOKS

www.readersdigest.co.uk

The Reader's Digest Association
Limited 11 Westferry Circus
Canary Wharf London E14 4HE

For information as to ownership of
copyright in the material of this
book, and acknowledgments, see
last page.

Printed in France
ISBN 0 276 42590-1

READER'S DIGEST CONDENSED BOOKS

Selected and edited
by Reader's Digest

CONDENSED BOOKS DIVISION

THE READER'S DIGEST ASSOCIATION LIMITED, LONDON

CONTENTS

When journalist Jo Harper interviews explorer Douglas Marshall she quickly comes to share his fascination with the ill-fated Franklin Expedition of 1845. Although Jo does not know it, those same icy wastes that defeated Franklin and his men are destined to bring about her own darkest hours. A captivating tale of Arctic adventure and a family's journey to forgiveness and reconciliation.

PUBLISHED BY BANTAM PRESS

The Californian police are grappling with the case of Lara Gibson, victim of an apparently motiveless murder. They have a hunch the killer hacked into Ms Gibson's computer before luring her to her death. If so, he's going to prove impossibly elusive—unless they call on the skill of a brilliant hacker already in custody for computer crime. A roller-coaster ride of a thriller that takes the reader into the dark heart of the Internet.

PUBLISHED BY HODDER & STOUGHTON

WARLOCK

Wilbur Smith

Storm clouds are gathering over the House of Tamose, the ruling dynasty in Ancient Egypt. Plague, war and treachery threaten to destroy fourteen-year-old Prince Nefer's future and bring down his royal line. Can the boy's one great ally, Taita the warlock, save him through his cunning and magic power? The splendour and magnificence of Ancient Egypt are brought to vivid life in this latest block-buster by one of today's great storytellers.

PUBLISHED BY MACMILLAN

SUZANNE'S DIARY FOR NICHOLAS

James Patterson

Katie Wilkinson is eleven months into a love affair with Matt, the most wonderful man she's ever met, when, abruptly, he calls off their relationship. All he offers, by way of explanation, is a diary. As Katie turns its pages, however, she is amazed by the story it tells and filled with understanding of Matt's situation. A moving love story by a best-selling American author.

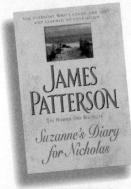

PUBLISHED BY HEADLINE

THE ICE CHILD

Elizabeth McGregor

What happened to the intrepid members of the Franklin Expedition that set sail from London, in 1845, on a journey into the unknown? That question has always haunted explorer Douglas Marshall, and time after time he has returned to the Arctic in search of answers.

Now fate has brought Jo Harper, a London journalist, to Marshall's door. As she, too, becomes fascinated by Franklin's brave quest, she cannot possibly foresee how it will acquire profound and surprising significance in her own life . . .

 PROLOGUE

The great white bear lifted her head, narrowing her eyes against the driving Arctic snow. She looked back along the rubble ice to the cub that followed her, waiting for him in the white-on-white landscape.

All around her, the ice of Victoria Strait groaned as it moved, compressed by the pressure that flooded from the Beaufort Sea, forcing its way through Melville Sound towards the Northwest Passage.

It was desperately cold. Colder, certainly, than a man could tolerate for long. But the bear did not register the temperature, padded as she was by four inches of fat and insulating fur. She was in her country, her kingdom, impervious to any law but her own.

The polar bear had mated on the ice floes of Peel Sound last May. She had been an exceptional and solitary traveller, swimming all that season, rarely resting on the ice. She had crossed the Arctic Circle opposite Repulse and was spotted by a marine mammal research team as she crossed the old whaling routes in March. On most days, she could swim fifty miles without a rest, churning through the ice at six miles an hour.

In December she had given birth for the first time, in a snow den deep underground. Her cub weighed less than a pound at birth, and fitted neatly into her curled paw; but by April he had grown to twenty-six pounds.

It was August now, and the light was beginning to change. And she had felt for days that the angle of the light was subtly wrong. She had, perhaps, tracked too far west before denning. Her internal mapping seemed to have failed her, and in the first spell of real cold, she stood indecisively on the freezing floe.

There was something strange here.

She felt a thread of danger—a message transmitted in nerve impulses and scent. She wanted to turn back, to trek south, where her own kind was concentrated. But the cub was sick—too sick to travel far. Still watching him now, she saw him drop to the ground and lie passively in the snow.

She could feel the wreck underneath her, on the seabed below. It smelt, even now, after lying under the ice for 160 years, like man. The wooden and iron bulk had left its indissoluble human mark—this sense of *un*rightness, a dislocation in the frequencies. The echo touched the animal above.

She raised herself up on her hind legs, swaying, seven foot high at the shoulder, her immense forepaws extended in front of her. Then she dropped down to all fours, and turned back towards the cub. As she drew level with him, she wound her body round him, pushing him gently into her shoulder, until she felt his faint, warm breath against her.

PART 1: SPRING 1997
CHAPTER 1

It had begun in April, in the spring. The cherry trees had been in flower, and there was that first iridescent promise of summer showing in London's dusty haze.

When she thought about it now, Jo would see herself in that café on the corner of Bartlett Street, Gina at her side leafing through the newspaper. And she would link those two: the cherry trees, and the newspaper. The first day that she had ever given more than a passing thought to Douglas Marshall.

She was twenty-six years old, and had been guesting at *The Courier* for four years, where Gina was her editor. From time to time, Gina took it upon herself to see that Jo's life ran in a more ordered, less frantic pattern, and it was this concern that had found Jo, at midday on Good Friday, bundled into Gina's battered blue Citroën.

'It'll do you good to get out of London,' Gina had told her. 'You can't have another weekend cooped up in that flat.'

'I am not cooped up,' Jo had objected, defending the three rooms she could barely be described as living in. Most of her possessions were still in boxes six months after moving in.

'You want to take care of yourself.'

A roll of the eyes from Jo. 'Gina, I *do*.'

Gina glanced over again at Jo's profile and saw a stubborn little grimace of independence.

Whenever people met Jo, they would screw up their faces, trying to dredge up a name to fit the face. 'Don't I know you?' was the commonest opening gambit. Jo's photograph at the top of *The Courier*'s guest column pictured her sitting on a scattering of books and newsprint. The image had been taken from above so that, laughing, she was shown marooned in a little sea of paper.

If Gina had a characteristic expression, it was a sardonic smile below her rounded, you-don't-say eyes. Gina had propelled herself to features editor at *The Courier* by the time that Jo was taken on as a freelance, a babe-in-arms of twenty-two.

Perhaps it was Jo's sheer outlandishness that pleased her friend, the refusal to be deterred. Jo's career had been chequered, to say the least. She had dumped university and found her way into journalism by gate-crashing a rock-classics concert at the Edinburgh Festival. She had been spotted there by a morning TV show and hired to present their entertainment slot. Single-minded and outspoken, it was by this route that she had arrived one morning at Gina's desk.

Gina's first thought had been that Jo looked painfully young. She was five foot five, thin, antsy with impatience, quick to humour, quick to anger. Her smile hid a sharp, ironic mind. It had been quite a job to get her to sit down that first day, such was her enthusiasm to get going.

Sitting now in the city centre, Gina smiled to herself. Jo was stretched out in her chair, eyes closed and turned to the sun. For a second she looked the perfect picture of relaxation. Until she opened one eye, yawned, and tapped the broadsheet in Gina's grasp. 'What's the opposition say?' she asked, wriggling upright in her seat.

'Nothing radical,' Gina said. 'Except for that.' She held open the paper at the third page.

Jo shielded her eyes against the sun and looked at the article. There was a map of Greenland in the top right-hand corner—an indented coastline, and contour lines of mountains that ran down to the sea.

'You know Douglas Marshall?' Gina asked.

Jo had to think for a second. 'Give me a clue.'

'BBC 2. Archaeology. *Far Back*.'

'Ah,' Jo acknowledged, 'lots of running about with bits of pottery. Which one was Marshall?'

'The smiling one. The ships expert.'

'Oh, *him*.' Jo vaguely remembered a tall man, habitually dressed in a battered leather jacket. 'What's happened to him?'

'He's lost.'

'What—there?' Jo asked, glancing at the map. She took the page from Gina and skimmed the article. Douglas Marshall had been reported missing while on an archaeological expedition in one of the most inhospitable landscapes on earth. She sighed heavily. 'This guy's gone on some harebrained personal mission in a snowstorm, and now we're all supposed to go out and find him,' she said. 'They've actually sent a bloody frigate. What a waste of money.'

Gina frowned at her. 'You don't mean that.'

'I do,' Jo countered. 'What's he gone there for? Personal glory. Some obsession or other, I bet.'

'But he could be dying, Jo! We have to do something.'

'Send out the fleet?'

'Yeah, send out the fleet, why not? He's a British subject.'

Jo burst out laughing. 'What ho,' she said. 'Wave the flag.' She looked away, towards the traffic.

'So . . . what's the alternative?' Gina asked. 'Let him freeze?'

'Yes,' Jo said. And she almost meant it.

JO HAD ALMOST FORGOTTEN the conversation when she went into *The Courier* the following Tuesday. She put her head round Gina's door, just to wave hello.

'Hey, come here,' Gina called. 'Marshall's still missing. I want you to do a piece.'

Jo's gaze settled on her. 'You're joking. Not the madman.'

'I want you to go and talk to his wife. We haven't heard anything from Mrs Marshall.'

'His *wife*? Ah, Gina. No. I can't go steaming in there. I don't know a thing about him.'

Gina nodded briefly, the nod dismissing the objection. 'Here's Marshall's biography,' she said, handing Jo six stapled sheets. 'He's pretty up-front, but his wife likes to keep a low profile. Power behind the throne stuff. A lot of money. She's a trustee of the Exploration Academy. Rumoured to be a bit of a bitch.'

Jo raised her eyebrows, interested at last. 'Oh, yeah?' She leafed quickly through the document. 'I don't even know what he was looking for in ruddy Greenland.'

'Medieval settlements. Vikings and Eskimos.'

'Oh, thrilling.'

Gina ignored her. 'The archivist at the Academy in Cambridge is called Peter Bolton. He can see you at eight tomorrow morning.'

Jo held Gina's eye for a few long seconds before conceding. She knew the glint in her editor's eye too well to refuse. 'Great,' she grumbled, as she packed the papers together.

IT WAS A LONG WAY on the tube to Jo's flat. After a full day correcting copy and researching another piece, she was still not really interested in Marshall. Crammed into a carriage with a hundred other commuters, however, she glanced through his biography.

Douglas James Marshall, born Ontario 1957. Fellow of Blethyn College, Professor of Archaeology, special interest Victorian ship construction, Chairman Royal Commission 1989–92, author of *The Shipwreck Society* (1994), *Under the Mediterranean* (1996) . . .

Over the last couple of years Marshall had become the spokesman for the University Exploration Academy, and had been a regular on the BBC2 series. She could bring the title pictures to mind, but she couldn't visualise Marshall himself beyond a broad, blurred smile.

When she got home, Jo grudgingly read the newspaper article Gina had given her. Marshall had gone missing at a place called Uummannaq.

Frowning, Jo sat down and riffled through her old school atlas. *Uummannaq* . . . She couldn't even find it. The coastline of Greenland was mountainous and unforgiving. Surely at this time of year there would be ice packed deep in the fjords. She shuddered. She had never liked the cold.

She closed the book and replaced it on the shelf.

The expression on her face was impenetrable. She had lost both father and mother in the last five years, and the isolation was still fresh. Yet people like Douglas Marshall actually chose to exile themselves. She wondered what kind of family she would find, waiting for his return.

As she went through to the hallway, she caught sight of the fax machine. The light on it was flashing. She pulled the piece of paper out, and Doug Marshall's face stared back at her. On the top of the paper Gina had scrawled, *This is your man.*

It was not a great photo. Marshall's face was screwed up against bright sunlight. Impossible to guess his age from the shot. A frown into the camera, a backdrop of ocean. He was leaning on a white rail, holding something in one hand. It might have been a piece of iron, a metal rod, a wooden stick.

She sighed as she trailed into the bedroom. 'Oh, I'm going to love *you*,' she muttered.

THE UNIVERSITY EXPLORATION ACADEMY was housed in a Georgian building in the heart of Cambridge. Double glass doors led in to a large foyer. Pressing the doorbell, Jo could see a reception desk, with some sort of office behind, and glass-fronted cabinets.

A woman came out of the office. She smiled at Jo through the glass as she unlocked the door and ushered her in. 'He's upstairs. I'll tell him you're here.' She showed Jo to a chair in the hall.

Several minutes ticked past. Eventually, Jo got up and walked to the cabinets that were ranged against the far wall. Behind the glass of the first there was a silver spoon with a copper repair on the handle, the tattered remains of a small book, a few sepia photographs, a tiny piece of red tin. She peered at the photographs. Four men in uniform, only one of them youthful. They had the posed and rigid look of Victorians.

'Miss Harper?'

She turned. A man was standing at her shoulder. He was not more than five foot six, and was incredibly round. He held out his hand. 'Peter Bolton.'

She liked him on sight: he had the face of an enthusiastic schoolboy. He was breathing heavily from the exertion of walking downstairs.

'Come far?' he asked.

'London,' she said.

'Ah,' he replied, commiserating. 'Come with me.'

They went upstairs to his office, a typical academic's room, lined with shelves, books covering the floor, dust everywhere. They could just about get in by pushing hard on the door and picking their way over to two chairs marooned in a wash of files and paper.

'My phone hasn't stopped ringing,' he said cheerfully, shuffling some papers on his desk. 'I'm very popular all of a sudden.'

'Has Douglas Marshall been missing before?'

'No. Never.'

'I see,' she said. 'Have you known him long?'

'Over ten years.'

'Really?' she said. 'I'm sorry. You must be frantic.'

He nodded slightly. 'Yes . . . It's unlike Douglas. One tries not to be frantic, exactly.'

'But anxious?'

'Oh, yes.'

'And his wife?'

'Alicia?' He paused just a fraction too long. 'Yes, of course.'

Jo smiled. 'I would like to talk to her. Is that possible?'

To her surprise, Bolton blushed. 'No. No, I'm sorry . . . Alicia never gets involved in the public side. If you want to ask me about Doug's journey, anything about that . . .'

She let it go, temporarily. 'I might as well tell you that I know nothing about Doug Marshall and I don't understand this passion for Greenland.'

Bolton took a box file from one of the closest shelves. He opened it and took out a sheaf of papers. 'Take a copy,' he said. 'It's Doug's CV . . . a couple of articles he's written . . .'

She took the papers from him. 'Thank you.'

'The Inuit communities are where he started,' Bolton continued, 'because of Franklin. Franklin has been Doug's lifelong passion. Of course he's done other things—a considerable number of other things—but the Inuit and Franklin were the subject of his original doctoral thesis. Inuit. What we once called Eskimo. Or Esquimaux.' He spelled it out for her.

The phone rang. He picked it up.

Jo sat watching him. She had no idea at all who Franklin was. She felt her mind go blank and recognised it as her hitting-the-buffers feeling which came when her interest in a story waned.

Bolton started to flick the pages of his diary. His gaze drifted away, as he listened to the caller at the other end of the line.

Jo got to her feet. She took a piece of paper from her bag and scribbled on it, *Are you free at lunchtime?*

He nodded and wrote *1.30* on the page.

'Thanks,' she said.

Going back down the stairs, she stopped halfway. The world was looking for a man who couldn't be found. And the press were looking for a woman who didn't want to be found. 'We'll see about that,' she told herself.

She went over to the reception desk, and the same woman who had shown her in came over to her. Jo smiled. 'Mr Bolton's given me the address of Mrs Marshall, but I don't know Cambridge,' she lied smoothly. 'If I take a right from . . .'

The woman glanced down at the map that Jo was holding open. 'Oh, you can't get to it that way,' she said. 'Go down the A603. Cross over the bridge and carry on down towards the Eversdens.'

Jo took a gamble. She glanced at the map. 'And the house is at Little Eversden?'

'No. Pass the Eversdens, but don't go as far as Haslingfield.'

Jo gave her broadest smile. 'That's great.'

SHE DROVE OUT INTO A COOL, grey-on-green landscape. Roads that had been laid down for centuries crossed the flat fens. She always felt a little lost in the wide sweeps of East Anglia. The light was curious.

She passed a string of houses, bordering a narrow road. The village was there and gone in thirty seconds. Fine rain obscured her windscreen and she put the wipers on, negotiated a right-angled turn that appeared from nowhere. Ahead, she could see a church. She pulled in close to it, and looked again at the map. The Marshalls had to live somewhere close.

She drove on. The rain began in earnest, and the light grew dim. Just as she switched on the headlights, she saw a little black and white sign at the edge of a track: FRANKLIN HOUSE. She stepped on the brakes. It was worth a try.

IT WAS A BEAUTIFUL, mellow stone building, with a steep tiled roof. Jo guessed eighteenth, maybe early nineteenth century. A huge magnolia tree almost obscured the door. She rang the bell.

The woman who opened the door was in her early forties, and very tall. She wore a dark suit, and her dark hair was pulled back from her face. She was well groomed and, if not beautiful, certainly striking.

'Yes?'

'I'm looking for Mrs Marshall.'

'And you are?'

Jo held out her hand. 'Jo Harper. Have I got the right house?'

The woman ignored Jo's hand. 'What is it in connection with?'

'I've been speaking to Peter Bolton at the Academy.'

Alicia Marshall's face clouded. Her mouth turned down in an expression of distaste. 'He sent you here?'

'No, but I was speaking to him an hour ago. I'm from *The Courier*.'

The mention of one of Britain's most prestigious broadsheets sometimes eased the way into a conversation like this one. Jo expected to see a softening in Alicia Marshall's face.

Instead, the other woman began to close the door.

'I was wondering if you could tell me about this trip,' Jo said. 'Why your husband went . . . how you feel about such'—she hesitated under the searching gaze—'such adventures.'

For the first time Alicia Marshall smiled. 'Adventures?'

'Have you heard from your husband?'

'No.' The door caught a little on the flagstone floor of the hallway. Alicia pushed it hard.

'You've heard nothing at all since he left?'

'No. Now, please—'

Jo put her hand on the door frame. 'Are you separated?' she asked.

Alicia Marshall gave Jo a lingering look. 'You people,' she said, at last, contempt in her voice.

'Are you worried?'

'No.' Mrs Marshall stared pointedly at Jo's hand.

'Do you think he's alive?' Jo asked.

'I really have no idea.'

Astonished at her tone, Jo dropped her hand.

Alicia Marshall shut the door in her face.

For some time Jo remained where she was, staring at the heavy iron knocker. Behind her, the rain pattered down through the magnolia tree. She wondered what had happened here to make a wife seem so indifferent about a husband's life or death. Suddenly, she felt very sorry for Douglas Marshall. And very interested indeed in what had taken him away from home.

JOHN MARSHALL was dreaming. He could see his father out on the ice, a pinprick of black on a frozen ocean. Doug was saying something to his only son—something very important—with his head turned away, so that his words were swallowed in the vast, flat space.

John looked down. At his feet, outlined in the snow, were massive polar-bear prints. When he looked up, his father was gone.

Shock coursed through him. 'Dad!' he called. 'Dad!'

His voice barrelled away across the ice, silenced in seconds. Thin trails of blowing snow were already wiping away the tracks of both bear and father. The idea rushed in on him that he was lost, truly lost. He had vanished into the same empty gulf that his father had travelled before him, and there was no way back.

'John,' a voice said.

Slowly, he opened his eyes.

Amy Wickham was looking at him. Her hand lay on his arm. She was his own age, nineteen, five foot two, black-haired, sturdy. He had met her at the end of the spring term.

'You're bloody cold,' she said.

John winced, flexing the arm that had been out of the bed. 'I was dreaming,' he said. 'Warm me up, why don't you?'

She rubbed the skin of his arm, lowering her face to his.

'You smell good,' he murmured.

'I wish I could say the same for you,' she told him.

He smiled lazily. Evenings, he worked at a college bar and last night had been busy. He had been bought half a dozen drinks and now his head was aching.

As he lay back in bed, Amy considered his rumpled good looks with a smile. 'What were you dreaming of?' she asked.

He ran a hand over his face. 'Dad,' he said.

She looked down at him, her expression somewhere between concern and trepidation. She didn't know what to say to him about his father: Doug Marshall was so rarely mentioned that it was all uncharted territory for her. Having known John only a matter of weeks, she felt like a trespasser. She walked away to the window, twisting a strand of hair around one finger.

When she turned round he saw that her expression was serious.

'What is it?' he said. He sat up.

'It's not your father. There's no news. But your mother rang.'

John sighed, and dragged himself out of bed. He picked up his jeans from the floor where he had thrown them last night. He didn't ask what Alicia had said.

'Didn't you hear the phone downstairs?'

'No.'

'It was ringing when I came through the door. There's some reporter from *The Courier*, trying to do a family piece on you. A woman called Jo Harper. Your mother wants you to go home and not to talk to her.'

'I don't want to talk to anyone anyway,' John said. He pulled a sweater over his head.

Amy had walked over to his computer, and was leafing through some print-outs. 'What's this?' she asked. She was holding up a picture, turning it this way and that, trying to make out the detail.

'Ice drift,' he told her, taking the printed page from her and tracing the image with a fingertip. 'Lancaster Sound.'

'Yeah?' she asked.

'You remember I told you about this group of eighteen people going after Franklin relics? The Canadian historians? This is from their website.'

'Right.'

He smiled at her and slung his arm round her neck from behind, holding the page in front of her face. 'Pretend you give a damn. Big story,' he said. 'Big historians chasing big Victorian ship, big ship disappeared, men disappeared, never seen again. Lots of cash and kudos for guy finding wreck.'

She feigned a yawn. '*So* boring.'

He released her. 'No imagination,' he said. 'That's your trouble.'

She shrugged. 'I'm mathematics, remember? *You're* archaeology.' But a second print-out, a photograph, caught her eye. 'Oh, sweet!' she said.

It was a picture of a polar bear way out on the blue-white ice, with turquoise shadows, a slanting, blinding sun.

John sighed resignedly. 'That's not sweet. That's the world's largest land carnivore. A killing machine.' He pulled the picture away from her grasp. 'See the crescent-shaped scar on her face?' he said. 'This maritime history crew have got a photographer with them, a guy called Sibley. He takes shots like this—grizzly, caribou, white bear. They call this one the Swimmer because she swims a hell of a long way.'

Amy looked at the photo again. 'Look at her feet. The size of them! Aaah. They're just cuddly feet.'

This time, John didn't even hear her. According to the website, this enormous predator was following the course of Franklin's ships almost mile for mile. It was eerie.

Amy picked up her bag. 'John,' she reminded him, 'your mother told you to go home. Right now. Today.'

John tore his gaze from the paper in front of him, flung it onto the desk and rubbed a hand through his hair. He gave a little-boy grin, all innocence and charm. 'But I don't want to go home.'

JO WAS DRIVING BACK to the Academy when her mobile phone rang on the passenger seat.

'Jo? It's Gina. Where are you?'

'Driving into Cambridge.' There were traffic lights ahead, turning red. Jo eased her foot onto the brakes.

'Drive back out of Cambridge,' Gina said. 'Come back here.'

'Why?'

'I've had Mrs Marshall on the phone. She's furious.'

'But I was politeness itself. You should have heard me. I didn't even get over the doorstep.'

'Peter Bolton rang me too.'

'But he was perfectly OK!'

'Not now.'

'She came to the door, I didn't argue . . .'

'She's a trustee of the Academy, remember?' Gina said. 'A benefactor, no less.'

'So we aren't allowed to ask her anything?'

The car behind blew its horn. The lights had changed.

'It's not worth it. Leave it,' Gina told her.

There was an opportunity to take a right turn, towards the southbound motorway. Just for a second Jo hesitated, then she put her foot on the accelerator and made for the city centre.

SHE GOT TO THE DOORS of the Academy at one thirty. Peter Bolton was coming out. When he saw her, his face fell a mile.

'Can I speak to you?' she asked. He was walking down the steps, not stopping for her.

'Mr Bolton?'

He did stop then, and looked at her. 'You lied to my assistant. I did not give you Mrs Marshall's address.'

'No. I'm sorry.'

He looked exasperated. 'You can't ride roughshod over people.'

'I didn't ride roughshod!' Jo objected. 'She seemed to know nothing about what her husband is doing. Were you aware of that?'

He opened his mouth to say something, then evidently thought better of it. 'Nice try,' he said.

'Is Doug Marshall's visit to Greenland a state secret?'

'Yes.' He gave the ghost of a smile.

'It's about Mrs Marshall's privacy?'

'Yes.'

'Has Douglas Marshall gone missing because of his marriage?' Jo persisted.

This was the idea that had been preying on her mind. One of those out-of-the-blue hunches, the result of putting two and two together. Douglas Marshall in a life-threatening situation, just not wanting to come home. Seeing no *point* in coming home.

Peter Bolton laughed out loud. 'No, no, no. What is it about his marriage that so fascinates you?' he asked.

'But—'

'You really must excuse me,' he said.

She watched him cross the road and walk away. Thought about Alicia. Thought of her smiling, laughing, opening her arms to welcome her husband home, with a meal waiting, a warm bed. No, it did not compute. Alicia Marshall's face had been colder than Greenland.

Jo shrugged. There was nothing here, other than that Douglas and Alicia Marshall had a terrible relationship, which enabled him to go ice-hopping at regular intervals without regret.

Yet she wondered.

Most of all, she wondered who Franklin had been, why he had become, by Bolton's own admission, the passion of Marshall's life.

CHAPTER 2

The bear lifted her head.

She was alone on hard-packed floe, and the weather was startlingly clear. Ice crystals in the atmosphere created a double sun, a central light source, with a circle of glowing satellites. She could hear the plane and turned towards the drone of its engine.

The Twin Otter was flying low. Richard Sibley, swathed in layers of expedition clothing, sat forward, waiting to take photographs through the copilot's window. When conditions were right, and luck was in, it was possible to take the kind of shots that kept him in business. He was one of only a handful of Arctic specialists—you needed to be more than a little crazy to endure subzero work.

Rippled ridges of land swept beneath him. The colours were hypnotic: grey ridges of stunted vegetation, threadbare lichen, striped with snow. On the ground the thermometer was at minus 30; it would freeze his flesh in seconds.

It was just then, as they crossed the indeterminate border between land and icebound ocean, that he saw the bear, standing stock-still, the crescent scar on her forehead. His heart skittered through several uneven beats.

They passed over her twice. She might have been carved from stone, her fur shimmering in the oblique light. It was as if she had materialised from nowhere.

He ran out of film as they made the third pass. Cursing, he reached for another camera, and only then did he see that she had turned away. She was facing down the Sound, looking south.

He had that last sight of her, head slowly swinging from side to side as if seeking a scent, and then he lost her in the glare of the ice.

AT HALF PAST SEVEN the next morning Jo was at *The Courier*.

Balancing a coffee cup, that morning's edition and her shoulder bag, she invaded Gina's office, and sat down on the corner sofa and began to unload the contents of her bag. As well as the photocopied sheets on Doug Marshall that Gina had given her, she'd brought several dog-eared magazines, sheaves of cuttings and four videotapes. She grabbed one, crossed to Gina's TV and slotted it home.

After a moment's static, the opening titles of *Far Back* appeared. Jo picked up the tape case and checked the black scrawl along its spine. *Episode 4. Maritime London, Douglas Marshall.*

She pressed up the volume on the remote. Doug Marshall came into shot, standing on London Bridge on a winter morning. Jo remembered now the thick thatch of sandy hair, the tall, almost awkwardly long-limbed body. And the smile.

'When I was a kid,' Marshall began, 'I didn't much like boats. The thing I wanted for my ninth birthday was a massive bike with a racing saddle.' His grin became broader. 'But there you go. I got a book about a boat. It was called *Arctic Explorations*.'

Jo pulled both knees up to her chest and wrapped her arms round them.

'On the spine,' Marshall said, 'there was a guy dressed in fur using a saw to cut through ice to get to a seal swimming underneath.' He started to laugh. 'That was more like it—going after a seal with a saw.' He shrugged. 'Nine-year-old boys are like that.'

Jo smiled.

Marshall was gesturing along the length of the Thames in front of him. 'You see an empty river now,' he said, 'compared to what it was in Franklin's time. Sir John Franklin, who set out from this same river in 1845, would have known a city where every language of the world was spoken and every commodity that could be traded changed hands. The West India Docks were half a mile long and berthed six hundred ships.'

Marshall turned back to the camera. 'Vanished,' he said. 'Like Franklin himself, and the greatest maritime nation on earth.'

The office door opened. Gina paused a moment before she came in and took off her coat. 'Make yourself at home,' she observed mildly.

Jo smiled. 'Hello,' she said. 'Sorry. Won't be long.'

Gina hung the coat up. 'What're you doing?'

Jo waved the tape case at her. 'I got these from a guy at the BBC this morning,' she said. 'Ever heard of John Franklin?'

Gina considered. 'No.'

Jo reached for the nearest sheet of paper on Gina's couch. 'You wanted me to find out about Marshall, so I found out about Marshall,' she said. 'You know what really drives him? Some Victorian explorer called Franklin. He went to the Arctic in 1845 to find the Northwest Passage. He set out with two enormous ships and a hundred and thirty-odd men, and they all disappeared.'

'Excuse me,' Gina interrupted. 'Did you miss a day? The one where I asked you to stop chasing up Marshall? There is no angle on this story, Jo.'

Jo smiled and shoved the papers in Gina's direction. 'Look at those,' she said.

Gina glanced at a print-out from an Internet search engine. 'Franklin, Sir John,' she read. Her index finger traced the entry. 'Born 1786, Arctic explorer . . . command of an expedition in 1845 . . . forty expeditions were sent to look for traces—'

'Forty,' Jo repeated. 'Victorian England went crazy trying to find him.' She flicked the tape on again.

Now Douglas Marshall was standing in central London, near Admiralty Arch, his fingers tracing a bronze plaque, memorial to Franklin's crew. 'The Victorians had an obsession with finding the

Northwest Passage,' he said, 'that elusive route over the top of the world. They were convinced that if any generation was destined to conquer the route it was them. What was the passage, after all?' Marshall asked. 'Just a few short miles of ice that had to be crossed during the months of darkness, in the face of the strongest sea currents on the planet. The finest nautical minds of the age talked about it as if it were an afternoon jaunt. So,' Marshall sighed, 'they sent their best. They assembled the finest ice masters, Royal Marines, able seamen, stokers, sailmakers, blacksmiths, carpenters, doctors and engineers, and Sir John himself—a mere slip of a lad at fifty-nine— and Her Majesty's Ships *Erebus* and *Terror* sailed from Greenhithe on May the 19th, 1845. The best-equipped polar expedition that ever set sail.'

Music swelled over the sound of Marshall's voice, and his image dissolved into a shot from the prow of a masted boat.

'The ships were low in the water, weighed down with equipment and food. They had over thirty-two thousand pounds of beef, thirty-two thousand pounds of pork, thirty-three thousand pounds of preserved meat, three thousand six hundred gallons of spirits, seven thousand pounds of tobacco, and two thousand seven hundred pounds of candles.'

'That's some stack of victuals,' Gina murmured.

'Although they were barque-rigged sailing ships,' Marshall continued, 'they both had railway steam locomotives below decks, specially adapted for the trip and stripped of their front wheels. They still weighed fifteen tons apiece.' He smiled, shaking his head at the improbability of it. 'And just to add to the weight, the ships' hulls were blanketed with iron to protect them against pack ice.'

The soundtrack rose with the noise of a fierce gale.

'On July the 4th, the ships restocked at Greenland,' Marshall said. 'They were seen by the whaling ships *Enterprise* and *Prince of Wales* on the 28th, as they entered Lancaster Sound. But neither they nor any of their crew were ever seen again.'

Jo stopped the tape and turned to Gina. 'It's what he chases,' she said. 'He's been looking for those ships for years. He found a canister from one of them.' She leaned over and tapped the papers she'd given Gina. 'It's in there somewhere. Both ships had little copper canisters that the crew wrote messages for, which were then sealed up and thrown overboard. They were a kind of marker. But only one was ever found, in Greenland. Until Douglas Marshall found another one four years back. Do you think he went to Greenland looking for another canister?'

Gina looked steadily at her. 'Did you see this?' she asked. She took that morning's copy of *The Courier* and flipped it open to an article with a photograph of a Royal Navy helicopter.

BLIZZARDS FORCE SEARCH TEAMS BACK

The overnight search for the British scientist Douglas Marshall and his Inuit guide was last night called off until first light, following the worst weather conditions in living memory.

Marshall, 39, Professor of Archaeology at Cambridge's Blethyn College, went missing four days ago in the Uummannaq Fjord in northwestern Greenland . . .

'They'll never find him out there,' Gina said.

Jo said nothing. She was rereading the article.

'I see the angle,' Gina said. 'The vanishing explorer. He's relived his hero's life.'

To her surprise, Gina saw Jo colour. The younger woman turned the page and carefully folded the newspaper. Then she walked over to the window.

As she looked at Jo's turned back, Gina frowned. Then a light dawned on her face and her expression was all astonishment. She got up, moved round her desk, and drew level with Jo. 'You wanted him to freeze, remember?' she said.

Jo's expression betrayed no emotion—not a flicker—as she gazed at the river.

JOHN MARSHALL let himself into his father's third-floor flat in Cambridge. There was mail behind the door, almost two weeks' worth. He put it on the first flat surface to hand.

The air smelt musty. There was a single bed in one corner of the main room, covered with a red throw, a couch that had seen better days and a gas fire hooked onto the wall. In the opposite corner to the bed was a kitchen area.

His father had lived in this high Victorian block, looking out over Parker's Piece, for five years, although Alicia, John's mother, would deny it. She pretended that Doug still lived at home at Franklin House. She had Doug's clothes on the right-hand side of the wardrobe in her bedroom. She still slept on one side of the bed, with

Doug's side turned down. There were books on his bedside table.

John sat down at the desk under the window, and tilted the chair backwards, running his fingers over the arms. 'He's coming back,' he told the views of Parker's Piece.

Last night John had gone home, but only after trying to get out of it. He had rung Alicia, trying to find a good excuse.

'You ought to be here.'

'I have classes.'

'No one would expect you in class. You ought to be here,' she'd repeated.

So he had gone, hitched a lift to the village.

She had been waiting for him as he opened the door. 'Darling,' she had said, holding out her arms.

He'd given her a kiss.

'Are you hungry?'

'Don't worry.'

'I do worry.'

They had eaten a meal in silence. It was an atmosphere he had grown used to in that house.

It was hard to say when the war between his parents had begun. He remembered his mother as constantly moving, and constantly talking. His father would be there at odd times—bleary-eyed and monosyllabic in the morning, or turning up very late, carrying his cases up the stairs.

'Your father is travelling,' Alicia would say. He could still recall when she said it with warmth in her voice. Pride.

He'd always wanted to go with his father. 'What's he doing?' he'd asked.

'Diving in water to find buried things,' she'd say.

There were trips in the UK, too, on which Alicia had accompanied her husband. Portland, Lyme Bay. What age had John been then? Seven? Eight? Memories of sitting in a windswept cliff hotel.

One day at Lyme, Doug had taken his son out on the dive boat. It was John's initiation into marine work. A gift and a test. John had been fired up to show his father what he could do. He'd promised to help check the equipment, watch the tank's oxygen level. He had wanted his father to be proud.

It could not have gone worse. He'd thrown up for five solid hours.

'We've got to make a sailor of you,' Doug had told him. 'Look at the state of you.' He'd laughed. 'You stink, my man.'

I hate you. John had thought, an eight-year-old's grief welling up.

When he was ten, Doug took John to see the wreck of *Mary Rose*, the royal yacht of Henry VIII.

'I knew some of the crew who raised her,' Doug told him, as they went through the Royal Dockyards at Portsmouth. They looked in the museum at the remains: the worsted clothing, the bronze muzzle-loading guns, the arrows and yew longbows.

His father had stood, deep in thought, for some time before one of the displays. John had wanted to hold his father's hand. He tried hard to resent him and all the times he had not been at home, and all he could find in his heart that day was an overwhelming hope that his father would put his arm round his shoulder. He wanted to bring Doug back from wherever he had drifted to.

But his father never really came back to them at all. Even when he was home, he would be immersed in some private, inner picture. He would be at the wreck of *Lord Western* in British Columbia, or in Egypt on *L'Orient*, which was blown to her death by Nelson in 1798.

When John reached sixteen, he no longer wanted to go anywhere with Doug. He'd given up on ever commanding his father's atten-tion. He'd accepted, with adolescent bitterness, that he was some-where on the sidelines of Doug's life, that he came maybe second, maybe third, maybe fifth, sixth or, worse, after dozens of sea-covered ships. He came after Franklin, he suspected—the Franklin enigma that constantly preoccupied his father. He suspected he meant less to Doug than Franklin or Crozier, Franklin's first officer. Crozier, the one who had supposedly survived for a long time after Franklin, who had lived out on the ice after the ships sank. The hero Crozier, trying to command over a hundred dying men after *Erebus* and *Terror* went down.

He grew hot, stifled by the idea of those men who lived in his father's heart. 'I'm alive,' he wanted to say. 'I'm not a dead hero. I'm alive!'

That was when the thought of eclipsing his father's achievements had first come to him, he supposed. It was a secret he'd nourished silently for some years now. He dreamed of finding what his father had never been able to find: some relic of the Franklin expedition, some astonishing clue. Perhaps then his father would respect him, for the first time.

He sighed deeply now, rubbing his hands over his hair.

The doorbell rang.

Startled, John went over to the window and looked out.

A girl was standing on the step below. He opened the window. 'Yes?' he called.

She looked up. 'I'm trying to find John Marshall,' she said.

He stared down at her. His first thought was that the upturned face was not English. In fact, it was like no other face he had ever seen.

'Wait there,' he called. He ran down the stairs two at a time and opened the door to her.

She was smiling, standing half on and half off the step.

He could do nothing but stare at her. She was a little taller than him, perhaps five foot ten. She had dark hair, tied back in a loose ponytail. Suddenly he felt incredibly awkward and stupid. How could he say to her, 'You're like the women in the books.' She wouldn't know which books. She wouldn't know about the Arctic explorers Kane or McClintock, or any of the others. And yet . . .

'I'm at King's College,' she said. She held out her hand to him. 'My name is Catherine . . .'

'John Marshall,' he replied, grasping her fingers.

He held on too long; she glanced down at their hands. Releasing her at once, he blushed beetroot red. This was what it was like, he thought, to be faced with your own fantasy. Here was a woman from the McClintock and Kane journals, an Inuit girl with a black snake of hair down her back, looking at him with the same kind of knowing expression that he had seen in photographs from the last century. Fantastic. Impossible.

'I'm sorry,' he said. 'You really remind me of someone. People. Some people I've read about.'

Stop gabbling, he told himself silently. Stop it, before she turns and runs.

But the girl did not run. 'My name is Catherine Takkiruq,' she told him. 'Could I talk to you about your father?'

AT ELEVEN that same morning, Jo was in Westminster Abbey, standing in line at the ticket desk.

The queue moved forward and Jo asked the attendant behind the counter where the John Franklin memorial was.

'Round to your left, first on the left.'

She followed the crowds. The roof soared above a wealth of gilt and marble; voices were hushed by the sheer size. Jo fished some papers about Franklin out of her bag.

The print-out was from an American university; their history faculty was manned, apparently, by Franklin obsessives. They had listed every name from *Erebus* and *Terror* and next to each name was a brief biography.

Lieutenant Graham Gore, entered the Navy in 1820. Took part in the Chinese war . . . portrait in the Royal Naval Museum . . . Harry Goodsir, assistant surgeon and naturalist . . . Captain Francis Rawdon Moira Crozier, born in County Down in 1796, second-in-command, an authority in terrestrial magnetism . . . James Reid, ice master, a whaling captain . . . And there were boys, two on each ship.

She bunched the papers together and walked on, looking to the left for the little chapel. When she found it, she went in and passed Franklin without seeing him. She turned at the end and came back. Only then did she notice, halfway up the wall, the modest marble bust of the commander staring out into the abbey. Below him, *Erebus* and *Terror* were shown with their rigging weighed down with ice.

She read the small, neat lettering. *To the memory of Sir John Franklin. Born April 16, 1786 at Spilsby, Lincolnshire. Died June 11, 1847 off Point Victory in the frozen ocean, the beloved Chief of the Gallant Crews who perished with him in completing the discovery of the Northwest Passage.*

There was another inscription on the edge of the marble: *This monument was erected by Jane, his widow, Who, after long waiting, and sending many in search of him, Herself departed to seek and find him in the realms of light July 18, 1875, aged 83 years.*

There was a lump in Jo's throat. Jane Franklin, his wife. Who had waited for him for thirty years.

At the base of the memorial, a second plaque had been added: *Here also is commemorated Admiral Sir Leopold McClintock, Discoverer of the fate of Franklin.*

She glanced down at the photocopied sheets. There were so many names. Graham Gore . . . Harry Goodsir . . . Francis Crozier . . .

All those people, she thought, dying for England. She felt something rise in her chest, a reaction against the waste of life. They had taken boys, too, for God's sake, into subzero temperatures for years on end. And for what purpose? No ships ever went north of Canada or Alaska now, from west to east, or vice versa. It was all blocked off with ice. It was pitch-black half the year. You couldn't defy one of the world's greatest natural forces with a couple of ships.

Jo turned away, into the crowd.

CHAPTER 3

In 1845 Augustus Peterman was twelve years old. He stood at the dock at Greenhithe and shivered, not because he was cold: it was May, and the day was warm. It was the sight of the ship that had set him trembling. Towering over him, wide in the beam, *Terror* was breathtaking. His heart pounded with ecstasy.

'Is she big enough?' a man asked him.

He leapt back, ashamed at having been seen. 'Yes, sir.'

It was an officer. He daren't look up from the breeches to the face, but the voice had an Irish accent.

'Seen the bow?' the man asked.

'No, sir.'

A firm hand landed on his shoulder and walked him forward. Augustus caught sight of *Terror*'s armouring, which reached back twenty feet from the stem.

'Know what's under that?'

'No, sir.'

'Three inches of English oak doubled with two layers of African oak, overlaid with Canadian elm.' The man slapped his back. 'That is *Terror*,' he said. 'That is what a British ship is made of.'

Augustus grew hot. His mother would be looking for him. She would be furious, and she had a quick temper. But he couldn't say that to this officer.

'Who are you?' he was asked.

He spoke his name.

'Look up at me, lad.'

Augustus obeyed. He saw a handsome face, clean-shaven, blue eyes, with sandy-coloured hair, gold fringing on the jacket, a double row of buttons.

'You are Thomas Peterman's son. Your uncle recommended you.'

'Yes, sir.'

The man nodded. 'Your father was a fine seaman.'

Gus said nothing. His father had been dead for four years, and he could barely remember him. He knew only that his father had gone down by Home Bay in the Davis Strait. The harpooner of number two boat had delivered his blow, and the whale had suddenly lunged upwards, capsizing the boat. His father had been killed instantly.

Suddenly the officer squatted down on his heels. He looked up into Gus's face and held out a hand. 'I am Francis Crozier,' he said.

Gus knew who Francis Crozier was, and the realisation dried the words in his mouth. Crozier was second-in-command of the expedition, and captain of *Terror*. If *Terror* was every boy's dream of a ship, Crozier was every boy's dream of an explorer. He had been at sea since he was thirteen—thirty-six years. He had spent ten winters in the frozen seas. He had sailed the Atlantic, the Pacific and the Indian Oceans as well as the Mediterranean Sea.

It was unusual for a captain to notice a boy, less still for him to offer to shake his hand. Gus extended his own small palm. 'I am indebted to you, Augustus,' the Irishman said softly, 'for coming with us on this adventure.'

Gus tried to say something. It came out as a few stumbled syllables. He stood open-mouthed as Crozier walked away.

He was still standing like that when his mother found him. The first he knew of her was a stinging blow to the side of his head. Then she grabbed him by the wrist. 'I've been searching high and low,' she muttered. Then she took him to the long row of warehouses. There, his name was taken, he was given a pack, and she leaned down and kissed him roughly, just once.

As he stood on the dock, waiting to board, he wondered about the great white bears. Although Augustus had been out on nine whaling voyages, he had never seen a polar bear. It was rumoured they could be ten feet high at the shoulder and weigh as much as eight men. Would they see one on this voyage?

IT WAS MIDMORNING when Gus was taken down onto *Terror*'s lower deck. Only half the crew were there but it was already crowded.

The officers had cabins—tiny rooms, six feet long and five feet wide—but the seamen were more cramped still. Their quarters were forward, at the bow, taking up less than half the deck. Right in the centre of the smoky, dim berthing was the galley, where the cook-stove belched. Above Gus's head swung the galley tables, suspended on pulleys so that they could be winched down when the crew ate. Forward of the galley was the sickbay, which was packed with boxes of provisions.

The man who had brought him below was called Torrington, a

stoker. 'New to the navy,' he said, as the men looked up at them.

The nearest sailor looked them both up and down, 'You're a pair, then, Torrington.'

Torrington grinned at Augustus. 'I worked a couple of coasters. Steam, you see. I worked steam engine, not sail.'

'And you, boy,' the other man asked, 'what of you?'

'Whalers,' Gus said. 'Out of Hull.'

The man walked over to him. 'You're the boy the captain knows. Hand-picked, you are.'

'Yes, sir,' Gus said.

The man leaned down. 'You can call me Mr Smith,' he said. 'I'm a stoker.'

Torrington squeezed Gus's shoulder and smiled. 'Find yourself a berth.'

Gus put his canvas roll down in a corner. He pushed it hard up against a stack of cartons, all with the stencilled marking: *Soup and bouilli—Goldner's Patent Preserved Provisions—137 Houndsditch, London.*

'They cans got here yesterday,' another man told him. 'Supposed to have been here and stowed a month ago. But got here yesterday,' he grumbled. 'Now can't get them below.'

Gus didn't care. The high boxes were proof against draughts, and he could make himself a bit private, if he was careful, curled up. And the thought that this was a true navy ship, that it would have men aboard who knew botany and medicine, magnetism and trade, well, that made it a floating palace, a kingdom of the favoured and few. Franklin himself, whom Gus had not yet seen, had been Governor in the Australian colony of Tasmania, and was refined, religious and soft-voiced, they said, a man of many talented parts.

While he scrubbed the deck—his daily task—Gus thought of the difference between Crozier and Franklin. Crozier was a plain-speaking working seaman, they said. He knew the Arctic and the natives who endured their lives upon it, the Esquimaux. Crozier was a hunter who could bring down caribou and trap foxes. He was a singing man, Smith said, with a fine Irish voice. And Crozier could dance, play a penny pipe and tell good stories.

'Course,' Smith told him one night as they ate at the galley table, 'he'll never take command of a voyage, like Franklin.'

'Why?' Gus asked.

'He ain't no blue-blood gentleman.'

'He is too,' Gus objected.

Smith just laughed. 'He weren't brought up with a silver spoon,' he said. 'He's like the rest of us, ballast. Be he the best that ever were on the sea, though he bring his ship through fire and storm and monster, even find the Orient—you'll see—they'll not give him a knighthood like Ross. They'll not have him to see Her Majesty. Not Crozier.'

There was a silence round the table.

'I'm not ballast,' Gus said.

'We all are, boy,' Smith retorted. 'Think we'll partake in the glory when we get home? Think they'll hold any parade for yer? No, they won't. And neither will they for him.'

A couple of the seamen opposite nodded assent as Gus glanced round the table.

'Ballast,' Smith repeated, wiping his tin plate with his sleeve. 'Needful for a ship, boy. Make no mistake.'

THE VOYAGE across the Atlantic was stormy.

Erebus carried heavy sail, and the ship roared on through high seas, occasionally losing sight of *Terror*. On June 27 a thick fog came down as they rounded Greenland.

By next day the fog had cleared and the ships ran in a fine show up the Greenland coast. They saw the first ice, all they ever hoped to see, bergs floating in open water. The ice masters of each ship were out in navigation; Crozier was up on deck for hours.

On June 30 they crossed 66 degrees north. A small case was brought up from Crozier's cabin and the first of the cylinders unpacked. Gus saw it tossed into the sea, a little copper rod that soon faded away.

By July 4 they were in Disko. It was bedlam in port. Everything from the transport ships was unloaded and reloaded again onto *Erebus* and *Terror*. When it was all done, the ships were weighed low down in the water, groaning with foodstuffs and coal.

The weather turned fair; the sun beat down on them. Word went round the ships that the ice was far open to the west; the sea would be warmer than usual, the passage easier than anticipated. In less than eight weeks they would be in Alaska.

They sailed from Greenland on July 12.

The atmosphere in *Terror* was unlike anything that Gus had known in the hard business of whaling. There was a recital on the open deck one night; there was singing; there was a service and prayers. There was even dancing. The seas were bright and the icebergs beautiful, and they felt they were in God's ships on God's ocean, on the highest mission, with God's mercy and blessing. They were the most fortunate of men.

The only thing that spoilt Gus's sailing in these summer days was the sight of Crozier himself.

The officer stood late in the day, every day, looking forward from the very edge of the bow. And on the very day that they entered Lancaster Sound, Gus saw a strange expression on Crozier's face. Crozier hid it well as he came down and passed the boy. He even smiled then, and nodded at Gus, making a show of pulling at his cuffs and wrapping his coat closer around him. Gus watched him, worried for the first time. For the look in the captain's eye had not been confidence in God's mercy or excitement at the conquests they were about to make. It was fear.

THE PHONE RANG in the early hours of the morning.

Jo struggled up from sleep. 'Hello?'

'Jo, it's Gina.'

'God, Gina, it's nearly one. Where are you?'

'At work. Listen, they found him. Marshall.'

Suddenly, Jo was wide awake. 'Doug Marshall?'

'Your very man. Frozen like a fish finger, but alive.'

Thank you, God, Jo thought. 'And his guide?' she asked.

'Marshall broke a leg,' Gina told her. 'It was the Inuit guy that got through. Big hero stuff. They picked Marshall up an hour ago.'

Jo swung her legs out of bed. 'When's he due in England?' She could almost hear Gina smile.

'I'm going home,' Gina said. 'Chase your own story, girlfriend.'

THE NIGHT WAS BEAUTIFUL and John thought he had never seen one so lovely, but when he slipped as he came round the corner of Trinity Lane, just past the gates of Caius, he thought that maybe he was just drunk. He steadied himself on the wall. Ahead of him, she stopped and looked back. 'Got a stone in my shoe,' he said.

Catherine Takkiruq laughed softly, not fooled. 'Stand up and walk straight,' she murmured, half laughing, half reproving.

He did as he was told—or, at least, the best he could.

They emerged at last in his road, and stopped by the door to his flat.

'I'm going home from here,' Catherine said. She held out her hand.

He wanted to kiss her, not shake her hand. 'You can't leave me,' he said. 'I was going to show you the Franklin stuff.'

'Maybe another time,' she said.

A little bolt of panic shot through him. She would turn up this street, and he would never see her again. 'I never thanked you properly,' he said, 'for the news and everything.'

'You thanked me twenty times, John,' she said, 'and bought me four drinks. You thanked me all night.'

He caught her arm as she turned to go. 'I'm going there,' he told her, abruptly. 'Where you come from. King William Island.'

She prised his fingers from her wrist. 'I come from Arctic Bay, and I haven't lived there since I was six, remember?'

'I'm going there,' he repeated. 'My secret. Now you know it.'

She leaned against the wall. 'Thanks for telling me.'

'No,' he said. 'Thank *you*. Your dad, and all that, emailing you to tell me about Dad's rescue before the papers got it.'

'That makes twenty-one thank-yous,' she observed. But she was not impatient at all. 'François is Dad's cousin.'

'Yeah. Brave man. Saved Dad's life.'

'Maybe,' she said, smiling to herself.

'Come upstairs just for a second,' he said. 'I want to show you. Got a whole mass of stuff about your country. Then I'll see you home. Promise.'

She paused. 'One minute,' she murmured. 'OK.'

She followed him up the three flights of stairs. He fumbled with the lock. Then the door opened from the other side.

Amy was standing there. She flushed deeply at the sight of the other girl. 'Come in,' she said. 'I'm just going.'

John suddenly felt dead sober. 'Amy, this is Catherine Takkiruq,' he said.

'Is it?' Amy said. She had walked across the room, and picked up her bag.

'She heard about Dad and came to tell me,' he said.

'Did she?' Amy said. 'Jolly good. I thought I'd drop by and see how relieved he was,' she commented, stony-faced, looking directly at Catherine. 'I guess you beat me to it.'

'I'm sorry,' Catherine said.

'Don't be,' Amy said. 'You're welcome to him,' she added, and ran down the stairs.

'Amy!' John called. 'Amy!'

The slamming of the street door was the only reply.

'I think I'll go,' Catherine said.

'No,' he said. 'Please. Please come in. It's not like it looks. I didn't ask her here. I'm sorry for all this . . .'

Catherine's gaze was taking in the room: the desk flooded with paper; the Canadian Hydrographic maps above the desk; the photocopied picture of *Erebus*, cross-sectioned, that was taped to the wall by the bed.

He followed her eyes to the picture. 'She was a warship before they took her to the Arctic,' he said.

'I know,' she murmured.

He sat down on the bed. No girl had ever known what he was talking about before. The fact that Catherine Takkiruq knew exactly what *Erebus* was, struck something basic in him.

'You have hurt your friend's feelings,' Catherine said. She walked to the desk and picked up the first book to hand. '*The Barren Grounds of Canada*,' she read. She picked up another. '*A History of the Canadian West to 1871 being a History of Rupert's Land, the Hudson Bay Territory and the Northwest Territories . . .*' She sat down on the edge of the desk, without commenting.

'I meant what I said,' he told her. 'One day I'll go there. I'll find Franklin.'

'Find Franklin?' she echoed. 'How are you going to do that?'

'Maybe your father could help me.'

Her face clouded. 'So, this is why you talk to me all night,' she said. 'But my father lives hundreds of miles from King William Island and the Franklin sites. So you have wasted your time. My father couldn't help you.' She began to move towards the door.

He sprang to his feet. 'No, that's not it,' he said. 'I'm not trying to get to your father through you. Forget I said anything about him helping me. I'll get there on my own.'

She stood looking at him. 'People don't do that on their own,' she said. 'Now I know you're crazy.'

'So?' he said. 'I'm crazy. I'll find something that no one else has ever found. You can laugh all you like. I'll find a way.'

'John,' Catherine said, 'no one will ever find them. They are gone, all those Franklin crews and the ships. King William Island is in the middle of nowhere. It takes days to trek from Gjoa Haven to the west shore. And then what? You're going to walk through ice by yourself?'

'Ever since I was a little boy,' he said, without looking at her, 'I just wanted to get there ahead of him.'

'Who?' she asked.

He didn't reply.

She went over to him, touched his shoulder. 'John,' she asked, 'who are you really looking for?'

By way of reply, he took her hand. Then, very gently, he pulled her towards him and kissed her.

'Oh,' he said, and his eyes were full of tears, 'you really are so lovely.'

She smiled, moved by the sight of the tears yet not quite understanding them.

'Who do you look like?' he asked. 'Your father or mother?'

That evening she had told him a little of her background. Her father was Inuit, her mother an American working with an oil exploration company. They had separated when Catherine was six, and Catherine and her mother had moved to London. Since Catherine had won a place at Cambridge, however, her mother had moved back to Washington.

'My father is not very tall,' she murmured, answering John's question, 'and my mother is very tall.' She smiled. 'They were an odd couple.'

'Do they ever see each other?'

'Not now,' she told him. 'They email a lot. To argue.'

He smiled back at her. 'Like mine,' he said.

She considered him. 'You are like your father. You have the same eyes, I think. The smile. Very handsome.'

He lifted her hand and kissed it. The sensation of her skin against his mouth sent a charge through him. He took the hand from his lips, not daring to look into her face, rubbing his thumb gently, exploringly, over her long fingers, turning her palm up.

'You don't want to go to that cold, John,' she murmured. 'I think maybe there is a cold in your heart, and that is what you want to cure. A father and son—'

He stopped her by looking directly into her face. 'My father doesn't have a heart,' he said.

THE BEAR WAS OUT FROM Prince Leopold Island, close to Cape Clarence.

When ships had come past the Borden Peninsula in 1845, passing out of Lancaster Sound, Franklin would have seen the 1,000-foot mountains that almost walled in Arctic Bay. In season it was an area full of narwhal, killer whale, seal and walrus.

It was cold and clear today, minus 30, but felt warmer in the sunlight. The Swimmer had a male less than a mile behind her, a mature male of 1,100 pounds, who had avoided her when he had not picked up a trace of oestrus. The team had come out to tag her.

Richard Sibley sat behind the lead biologist, with the biologist's assistant and their researcher alongside him. The idea was to put radio telemetry collars on young females who had not yet had cubs. They would tranquillise her from the air, the biologist explained, once she had moved past open water. They didn't want their infamous Swimmer returning to the sea while sedated.

As they passed above her, the bear began to move. She was faster than a snowmobile, steady over the rucks of ice. They used a dart from a .22 calibre, leaning out of the helicopter's side door.

The Swimmer barely looked up, propelling herself faster, weaving a little as if to avoid the gun. When the dart connected with her flank, her speed never altered. She kept up the same even rhythm, a moving cloud against cloud, hypnotic in her unchanging, shimmering pace, her blue shadow matching her.

And then she slowed, her hind legs first showing the effect of the drug. She tried to keep running, front paws pulling, until she succumbed, lying prone on the ice, flattened to it, sunk into a deep sleep.

On the blinding white-blue of the snow they took blood samples and ran an electrical current to test her fat reserves, which indicated four out of five on the index. She had hunted well, fed well. They noted the extraordinary development of the hindquarters and shoulders. They tattooed her for permanent identification.

As this was done, Richard Sibley stepped back. He was experiencing the usual problems of taking photographs in subzero temperatures: his breath had coated the back of the camera with frost and the lens was in danger of icing over. He put it under his armpit and backed away, staring down at the collar on the bear. They had rolled her onto her side and her neck was extended along the ice. Her strength and beauty moved him.

He looked away, closing his eyes against the snow streaming along the ground. He tried to see a photographic pattern. He focused on the shape of the bear, the tableau she made with the emptiness of the backdrop. He snapped off a reel of pictures, moving in to take the detail of her head, ears and paws. Claws against ice. Collar against fur. The tattoo.

He could no longer feel his feet or hands. There was a warning numbness in his face, around his mouth. He got back into the helicopter, pressing his face into his coat sleeve, heaving warm breath into the angle of his elbow. He suddenly wanted to be gone, out of the Sound, back to Winnipeg. He felt a congestion in his chest until they were airborne again, and he looked back at the bear, now stirring on the snow. He felt he had invaded her, been party to a swift assault. And more than that, he felt she was better than they were, moving in a world he would never really know, possessor of some more permanent truth.

As they crossed Barrow Strait and made for Resolute, he shook away these thoughts, mentally preparing the text of the update he would put on the website, and the response he would write to a young man called John Marshall.

LATER THAT SAME WEEK, Jo sat directly behind the pilot in the Dauphin helicopter, wedged between John Marshall and the leading medical assistant. The sea was clear, but Jo couldn't look at it. She spent most of her time with her fingers crossed.

It was a bright day over the North Atlantic, the visibility limitless. A charitable weather system was sitting square on the southern tip of Greenland, giving them effortless flying. Jo glanced across at John Marshall. If anything, he looked sicker than her, his head tucked down. She nudged his arm. 'Like flying?' she asked.

He shrugged. He looked very much like his father: tall, rangy, sandy-haired. She wondered if, in private, Douglas's face wore this same expression, this guarded look. His public persona seemed to be full of charm and humour.

That morning, when she had first met John, he had been accompanied by one of the most beautiful girls Jo had ever seen. Introduced by John to Catherine Takkiruq, Jo had found herself self-consciously tugging down the bulky anorak she was wearing, standing very upright. Then she had grinned inwardly at herself: no amount of standing up straight was ever going to bring her up to Catherine Takkiruq's shoulder. She couldn't even find it in her heart to hate the girl for her astonishing good looks. Catherine seemed to be sweetness itself.

She nudged John's arm again now. 'Is your girlfriend Russian?'

He smiled, and shook his head. 'Canadian. Inuit,' he said.

Of course, she told herself. What other kind of girl would a Marshall man be interested in?

'She's amazing,' she told him.

His eyes said it all.

The Dauphin roared on. After a while, Jo dug into her pocket. She brought out a crumpled photograph of Doug and showed it to John.

'This photograph . . .' she said. 'Is this the canister he found?'

'Yes,' he said, and turned his head away from her.

She folded the paper and put it back into her pocket, puzzled at his continuing silence.

In the last few days she had found out about Doug Marshall's discovery, a find so momentous that it had made his professional name. She had found an article he had written: how he had stumbled across the canister while on a previous Greenland trip. Only two canisters from Franklin's ships had ever been found: one on the west coast of Greenland in July 1849; one by Doug Marshall, at Sarfannguaq, in August 1993. The canisters, thrown overboard at regular intervals during the journey—a kind of copper-wrapped paper trail—noted the ship's positions and the dates. The fact that the trail had gone dead had puzzled historians for years, until Douglas Marshall had picked up the second canister and found inside it the note from Crozier, Franklin's second officer. More than anything, Jo wanted to talk to Marshall about that note, Crozier's cryptic message, thrown from the second ship, *Terror*, in July 1845.

She glanced up to see the pilot looking back at her, with a thumb raised. Then he pointed down at the sea. Jo looked down in the direction of his finger and suddenly saw, far below them, the slim grey line of HMS *Fox*, a type-23 frigate of the Royal Navy. The Dauphin swung low, and Jo's stomach dropped a few hundred feet.

Minutes later, they were shepherded out on deck under the still-turning blades. Buffeted by the wind, Jo took the outstretched hand of the officer stepping forward to meet them.

'Good flight?'

'Great.'

Inside the hangar, she pulled off the wool hat she had been wearing.

The principal medical officer smiled at her. 'Anthony Hargreaves.'

'Jo Harper,' she replied. She looked behind her for John. 'This is Doug Marshall's son, John.'

The two shook hands. John said nothing.

'Is he OK?' Jo asked.

'We reset the leg last night,' Lieutenant Hargreaves told them. 'Nasty break.'

'Can we see him?'

'Any time.'

Jo looked at John. 'You first.'

'I don't mind,' he said.

There was a moment of awkwardness. Jo was embarrassed by John's apparent lack of concern. She had moved heaven and earth to get them both here and, from the first, his attitude had surprised her.

She had reached him in Cambridge the day after Doug had been found. His voice on the phone had been wary.

'You don't know me . . .' she had begun, after saying her name.

'My mother told me,' John had replied.

From this difficult start, he hadn't made it any easier for her.

'I'm trying to get a flight to the ship,' she'd said. 'I'd like to interview your father. I know someone in the department, and . . . well, I just wanted to know if you'd come with me.'

'I might,' he said.

She'd put the phone down with the conviction that John Marshall loathed her.

Still, less than twenty-four hours later, she rang him again. 'Someone on board needs blood,' she'd said. 'AB rhesus negative. We can hitch a ride.'

'Fine,' John had replied.

She had put the phone down thinking, If your father isn't more talkative than you, I'm sunk.

They went down now into the sickbay. It was a small cabin with barely enough room for a desk and a screened-off double bunk.

Jo's eyes strayed to a notice board on the wall. There was a photograph of a young girl there, not more than eight or nine years old. Seeing her glance, Hargreaves tapped the image with his finger. 'Daughter of one of the crew,' he told her. 'She has leukaemia. The whole ship was tested by the Norberry Trust when we were in port, for bone-marrow donation.'

'Oh,' Jo murmured. 'I'm sorry.'

Hargreaves walked over to the bunk and drew back the curtain.

Doug Marshall had evidently been asleep. As they moved up to the bed, however, he opened his eyes.

Jo's first thought was that he looked different from the photograph in her trouser pocket. 'You look younger than your publicity shot,' Jo told him, smiling and holding out her hand. 'Jo Harper.'

John briefly touched his father's shoulder, and moved back to the end of the bunk. 'All right?' he asked Doug.

'Been better,' Doug replied.

Jo looked from one to the other, embarrassed. 'How's the leg?' she asked Doug.

'Fine. Dunno how I did it. It was flat where I fell. I slipped on the easiest track in the world, and fell 150 feet.'

Jo smiled at him. She had half expected a show of bravado—*I was negotiating a really hard climb, and* . . . 'And this was a week ago?' she asked.

'Eight days,' he said.

She knew all this already, of course. But as she made small talk, she listened for her angle. 'You lay for eight days in snow?'

'I walked a bit. We found a place to shelter.'

Out of the corner of her eye, she saw John slump into a chair.

'You *walked* on the broken leg?' she asked.

'I got off the shore out of the water,' he said. 'That was all.'

She frowned. 'You're losing me. When did you get into water?'

'When I tried to get off the rocks,' he said.

She gaped at him, then started to laugh.

'It wasn't so bloody funny at the time,' Doug admonished her.

'You fell from a flat, straight track a hundred and fifty feet onto rocks by water, and then fell into the water?' she said.

Doug started to laugh himself. At last she recognised the TV face, creased in a fan of laughter lines. 'Just dress it up a bit for the paper, will you?' he said. 'I don't want everyone knowing.'

'I'll do my best,' she promised.

Hargreaves had gone to the door to answer a knock. He came back carrying a tray. 'See if you can take this, Doug,' he said to Marshall, holding out a cup of tea.

Sitting back in a chair beside Doug, Jo saw his eyes flicker to his son. She caught John looking at her and saw that he felt rebuffed. She had come between them, she realised. This was an opportunity for John to talk to his father and she had stepped in the way. 'John,' she said, 'come and take this chair next to your dad.'

He didn't move. 'I'm all right,' he mumbled.

Doug drank slowly, with Hargreaves holding his head, and Jo saw how much of an effort it was for him. To cover the silence, she said, 'What do you think it meant, the note in the copper cylinder?'

Doug nodded to Hargreaves to take the cup and looked at her. 'Cylinder?' he repeated.

'I've been reading your article, "Finding Franklin".'

'Well,' he said. 'Thanks.' He smiled at her, as if really seeing her for the first time. 'Are you interested in Franklin?'

'Yes,' she said.

'I don't believe you,' he said. 'Women aren't.'

She was affronted. 'Let's say I was hooked,' she told him.

Their eyes met briefly.

'You wouldn't have believed that note,' he said. 'We took the canister to the National Maritime and opened it. You wouldn't think a piece of paper could survive more than a century in the ice but it did. There was no discoloration at all. Just Crozier's handwriting as if it had been written yesterday.'

'It must have been eerie,' Jo observed quietly.

'It was. They wintered the first year at a place called Beechey Island,' he said, his voice low. 'Then they tried to sail along Lancaster Sound and into Barrow Strait. But the ice was there. The ice stopped them again. Three died that winter . . .'

The medical officer looked at his patient. 'Hey, Douglas,' he said. 'Tired?'

'The stately ships go on,' Doug muttered, 'but it came true. They were dead men . . .'

And, while they watched him, he fell asleep.

HARGREAVES LOANED HER his cabin to write and email the article.

'Come with me,' she told John. 'Maybe you can help me.'

Doug's son followed her, grudgingly, like a sulky child. Jo wondered if it was her, or him, or just that he was an archetypal teenager. She closed the door of her cabin and watched him perch, folded up awkwardly like a crane, legs tucked under himself, arms over knees. Nineteen was still teenage. Just.

'How do you think Doug is?' she asked him.

'He'll survive,' he responded. 'He always does.'

She had been booting up the laptop. The comment stopped her. 'Is everything OK with you?' she asked.

'Sure,' he said.

She made a stab in the dark. 'I bet you don't see much of him.'

'Other people see more of him than I do,' he answered.

Their eyes met. *Ouch. There's the nerve.*

'You're doing archaeology, too.'

'Yes.'

She glanced at the glowing blue screen in front of her. The blank page. 'Where should I start?' she asked.

There was no reply.

'Do you think your father identifies with Franklin?' she asked.

At last a spark of interest showed in John's face. 'Franklin?'

'Yes.'

He grinned. 'No. It's Crozier he'd like to find.'

'Crozier, who wrote the message in the canister?'

'Yes.'

'A message in a bottle,' Jo mused. 'Sort of romantic.'

John made a dismissive, huffing sound.

'Not romance, then?'

'That's what some say. The bit Crozier wrote at the bottom of the page, "the stately ships go on", they think that was for Sophia, Franklin's niece. Crozier proposed to her and she rejected him.'

'Oh,' Jo said. 'Poor man.'

'Do you know what that poem says?' John asked.

'No,' Jo admitted. 'Who wrote it?'

He raised his eyebrows. 'You don't know Tennyson?'

Jo held up her hands. 'I'm a philistine.'

John managed a small smile. He leaned back against the bulkhead and began to speak, his voice low.

> '*And the stately ships go on*
> *To their haven under the hill;*
> *But O for the touch of a vanished hand,*
> *And the sound of a voice that is still!*
>
> *Break, break, break*
> *At the foot of thy crags, O Sea!*
> *But the tender grace of a day that is dead*
> *Will never come back to me.*'

They looked at each other. She saw it then, briefly, acutely, in his face; saw that he had tried to hide it. Rejection.

'Who did you lose, John?' she asked.

He hesitated, then, to her surprise, he suddenly got up and wrenched open the door. He went, without looking back.

CHAPTER 4

In October the moon was beautiful to see, bold and luminously bright. Sometimes Gus stood on *Terror*'s deck and watched her. It was strange to think of them being so far north that the moon never set. The shore of Beechey Island was lit constantly by the same glorious glow, and the ships, sealed motionless in their winter harbour, seemed to be merely flat, pen drawings on a page. Gus had always hated going to bed in the dark, but somehow that old fear had left him. Thank God, because he was going to be in the dark now—twenty-four-hour, relentless dark, with only this occasionally luminous moon—for weeks to come.

By October the crews had arranged the ships for the winter ahead. The mooring was sheltered. The fires and ventilation fixtures below were able to keep a mean temperature on both *Erebus* and *Terror* of 60 degrees, which was comfortable and warm.

Since July they had sailed along Lancaster Sound and into Wellington Channel, further north than Gus had ever been. Aboard *Erebus*, Commander Fitzjames was as keen as Sir John to skip forward at a good pace, because he believed that Wellington was a route westwards. A rumour flew round the crews that Fitzjames had said they might find the passage most presently, and be through it in less than three weeks.

It was on August 8 that they saw the first walrus. And the first icebergs.

Gus was sitting below when John Torrington came down to tell him, 'We'll have a storm. It'll push us further on.'

Gus was worried for Torrington. He had not seemed right for more than two weeks. Gus thought he was thin; his face showed white ridges under each eye.

'Go up and see the walrus,' Torrington said to him now.

Gus ran up on deck.

A large number of walrus were within twenty feet of the ship, shaking their heads. But it wasn't the walrus that caught Gus's attention. It was the sight of the sea ahead, which before had been flecked with small floes, and was now—only two hours since he had gone below—streaming with denser ice. There was no open sea now.

Later that night, the gale came up fast.

The noise woke Gus. The ship heaved, dancing curiously in the current, as if unseen hands were tugging at the stern. By three in the morning the wind was blowing like a hurricane and ice was driving through the strait. There was no more sleep. The sea was furious; the feel of the ice-laden air scythed through both ship and man. They lost sight of *Erebus* in the indigo-green mountains of the ocean.

It was eight in the morning when *Erebus* came back into view, ahead of them still, between enormous bergs. Gus whispered a prayer. Surely God would not let them die before they had really begun. Each man waited in silence, expecting at any moment to see their sister ship crushed, as the bergs pushed in opposing directions. On the shore side, the ice tables were grinding together in masses, and they had no choice but to slip helplessly alongside the floes, each mass of ice depositing ice on deck as they were buffeted.

Only the sudden appearance of a passage of clear water saved them both; *Terror* managed to make fast to the sconce of a low water-washed berg, and the ice hauled them forwards like a race-horse, the sea crashing over it and the ship, running at high speed down the channel.

Never had Gus seen ice come so rapidly. Only the day before they had been talking of three weeks until they saw the other side of Canada; now they were at the mercy of the oncoming winter. It was as if their optimism had been months before: this was another landscape, another world.

It was decided to make back for Beechey Island, to the little bay that would protect them for the winter. What Sir John and Commander Fitzjames made of the shock of the sea change, the boy did not know. Nothing more was said of running to the Pacific in three weeks. The men accepted the long, dark wait ahead.

WHEN THEY FIRST BERTHED in the bay in October, the shoreline of Beechey Island was still visible. It was a grey place, a beach of shattered limestone crumbled to silvery gravel. In sunlight, Beechey could be arresting in its emptiness, arched over with a brilliant blue sky. A spit of land connected it to the greater mass of Devon Island, a square block rising from the ocean. A few hundred yards back from the shore, cliffs almost 500 feet high dominated the bay.

Very soon, the crew had built an observatory, a carpenter's shop, a forge, washing places and a large storehouse on the shore, within easy reach of the ships. They unloaded provisions into the store-house, and Sir John allowed the making of a shooting gallery to aid the men in their hunting skills. Gus hoped that someone would teach him to shoot, and Torrington said that he would try. They walked out on the very first Sunday after the gallery was made and, leaning on the boy's shoulder, Torrington said that they would make fine marksmen and shoot bears together by the light of the midnight sun next May.

But only two days later Torrington was confined to bed in the sick-bay. No one would say what the matter was, and Gus dared not ask. They took food in to Torrington and he refused it.

Outside, the temperature fell rapidly and the ships stopped rising and falling with the waves. They were soon in the unbreakable embrace of ice, captured for months to come.

Gus was standing outside the sickbay when the assistant surgeon, Mr Macdonald, came out one evening, a week after Torrington had been confined.

'Sir,' he ventured. 'Is Mr Torrington well yet?'

Macdonald paused. 'No,' he said, at last. 'He is no better.'

The officer called the galley cook over, and spoke softly to him. The cook went back and brought several of the lead-soldered Goldner tins from the stores. Macdonald selected two or three. 'Meat,' Gus heard him say, 'and make sure he keeps it down.'

Fear gave Gus courage. 'Is it the consumption?' he asked.

He read the answer in Macdonald's face.

TWO WEEKS AFTER COMING to Beechey, Gus helped lay the road to *Erebus*. The two ships were barely 100 yards apart.

They drove rows of posts into the sea ice, so that anyone passing between the ships, even in a storm, would be able to see the way. On one side, the posts were strung with rope; on the other, they laid lumps of limestone in a line. After the road, they made fire holes—backbreaking work. The holes needed constant attention to stop them freezing. Seawater must be available to put out fires, and the holes could not be allowed to close.

Slowly the sun went down. The snow began. They used it on the decks, packing it down hard for insulation and scattering sand over the top to get a foothold. It formed drifts right up to the ship's rails and over the top. But by far the most insidious were the silent snow-storms that dumped huge quantities on them in the darkness, stealthily, silently. Gus soon tired of running about in it as he passed, working, from the ship to the island. It became something to be mastered and fought, clogging his footsteps, crusting his clothes.

CHRISTMAS CAME. On December 21 the captain, upon making for the shoreline observatory, asked Gus to go with him. Nothing was said while they traversed the ice road. On entering the storehouse, Crozier simply indicated the stove, glimmering with its dwindling supply, and Gus set to, shovelling anthracite to feed the blaze.

Crozier, clothed in sealskin pants and coat, with a dogskin cap, sat down on a box and prepared to take his readings; the thermometer read 10 degrees below. 'We are warm in here, Augustus,' he murmured.

'Aye, sir,' he said, watching the reading.

The magnetometer was perched on a pedestal of frozen gravel; stretching out from it was a telescope. Every six minutes, Crozier made a note of the arc and recorded the reading in his memorandum. After a while, he glanced up. 'At home they are filling the churches as well as the fires,' he murmured. 'What will your mother do, without you?'

Gus didn't give it much thought. 'I have a brother who can fetch and carry,' he said. 'He is six now.'

Crozier smiled. 'She will miss you in terms of labour?' he said. 'More than that, I think.'

Gus considered. He did not think that his mother would miss him. He had four brothers and three sisters. His two elder brothers were at sea, like him. His sisters, when not at school, picked rags, sorting them for sale. Christmas in his house was a hand-to-mouth nightmare. 'They will think of us,' he said.

'Are you happy to have come here, Gus?' Crozier asked.

It was a curious question. Men did not ask each other if they were happy. Many complained; they complained of the lack of light, the rats, the cold. On the other hand, when they were in a good temper, they sang; they had races around the ship, with prizes for the fastest man; they aided each other in the worst jobs. But they did not ask each other if they were happy.

'Yes, sir,' Gus replied. 'Very happy.'

IT WAS NEW YEAR'S DAY when John Torrington died. Gus had spent New Year's Eve with him.

Torrington was stretched out on a bed that had been made for him; a great concession, for only the officers had beds. Two oil lights burned next to him. The Bible was folded on his chest. He stroked it. 'Eighteen forty-six, Gus,' he said, 'And I shall be twenty-one.' He turned his head.

Gus's heart dropped as he saw how wasted Torrington had become.

'Have you a sweetheart, Gus?' Torrington asked.

Gus coloured fiercely. 'No, sir.'

Torrington nodded. 'Nor I,' he murmured, and felt for Gus's hand. His fingers were long. Someone had scrubbed his skin so that you could hardly see the coal dust any longer. Gus could see every small bone. The knuckles looked huge and ungainly.

'Look under the bed,' Torrington said.

Gus did as he was told and found a small tin box.

'Open it.'

There was a letter inside it, and a key, a little book of verse and a leather purse.

'Take it,' Torrington said, 'and give it to my mother.'

Gus didn't know what to say. This man, above any except perhaps the captain himself, had been kind to him, talking to him as if he were an equal and not the lowest of the crew.

Gus started to cry. He choked on his tears, and laid his head on Torrington's bed.

It wasn't for some seconds that he realised there was a noise other than his own gasping. In sudden horror, he lifted his head to see Torrington with blood at his mouth.

Gus leapt to his feet. 'Mr Macdonald!' he cried. 'Mr Macdonald!'

FOR TWO DAYS, the ship's carpenters constructed the coffin. At midday on January 2, Torrington's body was brought on deck.

He had been washed, then dressed in his cleaned shirt and trousers. He was laid carefully in a sweet-smelling bed of shavings that filled the coffin, his head resting on a larger mound of the same.

They nailed down the lid, wrapping the whole in a wool blanket, and draping the bier with a flag. They lowered him down the side of the ship, and went out in a line across the ice, torches lighting their way. Halfway across, they paused, waiting for a second line of torches and Sir John Franklin himself, muffled, coated and capped, his head bent against the snow that was falling.

Captain Crozier fell in at his side, with Commander Fitzjames and the two surgeons. Behind them came the men who would fill the grave. The service was brief in the biting wind.

During the following week a curious atmosphere fell over the ships. The officers continually ferried between *Erebus* and *Terror*; there was much discussion in their quarters and in the mess.

To all the men's surprise, on the fifth day after Torrington was buried, Franklin ordered that the storehouse be unlocked and three boxes of Goldner's Provisions opened. A few from *Erebus* were ordered to take the boxes to the northeast slope of the island, and there open the entire stock of tins in each box. It was said that Sir John had the tins emptied, then stacked neatly in rows, more than 700 in all, and the meat that had been in them was taken away further still, and covered with snow.

Gus did not know what to make of it. He had eaten from the tins himself, as everyone had. Vast quantities of their provisions were tinned, all painted red outside, and stamped with the words *Goldner's Patent*. How could there be anything the matter with the tins? They were lead-soldered tight. The food could not decay.

When he asked one of the Marines, the man shrugged. 'They found a bad box, I suppose,' he said.

'Did something in the tins kill John?' Gus persisted.

The man laughed in the boy's face. 'Cold and consumption killed Torrington.'

Gus turned away, went below, took up the Bible that Torrington had left. In an hour, he had forgotten the leering face. But he didn't forget the 700 tins, taken away.

A bad box, he thought. One bad box.

THREE WEEKS PASSED before Jo saw Doug Marshall again. In that time, April turned into May and the two chestnut trees on Jo's street came into flower. One morning she found herself staring at them, thinking what spring might look like in Cambridge.

She phoned him. 'Hi, it's Jo Harper.'

'Hello, Jo. I see you sold the story.'

'I sold it everywhere,' she said. 'All over the world.'

'Congratulations,' Doug said.

'I wondered if . . .' She bit her lip. She felt sixteen, embarrassed, tongue-tied. 'Look, I owe you lunch, at least.'

'For what?'

'For the story. For being a national treasure. Everybody loves you.'

He laughed. 'I'm beating them off with sticks.'

'If I drove up, say, tomorrow?'

'Feel free.'

They fixed a time; he told her his address. When she put down the phone, she grinned, then caught sight of herself in the mirror in the hallway. 'It's just lunch,' she told her reflection.

EARLY THE NEXT DAY, she went straight to the Academy.

A student, sitting behind the visitors' desk, put a call through to Peter Bolton. When at last he appeared in reception, Jo stood up, extending her hand.

'You're very persistent,' he said thinly.

'Could we start again?' she asked. 'I promise not to harass Alicia. Cross my heart.'

Bolton smiled and nodded down at the copy of *The Courier* that she was carrying. 'You did a nice job. Thanks for the publicity.'

'Look, I . . .' She glanced at the exhibit cases. 'The last time I was here, I think you had Franklin pieces?'

'Yes, we do.'

'Would you explain them to me?' She blushed a little.

'You got the bug.'

'The paper had a lot of enquiries.'

'Yes, so did we.' He spread his hand. 'This way.'

The exhibit case was just as she remembered it; the sepia photographs, the tiny piece of red tin, the silver spoon.

'They wintered in Beechey Island between 1845 and 1846,' Bolton said. 'They left in a hurry, leaving behind hundreds of artefacts.'

'Why the hurry?'

Bolton shrugged. 'The most popular theory is that the ice suddenly broke, and they had a favourable current.'

'What kind of things did they leave?' she asked.

'Things like rings of stones to hold down tents, empty meat and soup tins, bottles. And two fragments of paper. One had on it the name of the assistant surgeon to *Terror*, Mr Macdonald. Only that. The other said, "To be called . . ."'

'But how did paper survive?' Jo asked.

'The Arctic is like no other landscape,' Bolton told her. 'An item left there, even paper if sufficiently protected, will simply stay put for hundreds of years. There's nothing to disturb it, you see. And the permafrost preserves them. Like Torrington.'

Jo glanced up at him. 'Torrington?' she asked.

'Petty Officer John Torrington, leading stoker on *Terror*. His grave is on Beechey. His, and that of two others from the expedition. John Hartnell and William Braine.'

Jo remembered Doug's words on board HMS *Fox*. *Three died.*

'They've been exhumed and examined by a team led by an anthropologist, Owen Beattie,' Bolton told her. 'Their burials and bodies provided amazing information, not just about the expedition, but about medical science in the nineteenth century.'

'Like . . .?'

Bolton shrugged. 'Hartnell had had an autopsy. No one had ever seen evidence of such a thing before.'

'And the ships' surgeons would have done that?'

'Yes,' Bolton said. 'It was probably Harry Goodsir. He was the assistant surgeon on *Erebus*.'

'Would that mean Hartnell's death was a surprise?'

'Yes, probably.'

Jo shivered. 'Tell me about Torrington,' she said, trying to rid herself of the uncomfortable feeling in the pit of her stomach.

'Torrington died of tuberculosis and pneumonia,' Bolton said. 'He was only twenty.'

'And did Hartnell and Braine die of TB, too?'

'Ah,' Bolton said. 'This is where it gets interesting. Braine was a tough fellow. A Royal Marine, a man used to privations, used to a hard life, used to the sea. He'd survived much worse than this. Yet he weighed only six stone. He was emaciated, a starvation victim.'

'But they had all those provisions. Thousands of cans. Enough for years . . .'

'That's right.'

She stared at him. 'So how could a man die of starvation, with all that food aboard?'

'Both Braine and Hartnell had TB, like Torrington,' Bolton said quietly. 'But it was the speed with which it took hold. In all probability, they were weakened already.'

Jo frowned. 'By what?' she asked.

'They were poisoned,' Bolton replied.

Jo WALKED OUT into the fresh air, taking deep lungfuls as she walked alongside Midsummer Common. It was a lovely morning, the air very still, the sounds of the city muted.

She stopped at a florist's and bought an enormous bunch of pinks. She had no idea how Doug Marshall would react to being bought flowers, and she didn't really care. They were as much for herself as for him. She had to have their scent in her arms to banish the images of Torrington and Hartnell.

Doug answered the ring on the bell immediately. 'Come up,' he said through the intercom. 'The door's open. Three flights of stairs.'

He was sitting on the couch, with his leg propped on a stool.

'Well,' she said, 'you're looking fine.'

'I feel OK,' he said.

She shifted from one foot to the other before she realised that she still had the flowers in her arms. 'These are for you,' she said. 'I'll put them in water.'

'Thank you. Can you make tea while you're there?'

'No problem.'

As she waited for the kettle to boil, she said, 'This must be really difficult for you.'

'Friends come in,' he told her. 'One of the secretaries has taken pity on me. She shops.'

'I was surprised when you gave me the address,' she said. 'I thought you'd be at Franklin House.'

'Franklin House isn't my home,' he said. 'My wife lives there. We've been separated for five years.'

'I'm sorry,' she said. She turned to make the tea, feeling awkward.

Doug was sitting back. Glancing in his direction, she caught a fleeting look of pain. 'Is there some medication you want now?' she asked as she brought the tea over.

He paused a minute, then made a submissive gesture, spreading his hands. 'Damn it, I thought I'd fool you. Top drawer, next to the couch.'

She took out the bottle, gave it to him, and got him a glass of water.

He swallowed the tablet. As he passed the glass back to her, his hand brushed hers. She felt herself blush. What's this? she thought. I haven't blushed since I was twelve.

She busied herself with the tea, hoping he hadn't noticed, and sat down opposite him. 'I've just been hearing about Owen Beattie.'

'Ah,' Doug said. 'Brilliant. Beechey Island.'

'And the lead soldering on the tins from Goldner.'

'Who's this from?'

'Peter Bolton. I've just been down to the Academy.'

'Why? For an article?'

'No,' she said. 'I'm curious.'

'Never met a woman curious about Franklin,' he said.

'You told me that on the ship.'

'Did I? I'm sorry, Jo. I don't remember much of what we said on the ship.'

'You were pretty well out of it,' she said. 'Tell me about the cans. The provisions. This lead poisoning.'

Doug leaned back on the couch, pulling a face. 'Good old Stephan Goldner,' he muttered. 'The grim reaper.'

'He supplied all the tins to the expedition?'

'Every one.'

'And all the cans were contaminated?'

Doug nodded. 'And they got worse the longer they were left before they were opened. Beattie found a huge quantity of lead in Torrington's bone and hair, from four hundred and thirteen to six hundred and fifty-seven parts per million. In a culture that isn't exposed to lead, you might find, say, thirty parts per million.'

'Jesus,' Jo breathed. 'And . . . all from the cans?'

Doug shifted again in his seat. 'Well, Victorian society was lead saturated,' he conceded. 'For instance, all their tea was wrapped in lead foil. And they had pewterware, and lead-glazed pottery. All those things could contaminate. But it was the tins that did for them all. The meat was probably not only tainted with the lead solder used to seal them but with all kinds of toxic stuff. Botulism, for a start. Victorian slaughterhouses and food preparation left a lot to be desired. When they opened Braine's body they found *clostridium botulinum*, a bacteria that flourishes in badly processed foods. It's the family of bacteria that causes tetanus and gangrene.'

'My God,' Jo said, shocked.

He gave her a small smile, and hesitated. His gaze slipped over her, as if he were seeing her in a slightly new light. She saw the spark of interest, and her stomach tightened. A flush spread to her face. Something that Gina had said one night while they shared several bottles of Beck's sprang to mind: 'You'll fall, girl, and when you do'—she'd wagged her finger—'you'll fall *hard*. You wait. Trust me. I know.'

At the time Jo had thought little of it. She could get a man if she wanted, she reasoned. She just didn't want. And when she *was* ready, it would be on her terms, not his.

Suddenly she leaned forward. 'Do you mind me asking how old you are?'

'I was forty last week,' he told her. 'Why? How old are you?'

'Twenty-six.'

Doug nodded, a small smile on his face. 'So . . .'

'Nothing.' The blush came back with a vengeance. She moved to a safer subject. 'So, what do you fancy for lunch?'

His laughter was interrupted by the ringing of the doorbell. A few seconds later they heard one of the other tenants go down the stairs, hold a muffled conversation on the threshold, then a second set of footsteps coming up to Doug's flat.

Alicia appeared in the doorway. The first thing that occurred to Jo was that she looked even more glacial than she had a month ago. Her make-up was faultless. She wore a linen suit and carried a large leather portfolio. On one arm was a little woven basket with a cloth tucked tidily over its contents. Her gaze travelled slowly over her husband, then on to Jo.

'Hello,' Jo said.

Alicia didn't reply. Instead, she walked over to Doug and kissed his cheek.

'This is Jo Harper,' Doug said.

'Yes, I know,' Alicia replied. 'How are you?' she asked him.

'I'm fine. Alicia, this is Jo Harper.'

'You don't look fine,' she said. 'You look dreadful.'

'What are you doing here?' Doug asked.

Alicia smiled tightly. She turned her head in Jo's direction. 'More to the point, why are *you* here?' she asked Jo.

Doug stiffened visibly. 'Alicia—'

'I read your piece,' Alicia said. 'Unpleasantly sensationalist.'

'Really? Luckily I don't care one way or the other,' Jo told her. 'We're just going to lunch. Would you like to come?'

'Lunch?' Alicia said. 'He can't get down the stairs.'

'I can help him,' Jo said.

'It won't be necessary,' Alicia announced. 'I brought some lunch with me.'

'I'm going out,' Doug said.

'No,' Alicia said. 'Not unless you're coming home.'

'For heaven's sake,' Doug said.

Jo stood and picked up her bag. 'I'll go, I think.'

'No,' Doug said, holding up his hand. 'I'm going out to lunch with her,' he told Alicia. He was struggling to get up, casting about him for his walking stick.

'Don't be so absurd,' Alicia said. 'How do you think you'll get him downstairs? Don't you realise he hasn't been out of this room since he got back?'

'Why don't you leave me alone?' Doug said to her. 'Jo . . .'

Jo took a step forward. She put her hand on Doug's arm. He gave her a look that was almost plaintive. For a second, she thought that he was actually going to say, 'Don't leave me.'

'I'll catch you some other time,' she said.

'I'll show you out,' Alicia said.

'Thanks,' Jo told her, 'but I can find my own way.'

THEY WERE UNDER SAIL, heading south in the Arctic summer. It was August 1846, and Gus was ill. He didn't know when it had started, but he knew that he was thinner, and he didn't look at his wrists and hands any more, hiding them under the cuffs of his shirt. His hands did not belong to him. They belonged to John Torrington.

He was so tired, too; tired enough not to follow where they were since leaving Beechey at a run one morning in July, scattering possessions, leaving behind even the stacks of tins in careful rows, which some of the men had intended to use for target practice. Worst of all, to Gus's lasting dismay, as he charged down to the shore, he had dropped the key from Torrington's little box, the key that he had promised to take to Torrington's mother.

As they sailed, he did not feel inclined to work, although he had formerly been so proud of all he could do. On some days he was in good spirits. On other days, the worst fatigue swept him under. Once his stomach cramped and he longed for plain milk from home, for any taste that was not metal, or salt.

He thought, perhaps, that salt did not agree with him. But that was ludicrous. How could salt not agree with a sailor? Yet he seemed better when they did not eat the salted pork in the rations, and when they had feasted on birds that had been shot on Beechey.

The ice had cracked on the last day of July. They heard an explosion out to sea, as if God had mined his own white landscape and blown it to pieces. There had been a flurry of activity, with officers on deck and signals passing between ships.

'Ice moving!' Gus heard as he clambered up on deck. It was Crozier's voice.

They came out into the Barrow Strait, the area where the ice had impeded them last year, and the wind rose. *Erebus* and *Terror* ploughed forward and picked up speed. Movement! Glorious movement! They entered Peel Sound, overjoyed to find this unknown strait going directly south.

'Now we're for the Pacific,' the men said.

There were no icebergs to be seen. Only the beautiful sea with its many wonderful colours. The relief from the grey and white of Beechey was like a drug. Blue, blue ocean—cobalt and aquamarine and deepest royal blue—rushed past them.

They had been sailing out of Beechey for less than a week when they saw the ice again. Bergs started to appear far to the south, and Thomas Blanky, *Terror*'s ice master, was constantly on deck looking for safe passage.

'See that floe,' Blanky said. 'Old pack.'

'Old pack' meant a chunk of ice, perhaps as large as a house, with snow still stacked on top of it, and tidemarks all around it. This was ice that had been packed tight for many winters, and that had been freed by the extraordinary warmth of the last weeks.

Still keeping a swift pace, despite the ice, *Erebus* and *Terror* covered almost 250 miles.

'Land!' came the cry.

All hands rushed to the side. Just visible in the distance was a dim outline.

'What is it?' Gus asked.

'King William Land!' was the reply.

Gus immediately looked to Blanky and to Crozier, who were upon the bridge. Blanky was not looking south, but back to the northwest, to the large stretch of sea guarded by Gateshead Island. They had passed the entry to it forty-eight hours before. As Gus followed Blanky's gaze, he saw how much white was piled in the sea in their wake—more white now than blue.

We're being closed in again, flashed through the boy's mind. But he shoved the idea away. It didn't matter if the ice closed in behind them, as long as it kept open in front. King William Land, he knew, was not far from the channel called Simpson Strait. If they passed King William they would be in Simpson. And Simpson was past halfway, much closer to the Pacific than the Atlantic. The glimpse of King William was a glimpse of salvation. Better not to look back.

At six in the evening, the ships hove to. Clouds were gathering on the horizon, but the sea was calm. Crozier came on deck, with Lieutenants Little and Hodgson; the ice master, Blanky; and the captain's steward, Jopson. Jopson grabbed Gus by his shoulder, hauling him to the rail.

The boy shrank under Crozier's inspection. 'Augustus,' Crozier said, 'you're coming with me. I want you to see Mr Goodsir.'

They went down through the single hatch to the lower deck, and through a narrow tunnel with little light. At the end was the officers' mess. Jopson opened the door and stood back to let Crozier, Little, Hodgson and Blanky enter. 'Stay here,' Crozier said to Gus. 'Wait until Mr Goodsir comes to you.'

Gus peered through the crack of the door. Under the circular glass skylights, his face ghostly in the bluish tone, sat Franklin himself. Gus had never seen the great man as close as this before. Franklin was looking at maps spread on the table; Gus noticed the drooping skin around his eyes. He looked far more than his sixty years.

The officers were already talking. As Gus watched, Franklin interrupted. 'There is no choice,' Franklin said. 'Poctes Bay may well provide ample wintering. But we are not looking for winter quarters.'

Franklin's finger was resting on the Admiralty North Polar chart. On it, King William Land was clearly marked in their vicinity; but its southern coast was not known. All that could be known for certain was that, from where they were anchored now, straits passed to either side of King William; to the east was James Ross Strait, to the west Victoria.

'There is no way out down James Ross Strait,' Franklin said.

'I am not convinced, sir,' Crozier murmured. 'I am sorry.'

A small murmur went round the other officers and a look passed between Crozier and Blanky.

'Expand upon your theory,' Franklin said.

Crozier turned the chart towards him. 'Here at the southernmost tip, we assume the isthmus between King William and Boothia,' he said, quietly. 'Ross assumed such a link. But it is an assumption.'

Franklin waved his hand. 'And you think there is no isthmus, and the way is clear to Victoria, to the west? That King William is an island?'

'Yes, sir. It may well be so. However if we went east, we could find our way through as effectively as if we went west,' Crozier said. 'And we may not meet such heavy ice.'

Franklin considered Crozier for some time. At last, he said, 'There is no gamble in going west. There is a gamble—the gamble that we will meet the isthmus—in going east.'

'But there *is* a gamble in going west,' Crozier said.

'Name it,' Franklin retorted.

Crozier glanced at Blanky. The ice master had sailed with the same Ross for whom this strait was named.

'I know nothing more than the next man,' Blanky replied, 'as to whether east is a dead end or not. But with respect, Sir John, I do know the ice. And we have ice coming hard from Victoria. There may not be such ice on the other side.'

Franklin smiled. 'We have railway locomotives below deck, man.'

'Not even they will break through what is to come,' Blanky said.

Franklin turned to James Reid, the *Erebus* ice master. 'What say you, Mr Reid?'

'There is old ice coming past us,' he said, finally. 'But Victoria is the shortest and most direct route.'

Franklin smiled again. 'Exactly,' he said. 'We can outpace the ice before it becomes solid.'

Crozier visibly blanched. Blanky looked away.

'We have in our ships the most powerful methods of breaking through even compacted floe,' Franklin said. 'We must seize our chance now. There may be less than two weeks before Mr Blanky's predictions come true.'

There was a murmur of consent from everyone present. Except for Crozier. 'Sir,' Crozier said, 'steam will not get us through Victoria Strait. Had I commanded this expedition, I should have refused to sail depending upon steam. If we hope it will bring us through Victoria Strait, we are wrong. The ice will close in upon us before we have passed King William. Long before.'

It was almost insubordination. The officers froze.

Gus saw a little spot of colour on each of Franklin's cheeks. 'But you are not commanding this expedition,' he said. 'We shall sail on through Victoria Strait and reach Simpson before the week is out. And we shall blast our way, if necessary, through ice. With God's will, we shall see the Pacific before winter comes. And that, Mr Crozier, is my final word on the subject.'

IT WAS FRIDAY NIGHT. Jo was fast asleep on her couch, and the comedy tape she had rented was entertaining thin air. She was dead to the world, when the doorbell rang.

She woke up and tried to think where she was. She squinted at her wristwatch. Nine forty. She rubbed her eyes, wondering who the caller was.

The doorbell rang again. She turned off the TV.

'Who is it?' she called.

'Doug,' came the answer.

She stared at the door in surprise. Then she got up and rapidly undid the lock and chain.

He was leaning on the outside wall just by the steps. Even in the sulphur shadow of the streetlights, he looked grey.

'My God,' she said. 'What on earth are you doing here?'

'I'm on a half-marathon,' he said.

'You what?'

'A joke. Jo, if you don't let me in, I can't guarantee I won't fall down.'

She jolted. 'I'm sorry. You just gave me a shock . . . Come in. Are you OK? Let me help you.'

By a series of stumbles, she got him to the couch. 'Thank the Lord,' he muttered, collapsing into the seat.

'You look awful,' she said. 'What possessed you?'

'Insanity,' he told her.

'Do you want a drink?' she asked.

'What have you got?'

'I've got a bit of brandy.'

'You persuaded me,' he said.

She went to the kitchen, laid a tray, took in the drinks.

She put the tray on the carpet. He drank the brandy and colour gradually returned to his face.

'How did you get here?' she asked.

'A friend gave me a lift to Charing Cross. I got a hotel room. Taxi from the hotel.'

'Just to see me?'

'Just to see you,' he said. 'To apologise.'

'To apologise for what, exactly?'

'Alicia. I should have thrown *her* out, not you.'

'You didn't throw me out,' she reminded him. 'I walked.'

He fisted his hand around the stem of the glass. 'She is such a steamroller.'

'It doesn't matter, Doug.'

'It does,' he said. 'The least I could have done—'

'You can't throw your own wife out,' she told him. 'She loves you.'

'She doesn't love me,' he told her. 'She's parasitical. I filed for divorce two months ago. I can't tell you what the last five years have been like.'

Jo fiddled with the edge of the tray. It didn't feel quite right to sit condemning Alicia in the other woman's absence. 'How did you meet?' she asked.

He smiled. 'Now you're asking ancient history,' he said. 'College. Lancaster. Alicia took economics and politics.'

'Fearsome.'

'She always was. Alicia decided we would get married,' he continued. 'She suggested the postgraduate degree. She seemed to think I had a bright future.' He put the glass down, remembering. 'We moved south, she got a job, supported my studies . . .'

'And you got married.'

'Only when John was on the way. I think she planned her pregnancy, although she denies it now. I had met someone else and was thinking of telling Alicia, breaking it off . . .'

'And then Alicia told you she was pregnant?'

'Yes.' Jo met his eye. 'I know,' he said, 'but I couldn't let her down.'

Jo gave a little shrug. 'It sounds a little like blackmail. What did the other girl say?'

'She was devastated. Really devastated. I was so torn, I didn't know what to do.'

'Did you love her?'

To her surprise, he blushed deeply. 'Very much. But I couldn't leave Alicia,' he replied. 'John was born. The girl got married to someone else and moved away.'

'But with John around, things must have got better?'

He looked up. He had been staring at the floor. 'Things never got better. I didn't love the woman I'd married. I just worked, and she worked, and she did the lion's share of bringing John up. We limped along. It's not a very attractive story.'

Jo shifted, and crossed her legs.

He glanced at her. 'Jo,' he said, 'I didn't mean to tell you my life story. I just wanted you to know I was sorry. I ought to go. You're tired.'

'I am not.'

He smiled at her. 'That's right,' he said. 'I was forgetting. You're twenty-six. You don't get tired.'

She gave him a wry grin. 'I get shattered like any normal person. But not tonight.'

He looked hard at her.

'I'm not tired tonight,' she repeated.

A look coursed across his face: pure astonishment.

She knelt in front of him and, carefully avoiding the injured leg, leaned forward and kissed him.

She thought that she had done with it all a long time ago, the fantasy picture of the prince in the fairy tale. And all this time, there had been a knight waiting in the wings.

She looked at him, and saw everything that had just passed through her own mind reflected in his face. My God, she thought. There are still miracles.

He hugged her to him, pressing his face into her shoulder. She felt his chest heave, his arms tighten around her. 'I didn't know,' he murmured. 'I didn't know.'

She leaned back a little, and looked him in the face. 'Neither did I,' she told him. 'But . . . I know now.'

THROUGH THE STORM, the great bear slept peacefully. She had closed her ears to the howling blast of the gale. Cold couldn't touch her. She was fat with seal, and craved sleep.

Her mate was lying ten feet from her. For the past few days he had been shadowing her, mesmerised by the smell of oestrus in her urine. They had mated that day. Over and over again, they consummated their union on the ice. The long Arctic day was calm; they roamed the broken floes, stopping from time to time to assess the current. Towards evening, the male had killed a bearded seal.

The ice storm lasted until the morning, when it stopped as suddenly as it had begun. For a while, nothing stirred in the featureless landscape, where the newly sprung carpet of grasses and saxifrage had been swallowed up. Then the female got to her feet slowly, and shook her body free of snow. She raised her head and scented the frozen air. The light blazed in the white-blue sky. In a few more hours, the colours of the Arctic spring would begin to emerge again. The low, smoothed rocks, where she had been lying, would reveal their bright orange lichen. Everything would look as it had looked earlier.

But the Swimmer, beginning to walk now, felt a change. During her sleep, she knew that something had altered.

She did not look back at the sleeping giant behind her. Her mate wouldn't wake for another hour. By then, she would be far away. It was unlikely that she would see him again.

ALICIA SAT in the conservatory of Franklin House and looked down at the letter, frowning.

'What do you think?' John asked. 'Richard Sibley is a very good photographer,' he said. 'He has a great reputation.'

He and Catherine were seated opposite his mother: the low table, with the neatly laid tea tray, was between them.

Alicia took off her reading glasses and laid the letter down among the cups. 'Let me get this absolutely right,' she said. 'You want to go to Canada during the summer vacation to work with this man.'

'He's offered me a job for six weeks.'

'I can't understand why he should want to do that,' Alicia replied.

John took a deep breath. 'Because I've been writing to him.'

Catherine laid her hand on John's arm. 'Because you have been nagging him day and night,' she said, smiling.

He smiled back at her; looked at his mother.

Alicia was not smiling.

'Mother,' John said, 'it's an experience. A huge number of bears congregate in that area.'

Suddenly Alicia got to her feet. Tension was spelt out in her rigid shoulders. She gazed at the garden beyond the windows. 'It isn't as if your course has anything to do with Arctic civilisations,' she said.

Now John stood up, too. 'It isn't about coursework. It's something different. I want to go.'

Alicia met his gaze with a stony expression. 'Following some pointless crusade, the same as your father. And you come here asking me to finance it.'

Catherine now got to her feet. She walked to John's side. 'It's nowhere near the Franklin sites,' she said.

Alicia's expression hardened. 'John is only interested in this particular place and this particular job because the man is chasing a bear *that has been seen on Franklin sites*.' She folded her arms in triumph. 'Oh, you think I don't understand. Perhaps you think I'm unable to call up an Internet site when you tell me a person's name. I know full well who Richard Sibley is, and his connection with Franklin, and his obsession with this particular bear.'

John snatched up the letter. 'I knew you wouldn't get it,' he said.

'And to think that I haven't heard enough of Franklin in my lifetime.' She stepped closer to her son. 'What has your father ever achieved in searching for them?' she asked softly. 'One copper canister. Why do you want to compete with him?'

'I'm not competing with him,' John retorted, colouring suddenly. He turned on his heel and slammed out of the room. Catherine picked up her shoulder bag and followed John, who was now out in the hallway, dialling a cab.

'Don't leave her like this,' Catherine said.

'I'm only asking for an air fare.'

'She doesn't like to lose you.'

The cab firm answered. He gave them the address and replaced the receiver. 'This bloody stifling house,' he muttered.

'She adores you.'

She was struggling with the idea that Alicia might be right. John could dress up the Sibley offer as a new venture, but it was really the old venture, the old obsession. Catherine knew how much John wanted to outdo his father.

'You could try asking your father for the fare,' Catherine observed.

John clapped a hand to his forehead, totally exasperated. 'Did he ever listen to anything I've wanted?' he demanded. 'Do you think there's a hope in hell of him listening now, now that this woman is monopolising him?'

Catherine bit her lip for a second, before replying. 'For what it's worth, I think Jo Harper is nice. And she's making your father very happy.'

'Oh, yeah,' John replied viciously. 'Happy. Great.' He wrenched open the door and went onto the drive.

Catherine followed him. 'You're surely not jealous of your father's happiness?'

He stopped, stared at the ground. 'What do you think I am?' he said. 'If he's happy, fine. Why should I care?'

She looked at him intently. 'I think you do care very much.'

'Who asked you to be an amateur psychiatrist?' he growled. 'Especially such a bad one.'

'I don't think I'm wrong. You don't want to get to Beechey Island because of Franklin or this bear. You want to get to *him*. That is what it is.'

'Don't tell me what my bloody motives are, all right? Don't be like her.' And he jerked his finger back to the house.

'It's because we love you,' she said simply. 'Just as your father loves Jo Harper. Just as you love him.'

He stared at her. Then he walked away, to meet the cab at the gate to the road.

As THEY ENTERED the strait panic set in. The first thing that Franklin ordered was steam: the locomotive engines roared below, and at first the ships broke through the gathering ice, cracking it like gunshots. The sun was high, the wind strong; the ships plunged through ice and waves alike.

Terror sailed in *Erebus*'s wake, and barely had *Erebus* found her way through, when they saw the ice re-forming behind her. They plunged into it, each man with a single hope in his heart. *Just through these miles. Just through this strait. There will be free water on the other side.*

The ice did not surrender silently to them. It whistled and whined and thundered; sometimes it grumbled low, as if there were some sea monster beating the underside of the ship.

The more *Terror* rolled, the more steam was called for. The belching from the funnel cut a black channel through the white light. There was electric-blue water, and streams of floating pack, but beyond that the whole world was white.

At one o'clock, Gus was sent below. They needed more men with the stoking. It was like Hades down there, so hot that they worked naked to the waist. Gus ran as fast as he was ordered, feeling the dust coating his throat. They worked relentlessly, until sweat ran into their eyes and they had to be replaced by others because they couldn't breathe any more in the blazing pit.

As Gus staggered out, he felt the ship wrench.

'Mother of God,' said one man. 'She's going over.'

Terror lifted up. An enormous boulder of ice had pressed her suddenly and hard. They felt her lose contact with the water, and for long minutes she skirted along the ice. No one glanced at anyone else. Then the pressure eased and *Terror* dropped down. Although Gus knew about ice relaxations, this had not been like the others they had felt. The blow from the ice had felt massive.

Six men from each ship were sent down onto the floes ahead. For two hours, they hacked at the ice. It was a deadly business. The men slithered and slipped at their task, working with axes like black demons under the prow of each ship.

Gus sat in misery below while *Terror* groaned and jolted. They were going to be stuck here another winter. They would surely starve.

Another winter in the strait would bring them into the third year, and, in truth, they did not have enough food for another twelve months. And not enough coal to cook it. Not having shot as much game as they had anticipated on Beechey, they would depend, from now on, entirely upon the tins and hard tack, and salt pork. Gus hated the tins. They never saw meat, but they had plenty of the soups—parsnip, carrot, potato. He had never liked vegetables and he had to hold his breath to swallow it.

He put his head in his hands, covering his eyes.

'Franklin is out,' a man said.

Gus opened his eyes. 'On deck?'

'You can hear him shouting.'

Gus crept up the ladder. Skittering round the starboard side, he saw the officers, Blanky among them. *Erebus* was perilously close. The ice was screaming, grinding, keening. And it was true: Franklin himself was on the deck of *Erebus*, and he was shouting, his voice as wild as the ice. It was the kind of noise a man would make in the throes of a last despair.

There was a sudden flurry on *Terror*. The ship lurched. Ice sheered upwards between the two ships, a great white solid fountain. Particles showered the deck, landed on Gus's shoulders and face. He heard a cry go up. 'Dear Mother of God and all the angels!'

They all turned to look. About a quarter of a mile to stern, they saw the pack behind them suddenly pile up, as if the enormous weight of the ice were nothing more than paper cards. It crumbled and fell, rose up again and fell, and with every falling and climbing, greater layers of floe lay in huge blocks at the feet of the newly forming berg. Something massive was pushing it from behind. And it was coming straight for them.

'Our Father,' Gus stammered, 'who art in heaven . . .'

It was 200 yards away.

It was 100 yards away.

It was taller than the ship, a white rock wall, a fortress.

'Dear Jesus,' a man said, at his side.

The grinding, crashing, whining of the approaching ice wall abruptly stopped. There was unearthly silence. Between *Erebus* and *Terror* a broken landscape of ice had appeared, and both ships, tilting in opposite directions, lay skewered on its surface. And overhanging them both was the mountain that towered eighty feet in their wake, not more than fifty yards away. It had stopped.

'Captain Crozier, sir!'

The voice broke the silence. Every soul on both ships could be heard to breathe out suddenly. They were still alive.

Crozier was at the rail. The first mate of *Erebus* was barely twenty feet away. 'What is it?' Crozier shouted.

'Mr Franklin, sir!' the man babbled. 'Sir John is taken.'

IT WAS SIX IN THE EVENING before Crozier called the crew together.

'Sir John has suffered an apoplexy,' he said. 'He is recovered. There is nothing to worry about.'

They heard the difference in him. They looked at each other, and back at the captain, who had predicted this day: that they would meet the huge ice currents flowing down the strait—that there would be no getting through them.

Crozier did not give the speech that they had expected. He did not say that, tomorrow, they would try to break the ice again. He did not say that it was only temporary, or that a distant way might yet be seen and attempted. In short, he neither encouraged them, nor said that he had been right, and Franklin had been wrong.

He said nothing at all, other than issue a double portion of rum and tobacco, then went below, to his quarters.

CHAPTER 5

The snow was falling in Cambridge. It had begun during the night, a softly moving curtain drifting across the country. By the time Jo woke at seven, it covered the city streets.

It was six months now that she had been living with Doug.

She pressed the length of her body to his, wrapping her arms around him. He murmured in his sleep and stroked her hands.

It was almost Christmas; today was December 22. Six months ago she had been alone in the flat in Fulham that now stood empty. She didn't know if she should sell or wait; she hardly trusted what had happened to her.

She turned onto her back, gazing up at the ceiling. The house was narrow and old, a four-storey Regency building, with a cellar, a cramped back kitchen, a luxuriously broad sitting room on the first floor, and this bedroom at the top, tucked under the roof. Doug had brought her to it only last month.

'Do you like it?' he'd asked, as they stood in front of it.

She'd gazed up at the tiny frontage, and noticed that the small leaded panes of the top windows caught the various tones of the sky, and were speckled white and blue.

'I want to buy it,' he'd told her. 'For us.'

'You don't have to support me,' she'd said.

He'd sighed. 'I *want* to support you.'

'Thank you,' Jo had said, 'but I don't want to be a kept woman.'

'Kept woman?' he'd repeated, perplexed. 'What year is this? Nineteen hundred and two?'

'Quite. There you go.'

He'd shaken his head. 'Look, it's a place to live, better than my flat. I thought you'd like it.'

'I love it,' she'd said. 'But don't let's change. I don't want to move.'

'The world won't fall down if we cart our belongings four streets across town.'

She'd looked at him. 'I don't want to be bought things.'

'I'm not buying it for you, you silly tart,' he'd replied equably. 'I'm fed up of living in three rooms, and I want a study. And there's the other thing. We need more space.'

She'd smiled at what had become their softly spoken catchphrase recently. 'Yes, the other thing.'

He'd looked into her face, considering her. 'We won't break,' he'd said quietly. 'We're not that fragile.'

Since that first night at her flat in May, they had barely been apart. Jo couldn't remember what it was like to be without him; they had fitted together seamlessly, without any of the half-expected strains of adjustment. For the first month, during the absence from work imposed by his leg, he had lived with her in Fulham. When it was healed, he went back to Cambridge, and she went with him. She worked as well in Cambridge as in London, going down to London, work and Gina by train a couple of times a week.

In everyday things they were not alike: he was a practised housekeeper, Jo lived in a habitual mess. It was at some deeper level that they were moulded from the same material. They were wanderers both, and they tended to bend rules. They were of different generations; they looked nothing like each other; they inhabited different worlds. And yet they were the same.

Jo smiled now at her thoughts. She gently stroked the centre of Doug's back. He woke up.

'It's snowing,' she said.

He rolled onto his side and looked at her. 'Is it?' He glanced at the bedside table. 'What time is it?'

'Almost eight.'

They looped arms, lying in the bed. 'They'll all make an excuse not to get here, if it's snowing,' he said.

'Not Gina,' she said. 'Gina will single-handedly shovel her way up the M11. And John will come. Catherine will make him.'

They smiled, but suddenly Doug's mood faded. 'We should have told Alicia,' he said. 'I've got a bad feeling.'

Doug had seen his wife only once since May. In July, a couple of days after Jo had moved into his flat, he'd gone to Franklin House one morning. He'd turned up again at lunchtime, looking almost ill. 'What's the matter?' she asked him. 'What've you been doing?'

'I've been to see Alicia,' he said. He held out a letter to her. It was his decree nisi. 'I knew she would have got hers today.'

They sat down on the couch, side by side, sunlight filling the room.

'What did she say?' she asked.

'The usual rubbish,' he told her.

'She'll never let go of you,' Jo replied.

'She'll have to,' he said. 'I want us to get married.'

There was a moment of silence. 'You don't want to get married so soon after the last,' Jo murmured.

'I do. It's the only thing I want. Marry me next month.'

'No.'

'Christmas, then.'

She smiled at him. 'A second wife years younger than you,' she said. 'The same generation as your son, who hates me.'

'John doesn't hate you,' he said. 'He's just mixed up.'

She narrowed her eyes. 'He's jealous, Doug,' she said, 'of you and your time.'

Doug shook his head. 'I lost a lot of years with him,' he said. 'I'm not going to lose them with you as well.'

'Oh, Doug . . .'

'I'll get him back,' he assured her. 'I'll do my damnedest. But I'm not losing you. I want you to marry me. Say you will. At Christmas.'

The scent of the old English roses that Jo had brought the day before flooded the room. She remembered that, above anything else.

THEY ARRANGED to meet Gina, John and Catherine at the Preston Arms before the ceremony at Shire Hall. They walked there, heads down against the still-blowing snow, more sleet than snow, and settling on the already transformed roads. When they arrived they stood in the doorway, shaking the snow from their coats.

They looked up and saw Gina, her arms outstretched.

Jo hugged her. 'How in hell did you get here?'

Gina smoothed her hair, smiling. She was perfectly turned out in a red suit and red shoes with killer heels. 'I read the weather forecast yesterday and drove up last night. I got here about midnight. Come and have some champagne.'

They went into the next room. An ice bucket and five glasses were already on the table.

Doug glanced down at the glasses. 'Shall we wait for John?'

Jo shot him a sympathetic look. She knew that he was making an effort to do it right and not upset his son.

Ever since they had told John that they were getting married, he had been very formal with them.

'He makes me feel like a scientific specimen,' Jo had said to Doug. 'He acts like he's preparing a paper on us.'

Doug had shaken his head. 'I don't understand any more than you do,' he'd replied. 'He freezes me out.'

'Well, don't let him. You two have got to get round this.'

He'd given her a crooked smile. He just didn't know where to start, what to say. And John wasn't about to help him.

'Well,' Gina said now, 'you look good. Both of you. An hour from now, Mr and Mrs.'

'Yes,' Jo said. She couldn't help a grin.

Gina touched Jo's knee. 'Have you told John?' she said.

At the same moment the door opened. John and Catherine stood in the doorway, Catherine dazzling in a white sheepskin jacket, John less so in jeans and a Barbour.

Doug walked forward, hand extended.

'Told John what?' John said.

Doug let his hand slip from his son's weaker grip. He kissed Catherine. 'Come and sit down. Let me open this bottle.'

'Great,' Catherine said. She gave John a warning look. Then she kissed Jo's cheek.

'Let me introduce you two,' Jo said. 'Catherine, this is Gina, my editor at *The Courier*. Gina, this is John's partner, Catherine.' The two shook hands.

John walked over to the table. He hadn't kissed Jo. He watched Doug peel off the foil on the champagne. 'Is there news?' he asked, very levelly. Very pointedly.

Doug's eyes flickered, just once, to Gina. Then he uncorked the Bollinger and filled the glasses. 'We're . . . well, starting a new venture,' he said. 'In every way.'

Jo had been looking hard at John. There was a hitch of silence.

'I'm getting another series of *Far Back*,' Doug said.

'They offered you another series because of the Greenland fiasco?' John said.

Doug flinched at his choice of words. 'I suppose.'

'We're doing it together,' Jo said. 'He hired me to carry bags.'

The weak little joke fell flat.

'I see,' John said. 'The reporter who got her man because of Greenland, flying out to meet him . . .'

'That was all hype,' Jo countered. 'I never said all that about moving heaven and earth to meet him. The paper put that in.'

'Well, it doesn't matter,' Doug said.

'It's eleven fifteen,' Gina murmured.

Catherine stood up.

'So,' John said, 'you'll be travelling. To Greenland?'

'Yes, Greenland . . .'

'And Victoria Strait?'

Doug jolted a little, as if John had hit a nerve.

'You're chasing Franklin,' John said.

'Look, John,' Jo said, 'we want you in on it. Of course we do. We know it's your passion.'

John's chin suddenly tilted upwards. 'It's always someone else going with you,' he said to Doug.

'John . . .' Doug began.

'No, fine,' his son continued. 'That's OK. I'll show you.' He turned on his heel and walked out of the room.

'John!' Catherine called.

'Doug, go after him,' Jo begged.

'I will not,' he said.

Jo pulled on his arm. 'Go after him right now. Bring him back.'

'To say what?'

'It's what he's dreamed of,' Catherine said.

Jo looked at her. 'I know. Doug told the TV people he wanted John in on this. Right from the beginning. His name's on the project.'

Catherine frowned briefly. 'Maybe . . .'

They all waited. 'Maybe what?' Doug prompted.

Catherine shook her head.

'He doesn't want to do it with me,' Doug said. 'Is that it? He wants to best me in some way.'

Jo stepped up close to him. She put her hand on his arm. 'Doug,' she said, 'go and find him. We need to sort this out. Now. Please.'

Doug looked shaken, hurt. He patted Jo's shoulder, almost absentmindedly. 'Let's get married,' he said. 'If he can't swallow down this envy, that's his problem.'

Jo's expression hardened. 'We are not getting married without your son as your witness,' she said firmly.

He stared at her. 'But we'll be late for our own wedding!'

'Fine,' she told him. 'So you'd better start now.' She kissed him, softly, on the mouth. 'Time's wasting,' she said.

He went out of the door, with a single backward glance.

They followed him into the snowy street. John was nowhere to be seen. Doug jogged to the end of the pavement, slipping a little on the icy slush under his feet.

The three women made their way in his direction.

'There he is,' Gina said.

Doug had already seen his son on the other side of the street. He ran across the road, dodging a van to reach him.

They talked a moment. Doug caught hold of John's arm. John looked hard at his father, listened, then wrenched away. Doug tried to grasp his son's hand. Misinterpreting the gesture, John pulled away, oblivious to the fact that he was now standing in the road. Doug's fingers glanced off his son's arms, trying to draw him back out of harm's way.

'Doug!' Jo shouted.

Doug turned to look at her.

The lorry was coming down the hill quite soundlessly. Jo registered the massive tyres turning without purchase over the ice, and the back wheels moving out, pulling the vehicle sideways on. There was a screech of brakes from vehicles on the other side of the road who saw the obstacle rushing towards them. Fourteen tons of container bounced against the kerb, mounted the pavement and smashed against some traffic lights.

It won't hit them, Jo thought.

Doug pulled John towards the pavement where the women were standing. Relief was in his look.

But none of them saw the car.

Coming full pelt along Chesterton Lane, it was driven by a boy who had passed his test only five months before. The lad had never driven in snow; his assessment of the scene ahead of him was misjudged. He actually put his foot down to overtake a stalled car in the centre of the road, and only saw the lorry as he rounded the car.

He didn't see Doug and John until it was too late.

GINA STOOD in the hospital corridor and watched the afternoon light fade. It was three o'clock. The snow had stopped at midday.

Hearing a noise behind her, she turned round to see Jo emerging from the Ladies. She looked ashen. 'Are they ready?' Jo asked.

'Yes,' Gina said. She took her friend's arm.

It was only a few yards away, but it seemed a very long distance to the chapel.

Doug's body lay on a white-sheeted trolley by a small altar. Even from where she stood, Gina could see there was no mark on his face. On either side of him were two great bouquets of flowers.

'I can't,' Jo said.

John was sitting with Catherine on the second row of seats. Hearing Jo's voice, he stood up and faced her.

The bruise over his right eye was turning black. A deep scratch ran the length of his face. In the last moment, Doug had spun him out of the line of the speeding car. John had been unconscious for five minutes, waking to hear the sound of the ambulance siren, and to see Jo on her knees, trying to wake his father.

Jo stared at the boy in front of her. Beside John, Catherine was pale, her eyes reddened, her arms crossed tightly across her chest.

Jo walked towards him, and hesitated.

'I'm sorry,' John said.

'You killed him,' she said. 'You killed him with your jealousy.'

John reeled back.

'I'll never forgive you,' Jo said. 'Do you understand?'

Gina turned Jo away, pulled her into her own body, held her.

John walked away, down the echoing aisle. Catherine ran after him. 'Let me come with you,' she said.

He stared at her. Tears were in his eyes. 'She's right!' he cried.

'No, John, she didn't mean it . . .'

He pulled savagely away from her. 'Well, I do,' he whispered. 'Keep away from me.' He opened the door and they heard his footsteps, walking then running.

Jo slumped against Gina's shoulder, and they edged together towards the chairs, where Gina sat her friend down.

'It's all right,' Gina said. 'It's OK.'

Jo looked at her slowly. 'It's not all right,' she said.

'No,' Gina said. 'I didn't mean . . . God, Jo, I don't know what I mean.'

Jo's gaze trailed away to the snow beyond the glass. 'It's the other thing,' Jo said quietly. A ghostly smile came to her face.

'What other thing?' Gina asked.

'It's not all right, because I'm going to have his baby.'

THE BEAR HAD SPENT a long time trying to find the right place. She was looking for fine and hard-packed snow. When she finally came upon a bowl-shaped slope, she began to dig, progressing quickly through the drift with her massive, raking claws, until she had made a narrow doorway. She worked upwards, making a rounded chamber about eight feet long and six feet wide.

This would be her home through the winter, the place where she would give birth. Inside, the temperature was pleasant, 40 degrees warmer than the tundra outside. She scuffed the den floor until she was comfortable, then lay down to sleep.

The faultless machinery of her body ticked slowly as, week after week, she lay isolated from the world. Her temperature and heartbeat were lower than normal, and she passed into the suspended animation of hibernation, neither eating nor drinking, while her fat was metabolised. In this dreamlike state, her cub grew inside her.

He was born in December, a tiny scrap of life. As a male polar bear his bodyweight ought to rise to between 1,200 and 1,500 pounds. His kind were the largest carnivores on earth. And yet, at birth he weighed just over a pound. He was blind and deaf, his body barely covered in thin wool. Following instinct, he suckled his mother's milk, luxuriously rich at 31 per cent butterfat and 12 per cent protein.

Outside, the sky flickered with the spectres of the aurora borealis. But the mother and cub saw nothing of the flames and mists that billowed across the heavens. The mother bear wrapped her cub in her embrace, surrendering to sleep.

When four months had gone by, the mother roused herself to dig a tunnel to the world. It was April and her cub had grown to the size of a small dog, and was lively and inquisitive.

At first, the light blinded him. He waited at the entrance while his mother, still drowsy and moving in slow motion, walked away from the den and began to scrape the snow from the ground. When she found the frozen mosses and algae, she ate them ravenously.

But, for a while, food was not her priority. She remained near the den, watching her cub's tentative explorations. He played in the newly found expanse stretching out in front of him, but eventually he returned to his mother's side. She was his only protection under the ice-white sky.

PART 2: JUNE 2000
CHAPTER 1

The sun was shining into Jo's bedroom. She woke suddenly and looked at the clock. It was 6.00am. She pulled on her dressing gown and went out along the landing and into the room that now belonged to her son.

Sam was fast asleep, the blankets in a heap around him, his blue teddy bear clutched in his fist. She reached out and gently stroked his forehead and hair.

After a moment, Jo went downstairs to the kitchen, where she made herself tea. With the hot cup in her hands, she stepped outside into the garden. As always, in these first few, silent moments of the day, she stood still, closing her eyes, letting herself drift.

When she and Doug had first moved here, the garden had been the bleakest square of untended grey grass. In December it had disappeared under snow that froze England for six weeks. But she recalled vividly the first day that she had walked out into it, a March morning. The snow had gone, and the grass was growing. She had suddenly realised that the malnourished-looking tree in the corner was actually a lilac and the twisted net of vines on the wall was a clematis.

She came back to life with the garden. It was a long, slow journey.

When Sam was born in June of that year, she had taken him out onto the lawn when she came home, and had sat with him in her arms in the shade of the lilac. By then, the clematis had already flowered and was a sheaf of green leaves. Oblivious to Gina's anxious fussing—rearranging of chairs and parasol—she had lowered her face into Sam's body, inhaling the newly bathed scent of him and feeling the sunlight on her neck and back, its tender warmth. She had felt flooded with feeling—a feeling that there was some sort of connection, some sort of thread that passed out from them both into the greater world. It had been like a hand brushing her hair, a name whispered in her ear.

She opened her eyes now to the brightening day. She finished her tea, and walked back into the house, up the stairs to Sam's bedroom.

He was lying awake now, staring into space.

She knelt down. 'Hey, soldier,' she murmured, and stroked his face. 'We've got your party to organise. Wake up.'

A smile transformed his face. His birthday had been several days before, but the party was today, Sunday.

'Come on, Sam,' Jo said. She held out her arms. 'Breakfast.'

He turned away from her, shoving a piece of Duplo in his mouth. She pulled on his T-shirt. And stopped. 'Hey,' she murmured, 'what's this?' The bruise at the base of his spine was large and odd-looking. 'What did you do?' she asked him. 'Does it hurt?'

Sam wriggled away.

Still frowning a little, she managed to grab and lift him, taking his well-padded weight against her as she stood up. She pressed her lips to his neck and blew a raspberry. Squealing with delight, he looked at her. Doug's smile. Doug's eyes.

'Hungry?' she asked him.

'Yeay,' he told her.

She grinned, hoisting him onto one hip. 'Nothing much wrong with you, is there?' she said.

BY ELEVEN O'CLOCK she was standing in the kitchen, which was completely cluttered with pans, dishes and mixing bowls. When the doorbell rang, she ran along the hall, licking chocolate mixture from her fingers.

Catherine was on the doorstep.

'You came,' Jo said, hugging her. 'Oh, thank you.'

As Catherine took off her coat, Jo poured her coffee.

'Where's Sam?' Catherine asked.

'Asleep on the couch,' Jo told her. She sat opposite Catherine, and smiled at her over the rim of her cup.

After Doug had died, Jo hadn't seen John's girlfriend for six months. The first two Jo had spent with Gina in London. She had been afraid to go home, back to the Lincoln Street house. Instead she had thrown herself into work with a feverishness that had worried her friend. Gina knew that Jo barely slept, and so it had been hardly any surprise when she had woken up one morning to find Jo crouched on the floor of her room, weeping helplessly. Having tried to run herself into the ground to avoid her grief, she had finally given in to it.

There had followed a week of utter despair. Gina nursed her through it. Jo barely ate, but she slept fourteen hours a day. Afterwards, she had emerged looking like a battle survivor, pale, fragile and painfully thin, but with a cold clarity back in her face.

In March, Jo went back to Cambridge. And early in the spring she had tried to contact both John and Catherine. She met a dead end in both cases. John had moved from his flat, leaving no forwarding address. Frustrated, Jo had written to John care of Franklin House. She wanted to repair the gulf between them. But her letter had been returned to her. Catherine, too, had moved from her student hall of residence.

But one morning in May, in a bookshop in the city centre, she came across Catherine sitting in the coffee shop.

For a second Jo was transfixed. Catherine was as lovely as ever, her thick black hair pulled upwards in a pleat. She had a book open in her lap, and a pile of others stacked by her feet. Then Catherine glanced up.

'Hello,' Jo said, coffee cup in hand.

'Hello,' Catherine responded.

They stared at each other. For a moment, Catherine's eyes strayed to Jo's stomach. 'Do you need a hand?' she asked.

'No. Thanks. I'm fine,' Jo told her. 'Am I disturbing you?'

Catherine shook her head. She cleared the pile of books out of Jo's way.

'You're taking your finals,' Jo said, once she had got herself seated.

'Yes,' Catherine replied. 'I come here to get some peace.'

Jo stirred her coffee, embarrassed. She didn't quite know what to say. 'I tried to contact you,' she said, finally. 'They told me you'd moved.'

'I got a cheaper room, with a girlfriend,' Catherine said. 'I tried to phone you. Someone said you'd gone to London.'

'I did,' Jo told her. 'For a while.'

They gazed at each other.

'Do you know where John is?' Jo asked.

Catherine's eyes suddenly filled with tears.

'Oh,' Jo said, 'I'm so sorry. If only you knew how sorry I am. I've tried to reach him.'

Catherine waved her hand. 'It's not your fault. He's not at home. He disappeared.'

Jo stared at her aghast.

'He stayed with his mother after the funeral,' Catherine said. 'But in the New Year, he left.'

'Oh my God,' Jo said. 'I've done this with what I said to him.'

Catherine leaned forward, reaching for Jo's hand. 'No,' she said adamantly. 'I really don't think that.'

Jo gazed at her. 'Alicia thinks it,' she murmured. 'She blames me.'

'Alicia is very bitter,' Catherine said. 'She is the kind of person who looks for someone to blame.'

'And she's found me,' Jo said. 'Not just for John but for Doug's death, because he was with me. Marrying me.'

Catherine bit her lip. 'I sometimes think she drove John away,' she continued. 'Then I think, it's not just Alicia . . . it's not just what you said . . . He is just lost.'

'Has he written to you?' Jo prompted.

'No,' Catherine said. 'I've heard nothing at all.'

'I'm so sorry,' Jo said.

At last Catherine raised her head. 'I thought you must still be in London. Maybe with Gina?'

'Yes, I was,' Jo told her. 'But I wanted Doug's child to be born here, in the place he had chosen.'

Catherine nodded. 'There is some happiness to come for you, Jo.'

Jo looked down. 'I don't know what kind of mother I'll make. I don't know much about babies.'

Catherine gazed back at her with her smile of infinite patience. 'I can help you, Jo. If you would like,' she replied. 'I have a research place, here in Cambridge, for two years.'

'Well.' Jo didn't like to impose. 'Maybe baby-sitting sometimes.'

Catherine placed her hand, very gently and fleetingly, on Jo's stomach. 'I mean *help*,' she said. 'For Doug.'

In that moment their alliance was forged.

THE PARTY BEGAN at three, but, long before that, Gina arrived. She held out her arms to Jo and hugged her.

'You're looking fantastic,' Jo said.

'And you're looking thin,' Gina said. Her husband of almost one year, Mike, was standing beside her on the pavement.

The sight of Mike always made Jo want to laugh. It was his size: at six foot six and seventeen stone, most of that muscle, Mike was your archetypal rugby player, and *The Courier*'s sports correspondent. They had been married last September, in a wonderful, joyful celebration, where the bride smiled fit to burst through the whole ceremony, and the groom shed several tears. When Jo had come home that night, she found that a little of Gina's bliss had rubbed off on her, and she went to bed smiling, remembering with pleasure what love could be like.

She watched Mike now as he stepped over the threshold. He almost filled the narrow hallway as he kissed Jo's cheek enthusiastically. 'How are you?' he asked.

'I'm good.' She stopped. 'What in heaven's name is *that*?'

He was pulling a parcel behind him, an enormous triangle shape, wrapped in yellow paper. Before he could reply, Sam appeared at the back door. 'Sam!' Gina called. 'Come and rip something up!'

She swept Sam up in her arms and kissed him.

'Take it into the garden,' Jo suggested.

They went out onto the lawn, where Sam tore the paper from the present. It was a trailer with a giant pivoting arm for his tractor.

'You can hook stuff up,' Mike said.

'Mike, it's great. Thanks so much,' Jo said.

Sam was concentrating on piling his toy cars into the back when the doorbell rang.

'I'll get it,' Catherine said.

The garden filled as the other guests arrived. Jo had invited the mothers from her antenatal classes. Even Eve, the health visitor, was there. Soon, the grass was packed with little bodies and strewn toys.

'How are you doing?' Gina asked Jo, in a quieter moment. They watched Sam balancing bricks on his tractor seat.

'Can't complain,' Jo told her.

It was their usual coded conversation about money. Gina worried that Jo had none. Jo reassured her that work was flowing. Gina knew that meant Jo worked all hours, fitting it around childminders.

After Doug's death they had found that his financial affairs were in a mess. In the midst of the hassle of buying the house only six weeks before, the solicitor told Jo he had advised Doug to redraw his will, which was ten years old and left everything to Alicia. Doug had promised to do so—in fact, he had written out a draft document at home that made it clear that Jo was the new beneficiary. But it had never been signed.

Alicia had laid claim to half of the Lincoln Street house—the half in Doug's name—and all his savings. Jo had been too shocked to take it in. It was Gina who had waded in on her behalf, hiring a firm of solicitors to see Alicia off.

But Alicia had not been ready to be seen off. She had dug in her heels, citing John's precedence over any offspring that Jo might produce. At the end of eleven months, she had graciously accepted Franklin House and Doug's savings. Jo was awarded the whole of the Lincoln Street house. *Finito*.

Gina looked at Jo now: her friend was leaning her head on the garden wall, shading her eyes against the sun, listening to Catherine and Mike's conversation alongside her.

Then there was a sudden scream. Sam, who had been balancing in the back of the new trailer, had toppled out of it.

'Oh my God,' Jo breathed. 'Sam!'

She dashed across the grass. Sam was lying crookedly, one leg still on the trailer side, the rest of him on the grass. He looked up at Jo with an expression of surprise, then began to cry.

One of the mothers who had been sitting close by had run up, too. 'He hit his head on the tractor,' she said.

'Sam,' Jo cried. She knelt down and picked him up. 'It's OK,' she murmured. 'It's all right now.' She pushed his hair back from his forehead and saw a small cut above his eyebrow.

'Bring him into the house,' Eve said, appearing at her side.

A little procession of people went in, Sam and Jo, Catherine, Eve, Gina and Mike, and sat down. Catherine brought a box of antiseptic wipes. Jo wiped Sam's forehead.

Eve, meanwhile, was looking him over. 'No broken bones,' she said. 'He's fine. Let him rest a second, get his breath back.'

Gina brought a feeder cup of orange juice. Sam grabbed it and drank greedily.

'Maybe a little quiet,' Eve said. 'Five minutes' peace.'

Gina took the hint. 'I'll make some coffee,' she said. She pulled at Mike's arm.

When the door was closed, Jo sat back. Sam wriggled a little in her lap. Then, bored, he turned over onto his stomach, slipped down onto the floor, and bumped his way slowly on his bottom, as if tired, over to the window.

Jo looked over at Eve, smiling. The other woman's expression halted her in her tracks.

'Jo,' Eve said quietly, 'how long has Sam had those bruises?'

IT WAS ALMOST TWO YEARS since *Erebus* and *Terror* had left Beechey Island. They would never float in water again. They were ice, part of an endless white landscape.

Gus had asked one of the Royal Marines, Mr Daly, what the name *Erebus* meant.

'It's a name for our predicament, to be sure,' Daly said. '*Erebus* means darkness, boy. The place between heaven and hell.'

It was March now, 1848, the year that Gus would be fifteen. He had grown out of his clothes. For a while, he wore a pair of trousers that one of the sailmakers had made for him: too long and too wide. He had been a figure of fun, but he did not really mind. No, it was not the trousers that bothered him, but the jacket. It seemed to him that his arms were too long for the rest of his body. He felt monstrous. His knees ached and felt huge; his feet were splayed.

There were other things wrong, too. Everyone had something wrong. Some of the men had the first signs of scurvy—bleeds under the skin, and their teeth affected. The surgeons prescribed lemon juice, sweetened with sugar.

With a few of the men the problem was not physical illness so much as the dark, the winter. It had shocked Gus to see that the prospect of another winter really disturbed a handful of the sailors. Two of the men on *Terror* had run away from the ship, into a howling blizzard. The temperature was 30 degrees below zero.

They found them two days later, about half a mile from the ship. One lay on his front, curled, defending his face with his hand. The other lay on his back, his arms raised in the air, his knees drawn up. They were frozen solid; and they buried them where they lay.

It had been in May of last year that Franklin had ordered a search party to go out to King William to find the passage that would take them home. He named Lieutenant Gore and Mr des Voeux, and six other men from *Erebus*.

Every man's heart rested with that team. Mr Gore's task was to find a little channel somewhere out there in the endless white monotony. A small stretch of clear water, that's all they wanted. A little blue water. A fresh current. A chance.

The team left the ships on May 24, 1847. Gus watched them go. He would have liked to be with them, the handpicked few who were loaded down with two sledges packed with calico tents and poles, blanket sleeping-bags, food, cans of spirit fuel, guns, powder and shot. Of course, Franklin had chosen the toughest of the crew, the biggest. Gus knew he was too thin to pull a sledge for long in such conditions.

The crew on *Terror* saw the men make the first climb of many; slithering back as often as they lurched forward; they saw the little black dots that were their comrades ascend an ice wall. It took an hour before they vanished over the other side.

They waited for them as patiently as they could. 'They'll not cover more than two miles a day,' it was said. Gus reckoned on his fingers that that meant they would be gone twenty days. Perhaps a month. A month would bring them to June. Surely, in June, there would be some little sign of the ice cracking.

On June 10—Gore had been gone fifteen days—word came from *Erebus* that Franklin was not well. The men were not too concerned because ever since the apoplexy attack Franklin had rarely been seen on deck. He would come up for the religious services, but he was not the man he had been eighteen months before. One hand would tremble sometimes; once, Franklin took a long time ascending the steps.

His stewards rallied round him like housemaids. They served him his four-course meals twice a day; they gave him hot water and soap to wash, and kept his cabin warm. And so, when he first fell ill, everyone thought it was a passing infection that would clear.

If the crew could have seen what was happening in Franklin's quarters, they would have been less confident.

The captain had dined as usual on the night of June 9. He had been served soup, meat with vegetables, raisins, and a little cheese. Of course, the meat was tremendously salty, and the potatoes bland, but it was a full meal. Franklin had consumed everything, had a glass of Scotch ale, and retired to his bed.

Early in the morning, Franklin called the surgeons. He told Stephen Stanley and Harry Goodsir that he had stomach cramps, and they administered dogwood bitters. Half an hour later, Franklin took brandy, and all was quiet for the morning.

Yet that night, Franklin complained that he could not feel one side of his face. Opium was given, to help him sleep.

Then, during the night all hell broke loose. On *Terror*, the first that was known of it was that Crozier was called to *Erebus*. It was three in the morning. At four, Mr Macdonald was sent for, and John Diggle, the ship's cook.

Then, at five in the morning, Franklin sat upright in his bunk, with one hand fisted against his chest. And he died like that, without any sound. It was over in a matter of seconds.

At first no one knew what to do. The deaths of Torrington and the others, while a blow, had not been a shock. But no senior officer had ever died on an Arctic expedition. These were men raised in comfort and kept apart from their working-class fellows. Their lives were so different from those of the men—they were so protected from the ravages of temperature, exhaustion and diet that the crew underwent.

It was decided to bury Franklin that day, out on the ice.

As the officers gathered in the Great Cabin of *Erebus* afterwards, the controversy over what had killed their commander raged.

'It is something in the cans,' Crozier said softly.

'But what? Sir John died of heart failure,' Fitzjames said. And he looked at Stephen Stanley.

Stanley, the senior surgeon of *Erebus*, had trained at the Royal College of Surgeons, and there was little he had not seen. But, for all his experience, Stanley had not seen a case like Franklin's. He had dimly heard of something like it, however. 'Sir John did die of heart failure,' he agreed. 'Of a congestion of the heart already present from his first attack last year . . .'

'But?' Crozier prompted. They had all heard the hesitation in Stanley's voice.

'But the intestinal cramping and the paralysis . . .'

'Botulism,' Goodsir said quietly.

Stanley nodded his agreement.

'Botulism?' Crozier repeated. 'What is that?'

'It is a fast-acting poison, and they say it is caused by eating preserved meat. No one knows how it can be prevented,' Stanley said.

'But all the food is boiled,' Fitzjames commented.

'What did Sir John last eat?' Crozier asked.

The officers' cook, Richard Wall, was brought in. He was flushed as he stood in front of them.

'I washed everything,' he said, when questioned. 'My stoves are clean, sir. You may examine them.'

'What did Sir John eat two nights ago?' Crozier prompted.

'The officers ate roasted beef from the tins. But Sir John ate pork.'

'He ate a different meat from the rest?' Crozier asked.

'Yes, sir. He expressed a wish for pork.'

'And the pork was boiled, the same as the beef?' Crozier said.

'Yes, sir . . .'

'All right, Wall,' Crozier said. The man was dismissed.

Inside the Great Cabin, Crozier rubbed his eyes with one hand. 'Is it your opinion, Mr Stanley,' he asked, 'that this disease could be present in the tins of pork?'

'I don't know, sir,' he said.

Abruptly, Crozier stood up. Every man there looked at him: an Irishman whose bearing was not that of an officer such as Fitzjames, but who now was promoted to lead them all.

'No man is to eat any more of the pork until every tin has been examined for damage,' Crozier said. 'We will continue to eat the beef.' He drew his coat around him.

The officers withdrew.

Crozier watched them go; then, left alone in the cabin, he paced. He could not rid himself of the idea that something else was wrong with the tins. When he looked at the crew, he could not help thinking that they seemed too pallid, too irritable, too easily tired.

When a man fell very ill, as Torrington had done, and they gave him officers' rations from Goldner's tins, he seemed to get worse, not better. And Crozier had noticed something else. Men like himself, who did not always relish meat and preferred the pickled fish or vegetables, seemed to be much better, in spirit, than their colleagues.

Why should that be? He could not shake the fear that some invisible enemy was among them, weakening them by degrees.

His fingertips trailed along his books. Shakespeare's sonnets. Spenser's *Faerie Queene*. Tennyson and Wordsworth. He had been thinking of Sophia, Franklin's niece, all day. He had been thinking of that canister, and his message. 'And the stately ships go on.' What had possessed him to do such a thing? It was not a pretty poem. It was full of despair.

But it had been perhaps a gentlemanly thing to write that message. If the canister was picked up, and returned to Lady Jane Franklin, and her niece read the inscription, Sophia would realise he was speaking of her. He had said the same line to her, half in humour, on the day that she had refused him. 'Well,' he had said, 'my stately ship shall go on, Sophia. I shall be a lone sailor.'

He had pressed his case too fast, he knew. If he had waited, perhaps another year, she might have accepted him. He should not have written the line. She would be angry with him for that, when he returned.

As he held the volume of Tennyson in his hand, there was a knock at the door. Surprised, he turned round. It was Stanley.

'What is it?' he asked.

Stanley came in and closed the door behind him. 'I am thinking of Lieutenant Gore,' he said, his face grim. 'What, of Goldner's provisions, did Lieutenant Gore take with him?'

IT WAS JUNE 22 when Gore's party returned. They had marched to the coast of King William Land, a distance of four miles from the ships. It had taken four days. Gore had left a note, which gave the position of the ships, in a stone cairn on May 28. He had put it in a canister and secured it with solder.

After leaving the note at the cairn, Gore had marched south for twelve miles and reached the south side of Back Bay. He saw that Victoria Strait did indeed continue to the west, as Franklin had said, and that, if the ice melted, there was a wide way forward.

On June 11, the very day that Franklin had died, the party turned back for the ships, and by way of celebration they cooked themselves a meal, opening the second case of Goldner's tins.

Lieutenant Gore died three days later, on June 14.

When Crozier met the returning men out on the ice, Gore's body and those of two others were being pulled behind the survivors on a second sledge.

EARLY ON TUESDAY morning Jo saw her doctor. She had been there only the day before, on Eve's insistence, for a blood sample to be taken from Sam. 'It's a precaution, that's all,' Eve had told her.

As she drove into the car park, Sam was grizzling. She got him out of the car and hoisted him onto her shoulder. 'Be good now,' she whispered. 'Show Dr Jowett what a good boy you can be.'

When she went into his office Dr Jowett smiled and stood up. He indicated the chair to one side of the desk. Jo sat down, with Sam cradled in her lap.

'How has Sam been?' Jowett asked.

'Fine,' Jo said. It was a reflex action, a defence. 'Well,' she relented, 'not exactly fine. All the usual baby things.'

Jowett glanced at his notes. 'We had a chest infection a couple of months ago,' he said. 'An ear infection . . .'

'The usual baby things,' she repeated.

'Right,' he said.

She stared at his profiled face. Suddenly she saw a pulse beating in his throat. He's afraid, she thought. He's afraid to tell me.

'What is it?' she asked.

'Jo,' he said, 'I'm afraid that Sam is a sick little boy.'

All she could think of, at that moment, was that she had been right. 'Is it the blood test?'

'Yes.' Jowett shuffled Sam's notes. 'He has a deficiency in his blood. A low platelet count. Low red count, too.'

Instinctively, she tightened her grip on Sam. 'What does that mean?'

'Well,' Jowett said, 'it means that the body is fighting something. It might be a viral infection, a disorder of the immune system, a dozen things. Whenever we have a serious illness, our body fights back. It has to produce the right kind of blood. At the moment, Sam's blood isn't doing that.'

'And did that cause the bruising?' she asked.

'Perhaps. We need to do more tests, a full blood count and a blood film report, and a chromosome analysis.'

She shook her head. 'Just for a bruise . . .'

'You need to take Sam to the hospital,' Jowett was saying. 'I've made an appointment for you this morning.'

She tried to concentrate. 'Now?' she asked.

'Yes. Straight away. You go to the haematology department.' He handed her a piece of paper. On it he had written the address of the department, the road and gate number she should use.

She looked at the paper. 'Straight away,' she repeated.

'Yes.'

She stood up in a daze. 'Low blood count,' she said. 'That's what you have when you get leukaemia.'

Jowett got up and walked towards her, put his hand on her shoulder. 'It might be one of several things, not necessarily that.'

It was as if the ground had just dropped out from under her. 'He's not that sick,' she said. 'He's OK, really.'

'Good,' he replied. 'Then we'll prove it today.'

As Jo LEANED HER HEAD against the glass of the hospital window and looked out, she wondered if the day would ever really end. It had lasted centuries already.

As soon as she had come into the ward with Sam, he had been hooked up to a drip and given a blood transfusion. She had held on to his hand and soothed him. He cried and scratched at the needle in his arm, flung his head from side to side.

Halfway through the morning, they had sedated Sam, and he had slept, a frown on his face.

'Mr Elliott will see you this afternoon,' the ward sister told her, at about one o'clock. 'He's the consultant.' She patted Jo's shoulder. 'He's very good with the children.'

I hope he's very good with the parents, Jo thought.

They took Sam's details. His date of birth; what kind of birth it had been; what illnesses he had had; his height, weight. They took more blood. Jo watched the vials fill up. How could a child in trainer pants go through this? It was a sick joke. She screwed her eyes shut, willing tears away. He wouldn't wake and see her crying. Her fingers smoothed through his hair.

The consultant arrived two hours later. He came to stand by the bed where Sam was now awake and sitting up, eating ice cream. 'Hi, Sam,' he said. 'That looks good.'

Sam stared at the stranger, spoon poised halfway to his mouth.

The man smiled and held out his hand to Jo. 'My name is Bill Elliott,' he said.

'Jo Harper.'

'Nurse Stevens would like to sit with Sam, if I could talk to you? We won't be long.' He stood back, indicating the way to a room across the corridor.

Jo kissed Sam's forehead. 'Back in a minute,' she said.

'We'll keep the door open,' Elliott told her. 'He'll be able to see you.'

In his office, Jo glanced at Elliott's desk, and a framed photo standing there, a picture of him with his wife. They had three children, it seemed. Two girls and a little boy of about Sam's age.

'We have the results of some of the tests,' Elliott said. He leaned forward, hands clasped.

'Just tell me,' she said. 'Please.'

'Sam has a problem with his blood,' Elliott said. 'Let me try to explain a bit. Blood is made in the bone marrow. About three million red cells and about a hundred and twenty thousand white cells are produced every single second.'

'I see,' she murmured.

'We have several kinds of blood cell in our bodies,' Elliott told her. 'Lymphocyte T-cells—they control immunity, kill viruses. Lymphocyte B-cells—they make antibodies. Granulocytes—mainly neutrophils—they fight infection and kill bacteria.' He smiled a little. 'Too complicated?' he asked.

'No, no,' she said, frowning. 'Go on.'

He nodded. 'Then there's monocytes,' he continued. 'They work at antibody production, among other things. The red cells carry oxygen, and the platelets help clotting. All these different cells have different life spans. Red cells live for about four months after they leave the marrow, neutrophils for a few hours, platelets for a few days. Because white cells and platelets go so quickly, they can't easily be replaced by transfusion.'

She took a deep breath. 'Has Sam got leukaemia?' she asked.

Elliott waited a beat. 'We need to do more tests,' he said. 'I would like to do a bone-marrow biopsy tomorrow.'

'But has he got leukaemia?'

'No,' Elliott told her. 'I don't think Sam has leukaemia.'

She stared at him for a second, then gave an almighty sigh. 'Oh, thank God,' she said. She covered her face, and felt Elliott's hand on her knee. He was giving her a tissue. She wiped her eyes and face. 'You just don't know how relieved I am. All day today, I thought . . .'

'I think that Sam has got aplastic anaemia,' Elliott said.

She blew her nose. She was half laughing. 'Anaemia,' she said. 'Just anaemia. You can cure that, can't you?'

A spasm crossed Bill Elliott's face, a reflex of real pain. Jo stopped, the tissue pressed to her mouth for a second. Then her hand dropped slowly into her lap. 'You can cure that, can't you?' she repeated.

'Mrs Harper. Look, we need to talk again tomorrow. These tests have to be done several times. We have to make sure. It's been a long day,' he said, and rose to his feet. 'You go home and get some rest. Let Sam get some rest. We need you back here in the morning.'

She remained where she was. 'Aplastic anaemia,' she said. 'Tell me about it. It's not what I thought, is it? Not something simple?'

'Aplastic anaemia,' he said slowly, 'is a serious illness, as serious as leukaemia. It's a life-threatening illness,' he said.

Jo took a long, deep breath. Her heart was thudding, each beat a blow in her chest.

'I'm very sorry,' Elliott said gently.

'Aplastic anaemia. I've never heard of it.'

'It's a rare disease,' he was saying. 'We get maybe a hundred, a hundred and twenty cases a year in the UK. The number is rising. We might find that Sam also has an immune-system problem. Sometimes they go hand in hand.'

She thought. Then, 'When I was pregnant, his father died,' she whispered. 'Could the shock have done something to him?'

'It's unlikely. Don't think that way. It's not your fault.'

'But it must have come from *somewhere*.'

Elliott spread his hands. 'We're just guessing,' he said. 'We suspect things like radiation, or benzene, or antibiotics—'

'Antibiotics?' she repeated, aghast. 'Sam's had several courses, for his chest infections.'

'We just don't know. That might be the cause, it might not. It just suddenly starts. The patient gets tired and pale; they bruise easily. Sam's bruises are very characteristic. They're caused by a low platelet count. People with aplastic anaemia don't produce good blood cells. When we look at the bone marrow under a microscope we see a large number of fat cells instead.'

She put her hands to her face. 'I don't understand,' she said. 'I can see he's tired, he's bruised. But he runs about.'

Elliott nodded. 'I know,' he said. 'But the blood film report is really clear. Aplastic anaemia looks very distinctive on a blood film.'

'But you'll double-check,' Jo said.

'Of course,' he told her. He put his hand, briefly, on hers. 'We'll do an aspiration. Sam will need just five minutes' anaesthetic in the morning. We take a little marrow from his hip.'

Jo shuddered involuntarily.

'The good news,' Elliott added, 'is that, ten years ago, seventy per cent of people with this died. Now, the same percentage lives. We're breaking new ground all the time. New drug protocols . . .'

'Is that what you would do for Sam?' Jo asked. 'Drugs?'

'Sam would be started on immuno-suppressive therapy,' Elliott said. 'He would have ALG—anti-lymphocyte globulin. That knocks out T-cells. And cyclosporin. That inhibits T-cells.'

'And these T-cells could be doing the damage?'

'T-cells will attack the marrow. The body turns on itself. We try to stop it.'

Jo tried desperately to get her head round the idea that Sam's own blood was attacking him. 'What if it doesn't work?'

'Occasionally the marrow regenerates and starts working again of its own accord. We take blood weekly to see how Sam's doing. We give him blood and platelets . . . We try to think positive . . .'

'But what if that doesn't work?' Jo looked Elliott in the eye.

'Think positive,' he repeated kindly.

# CHAPTER 2

That summer of 1847, a camp was established on Cape Felix, on the shore of King William Land, four miles from *Terror*. The shore party was made busy setting traps; collecting magnetic observations; cutting deep fishing holes in the ice.

Gus had begged to be brought here, even though it was less than a week since he had been bled on the ship. The men had told him that bleeding would do him good, but he did not know if they were right.

Early one morning, half the shore party had left the tents and trekked for a mile following the trail of reindeer. Gus was desperate to be with them, to be allowed to fire a rifle. They had not got far, however, before a fog came down, obscuring everything.

They had turned back, but the fog got worse, and Gus, bringing up the rear, had lost his bearings. He could hear the voices of the men ahead—and several times they turned back for him—but he fell and, getting up, had lost them. Their voices seemed to come from all directions and he floundered around before having the sense, finally, to scoop out a hollow in the snow, piling it around him. For a while, he slept. Once, thinking he woke, he looked up through the mist and saw a face—pretty, female. Even with the tattoos that ran from the corners of her mouth to the corners of her eyes, she was lovely.

They found him again at midday. 'Augustus!' cried a man's voice.

He screwed up his eyes against the distant glare of the horizon.

'He's here, sir! Here!'

Four men were approaching. He squinted to see the faces. The first was John Handford, one of the able seamen. He dropped to his knees. 'Where have you been, boy?'

A second face loomed out of the greyness. 'Is it he?'

'Aye, sir. Frozen.'

'Get him up. Carry him,' said Irving, one of the lieutenants.

Handford hauled Gus onto his back.

'There are tracks,' Irving said, peering at the ground. 'That's a human print.' He turned Gus's face towards him. 'Has there been someone here?' he demanded.

'A girl,' Gus breathed.

THERE WERE TWELVE OFFICERS and forty men in the camp on Cape Felix. They had set up three tents. Boarding poles were used as tent poles, while bearskins and blankets lined the interiors. Fireplaces were made near each tent.

Crozier had ordered that Cape Felix should be self-sufficient, and use no tinned goods. He organised fishing parties and took the hardiest men further inland where they trapped foxes and found ptarmigan. 'You'll be better for it,' he had told them. 'The native Indians do not have scurvy. We shall copy them. We shall find how they survive.'

It had been an unwelcome gospel. Most of the men did not want to live as the Esquimaux lived. They were English; they were not savages. They had been taught since childhood that Christian man had a duty to convert the unknowing tribes of the earth to his knowledge. To live as a native was to rescind that understanding. But they could not disobey Crozier.

'When the Esquimaux, who some call Inuit, eat, they do not bother, necessarily, with fire,' he had told them. 'They eat raw venison and salmon.'

They had not believed him. Surely Crozier was becoming mad, they said. And yet the diet did make a change in them. Those men that had been suffering scurvy began to improve.

'You must eat the fish,' Crozier had told Gus. 'Even the entrails, guts, gills and heads. You must eat it all, Gus.'

He spat out the bones, though. He couldn't stomach them.

Gus was brought back to camp by one o'clock. They lit a fire and sat him in front of it, wrapped in bearskins.

Crozier came to see him. 'Now, Augustus,' he said, 'are you mounting an expedition of your own?'

'I fell down,' Gus said. 'I'm sorry, sir. I fell asleep.'

'You are lucky to be alive.'

'I saw a woman,' Gus said. 'She had a tattooed face.'

Crozier paused, frowned. 'What kind of tattoo?'

'In lines like the lines when we smile,' Gus said.

'And was she real?'

'I don't know, sir.'

Crozier remained looking intently at him. 'An Esquimau woman?'

'Yes, sir.'

Crozier nodded. He got to his feet and stayed looking down at the boy for a moment, before walking away.

They raised a cairn that morning. It was set on a small hill, the highest point, Crozier thought, for many miles. It took some time to haul the stones from the surrounding ice-cracked land. Crozier sat upon the largest slabs that formed the base, in order to write the record that would be put inside the cairn.

> June 25, 1847
> HM Ships Erebus and Terror
> Party consisting of twelve Officers and forty men journey from here June 26 south in continuation of the exploration made by Lieutenant Gore.
> Sir John Franklin died on June 11, 1847 and Lieutenant G. Gore on June 14, 1847, the total loss to date two Officers and seven men.
> Ships beset in unseasonably heavy ice at Latitude 70 degrees 05' N, longitude 98 degrees 23'W.

They built up the cairn five feet high, and on the top they placed a bottle, into which Crozier sealed the note. The bottle was covered, then, with further stones.

They turned and went down the hill, and as they drew closer to the tents they saw their first Esquimaux.

Crozier saw Augustus, still sitting by the fire, humped over with the skins, his face peering out at the group of natives walking towards him. One of the seamen rushed out of a tent, carrying a rifle.

'Stop!' Crozier called.

The silence of the camp was profound: suddenly Crozier was acutely aware of the thousands of miles, that stretched in every direction, with this little band of Englishmen at its centre, stranded, cold and ill, with their little cache of skinned fox and plucked birds. By contrast, the band that faced them now were well fed, well clothed, at ease. And curious.

Three men came up to Crozier. At their back, their team of dogs watched, alongside the women and children. The men had cropped dark hair, with a single lock hanging down at each side of the face.

Crozier repeated the few words he knew. '*Kammik-toomee*. We are friends.'

The Esquimaux grinned. They advanced on him, all talking at once. The first man reached out and, with a dark brown finger, tapped Crozier on the chest. He was grinning from ear to ear. He turned round and called to those behind him. Men, women and children all ran forward.

'Mr Irving,' Crozier said, 'go and get the chest in the tent.'

A woman to Crozier's right walked straight past him and into the nearest tent. Two of the crew went after her. Fifteen seconds later she emerged carrying tobacco pouches and some of the timber stored for fuel.

'Watch them,' Crozier said. 'Stand by the tent doors. Don't touch them.'

He opened the box that was brought to him. The Inuit peered down into it, still grinning.

'Needles and knives,' Crozier said. He showed the needles in the flat of his palm.

The men ignored the needles. They touched the knife blade.

Gus sat stock-still. He looked from the strange, weather-beaten faces of the Inuit to Crozier's. The captain's eyes were raw and inflamed. Gus saw, for the first time, how sick the Europeans looked next to these seemingly indestructible natives. The whites of their eyes were brilliantly clear and white.

A package brought from the Esquimaux sledges was unwrapped. The men directly behind Crozier stepped back but Crozier did not move. 'Blubber and seal meat,' he said. 'Frozen salmon.'

The children were running round the camp, pulling up stores and turning them over.

'They have no fear,' Irving said.

'They have nothing to be afraid of,' Crozier said. 'Your rifle is no more than a stick. They have never seen a gun before. They may not have seen a white man before.'

As if to demonstrate that he was right, the women had gathered round Gus. They stroked his face.

'It's her,' Gus called.

'Let her look at you,' Crozier said. 'It's all that she wants to do.'

Gus was enthralled. He had never seen such eyes, almost ink-black. A face framed with sumptuously thick, oily dark hair. The girl was his own age, and she wore a caribou-skin jerkin and trousers with white fur edging. She pushed back the hood to show the tattoos that Gus remembered: extraordinary henna-brown lines in arcs on her cheeks and radiating along her chin.

The packages from the sledges had been hauled to Crozier's feet. There was plenty of meat, all raw. The man who had tapped Crozier's chest deftly took the knife and pushed it into his sleeve. The women took the needles and wood.

The girl had not left Gus's side. After suffering her stroking and prodding his face, he finally got to his feet, stumbling a little. She gripped his arm, pointing at the sledges, laughing.

'Aye,' Gus said, 'but they're not like ours.'

The Esquimau sledges were neat and slim. They were more than twenty feet in length, Gus estimated; and less than two feet wide. Sealskin line was threaded through holes in the runners and passed over the ends of wooden crossbows. They looked lithe and flexible. By sharp contrast, the sledges hauled from the ships were two refurbished lifeboats with runners attached to them, wooden, broad and heavy.

The girl went down to the sledges, looking over her shoulder. There was a lot of gesturing and talking. Something was lifted from the first sledge, cradled in the girl's arms, and brought back to Gus.

They were puppies. Two barely weaned huskies stared back at him. The girl bundled them out of her arms and into his.

'Captain!' he called.

But before Crozier could reply, there was an explosion.

The Esquimaux froze. One of the Marines closest to the first tent was standing with his gun raised in the air, the barrel slightly smoking. In front of him stood an Esquimau woman, her hand still outstretched. She stood, dumbfounded and stock-still.

Irving was first at the Marine's side. 'She tried to take it off me,' the man said.

The woman raised her outstretched hand to her head. The hood of her jerkin was marked with a scorched brown line: she took her hand down and looked at it. Blood fell on the snow.

'She's wounded,' Irving called. 'She is bleeding.'

The women were crowding around. They took down the woman's hood and explored her head, her face, her neck.

The girl next to Gus turned to look at him, eyes wide with fear. Then, turning on her heel, she fled full pelt across the ground, flinging herself onto a sledge. The women followed.

'I told you not to shoot,' Crozier shouted to the Marine.

'I didn't shoot, sir. She pulled the gun.'

They watched, helpless, as the sledges were manned. The dogs bounded forward under the cut of the whip. From the rear of the last sledge, Gus saw the girl stare back at him.

Crozier threw the chest that he still held to the snow. 'God damn it!' he cried.

Not a man moved. No one had heard him utter an oath before.

They stared at him, while the full significance of the gunshot dawned on them. It had been the first time in over two years that the crews had seen other living human beings. It was the first time that they had been given fresh meat for which they had not had to fight with every ounce of their strength. More terrible still was the knowledge that they had frightened away the first sweet human kindness that had been shown to them.

CATHERINE RANG THE DOORBELL of the house in Lincoln Street that night. She had made a detour on the way home to see what the doctor had said about Sam.

The hall light came on and Jo opened the door. Whatever Catherine had been about to say froze in her throat. Jo looked drained, white.

'Jo,' she said, 'what on earth's the matter?'

Jo said nothing. She left the door open and went upstairs without a word. Catherine closed the door and followed.

The bedrooms were on the third floor. As she reached this landing, Catherine saw a light in Sam's room. Jo was sitting on the floor opposite his bed. Sam was asleep, only his head showing above the coverlet.

'What is it?' Catherine repeated. 'What happened?' She sat down beside Jo.

Jo's lip trembled. 'Do you know where John is?' she asked.

Catherine stared at her. 'John? No. I haven't heard from him at all.'

Jo put her head in her hands. 'I've got to find him.' She dissolved into tears.

Catherine reached forward and took her in her arms. 'What happened today?'

Jo didn't reply. Tears coursed silently down her face. The last time Catherine had seen her in this state was at Doug's funeral.

'Come downstairs,' she whispered. 'Talk to me.'

'I can't,' Jo said. 'I can't leave him even for a minute.'

'Can't leave Sam?' Catherine said. 'Why not?'

'He has to be watched all the time,' Jo said. 'He can't be allowed to cry or have a nightmare, or have a tantrum, or fall down. He can't be allowed to cycle down the path. We can't let him try to climb . . .'

Catherine was confused. 'But why not? What did the doctor say?'

Jo put her head in her hands. 'Have you ever heard of aplastic anaemia?' she asked.

'Aplastic what?' Catherine echoed. 'No.'

Jo gave a ghost of a smile. 'No, neither had I,' she replied.

'Aplastic anaemia.' A nightmarish feeling shot through Catherine, a kind of terror. 'The blood.'

'The bone,' Jo said. 'The bone marrow.'

Catherine swallowed. 'And Sam's got this? A failure of the bone marrow?'

'Yes,' Jo said. 'He has to go back to the hospital in the morning,' she continued. 'Oh Christ . . .'

Catherine looked at Sam helplessly, then back at Jo.

'We have to find John,' Jo whispered. 'We must.'

'Why?' Catherine said.

Jo stood up unsteadily. 'Things can be done to stop it, temporarily, if we're lucky. There's blood, and steroids—a thing called cyclosporin. But he's very sick, Catherine.'

Catherine got up too. She couldn't speak at all now.

But Jo had lifted her chin, and Catherine saw a faint glimmer of hope in her expression. 'There's something called stem cells,' Jo said. 'I can donate stem cells, as his mother . . . They take them out of my bloodstream and they freeze them,' she continued. 'To use if nothing else works.' Her face went very pale. 'But I would only be a half match for him. Even if I did all that, the chances of it working are small.'

'Oh, Jo,' Catherine whispered.

Jo gripped Catherine's arm. 'But there's something else,' she said. 'There's a bone-marrow transplant. And the closest matches are siblings. Brothers.'

'But, Jo,' Catherine whispered, 'John is a *half*-brother.'

'It lowers the chances of a match,' Jo said, 'but—'

'There are bone-marrow registers,' Catherine said, suddenly. 'I've seen them on television.'

'The registers can search the world over, and never find a match at all,' Jo said. 'But John and his father and Sam might share the same tissue type. A haplo-type. If it was rare, and if Alicia and I had the same *common* haplo-type . . . then we'd all match, and John would match Sam, and he'd be close enough to save Sam.'

Catherine felt a tightening in the pit of her stomach, a dread. 'Jo,' she said slowly, 'that's an awful lots of *ifs*.'

'Yes,' Jo said. 'I know.'

'How likely is it that John, Doug and Sam share the same tissue type, this—'

'Haplo-type. They might. It's possible.'

'OK,' Catherine said slowly, 'so father and sons share the same rare type. But you and Alicia—'

'That's possible too,' Jo said. 'Ten per cent of the population have the same haplo-type, and if Alicia and I had the same . . .'

'John would be a match for Sam.'

'Yes.'

'Oh, dear God,' Catherine whispered.

'But it's *possible*,' Jo insisted.

Quickly, Catherine put her arms around her, holding her tightly. 'I'm here now,' Catherine said. 'I'll help you, Jo.'

Jo shuddered. 'I know it's a long shot,' she whispered. 'But you see, don't you, Cath? You understand? If there isn't another donor, John would be the only hope that Sam had left.'

IT TOOK ANOTHER HOUR, but Catherine managed to get Jo downstairs after they had found the baby alarm that Jo hadn't used in six months, and plugged it in in Sam's room.

Catherine made Jo sit in the kitchen while she heated soup. Then she sat next to her and held her hand. 'Maybe Alicia knows.'

Suddenly Jo stood up and went to the phone. 'I'll ring her.'

Catherine stopped her. 'She won't speak to you,' she told Jo. 'Let me try.'

The phone rang for some time before Alicia answered.

'Mrs Marshall?'

'Yes?'

'It's Catherine Takkiruq. I am trying to find John.'

'John,' the other woman repeated. 'Why?'

Catherine paused, acutely aware of treading carefully. To mention Jo's name would be a red rag to a bull. 'I wondered how he was.'

'If he hasn't written to you, I shouldn't think he wants you to know,' Alicia replied.

Catherine frowned. 'Has he written to you?' she guessed.

'I can't see it's any of your business,' Alicia said. 'Together with that Harper woman, you drove him away.'

'That's not true!' If anyone had driven John away, it had been Alicia with her endless self-pity. Catherine never once heard Alicia voice any appreciation of John's despair.

'I have nothing more to say to you,' Alicia said now.

Catherine forced herself to keep calm. 'Please, Mrs Marshall. It's very important . . . Do you know where John is?'

But she was listening to a dead line. Catherine handed the phone to Jo to let her hear the disconnection, then hung up.

'Oh God,' Jo groaned. 'How are we going to get through to her? Do you think she knows where John is?'

'If she does,' Catherine said, 'she's never going to tell us.'

THE UNSEASONAL STORM in the strait had swept east, and the bear was walking on the fringe of the sea ice now. Occasionally she would look back, sometimes seeing the cub standing still. This confused her. It was as if he were travelling away from her, focused on some distant object that was invisible to her.

Her instinct was to go south. She wanted to teach him to swim. But it was not good here, not good halfway down the great, swift-running gulf of water. She hated the tremor from under the sea, the old imprint of fear, the trace of some dark memory on the edge of ice and land. She grunted now as she came to the top of the rise, then stopped dead in her tracks.

She saw strips of darker colour on the ridge. They were attached to old bones. There was no flesh left on them, but the stuff that blew about them was dark: strips of wet cloth. She tasted them before throwing them to one side. Not seal. She pushed the material aside and nosed at the objects next to the skeleton. Red-painted tins.

Nothing at all, less than nothing to her. She sat up on her hindquarters, and gave a braying call.

The cub came slowly after her, picking his way over the long-dead human debris.

EARLY THE NEXT DAY Alicia left Cambridge. By six forty-five she was on the outskirts of London, negotiating the M25, and was on the M3, heading south, by half past seven.

By nine she had left the motorway and taken the long road across the tops of the Wiltshire Downs, passing south of Salisbury Plain through Cranborne Chase, and emerging into the Blackmore Vale.

The letter lay beside her on the seat. She looked down at the address. Hermitage Farm, Cerne Magna.

It was almost midday by the time she found it, tucked under a chalk ridge with no sign to point the way, and only a huddle of decaying outbuildings betraying its working past.

No one seemed to be about. Alicia walked through the yard, and, following the sound of voices, towards a stone wall bordering a field. 'Good morning,' she said.

The girl who was sitting on the other side looked over her shoulder. 'Hello.'

'I'm looking for John Marshall. Is he here?'

'Well, he's somewhere about, I suppose.' She stood up and looked Alicia up and down. 'Are you from the university?'

'I'm John's mother,' Alicia said.

The girl's mouth dropped open. 'This way,' she said.

They walked to where half a dozen people were working on the excavation of an Anglo-Saxon settlement.

'Ken,' the girl said, 'someone for John Marshall.'

The man nearest her offered Alicia his hand. 'Ken Bryant.'

'Hello,' Alicia said. 'I'd like to see John.'

Bryant hesitated.

Alicia frowned. 'John *is* here?'

'Yes . . .'

'Do you know he's been missing for more than two years?' she said. She hadn't meant it to sound like an accusation but, nevertheless, it came out that way.

'We don't ask for life histories when they arrive. I'm sorry.' Bryant glanced at the crew behind him. 'Would you like to sit down over here?' he said quietly.

He walked her over to a table and chairs. Brushing the dust from the canvas seats, he settled one on level ground and waited until Alicia was comfortable. Then he sat down next to her. 'You see, John has . . . Well, to say he worried me . . .'

'What's the matter?' she asked. 'Is he ill?'

'No, no,' Bryant responded. 'Not as such.' He gave her a sympathetic look. 'Mrs Marshall,' he said, 'John lives up here, on site. He arrived with a tent, and he lives here. Camps here.'

'Don't you all?' she asked.

'Some do,' he replied. 'But John took himself off, out of our sight. He . . .' Bryant gazed at her. 'He just doesn't talk.' He stopped, and pointed up a slope, in the direction that she might find him, evidently deciding to say nothing more. 'You'll see for yourself.'

JOHN WAS LYING on his back on a stretch of open downland. The sun was hot on his face, and he stared into the sky. He liked to come up here. It was quiet. He would often come here alone, at night. He had got used to it. It wasn't far enough away, of course. But, then, nowhere was far enough away.

'John,' said a voice.

He looked up, shading his eyes.

'Hello,' Alicia said.

He stared at her, then scrambled to his feet.

'Aren't you going to give me a hug?' she asked.

He hung back for a second, but then walked over to her and opened his arms. She returned his embrace, resting her head briefly on his shoulder. 'Oh, John,' she whispered.

He stepped back. She held him at arm's length and looked him over. 'Look at you,' she murmured.

He was filthy, as if he hadn't washed in days. Alicia tried not to show her dismay. She wanted to take him home immediately, but she forced herself to stay calm. 'I think I'll sit down,' she said, and perched on the grass. He sat down alongside her. 'How are you?' she asked.

'Fine.'

She swallowed hard. 'Your letter,' she said. 'I can't . . .' She stopped. She took a handkerchief out of her bag and pointedly wiped her eyes. 'You've broken my heart,' she whispered.

There was no response.

'John,' she said. 'Two years. What did I do to deserve that?'

'I'm sorry,' he mumbled.

'I was worried absolutely sick, John.'

He turned towards her. 'Look,' he said, 'I am going to Canada, so if you've come here to stop me, it's been a wasted journey.'

'Who am I to stop you?' she said. 'As if I could. I'm only your mother. The person who cares most for you in the world.'

He plunged his face into his hands. 'Oh, please, not that,' he muttered. 'If you care that much, you'd be glad I was doing what I wanted. I'm going to Canada to work with Richard Sibley. He's going to Gjoa Haven this summer.'

'And what are you doing for money?' she asked.

'I've got the air fare. I've saved it.'

'I would like to have you at home for a while.'

'No, Mother.'

'I don't know why you went away,' she continued.

'I had to,' he said. He rubbed his hands over his face, then wiped his eyes with the sleeve of his sweatshirt. 'I kept thinking about the accident.' He got to his feet.

'I don't understand,' she said.

He shook his head, grimacing. 'No,' he muttered. 'You don't understand. I tried to tell you. You just wouldn't listen to me.'

'But—'

'It was my fault.'

Alicia stared at him. 'The accident? It was not!'

'Yes, it was. You weren't there. He wouldn't have been in the road at all if it hadn't been for me.'

'And you wouldn't have been there if it hadn't been for her,' she said. 'Jo Harper. Have you thought of that?'

He looked up. 'Where is she?' he asked. 'Do you know?'

'I haven't the faintest idea,' she lied.

'Is Catherine still in Cambridge?'

'John,' Alicia said, 'it's in the past. Everything. Come home,' she said. 'Have you any idea what it's been like for me?'

He stood up and started to walk. 'I've got to work,' he said. 'This was my lunch break.'

She got to her feet and ran after him. 'John,' she called. She grabbed his arm.

Slowly, his entire face flushed. 'You don't understand,' he said. 'You never will. All you think of is yourself. I left Catherine, too. Did you ever think about that? I loved her. I still love her.'

'Then . . .' Alicia wavered. 'Come home. I'm sure we could find her.'

'I can't do that!' he shouted. 'I killed him! Jo was right. I killed him. I saw it in Catherine's face when we went to that chapel.'

'No,' Alicia whispered. 'No, you're wrong.'

'I'm not wrong,' he said. He tore himself out of her grasp. 'I've tried to escape it for two years. Get away, and not think about it. Go to some of the places *he* went to. But he wasn't there. There's only one place on earth that he can be.'

Alicia was aghast. For the first time she saw the depth of her son's pain, and it frightened her as nothing had ever frightened her before.

'Oh, John, darling—'

'Don't *darling* me!' he shouted. 'I can't go back. I can't see people like Peter Bolton, or Catherine. I don't want to see it in their faces.'

'But you won't,' she objected. 'They don't think that you killed anyone, John.'

He stared at her. 'They do,' he said. 'And even if, by some bloody miracle, they didn't, *I* would know. *I would have it in here*,' he said. Tears came to his eyes; they began to fall. Distraught, he covered his face with his arm.

'John,' Alicia murmured, 'please, we'll see someone. A grief counsellor. They would help, I know they would.' She was wringing her hands. 'He was your father, it's right to feel terrible, you wouldn't be human if you didn't—'

He laughed suddenly. A crooked, mirthless grin was on his face. 'Human?' he said. 'I'm not human. I left the human race. I'm out in the cold.'

She felt an awful wrench in her chest. Never had she felt an emotion like it. 'John, dear,' she said. 'That's not true. You're my son. Please come home with me.'

He turned and looked at her. She met his eyes, and saw that she had lost him.

'I have something to do,' he said. 'Something to finish.' He started to walk down the slope. 'Go home, Mother,' he said. 'Go home.'

JO DREAMED the same thing, over and over again. She was on a roller-coaster ride. Gradually, as the car rose up the steep incline, she could see the tops of trees. Then she would see Sam, passing on a parallel track, just out of her reach. At that second, she would plunge down, seeing the world flash past in a riot of colour. She would be thrown forward, out of her seat, into a vast space, to drop with increasing speed until she knew, with absolute certainty, that she would never stop falling.

The ride was almost the same in her waking world. She had no control any more. She wanted to have a day, an hour, to think. She wanted so badly to get off this roller coaster. But there was no time. And there were no choices.

She had come to London, and was staying with Gina. Sam had just finished a course of drugs designed to knock out the lymphocytes in his system, and the T-cells attacking his bone marrow.

He had cried on the first day; his tears wore him out. He had stared at Jo with a blotched, miserable face, his expression full of condemnation. Why are you doing this to me? She wished she could lie on the bed and take it for him. Hook herself up to the machines, the drips. 'Soon be better,' she'd reassured him.

She had hated herself for the lie. How could she know that? How could she possibly even begin to explain it to him?

Every day when she looked at herself in the mirror, she was faintly surprised to see the same old face staring back at her. She found it hard to believe that her pain wouldn't be obvious, like a scar. She almost expected to see something horrible, terrible . . . blood in her eyes, maybe. But she was the same. It was Sam who was changing.

He had to be kept away from sources of infection. He couldn't go to playschool any more. They couldn't take public transport anywhere. No crowds. No parties. No swimming pool. No garden. The heaven-sent patch she had tended for him had become fraught with danger. His diet had altered dramatically, too. He couldn't eat uncooked fruit or vegetables. His meals had to be boiled. No fresh milk. Only variety boxes of cereal that could be opened and consumed in one day. Packaged, boiled, tinned. It was like being on some long voyage where they couldn't get hold of fresh food.

The administration of the drugs had taken a week. The worst of all was the fitting of the Hickman line, a permanent line that went into his chest. The innocuous-looking plastic adapter plug hanging from his chest wall was well done; a glance betrayed little more than the plaster tape holding it in place. But when she saw it as he was brought back from theatre, something washed over Jo. It wasn't fright or revulsion. It was the knowledge that this was unalterable, that the world had turned, and could never turn back again.

They had put him back, gently, into bed, and his eyes opened.

'Hi, Sam,' she'd said, 'how're you doing?'

He had gazed at her, his bottom lip trembling. Then he became aware of the line. His fingers fluttered towards it, at the entry point under his arm. 'It's OK,' she'd tried to reassure him.

He'd stared at her. She saw utter trust in his face. 'Fix,' he'd whispered. 'Mummy, fix.'

Somehow, she'd managed to smile at him, fuss the bedclothes over him, stroke his forehead until mercifully he dozed.

Then she walked to the loo, shut herself in and wept in agony.

The treatment had started with a test dose for an hour. The ward had given her a leaflet about the drugs—like any medication, it listed the side effects as well as its benefits—and she'd shoved it out of sight, because the list of side effects was so long. At four o'clock in the afternoon he'd started receiving the main dose. Eighteen hours a day for five days, and, when the eighteen hours were finished, platelets, blood and antibiotics.

Around the third night or so she'd stopped crying. The tears were someone else's, anyway. They belonged to some gutless crying woman. God, how she hated that woman, that mother who wept when the drugs went into the Hickman. Her heart hurt inside her. Her ribs ached because she often held her breath without knowing it. She just sat, watching him.

But worse was to come, worse than the crying and complaining. Sam became silent, acquiescent, accepting. His eyes followed his mother. He would look at her with a complete faith that she could protect him. That was the worst of all.

AT THE END of the week, Elliott had told her that she needed to go for her stem-cell donation. 'It's a form of insurance,' he'd explained to her, sitting in his office. 'Here's what will happen. We give you a chemical that makes you overproduce stem cells. We harvest them and freeze them. They'll be there if we need them.'

'How?' Jo asked. 'How do you do it?'

'We put you on a machine,' Elliott said. 'The process is called apheresis. It just means separating the blood, your blood, into different components. You sit in a chair with a tube in both arms. It takes about four hours.'

'Oh,' she murmured. 'OK.' Her stomach had turned over.

'Five days beforehand we give you a drug by injection. It's called G-CSF. It's a growth factor. You have five doses over five days.'

'And what happens?' Jo asked. 'How will I feel?'

'Everyone reacts differently,' Elliott said. 'We're making your body mirror the effect of fighting off a virus. So you'll maybe get flu-like symptoms. You might get bone pain. That's a good sign. It means the bone marrow's expanding, making so many stem cells they spill over into the blood. Now's the time to catch those cells while they're circulating round in you.'

Jo considered. She began to see the skill of it all. Taking her own cells out of her, wiping them free of the blood, putting it back. It was so clever, and it was something she could do—she who had felt so helpless standing at Sam's side. She smiled, and looked up.

Elliott relaxed back into his chair. 'Well, hello,' he said.

She raised an eyebrow. 'What?'

'A smile,' he said. 'The first I've seen.'

'I used to do it a lot'—she shrugged—'used to be pretty good at it.'

'Do it some more,' he told her. 'You'll need that skill again.'

SHE WAS SITTING now in University College Hospital, London. Gina was beside her. It was the day of the first stem-cell donation. Next to them stood one of *The Courier*'s photographers. Jo had asked for this favour, and there hadn't been a moment of hesitation on Gina's part. Could *The Courier* run an article on what Jo was doing? Could it print a photograph? Could it say how important it was that Sam find a donor?

'Of course,' Gina had said. 'It's news, isn't it?'

Gina was already seeing the shout line: 'The most desperate rescue of all'. A picture of Jo wired up to apheresis.

'You'll stay with us when you come,' Gina had said.

'It can only be overnight,' Jo told her. 'Cath is with Sam. I have to get back.'

'No problem. See you soon.'

Yet the phone calls hadn't prepared Gina for Jo's appearance when she stepped off the train. Her jacket hung off her shoulders. Her skin was pale. Only the hug was the same: full of defiance.

'Down to fighting weight, I see,' Gina had observed.

Jo had raised a clenched fist. 'You'd better believe it.'

The call came through at eight thirty the next morning. *The Courier* had been on the newsstands for less than three hours.

Gina and Jo were in Gina's office, when Gina picked up the phone. 'Features.' There was a pause. 'I see,' she murmured. 'Yes. Hang on a moment.' Gina put her hand over the receiver. 'Do you know an Anthony Hargreaves?' she asked Jo. 'From HMS *Fox*?'

Jo thought. 'The principal medical officer who treated Doug,' she said. 'Yes, of course.'

Gina smiled. Wordlessly, she handed Jo the receiver.

'Miss Harper? Anthony Hargreaves.'

'Hello,' she said. 'How are you?'

'More to the point, how are you?' he asked. 'I read your piece. I'm so sorry about your son. I just wanted to say . . .' He paused. 'You said in your article how Sam needed a bone-marrow donor.'

'Yes,' she said.

'Well . . . Have you talked to the James Norberry Bone Marrow Trust? They keep a register of people who've offered to donate.'

'No,' she said. 'Should I?'

'Doug and John went on their register,' he said.

Jo sat down on the nearest chair. 'They what?'

'Don't you remember? We had a whole-ship screening. It was a recruitment drive for donors. One of the men on the ship—'

'The little girl on your notice board,' Jo breathed.

'That's right,' he said. 'Chrissie Wainwright. She was the daughter of one of the crew. She had leukaemia.'

'I remember,' Jo murmured.

'Well, Doug was tested, as you know, and he suggested that his son be tested, too,' he told her. 'We managed to get the bloods out with the next flight. They went to the Norberry Trust.'

'He never told me,' Jo said.

'He would have been given a donor ID card. If you can't find it, the Trust would have the records.'

'I'll get in touch with them,' Jo said.

'I don't think they would tell you the names of their donors,' Hargreaves responded, 'but John might be in touch with the Trust. He might have told them where he is now.'

'And they would know,' Jo said, 'if John is a match.'

'Probably,' Hargreaves said.

'Oh God,' Jo breathed.

When she had thanked him and said her goodbyes, she put the phone down and stared at Gina.

'Is it good news?' Gina asked. 'What did he say?'

Jo remained where she was. 'Have you got a phone directory?' she asked, after a second or two.

'Of course,' Gina said. She fished it out of her desk drawer. 'Who do you want to find?'

'The James Norberry Trust.'

Gina flicked through the pages. 'Here it is,' she said. 'Tarrangore Street.'

'I've got to go and see them,' Jo said.

Gina sprang up from her desk. 'Whoa,' she said. 'Hold on. You've got to be at University College Hospital at three.'

'So?' Jo said. 'I've got hours.'

'What are you going there for?' Gina said. 'What is it? A bone-marrow register? Those people don't talk to the public.'

'I'm not the public,' Jo said. 'I'm a patient's mother. I want to know where John is. Hargreaves says they might know.'

'If they know, it's between John and them,' Gina pointed out. 'They're not going to tell you.'

'Yes, they will,' Jo said defiantly. 'They have to. If they've found him and he says no, I can go and see him, wherever he is. I can persuade him. He may be messed up and guilty and lonely and afraid. I can apologise for calling him a killer, for a start.'

'You didn't mean it,' Gina said.

Jo eyed her sadly. 'I did mean it. I meant it from the bottom of my heart. I believed it. But I don't believe it now.'

Gina held her arm gently. 'Why don't you wait?' she said. 'Elliott will tell you soon enough if a donor's been found.'

Jo pulled away from her. 'I can't wait, Gina,' she said, already halfway out the door. 'If there's a fraction of a chance that I could speed this up, I have to do it.'

THE JAMES NORBERRY TRUST was nearly invisible. Jo got out of a taxi to find herself in a busy street, and the trust was nowhere to be seen. She found it at last, a single doorway sandwiched between a video store and a launderette. She pressed the keypad on the wall. 'James Norberry,' said a voice.

'My name is Harper,' Jo replied. 'I need to talk to someone about a donor.'

There was a pause, then the door unlocked.

She made her way up a flight of stairs. At the top, a pair of glass doors led to a reception desk.

The receptionist looked up as Jo walked in. 'Miss Harper. I recognise you from the paper. I've buzzed Mrs Lord. Here she is now.'

Jo turned to see a woman who had come from another office. Small, slight and dark, she held out her hand to Jo. 'Hello. I'm Christine Lord.'

'Jo Harper. I want to talk to you about a donor on your books.'

'OK,' Christine said. Jo followed her to an interview room.

'His name is John Marshall,' Jo began. 'He and his father, Douglas Marshall, came onto the register about three years ago. Are they on your list?'

'I can't tell you that.'

Jo took a deep breath. 'Douglas Marshall died in a road accident,' she said.

'I know that Douglas Marshall died,' Christine said. 'I remember reading about it at the time.'

Jo nodded. 'Well, after his death, his son John moved out of his Cambridge flat. Has he contacted you with some other address?'

Christine was listening, hands clasped on the tabletop. 'Everything we do is between us, the donor and the transplant surgeon,' she said. 'We have to protect identities.'

'This isn't a normal case,' Jo objected.

'With the greatest respect, every case we have is abnormal. Everyone is an emergency.'

Jo felt like screaming that Sam wasn't like anyone else, but, just in time, saw how illogical that was. In this room, Sam was exactly like everyone else.

'If a match comes up, we have contact officers, whose job is to try and find missing names,' Christine said.

Jo leaned forward. 'Is your contact officer looking for John Marshall?' she said. 'Have they found him?'

'I'm sorry, but—'

'Oh, please don't tell me that you can't tell me that!' Jo cried. 'His half-brother is dying. You *can* tell me!'

Christine shook her head. 'I can't tell you, Miss Harper,' she said gently, 'not because I don't want to, but because I'm legally constrained not to.'

Jo put her head in her hands.

'Donors must be protected,' Christine went on. 'They must be sure that no one will ever come knocking at their door demanding they give bone marrow.' She reached behind her to a desk and took out a piece of paper. 'There is something I can offer,' she said. 'If ever John Marshall contacts this office,' she said, 'I could forward a letter to him.'

Jo gazed at the paper. 'You'd do that?'

'I can't guarantee anything,' Christine said. 'But I could keep your letter here. If we ever did get in touch with John Marshall, I could tell him that there was a letter here from you. But I would only pass it on if he specifically asked me to do so.'

'Thank you,' Jo said.

She took half an hour to sit, alone, in the interview room, and compose what she wanted to say to John.

John, please forgive me for the terrible thing I said to you. I'm so very sorry. We badly need your help now. If you can come home, or need help to do so, please get in touch.

She wrote her telephone number and email address on the bottom, sealed the envelope, and went back to reception.

'If you ever hear . . .' Jo said.

'We'll do our best.' Christine put the letter in her pocket.

Jo paused. 'I don't suppose you'll tell me if there are any matches, even if it isn't John?'

'As soon as there are matches we tell the transplant surgeon,' Christine said. 'Even then, the surgeon will know only the donor's identity number, not his name. But I can assure you, whenever we have a positive result, none of us here wastes a moment.'

'OK,' Jo murmured. 'Thanks. Well . . . goodbye.'

'Goodbye, Miss Harper. Good luck.'

Christine Lord listened to Jo's footsteps on the stairs, then she went back into her office and sat down at the computer. That very morning, the James Norberry Trust had received a request for a match for a two-year-old boy. He lived in Cambridge, and he was not responding to treatment. Christine ran through the patient details. At the top of the search request form, a box asked if the search was urgent. *Yes*, the doctor said.

> *Date of birth:* June 11, 1998.
> *Sex:* Male.
> *Race:* Caucasian.
> *Diagnosis:* Severe aplastic anaemia.
> *Name:* Samuel Douglas Marshall.

With practised speed, Christine transferred the serology and DNA details onto the system. When the information was complete, she switched the computer to search mode.

It was an awe-inspiring process. There were over 2 million donors to search worldwide. Each search was focused on exactly the same components: the HLA antigens in the blood. Twenty-four possible antigens had been identified to date and more than 600 million different combinations of HLA antigens were theoretically possible. And through those 600 million the search engines went roaring away, chasing the matches down ever-narrowing tunnels of probability.

It was a miracle that any transplant worked, such were the gigantic odds stacked against it. And yet they did work. And, when they did, they transformed very sick people into well people, and grieving families into joyful ones.

Christine Lord rested her head on her hand and waited.

Six hundred million combinations. Two million donors. One little boy in an isolation unit in Cambridge. Samuel Douglas Marshall needed to share his father's rare haplo-type with his half-brother. Jo Harper needed to share a different haplo-type with John Marshall's mother.

Christine put the chances at 20 million to one.

CHAPTER 3

April 17, 1848. Crozier stood alone on the ice. A hundred yards from the ships, he looked at them with a full heart. His fate had been tied to *Terror* for nine years. He had seen two ice continents in her. He had crossed thousands of miles in her. He knew her better than he knew any man alive. She was his partner, his pride. But no matter how much she meant to him, he had to leave *Terror* now.

He looked down at his hands. It was a mild day, only 10 degrees below freezing, and he had ventured to remove his gloves. He lifted his hands closer to his face. The bruises had even begun on the fleshy mounts of his palms and around his thumbnails. On his knuckles were cuts that were neither cold sores nor injuries, but a curious, creeping disintegration.

The truth was that they were dying. Even the best of them. Even the Marines. Even the ice masters. Even him.

The worst of the scurvy had started last year. No one knew, not even the doctors, exactly what caused it. That it was something to do with diet they knew, and that fresh meat and the daily ration of lemon juice could keep it at bay.

Scurvy was feared, but expected. When a man became tired, when he bled under the skin, his gums became swollen and his teeth loose, sailors recognised it for what it was. Sufferers became breathless at the slightest exertion; mental work—the writing of a journal, the making of calculations—became a mountain to climb. Crozier knew that his own mind wandered. Often, he could hardly form complete sentences.

They still had three months' supply of lemon juice left, but Crozier was sure it had lost whatever qualities it had once had to prevent the disease. It had been frozen and thawed perhaps a dozen times. Maybe the freezing did something to it. He didn't know.

He looked up and saw Fitzjames coming towards him across the ice. Once tall, dark, striking, Fitzjames had been called the handsomest man in the navy. Now he seemed to have shrunk. His shoulders were hunched, his steps sluggish, and as he drew close to Crozier, no man alive could have described his face as handsome. Fitzjames had had pneumonia in the last few weeks. The surgeons claimed they had eradicated it, but Crozier could hear Fitzjames's breathing from yards away—rattling ominously.

'What are the results?' Crozier asked. That morning he had asked Fitzjames to check the remaining supplies.

'Not good,' Fitzjames told him. 'We have ten days of coal for steam.'

'And for cooking?'

'It might last the summer.'

Crozier beat his fist impotently against his hip.

Today was the first calm day in four weeks. For the last month they had been in the grip of one storm after another. No one had got out to set traps. Only a handful of men had managed to cut holes in the ice to catch fish. And so, in the very season when they ought to have used less fuel and less canned food, they had run through their supplies at double rate. They had only ever been equipped for three years. And the three years had finished.

Crozier knew that there was no time to lose. They could not stay on board the ships. Their only hope was the fresh meat that lay to the south of them. They would have to leave, to turn their backs on their security before it became their tomb.

'That's not all,' Fitzjames said. 'It's not the worst.'

Crozier glanced up at him. 'Not all?' he repeated.

'We inspected every last carton of Goldner's supplies,' Fitzjames said. 'There are blown cans in every case.'

They stared at each other.

'Dear God,' Crozier muttered. 'How many have we left?'

'Eighty-two tins of meat and a hundred soup.'

At half rations, that meant they had barely enough food for seven weeks. Seven weeks took them to the end of June. Last year, nothing had moved here in June. Not a single fracture of the ice. They could not afford to take that gamble again. He had to take his men to wherever the ice might thaw. South. It was the only direction. They would go towards the passage that Gore claimed to have seen on his final journey.

He looked at Fitzjames. 'I am sorry, James,' he said.

Fitzjames gazed back at him. He knew the march must begin. But not a flicker of emotion passed over the younger man's face. He had had difficulty negotiating the 100 yards between them and the ships. His face was livid with sores, especially at his mouth. Fitzjames was not fit to walk a mile.

'There is no choice,' he said.

Crozier touched his arm. Together, they walked back across the ice.

GATHERED ON THE DECK of *Erebus* were 105 men. In the past three years they had lost twenty-five of their number, including Franklin. For a moment, Crozier searched out the face of Augustus Peterman. Gus was tall now, wiry, little more than skin and bone. His mother wouldn't recognise him, Crozier thought. The boy was a man.

He let his gaze run over the others. 'When we began this journey,' he told them, 'we did so with every hope of success. That we floundered in the ice I need not tell you; it is you who have known and lived what no other man has, no sailor before you.'

They waited, listening, not a man moving. He supposed they knew what he had to tell them.

'I could not have asked more of you,' Crozier said. 'I salute you, as your country salutes you, for your fortitude.'

Silence. Not even the ice pack shifted.

'We will abandon both ships in the morning,' Crozier said. 'We will load three boats. We will make for the Backs Fish River.'

There was a murmur. Backs Fish River was 210 miles south. They could not haul boats more than a mile or two a day. Even if every man was fit and strong, they would not make the river for at least 150 days.

'Backs Fish River is a tortuous route, I know,' Crozier told them. 'But when we reach it, it will still be summer. There will be no ice on the river, which is at a more southerly latitude. Sir George Back recorded that there were large numbers of deer, musk ox and birds at the river mouth. There we can eat our fill. And I am confident that we will be met on the river by scouts from the Hudson's Bay Company, who will be sure to set out for us if there is no news of us by this spring.'

The murmurs continued: not all of them placed so much faith in Hudson's Bay.

'I'll not lie to you,' Crozier said, leaning forward. 'We are in desperate straits. Our only hope is south, and to go south is certain death for some. Yet to stay here is certain death for us all. If this summer is the same as last, there will be no food here, and no breaking of the ice.'

There was no more murmuring.

'We take three boats,' Crozier said, 'each mounted on oak sledges. We take awnings and sail and weather-cloth and paddles, food and clothing, gunpowder, guns and fuel.' He paused, emotion flooding him, threatening to break the steadiness of his tone.

Each man's thoughts fled to wives or parents, or children. They thought of Easter; in three days' time, both the churches and the alehouses would be full. They thought of spring in England.

Crozier stared southwards, into the ice-blue day. He deliberately did not look at Fitzjames, or any of the officers standing at his side.

'We leave the finest vessels in the world to God's mercy,' he said softly, 'and we commend ourselves to His care.'

AT EIGHT THIRTY the next morning, Catherine was waiting in the hall of the University Exploration Academy, gazing through the glass doors. When Alicia arrived, she stepped forward. 'Mrs Marshall . . .'

Alicia stopped. 'You,' was all she said.

The doors behind them opened. Other people came in.

'Excuse me,' Alicia said. 'I have a trustees' meeting to attend.' She began to walk away.

Catherine ran after her. 'Is John still in this country?' she asked.

Alicia had got to the foot of the stairs. 'Who gave you permission to be in here?' she said.

Catherine searched through her shoulder bag, took out a little wallet and opened it. There was a photograph of Sam inside. She pulled it from the plastic casing and held it out.

Alicia froze. 'Who sent you?' she said.

'I came by myself,' Catherine said. 'Do you know this little boy?'

'The Harper woman,' Alicia said. 'That's who.'

'His name is Samuel Douglas Marshall,' Catherine said. 'He's only two. He's very sick. He has an illness called aplastic anaemia.'

Alicia seemed to flinch.

'He was in the newspapers,' Catherine said. 'Did you see his mother? She was in *The Courier*, an article—'

Alicia's face drained of colour. She snatched at Catherine's elbow and dragged her to one side. 'What makes you think,' she hissed, 'that I would want to see this child's mother?'

'He's very sick,' Catherine repeated.

Alicia's grip tightened. 'I have a son too,' she said. 'And I had a husband. Perhaps you've forgotten that. This child's mother took him away. She accused my son of murdering my husband.'

Catherine blanched and tried to pull her arm away. She pressed Sam's photo to her chest and took a long time to reply. 'People say a lot of things when they are hurt. They regret it afterwards, just as Jo has regretted it,' she said. 'John didn't leave just because of what Jo said. He stayed after the funeral, didn't he? But in the end, he couldn't bear it. And that has nothing to do with you, or me, or Jo. It's to do with John and his father. That's why he went, and all our love can't bring him back until that is resolved, Mrs Marshall.'

For a second, Catherine saw that her words had hit home. Just for the briefest flash, she glimpsed a realisation in Alicia's face.

'Won't you forgive her?' she asked. 'What John carries in his heart is not Jo's fault.' She paused, then added, 'And she is very sorry.'

Alicia raised her eyebrows. 'Oh, is she?' she said sarcastically. 'Well, that makes everything perfectly all right, then.'

'I don't know very much about your husband,' Catherine admitted, 'but I know about your son, Mrs Marshall. I know how much he loved his father.'

'You know nothing at all,' Alicia said, releasing her grip on Catherine.

Catherine's face flushed. 'Did you read the newspaper article?' she asked.

'No.'

Catherine looked at Alicia closely. 'I don't believe you,' she responded. 'I think you read it, but you still don't understand. Sam is very sick.' She held up the photograph.

Alicia's mouth trembled slightly.

'He's a sweet little boy, isn't he?' Catherine said. 'His father's eyes.' She pushed the photo under Alicia's nose. 'Except you can't really see his eyes very well just now. He's taking drugs to try to cut infection. His eyes are swollen,' she said, 'and he cries a lot, but we try not to let him cry too much, because a child with aplastic anaemia mustn't raise his blood pressure. His system's breaking down. He has nothing to fight injuries to himself. Nothing to combat bleeding.' She grabbed Alicia's arm and tried to shake her. 'You understand what I'm saying?' Her voice wavered. 'He's dying, your husband's son. And his mother—this person you call the Harper woman, you know what she's doing right now? She's sitting with her son, trying to make him drink milk. He can only drink one kind of milk, and he doesn't like it, and she's been sitting with him since five o'clock this morning, and he's been sick, vomiting, and the doctor has been to him, and he has had an injection, and now . . .' Catherine gasped for breath. She steadied herself against the wall. 'This . . . *Harper woman*,' she whispered, 'is trying to keep her son alive, and she doesn't know how to do it.'

There was a silence for a moment.

'You think I don't understand that,' Alicia murmured.

Catherine looked at her. 'I'm sorry,' she said, 'but . . .' She pushed the hair back from her face. 'Sam is the only brother that John will ever have,' she said.

The two women stood face to face. A small knot of people had gathered nearby, unsure as to whether they ought to intervene.

'This little boy needs his brother,' Catherine said.

'I don't know where he is,' Alicia said.

Catherine almost screamed in frustration. 'Don't lie to me!'

'I don't know where he is,' Alicia repeated, her voice rising.

Catherine looked down the hall. There, in the cabinets, she could see the Franklin artefacts from King William Island, the sepia image of Crozier. She looked back at Alicia. 'Has he gone to Gjoa Haven?' she asked. 'Is that where we should look?'

Alicia did not respond.

'Gjoa Haven,' Catherine repeated. 'It's a small town in a place called King William Island, in the Arctic.'

Alicia dropped her eyes to the floor.

'Don't you see?' Catherine whispered. 'We are all afraid. We have all lost someone. Please, Mrs Marshall,' she added softly, 'don't let us lose anyone else.'

Alicia turned her back, and walked on up the stairs.

Catherine watched her until she was out of sight, slow tears running down her face.

THE CITY WAS HEAVY with heat. It was Sunday morning, barely eight o'clock. As Bill Elliott walked down Senate House Passage, he thought that he had never known Cambridge this warm in August. It might have been midafternoon: you could feel the humidity and the pressure in the air.

Jo had said to come early. But when he got to the house, the curtains were still drawn on the floors above. He didn't like to knock: he knew what kind of night they might have had, and how precious sleep was. He had turned away and started to walk instead, to kill an hour in the quietest part of the day.

He had seen Jo last week, at the hospital. She was no longer the twenty-something who had paced his office that first day, demanding what the problem was. She was weary now, and the attitude had gone. She had lines around her eyes. She had cut her hair short. The style didn't really suit her. It revealed the nakedness of her eyes, the high cheekbones. 'You must eat,' he'd told her.

'I do,' she'd said. He didn't believe her.

He skirted the entrance to King's College Chapel, glancing up at its ethereal face, a triumph of grace. He wished Jo Harper were alongside him now so that he could stop and show her this product of man's faith.

He went down to the River Cam and stared into the bottom of the muddy water. He thought of Sam, mesmerised by the electric fan they had brought alongside his bed during the last transfusion. Small things could distract the child now; illness and isolation were tiring, draining, confining.

Last month Jo had brought a photograph album into the hospital. She had been trying to distract Sam with it, and when Elliott had come in, she had shown it to him. 'This is Sam and John's father,' she had said, shyly. 'The owner of the rare haplo-type, the awkward cuss.' She'd handed him the pictures with pride. Douglas Marshall on a beach somewhere. Douglas Marshall on an icy shoreline. 'He had a fixation with Franklin,' Jo had said. 'He passed that to his son, too.'

The name had been in the news so much recently, as a result of Jo's *Courier* article, that Elliott knew the story backwards. Jo and Catherine Takkiruq were so sure that John had gone to King William Island that Canadian newspapers had carried Sam's story.

But John hadn't come back.

Elliott had witnessed Jo's savage disappointment. He longed to tell her what he knew—but professional guidelines forbade it. He was not supposed to disclose if a donor had been found, let alone if John was a match. Jo was pursuing John with metaphorical fingers crossed, but she didn't know for sure. No one did, except the Norberry Trust, and himself. And that knowledge weighed heavy.

Elliott turned and went back to Jo's house, arriving at ten minutes to nine. The TV crew had arrived and, as he looked in through the open door, he could see Jo down the hall, Sam on her hip, his head on her shoulder. She glanced round as she heard his footstep.

'Hello, Bill,' she said, smiling. 'You nearly missed our big moment. We decided on the garden,' she said, and gestured towards the back of the house.

The chairs were set on the lawn, under the lilac tree.

'Looks very professional,' he said.

'Yes,' she murmured. 'Hope I don't fluff it.'

He touched her arm as he looked at Sam, who stared at him silently. He ran his finger down the boy's cheek. Jo looked at Elliott, her expression unreadable as she turned and walked into the garden.

'We're ready for you,' the director said.

Jo sat down on the chair facing the camera, rearranging her skirt, and making sure that Sam was comfortable.

'Ready?'

'Yes,' Jo said.

'Turning,' someone called.

Jo lifted her face to the camera. 'This is my son,' she said, smiling. 'His name is Sam. Just under three months ago, we found out Sam was ill.'

Bill Elliott found a lump coming to his throat.

'Like any two-year-old,' Jo continued, 'Sam likes to get into all sorts of trouble.' She stroked his shoulder. 'And, like any mother, I'm used to getting him out.'

There was an awful silence in the garden, as Sam looked directly into the lens. Not so long ago, he had been a handsome, mischievous little boy with a thick head of straw-coloured hair and startlingly blue eyes, but the face that would reach into every home the following weekend was not handsome or mischievous. He had lost a great deal of hair. His skin was yellow. Worst of all was the look in Sam's eyes. Bill Elliott had seen it a thousand times before. It was filled with the knowledge of pain. He looked down at the ground, frowning, hoping no one would see his tears as he rubbed them away.

'But this time I can't get Sam out of trouble,' Jo was saying softly. 'He's got something called aplastic anaemia. Sam needs a bone-marrow transplant.' She paused. She, too, seemed to be struggling with her emotions. The crew looked at each other.

Eventually Jo raised her head. 'That's a pretty bad position to be in,' she said. 'Sam needs a donor. A bone-marrow donor.'

She glanced at the director. He was making a sign at her, to demonstrate that she should carry on, and that images would be overlaid at this point.

'This is John Marshall,' she said. 'He's Sam's half-brother. It's just possible that John could be a bone-marrow match for Sam.' She gave a hesitant smile. 'The problem is that we don't know where John is, and we wonder if you could help us. John is an archaeology student. He used to live in Cambridge.'

The director's hand made a slicing motion. The camera was back on Jo.

'Sam and I would like to ask you today if you have seen John Marshall,' Jo said. 'He might be in this country, or abroad. He's tall, and fair-haired, and he . . . well, he looks quite a bit like his father, Douglas Marshall. The James Norberry Trust matches up bone-marrow donors to patients like Sam, and John Marshall was registered with the trust.'

Sam leaned back in her arms and, as if on cue, gazed up at his mother.

'If you think that you could be a donor, or if you think you have seen John Marshall, please contact the number at the bottom of the screen today. And thanks very much.' She paused. 'Thanks.'

THEY WERE FINISHED by half past nine. Bill Elliott had made his thirty-second shot with Jo. Between the beginning and the end of her appeal, there would be other shots of him in his office. Cut in between both Jo and Elliott and the images of John would be the work of the Norberry Trust. The item was due to be screened the following Sunday, in the traditional appeal slot just before the early evening news.

'You did well,' Jo said, as she and Bill sat together after the crew had left.

'Not if you saw the stuff they took yesterday,' Bill said. 'They showed me the rough cut . . . I walk like a duck.'

Jo began to laugh. 'You do not walk like a duck,' she said.

He saw her eyes trail up to the bedroom window above them, from where Sam could be heard fretting.

'His temperature is all to hell,' she muttered.

'I ought to go,' he said.

She moved to the door of the house, which led through to the kitchen.

'Jo,' he said, 'you know that if they find a match you must go to Great Ormond Street for the transplant.'

'I'm glad you believe in a match,' she said.

'You have to believe it,' he said. 'Plan for it.'

'Excuse me if my faith is a little thin,' she said.

'You know what my ward sister tells me?' he offered. 'When you face a crisis, it's like a furnace. You go in flesh and you come out steel.'

'I hate that stuff,' she muttered. 'God makes burdens for the broadest backs. All that ridiculous sanctimonious crap. Have you looked at Sam? Do you blame me?' She glared at him. 'You know, Catherine has a faith,' she said. 'And it looks like you have.'

'Yes,' he said.

'Well, tell me,' she said, 'how do you do that? I don't get it. Catherine watches Sam as much as I do. And she just . . . she just doesn't get angry.'

'And you're angry,' he said.

She advanced on him, eyes blazing. 'Bloody right I'm angry,' she said. 'You want me to think there's some logic behind all this? You want me to pray? Ask Him for help?' Her mouth trembled. 'I can't ask Him. I can't pray any more.'

They stood, face to face. Bill Elliott had the intelligence to say nothing. He tried to touch her, but she didn't see him. Instead, she caught sight of the coffee cups, waiting to be washed. She snatched up the nearest and threw it at the wall.

'Jo,' he said, flinching as the pieces scattered over the floor.

'Nothing will happen,' she sobbed. 'John won't be a match, he'll never come back. Sam is going to die.'

'You mustn't believe that,' he said. 'Sam will sense it.'

'I can't help it,' she cried. He saw the devastation in her face. 'I can't bear another day of watching him go from me. I can't do it any more. And all this talk of John. I'm just clutching at straws.' She plunged her head into her hands. 'He isn't a match,' she groaned.

'He is,' Elliott said.

She lifted a tear-streaked face to his. 'What?'

'John *is* a match,' he repeated. 'Christine Lord told me last week.'

She stared at him, open-mouthed. 'She isn't allowed to say,' she murmured. 'Neither are you.'

'No, not really,' he agreed, 'but pressure gets to all of us.'

'He's a match,' she echoed. 'How good a match?'

'Almost perfect.'

'Perfect . . .' she breathed.

He took a scrap of paper out of his pocket. He had written a number on it. AZMA 552314. He pressed it now into Jo's hands. He had a desperate urge to take her in his arms, to give her strength, to take the pain from her. But he stopped himself. 'This is the donor number of the match,' he said. 'Among John's things will be a donor card with that number. If you ever wanted to double-check, that would be your proof.'

'A match.' She closed her fist over the paper, still looking at him. 'Oh . . . thank you so very much,' she whispered.

CHAPTER 4

The snow had been falling softly for days, heavy with thick flakes. It was rare to have such a prolonged snowfall. In any one year, the falls in the Arctic might not be more than four or five inches. But 1848 was not a year like any other year. This was the year that the Esquimaux would call *tupilak*. The ghost. Nothing lived in it. Or, at least, nothing lived in it for long.

Three and a half months before, the men of *Erebus* and *Terror* had come across four miles of ice ridges between them and the King William coast.

A team of men from the first sledge party went first, trying to flatten the ice with spades and picks, to make a channel through which to haul the boats. Once done, a dozen men were attached to the front of the boat with harnesses and ropes; the remaining eighteen men were stationed on either side and at the back. The boats on their wooden runners were hell to pull, let alone lift. The contents, wrapped in tarpaulins and secured with rope, might as well have been blocks of marble. The sweat broke out on their skin, and froze. The sun goggles cut into their faces.

It took an hour and a half to negotiate the first ridge. By the time they stood on the summit, it was one in the afternoon. And as each man laboured to the top, he fell silent, for there was nothing to see but another ridge, and another, and another.

They descended the ridge, heaving and leaning backwards on the ropes to prevent the boats careering down on their own. As soon as they reached the bottom, they walked hardly ten paces before they started to climb again.

It was six o'clock before they stopped for the night.

They put up the tents, muscles aching, lungs scorched with effort. Everything they touched froze to their fingers; within minutes the canvas tents were rigid. The cooks brewed tea from a fire that took an age to take light. The men ate lukewarm *bouilli*, stewed meat, from tins, and raisins that they had to keep in their mouths before the fruit thawed. Crozier recorded a temperature of minus 32 degrees that night.

It was four days before they reached King William. It was almost as if Fitzjames had waited to get there. For the last mile he had been carried in the boat, and when Goodsir, the surgeon, came to see him once they had erected the first tent, he looked peaceful.

'James,' Goodsir said, 'can you hear me?'

Fitzjames barely opened his eyes. 'I am tired,' he said.

'Don't sleep.' With his own hands numbed beyond feeling, the surgeon chafed Fitzjames's hands, chest and arms. Outside, the wind picked up. The last party was having trouble pitching their tent. Goodsir could see two men sitting on their sledge, heads drooping.

He looked back at Fitzjames. In the short interval since he had looked away, the man had died.

They buried him in the morning, using precious energy to cut down through nine inches of ice to lower him into the scant water of the shoreline, the ground behind them being too hard to dig.

FINDING THE CAIRN left by Gore the previous year, they had unearthed his message, and added their own. Fitzjames had insisted upon writing the account; it had taken him almost an hour. Crozier had indulged him the time, and was glad, now, that he had.

> *April 25, 1848*
> *HM Ships* Terror *and* Erebus *were deserted on April 22, five leagues NNW of this, having been beset since September 12, 1846. The Officers and crews consisting of 105 souls—under the command of Captain F. R. M. Crozier here—in Latitude 69 degrees 37' 42", Longitude 98 degrees 41'. Sir John Franklin died on June 11, 1847 and the total deaths in the expedition have been to this date nine Officers and fifteen men.*
> *James Fitzjames, Captain, HMS* Erebus.

When Fitzjames had finished, Crozier had squeezed a few words at the very bottom of the page: '*F. R. M. Crozier, Captain and Senior Officer. And start on tomorrow 26th for Backs Fish River.*'

THE JOURNEY ALONG the King William coastline had been little better; they made an average of two miles a day, and the temperatures were up, almost 10 below.

Augustus Peterman had been the lead man on the first sledge, and only relinquished his place at midday.

'You did well,' Crozier told the boy.

Gus looked at him with empty eyes.

Having changed men, the team tried to get the sledge started again, but it was hard. The snow was knee-deep, and the weight of the load drove the runners into it. Both Gus and Crozier joined the team at the back, pushing and heaving until the forward runners lifted slightly, and the men leaned hard on the traces, hauling with their bodies at a 30-degree angle to the ground.

No one commented any more at an officer doing the men's work. An idle pair of hands could not be tolerated.

Once they were moving, Gus stood up. He passed his hands over his eyes.

Crozier looked hard at him. The lad's eyes were running with water, smarting at the snow. The cold made the eyes stream, the head pound. 'Where are your goggles?'

'I can't wear them, sir. When I get warm, the sweat makes my eyes sting, and then, when I'm not pulling, the sweat ices.'

'If you walk without them, you will get snow blindness, and then someone will have to lead you,' Crozier pointed out.

'I don't care,' Gus whispered.

'Put them on,' Crozier ordered.

Gus did so with exaggerated slowness. When he had finished, he looked at the crews ahead. 'How many are there?' he asked.

Crozier frowned at him. 'How many what?'

'Men, sir.'

'On this team? Thirty-one, Gus.' Crozier took his arm, worried by the question and by the dead note in Gus's voice. 'Walk with me,' he said.

Gus did as he was told.

Crozier pushed the boy in front of him, and began to talk, as their boots sank into the drifts. 'It's not so hard to survive here.' He watched Gus's swaying gait. 'Think what you'll do when you get home.'

The boy was silent.

'Men have lived through worse than this,' Crozier said. 'Ten years ago, British ships were beset in Baffin Bay. The ice held them just as it held us.' Crozier touched Gus's shoulder. 'Every single ship of that group reached England,' he said. 'Three years before that, the *Shannon* out of Hull . . .'

Gus looked at him wearily. 'I knew the mate of the *Shannon*,' he said. 'Sixteen men and three boys were swept away. And when the two Danish brigs found the rest, there was no water and no food.' He stared into Crozier's face. 'I knew that man, in the public houses,' he said. 'He never went out on the boats again. He drank. He said it was his thirst. He had . . . a thirst.'

Crozier pulled up Gus's drooping head. 'But he lived,' he insisted.

'Aye,' Gus muttered. 'There was a life.'

Crozier shook him hard. 'What a man does with his life is his own affair,' he said. 'We all have choices in what we do, whether we live out our days drowning the memory, whether we stand up to fight again. That is God's gift to us. Our freedom to choose.' He turned Gus to look at the struggling crew ahead of them. 'Look hard at those men, Gus,' he said. 'God will not give life back to every one of them. But we must live out that life to its last breath. We don't despair of a gift like that.'

Gus's mouth trembled. He was struggling not to cry.

Crozier lowered his voice. 'Can you walk on?' he asked gently.

'Yes,' Gus said.

'We'll walk on to Backs River,' Crozier told him. 'All the way.'

'Yes,' Gus whispered.

Crozier patted his back. 'Good lad.'

DURING THAT NIGHT, the tenth away from the ships, there was no snow and no storm. A perfect silence fell upon the camp. Gus lay with the sick. Goodsir had put him here, at Crozier's instruction, but he tried not to think that he could be as bad as those men around him. His teeth ached, and his mouth was sore, but he was not like Kinningthwaite, who had been laid on his side and stared at Gus with glassy eyes.

'Kinningthwaite,' Gus whispered. 'Are they back?'

The man's gaze flickered.

When Gus had been given the task of feeding him, Kinningthwaite had told the boy that there were people at his shoulder.

'What people?' Gus had asked.

'Dead,' Kinningthwaite said. He had given a horrible smile.

Gus shrank away from him, spoon and cup hovering in his grasp. 'They're not dead, Joshua. They are us. We are alive. We'll be fifty miles south of Point Victory tomorrow,' he added. 'We have come sixty-five miles.'

'Count them,' Kinningthwaite said.

Gus couldn't look at him any more. He counted. He counted all day. Was it a sign of this sickness? he wondered. Sometimes the team looked like five men, and sometimes they looked like fifty, and sometimes one man had more than one face. How many were left?

After you stopped being pierced by the cold, you began dreaming while you walked. You heard voices. He heard the voices of the women that his mother knew, as they hung washing on lines between houses, or cleaned their doorsteps. He heard his mother singing. He became her child again, cradled in her arm in the fireside chair. He remembered being two or three years old, and warm in his mother's lap, while heat or rain or sleet hammered in the street.

He lay down in the tent in the dark now, put his face into the blanket and cried. They were all alone, each man cast adrift, each man singly pursuing his Maker.

BY JUNE THEY HAD reached Terror Bay. In the six weeks it had taken them to get there, they had lost twenty-eight of the original 105.

As they neared the southwest corner of King William, they could not bury the last three that died. A fierce northwesterly wind was blowing and those who remained had no strength. Instead, they wrapped the men in blankets, and scraped snow and stones over them. The bodies were already frozen as they said the last words over them.

Crozier had almost lost sense of where they were by the time they pitched camp fifty miles south of Point Victory. Ten more had died where they fell—in one morning, four within the space of an hour. Turning over one of the bodies, Crozier had seen the bloated, blackened mask of the scurvy. Exertion brought the blood to the face, and there it coagulated and filled the flesh. There was nowhere for it to go, it seemed. Circulation simply broke down. It was shameful, Crozier thought—sometimes they were too tired to care about the dead. Cold and lethargy had atrophied their emotions; they had no grief left.

They would look back, and realise a man was down. They would stop, and watch. Someone might go back to him, but it was hopeless. Once down, they were dead.

At Point Victory, Crozier felt a huge sense of weariness seep into his bones. Around him, he could see that the rest of the men were fading. Of the sixty-seven remaining, perhaps three or four did not move with the same clumsy slow motion he felt in himself. Their efforts at pitching tents and setting up sleeping quarters were terrible to witness. It took twice the time it had when they had set off from the ships.

The whole landscape was still one long sheet of ice. Hard to conceive it, but it was summer. The gneiss and limestone of the land should be not only showing through the ice but in full view. He ought to have been able to feed the men on the lichens that were supposed to cover most of the ground. They should have had hunting parties bringing down the deer that were reputed to move across this peninsula. But there was nothing. No ground, no lichen, no deer. No thaw at all.

HE BROUGHT OUT his charts and laid them, with difficulty, on the single narrow chest that he had brought with him.

He tried to calculate how many days it would take to get to Backs Fish River. At one and a half miles a day, now that they were so slow, they might reach Backs Fish River in a month. No man knew what lay to the west of the Backs Fish River, except that it was a strait of some kind. If they were still able to launch boats, they might take advantage of what sea currents there were, and sail directly towards the Pacific. With luck, they would find enough fresh fish and game at the mouth of the river to sustain them.

He stared out of the tent and considered. Finally he called in Goodsir. Standing in the evening light, he thought that, of any of them, Harry Goodsir was the worst. He shuffled with a broken gait, bent over at the waist.

'How many can walk to Backs Fish?' he asked him.

'None.'

'Harry . . .' Crozier said gently. 'We must go on. An estimate.'

Goodsir shrugged. 'Twenty.'

'How many are we now?'

'As of this evening, sixty-four.'

They contemplated each other.

'I want you to make a hospital tent,' Crozier told Goodsir. 'We will leave you with as much as we dare. I want you to stay here with Macdonald. Stanley and Peddie will come with me.'

Crozier looked at the pathologist with a passion for natural science, who had so enthused at the prospect of Arctic exploration.

Goodsir's expression was almost blank. 'Mr Stanley is too sick to walk, sir.'

THERE WAS NO NIGHT now. From May to July, twenty-four hours of sunshine was the great bear's world. She stood now on the edge of Simpson Strait, her head hung low with exhaustion.

She had no idea if the cub was alive or dead. She had not been able to feed him. The seals were far out in the water, and she had had no luck in pursuing them. She had walked 108 miles, and she no longer knew the purpose of her movement. The cub lay on the rocky shoreline. She regarded it with dull perplexity, until a movement in the water distracted her. Offshore, an adult male was still hunting.

The female had no wish to cross the male's path. She lay inert, her cub at her back, waiting for the male to pass up the strait.

It was midnight when he came ashore. The smell woke her. She lifted her head and saw him walking towards them. In a moment, she was on her feet. The male skirted her, scenting the cub. He would have no compunction in killing it, if he could get close enough, and, as he suddenly increased his speed, the female charged him. She took him in the shoulder, tearing his flesh and drawing blood. Surprised, but not deterred, he backed away, head still low, signalling his aggression. She stood her ground. This was a battle of instinct for the survival of her own line. She would fight to the death for her cub.

Her second charge was harder than the first, expending most of her energy. She pounded his shoulder with her forelegs, as he snapped at her head, trying to find the softer spot below the jaw. She was a greater challenge than he had anticipated, and he only managed to hold on to her for seconds. He backed away, grunting, his eyes on the body of the cub. Then, his pain registered. He assessed her, as the blood coloured his pristine coat, then, as quickly as he had come, he walked away.

She watched him until he eased back into the ocean, heading out to the harder ice floes.

It took her almost an hour to rouse the cub before they walked on. As she made the first few steps, she was aware of the new sensation at the base of her throat. But she ignored it. It was of no importance.

SINCE JO'S SUNDAY evening broadcast, all hell had been let loose. The five-minute TV appeal had begun at six twenty. The first two minutes outlined the James Norberry Trust; then pictures of Doug Marshall came onto the screen. Excerpts from his series reminded viewers of the personality that had earned the series' high ratings.

Next came Sam at his first birthday, hands plunged into lime-green jelly, face transformed with delight.

And then Sam was shown as he was now, face swollen, arms bruised. Pasty-coloured, listless.

The phones had begun to ring at the James Norberry Trust after the first of Doug's pictures went up. By midnight on Sunday the trust had received 4,800 calls from potential donors. By Wednesday, the figure had become 26,000.

The Courier, too, was swamped. It had run a front-page picture of John on the Friday, and by the following week the post was full of letters from people who claimed to have seen Doug's son. Unfortunately, it appeared that he was in several places at once: in Thailand, in New Zealand. And all over England.

Gina had done her share of the letter-opening, painstakingly reading each one. Just in case.

This morning, drumming her fingers on her desk, Gina thought for a while. She had heard all about John's passions and preoccupations from Jo; they had discussed him countless times. Ignoring the fact that she had a meeting scheduled for five minutes ago, she logged on to the Internet and searched for *polar bear*.

Alta Vista came up with dozens of sites. Choosing one at random, she spent ten minutes gazing at the explanation of how global warming was shrinking the polar bear's habitat. Then she scanned through the Net for the Canadian Hydrographic Service, and brought up the weather conditions in the area that fascinated John: King William Island and Lancaster Sound. They showed impossibly complicated shallow- and deep-water images, and networks of tiny islands. If John ever tried to get there, he would put himself completely out of reach, she thought. Victoria Strait was about as isolated as any place on earth could be, frozen in for eleven months of the year, not navigable by any normal shipping.

She rested her chin in the palm of her hand and stared at the screen. 'Come back,' she whispered, to the empty office. 'For God's sake, John. Come back.'

WHEN SHE LEFT work Gina went straight to Great Ormond Street Children's Hospital, where Sam had been transferred, so that he could be ready at a moment's notice for the transplant, as soon as John was found.

Gina found Catherine and Jo in the corridor outside Sam's ward. 'How is he?' she asked.

'Sleeping,' Catherine said.

'He's just had another platelet transfusion,' Jo said. She looked at Gina with an expression tinged with fear.

'What is it?' Gina said. 'There's something else. What?'

Catherine put her hand on Jo's shoulder. 'It's the latest tests,' she said. 'His neutrophils are zero point one. Platelets eleven.'

The three of them had got used to this shorthand. Sam had a blue sheet that was filled in daily, a record of his blood results. It obsessed them all.

'Neutrophils zero point one,' Gina repeated slowly. She knew the neutrophils were the cells that fought infection in the body. A normal level was anything between 1.5 and 8.5 per cubic millimetre.

'It can go to zero,' Jo murmured. 'They record zero all the time. The ward sister told me.' She raised her eyes to Gina's, pleading.

'The platelets,' Gina whispered. 'What happened to the platelets?'

She saw that Catherine's eyes were filled with tears, and that the girl was struggling not to let Jo see. No one said a word. They all knew that the normal level for platelets was between 150 and 400. Sam's was 11.

Oh, sweet Lord, Gina thought. Less than 10 per cent of what he needed, minimum. Would they still do the transplant if he got worse? she wondered. Surely he wasn't strong enough to survive the preparatory chemotherapy if this carried on. He'd die in the isolation ward while he waited for the bone marrow.

He's going to die anyway, a voice said inside her head. She clasped Jo's hands, and to her shame, started to cry. She was supposed to be stoic. Jo's support. But still . . . 'Oh, Lord,' she said. 'Lord, please.'

Jo stiffened. Suddenly she got up, wrenched her hands from Gina's grasp. 'It doesn't matter if John gets here. He'll be too late.'

'No, he won't,' Catherine said.

'Sam won't make it,' Jo said. 'He's too sick.'

'Don't say that,' Gina told Jo. 'Don't even think it.'

'Why don't you both stop lying to me?' Jo cried. 'He's not responding to anything. The drug treatment did nothing at all.' She turned away from them, pressed both hands to the window glass. 'His body's given up already. He's gone through to some other place,' she whispered. 'He's fighting his dragons all alone in there, and I can't get through to him.' She took in a great gasp of air, a grieving sob.

Gina promptly turned her round. 'Listen to me,' she said. 'He's not going to die, Jo. He'll get the bone marrow. We'll pull him through that door, we'll get him back.'

Jo dropped her head. 'Oh, Gina,' she murmured.

As ALICIA WALKED out onto King's Parade, she saw John. She stopped dead in the hurrying crowd. Then, with a thud of her heart, she realised that someone had enlarged a college picture of him and pinned it in a café window. Getting closer, she saw a red banner stuck across the lower half. *Have you seen John Marshall?*

He was everywhere. She no longer took *The Courier* because of the relentless campaign they had been running. She had thought of ringing them up to complain. She was John's mother, and yet no one had ever consulted her. It was as if Jo and Sam Harper were the only mother and child in the world.

She drove home in a daze. When she turned into the drive, she saw the evening paper in the letterbox. She got out of the car, pulled it out and stared at the front page. A small paragraph at the bottom caught her eye.

Sam Marshall, the local boy who continues to fight a life-threatening illness, was yesterday transferred to Great Ormond Street Hospital in London to prepare him for a bone-marrow transplant from his half-brother.

Blood rushed to Alicia's face. Wrenching the keys from the ignition, she rushed indoors and grabbed the phone from the table in the hallway. She dialled the paper's number.

'*Evening Clarion.*'

'I want the editor,' she said. She waited impatiently, stabbing her keys on the wood panelling.

'Ed Wheeler.'

'This is John Marshall's mother,' Alicia said. 'I suppose you know who I am?'

'His mother,' the editor repeated. 'Miss Harper?'

'No,' Alicia retorted, furious. 'I'm *John* Marshall's mother.'

'Oh,' he said. 'Sorry. What can I do for you?'

'Your paper tonight. The front page. Where is he?'

'I'm sorry. Who?'

'John. My son,' she snapped. 'It says in the paragraph that the boy's been transferred to London for his transplant. If he's getting the transplant, they must have the donor.'

Light seemed to dawn in the editor's mind. 'Oh, no,' he said. 'My apologies if that's misleading. That was the reason for the transfer, but they haven't found his stepbrother.'

She stared at the receiver, incensed. 'So don't print a story with half the facts. They haven't found him. If anyone could find him, it would be me.' The words were out before she could stop them.

The editor almost jumped down her throat. '*You* could find him?'

She tried to backtrack. 'I simply want to make the point that there is more than one mother who has lost a son in this.'

'Do you know where he is?' the editor repeated.

Furious, she slammed the phone down.

Everything she had had fallen apart. The phrase blasted through her mind. She was a wealthy woman, she was well respected, she was influential. And yet she couldn't control her own life. She groaned, went to the sitting room, and slumped down in the nearest armchair, switching on the TV with the remote.

It was the local evening news programme. She passed her hand over her eyes, irritated by the tragedies of the rest of the world. When she took her hand away, Doug's face was looking back at her.

Alicia sat forward. Jo and Sam came on the screen, Jo sitting underneath the lilac tree, Sam in her arms. The voice-over went on.

'Sunday's screening of the TV appeal has produced the most astonishing response to the James Norberry Trust. To date . . .'

The breath seemed to have stopped in Alicia's body. Unable to look at Jo, she stared at the child. He looked so like John at the same age: he even had that lopsided look to his mouth when he was concentrating, that so resembled a smile.

But the boy in Jo Harper's lap was not really smiling, she saw. His eyes were fixed on his mother, as if she held an important answer to something. She looked at his fingers, knotted in Jo's.

Alicia switched off the set, and leapt to her feet. She went into the hall, wrenched open the front door and stepped out into the drive, taking deep breaths. She was shaking from head to foot.

The garden was in full bloom. She stared at the flowers that she had tended all year and dropped to her knees on the closely mown grass. 'Oh God,' she moaned. 'What have I done?'

All her life she had fought to make things happen. She had fought to get Doug; she had fought to keep him. She had kept John near her, when Doug became increasingly distant, suffocating her child emotionally. And she had nagged him. God, how she had nagged him. She used to phone John daily. Insisted on knowing where he had been, and who he had been with. When he started to break away, when she could see how much he wanted his father's attention, not hers, she had pressed down harder to make him feel guilty. And now she had lost them both. Husband, son.

All that she had was isolation. And fear. She loathed the world that she thought had taken John from her and the woman to whom Doug had given his love. She hated a small, sick child. That was where her so-called loving had brought her.

Jo Harper was admired and respected. Look how Catherine had stood by her. Look at those television pictures. Even the doctor seemed struck with Sam's mother. The TV crew, the people at *The Courier.* There was nowhere you could go that didn't show how strongly people felt for her. Because she was loved. Genuinely loved.

Doug had loved Jo as he never loved her. It had been written plainly in his face. Now he was alive again in Sam. In twenty years' time there would be another Doug Marshall walking around. Samuel Douglas Marshall . . .

If he lived.

Alicia walked slowly back to the house.

She opened the drawer in the front of the hall table and took out a bundle of papers with John's only two letters to her in the past two years. In the same pile of papers was a small, cream-coloured card. She put it, with John's last letter, in her handbag. Then, she picked up the car keys and went out of the house.

IT WAS MIDNIGHT. At Great Ormond Street Jo was asleep on the sofa bed at Sam's side. The lights in the corridor were turned down.

Woken by a movement, she surfaced slowly from sleep. For a moment, all she saw was the pool of moonlight on the floor. Then she sat bolt upright.

Alicia was standing at the door. 'Hello, Jo.'

Jo stumbled to her feet.

'He's such a little boy,' Alicia said. 'I didn't realise . . .'

Jo followed Alicia's gaze. Sam was sedated now. He lay peacefully, like an angel, his face smoothed by sleep. Alicia stretched out her hand and touched his face.

In an automatic gesture of protection, Jo went to Sam's side, and took his hand. 'What are you doing here?' she asked.

'I brought something,' Alicia said. She fumbled with the catch of her handbag. At last she brought out a card. She gave it to Jo. 'The James Norberry Trust', said the lettering across the top. And John's name. And the number. *AZMA 552314.*

Jo didn't need to go to her own bag to know that this was the number that Bill Elliott had given her. John's donor number.

'There's something else,' Alicia said. She had a letter in her hand. 'John wrote to me. I went down to see him. He was leaving, I couldn't stop him. I—' Her voice broke. 'If it would help you,' she said, 'this is where he's gone.' Richard Sibley's address was printed along the top.

Jo took the page and gazed at it.

Suddenly Alicia turned away. She had got to the door when Jo rushed over to her, John's letter still in her hand. She touched Alicia's shoulder and, just for a second, the two women stared into each other's eyes. Then, Jo flung her arms around her.

'Forgive me.' Alicia was weeping quietly. 'Please forgive me.'

WHEN HE GOT to the rock, Gus was too tired to sit. He lay down with his face on the ground and his arm resting on the stones. There was no more snow, no sleet, not even the wind laden with the fine grains of ice. In fact, the temperature was above freezing. He stared out over Simpson Strait.

They had left the ice behind, and had emerged, last week, close to Latitude 68. The sea was unfrozen here, carrying its burden of grey floes from the great choked fields where they had left the ships. So many miles south, the ocean had freed itself at last of that solid embrace. King William was an island. The Northwest Passage existed. But there was no one to care. Least of all the four men of the *Erebus* and *Terror* who were still alive.

At last, Gus raised himself and pulled one or two of the larger stones towards him; lifting them was beyond his strength. Then, he got the copper canister out of his pocket. They had pushed the message into it.

> *August 11, 1848*
> *HM Ships* Erebus *and* Terror.
> *1 Officer, 3 crew remaining.*
> *Final cairn constructed Latitude 68 degrees 15', Longitude 97 degrees 30'.*
> *Awaiting Hudson's Bay scouts.*
> *F. R. M. Crozier, Captain and Senior Officer.*

Gus put the canister on top of the larger stones and scraped pebbles over it. The effort made him want to weep. Soon the container was covered, and he knew no one would ever find it. So much for the final cairn that Franklin's crews would make, he thought.

Two hundred yards away, they had pitched their last tent. Looking back now, Gus could see how badly it had been done. The tarpaulin was not taut, and the edges had not been weighted properly.

Slowly, Gus scraped at the closest rock with his fingernail. The acid-green covering came off in dry flakes. He put it on his tongue. His mouth hurt badly; even the lichen flakes were hard to move around in it. Yesterday, they had shot a bird. They had tried to chew the flesh, but their gums were so swollen that their mouths bled fiercely.

Gus got to his feet. He set off down the slope at a snail's pace. When he had last summoned the courage to look at his feet, his toes had been black. Also, he had lost sensation from just below the ankle in his right leg.

At the tent on the shoreline, he knelt down. He didn't want to go into the tent. He didn't want to know what was being said in there. Those prayers and absolutions.

They weren't going to recover. They would die in a few days.

Gus looked across the water, at the blur of grey beyond the sea. Across the strait was Canada. Hundreds of miles away in that direction were the Hudson's Bay outposts: Fort Churchill, Fort York, Severn Fort, Albany, Moose Fort. There were settlements there. But he would never go to them. He would never get on a ship again. He felt glad of it. He felt glad at the prospect of ceasing to exist. Never walking again. Never breathing. Never waiting to see the last dying flicker in a man's eye.

Then, across the strait, he saw movement. He thought his eyes must be deceiving him. He thought it was just the endless ice, turning over in the current. He thought it was the sea itself, at first. And then he saw that it was men.

As the Esquimaux approached the camp, the four men in front glanced at one another. They were tempted to pass by. They knew that white men came into this country, but none had seen white men before.

Tooshooarthariu stepped a little way forward. There was something alongside the tent that intrigued him. He could see a man on the ground, and an older one standing above him.

He lifted his hand.

Slowly the standing man returned the gesture. Then he walked towards him.

Teekeeta and Owwer shrank back, and Mangaq turned swiftly on his heel, ready to run. He signalled to his wife; they hauled the sledge round.

Tooshooarthariu could see that the hunger that had plagued his own family all winter had struck hard in the man before him. The man was a strange colour. His forehead was crosshatched with different shades: a curious, ugly blue, a grey, dead white. His cheekbones, too, looked white. But the mouth was black, the teeth yellow, flecked with blood.

The man began to speak.

Tooshooarthariu didn't understand the language, but he understood that the man had come from the north—he waved his arm behind him—and that there were boats, large boats. The man counted, holding up one finger and then pointing at his chest. He repeated the gesture. One man. Two, three. The hands flew. Many men.

The Esquimaux looked disbelievingly at the tent. There were not many men now, that was obvious. How could there ever have been many men walking from the ice?

The white man was thin—you could see that, even if you didn't look at the awful face. He didn't stand straight. The younger one behind him was standing now, and was a little taller.

'They're hungry,' Owwer whispered at his back.

The Esquimaux walked away, back to the women.

The first thing that his wife said was that there was not much seal. It was as if she had read her husband's mind.

'We haven't enough to feed them,' she told him.

'They have killed birds,' Owwer said. 'Let them wait for more.'

He stared at the tent. How many men would it hold? Maybe ten. If they gave them meat for ten men they would have nothing left for themselves.

'What is their sickness?' his wife asked.

'I don't know,' he told her.

She inclined her head to their children. 'We don't want their sickness,' she said. Yet her gaze trailed back to the white boy, who could not have been more than sixteen. She gave a half-smile, before lowering her face and covering it with her hand. Despite his mottled skin, she could see that he was fair.

Tooshooarthariu looked again at the sorrowful little tent, and he wondered what ships the men had come on, and where they were. He wondered if they were lying. Hundreds of men. Tall ships. If they were telling the truth, where were the rest? He wished he knew. He wished he understood.

The older white man sat down suddenly on the shore, as if the breath had been knocked out of him. Tooshooarthariu saw the blunt hopelessness in his eyes. Whatever had happened, he thought, it came down to the same fact. He couldn't walk past them with seal meat in the bags.

'Give them meat,' he said.

TWO MORNINGS LATER, the sea looked very blue. The air was amazingly sweet. Just for a second, Gus thought of gardens. At his side was the seal meat the Esquimaux had left. The night before, he and Crozier had eaten barely half a dozen mouthfuls. It had been too rich, and very hard to chew. They had tried their best. They had said nothing. There was nothing left to say.

Early in the morning Francis Crozier died.

It took Gus a long time to get the blankets from the tent and wrap the body. The effort exhausted him.

At the very end, he couldn't remember a single prayer, and he couldn't weep. He sat with his hands resting on the body. Then, he lay down at Crozier's side, and waited to follow him.

CHAPTER 5

The rain had stopped. The day was dull, but visibility was clear. The bear lay on her stomach, all four legs splayed out, her head propped up slightly on the stones.

She had been dreaming for hours. She had swum under ice ceilings, swept clean of snow, that filtered light through the ocean, filling the depths with curtains of colour. She had filled her senses with the power of the current, the fierce cold beauty of the ice-covered sea.

She had tracked hundreds of miles along the shoreline, and had seen the irrepressible return of life each year: the bearberry, whose leaves turned bright red in the autumn; the cloudberry, with its creamy consistency; the lichen—the oldest plants on earth, and virtually indestructible; the flush of wild flowers—pink-flowered fireweed, poppies, white mountain avens, blue forget-me-nots.

She knew the huge concentrations of birds: snow geese; long-tailed jaegers; killer hawks; black-legged kittiwakes. She knew the changing patterns of the sky, the dazzling brightness of snow reflected on the underside of clouds. The blue-white of Arctic haze, carrying ice crystals; the optical illusions of sun pillars and halos.

She had their image in her head and heart. They carried her now, on her final journey.

THE HELICOPTER SWUNG low over the beach, making its fourth run along that section of coast.

'There!' Richard Sibley shouted. 'By the gravel ridge!'

It was four days since he had got back to the office in Winnipeg. He had been filming grizzly above Khutzeymateen, and returned home to find his sister snowed under with emails, and John Marshall sitting among the chaos, a holdall at his feet.

An Inuit guide had spotted the bear from a canoe. He had come back to Gjoa Haven to spread the word of the adult female, apparently dead, a wound showing at her throat.

Within minutes the message had gone down to Sibley. 'We have the Swimmer onshore here. Do you want a last picture?' He surely did.

He had originally planned to come north to Gjoa Haven in the summer, to shoot the Arctic char fishing. When he invited John Marshall here again, he had said that he would be on King William Island around August.

John had sent him one letter in reply. It had contained the date of his arrival and the flight number.

He hadn't had much time to talk to the boy and, anyway, in truth it seemed that John was no conversationalist. He kept himself to himself, even on the long journey up to Gjoa.

They had come out yesterday, but seen not a trace of the bear, even with a guide alongside them. Sibley had woken this morning in a bad temper, irritated at the expense of a second flight. 'She'd better be there this time,' he'd told John, over breakfast. He had dug a heap of letters from his bag and was sifting through them. At one, he stopped. 'Know someone called Gina Shorecroft?'

'No,' John told him.

Sibley passed the message across, a handwritten note taped to an email by Sibley's sister. 'Says it's urgent,' he'd said.

John looked at it, then put it in his pocket.

'Who is Jo Harper?' Sibley asked. He quoted the email. '"Jo Harper needs to talk to you."'

John got up. 'She's talked to me before,' he answered. Seeing Sibley's puzzled expression, he shrugged. 'I'll ring tonight,' he said. 'It's the middle of the night there now.'

THE HELICOPTER came down 100 yards from the shore. Their guide, Mike Hitkolok, got out first. 'You stay behind me,' he told them. 'We see what's she's doing, OK?'

They nodded their agreement.

Sibley had handed a pack of equipment to John, and they both edged onwards with the cameras. When they got to the first of the gravel rises, Mike went over it first. They watched him carefully. There was no sight of the bear from this angle.

'John,' Sibley said softly, 'if she's not dead, if she moves, you run, OK? We're back in that machine.'

'OK,' John said.

Down the slope, they saw Mike wave to them.

They went down cautiously, to within twenty yards.

Mike stood guard on top of the nearest rill.

'She dead?' Sibley called.

'Dead, yeah,' came the reply. 'No movement.'

They eased on, until at last they saw her, curled in a foetal position. Blood stained her chest. Sibley flexed out the tripod and took some time to position it.

When he had done so, he was surprised to see that John had moved forward. 'Hey, son,' he said.

John was walking at a steady pace.

'What the hell?' Sibley muttered. He had set the handheld video running.

'Stay up,' Mike shouted, meaning stay upwind. Just in case.

Through the lens, Sibley barely saw what happened next. The flash of movement was so sudden that the shock sent the video slithering in his grasp. It slipped from his eyes, and while automatically raising it again, he saw Mike Hitkolok raise the rifle to his shoulder in one swift movement.

John didn't cry out. He didn't run. As the bear launched herself forward, he remained where he was, as if frozen to the ground.

The shot was earsplitting. The bear staggered, a ghastly sight, coat stained with blood, teeth bared. Barely six feet from John, she fell down dead.

It was only then that Sibley dropped the camera. He started to run full pelt down the slope. Mike was ahead, shouting John's name.

They got up to him, and spun him round.

'You bloody fool!' Sibley yelled. 'What did you think you were doing? You got a death wish, or what? I told you not to move!'

But the words glanced off the boy like weightless blows.

John Marshall was staring past them, past the body of the female, to the pit where she had lain.

'She's got a cub,' John whispered. 'She was protecting the cub.'

THEY PICKED UP JO at midday the next day, outside Great Ormond Street Hospital. As she walked out under the white canopy of the front doors, Gina and Mike got out of the taxi to exchange places with her. Jo almost fell into Gina's arms.

Catherine got out of the cab. 'You don't have to come with me,' she told Jo. 'I'll get to Heathrow by myself.'

'You won't,' Jo said. 'If I could, I'd go all the way with you. Not just to the airport.'

'We know,' Gina murmured.

'I'll be back with Sam as soon as I can,' Jo told her.

'We won't stray,' Gina replied. 'I've got your mobile number. Go.'

Jo kissed her and hugged Mike. She and Catherine got back into the cab. They waved out of the back window, then, as the cab pulled away from the pavement, Jo turned to Catherine. 'You've got everything?'

'Yes, don't worry.'

'What time does the flight leave?'

'Three thirty. Plenty of time.'

'And from Calgary . . .'

'To Edmonton. And the next day I go on to Gjoa Haven. I'll be there at half past one in the afternoon,' Catherine said. 'I'll ring.'

'And your father takes another day?' Jo asked.

Catherine nodded. 'He'll be there twenty-four hours after me. It's a long way.'

Suddenly Jo gripped her hand. 'I can't believe this is happening,' she said. 'First John's there. Then he's not.'

Catherine put her arm round Jo. 'We'll find him.'

'For God's sake, promise you won't go out after him without your father, and this Mike Hitkolok. Don't do anything dangerous.'

Catherine smiled. 'I promise you,' she said.

They locked hands.

Gina had had a call yesterday evening from Richard Sibley. Yes, John had come to Gjoa Haven with him, he told her. Yes, they had found the bear and they had come back to Gjoa together. But, no, he didn't know where John was.

'I'm sorry?' Gina had said, afraid she had misheard him over the crackling static of the line.

'We came back. He went to his room,' Sibley shouted down the line. 'When I went to find him, the email with your number was on his bed. But John had gone.'

'Gone?' Gina had echoed. 'Gone where?'

'He'd taken a freighter canoe,' Sibley replied, then, after a pause. 'And, Mrs Shorecroft . . .'

Gina had waited, eyes squeezed shut.

'Somebody here from CBC told me about Sam. I'm sorry.'

'You didn't know?' Gina breathed, her heart sinking.

'There was nothing on the email to tell us.'

'It was on your national network!' she protested.

'We never saw it,' Sibley replied. 'We were nowhere near a TV.'

'I can't believe this,' Gina said.

'I don't know why he would go,' Sibley told her. 'The bear was a shock, but—well, in all honesty, Mrs Shorecroft, he didn't seem too upset at all. John . . . seems like he's got a heavy burden,' Sibley said, at last. 'You know what I'm saying, Mrs Shorecroft.'

'I know,' Gina replied, eventually. 'It's a long story, Mr Sibley. A very long, sad story.'

THE TAXI WAS COMING down the Mall now, to the Franklin Memorial at Waterloo Place, the bronze plaque that showed Crozier reading the memorial service over Franklin's body.

Strange, Jo thought. Less than three years ago, she had never heard of Franklin. The endurance of the *Erebus* and *Terror* crews had meant nothing to her. And yet, here she was, on the same kind of journey into white space.

There were no maps for where she was going. There was no one to show you the way as you stood at the door of an isolation unit and went through it with your son's hand in yours. People told you there was a way through, but no one knew for sure. You just had to go, make the leap. Push yourself forward into the unknown.

And somewhere now, on the other side of the world, a young man was making the same journey as Franklin, because he had become hooked on the idea that absolution was somewhere down that line. He couldn't know what he was doing any more than she did. He was just as lost.

And she and Sam were tied to him, being dragged into that landscape. A place of death.

God, no, she thought, as her stomach turned over. Don't think that. It *won't be* a place of death any more. We'll all come to life there.

Jo shut her eyes, the familiar names of the dying crews of *Erebus* and *Terror* fixed in her head. Doug had told her the story in the weeks when he had been negotiating the contract for the new programme. They had sat down among the packing cases, nearly ready to move into Lincoln Street, and roughed out the treatment for the first few episodes.

She thought now of the names she had pushed to the back of her mind for months. Leopold McClintock. Searching in 1859 along the coast of King William Island, he had found the body of Harry Peglar, captain of the foretop in *Terror*. They could still make out his double-breasted jacket of fine blue cloth edged with silk braid, the greatcoat and blue and white comforter round his neck. Around his skeleton lay personal fragments: a comb, coins, a pocket book. Nothing had disturbed the body in eleven winters.

McClintock's crew also found a lifeboat resting on a sledge and pointing north, as if it had been left there as the few remaining men marched back towards the ships. Perhaps they were the last few who had not died. Doug thought that a decision had been made to try to get back to *Erebus* and *Terror,* because there was at least greater shelter there. But the small band hadn't got far. The boat was ridiculously heavy. When it was found, inside it, besides two skeletons, were boots, towels, soap, sponges, a gun cover, saws, files, bullets, knives, bayonet scabbards, and even books. In the back of the boat McClintock unearthed spoons, forks, watches, paddles, tins, tobacco, tea and chocolate. There was no meat or biscuit of any kind. And no fuel. Writing about the discovery afterwards, McClintock had said that everything in the boat was an accumulation of dead weight, of little use.

No one ever knew who the two men were who had been left with the boat. One, McClintock said, was crouched in the bow. He had been a young man. Under the after-thwart lay the second man. Older and larger, he sat propped up, swathed in furs, with a double-barrelled gun on either side of him, loaded and cocked, and levelled muzzle upwards against the boat's side.

These two had always fascinated Doug. As had Crozier himself. The shadowy figure that John seemed to be chasing. All that had ever emerged about Crozier was the testimony of the Inuit natives, the people who had once been called Esquimaux. There were legends among them that Crozier had survived for years, living among them, eventually working his way westwards towards Hudson's Bay. Stories abounded of him being nursed back to life over the winter of 1849, and of him eventually making his way up Backs Fish River, or out towards Repulse Bay. Some Inuit women even teased the Europeans years later by saying they had children descended not only from Crozier but from Franklin himself.

What was certain among all this mixed testimony was that Crozier was definitely seen on the southernmost tip of King

William Island in the summer of 1848. He met a group of Inuit then, and begged for seal meat for his starving men. What was also certain was that neither he nor any of his crew were seen again after that last meeting. The ships—those huge technical masterpieces of Victorian Britain—had sunk or been driven onto the shore by the storms of subsequent years and had broken up. They, like the men aboard them, had disappeared as if they had never existed.

Jo shuddered as the taxi pulled into the airport terminal. What if John never comes back? she thought, watching Catherine's profile. Lady Jane Franklin had mourned for nearly thirty years after Franklin had disappeared, she knew. Suddenly, she wished desperately that Catherine should never know what it was to live the rest of her life, like Franklin's wife, without knowing what had happened to the man she loved.

WHEN JO AND CATHERINE got out of the cab at Heathrow Airport, they were in for a shock. The first person Jo saw was a news reporter, running towards her, with a cameraman in close pursuit.

'Meridian News,' said the woman. 'Have you heard any more about John Marshall?'

'No,' Jo said, flinching at the camera light.

'How is Sam, Miss Harper?' Another voice.

'He's OK. Stable.'

'Are you going out there?'

'No,' Jo said. 'Miss Takkiruq is going. She knows the area.'

The microphone turned in Catherine's direction. 'If he's there anywhere, we'll get him,' Catherine said.

Jo reached out a hand towards the reporter. 'I want to make one thing clear,' she said. 'John doesn't know why we're looking for him.' She tried to steady her voice. 'If we find him, and he decides to come back, that'll be wonderful.' She looked directly into the camera. 'But if we don't get to him in time, or . . . or whatever happens,' she added, 'it's not his fault. Please remember that.'

IT WAS TWO FIFTEEN before they got Catherine's luggage checked through. She stood at the departures gate, gripping her tickets.

'Hug Sam for me,' she said.

'I will.'

'His count was better today.'

'Yes.'

Jo glanced at the computer screen, where the number of Catherine's flight showed green. Boarding, Calgary, Gate 79.

Jo wrapped her arms around Catherine. 'Please take care of yourself,' she whispered.

'I'm going to bring him back, Jo,' Catherine said. 'We'll walk back through those gates. I promise you.'

She kissed Jo's cheek and walked away.

Watching her, Jo felt an almighty wrench in her chest. She wanted so much to go with her, to step off that plane in Gjoa Haven. To walk out with her wherever she was going.

And she wanted to be in Great Ormond Street, to watch the next transfusion, to will the blood through the lines, to stare at Sam's pulse, that little blue spot under the skin on his arm. That was her signal of life. While the vein there flickered, he was still with her.

God, it was so much to ask for. The life of a child. The life of John Marshall. Two lives, in a world of daily destruction. The weight of it pressed down on her. She could just see Catherine at the departures gate, her tall frame, her dark hair. She was so frightened that Catherine should be going alone. That she wouldn't come back.

And then, she saw him. Doug was just to the left of Catherine. Jo saw him in profile, his grey bag slung over one shoulder. He was gazing round the crowds, looking for someone. 'Doug . . .'

He turned. First to Catherine. Then, he looked towards her. She met his eyes, saw the message in them. *I'm going with her. I'll be there.*

She blinked; he vanished. Catherine looked back, once, and raised her hand. Then she was lost in the crowd.

Jo stared at the place where Doug had been.

'Dear God,' she prayed, letting go of all her previous bitterness, 'dear God, please, please help us.'

An overwhelming feeling suddenly swept over her. A warm sensation, an unmistakable note of connection. She felt Doug so close to her that she had the touch of his lips on her face.

STARVATION COVE. Maconochie Island. John had seen it before in his dreams, although his dreams had always been high with colour: stark blues and orange, backlit ice that glowed in low light; green-blue ocean, Arctic poppies, saxifrage. In the last two days he had realised that there was no colour here.

He stood on the highest piece of land he could find. It was midday. There was nothing at his back but the moonscape of the peninsula.

Water lay everywhere. Run-off from the ice had left hundreds of pools among the rock.

He looked east. The land was perfectly flat for as far as the eye could see. There was no movement, no vegetation. As he turned his body, every muscle protested. He had walked thirty-five miles in three days, and his legs burned. He had pitched his tent, but he had made a poor job of it. The tent door flapped. He felt an overwhelming urge to pull it down.

Out there, to the east, the inlet broadened. Maconochie Island was probably half a mile away. On the map that had been pinned to his wall in Cambridge, the island was a small white oval, fringed on its western side with sand and gravel dunes. And it was the same today. A bleached horizon, with fog rolling. White on grey, grey on white.

John sat down on the shore. He curled up on the ground, the last of his energy gone, oblivious to the 7-degree temperature and the ever-present thick cloud of mosquitoes. His face was swollen with bites. It didn't matter. The pain was no longer real. Like his thirst, it had become background buzz.

He rolled onto his stomach, plunging his hands into the stones underneath him. A cool salt breeze blew over him.

Lieutenant Schwatka had called this Starvation Cove when he came looking for Franklin in 1879. He thought he had found survivors then. He listened to the Esquimaux and heard them tell him about finding bodies, and watches, and guns, and gunpowder.

Some said Crozier had got as far as Montreal Island, but John had always doubted it. No . . . it was here. He had died here.

John turned on his side and opened his eyes. After leaving the boat from Gjoa Haven on the coast, the walk had been cleansing. He was grateful for the hardness of it, because it had filled his head. It had rained the second night, and when he woke up water had got into the tent somehow; he had found that he was wet through. He had got up and moved on, seeing ice far out in the channel. Another month, and the weather would start to close in again.

He pushed himself to a sitting position now, and waited. Suddenly, his father sprang into his mind. His father talking to Jo Harper. John had wanted to tell him about Catherine but never could put it into words. That was his problem: words closed in his throat. He couldn't reveal himself. Only Catherine had seen the face he hid, had known his desperation, wanted his love. She had taken the obsessions, accepted him.

He couldn't look into her face after Doug had died. He couldn't bear the patient forgiveness and understanding. He didn't forgive himself. Why should she? He had nothing to give anyone. And yet she would have walked with him this far.

He put his hand up to his face, wondered where the water had come from, then realised that it was tears.

THE DAY ROLLED DOWN towards evening. The rain came suddenly, the wind picked up and drove the needles of cold into his face. He could no longer see the ice on the ocean, the pitted terrain at his back. Disorientation took hold of him.

He had found himself on his hands and knees, and he couldn't remember what he was looking for. He had somehow cut himself on the palm of one hand, looking for something. The rounded, cylindrical shape he thought he'd felt.

He lay in the door of the tent now, motionless. Somewhere out there in the sea was *Erebus*. She would have drifted. Perhaps she had brought *Terror* with her. The Inuit said that one of the ships had been broken up on the shore of King William, pushed there by ice. They had found the other almost intact, further south, and they had boarded her, and found a man's body, and a ladder stretching down to the ice, and the footprints of two other men. They had gained access by tearing away part of the hull. They carried off what metal they could, and then found that the ship was sinking, because they had weakened the hull around the water line.

She went down within the day. Somewhere at the bottom of the sea were the remains. His father had always said what a coup that would be, the dive of his life—to go down to the wreck of *Erebus* or *Terror*.

John got to his feet and stared out at the ocean. He looked at the blue on grey, and the light sky devoid of stars.

'Dad,' he said, the word drowned by the sound of the water. He sank to his knees in the grainy shale of the beach. 'I can't find you,' he whispered. 'Dad, help me. I can't find you.'

THE SOUND OF THE BOAT came late at night. It was only the persistence of one person that had brought them this far. The boat ground up on the shingle. Three people got out, two immediately hauling the canoe up onto land. They turned their faces from the onslaught of the wind, shoulders hunched. He heard their voices—surely ghost voices—torn and scattered by the gale. The third figure looked up the slope, and began to run towards him. He strained through a fevered sleep to see her coming through the torrent towards him.

As she knelt beside him, she pushed back the hood from her face, and he saw the water, the driving rainfall of the storm, streaming through her hair. That hair, black in his hand, that rope of hair . . .

'John,' she called 'John . . .'

He closed his eyes, grateful that she had come to him in this most terrible dream.

She put her arms round him. She lifted his head.

'It's too far,' he said. 'Too far to go back.'

'It doesn't matter how far,' she told him. 'We'll go there together.'

CATHERINE HAD BEEN gone five days.

Gina was standing in the ward in Great Ormond Street. They had put Sam in a screened-off bed; Jo was next to him, propped up in the big green armchair. She was asleep, her head on one side, and Sam's teddy bear was in her hand.

The TV set was on, but with the sound turned down. Gina stepped forward, momentarily drawn by the image. The familiar BBC logo of the evening news had been replaced by the face of the newsreader, and in the top left-hand corner of the screen an image of a helicopter hovering above a grey landscape, a knot of people on the ground below it.

At that very second, Jo woke up. Following Gina's gaze, she turned to the screen. 'My God,' she breathed.

Now there was a camera shot taken from a moving plane. The first snatched image showed a patch of blue against the grey. It was a small tent, pitched between pools of water, stranded on an isthmus of land.

Next image, a map: Gjoa Haven marked as a red spot in the north, Pelly Bay to the east, Cambridge Bay to the west, the long stretch of King William in between. And the tent again, closer this time, the plane flying lower. Then, faces. Catherine, mobbed on an airport strip, her father at her side. Joseph Takkiruq's brown face and piercing black eyes. Catherine lifting her hair out of her eyes with one hand, grinning.

Jo leapt forward for the volume control. ' . . . found alive after five days' search in this most unforgiving of landscapes, and a worldwide publicity campaign lasting more than two months . . .'

The crowd was parting. Behind them was a medevac stretcher.

'Oh God, oh God!' Gina cried.

The commentary swept over them. They heard probably half of it. At that same moment, both phones on the ward sister's desk down the corridor began to ring.

' . . . this double rescue, on the same day that the polar bear cub was airlifted to Manitoba . . .'

Now Catherine was on screen again.

'Miss Takkiruq! How is John?'

'He's OK,' she replied. 'Exhausted. But OK . . .'

'Can you show us what was found?'

'I can,' she said. They saw Catherine dig into her parka pocket. She brought out a small copper canister, greened over with verdigris.

Jo uttered a small, astounded cry.

'It was underneath him,' Catherine was saying. 'Under his arm.' She smiled broadly and looked at the item in her hand. 'Francis Crozier,' she murmured, 'Captain of Her Majesty's Ship *Terror*, August the 11th, 1848.'

In the hospital room, Jo and Gina flung their arms round each other.

On screen, they saw Catherine put her hands over her ears in renewed protest at the volley of noise around her.

Jo rushed to Sam, who was now awake, and kissed him.

Catherine had grabbed the nearest microphone. 'Can I say something?' she asked. 'I have a message for Jo Harper in London.'

Across the bed, Gina gripped Jo's arm.

They saw Catherine hold up the canister. 'Hey, Jo,' she said softly, to the camera, 'miracles do happen, after all. Tell Sam his brother is coming home.'

POSTSCRIPT

The Tundra Buggy in Churchill Bay, Manitoba, was raised ten feet from the ground, but the bear, stretched to full height, still reached the window. Those in the vehicle moved back instinctively, seeing the massive head intruding almost into the cab, its teeth fastened on the window edge. But the child did not move.

Of all those in the buggy, perhaps his mother should have been the most afraid. But Jo Harper stood back with Bill Elliott to watch this most extraordinary meeting.

It was John Marshall who stepped forward. He sat beside his half-brother, taking him on his knee, next to Catherine. 'What shall we call him, Sam?' he asked, wrapping his arms round the four-year-old boy.

'Swimmer,' Sam replied.

'You think he can swim?' Catherine said, smiling.

'Miles and miles,' Sam told her.

'Like his mother,' John agreed.

The bear turned away and dropped on all fours on the snow-swept plain. It seemed to hesitate, and then it moved away, walking north-west without looking back. The first great white bear to be released from captivity back into the wild.

John stood up with Sam. They followed the Swimmer as far as they could see it along the observation deck. Then John turned to Jo, held out his arms, and hugged her. They stood there for some time, Sam wedged between them.

'Do you think it'll survive?' Jo murmured.

'Yes,' John replied, with conviction. 'The impossible happens here.'

Running back to the window, Sam pulled off his mittened gloves and pressed his palm to the cold pane. As he took his hand away, a perfect impression was left. Taking off his own glove, John superimposed his hand on Sam's. Over John's, Jo placed her own.

When they took their hands down, three interwoven prints patterned the window.

And, beyond them, the track of the polar bear stretched away.

SOME STORIES ARE TRUE, and some are fantasy. Some journeys are dreamed of, but never made.

And some, like Sam Marshall and Augustus Peterman, travel a long way through the dark on paths that no other man could ever know.

To reach the light at last.

ELIZABETH McGREGOR

With over a hundred short stories, several TV scripts and six psychological thrillers to her name, Elizabeth McGregor is no newcomer to the world of fiction. But with *The Ice Child*, a book she was inspired to write after reading letters written by members of the Franklin Expedition of 1845, she is set to break into the big time.

Before becoming an author, she had a variety of unsatisfactory jobs. Armed with a BA in Literature from Lancaster University, she initially worked in the civil service and became 'hopelessly bored but solvent' processing Treasury finance applications for the Department of the Environment. Then, following the birth of her daughter and various moves up and down the country, necessitated by her husband's career, she dabbled in antique dealing, however she says that she proved 'utterly ineffective and very nearly bankrupt—I liked the stuff too much and kept most of it!' Finally, she became a teacher of creative writing.

'I started writing in a serious way when when my daughter was just under a year old. I entered a *Woman's Own* short-story competition, wrote a story in a day and, to my amazement, it won! *The Ice Child* was the next great turning point in her career. She wrote it in just two short weeks. 'I have stuck to fact wherever possible, but all the conversations described can only be conjecture. No ships' logs were ever found—similarly, only one copper canister. There was no one called Augustus Peterman on *Terror*. There were no boys below the age of seventeen. Yet boys of Gus's age were regularly taken on other vessels. I wanted to develop the tragedy through a child's perception, so I hope this slight stretching of the facts will be excused.'

She revels in the book's success. 'Written at a traumatic time when my twenty-year-old marriage was coming to an end, and mother died, its success still feels like a dream. I keep thinking I might wake up from it all!'

> THE BLUE NOWHERE
> JEFFERY DEAVER

> In the 'blue nowhere', the
> infinite reaches of cyberspace,
> hackers rule supreme. No
> computer is secure; no one's
> privacy is guaranteed.

> Which means that a serial
> killer called 'Phate', who
> infiltrates and takes control of
> his victims' computers, poses
> serious problems for
> Detective Frank Bishop and
> his colleagues at a Computer
> Crimes Unit in California.

> How can they catch a
> merciless and brilliant criminal
> able to disappear at the speed
> of light, leaving no trace?

0000001 / ONE: THE WIZARD

The battered white van had made her uneasy.

Lara Gibson sat at the bar of Vesta's Grill on De Anza Boulevard in Cupertino, California, gripping the cold stem of her martini glass and ignoring the two young men standing nearby, casting flirtatious glances at her.

She looked outside again, into the overcast drizzle, and saw no sign of the windowless white van that, she believed, had followed her from her house to the restaurant. Lara slid off the bar stool and walked to the window to investigate more closely. The van wasn't in the restaurant's parking lot. Nor was it across the street in the Apple Computer lot, which would've been a logical place to park to keep an eye on her—if the driver had in fact been stalking her.

No, the van was just a coincidence, she decided—a coincidence aggravated by a splinter of paranoia.

She returned to the bar and glanced at the two young men who were alternately ignoring her and offering subtle smiles.

Like nearly all the young chip-jocks—or hardware developers— here for happy hour they were in casual slacks and tie-less shirts and wore the ubiquitous insignia of Silicon Valley—corporate identification badges on thin canvas lanyards round their necks. These two sported the blue cards of Sun Microsystems. Others represented Compaq, Hewlett-Packard and Apple, not to mention a slew of start-up Internet companies which were held in some disdain by the venerable Valley regulars.

At thirty-two, Lara Gibson was probably five years older than her two admirers. Although as a self-employed businesswoman who wasn't a geek—connected with a computer company—she was easily five times poorer. But that didn't matter to these two men, who were captivated by her exotic, intense face, surrounded by a tangle of raven hair, and the tight, black sleeveless top that showed off her hard-earned biceps.

She figured that it would be two minutes before one of these men approached her and she missed that estimate by only ten seconds.

The young man gave her a variation of a line she'd heard a dozen times before. *Excuse me but, hey, would you like me to break your boyfriend's leg for making a beautiful woman wait alone and, by the way, can I buy you a drink while you decide which leg?*

Another woman might have felt threatened, another woman might have stammered and blushed. But those would be women weaker than she. Lara Gibson was 'the queen of urban protection', as the *San Francisco Chronicle* had once dubbed her. She fixed her eyes on the man's, gave a formal smile and said, 'I don't care for any company right now.' Simple as that.

He blinked at her frankness and returned to his friend.

Power . . . it was all about power.

That damn white van had brought to mind all the rules she'd developed as someone who taught women to protect themselves in today's society. Several times on the way to the restaurant she'd glanced into her rearview mirror and noticed the van thirty or forty feet behind. It had been driven by some kid. He was white but his hair was knotted into messy brown dreadlocks. He wore a combat jacket and, despite the overcast and misty rain, sunglasses.

Lara found herself absently fondling the can of pepper spray she kept in her purse. She glanced at the wall clock. Quarter past seven. Her friend, Sandy, was fifteen minutes late. Not like her. Lara pulled out her cellphone but the display read NO SERVICE.

She was about to find the payphone when she saw a young man enter the bar and wave at her. She knew him from somewhere, but couldn't quite place him. His trim, but long, blond hair and the goatee had stuck in her mind.

'Hey, Lara.' He walked up and shook her hand, leaned against the bar. 'Remember me? I'm Will Randolph. Sandy's cousin? Cheryl and I met you on Nantucket—at Fred and Mary's wedding.'

That's where she recognised him from. He and his pregnant wife had sat at the same table as Lara. 'Sure, Will. How you doing?'

'Good. Busy. But who isn't around here?'

His plastic neckwear read Xerox Corporation PARC. Xerox's legendary Palo Alto Research Center. She was impressed.

Will flagged down the bartender and ordered a light beer. They chatted and the beer arrived. Will continued, 'Sandy asked if I'd stop by and give you a message,' he said. 'She tried to call you but couldn't get through on your cellphone. She's running late and asked if you could meet her at Ciro's in Mountain View. She made a reservation at eight.'

'You didn't have to come by. She could've called the bartender.'

'She wanted me to give you the pictures I took at the wedding. You two can look at 'em tonight and tell me if you want any copies. They're out in my car.' He paused and smiled as if he had a secret to share. He pulled his wallet out and flipped it open to a picture of himself, his wife and a very tiny, ruddy baby. 'Last week,' he said proudly. 'Claire.'

'Oh, adorable,' Lara whispered. 'How's Cheryl?'

'She and the baby are fine. There's nothing like it . . . But, I'll tell you, being a father totally changes your life.'

'I'm sure it does.'

Lara glanced at the clock again. Half past seven. It was a half-hour drive to Ciro's. 'I better get going.'

Then, with a thud of alarm, she thought again about the van.

And the dreadlocks.

Will gestured for the bill and paid.

'You don't have to do that,' she said. 'I'll get it.'

He laughed. 'You already did.'

'What?'

'That biotech fund you told me about at the wedding. The one you'd just bought? I got home and bought a load of it . . . So . . . Thanks.' He tipped the beer towards her and, draining the bottle, he stood up. 'You all set?'

'You bet.' Lara stared uneasily at the door as they walked towards it. She recalled another rule of urban protection: Never feel too embarrassed or proud to ask for help.

'Will, I think somebody followed me here to the restaurant. Some kid.'

Will looked around. 'You see him?'

'Not now.'

He asked, 'You run that web site, right? Advising women how to protect themselves.'

'That's right.'

'You think he knows about it? Maybe he's harassing you.'

'Could be. Will . . . Would you mind, after we get the pictures, walking me to my car?'

Will smiled. 'Of course not.'

They walked along the sidewalk in front of the restaurant and she checked out the Saabs, BMWs and Lexuses. No vans.

Will nodded towards his car in the back parking lot, a spotless silver Jaguar.

Did *everybody* in Silicon Valley have money except her?

He dug the keys out of his pocket. They walked to the trunk. 'I only took two rolls at the wedding. But some of them are pretty good.' He opened the trunk, paused and looked around the parking lot. She did too. It was completely deserted.

Will glanced at her. 'You were probably wondering about the dreads.'

'Dreads?'

'Yeah,' he said. 'The dreadlocks.' His voice was flatter, distracted. He was still smiling, but his face was different now. It seemed hungry.

'What do you mean?' she asked calmly but fear was detonating inside her. She noticed a chain was blocking the entrance to the back parking lot. And she knew he'd hooked it after he'd pulled in—to make sure nobody else could park there.

'It was a wig.'

Oh, my Lord, thought Lara Gibson, who hadn't prayed in twenty years.

He looked into her eyes, recording her fear. 'I parked the Jag here a while ago then stole the van and followed you from home. With the wig on. You know, just so you'd get edgy and paranoid and want me to stay close . . . I know all your rules—that urban protection stuff. Never go into a deserted parking lot with a man. Married men with children are safer than single men. And my family portrait? In my wallet? I hacked it together from a picture in *Parents* magazine.'

She whispered hopelessly, 'You're not . . . ?'

'Sandy's cousin? Don't even know him. I picked Will Randolph because he's somebody you *sort of* know, who *sort of* looks like me. Oh, and you can take your hand out of your purse.' He held up her canister of pepper spray. 'I got it when we were walking outside.'

'But . . .' Sobbing now, shoulders slumped into hopelessness. 'Who *are* you? You don't even know me . . .'

'Not true, Lara,' he whispered, studying her anguish. 'I know everything about you. Everything in the world.'

THOMAS FREDERICK ANDERSON was a man of many names.

Tom or Tommy in his grade-school days. Stealth when he'd been a high-school student in Menlo Park, California, hacking on TRS-80s and Commodores. CryptO when he'd worked for the security department of AT&T, tracking down hackers and phone phreaks and call jackers. Nowadays he was usually called either Dr Anderson—when introduced at computer conferences—or just plain Andy. In official records, though, he was Lieutenant Thomas F. Anderson, chief of the California State Police Computer Crimes Unit, the CCU.

The lanky man, forty-five years old, with thinning curly brown hair, now walked down a chill, damp corridor beside the podgy warden of the San Jose Correctional Facility—San Ho, as it was called by perpetrators and cops alike. A solidly built Latino guard accompanied them.

They continued down the hallway until they came to a door. The warden nodded. The guard opened it and Anderson stepped inside, eyeing the prisoner.

At twenty-nine, Wyatt Gillette had the hollow face of a man who was six foot, one inch tall and weighed 154 pounds, a man about whom people were always thinking, Somebody should fatten him up. He was very pale—he had a 'hacker tan' as the pallor was ironically called. His hair was dark, nearly black, and was filthy, as were his fingernails. Gillette apparently hadn't showered or shaved in days.

The cop noticed an odd look in Gillette's dark brown eyes; he was blinking in recognition. 'You're . . . Andy Anderson?'

'You know me?'

'I heard you lecture at Comsec a couple of years ago.'

The Comsec conference on computer security was limited to law enforcers; but Anderson knew it was a national pastime for hackers to try to crack the registration computer and issue themselves admission badges. Only two or three had ever succeeded.

'How'd you get in?'

Gillette shrugged. 'I found a badge somebody dropped.'

Anderson nodded sceptically. 'What'd you think of my lecture?'

'I agree with you: silicon chips'll be outmoded faster than most people think. Computers'll be running on molecular electronics. That means users'll have to start looking at a whole new way to protect themselves against hackers.'

'Nobody else felt that way at the conference.'

'They heckled you,' Gillette recalled.

'But you didn't?'

'No. I took notes.'

The warden leaned against the wall while the cop sat down across from Gillette and said, 'You've got one year left on a three-year sentence under the Federal Computer Fraud and Abuse Act. You cracked Western Software's machines and stole the source codes for most of their programs, right?'

Gillette nodded.

The source code is the brains and heart of software, fiercely guarded by its owner. Stealing it lets the thief easily strip out identification codes then repackage the software and sell it under his own name. If an unscrupulous hacker had stolen Western Software's codes he might have put the billion-dollar company out of business.

Gillette pointed out: 'I didn't do anything with the codes. I erased them after I downloaded them.'

'Then why'd you crack their systems?'

The hacker shrugged. 'I saw the head of the company on CNN. He said that their network security systems were foolproof. I wanted to see if that was true.'

'Were they?'

'As a matter of fact, yeah, they were foolproof. The problem is that you don't have to protect yourself against fools. You have to protect yourself against people like me.'

'Well, once you'd broken in why didn't you tell the company about the security flaws? Do a white hat?'

White hats were hackers who cracked into computer systems and then pointed out the security flaws to their victims. Sometimes for the glory of it, sometimes for money. Sometimes even because they thought it was the right thing to do.

Gillette shrugged. 'It's their problem.'

'Why'd the feds come down on you so hard?' Anderson asked. If a hacker doesn't disrupt business or try to sell what he steals the FBI rarely even investigates, let alone refers a case to the Attorney General.

It was the warden who answered. 'The reason is the DoD.'

'Department of Defense?' Anderson asked.

The warden explained, 'The Pentagon thinks he wrote some program that cracked the DoD's latest encryption software.'

'Their Standard 12?' Anderson gave a laugh. 'You'd need a dozen supercomputers running for six months to crack a single email.'

Standard 12 had recently replaced DES—the Defense Encryption Standard—as the state-of-the-art encryption software government agencies used to encrypt secret data.

Anderson continued, 'But even if he *did* crack something encoded with Standard 12, so what? *Everybody* tries to crack encryptions.'

There was nothing illegal about this as long as the encrypted document wasn't classified or stolen. In fact, many software manufacturers offer prizes to anybody who can break documents encrypted with their programs.

'No,' Gillette explained. 'The DoD's saying that I cracked into their computer, found out how Standard 12 works and then wrote some script that decrypts a document in seconds.'

'Impossible,' Anderson said, laughing. 'Can't be done.'

Gillette said, 'That's what I told them. They didn't believe me.'

Anderson knew he himself couldn't have done it; he didn't know *anybody* who could. But maybe Gillette *had*. After all, the cop was here now, hat in hand, because Gillette was a wizard, the term used by hackers to describe those among them who've reached the highest levels of skill in the Machine World.

There was a knock on the door and the guard let two men inside. The first one, fortyish, had a lean face, dark blond hair swept back and frozen in place with hairspray. Honest-to-God sideburns too. He wore a cheap grey suit. His overwashed white shirt was far too big for him and was untucked. He glanced at Gillette without a splinter of interest. 'Sir,' he said to the warden in a flat voice. 'I'm Detective Frank Bishop, State Police, Homicide.' He nodded an anaemic greeting to Anderson and fell silent.

The second man, a little younger, much heavier, shook the warden's hand then Anderson's. 'Detective Bob Shelton.' His face was pockmarked from childhood acne.

Anderson didn't know anything about Shelton but he'd talked to Bishop and had mixed feelings concerning his involvement in this case. Bishop was supposedly a wizard in his own right though *his* expertise lay in tracking down killers and rapists in tough neighbourhoods like the Oakland waterfront and the infamous San

Francisco Tenderloin. He knew nothing about computers.

Anderson had also heard that Bishop didn't want to be working with Computer Crimes. He'd been lobbying for the Marinkill Case— so named by the FBI for the site of the crime: several days ago three bank robbers had murdered two bystanders and a cop at a Bank of America branch in Marin County and had been seen headed east, which meant they might very well turn south towards Bishop's present turf, the San Jose area.

'You gentlemen want to sit down?' asked Anderson.

Bishop shook his head and remained standing. He tucked his shirt in then crossed his arms. Shelton sat down next to Gillette. Then the bulky cop looked distastefully at the prisoner and moved to the other side of the table. To Gillette he muttered, 'You might want to get cleaned up sometime.'

The convict retorted, 'You might want to ask the warden why I only get one shower a week.'

'Because, Wyatt,' the warden said patiently, 'you broke the prison rules. That's why you're in administrative seclusion.'

Anderson didn't have the patience or time for squabbles. He said to Gillette, 'We've got a problem and we're hoping you'll help us with it. Last night a woman was abducted from a restaurant in Cupertino. She was murdered and her body found in Portola Valley. She'd been stabbed to death. She wasn't sexually molested and there's no apparent motive.

'Now, this victim, Lara Gibson, ran a web site and lectured about how women can protect themselves. She'd been in the press a lot and on TV. Well, what happens is, she's in a restaurant and this guy comes in who seems to know her. He knows all kinds of information about her, the bartender said. Friends, social engagements, what she does, what stocks she owns.'

'He social engineered her,' Gillette offered.

'How's that?' Shelton asked.

Anderson knew the term but he deferred to Gillette, who explained, 'It means conning somebody, pretending you're somebody you're not. The more facts about somebody you can feed back to them, the more they believe you and the more they'll do what you want them to.'

Anderson continued, 'Now, the girlfriend Lara was supposed to meet—Sandra Hardwick—said she got a call from somebody claiming to be Lara's boyfriend cancelling the dinner plans. She tried to call Lara but her phone was out.'

Gillette nodded. 'He crashed her cellphone, then turned himself into somebody she'd trust, and he did it with information he got from her computer?'

'Exactly.'

'Did she have an online service?'

'Horizon Online.'

Gillette laughed. 'You know how secure that is? He hacked into one of their routers and read her emails.' The hacker shook his head, studied Anderson's face. 'But that's kindergarten stuff. There's more, isn't there?'

'Right,' Anderson continued. 'We went through her computer. Half the information the bartender heard the killer tell her *wasn't* in her emails. It was in the machine itself.'

Gillette's eyes narrowed. Anderson could see he was interested.

'The bottom line is that we think there's some kind of new virus the killer used to get inside her machine. The thing is, we can't find it. We're hoping you'll take a look.'

Gillette nodded, squinting as he looked up at the grimy ceiling. Anderson noticed the young man's fingers were moving in tiny, rapid taps. At first the cop thought Gillette had some nervous twitch, but then he realised he was unconsciously typing on an invisible keyboard—a nervous habit, it seemed.

The hacker lowered his eyes to Anderson. 'How'm I going to find something you couldn't?'

'I need a hacker. You walked around inside every machine in Western Software, even places the *chairman* didn't have access to.'

Gillette asked Anderson, 'So what's in it for me?'

'What?' Bob Shelton stared at the hacker. 'A girl got murdered. Don't you give a shit?'

'I'm sorry about her,' Gillette shot back. 'But the deal is if I help you I want something in return. I want a machine.'

'No computers,' the warden snapped. 'No way.' To Anderson he said, 'The judge issued an order that he can't go online.'

'I won't go online,' Gillette said. 'I'll stay on E wing, where I won't have access to a phone line.'

The warden scoffed. 'You'd rather stay in administrative seclusion—'

'Solitary confinement,' Gillette corrected.

'—just to have a computer?'

'Yes.'

Anderson asked, 'If he were to stay in seclusion, so there was no chance of going online, would that be OK?'

'I guess,' the warden conceded.

The cop turned to Gillette, 'It's a deal. We'll get you a laptop. But only *after* you analyse the Gibson woman's computer. We'll get it over here in the next hour.'

'No, no, no,' Gillette said firmly. 'I can't do it here.'

'Why not?'

'I'll need access to a mainframe—maybe a supercomputer. I'll need tech manuals, software.'

Anderson was debating with himself when the warden asked, 'Can I see you gentlemen up the hall for a minute?'

IT HAD BEEN a fun hack.

But not as challenging as he would've liked.

Phate—his screen name, spelt in the best hacker tradition with a *ph* and not an *f*—now drove to his house in Los Altos, in the heart of Silicon Valley.

He'd been busy this morning: he'd abandoned the white van that he'd used to light the fires of paranoia under Lara Gibson yesterday and ditched the dreadlock wig of the stalker and the chip-jock costume of Will Randolph. He was now someone entirely different.

Not his real name or identity, of course—Jon Patrick Holloway, who'd been born twenty-seven years ago in Upper Saddle River, New Jersey. No, he was at the moment one of six or seven fictional characters he'd created, complete with driver's licences and social security cards and all the telltale documentation that is so indispensable nowadays. He'd even endowed his cast with different accents and mannerisms, which he practised religiously.

Who do you want to be?

Phate's answer was: pretty much anybody in the world.

Reflecting now on the Lara Gibson hack, he decided it'd been just a bit too easy to get close to someone who prided herself on being the queen of urban protection.

And so it was time to notch the game up a bit.

Phate's Jaguar moved slowly through morning rush-hour traffic. To the west the Santa Cruz mountains rose into the spectres of fog slipping towards the San Francisco Bay. This spring had been rainy and the flora was a rich green. Phate, however, paid no attention to the expansive scenery. He was listening to a play on his CD player—

Arthur Miller's *Death of a Salesman*. Occasionally his mouth would move to the words (he knew all the parts).

Ten minutes later, at 8.45am, he was pulling up in the garage of his large, detached house in the Stonecrest development in Los Altos. He noticed a drop of Lara Gibson's blood in the shape of a comma on the otherwise immaculate garage floor. Careless to miss it earlier. He cleaned the stain then went inside, locking the door.

The house was new, only about six months old, and smelt of carpet glue and paint. The room was expensively furnished and displayed dozens of pictures of Phate and a blonde woman, posing at the beach, dancing at their wedding. Other pictures showed the couple with their two children. Vacations, soccer practice, Christmas and Easter celebrations.

Neighbours who'd come calling to welcome him to the neighbourhood would stand in the front hallway and see evidence of an upper-middle-class family living the comfortable life that chip money has provided for so many people here in the Valley.

Hey, nice to meet you . . . Yeah, that's right—just moved in last month. I'm with a dot-com start-up over in Palo Alto. They brought me and half the furniture out from Austin early, before Kathy and the kids—they'll be here in June after school's over. You know, I'd ask you over for dinner, but Kathy's the social director . . . and a lot better cook than me. OK, you take care now.

And the neighbours would pass him the welcoming wine or cookies and return home, never guessing that the entire scene had been as fake as a movie set.

Like the pictures he'd shown Lara Gibson, these snapshots had been created on his computer. The house was a façade too; the living room and hall were the only fully furnished rooms. In the bedroom was a bed and a lamp. In the dining room—Phate's office—was a table, lamp, two laptop computers and an office chair. If need be, he could walk out the door and leave everything behind.

He now walked into the dining room and sat down at the table. He turned on a laptop.

The screen came to life, a C: prompt flashed on the screen and, with the appearance of that blinking symbol, Phate rose from the dead. *This* was his reality, the world inside his monitor.

He keyed some commands and, with an excited churning in his groin, heard the rising and falling whistle of his modem's sensual electronic handshake. He was connected to the Net and checked his email. He would have opened any letters from Shawn right away but there were none. He exited the mail reader and then keyed in another command. A menu popped up on his screen.

Trapdoor

Main Menu

1. Do you want to continue a prior session?
2. Do you want to create/open/edit a background file?
3. Do you want to find a new target?
4. Do you want to decode/decrypt a password or text?
5. Do you want to exit the system?

He scrolled down to 3 and hit the ENTER key.
A moment later the Trapdoor program politely asked:

Please enter the email address of the target.

From memory he typed a screen name and hit ENTER. Within ten seconds he was connected to someone else's machine, looking over the unsuspecting user's shoulder.

Lara Gibson had been a fun hack, but this one would be better.

'HE MADE THIS,' the warden told them.

The cops stood in a confiscation room in San Ho. Lining the shelves were drug paraphernalia, Nazi decorations and handmade weapons, even a few guns. What the warden was now pointing out, though, was nothing so clearly deadly. It was a wooden box filled with a hundred strips of bell wire, which connected dozens of electronic components.

Andy Anderson laughed and whispered, 'My God, it's a computer. It's a homemade computer.' He leaned forwards, studying the simplicity of the wiring, the perfect twisting of the solderless connections, the efficient use of space. It was rudimentary, yet astonishingly *elegant*.

'I didn't know you could make a computer,' Bob Shelton offered.

'Gillette's the worst addict I've ever seen—and we get guys in here've been on smack for years. Only *he*'s addicted to computers. He built this just to get on the Internet,' said the warden.

'It's got a modem built in?' Anderson asked, still awed by the device. 'Wait, there it is, yeah.'

'You *think* you can control him,' the warden continued, 'but people like him are just like alcoholics. You know about his wife?'

'He's married?' Anderson asked.

'Was. He tried to stop hacking after he got married but couldn't. Then he got arrested and they lost everything paying the lawyer and court fine. She divorced him. I was here when he got the papers. He didn't even care.'

He handed a battered manila folder to Anderson. 'Here's the file we've got on him.'

Anderson flipped through the file. The prisoner had a record going back years. The juvenile detention time for what hackers call phreaking, breaking into phone company switches—which are nothing more than huge computer systems—to make free calls or just to enjoy the challenge. He'd also been questioned in connection with twelve major hacking incidents over the past eight years.

His behaviour wasn't, however, exclusively felonious. Gillette had worked for a number of Silicon Valley companies and invariably had received glowing reports on his programming skills—at least until he was fired for missing work or falling asleep on the job because he'd been up all night hacking.

Then Anderson did a double take. He was looking at a reprint of a magazine article that Wyatt Gillette had written. The article was well known and Anderson recalled reading it when it first came out but had paid no attention to who the author was. The title was 'Life in the Blue Nowhere'. Its theme was that computers are the first technological invention in history that affects *every* aspect of human life. There are many benefits to this but also many dangers. The phrase 'Blue Nowhere' was replacing the term 'cyberspace'. 'Blue' referred to the electricity that made computers work. 'Nowhere' meant that it was an intangible place.

Andy Anderson also found photocopies of dozens of heartfelt letters requesting leniency in sentencing, sent to the judge by Gillette's father, an American engineer working overseas. The hacker's mother had passed away, but it sounded like the young man and his father had an enviable relationship.

Anderson was surprised. Most hackers came from dysfunctional families.

He handed the file to Bishop, who read through it absently.

'I'm just giving you fair warning,' the warden urged. He nodded at the homemade computer. 'If you want to go ahead, be my guest.'

Anderson looked towards Bishop. 'What do you think, Frank?'

The lean-faced detective tucked in his shirt again and finally put together several complete sentences. 'Well, sir, I think we should get him out and the sooner the better. That killer probably isn't sitting around talking like us.'

ON THE EASTERN EDGE of Silicon Valley a podgy fifteen-year-old pounded furiously on a keyboard. He peered through thick glasses at a monitor in the computer room at St Francis Academy, a private boys' boarding school in San Jose.

Jamie Turner had never been given a grade below a 92 in his life and, even though there were two months to go until the end of term, he had completed the required reading for all of his classes. He had read the Harry Potter books five times each, *Lord of the Rings* eight times and every single word written by computer/science-fiction visionary William Gibson.

Outside on the soccer field his classmates were shouting, laughing, scoring goals, racing back and forth. Jamie was supposed to be outside and Booty wouldn't like him hiding down here.

But Booty didn't know.

Not that Jamie disliked the principal of the boarding school. Not at all, really. It was hard to dislike somebody who *cared* about you. (Unlike, say, for instance, Jamie's parents. 'See you on the 23rd, son. Oh, wait, no. Your mother and I'll be real busy. We'll be here on the 1st or the 7th. Definitely then. Love you, bye.') It was just that Booty's paranoia was a major pain. It meant lockdowns at night, all those damn alarms and continual checking up on the students.

He even refused to let the boys go to harmless rock concerts with their older, responsible brothers.

But now Jamie was taking matters into his own hands. His brother Mark, a sound engineer at an Oakland concert venue, had told Jamie that if he could escape from St Francis that night he'd get the boy into the Santana concert. He could get out of his room, of course; that wasn't locked. And he could get into the school grounds, provided he could disable the fire alarm. But *they* were surrounded by a twelve-foot-high stone wall, topped with barbed wire. And there was no way to get over that unless he cracked the passcode to one of the gates that opened onto the street. Which is why he was now cracking the passcode file of Herr Mein Führer Booty, excuse me, Dr Willem C. Boethe, MEd, PhD.

It had been easy to hack into Booty's computer and download the file containing the passcode (conveniently named, *Security Passcodes*. Hey, *way* subtle, Booty!). What was stored in the file was, of course, an encrypted version of the password. Jamie's puny clone computer would take days to crack the code, so the boy was presently hacking into the Northern California Tech and Engineering College's computer lab.

He was greeted with this:

Username?

Jamie answered: User.

Passcode?

His response: User.

And the message popped up:

Welcome, User.

Hm, how about an F minus for security, Jamie thought wryly and began to browse through the machine's root directory. The school's supercomputer, probably an old Cray, was calculating the age of the universe. Interesting, but not as cool as Santana. Jamie nudged aside the astronomy project and uploaded a program he himself had written, called Crack-er, which started to extract the English-language password from Booty's files. He—

'Oh, hell.' His computer had frozen up *again*. He had no time for crashes, not today, with his 6.30pm deadline. Still, he jotted the occurrence in his hacker's notebook, as any diligent codeslinger would do, restarted the system and logged back online. He could—

'Mr Turner, Mr Turner,' came a nearby voice. 'What are we up to here?'

The words scared the hell out of Jamie. But he hit ALT-F6 on his computer just before Principal Booty padded up to the computer terminal in his crepe-soled shoes.

A screen containing an essay about the plight of the rain forest replaced the status report from his illegal cracking program.

'Hi, Mr Boethe,' Jamie said.

'Ah.' The tall, thin man bent down, peering at the screen. 'Studying the environment, are we? Good for you. But I can't help but notice that this is your physical education period. You should be out on the soccer field, inhaling that good California air.'

'Isn't it raining?' Jamie asked.

'Misty, I'd call it. Mr Lochnell has turned his ankle, so your team needs you. I expect to see you out there in fifteen minutes.'

'Yes, sir,' responded Jamie Turner. 'I just have to shut down the system.'

Coming out of the rain-forest window, Jamie started to type a status request to see how his Crack-er program was doing on the passcode file. Then he paused, squinted at the screen. The type on the monitor seemed slightly fuzzier than normal. And something else: the keys were a little sluggish under his touch.

He guessed the trouble was a bug in the system folder, maybe a graphics accelerator problem. He'd check that later.

SEVERAL MILES AWAY, Phate was looking at exactly what Jamie Turner was seeing on his monitor in St Francis Academy.

This particular character in his game had intrigued Phate from the first time he'd invaded the boy's machine, and Phate had spent a lot of time browsing through Jamie's files. He'd learned as much about him as he had about the late Lara Gibson.

For instance: Jamie Turner hated sports and excelled at mathematics. He was a MUDhead—meaning he spent hours in the Multiuser Domain chat rooms on the Internet, excelling at role-playing games. He was also a self-taught programmer who had designed his own web site and come up with an idea for a new computer game that clearly had commercial potential.

The boy's biggest fear—reminiscent of Lara Gibson's paranoia— was losing his eyesight; he ordered special shatterproof glasses from an online optician.

Jamie Turner, Phate had concluded, was brilliant.

The boy was also just the sort of hacker who'd one day be Phate's downfall. It wouldn't be the police who brought him down, or corporate security people. It'd be a young punk hacker like Jamie.

This was why he had to stop little Jamie Turner from continuing his adventures in the Machine World. And Phate planned to stop him in a particularly effective way.

He now scrolled through more files. These, which had been emailed to him by Shawn, gave detailed information about the boy's school—St Francis Academy.

The security was extensive because the school had been the scene of a break-in several years ago in which one student had been killed. The principal, Willem Boethe, had vowed not to let that happen again. He had renovated the entire school and turned it into a fortress. Windows and doors were alarmed. You needed passcodes to get in and out of the gates in the surrounding compound.

Getting inside the school was just the kind of challenge Phate enjoyed. It was a step up from Lara Gibson—moving to a higher, more difficult level in his game. He could—

Phate squinted at the screen. Oh, no, not again. Jamie's computer—and therefore his too—had crashed. This was the *one* bug in Trapdoor. Sometimes his machine and the invaded computer would simply stop working. Then they'd both have to reboot—restart— their computers and go back online. It resulted in a delay of no more than a minute or so, but to Phate it was a terrible flaw. Software had to be perfect, it had to be *elegant*. He and Shawn had been trying to fix this bug for months.

A moment later he and his young friend were back online and a small window appeared on Phate's monitor.

> Target subject has received an instant
> message from MarkTheMan. Do you want
> to monitor?

That would be Jamie Turner's brother, Mark. Phate keyed *Y* and saw the brothers' dialogue on his screen.

> MarkTheMan: Still on for tonight?
> JamieTT: You bet. Santana RULES!!!!!
> MarkTheMan: See you across the street by the north gate at 6.30. You ready to rock n roll?

Phate thought, You bet we are.

WYATT GILLETTE PAUSED in the doorway and gazed around him at the California State Police CCU. He felt as if he'd been transported back in time. 'It's a dinosaur pen.'

'Of our very own,' Andy Anderson said. He then explained to Bishop and Shelton, neither of whom seemed to want the information, that in the early computing days huge computers like the IBM mainframes were housed in rooms like this, called dinosaur pens.

The pens featured raised floors, beneath which ran massive cables called 'boas', after the snakes they resembled (and which had been known to uncurl violently at times and injure technicians). Air conditioner ducts crisscrossed the room—the cooling systems were necessary to keep the massive computers from overheating and catching fire. In the central work area, a dozen modular cubicles had been assembled. There were eight Sun Microsystems work stations, several IBMs and Apples, a dozen laptops.

'You can rent these old data-processing facilities for a song,' Anderson explained to Gillette. He laughed. 'The CCU finally gets recognised as legit and they put us in the low-rent district of San Jose and give us digs that're twenty years out of date.'

'Look, a scram switch.' Gillette nodded at a red button on the wall. A dusty sign said EMERGENCY USE ONLY. 'I've never seen one.'

'What's that?' Bob Shelton asked.

Anderson explained: the old mainframes would get so hot that if the cooling system went down the computers could catch fire in seconds. With all the resins, plastic and rubber the gases from a burning computer would kill you before the flames would. So all dinosaur pens came equipped with a scram switch which shut off the computer and dumped halon gas on the machine to extinguish the flames.

Andy Anderson introduced Gillette, Bishop and Shelton to the CCU team. First, Linda Sanchez, a short, stocky, middle-aged Latina in a lumpy tan suit. She was the unit's SSL officer—seizure, search and logging, she explained. She was the one who secured a perpetrator's computer, checked it for booby traps, copied the files and logged hardware and software into evidence.

'Any word, Linda?'

'Not yet, boss. That daughter of mine, she's the laziest girl on earth.'

Anderson said to Gillette, 'Linda's about to become a grandmother.'

'A week overdue. Driving the family crazy.'

'And this is my second in command, Sergeant Stephen Miller.'

Miller was older than Anderson, close to fifty. He had bushy, greying hair, sloping shoulders, and a bearish pear-shape. Gillette guessed he was from the second generation of computer programmers—men and women who were innovators in the early seventies.

The third person was Tony Mott, a cheerful thirty-year-old with long, straight blond hair and sunglasses dangling from a green fluorescent cord round his neck. A crash helmet sat on his desk, snowboarding boots in the corner. He represented the latest generation of hackers: risk-takers, equally at home hacking together script at a keyboard and riding his mountain-bike at competitions. Gillette noticed too that of all the cops at CCU Mott wore the biggest pistol on his hip—a shiny silver automatic.

Then Gillette's eyes slipped to erasable whiteboards against the wall, apparently used for listing clues. A photo was taped to one. He couldn't make it out and walked closer. Then he gasped and stopped in shock. The photo was of a young woman naked from the waist up, bloody and pale, lying in a patch of grass, dead.

Gillette had played plenty of gruesome computer games—Mortal Kombat and Doom and Tomb Raider—but those games were nothing compared to this horrible violence against a real victim.

Anderson said, 'We've got to get moving on this . . . Now we're taking a two-prong approach to the case. Detectives Bishop and Shelton are going to be running a standard homicide investigation. CCU'll handle the computer evidence—with Wyatt's help here.' He glanced at a fax on his desk and added, 'We're also expecting a civilian consultant from Seattle, an expert on the Internet and online systems. Patricia Nolan. She should be here any minute.'

Mott handed Frank Bishop an envelope. 'This came for you ten minutes ago. It's the preliminary crime scene report.'

Bishop brushed at his stiff hair with the backs of his fingers. Gillette could see the tooth marks from the comb very clearly in the heavily sprayed strands. The cop glanced through the file but said nothing. He handed the thin stack of papers to Shelton, who read for a few moments then looked up.

'Witnesses report the perpetrator was a white male, medium build and height, blond hair, goatee, late twenties, early thirties. Looked like every techie in there, the bartender said.' The cop walked to the whiteboard and began to write down these clues. He continued, 'ID card he was wearing said Xerox Corporation PARC, but we're sure that was fake. There were no hard leads to anybody there. The killer probably used a military KA-BAR knife.'

Tony Mott asked, 'How'd you know that?'

'The wounds're consistent with that type of weapon.' Shelton turned back to the file. 'The victim was killed elsewhere and dumped by the highway.'

Mott interrupted. 'How'd you tell *that?*'

Shelton frowned slightly, apparently not wishing to digress. 'Quantity of her blood found at the scene.' The young cop's lengthy blond hair danced as he nodded and seemed to record this information for future reference.

'Crime scene picked up his beer bottle. The bartender remembered that the perp wrapped his beer bottle in a napkin and one of the techs found it in the trash. But we printed both the bottle and the napkin and came up with zip. The lab lifted some unknown kind of adhesive off the lip of the bottle..'

Frank Bishop finally spoke. 'Might be glue for a fake beard.'

Gillette agreed. 'A good social engineer always dresses for the con.'

Shelton called homicide headquarters and arranged to have the adhesive checked against samples of theatrical glue.

Gillette realised that nobody had been standing close to him. He eyed everyone else's clean clothes, shampooed hair, grime-free finger-nails. He asked Anderson, 'I don't suppose you have a shower here?'

Anderson tugged at the lobe that bore the stigmata of a past-life earring and broke into a laugh. 'I was wondering how to bring that up.' He said to Mott, 'Take him down to the employee locker room. But stay close.'

The young cop nodded and led Gillette down the hallway. He chattered away nonstop, telling Gillette about the recent formation of the Computer Crimes Unit. They'd only been in existence for less than a year.

'Why'd *you* get into it?' Gillette asked him. 'CCU?'

'Hoping for a little excitement. I mean, I love machines and guess I have a mind for 'em, but sifting through code's not quite what I'd hoped.'

'Is Linda Sanchez a geek?' Gillette asked.

'Not really. She's smart but machines aren't in her blood. She was a gang girl down in Salinas. Decided to go to the academy. Her partner was shot up pretty bad in Monterey a few years ago. Linda has kids, so she figured it was time to move to a quieter side of the business.'

'Just the opposite of you.'

Mott laughed. 'I guess so.'

As Gillette towelled off after the shower and shave, Mott placed an extra set of his own workout clothes on the bench for the hacker. T-shirt, black sweatpants and a warm-up windbreaker.

'Thanks,' Gillette said, donning the clothes. He felt exhilarated, having washed away one particular type of filth from his thin frame: the residue of prison.

On the way back to the main room they passed a small kitchenette. There was a refrigerator and a table on which sat a coffeepot and a plate of bagels. Gillette looked hungrily at the food. Then he eyed a row of cabinets.

'I don't suppose you have any Pop-Tarts in there.'

'Pop-Tarts? Naw. But have a bagel.'

Gillette walked over to the table and poured a cup of coffee. He picked up a raisin bagel.

'Not one of those,' Mott said. He took it out of Gillette's hand and dropped it on the floor. It bounced like a ball.

Gillette frowned.

'Linda brought these in. It's a joke.' When Gillette stared at him in confusion the cop added, 'Don't you get it?'

'Get what?'

'What's today's date?'

'I don't have a clue. The days of the month aren't how you mark time in prison.'

'April Fool's Day,' Mott said. 'Those bagels're plastic. Linda and I put 'em out this morning.' He opened the cabinet and took out a bag of fresh ones. 'Here.'

Gillette ate one quickly. Mott said, 'Go ahead. Have another.'

Another followed, washed down with gulps from the large cup of coffee. They were the best thing he'd had in ages. Mott helped himself to a carrot juice from the fridge and they returned to the main area of CCU.

Gillette looked round the dinosaur pen, his mind churning. A thought occurred to him. 'April Fool's Day . . . so the murder was March 31st?'

'Right,' Anderson confirmed. 'Is that significant?'

Gillette said uncertainly, 'It's probably a coincidence.'

'Go ahead.'

'Well, it's just that March 31st is sort of a red-letter day in computer history.'

Bishop asked, 'Why?'

A woman's gravelly voice spoke from the doorway. 'Isn't that the date the first Univac was delivered?'

THEY TURNED TO SEE a hippy brunette in her mid thirties, wearing an unfortunate grey knitted sweater suit and thick black shoes.

Anderson asked, 'Patricia?'

She nodded and walked into the room, shook his hand.

'This is Patricia Nolan, the consultant I was telling you about. She's with the security department of Horizon Online.' Horizon was the biggest commercial Internet service provider in the world, larger even than America Online. Anderson explained, 'Horizon called us when they heard the victim was a customer and volunteered to send somebody to help out.'

The detective introduced her to the team and studied her. The designer glasses didn't do much to make her masculine, plain face any more attractive. But the striking green eyes behind them were piercing and very quick—Gillette could see that she too was amused to find herself in an antiquated dinosaur pen. Nolan's complexion was doughy and obscured with thick make-up. Her thick, unruly hair fell awkwardly into her face.

'What were you saying about Univac?' Tony Mott asked after hands were shaken.

Nolan filled in, 'March 31st, 1951. The first Univac computer was delivered to the Census Bureau for regular operations.'

'What was it?' Bob Shelton asked.

'It stands for Universal Automatic Computer,' said Nolan, 'and it was one of the first modern mainframe computers. It took up a room as big as this one. Of course, nowadays you can buy laptops that're faster and do a hundred times more.'

'Maybe our perp's got a theme of some kind,' Mott suggested. 'I mean, a milestone computer date and a motiveless killing right in the heart of Silicon Valley.'

'Let's follow up on it,' Anderson said. 'Find out if there're any recent unsolved killings that fit this M.O. in other high-tech areas. Try Seattle, Portland, Chicago's Silicon Prairie, and the Dulles Toll Road corridor outside of D.C.'

Tony Mott keyed in some information and a few minutes later he got a response. He read from the screen and said, 'Got something in Portland. February 15th. Two unsolved killings, similar M.O. to here—both victims stabbed to death. Perp was believed to be a white male, late twenties. Didn't seem to know the victims and robbery and rape weren't motives.'

'February 15th?' Patricia Nolan glanced at Gillette. 'ENIAC?'

'Right,' the hacker said, then explained, 'ENIAC was the Electronic Numerical Integrator and Calculator.' Like all hackers he was an aficionado of computer history. 'It was similar to Univac but earlier. The dedication date was February 15th.'

Another message arrived and Mott read the screen. 'About eighteen months ago a diplomat and an army colonel—both of them with bodyguards—were killed in Herndon, Virginia, August 12th and 13th. I'm ordering the complete files.'

Anderson wrote this on the whiteboard and looked at Gillette with a raised eyebrow. 'Any clue?'

'IBM's first PC,' the hacker replied. 'The release date was August 12th.' Nolan nodded.

'So he's got a theme,' Shelton said.

Frank Bishop added, 'And that means he's going to keep going.'

The computer terminal where Mott sat gave a soft beep. The young cop leaned forward. 'We've got a problem. The case files at VICAP on the Portland and Virginia killings're missing. The note from the sysadmin says they were damaged in a data-storage mishap.' The sysadmin was the systems administrator.

Linda Sanchez, eyes wide, gasped. 'You don't think . . . I mean, he *couldn't've* cracked VICAP. Nobody's ever done that.' The letters stood for the Department of Justice's Violent Criminal Apprehension Program.

'This is getting scary,' Mott said.

Anderson mused, 'But what's his motive?'

'He's a goddamn hacker,' Shelton muttered. '*That's* his motive.'

'He's not a hacker,' Gillette said.

'Then what is he?' Shelton persisted.

Gillette didn't feel like educating the difficult cop. He glanced at Anderson, who explained, 'A true hacker breaks into somebody's machine just to see if he can, it's a curiosity thing. The hacker ethic is it's OK to look, but don't touch. People who break into systems as vandals or thieves are called "crackers". As in "safecrackers".'

'I wouldn't even call him that,' Gillette said. 'Crackers maybe steal but they don't hurt people. I'd call him a "kracker" with a *k*. For killer.'

'Cracker with a *c*, kracker with a *k*,' Shelton muttered. 'What the hell difference does it make?'

'A big difference,' Gillette said. 'Spell "phreak" with a *ph* and you're talking about somebody who steals phone services. "Phishing"—with a *ph*—is searching the Net for someone's identity. Misspell "wares" with a *z* on the end, not an *s*, and you're not talking about housewares but about stolen software. When it comes to hacking it's all in the spelling.'

Shelton shrugged and remained unimpressed by the distinction.

Linda Sanchez turned to Gillette. 'I've secured and logged everything in Lara Gibson's machine.' She handed him a floppy disk. 'Here's a boot disk.'

This was a disk that contained enough of an operating system to 'boot up', or start, a suspect's computer. Police used boot disks, rather than the hard drive itself, to start the computer in case the owner—or the killer, in this case—had installed some software on the hard drive that would destroy it.

'I've been through her machine three times now and I haven't found any booby traps, but that doesn't mean they aren't there. I guess you know what to do from here.'

'Yep.'

She said, 'Good luck. The lab's down that corridor there.'

The boot disk in hand, Gillette started towards the hallway.

Bob Shelton followed.

The hacker turned. 'I don't really want anybody looking over my shoulder.'

'It's OK,' Anderson said to the homicide cop. 'The only exit back there's alarmed.'

Shelton wasn't pleased, but he acquiesced. Gillette noticed, though, that he didn't return to the main room. He leaned against the hallway wall near the lab and crossed his arms sulkily.

Inside the analysis room Gillette looked at Lara Gibson's computer. It was an unremarkable, off-the-shelf IBM clone.

He sat down at a work station and wrote a kludge, a program intended to solve a particular problem. He named the program 'Detective' then compiled and copied it to the boot disk Linda Sanchez had given him. He inserted the disk into the floppy drive of Lara Gibson's machine and turned on the power switch.

Wyatt Gillette's thick, muscular fingers slid eagerly onto the cool plastic of the keys. He positioned his fingertips, callused from years of keyboarding, on the tiny orientation bumps on the F and J keys. The boot disk went straight to MS-DOS, the famous Microsoft Disk Operating System, and a white C: prompt appeared on the black screen.

His heart raced as he stared at the hypnotically pulsing cursor.

Then, not looking at the keyboard, he pressed a key, the one for *d*—the first letter in the command line: detective.exe, which would start his program.

In the Blue Nowhere, time is very different from how we perceive it in the Real World and, in the first thousandth of a second after Wyatt Gillette pushed that key, this happened:

The voltage flowing through the circuit beneath the *d* key changed ever so slightly, and the code for the letter *d* was directed by the keyboard processor into the computer's basic input-output system—the BIOS—which translated the letter's keyboard code for the *d* into another one, its ASCII code, which was then sent into the computer's graphics adapter. The adapter converted the code to a digital signal, and electron guns located in the back of the monitor fired a burst of energy into the chemical coating on the screen. Miraculously, the white letter *d* burned into existence on the black monitor.

All this in a fraction of a second.

And in what remained of that second, Gillette typed the rest of the letters of his command and hit the ENTER key.

More type and graphics appeared, and soon, like a surgeon on the trail of an elusive tumour, Wyatt Gillette began probing carefully through Lara Gibson's computer—the only aspect of the woman that had survived the vicious attack, that retained at least a few memories of who she had been and what she'd done in her brief life.

HE HAS A HACKER'S SLUMP, Andy Anderson thought, watching Wyatt Gillette return from the analysis lab. Machine people had the worst posture of any profession in the world.

It was nearly eleven o'clock. The hacker had spent only thirty minutes looking over Lara Gibson's machine. He sat down in a swivel chair and flipped open his notebook. 'There's something odd going on. The killer *was* in her computer. He seized root and—'

'Dumb it down,' Bob Shelton muttered. 'Seized what?'

Gillette explained, 'When somebody has root that means they have complete control over machines on a computer network.'

Anderson added, 'When you're root you can rewrite programs, delete files, go online as somebody else.'

Gillette continued, 'But I can't figure out how he did it. There's not a trace of any kind of software on her machine that would let him get inside.'

Glancing at Bishop, he explained, 'See, I could load a virus in your computer that'd let me seize root on your machine, but in order for it to work I have to actually *install* the software on your computer and activate it. I could send you an attachment to an email, say, and you could activate it by opening the attachment. But there's no evidence that happened. No, he seized root some other way.'

'Then how do you know he seized root?' Linda Sanchez asked.

'I hacked together this kludge.' He handed Anderson a floppy disk. 'It's called Detective. It showed me that a lot of bits of pro-grams'd been moved to places on the hard drive that make sense only if somebody was going through her computer.'

Shelton shook his head in confusion.

But Frank Bishop understood. 'You mean, it's like you know a burglar was inside your house because he moved furniture.'

Gillette nodded. 'Exactly.'

Andy Anderson—as much a wizard as Gillette in some areas—hefted the thin disk in his hand. He couldn't help feeling impressed. Throughout the world there were tens of thousands of code crunchers—people who happily churn out software for mundane tasks—but only a few have the vision to conceive of script that's *elegant*, the highest form of praise for software. He had looked through some script in Gillette's file. The young man was just such a codeslinger.

He turned back to Gillette. 'So the bottom line is he got into her system thanks to some new, unknown program or virus.'

'Basically, that's it.'

'Could you find out anything else about him?' Mott asked.

'Only what you already know—that he's been trained on Unix.'

Unix is a computer operating system, just like MS-DOS, though it controls larger, more powerful machines than personal computers.

'Wait,' Anderson interrupted. 'What do you mean, what we already know?'

Gillette frowned. 'When the killer was inside her system he keyed some Unix commands—he must've entered them by mistake before he remembered her machine was running Windows. You *must've* seen them in there.'

Anderson looked questioningly at Stephen Miller, who'd apparently been the one analysing the victim's computer in the first place. Miller said uneasily, 'I noticed a couple lines of Unix, yeah. But I just assumed she'd typed them.'

'She's a civilian,' Gillette said, using the hacker term for a casual computer user. 'I doubt she'd even heard of Unix, let alone known the commands.'

'I didn't think, sorry,' the bearish cop said defensively.

Here was yet another mistake Stephen Miller had made, Anderson reflected. In the short time that Miller had been at CCU, this had been an ongoing problem. In the 1970s Miller had headed a promising company that developed software. But his products were always one step behind IBM's, Digital Equipment's and Microsoft's and he eventually went bankrupt. After his company went under, he drifted into computer security and finally applied to the state police. He wouldn't've been Anderson's first choice for a computer cop. Still he put in the longest hours in the department and took work 'home', that is, to some of the local university computer departments, where friends would let him run CCU projects on state-of-the-art supercomputers for free.

'What's that mean for us?' Shelton asked. 'That he knows this Unix stuff.'

Anderson said, 'It's *bad* for us. Hackers who use Windows or Apple systems are usually small-time. Serious hackers work in Unix.'

Gillette concurred. He added, 'Unix is also the operating system of the Internet. Anybody who's going to crack into the big servers and routers on the Net has to know Unix.'

Bishop's phone rang and he took the call. Then he sat down at a nearby work station to jot notes. He sat upright; no hacker's slouch here, Anderson observed. When he disconnected Bishop said, 'Got some leads. One of our troopers heard from some CIs.'

It was a moment before Anderson recalled what the letters stood for. Confidential informants. Snitches.

'Somebody named Peter Fowler, white male about twenty-five, from Bakersfield's been seen selling guns in this area. Been hawking KA-BARS too.' A nod at the whiteboard. 'Like the murder weapon. He was seen an hour ago at some park a quarter-mile north of 280.'

'Hacker's Knoll, boss,' Linda Sanchez said. 'In Milliken Park.'

Anderson nodded. He knew the place well and wasn't surprised when Gillette said that he did too. It was a deserted grassy area near the campus where Stanford computer science majors, hackers and chip-jocks hung out.

'I know some people there,' Anderson said. 'I'll go check it out when we're through here.'

Bishop consulted his notes again and said, 'The report from the lab shows that the adhesive on the bottle *is* the type of glue used in theatrical make-up. There's only one store in the immediate area, Ollie's Theatrical Supply on El Camino Real in Mountain View. They sell a lot of the stuff, but they don't keep records of the sales.'

'Now,' Bishop continued, 'we might get a lead on the perp's car if we question all the employees in the office building across the street from Vesta's, the restaurant where he picked up the Gibson woman.'

Anderson said to Bishop, 'You want to check that out while I'm at Hacker's Knoll?'

'Yes, sir, that's what I had in mind.' Bishop took another look at his notes. 'Some crime scene techs found a receipt for a light beer and martini in the trash bins behind Vesta's. They've lifted a couple of prints. They're sending 'em to the bureau for a state-by-state search, West Coast first, California, Washington, Oregon and—'

'No,' Gillette said. 'Go east to west. Do New York first.'

'Why?' Bishop asked.

'Those Unix commands were the East Coast version.'

Patricia Nolan explained that there were several versions of the Unix operating system. Using the East Coast commands suggested that the killer had Atlantic seaboard roots. Bishop nodded and called this information into headquarters. He then glanced at his notebook and said, 'There's one other thing. It looks like the perp's missing the tips of most of his fingers. He's got enough of the pads to leave prints but the tips end in scar tissue.'

Gillette shook his head. 'Callus.' He held up his own hands. The fingertips were flat and ended in yellow calluses. 'It's called a "hacker manicure",' he explained. 'You pound keys twelve hours a day, this is what happens.'

Shelton wrote this on the whiteboard.

'What I want to do now,' Gillette went on, 'is to go online and check out some of the hacking chat rooms. What the killer's doing is going to cause a big stir and—'

'No, you're not going online. Those're the rules. You stay offline.'

'Wait a minute,' Shelton said. 'He *was* online. I saw him.'

Anderson's head swivelled towards the cop. 'He was?'

'Yeah, in that room in the back—the lab. I looked in on him when he was checking the victim's computer.' He glanced at Anderson. 'I assumed you'd OK'd it.'

'No, I didn't.' Anderson asked Gillette, 'Did you log on?'

'No,' Gillette said firmly. 'He must've seen me writing my kludge and thought I was online.'

Anderson could have checked out the log-in files of the CCU computer to find out for certain. But he decided that it didn't really matter. Gillette's job here was finished. He picked up the phone and called HQ. 'We've got a prisoner here to be transferred back to the San Jose Correctional Facility.'

Gillette turned to him, dismay in his eyes. 'You *can't* send me back.'

'I'll make sure you get that laptop we promised you.'

'No, you don't understand. I can't stop now. We've got to find out what this guy did to get into her machine. The chat rooms, the hacker sites . . . there could be a hundred leads there. People *have* to be talking about software like this.'

Anderson saw the addict's desperation in Gillette's face, just as the warden had predicted.

The cybercop pulled on his raincoat and said firmly, 'We'll take it from here, Wyatt. And thanks again.'

HE WASN'T GOING to make it, Jamie Turner realised. The Cray wasn't going to spit out the decrypted password in time. It would take, he estimated, another two days to crack the code.

He thought about his brother, about the Santana concert—all just out of reach—and he felt like crying. It was nearly noon and he was sitting in the computer room, still in his damp soccer kit. He began to type some commands to see if he could log on to another of the school's computers—a faster one, in the physics department. But there was a long queue of users waiting. Jamie sat back and, out of frustration, not hunger, wolfed down a packet of M&M's.

Maybe he should just forget the whole thing, go hang with Dave or Totter or some of the guys from French club.

Then something happened.

On the screen in front of him the root directory of the college's computer suddenly appeared. The computer dialled out to one outside the school. The machines electronically shook hands and then Booty's password file was transferred to the second computer.

Jamie Turner was very savvy in the ways of computers, but he'd never seen this. The only explanation was that the college's computer had some kind of arrangement with other computer departments so that tasks that took a long time were automatically transferred to speedier machines. What was totally weird was that the machine Jamie's software had been transferred to was the Defense Research Center's supercomputer in Colorado Springs, one of the fastest computer systems in the world. It was also one of the most secure and was virtually impossible to crack (Jamie knew; he'd tried it). Ecstatic, he peered at the screen and saw that the DRC's machines were cracking Booty's passcode at a blistering rate.

Jamie turned to the second hack he needed to complete before the Great Escape. In less than sixty seconds he'd transformed himself into a middle-aged overworked service tech employed by West Coast Security, Inc, who'd unfortunately misplaced the diagram for a Model 8872 alarmed fire door he was trying to repair and needed some help from the manufacturer's technical supervisor.

The man was all too happy to oblige.

UNKNOWN TO THE SYSADMIN at the Defense Research Center the huge computers were presently under his root control and were burning about $25,000 of computer time for the sole purpose of letting a sophomore in high school open a single locked gate.

Phate had seen at once that the first supercomputer Jamie had used wasn't going to spit out the passcode in time for the boy's six thirty rendezvous with his brother. The DRC's array would easily crack the code before the deadline.

Phate's machine beeped and a box flashed onto the screen, alerting him that he'd received an email from Shawn.

He felt the pang of excitement he always did when Shawn sent a message. This reaction struck him as significant, an important insight into Phate's—no, make that Jon Holloway's—personal development. He'd grown up in a household where love was rare, and he knew that he'd developed into a cold, distant person. And yet the depth of what Phate felt for Shawn proved that he had within him a vast well of love.

He read the stark words of the email and his breath grew rapid.

The police knew about the killings in Portland and Virginia. He glanced at the second paragraph and got no further than the reference to Milliken Park.

He now had a real problem.

Ten minutes later Phate's Jaguar was speeding onto the freeway.

NORMALLY HACKER'S KNOLL would be crowded with young people swapping software and tales of their cyber exploits. Today, though, the cold April drizzle had emptied the place.

Andy Anderson parked, pulled on the rumpled grey rain hat his six-year-old daughter had given him as a birthday present, and climbed out of the car. He hurried through the grass, as streamers of rain flew from his shoes. He was discouraged by the lack of possible witnesses, but there was a covered bridge in the middle of the park; sometimes kids hung out there when it was rainy or cold.

As Anderson approached he saw that the bridge too was deserted.

He paused and looked around. The only people here clearly weren't hackers: an elderly woman was walking a dog, and a businessman was making a cellphone call under the awning of one of the nearby Stanford University buildings.

Anderson recalled a coffee bar in downtown Palo Alto where geeks gathered to swap tales. He decided to try the restaurant. Then he saw movement nearby.

Fifty feet away was a young man, walking furtively and looking around uneasily, clearly paranoid. The man's jacket fell away for a moment and Anderson could see, protruding from the waistband of the man's jeans, the knobby hilt of a KA-BAR knife.

Anderson ducked behind a thick stand of juniper, his heart pounding like a pile-driver. This was Lara Gibson's killer. He was in his twenties, had blond hair and was clean shaven; the beard he'd worn in the restaurant *had* been fake.

Anderson made a call to the state police's Field Operations Central Dispatch and requested immediate back-up. 'Four-three-eight-nine-two,' he whispered. 'I've got a visual on a suspect in a homicide. I'm in Milliken Park, Palo Alto, southeast corner. Suspect is armed.'

The dispatcher asked him to hold on. Anderson stared at the killer, squinting hard, as if that would keep him frozen in place.

'One moment, four-three-eight . . . OK, be advised, ETA is in twelve minutes.'

'Can't you get somebody here faster than that?'

'Negative, four-three-eight.'

Just then the man began walking again. He left the bridge and started down the sidewalk.

'He's on the move, Central, heading west through the middle of the park. I'll stay with him and keep you posted on his location.'

'Copy that, four-three-eight. CAU is on its way.'

CAU? he wondered. What the hell was that again? Oh, right: closest available unit.

Hugging the trees and brush, Anderson moved closer to the bridge, keeping out of the killer's sight. What had he come back here for? To find another victim? Anderson glanced at his watch. He was used to a very different kind of police work: stake outs conducted sitting in vans, staring at the screen of a Toshiba laptop. He hadn't had his weapon out in a year.

Then he remembered: his weapon.

He looked down at the chunky butt of his Glock. He pulled it off his hip and pointed it downwards, finger outside the trigger, as he vaguely remembered he ought to do.

Then, through the mist, he heard a faint electronic trill.

The killer had got a phone call. He pulled a cellphone off his belt and held it to his ear. Glancing at his watch, he spoke a few words. Then he put the phone away and turned back the way he'd come, walking quickly along the path, hands in his pockets.

Hell, he's going back to his car, the detective thought. I'm going to lose him . . .

Ten minutes till the back-up gets here. *Jesus* . . .

Andy Anderson had no choice. He was going to have to make an arrest alone. He now moved closer to the killer. They were paralleling each other on opposite sides of a row of tall boxwood. Anderson kept low and squinted through the rain. He got a good look at the killer's face. Except for the knife in his hidden hand, the man looked benign, almost friendly.

The detective wiped his hand on his shirt to dry some of the rain and gripped the pistol more firmly. He continued on. This was a hell of a lot different from taking down hackers at a public terminal in the mall or serving warrants in houses where the biggest dangers were the plates of putrid food stacked next to a teenager's machine.

Closer, closer . . .

Twenty feet further on, their paths would converge. Soon Anderson would have no more cover and he'd have to make his move.

Anderson thought of his wife and daughter, how completely out of his depth he was here. Just follow the killer back to his car, he thought, get the licence plate and follow as best you can.

But then he thought of the deaths this man had caused and the deaths that he'd cause again if not stopped. And this might be their only chance to stop him.

Ten feet.

Eight . . .

A deep breath.

Watch the hand in the pocket, he reminded himself.

A bird flew close—a gull—and the killer turned to look at it, startled. He laughed.

And that was when Anderson burst from the bushes, shoving the pistol towards the killer, shouting, 'Freeze! Police! Hands out of your pockets! Now!'

Anderson tensed. But then he got a clear look. The man held a rabbit's foot. A lucky key-ring.

'Drop it.'

He did.

'Lie down on the ground and keep your arms spread. Do it,' Anderson shouted in a quaking voice.

The killer lay down on the ground. Anderson was kneeling over him, shoving his gun into the man's neck. As he put the cuffs on, he realised that he'd forgotten the Miranda warning. He found the card in his wallet and read the words stiffly.

The killer muttered that he understood his rights.

'Officer, you OK?' a man's voice called. 'You need any help?'

Anderson glanced behind him. It was the businessman he'd seen under the awning.

'No, no, everything's under control.' Anderson turned back to his prisoner. He holstered his weapon and pulled out his own cellphone to report in. The call wouldn't go through. He glanced at the screen. NO SIGNAL. That was odd. Why—

And in an instant of pure horror he realised that no street cop in the world would've let an unidentified civilian get behind him during an arrest. As he started to turn, the businessman grabbed his shoulder and the detective felt an explosion of pain in his back.

Anderson cried out and dropped to his knees. 'No, please, no . . .'

The man crouched down next to him.

'*You're* the one,' Anderson whispered to the businessman. 'You killed Lara Gibson.' His eyes flicked to the man he'd handcuffed. 'And *he's* Peter Fowler.'

The man nodded. 'That's right.' Then he said, 'And *you're* Andy Anderson.' The awe in his voice was genuine. 'Amazing . . . Andy Anderson. You're a *total* wizard.'

'Please . . . I've got a family! Please.'

Then the killer did something odd.

Holding the knife in one hand, he touched the cop's chest with the other. He slid his fingers up slowly, counting the ribs beneath which his heart was beating so very quickly.

'Please,' Anderson pleaded.

The killer paused and lowered his head to Anderson's ear. 'You never know somebody the way you know them at a moment like this,' he whispered, then resumed his eerie reconnaissance of the cop's chest.

At 1.00pm, a tall man in a grey suit walked into the Computer Crimes Unit. Two uniformed state troopers were beside him. Their shoulders were damp from the rain and their faces were grim. They walked to Stephen Miller's cubicle.

The tall man said, 'Steve.'

Miller stood, brushed his hand through his thinning hair. He said, 'Captain Bernstein.'

'I've got something to tell you.' The captain spoke in a tone that Wyatt Gillette recognised immediately as the precursor to tragic news. Linda Sanchez and Tony Mott joined the group. 'We just found Andy Anderson's body in Milliken Park.'

'Oh,' Sanchez choked. She began to cry. 'Not Andy . . . No!'

Patricia Nolan had spent the past half-hour sitting with Gillette before he went back to San Jose, speculating about what software the killer might have used to invade Lara Gibson's computer. As they'd talked she'd opened her bag, taken out a small bottle and, incongruously, started applying nail polish. Now, the tiny brush drooped in her hand. 'Oh, my God.'

The door pushed open and Frank Bishop and Bob Shelton hurried into the room. 'We heard,' Shelton said. 'We got back here as fast as we could.'

'What the hell happened?' Miller asked, anger filling his voice.

Captain Bernstein said, 'We have a pretty good idea—there was a witness, a woman walking her dog in the park. Seems like Andy'd just collared somebody named Peter Fowler.'

'He was the weapons dealer we think supplied the perp,' Shelton said.

Captain Bernstein continued, 'While Andy was cuffing Fowler, a white male came up behind him, late twenties, dark hair, navy-blue suit. He stabbed Andy in the back, then in the chest, and then stabbed Fowler to death too.'

'Why didn't Andy call for back-up?' Mott asked.

Bernstein frowned. 'Well, now, that was odd—we checked his cell-phone and the last number he'd dialled was to Dispatch. But there was no record of Central receiving it.'

'The killer cracked the switch,' Gillette said. 'He hacked into the cellphone company's computer and had all of Andy's outgoing calls sent to his own phone. Probably pretended he was the dispatcher.'

The captain nodded slowly. 'What the hell're we up against?'

'The best social engineer I've ever heard of,' Gillette said.

Turning to Bishop, the captain said, 'Frank, I've OK'd that request of yours—for the Marinkill Case. The perps were spotted outside a convenience store ten miles south of Walnut Creek. It looks like they're headed this way.' He glanced at Miller. 'Steve, you'll take over what Andy was doing—the computer side of the case. The troopers here'll take the prisoner back to San Jose.'

'Look,' Gillette protested, 'don't send me back. You don't know how dangerous this man is! I have to—'

A look from the captain was all it took. The troopers cuffed Gillette and positioned themselves on either side of him—as if he were the murderer.

'Wait!' Gillette shouted just as he was about to be led out the door.

Bernstein gestured to the cops to get him out. But Gillette said quickly, 'What about Lara Gibson? Was *she* stabbed in the chest too?'

Bob Shelton glanced at the report on the Lara Gibson killing. 'Cause of death was a stab wound to—'

'The heart, right?' Gillette asked.

Shelton nodded. 'How'd you know that?'

'Because I figured out his motive.'

'Which is?' Bernstein asked.

'The killer's a MUDhead,' Gillette said. 'It stands for Multiuser Domain or Dimension. It's a bunch of specialised chat rooms—places on the Internet for role-playing games. Three or four years ago there was a big controversy about this game called Access.'

'I heard about that,' Miller said. 'A lot of Internet providers refused to carry it.'

Gillette nodded. 'The way it worked was that there was a virtual city populated with characters who carried on a normal life. But on the anniversary of a famous death—like John Kennedy's assassination or the day Lennon was shot—a random-number generator picked one of the players to be a killer. He had one week to kill as many people as he could.

'The killer could pick anyone to be his victim, but the more challenging the murder, the more points he got. A politician with a bodyguard was worth ten points, a cop fifteen. The one limitation on the killer was that he had to get close enough to the victims to stab them in the heart with a knife—that was the ultimate form of access.'

'That's our perp in a nutshell,' Tony Mott said. 'The knife, stab wounds to the chest, the anniversary dates, going after people who're hard to kill. He won the game in Portland and Virginia. And here he is playing it in Silicon Valley.' The young cop added cynically, 'He's at the expert level.'

'Level?' Bishop asked.

'In computer games,' Gillette explained, 'you move up from the beginner level to the hardest—the expert—level. Our killer's playing his own version of Access—a real-life version.'

Bishop whispered to Shelton, then turned to Captain Bernstein. 'I'd like to run this case, sir, and I want Gillette here to head up the computer side of the investigation in place of Miller.'

'I thought you wanted the Marinkill case.'

'I *did*, sir. But I changed my mind.'

Bernstein nodded reluctantly. 'OK, you got the case. You'll have full tactical and crime scene back-up. Good luck, Frank.'

After Bernstein and the troopers had left, Bishop asked Gillette, 'You were telling Andy that you thought you could find out more about how this killer got into Ms Gibson's computer.'

'That's right. Whatever this guy is doing has to've caused some buzz in the hacker underground. What I'll do is go online and—'

'Just do what you have to do, Gillette.' Bishop nodded to a work station. 'And give us a report in a half-hour.'

'Uhm.' Stephen Miller stirred.

'What is it?' the detective asked him.

Gillette was expecting the cybercop to make a comment about his demotion. But that wasn't what Miller had in mind.

'Andy said he wasn't ever supposed to go online. And then there's that court order that said he couldn't.'

'That's all true,' Bishop said. 'But Andy's dead and the court isn't running this case. I am.' He glanced over at Gillette with a look of polite impatience. 'So I'd appreciate it if you'd get going.'

IN PRISON, WHERE MOST inmates spend hours lifting iron, Wyatt Gillette had done only fingertip push-ups to stay in shape for his passion. Now, the plastic keyboard danced under his hammering as he prepared to go online.

Most of today's Internet is a combination shopping mall and amusement park. The point-and-click technology of the mouse can be mastered by a three-year-old. But the Internet of the true hacker is a wild, raw place, where hackers use complicated commands, telnet utilities and communications software stripped bare as a dragster to sail throughout the world at, literally, the speed of light.

One of the first skills hackers learn is the art of hiding software. Since you have to assume that an enemy hacker, if not the police or FBI, will at some point seize your machine, you never leave the only copy of your tools on your hard drive.

Most hackers store their stash in university computers because their security is notoriously lacking, but Gillette had spent years working on his software, writing code from scratch in many cases and it would be a tragedy for him to lose all that work.

So he cached his tools in a slightly more secure location. With a glance behind him now to make sure that no one was standing behind him and reading the screen, he typed a command. After a moment these words scrolled onto the screen:

Welcome to the United States Air Force
Los Alamos Nuclear Weapons Research Facility.
#Username?

He typed *Jarmstrong*. The computer then asked:

#Password?

He typed *4%xTtfllk5$$60%4Q*. This series of characters had been excruciating to memorise but it would take a supercomputer weeks to crack.

In three minutes he'd downloaded a number of files, including the famous SATAN program (the Security Administrator Tool for Analysing Networks), several breaking and entering programs that would let him grab root access on various types of machines and networks, and a cloaking program to hide his presence while he was in someone else's computer.

With these tools downloaded onto a high-capacity disk Gillette logged out of the Los Alamos site. He paused for a moment, flexed his fingers and then sat forward. Pounding on the keys with the subtlety of a sumo wrestler, he entered the Net. He began in the Multiuser Domains. No one, however, had played Access or knew anyone who had—or so they claimed.

From the MUDs he moved to the World Wide Web, searching through underground hacking sites, losing himself further and further in the Blue Nowhere, prowling through computers that might have been in Moscow or Cape Town or Mexico City.

From the Web he searched the Usenet—the collection of 80,000 newsgroups, in which people interested in a particular subject can post messages. He scoured the classic hacking newsgroups like alt.2600, and alt.binaries.hacking.utilities. He found references to dozens of newsgroups that hadn't existed when he'd gone to jail.

A snap under his fingers and on the screen he saw:

mmmmmmmmmmmmmmmmmmmmmmmmmmmmmmmmmmmmmmmmmmm

One of his powerful keystrokes had jammed the keyboard. Gillette unplugged it, tossed it on the floor behind him, hooked up another one and started typing again.

He then logged on to the Internet Relay Chat rooms, the IRC, and began searching through the BBs, the bulletin boards. Many were legitimate, but others—with names like DeathHack and Silent Spring—were the darkest parts of the online world, places to go for recipes for bombs and poisonous gases.

Following the leads—losing himself in web sites, newsgroups, chat rooms and archives. Hunting in the Blue Nowhere is like prowling through an ever-expanding universe, which contains not only the known world, but worlds past and worlds yet to come.

At 2.30pm Gillette emerged from the cubicle. His back was racked with fiery pain from sitting frozen in one place. Yet he could still feel the exhilarating rush from that brief time online and the reluctance at leaving the machine, which tugged him back fiercely.

'I've found something,' the hacker said, holding up a stack of print-outs.

'Tell us.'

'Dumb it down,' Shelton reminded. 'What's the bottom line?'

'The bottom line,' Gillette responded, 'is Phate.'

'Fate?' Frank Bishop asked.

Gillette said, 'That's his screen name. Only he spells it *p-h-a-t-e*.'

'What's his real name?' Patricia Nolan asked.

'I don't know. Nobody seems to know much about him—he's a loner—but the people who've heard of him're scared as hell.'

Bishop asked, 'Do you think he's the killer?'

Gillette flipped through the print-outs. 'Here's what I found. Phate and a friend of his, somebody named Shawn, wrote some software called Trapdoor. It's a program that somehow lets them get inside *anybody*'s computer.'

The hacker walked to one of the blank whiteboards and drew a chart. He said, 'The way information travels on the Net isn't like on a telephone. Everything sent online—an email, music, a picture—is broken down into small fragments of data called "packets". At the receiving end the web-server computer reassembles your request and then sends its response—also broken into packets—back to your machine.' Gillette pointed to his diagram and continued, 'The packets are forwarded through the Internet by these routers—big computers around the country that guide the packets to their final destination. Routers have real tight security but Phate's managed to crack into some of them and put a packet-sniffer inside.'

'Which,' Bishop said, 'looks for certain packets, I assume.'

'Exactly,' Gillette continued. 'When the sniffer finds the packets it's been waiting for it diverts them to Phate's computer. Once they're there Phate hides an application in the packets.'

'A *working* program?' Nolan said.

'Yep. Then he sends it on its way to the victim.'

Nolan shook her head. Her pale, doughy face revealed both shock and admiration. Her voice was hushed with awe as she said, 'No one's ever done that before.'

'What's this software that he sends?' Bishop asked.

'It's a demon,' Gillette answered.

'Demon?' queried Shelton.

'There's a whole category of software called "bots",' Gillette explained. 'Short for "robots". Once they're activated these programs run completely on their own, without any human input. They can travel, reproduce, hide, they can kill themselves.'

Gillette drew a second diagram, to illustrate how Trapdoor worked. 'Demons are a type of bot. They sit inside your computer and do things like run the clock and back up files. Routine work. But the Trapdoor demon does something a lot scarier. Once it's inside your computer it modifies the operating system and, when you go online, it links your computer to Phate's.'

'And he seizes root,' Bishop said.

'Exactly.'

'Oh, this is bad,' Linda Sanchez muttered. 'Man . . .'

Nolan twined strands of her unkempt hair round a finger. Her eyes were troubled, as if she'd just seen a terrible accident. 'So if you surf the Web, read a news story, read an email, pay a bill, listen to music, download pictures, look up a stock quotation—if you're online at *all*—Phate can get inside your computer.'

'Yep. Anything you get via the Internet might have the Trapdoor demon in it.'

'But what about firewalls?' Miller asked. 'Why don't they stop it?'

Firewalls are computer sentries that keep files or data you haven't requested out of your machine. Gillette explained, 'That's what's brilliant about this. Because the demon's hidden in data that you've *asked* for, firewalls won't stop it.'

Sanchez asked, 'Is there any way to tell if he's inside your machine?'

'Only little things—your keyboard seems sluggish, the graphics look a little fuzzy. Nothing so obvious that most people'd notice.'

'How did you find all this out?' Bishop asked.

Gillette shrugged. 'Pieced it together from these.' He handed Bishop the print-outs.

Bishop looked at the top sheet of paper.

To: Group
From: Triple-X

I heard that Titan233 was asking for a copy of Trapdoor. Don't do it, man. Forget you heard about it. I know about Phate and Shawn. They're DANGEROUS. I'm not kidding.

'Who's Triple-X?' Shelton asked.

'I don't have a clue,' Gillette said.

Bishop flipped through the rest of the print-outs, all of which gave some detail or rumour about Trapdoor. Triple-X's name was on several of them.

Nolan tapped one of the print-outs. 'Can we trace the information in the header back to Triple-X's machine?'

Gillette explained to Bishop and Shelton, 'Headers have information about the route the message took from the sender's computer to the recipient's. But I checked these already. They're fake. Most serious hackers falsify their headers.'

'So it's a dead end?' Shelton muttered.

'I just read everything quickly. We should look at them again carefully,' Gillette said, nodding at the print-outs. 'Then I'm going to hack together a bot of my own. It'll search for any mention of the words "Phate", "Shawn", "Trapdoor" or "Triple-X".'

Linda Sanchez was staring at the picture of Andy Anderson, his wife and their daughter on his desk. In a troubled whisper she said, 'So nobody who goes online is safe.'

Gillette looked into the woman's round brown eyes. 'Phate can find out every secret you've got. He can impersonate you or empty your bank accounts, give you a phoney lover and send your wife or husband copies of fake love letters. He could get you fired.'

'Or,' Patricia Nolan added softly, 'he could kill you.'

SITTING IN THE DINING-ROOM office of his house in Los Altos, listening to a CD of James Earl Jones in *Othello*, Phate was roaming through the files of the young character, Jamie Turner, and planning that evening's visit to St Francis Academy.

Thinking of the young student had brought back memories of his own academic history.

His teachers and counsellors had tried. They'd put him into gifted-and-talented classes and then *advanced* gifted-and-talented programmes but even those didn't hold his interest. And when he grew bored he became sadistic and vicious. His teachers stopped calling on him, for fear that he'd mock them and their limitations.

Busy with their own lives, his parents (Dad, an electrical engineer; Mom, a chemist for a cosmetics company) handed him off to a series of tutors after school. His fellow students of course disliked him intensely. He was the 'Brain', he was 'Jon the Head', he was 'Mr Wizard'. They teased and insulted him unmercifully.

And so to keep the pressure inside his whirling brain from blowing him to pieces he spent more and more time in the one place that challenged him: the Machine World. Since Mom and Dad were happy to spend money to keep him out of their hair he had the best personal computers that were available.

Still, though, it was obvious that the boy was on a downward spiral—his increasing reclusiveness, viciousness, and bad temper whenever he wasn't online. Then something happened.

The sixteen-year-old stumbled onto a bulletin board where people were playing a MUD game. This particular one was a medieval quest for a magic sword. He watched for a while and then shyly keyed, 'Can I play?'

One of the seasoned players asked, 'Who do you want to be?'

Young Jon decided to be a knight and happily killed orcs and dragons for the next eight hours. That night, as he lay in bed after signing off, he couldn't stop thinking about that remarkable day. All day long he'd been a knight. Maybe in the Real World he could be someone else too.

Who do you want to be?

He asked his parents if he could transfer to a different school for his junior year, and the next fall, among the eager students registering for classes at Thomas Jefferson High School for the Gifted was a particularly eager youngster named Jon Patrick Holloway. Transcripts showed his consistent B+ in all grades since kindergarten, counsellors' glowing reports described a well-adjusted child.

At Tom Jefferson he took up drama classes and several sports. He dated, went to dances, worked on homecoming floats just like everybody else.

At the age of seventeen Jon Holloway social engineered himself into one of the most popular kids in school.

He was so popular, in fact, that the funeral of his parents was one of the most widely attended in the history of the small New Jersey town where they were living. (It was a miracle, friends of the family remarked, that young Jon just happened to be taking his computer to a repair shop early Saturday morning when the tragic gas explosion took the lives of his family.) Jon Holloway had looked at life and decided that the only way he could survive was to see it as a MUD game.

And he was now playing again.

In the basement of his pleasant suburban house in Los Altos Phate washed the blood off his KA-BAR knife and began sharpening it. When he was finished, he wiped the blade clean. He replaced it in his locker and returned upstairs to find that his taxpayer dollars had been well spent; the Defense Research Center's supercomputers had just spat out the passcode to St Francis Academy's gates.

AFTER TWENTY MINUTES of poring over the print-outs from Gillette's search the team could find no other leads. The hacker sat down at a work station to write code for the bot that would continue to search the Net for him.

Then he paused and looked up. 'There's one thing we have to do. Sooner or later Phate's going to realise you've got a hacker looking for him and *he* might try to come after *us*.' He turned to Stephen Miller. 'What external networks do you have access to from here?'

'Two—the Internet, and then we're also hooked to ISLEnet.'

Sanchez explained the acronym. 'That's the Integrated Statewide Law Enforcement Network.'

'Is it quarantined?'

'No,' Miller said. 'You can log on from anywhere and get to the FBI, Secret Service, ATF, NYPD . . . even Scotland Yard and Interpol. The works.'

Mott added, 'Since we're a clearing-house for all computer crimes in the state, the CCU has root authority on ISLEnet. So we have access to more machines than anybody else.'

Gillette said, 'Then we'll have to cut our links to it. If Phate gets inside ISLEnet, it'd be a disaster.'

'But we use ISLEnet a dozen times a day,' Shelton protested. 'The fingerprint databases, suspect records, case files . . .'

Gillette said, 'You'll have to go to some other location to use it.'

'That's ridiculous,' Stephen Miller said. He glanced at Bishop imploringly.

The lean detective glanced down at his sloppy shirt tail and tucked it in. After a moment he said, 'Do what he says. Cut the connection.'

'One more thing,' Gillette said, 'from now on nobody goes online but me.'

'Why?' Shelton asked.

'Because I can sense if the Trapdoor demon's in our system.'

'How?' the rough-faced cop asked sourly. 'Psychic Friends' Hotline?'

Gillette answered evenly, 'The feel of the keyboard, the delays in the system's responses, the sounds of the hard drive. When you're a hacker you get the *feel* for machines.'

'Agreed,' Bishop said.

Shelton lifted his arms helplessly.

Bishop's phone rang and he took the call. He listened for a moment, picked up a pen and paper and started taking notes. After five minutes of jotting he hung up and glanced at the team.

'We don't have to call him Phate any more. We've got his name. Jon Patrick Holloway.'

'*Holloway*?' Patricia Nolan's voice rose in surprise.

'You know him?' Bishop asked.

'Oh, you bet. Most of us in computer security do. But nobody's heard from him in years. I thought he'd gone legit or was dead.'

Bishop congratulated Gillette, 'It was thanks to you we found him—that suggestion about the East Coast version of Unix. The Massachusetts State Police had positive matches on the prints.' Bishop read his notes. 'I've got a little history. He's twenty-seven, born in New Jersey. He went to Princeton, brilliant computer programmer, got a job at Sun Microsystems, left there and went to NEC. Then he went to work for Apple. A year later he was back on the East Coast, at Western Electric in New Jersey. Then he got a job with Harvard's Computer Lab.'

'Typical codeslinger,' Mott summarised.

Bishop nodded. 'Except all the while he'd been hacking at night and running cybergangs. The most famous was the Knights of Access. He founded that with another hacker, somebody named Valleyman. No record of *his* real name.'

Looking through his notes, Bishop said, 'The Knights were the gang that shut down nine-one-one in Oakland for two days.'

'Bastards,' Shelton spat out.

Bishop returned to his notes. 'Somebody snitched on him when he was working for Harvard. He'd been ripping off software and supercomputer parts and selling them. He jumped bail in Massachusetts and nobody's seen or heard from him for three or four years.' He glanced at Gillette. 'Can you change that bot of yours—the search program? And add the names Holloway and Valleyman?'

'Piece of cake.' Gillette began modifying his program.

Bishop picked up a marker and started transcribing his handwritten notes on the whiteboard.

Patricia Nolan nodded at the board, where the word 'Trapdoor' was written in black marker. 'That's the crime of the new century,' she said. 'Violation. In the twentieth century people stole your money. Now, what gets stolen is your privacy.'

'But on one level,' Gillette reflected, 'you've got to admit that Trapdoor's brilliant.'

A voice behind him said angrily, 'It sounds like you wish you'd invented this damn thing.' Gillette wasn't surprised to find that the speaker was Bob Shelton.

He replied evenly, 'I'd like to understand how it works, that's all. I'm curious about it.'

'Curious? You happen to forget he's killing people with it.'

'I—'

'You asshole . . . It's a game to you too, isn't it? Just like him.' He stalked out of the office.

No one moved for a moment. The team looked awkwardly at the whiteboard.

Bishop nodded for Gillette to follow him into the pantry, where the detective poured them some coffee.

'Look, about Bob Shelton . . . He had a thing happen a few years ago.' The detective sipped the coffee, glanced down at his blossoming shirt. He tucked it in again. 'Bob had a son.'

Had?

'The kid died in a car accident a few years ago. He was sixteen. Bob hasn't been the same since then. So try to cut him some slack.'

'I'll try. I'm sorry about that.' Gillette thought about the hours he'd spent in prison wishing he were still married, wishing that he and Ellie had had a child, wondering how he'd screwed up so badly.

'Appreciate that.'

ANOTHER *BEEP* on his machine.

Phate looked up from the architectural diagram he'd down-loaded—St Francis Academy and the grounds surrounding it—and saw another message from Shawn.

Phate opened the email and read it. Bad news. The police had dis-covered his real name. He was momentarily concerned, but then decided this wasn't critical; Jon Patrick Holloway was hidden beneath so many layers of fake personas and addresses that there were no links to him as Phate. Still, the police could get their hands on a picture of him. He'd have to use more disguises.

Anyway, what was the point of playing a MUD game if it wasn't challenging? He glanced at the clock: 4.15. Time to get to St Francis Academy for tonight's game.

'HERE, BROUGHT you this.'

Gillette turned. Patricia Nolan was offering him another cup of coffee. 'Milk and sugar, right?'

He nodded. 'Thanks.'

'I noticed that's how you like it,' she said. She sat down beside him, tugged at her ungainly knitted dress. Pulled the nail polish out of her Louis Vuitton purse again and opened it. Nolan noticed him looking at the bottle.

'Conditioner,' she explained. 'All the keying is hell on my nails,' she said. 'I could cut them short but that's not part of my plan.' There was a certain emphasis on the word 'plan.' As if she'd decided to share something personal with him—facts that he, however, wasn't sure he wanted to know.

She said, 'I woke up one morning earlier this year—New Year's Day, and I realised that I'm a thirty-four-year-old single geek girl who lives with a cat and $20,000 worth of semiconductor products in her bedroom. I decided I was changing my ways. I'm no fashion model but I thought I'd fix some of the things that could be fixed. Nails, hair, weight.'

'Well, you've got really nice nails,' Gillette said.

'Thanks. Really good thigh muscles too,' she said with averted eyes. (He decided that her plan should probably include a little work on flirtation; she could use some practice.)

She asked, 'You married?'

'Divorced.' Don't waste your time on me, lady, he thought. I'm a no-win proposition.

He nodded as Nolan told him about life at Horizon Online, which really was, she kept asserting, more stimulating than he might think (though nothing she said bore out that proposition), about Seattle and her tabby cat, about the bizarre dates she'd had with geeks and chip-jocks.

He absorbed all the data politely, if vacantly, for ten minutes. Then his machine beeped loudly and Gillette glanced at the screen.

Search results:
Search Request: 'Triple-X'
Location: IRC, #hack
Status: Currently online

'My bot caught a fish,' he called.

Triple-X was the hacker Gillette had tracked down earlier, the one who seemed to know a great deal about Phate and Trapdoor.

'He's in a hacking chat room,' Gillette said. 'I don't know if he'll give up anything about Phate to a stranger but let's try to trace him.' He asked Miller, 'I'll need an anonymiser before I log on. I'd have to modify mine to run on your system.'

An anonymiser, or cloak, is a software program that blocks any attempts to trace you when you're online by making it appear that you're someone else and are in a different location from where you really are.

'Sure, I just hacked one together the other day.'

Miller loaded the program into the work station in front of Gillette. 'If Triple-X tries to trace you all he'll see is that you're logging on through a public-access terminal in Austin. That's a high-tech area and a lot of Texas Uni students do some serious hacking.'

'Good.' Gillette returned to the keyboard, examined Miller's program briefly and then keyed his new fake username, Renegade334, into the anonymiser. He looked at the team. 'OK, let's go swimming with some sharks,' he said. And hit the ENTER key.

SILICON VALLEY is the land of fulfilment, the land of King Midas, where the golden touch, though, isn't the sly trickery of Wall Street or the muscle of Midwest industry but pure imagination, where some secretaries and janitors are stock-option millionaires and others ride the number 22 bus all night long because they can't afford to pay $3,000 a month for an apartment.

Many years ago, apricots, prunes, walnuts and cherries grew abundantly in this fertile land nestled south of San Francisco. The valley might have remained linked forever with produce, except for an impulsive decision in 1909 by a man named David Starr Jordan, the president of Stanford University. Jordan decided to put some venture capital money on a little-known invention by a man named Lee DeForest—the audion tube.

It was the type of innovation that the general public couldn't quite understand and, in fact, didn't care about one bit at the time it was announced. But Jordan and other engineers at Stanford believed that the device might have a few practical applications and before long it became clear how stunningly correct they were—the audion was the first electronic vacuum tube, and its descendants ultimately made possible television, radar, and computers themselves.

Once the tiny audion's potential was unearthed nothing would ever be the same in this green, placid valley.

Through the heart of this Promised Land, Jon Patrick Holloway, Phate, now drove southeast on the rain-swept 280 freeway. In the Jaguar's CD player was a recording of yet another play, Hamlet—Laurence Olivier's performance.

Reciting the words in unison with the actor, Phate turned off the freeway at a San Jose exit and five minutes later he was cruising past the brooding Spanish colonial St Francis Academy. It was 5.15pm.

He parked on a dusty commercial street, near the north gate, through which Jamie was planning on making his escape. Turning the volume up on his CD, he reclined the seat and watched people stroll and cycle along the wet sidewalk. They were no more real to him than the tormented Danish prince in Shakespeare's play.

He heard a voice, maybe his own, maybe not, reciting a slightly different version of a passage from the play. 'What a piece of work is a machine. How noble in reason. How infinite in faculty. In form, in moving, how express and admirable. In operation how like an angel. In access how like a god . . .'

He checked his knife and the plastic bottle containing a pungent liquid concoction, all carefully arranged in the pockets of his grey coveralls, on whose back he'd carefully embroidered the words 'AAA Cleaning and Maintenance Company.'

He looked at his watch, then closed his eyes again.

IN HIS PERSONA as Renegade334, Wyatt Gillette had been lurking—observing but saying nothing—in the #hack chat room.

He was learning about his prey Triple-X. He'd call out observations and Patricia Nolan would jot them down. The woman sat close to him. He smelt a very pleasant perfume and he wondered if this particular scent had been part of her make-over plan.

So far Gillette had learned this about Triple-X: he was currently in the Pacific time zone (he'd made a reference to cocktail happy hour in a bar nearby; it was nearly 5.50pm on the West Coast).

He was American, older and probably college educated (his grammar and punctuation were very good for a hacker). He was probably in a shopping mall, dialling in from a cybercafé (he'd referred to a couple of girls he'd just seen go into the lingerie store, Victoria's Secret). He had a huge ego and he tirelessly explained esoteric aspects of hacking to novices in the chat room.

Gillette was now almost ready to trace Triple-X.

If Triple-X's computer was hooked up to his Internet service provider over a standard phone line via a modem—a dial-up connection—Gillette could trace the call back only to the provider, and then the phone company's security people would have to trace the call from the service provider to Triple-X's computer itself.

Tony Mott snapped his fingers, looked up from his phone with a grin and said, 'OK, Pac Bell's set to trace.'

'Here we go,' said Gillette.

He typed a message and hit ENTER. On the screens of everyone logged onto the #hack chat room appeared this message:

Renegade334: Hey Triple how you doing.

Gillette was now 'imping'—pretending to be someone else, in this case a seventeen-year-old hacker with marginal education but plenty of adolescent attitude.

Triple-X: Good, Renegade. Saw you lurking.

In chat rooms you can see who's logged on even if they're not participating in the conversation. Triple-X was reminding Gillette that he was vigilant.

Renegade334: Im at a public terminal and people keep walking bye, its pissing me off.
Triple-X: Where you hanging?

Gillette glanced at the Weather Channel.

Renegade334: Austin, man the heat sucks.
You ever been hear.

Triple-X: Only Dallas.

Renegade334: Dallas sucks, Austin rules!!!!

'Everybody ready?' Gillette called. 'I'm going to try to get him alone.' Affirmative responses from around him.

Renegade334: Triple—How about ICQ?

ICQ (as in 'I seek you') was like instant messaging—it would link their machines together so that no one else would be able to see the conversation. A request to ICQ suggested that Renegade might have something illegal or furtive to share with Triple-X—a temptation that few hackers could resist.

Triple-X: Why?
Renegade334: can't go into it hear.

A moment later a small window opened on Gillette's screen.

Triple-X: So what's happening, dude?

'Run it,' Gillette called to Stephen Miller, who started the trace. Another window popped up on the monitor, depicting a map of Northern California. Blue lines appeared on the map as the program traced the route from CCU back to Triple-X.

Renegade334: thanks man. Thing is I got a problem and I'm
scared. This dudes on my case.
Triple-X: What, dude?
Renegade334: His names Phate.

There was no response.

'Come on, come on,' Gillette urged in a whisper. Don't vanish. I'm
a scared kid. You're a wizard. Help me . . .

Triple-X: What aobut him? I mean, about.

'Got his service provider,' Miller called. 'It's a dial-in service.'

'Damn,' Patricia Nolan muttered. This meant that a phone company trace was necessary to pinpoint the final link from the server to the computer where Triple-X was sitting.

'We can do it,' Linda Sanchez called. 'Just keep him on the line, Wyatt.'

Tony Mott called Bay Area online and told the head of the security department what was going on. The security chief in turn called his own technicians, who would coordinate with Pacific Bell and trace the connection. 'Pac Bell's scanning. It's a busy area. Might take ten, fifteen minutes.'

'Too long, too long!' Gillette said. 'Tell 'em to speed it up.'

Renegade334: I heard about this totally robust hack of Phates
I mean totally and I saw him online and I asked him about it
only he just dissed me. then Weird stuff started happening and
I heard about this script he wrote called trapdoor and now I'm
totally paranoyd.

A pause, then:

Triple-X: So what're you asking?

'He's scared,' Gillette said. 'I can feel it.'

Renegade334: this trapdoor thing, does it really get him in your
machine and you don't even know it.
Triple-X: I don't think it really exists.
Renegade334: I don't know man, I saw my files OPENING and
no way was I doing it. I freaked. I mean, totally.

'We've got incoming,' Miller said. '*He's* pinging *us.*'

Triple-X was, as Gillette had predicted, running his own trace to check out Renegade334. The anonymising program that Stephen Miller had hacked together, however, would make Triple-X's machine think Renegade was in Austin.

Another long pause. Then finally the hacker responded.

Triple-X: You oughta be freaked. I know Phate.
Renegade334: Yeah how?

'This guy is gold,' Tony Mott whispered. 'Ask him Phate's address.'
'No,' Gillette said. 'We'll scare him off.'
There was no message for a moment then:

Triple-X: BRB

Chat-room regulars have developed a shorthand of initials that represent phrases—to save keyboarding time and energy. BRB meant Be right back.

'Is he headed for the hills?' Sanchez asked.
'The connection's still open,' Gillette said. 'Maybe he just went to take a leak.'

He sat back in the chair, which creaked loudly. Moments passed. The screen remained unchanged. BRB.

Patricia Nolan opened her purse, took out her fingernail conditioner again and absently began to apply it.

The cursor continued to blink. The screen remained blank.

JAMIE TURNER WONDERED if maybe, thanks to computers, life had returned to an earlier, more spiritual time, like a place out of one of those books from the 1800s by Washington Irving or Nathaniel Hawthorne. Back then people believed in ghosts and spirits and weird stuff going on that you couldn't exactly see. Now, there was the Net and code and bots and electrons and things you couldn't see—just *like* ghosts.

The thought scared the hell out of him but he forced it away and continued down the dark corridors of St Francis Academy.

Think about Santana, think about hanging with your brother, think about what a great night you're going to have.

Then, finally, he came to the fire door, the one that led out into the grounds. He looked around. No sign of Booty, no sign of the other teachers who occasionally wandered through the halls like guards in some prison movie.

Dropping to his knees, Jamie Turner looked over the alarm bar on the door the way a wrestler sizes up his opponent.

WARNING: ALARM SOUNDS IF DOOR IS OPENED.

He unfolded a small sheet of paper, which contained the wiring schematic of the alarm that the door manufacturer's service chief had kindly sent him.

He took a deep breath.

Pulling on his thick glasses to protect his precious eyes, Jamie Turner reached into his pocket, pulled out the plastic case containing his tools, and selected a Phillips head screwdriver. He had plenty of time, he told himself. No need to hurry.

TRIPLE-X HAD finally returned.

> Triple-X: Sorry, dude. This guy had to ask me some shit about breaking screen saver passcodes. Some luser.

For the next few minutes Gillette, in his persona as the alienated Texas teenager, told Triple-X about how he defeated Windows screen saver passcodes and let the hacker give him advice on better ways to do it. The door to the CCU opened and Gillette glanced up to see Frank Bishop and Bob Shelton enter.

'Pac Bell says they'll have his location in five minutes,' Tony Mott said, listening into his headset. 'They're narrowing down the exchange. Looks like he's in Menlo Park or Redwood City.'

Bishop said, 'Well, how many malls can there be? Get some tactical troops into the area.'

Bob Shelton made a call and then announced, 'They're rolling.'

> Renegade334: man this phate dude, isnt their some thing I can do I mean to stop him.
> Triple-X: Phate is walking death, dude. Same with his friend Shawn. Don't go close to them. If Phate got you with Trapdoor, burn your drive and install a new one.
> Renegade334: Could he get to me do you think, even in texas? wheres he hang?

Triple-X didn't answer right away. After a moment this message appeared on the screen:

> Triple-X: I don't think he'd get to Austin. But I ought tell you something, dude . . .
> Renegade334: Whats that?

Triple-X: Your ass ain't the least bit safe in Northern California, which is where you're sitting right at the moment, you poser!!!!

'He made us!' Gillette snapped.

Renegade334: Hey man I'm in Texas.
Triple-X: 'Hey, man' no, you're not. Check out the response times on your anonymiser.

Triple-X logged off.

'Hell,' Gillette muttered. He explained what had happened. Triple-X had been tracing CCU's computer by sending out the same sort of tiny electronic pings that Gillette was sending to find *him*, but the hacker must've run a further test, which showed that the length of time it took the pings to get to and from Renegade's computer was far too short for the electrons to make the round-trip all the way to Texas and back.

This was a serious mistake—it would have been simple to build a short delay into the anonymiser to add a few milliseconds.

'Oh no!' the cybercop said, shaking his head when he realised his mistake. 'That's my fault. I'm sorry . . . I just didn't think.'

No, you sure as hell hadn't, Gillette thought.

They'd been so close.

In a soft, discouraged voice, Bishop said, 'Recall SWAT.'

Shelton pulled out his cellphone and made the call.

JAMIE TURNER STOOD UP and listened carefully. From far off down the halls of St Francis Academy he heard music, some shouting, laughter. He was leaving it all behind.

Easing the door open.

Silence. No alarms, no shouts from Booty.

The smell of cold air, fragrant with grass, filled his nose. It reminded him of those long, lonely hours after dinner at his parents' house in Mill Valley during the summer. His father saying, 'Go outside and play.' Like he was in kindergarten!

Well, Jamie hadn't gone outside at all. He'd gone *inside* and hacked like there was no tomorrow. That's what the cool spring air reminded him of.

It was then that the ghost got him.

Suddenly a man's arm gripped him painfully round the chest and a powerful hand covered Jamie's mouth. His other hand pulled the thick safety glasses off the boy's nose.

'What've we got here?' he whispered, tossing them on the ground and caressing the boy's eyelids.

'No, no!' Jamie cried, trying to raise his arms to protect his eyes. 'What're you doing?'

The man took something from the coveralls he wore. It looked like a spray bottle. He held it close to Jamie's face. What was—?

A stream of milky liquid shot from the nozzle into his eyes.

The terrible burn started a moment later and the boy began to cry and shake in utter panic. His worst fear was coming true—blindness!

Jamie Turner shook his head furiously to fling off the pain and horror but the stinging only got worse. He was screaming, 'No, no, no,' the words muffled under the hand over his mouth.

The man leaned close and began to whisper in the boy's ear but Jamie had no clue what he said; the pain—and the horror it represented—consumed him like fire in dry brush.

FRANK BISHOP and Wyatt Gillette walked through the old archway of the entrance to St Francis Academy, their shoes sounding in gritty scrapes on the cobblestones.

Bishop nodded a greeting to a detective, whose massive bulk filled half the archway. He and his partner had been first at the scene.

The detective led Bishop, Gillette and, behind them, Shelton, Nolan and Sanchez into the school proper. Gillette noticed no students in the corridors; maybe the teachers were keeping them in their rooms until parents and counsellors arrived.

Outside an open door were dozens of police officers and several medical technicians. The detective whispered something to Bishop who nodded and said to Gillette and Nolan, 'It's pretty unpleasant in there. The killer used his knife again—in the heart. But it looks like it took him a while to die. Why don't you wait outside?'

'I can handle it,' the hacker replied.

'It's OK,' said Nolan.

Detective Huerto Ramirez from Homicide in San Jose was the crime scene officer.

Bishop asked Ramirez, 'How old?'

'The kid? Fifteen.'

They walked inside the classroom.

Gillette stopped in shock. There was blood everywhere, an astonishing amount—on the floor, walls, chairs, the lectern. The body lay under a dark green rubberised blanket on the floor.

'What's the boy's name?' Bishop asked.

A woman police officer said, 'Jamie Turner.'

Frank Bishop walked into the classroom next door to the murder site, where a teenage boy sat clutching himself and rocking back and forth in a chair. Gillette joined the detective.

'Jamie?' Bishop asked.

The boy didn't respond. Gillette noticed that his eyes were bright red and the skin round them seemed inflamed. Bishop glanced at another man in the room. He was thin and in his mid-twenties. The man said to the detective, 'I'm Jamie's brother. Mark Turner.'

'Booty's dead,' Jamie whispered miserably and pressed a damp cloth on his eyes.

'Booty?'

'It was Jamie's nickname for him,' Mark explained. He nodded towards the room where the body bag rested. 'For the principal.'

Bishop crouched down. 'How you feeling, young man?'

'He had this knife. He stabbed him and Mr Boethe just kept screaming and screaming and I . . .' He lost his voice to a cascade of sobbing. His brother gripped his shoulders tighter.

'He all right?' Bishop asked one of the medical techs.

'He'll be fine,' she said. 'Looks like the perp squirted him in the eyes with water that had a little ammonia and Tabasco mixed in. Just enough to sting, not enough to do any damage.'

'Why?' Bishop asked.

'He told Jamie it was acid and that if the boy led him to where Mr Boethe was he'd give him an antidote. But if he didn't the acid'd eat his eyes away.'

The boy's hands shook and he started to cry.

'It's his big fear,' Mark said angrily, 'going blind. The bastard found that out somehow.'

'And it hurt so much! It really, really did . . . I told him I wasn't going to help him, but I couldn't help it. I . . .' He fell silent.

Bishop touched the boy's shoulder. 'You did just what I would've done, son. Don't you worry about it. Tell me, Jamie, did you email anybody about what you were going to do tonight? It's important that we know.'

The boy swallowed and looked down. 'My brother, I guess. And then . . .'

'Go ahead.'

'I kind of went online to find some passcodes and stuff. Passcodes to the front gate and instructions on how to dismantle the alarmed fire door. He must've hacked my machine and seen them.'

'You've been real brave, young man,' Bishop said kindly.

But the boy was beyond consoling.

The medical examiner's technicians took the principal's body away and the cops conferred in the corridor, Gillette and Nolan with them. Shelton reported what he'd learned from the forensic techs. 'Crime scene doesn't have much. A few dozen obvious fingerprints—they'll run those, but, hell, we already know it's Holloway. Ramirez has been pounding the roads with some troopers from HQ but nobody's seen anything at all.'

Bishop glanced at Nolan, Sanchez and Gillette. 'OK, let's secure the boy's machine and check it out.'

The assistant principal led the team down the dim corridor that led to the school's computer department. As they walked, Linda Sanchez made a call on her cellphone. She learned—Gillette deduced from the conversation—that her daughter still hadn't started labour. She hung up, saying, '*Dios.*'

In the basement computer room, Sanchez handed the hacker a boot disk but Gillette shook his head. 'As far as we know the Trapdoor demon hasn't self-destructed. I'm going to try to find out where it's resident in the system.'

Nolan looked around the damp, gothic room. 'Feels like we're in *The Exorcist* . . . Spooky atmosphere and demonic possession.'

Gillette gave a faint smile. He powered up the computer and loaded various applications—a word processor, a spreadsheet, a fax program, some games, some browsers, a password-cracking program that Jamie had apparently written (some very robust code writing for a teenager, Gillette noticed).

As he typed he'd stare at the screen, watching how soon the character he typed would appear on the monitor, listening to the grind of the hard drive to see if it was making any sounds that were out of sync with the task it was supposed to be performing.

Patricia Nolan sat close to him, also gazing at the screen.

'I can feel the demon,' Gillette whispered. 'But it's odd—it seems to move around.'

'OK . . . this is the most sluggish directory.' He looked over a list of files then gave a cold laugh. 'You know where Trapdoor hangs out?'

'Where?' Bishop asked.

'The Solitaire program.'

'What?'

'The card game that comes with almost every computer sold in America.'

Nolan said, 'That's probably why Phate wrote the code that way.'

Bishop shook his head. 'What happens if you erase Solitaire?'

Sanchez copied the contents of the hard drive from the computer Jamie had used and then Gillette deleted Solitaire. He noticed a faint delay in the delete operation, and he tested various programs again then laughed bitterly. 'It's still there. It jumped to another program and it's alive and well. How the *hell* does it do that?' The Trapdoor demon had sensed its home was about to be destroyed and had escaped to another program.

There was a blur of movement as the door to the computer room swung open fast, shattering glass. A raging cry filled the room. Gillette dived for cover just as a chair swung past his head and crashed into the monitor he'd been sitting at.

'Jamie!' the assistant principal cried sharply. 'No!'

But the boy drew back the heavy chair and slammed it into the monitor again, which imploded with a loud pop and scattered glass shards around them. Smoke rose from the carcass of the unit.

'It killed him and I'm going to kill *it*!' The boy shook with anger.

'Young man, you will calm down this instant!'

Mark, Jamie's brother, ran into the computer room. He put his arm around the boy, who collapsed against him, sobbing.

Sanchez surveyed the damage. She said, 'Central processor's OK. The monitor's all he nailed.'

Wyatt Gillette pulled a couple of chairs into the corner and motioned Jamie over to him. The boy looked at his brother, who nodded, and he walked over to join the hacker.

'I think that screws up the warranty,' Gillette said, laughing.

The boy flashed a weak smile but it vanished almost immediately.

After a moment the boy said, 'It's my fault Booty died. I hacked the passcode to the gate and the killer saw it and got in.'

There was more on the boy's mind, Gillette could see once again. 'Go on, tell me,' he encouraged softly.

The boy looked down and finally said, 'That man? He said that if I hadn't been hacking, Mr Boethe'd still be alive. And I should never touch another computer again because I might kill somebody else.'

Gillette was shaking his head. 'Jamie, the man who did this is sick. He said those things to you because he's afraid of you.'

'Afraid of me?'

'He's been watching you script and hack. He's scared of what you might do to *him* some day.'

Jamie said nothing.

Gillette put his arm round the boy's shoulders. 'You're good, Jamie. You're really good. There are *sysadmins* who couldn't run the hacks you did. Do you know what a white-hat hacker is?'

'Yeah. A good hacker who helps find bad hackers.'

'Will you be our white hat? We sure could use your help.'

The boy now seemed embarrassed he'd been crying. He angrily wiped his face. 'I don't know. I don't think I want to.'

The assistant principal spoke. 'OK, Jamie, it's time to get back to your room.'

His brother protested, 'He's not staying here tonight. We're going to that concert and then he can spend the night with me.'

'No. He needs written permission from your parents,' the assistant principal insisted.

'Loosen up, will you? The kid's had the worst night of his life and you're—'

'You have no say about how I deal with my students.'

Then Frank Bishop intervened. 'But *I* do. And Jamie's not staying here *or* going to any concert. He's coming to police headquarters and making a statement. Then we'll take him to his parents.'

The boy sighed and looked like he was going to start crying again.

Bishop glanced at the assistant principal and said, 'I'll take care of it from here.'

The man glanced distastefully at the detective and left the room.

After he was gone Frank Bishop smiled and said to the boy, 'Right, young man, you and your brother get on out of here. If you move fast you'll probably make the show.'

'But my parents? You said—'

'Forget what I said.' He looked at Mark. 'Just make sure he's back here in time for classes tomorrow.'

Mark Turner shook the detective's hand.

'Jamie,' Gillette called.

The boy turned.

'Think about what I asked—about helping us.'

Jamie looked at the smoking monitor for a moment. He turned and left without responding.

Bishop asked Gillette, 'You think he can find something?'

'I don't have any idea. That's not why I asked him to help. I figured that after something like this he needs to get back on the horse.' Gillette nodded at Jamie's notes. 'He's brilliant. It'd be a real crime if he got gun-shy and gave up machines.'

The detective laughed faintly. 'The more I know you, the more you don't seem like the typical hacker.'

'Who knows? Maybe I'm not.'

AT THE COMPUTER CRIMES UNIT the investigation stalled.

The bot's alarm that would alert them to the presence of Phate or Shawn on the Net hadn't gone off, nor had Triple-X gone back online.

Their hopes blossomed for a moment when a detective called in to say that he'd finally heard from the owner of Ollie's Theatrical Supply. The man had looked at the picture of a young Jon Holloway and confirmed that he'd come into the store several times in the past month. The owner couldn't recall exactly what he'd bought, but he remembered a brief exchange. He'd asked Holloway if he was an actor and, if so, wasn't it hard to get jobs? The killer had replied, 'Nope, it's not hard at all. I act every single day.'

A half hour later, at 9.30pm, Frank Bishop stretched and looked around the dinosaur pen.

The energy was low in the room. Linda Sanchez was on the phone to her daughter, who still wasn't in labour. Stephen Miller sat sullenly by himself, looking over notes, perhaps still troubled by the mistake he'd made with the anonymiser, which had let Triple-X get away. Gillette was in the analysis lab, checking out the contents of Jamie Turner's computer. Tony Mott was checking out details of Jon Holloway's background. Patricia Nolan was making phone calls and Bishop wasn't sure where Bob Shelton was.

Bishop's phone rang and he took another call.

Huerto Ramirez had compiled the preliminary crime scene report from St Francis Academy in record time. The murder weapon had again been a KA-BAR knife. The duct tape used to bind Jamie Turner was untraceable. They'd found plenty of Holloway's fingerprints— but they already knew his identity.

Bishop wrote these details on the whiteboard, but when he started to write 'Fingerprints', he paused.

Phate's fingerprints . . . troubled him for some reason . . .

He snapped his fingers. 'Phate didn't wear gloves.'

At Vesta's, when he'd kidnapped Lara Gibson, Phate had wrapped a napkin round his beer bottle to obscure his prints. At St Francis he hadn't bothered. 'That means he *knows* we have his real identity.'

The press hadn't mentioned his name, nor had that fact gone out online. It was all done verbally—over the phone.

'We have ourselves a spy, you think?' Linda Sanchez said.

Bishop's eyes fell again on the whiteboard and he noticed the reference to Shawn, Phate's mysterious partner. He tapped the name.

Nolan said, 'You're thinking Shawn's an insider?'

Tony Mott shrugged. 'Maybe he's a dispatcher at headquarters?'

'Or maybe,' a man's voice growled, '*Gillette* is Shawn.'

Bishop turned and saw Bob Shelton standing in front of a cubicle towards the back of the room.

'Come here,' he said, gesturing them towards the cubicle.

Inside, on the desk, a computer monitor glowed with text. Linda Sanchez looked over the screen. With some concern she said, 'You're on ISLEnet. Gillette said we weren't supposed to log on from here.'

'Of *course* he said that,' Shelton spat out bitterly. 'Know why? Because he was afraid we'd find this—' He scrolled a little further down and gestured towards the screen. 'It's an old Department of Justice report I found. Phate missed erasing this one.' Shelton tapped the screen. 'Gillette was Valleyman. He and Holloway ran that gang—Knights of Access—together. They *founded* it.'

'No,' Bishop whispered, brushing his sideburns with his knuckles. 'Can't be.'

Mott spat out, '*He* social engineered us too!'

Shelton muttered, '"Shawn" could be one of Gillette's screen names. Remember that the warden said they'd caught him going online. He was probably contacting Phate. Maybe this whole thing was a plan to get Gillette out of prison.'

Miller added, 'He was desperate to stay and help us, remember?'

'Sure he was,' Shelton said, nodding. 'Otherwise, he'd lose his chance to—'

The detectives looked at each other.

Bishop whispered, '—escape.'

They sprinted down the corridor that led to the analysis lab.

The room was empty.

Bishop ran to the end of the corridor and pushed into a storeroom at the back of the building.

He saw the fire door, which led outside into the parking lot. It was wide open. The fire alarm in the door-opener bar had been dismantled—just as Jamie Turner had done at St Francis Academy.

Bishop closed his eyes and leaned against the damp wall. He felt the betrayal deep within his heart, as sharp as Phate's terrible knife.

0000011 / THREE: SOCIAL ENGINEERING

He takes things apart.

Wyatt Gillette was jogging through the chill evening rain down a sidewalk in Santa Clara, his chest aching, breathless. It was 9.30pm and he'd put nearly two miles between him and CCU headquarters since he'd escaped.

He takes things apart . . .

Nature had cursed Wyatt Gillette with a raging curiosity mitigated somewhat by the blessing of a mind skilful enough to satisfy his obsession.

He lived to understand how things worked and there was only one way to do that: take them apart.

His mother would return home from her job to find young Wyatt sitting in front of her food processor, happily examining its component parts.

'Do you know how much that cost?' she'd ask angrily.

Didn't know, didn't care.

This had occurred when the boy was only five years old. Then came stereos and tape decks, the mysteries of vacuum tubes and circuit boards.

Next he discovered computers.

When Wyatt was eight his father, a tall man with the perfect posture that had been his legacy from his air force years, had taken him to a Radio Shack and told him he could pick out something for himself. 'You can get anything you want.'

'Anything?' asked the boy, eyeing the items on the shelves.

Anything you want . . .

He'd picked a computer.

It was a perfect choice for a boy who takes things apart—because the little Trash-80 computer was a portal to the Blue Nowhere, which is infinitely deep and complex, made up of layer upon layer of parts small as molecules and big as the exploding universe.

Gillette remembered the first time he cracked into a government computer and the first time he got busted for hacking. At seventeen, he was a juvenile, but he still had to do time. The judge was stern with boys who seized root of Ford Motor Company's mainframe when they should've been out playing baseball. But the most prominent memory was his first meeting with a hacker named CertainDeath, the username of Jon Patrick Holloway, in the #hack chat room. Their first online conversation lasted four and a half hours.

Initially they traded phone phreaking information. As far as they knew they were the only hackers in America who'd ever placed free calls from a payphone in Golden Gate Park to one in Red Square in Moscow.

From these modest beginnings they began prowling through corporate and government machines.

Soon other hackers began to seek them out to learn what the gurus had to teach. After a year or so, Gillette and Holloway realised that they'd become a cybergang—a rather legendary one, as a matter of fact. The 'Knights of Access'. CertainDeath was the leader and bona fide wizard, Valleyman the second in command.

Elana—Gillette's ex-wife, whom he'd met around this time—was a piano teacher and she said Gillette and Holloway reminded her of Beethoven, who could imagine his music so perfectly in his head that once he'd written it the performance was an anticlimax.

Recalling this, he now thought of his ex-wife. Unlike the Unix operating system, the relationship between him and Elana was something Gillette *couldn't* understand. He didn't know how to take it apart and look at the components.

In matters of love Wyatt Gillette was no wizard.

He now put these reflections aside and stepped under the awning of a shabby Goodwill store near the Sunnyvale town line. Once he was out of the rain he looked around him then, seeing he was alone, reached into his pocket and extracted a small electronic circuit board, which he'd had with him all day. When he'd gone back to his cell at San Ho that morning before Andy Anderson took him to the CCU office, he'd taped the board to his right thigh, near his groin.

Now in the pale, fluorescent light from the Goodwill shop he examined the circuit again and found that it had survived his jog from CCU just fine.

He slipped it back into his pocket and stepped inside the store.

He'd phoned earlier and discovered they shut at 10.00pm. Hurriedly he proceeded to pick out a change of clothing. In the best tradition of social engineering, he chose the sort of things he wouldn't normally wear.

He paid with money he'd lifted from a jacket in CCU and started towards the door. He paused and turned back to the assistant. 'Excuse me. Is there a bus-stop around here?'

The old man pointed to the west. 'Fifty feet up the street. It's a transfer point. You can get a bus to anywhere you want to go.'

'Anywhere?' Wyatt Gillette asked cheerfully. 'Who could ask for more than that?' And he stepped back into the rainy night.

THE COMPUTER CRIMES UNIT was mute from the betrayal.

Frank Bishop felt the hot pressure of silence around him. Bob Shelton was coordinating with the local police. Tony Mott and Linda Sanchez were also on the phones, checking leads. They spoke in quiet tones, reverent almost, suggesting the intensity of their desire to recapture their betrayer.

After Bishop, it was Patricia Nolan who seemed the most upset. She was attracted to the hacker. The detective wondered if this crush fitted a certain pattern: the smart but ungainly woman who'd fall hard for the charming renegade. For the fiftieth time that day Bishop pictured his wife Jennie and thought how glad he was to be contentedly married.

There were no leads. No one in the buildings near CCU had seen Gillette escape. No cars were missing from the parking lot, and no police cars reported seeing anyone fitting his description on foot.

Suddenly Tony Mott glanced at a computer terminal and leapt to his feet, shouting, 'Look!'

He ran to the terminal and started banging on the keyboard.

'What?' Bishop asked.

'A housekeeping program just started to wipe the empty space on the hard drive,' Mott said breathlessly, as he keyed. He hit ENTER then looked up. 'There, it's stopped.'

It was Linda Sanchez who explained. 'Almost all the data on a computer—even things you've deleted—stays in the empty space of your hard drive. It's easy to recover. The only way to completely destroy it is to run a program that "wipes" the empty space. It's like a digital shredder. Before he escaped Wyatt must've programmed it to start running.'

'Which means,' Tony Mott said, 'that he doesn't want us to see what he was just doing online.'

Linda Sanchez said, 'But I've got a program that'll find it.' She flipped through a box containing floppy disks and loaded one into the machine. Her stubby fingers danced over the keyboard and in a moment cryptic symbols filled the screen. Ten minutes later Sanchez smiled faintly and motioned her colleagues over to the terminal.

The screen contained a lot of gibberish, computer symbols and fragments of data and text that made no sense to Bishop. But among the fragments were references to a number of airlines and information about flights that evening.

'But how would he pay for the airfare?' Shelton wondered out loud.

'Are you kidding?' Tony Mott asked with a sour laugh. 'He's probably emptying *your* bank account right now.'

Bishop had a thought. He went to the phone in the analysis lab and picked it up, hit REDIAL.

The detective spoke with someone on the other end of the line for a moment. Then he hung up.

Bishop reported his conversation to the team. 'The last number Gillette dialled was a Goodwill store here in Santa Clara. The clerk said somebody fitting Gillette's description came in about twenty minutes ago. He bought a black trench coat, a pair of white jeans, an Oakland A's cap and a gym bag. He remembered him because he kept looking around and seemed really nervous. Gillette also asked him where the nearest bus-stop was. There's one near the store and the airport bus *does* stop there.'

Mott checked his pistol and started to rise.

'No, Mott,' Bishop said. 'You stay here. Or better yet go home and get some rest. You too, Linda.'

Mott shook his head, not at all happy about the detective's order. But he agreed.

Bob Shelton said, 'I'll call in Gillette's description to the Port Authority police. They'll cover all the bus-stops. But I tell you—*I'm* personally going to be at the international terminal to see the look in that man's eyes when I say hello.' The stocky detective cracked the first smile Bishop had seen in days.

PHATE SAT IN THE DINING ROOM of his house in Los Altos, listening to *Death of a Salesman* on his Discman.

Hunching over his laptop, though, he was distracted. He needed a new victim. He started reading through some of the articles from local newspaper web sites; there were stories about people like paranoid rap stars who travelled with armed entourages, politicians who supported unpopular causes and abortion doctors who lived in virtual fortresses.

He was trying to decide on his next victim. Who'd be more challenging than Boethe and Lara Gibson?

Then his eye caught a newspaper article that Shawn had sent to him about a month ago. It concerned a family who lived in an affluent part of Palo Alto.

HIGH SECURITY IN A HIGH-TECH WORLD

Donald W. is a man who's been to the edge. And he didn't like it.

Donald, 47, who agreed to be interviewed only if we didn't use his last name, is chief executive officer of one of Silicon Valley's most successful venture capital firms. While another man might brag about this accomplishment, Donald tries to keep his success, and all the other facts about his life, completely hidden.

There's a very good reason for this: six years ago, while in Argentina, he was kidnapped at gunpoint and held for two weeks. His company paid an undisclosed ransom for his release. Donald was subsequently found unharmed but he says he hasn't been the same since.

Donald is among a growing number of wealthy executives in Silicon Valley who are starting to take security seriously.

He and his wife even picked a private school for their only child, Samantha, 8, on the basis of its high-security facilities.

Perfect, Phate thought and went online.

The anonymity of these characters was, of course, merely a slight inconvenience and in ten minutes he'd hacked into the newspaper's editorial computer system and was browsing through the notes of the reporter who'd written the article. He soon had all the details he needed on Donald Wingate, 32983 Hesperia Way, Palo Alto, married to Joyce, forty-two, who were the parents of a third grader at Junípero Serra School, 2346 Rio Del Vista, also in Palo Alto. He learned, too, about Wingate's brother, Irving and Irv's wife, Kathy, and about the two bodyguards in Wingate's employ.

There were some MUDhead game players who'd consider it bad strategy to hit the same type of target—a private school, in this case—twice in a row. Phate, on the contrary, thought it made perfect sense and that the cops would be caught completely off guard.

He scrolled through the files again, slowly.

Who do you want to be?

WYATT GILLETTE'S BUS, which wasn't bound for the airport at all but was making local stops in Santa Clara County, had deposited him on a dark, empty street in the pleasant suburb of Sunnyvale, a good ten miles from the San Francisco airport.

As soon as he'd left the Goodwill store he'd pitched out those clothes and had stolen a tan jacket and blue jeans from the collection box in front of the shop. The canvas gym bag was the only purchase still with him.

He wasn't worried about recapture—he'd covered his tracks at CCU just fine, looking up international flight information then running EmptyShred to draw the attention of the team to the fake clues he'd planted about leaving the country.

But he was nervous as hell because of where he was now headed.

He walked north, away from El Camino Real, and soon the sound of traffic on that busy commercial street faded.

Ten minutes later he saw the house. He walked slowly, avoiding the glances of the few people on the street: a woman walking her dog. Two men hunched over a car's open hood.

As Gillette drew closer to the house—an old classic California bungalow—he stopped altogether.

Go ahead, he told himself. You have to do it. Go on.

A deep breath. What was he risking?

Everything, he thought.

He started forward, towards the house.

No more than three seconds later they nailed him.

The dog walker turned suddenly and sprinted towards him. A gun was in her hand and she was shouting, 'Freeze, Gillette! Freeze!'

The two men working on the car also drew weapons and raced towards him.

Dazed, Gillette dropped the gym bag. He raised his hands and backed up slowly. He felt someone grip his shoulder and he turned. Frank Bishop had come up behind him. Bob Shelton was there too, holding a large black pistol pointed at his chest.

'How did you—?' Gillette began.

But Shelton lashed out with his fist and struck Gillette squarely in the jaw. His head popped back and, stunned, he fell to the ground.

Bishop gave no reaction to the blow just delivered by his partner. He crouched, opened the canvas bag. He took out the circuit board. He turned it over and over in his hands.

'What is it, a bomb?' he asked with a lethargy that suggested he didn't think it was an explosive.

'Just something I made,' Gillette muttered, pressing his palm to his face.

Bishop stood, put it in his pocket.

'How?' Gillette asked again.

Bishop said, 'We *were* on the way to the airport but then I started thinking. If you'd *really* gone online and looked up where you were going, you'd've just *destroyed* the hard drive, not timed that program to run later. So, all it did was draw our attention to the clues you'd left about the airport.' The detective looked up the street. 'You know how we found out you were coming here, don't you?'

Of course he knew. They'd called the phone company and learned what number had been dialled from the phone in the lab *before* he'd called Goodwill.

'I should've cracked the switch at Pac Bell and changed the local-call records. I would've done that if I'd had time.'

Shelton said, 'You're Shawn, aren't you?'

'No, I'm not. I don't know who Shawn is.'

'But you were Valleyman, right?'

'Yes. And I was in the Knights of Access.'

'Christ,' the bulky detective continued, 'of *course* you're Shawn. You're him and you're on your way to meet Phate right now.' He grabbed the hacker by the collar of his cheap Goodwill jacket.

Gillette was shaking his head. 'No. I—'

Shelton continued, 'We've got tactical troopers surrounding the place. And you're going to help us get him out.'

'I have no idea where Phate is. But I'll guarantee you he's not in there.'

'Who is, then?' Bishop asked.

'My wife. That's her parents' house.'

'ELANA'S THE ONE I called,' Gillette explained.

'You're divorced, I thought,' Bishop said.

Gillette hesitated. 'I still think of her as my wife.'

'Elana,' Bishop said. 'Last name Gillette?'

'No. She went back to her maiden name. Papandolos.'

Bishop said to Shelton, 'Run the name.'

The cop made the call and listened, then nodded. 'It's her. This is her address. House owned by Irene Papandolos. No warrants.'

Bishop pulled on a headset mike to speak to Alonso Johnson, the head of the county tactical team. He said into his mouthpiece, 'Johnson? It's Bishop. We're pretty sure there're only innocents inside the house. Check it out and tell me what you see . . .' A pause of a few minutes. Then he listened into the microphone. He looked up at Gillette. 'There's a woman in her sixties, grey hair.'

'Elana's mother. Irene.'

'And a blonde in her mid-thirties. She's reading to two little boys.'

'Elana has dark hair. That's probably Camilla, her sister. She's got four kids.'

Bishop said into the microphone, 'Right, tell everybody to stand down. I'm releasing the scene.' The detective asked Gillette, 'What's this all about? You were going to check the computer from St Francis and instead you escaped.'

'I *did* check the machine. There was nothing that'd help us find him. As soon as I booted up, the demon sensed something—probably that we'd disconnected the modem—and killed itself. If I'd found anything helpful I would've left you a note.'

'Left us a note?' Shelton snapped. 'You make it sound like you're running to the 7-Eleven for cigarettes. You escaped from custody.'

'I just needed to see Ellie and I knew you wouldn't've let me go. I was going to call you from her house and have somebody come get me and take me back to CCU. I just needed some time to see Ellie.'

Bishop eyed the hacker closely then asked, 'Why's she living at her parents' house?'

'Because of me. She doesn't have any money. She spent it all on my defence. That's why I made that.' He nodded towards Bishop's pocket. 'It's a new kind of wireless modem that uses global positioning to link you to the best signal for data transmission. It—'

Bishop waved off the tech-speak. 'You made it? With things you found in prison?'

'Found or bought. Ellie can patent it, make some money.'

Bishop asked, 'Why didn't you tell us you were Valleyman?'

'Because you'd've sent me right back to prison. And then I wouldn't've been able to help you track down Phate.' He paused. 'And I wouldn't've had a chance to see Ellie . . .'

Shelton said angrily, 'So you were one of those assholes with Phate—sending out viruses and bomb recipes and shutting down nine-one-one?'

'No,' Gillette said adamantly. He went on to explain that for the first year or so Knights of Access *was* one of the world's premiere cybergangs but they never harmed civilians. 'The worst we did was write our own freeware and give copies away. So a half-dozen big companies lost a few thousand bucks in profit.'

But, he continued, he began to realise there was another person inside CertainDeath—Holloway's screen name back then. He was becoming dangerous. Gillette cracked Holloway's machine and found, to his shock, that Holloway had been writing deadly viruses—programs like the one that took down Oakland's 911 system. He downloaded the viruses and wrote inoculations against them, then posted those on the Net. Gillette also found stolen Harvard University software in Holloway's machine. He sent a copy to the Massachusetts State Police, and CertainDeath was arrested.

Shelton said, 'Let's get the scumbag back to San Ho. We've wasted enough time.'

'No, don't. Please! You've seen how good Phate is. You need somebody as good as me to stop him.'

'I know you're good, Wyatt,' Bishop said. 'But you also just escaped from my custody and that could've cost me my job. It's going to be pretty tough to trust you now, isn't it? We'll make do with somebody else.'

'You can't "make do" with somebody else—not when it comes to Phate. Miller and Nolan can't handle it. You need somebody who's been in the trenches.'

'Trenches,' Bishop said softly. The comment seemed to amuse him. He fell silent and finally said, 'I believe I'm going to give you one more chance.'

Shelton's eyes fluttered with dark resentment. 'Bad mistake.'

Bishop gave a faint nod, as if acknowledging that it might very well be. Then he said to Shelton, 'Tell everybody to get some dinner and some sleep. I'm taking Wyatt back to San Ho for the night.'

Shelton shook his head, dismayed at his partner's plans, but went off to do what he'd been asked.

Gillette said, 'Give me ten minutes with my wife. Ten minutes is all I'm asking.'

The detective took the hacker's wrist. But before the metal of the cuff closed around it, Gillette asked, 'Do you love your wife, Bishop?'

The cop said nothing for a moment. He looked up at the rainy night sky then put the cuffs away. 'Ten minutes.'

HE SAW HER FIRST in silhouette, lit from behind.

But there was no doubt it was Ellie. Her sensuous figure, the mass of long, black hair that reached towards her lower back.

The only evidence of the tension she'd surely be feeling was the way she gripped the doorjamb on the other side of the screen. Her pianist's fingers were red from the fierce pressure.

'Wyatt,' she whispered. 'Did they . . . ?'

'Release me?' He shook his head. 'I'm just out for a few days. I'm helping them find somebody—Jon Holloway.'

She muttered, 'Your gang friend.' Looking over her shoulder at her sister's children, she stepped further outside and pulled the door shut, as if she wanted to separate him firmly from her present life.

'I wanted to talk to you,' he said to her now.

'We have *nothing* to talk about, Wyatt. We had years to talk—but you had other things to do with your time.'

'Please,' he said, sensing that she was about to bolt back inside. Gillette heard the desperation in his voice but he was past pride.

'The plants've grown.' Gillette nodded towards a thick boxwood. Elana glanced at it and for a moment her façade softened. One balmy November night years ago they'd made love beside that very shrub while her parents were inside, watching election-night results.

'How's Camilla and the kids?'

Exasperated, Elana asked, 'What do you want, Wyatt?'

'I brought you this.'

He gave her a technical specification sheet for the circuit board and explained what it was. 'Find yourself a lawyer and sell it to one of the big companies. Compaq, Apple, Sun. Make sure they pay you a big advance up front. The lawyer'll know all about it.'

She looked down at the board but didn't take it from his outstretched hand.

There was more he'd wanted to say, so much more. Don't say it, he told himself. Do. Not. Say. It.

But he did. 'I love you.'

'No.' She held up a hand as if to deflect the words.

'I want to try again. I want to have a family with you.'

She walked to the door, opened the screen.

He blurted, 'Don't move to New York.'

Elana froze. She turned. 'New York?'

'You're moving to New York. With your friend Ed.'

'How do you know about Ed?'

Out of control now, he persisted, 'Are you going to marry him?'

'How do you know about him?' she repeated. 'How?'

Gillette looked down at the porch, at the spattering of rain on the deck paint. 'I cracked your online account and read your email.'

'You *what*?' She let the screen door swing shut. 'From prison? You hacked into my email from prison?'

'Do you love him?'

'Ed's none of your damn business.'

'Please—'

'Wyatt, Ed and I *are* going to New York. We leave in three days, and there's not a single thing you can do to stop me.'

'I love—'

'You don't love anyone,' she interrupted. 'You social engineer them.'

She walked inside, closing the door quietly.

He walked down the steps to Bishop.

Gillette asked, 'What's the phone number at CCU?'

Bishop gave it to him and the hacker wrote the number on the specification sheet and jotted, 'Please call me.' He wrapped the sheet round the circuit board and left it in the mailbox.

Bishop gave no reaction to what he'd just witnessed on the porch.

When they were inside the squad car Gillette said, 'I really don't want to go back to San Ho.'

'Well, I'm going back to CCU to look over the evidence and grab a few winks. And I didn't see any lockup there.'

Gillette said, 'I'm not going to escape again.'

Bishop didn't respond.

'I really don't want to go back to jail,' Gillette repeated. The detective remained silent and the hacker added, 'Handcuff me to a chair if you don't trust me.'

Bishop said, 'Put your seat belt on.'

THE JUNÍPERO SERRA SCHOOL looked idyllic in the early-morning fog.

The exclusive private school enjoyed a reputation for launching virtually all of its students to high schools of their (well, their parents') choice. The grounds were beautiful and the staff were paid extremely well.

At the moment, however, the school's receptionist wasn't basking in the benefits of her working environment; her eyes were filled with tears and she struggled to control the tremors in her voice. 'My God, my God,' she whispered. 'Joyce was just here a half-hour ago. She was fine. I mean, just a half *hour.'*

Standing in front of her was a young man, with reddish hair and moustache, wearing an expensive business suit. His eyes were red, as if he'd been crying too. 'She and Don were driving to Napa for the day, and one of those buses with migrant workers . . . it veered right into them. My brother broke his back.'

'Oh, God,' she muttered again. A grey-suited woman approached and the receptionist said, 'Mrs Nagler, Joyce and Don Wingate have been in an accident.'

'No!'

'It sounds bad.' The receptionist nodded. 'This is Don's brother.'

'I'm Irv Wingate, Mrs Nagler, Samantha's uncle. You're the director here, right?'

'That's right.'

'I met you at the spring recital last year.'

She nodded and shook his hand.

Wingate recapped the story of the accident. 'Kathy—that's my wife—she's up there now. I'm here to pick up Sammie.'

'Of course.'

But Mrs Nagler, sympathetic though she was, nonetheless ran a tight ship. She leaned over the computer keyboard and typed with blunt, polish-free nails on the keys. She read the screen and then said, 'You're on the authorised list of relatives to release Samantha to.' She hit another key and a picture popped up—the driver's licence photo of Irving Wingate. She looked up at him. It was a perfect match. 'Just one more thing,' she said. 'Your brother was very security minded, you know.'

'Oh, sure,' Wingate said. 'The password.' He whispered to her, 'It's S-H-E-P.' Mrs Nagler nodded in confirmation. 'That was Donald's first Airedale, Shep. We got it when he was twelve,' added Wingate.

Mrs Nagler said sadly, 'I know. We sometimes email each other pictures of our dogs.' She made a call, spoke to the girl's teacher and asked that the student be brought to the main reception area.

Irv said, 'Don't say anything to Sammie, please. I'll break the news to her in the car.'

'Of course.'

An Asian woman—presumably Sammie's teacher—led a skinny redheaded girl into the office. Mrs Nagler smiled and said, 'Your Uncle Irving's here.'

'Irv,' he corrected. 'She calls me Uncle Irv. Hi, Sammie.'

'Wow, you grew your moustache back like totally fast.'

Wingate laughed. 'Your Aunt Kathy said I looked more distinguished.' He crouched down. 'Listen, your Mom and Dad decided you could take the day off school. We're going to go spend the day with them in Napa.'

'Cool,' the girl said eagerly.

A few minutes later Samantha and Uncle Irv started out the door. The receptionist whispered to Mrs Nagler, 'Thank God she'll be in good hands.'

And Irv Wingate must've heard her say this because he turned and nodded. Still, the receptionist did a brief double take; the smile he offered seemed just a little off, like an eerie gloat. But the woman decided she was wrong and put the look down to the terrible stress the poor man had to be under.

'RISE AND SHINE,' the snappy voice said.

Gillette opened his eyes and looked up at Frank Bishop, who was shaved and showered and absently tucking in his stubborn shirt tail.

'I was up till four in the morning,' the hacker grumbled. 'I couldn't get comfortable. But that's not really a surprise, is it?' He nodded at the large iron chair that Bishop had handcuffed him to.

'It was your idea, the cuffs and the chair.'

'I didn't think you'd take it literally.'

'What's to take literally?' Bishop asked. 'Either you handcuff somebody to a chair or you don't.'

The detective unhooked Gillette and the hacker rose stiffly, rubbing his wrist. He went into the kitchen and got coffee and a day-old bagel. 'By any chance, you ever get any Pop-Tarts around here?'

'I don't know,' Bishop responded. 'I'm not much for sweets.' He sipped his coffee. 'Linda and Tony're on their way. Miller too. Linda's still not a grandmother. Patricia Nolan called from her hotel.' He held Gillette's eyes for a moment. 'She gave me hell for cuffing you to the chair. She said you could've spent the night on the couch in her hotel room. Make of that what you will.'

'Shelton?'

Bishop said, 'He's at home with his wife. Sometimes he just has to spend time with her—you know, because of that trouble I told you about before. His son dying.'

A beep sounded from a nearby work station. Gillette rose and went to look at the screen. 'Triple-X is online again,' he told Bishop. 'He's back in the hacker chat room.'

'We going to social engineer him again?'

'No. I've got another idea.'

'What?'

'I'm going to try the truth.'

'WHY WAS MRS GITTING upset?' Sammie Wingate asked.

'Who?' Phate asked absently. They were driving in an Acura Legend, which had been recently stolen but was duly registered to one of his identities.

'The lady at the front desk.'

'I don't know.'

'Like, are Mom and Dad in Napa already?'

'That's right.'

Phate didn't have a clue where they were. He wondered who'd feel the greatest level of panic: the parents of the missing child or the principal and teacher who'd released her to a killer?

'Ani, Ani, Ani, Ani, Animorphs. Who's your favourite?'

'Favourite what?' Phate asked.

'Favourite *Animorph*. I think Rachel's my favourite. She turns into a lion, it's totally cool.'

Phate listened as the girl kept up the prattle. His only comfort at the moment was the razor-sharp knife at home and the anticipation of Donald Wingate's reaction when the businessman received the plastic bag containing a rather gruesome present later that day. Phate himself would be the deliveryman, and this would earn him 25 points, the highest for any particular murder.

Phate glanced at the girl. Her perfectly done hair, the expensive watch, the shoes polished by someone else. Sammie wasn't like Jamie Turner, whom he'd been reluctant to kill because he reminded him so much of himself. No, *this* kid was like all the other little shits who'd made Jon Patrick Holloway's early life at school pure hell.

Suddenly a loud beeping filled the car and, as the girl continued to prattle on about morphing dogs or lions or whatever, Phate pulled the pager off his belt and scrolled through the display.

His reaction was an audible gasp. The gist of Shawn's message was that Wyatt Gillette was at CCU headquarters.

Phate felt the shock as if he'd touched a live wire. He had to pull off the road.

Gillette—Valleyman—was helping the cops! That's why they'd learned so much about him and were so close on his trail. Valleyman—whose brilliance in writing code approached and sometimes surpassed Phate's own. Valleyman—whose betrayal had destroyed Holloway's life.

'Uncle Irv, um, how come we're stopped here? I mean, is there something wrong with the car?'

He glanced at the girl.

'Well, Sammie, you know what—I think there may be. How about you take a look?'

'Um, me?'

'Yeah. Just see if the tyre's flat,' kindly Uncle Irv said. He unhooked the girl's seat belt, and pushed the door open.

Sammie got out and walked around the car. 'It looks OK to me,' she called.

'Good,' Phate called. And gunned the engine, racing forwards. The door slammed shut and the tyres sprayed Sammie with dust and gravel. She started to scream, 'Wait, Uncle Irv . . .'

Phate skidded onto the highway.

The sobbing girl ran after the car but she was soon obscured by a huge cloud of dust from the spinning wheels.

Phate, for his part, had stopped thinking about little Samantha Wingate the moment the door slammed. The shock and dismay of finding that Valleyman was among his adversaries was gone and had turned to electric excitement. Phate was now thrilled that the game he was playing had taken a dramatic twist, one that was familiar to anybody who'd ever played Access or other MUD games. This was the moment when the plot turns 180 degrees and the hunters become the prey.

RENEGADE334: Are you there, Triple-X?

'Come on,' Gillette encouraged in a whisper. 'Come on . . . Talk to me.'

Finally an ICQ window opened and Triple-X responded.

Triple-X: You're keying a lot better now. Grammar and spelling too. BTW, I'm launching from an anonymous platform in Europe. You can't trace me.

Renegade334: We're not trying to. I'm sorry about before. We need your help. I'm asking for your help.

Triple-X: Who are you?

Renegade334: You ever hear of Knights of Access?

Triple-X: EVERYBODY'S heard of KOA.

Renegade334: I'm Valleyman.

Triple-X: Right.

Renegade334: I am. Really.

Triple-X: If you are then tell me what you cracked six years ago—the big one, you know what I mean.

'He's testing me,' Gillette said. He typed:

Renegade334: Fort Meade.

Fort Meade, Maryland, home of the National Security Agency, had more supercomputers than anywhere in the world. It also had the tightest security of any government installation.

'Christ,' Mott whispered. 'You cracked Meade?'

Gillette shrugged.

Triple-X: How did you get through their firewalls?
Renegade334: We heard NSA was installing a new system. They loaded a patch to fix the sendmail flaw in Unix. That's when we got in.

The famous sendmail flaw was a bug in an early version of Unix.

Triple-X: Man, you're a wizard. Everybody's heard about you. I thought you were in jail.
Renegade334: I am. I'm in custody. But they're not after you. Don't worry. We're trying to find Phate—Jon Holloway. He's killing people.

A pause. Gillette typed invisible messages in the air for thirty seconds before Triple-X replied.

Triple-X: That man is sick, but what do you want from me?
Renegade334: Help finding him.
Triple-X: You have no clue how dangerous that psycho is. He could be in your machine right now, or mine, watching everything we're writing.
Renegade334: He's not. I could feel him if he was. And you could feel him too. You've got the touch, right?
Triple-X: True.
Renegade334: Do you know Shawn?
Triple-X: He hangs with Phate is all I know. Word is Phate couldn't hack Trapdoor together by himself and Shawn helped him.
Renegade334: Where is Shawn?
Triple-X: Got the idea he's in the Bay area. But that's all I know. I'm logging off. We've been talking too long.
Renegade334: We need your help. Please . . .
Triple-X: That's weird.
Renegade334: What?
Triple-X: I don't think I ever saw a hacker write please before.

The connection terminated.

STILL CRUISING through the Blue Nowhere like a dolphin in open sea, breaking the surface or nosing through dim vegetation on the impenetrable bottom, Wyatt Gillette's tireless bot sent an urgent message back to its master.

In CCU headquarters the computer beeped.

Search request: 'Phate'
Status: Posted message.

Gillette's face bristled with excitement. He called to Bishop, 'Phate's posted something.' He called up the message.

From: ‹phateicsnet.com›
To: Group
Subject: A recent character
Path:news.newspost.com!southwest.com!newscom.mesh.ad.j
p!counterculturesystems.com!larivegauche.fr.net!frankfrt.de.ne
t!swip.net!newsserve.deluxe.interpost.net!internet.gateway.net
!roma.internet.it!globalsystems.uk!
Remember: All the world's a MUD and the people in it merely characters.

Gillette downloaded a picture that was attached to the message. It slowly appeared on the screen.

'Oh, my God,' Linda Sanchez muttered, her eyes fixed on a terrible image. Lara Gibson was half-naked and lying on a tile floor. There were slashes on her body and she was covered with blood. Her dim eyes were gazing hopelessly at the camera. Gillette supposed that it had been taken when she'd had only a few minutes left to live. He—like Stephen Miller—had to turn away.

Bishop asked, 'That address? *Phateicsnet.com*? Any chance it's real?'

Gillette checked. 'Fake,' he said, not surprising anyone.

'So, it isn't any help to us,' the detective said.

'Well, this might be,' Gillette said. He leaned forward and tapped the line that was labelled Path. It identified the networks that Phate's message had made its way through to get to the computer server they'd downloaded it from.

'*That's* the network Phate's computer was actually connected to: *newsserve.deluxe.interpost.net*.' Gillette began to dig up more information about the company. 'Interpost is a chainer,' he said, shaking his head. He explained to Bishop why this was discouraging: 'It's a service that hides your identity when you send emails or post messages. They strip out your real return address and add fake ones. *Nobody* can find out who the sender is, even the police.'

'So we're dead in the water,' Bishop said.

'Not necessarily. I think that we ought to do some more fishing,' said Gillette. He loaded one of his own search engines into the CCU machine.

As the computer at the CCU was sending out Wyatt Gillette's search engine query, Phate sat in the Bay View Motel, a decrepit inn along a sandy stretch of commercial sprawl in Fremont, California. Staring at the laptop's monitor, he was following the progress of Gillette's search.

Within seconds the search engine had found dozens of sites in which Interpost was mentioned and was shooting their names and addresses back to the CCU computer. But the packets of data that made up this information took a detour—they were diverted to Phate's laptop. Trapdoor then modified the packets to insert its hard-working demon and sent them on their way to CCU.

Phate now got this message:

Trapdoor
Link complete
Do you wish to enter subject's computer? Y/N

Phate keyed Y, hit ENTER and a moment later was inside CCU's system. He went straight to a folder labelled PERSONNEL RECORDS— COMPUTER CRIMES UNIT.

The contents were—not surprisingly—encrypted. Phate pulled down a screen window on Trapdoor and clicked on Decrypt. The program went to work to crack the code.

As the hard drive moaned, Phate stood and fetched a Mountain Dew from a cooler sitting on the motel room floor. Sipping the sweet drink, he walked towards the window, and into shafts of brilliant sunlight that had momentarily broken through the storm clouds. The flood of jarring light agitated him and he pulled the shade down, then turned back to the muted colours of the computer screen, which were far more pleasing to him than God's palette could ever be.

'WE'VE GOT HIM,' Gillette announced to the team. 'Phate's inside our machine. Let's start the trace.'

'All right!' Tony Mott said, offering a deafening whistle of victory.

Ten minutes before, Gillette had had a thought: that Phate's message was a feint. The killer was setting them up. He'd posted the picture of Lara so he could find out CCU's Internet address and get inside their computer.

Gillette had explained this to the team and then added, 'And we're going to let him.'

'So *we* can trace *him*,' Bishop said.

'You got it,' Gillette confirmed. 'I'll transfer out all the real data to back-up tapes and load some encrypted files. While he's trying to decrypt them we'll track him down.'

'What if he's using an anonymiser?' Bishop asked.

'I doubt that. If I were him I'd be logging on from a payphone or hotel room, ready to run any minute.'

Gillette sat forward, staring at the screen. 'I've got his service provider!' he shouted finally. 'He's dialling into ContraCosta online in Oakland.' He turned to Stephen Miller. 'Get Pac Bell on it now!'

The phone company would complete the trace from ContraCosta online to Phate's machine itself. Miller spoke urgently to the Pac Bell security staff.

'Just a few more minutes,' Nolan said, her voice edgy. 'Stay on the line, stay on the line . . . Please.'

Stephen Miller stiffened and his face broke into a smile. He said, 'Pac Bell's got him! He's in the Bay View Motel—in Fremont.'

Bishop pulled out his cellphone and called Central Dispatch. 'Silent roll up,' he ordered. 'I want troopers there in five minutes.'

Tony Mott saw one more chance to play real cop. This time, though, Bishop surprised him. 'OK, you're coming along. Only stay to the rear.'

'Yessir,' the young cop said gravely and pulled an extra box of bullets from his desk.

Bishop nodded at Mott's belt. 'I think the two clips you've got with you'll be enough.'

'Sure. OK.' When Bishop turned away Mott slipped a furtive handful of bullets into his windbreaker pocket.

Bishop said to Gillette, 'You come with me. We'll stop by Bob Shelton's place, pick him up. Then let's go catch ourselves a killer.'

DETECTIVE ROBERT SHELTON lived in a modest neighbourhood of San Jose not far from the 280 freeway.

Frank Bishop pulled up to the house. He didn't get out immediately but appeared to be debating. Finally he said, 'Just want to let you know, about Bob's wife . . . Their son dying in that car crash? She never really got over it. She drinks a bit too much. Bob says she's sick. But that's not what it is.'

'Got it.'

They walked to the house. Bishop pushed the doorbell. There was no ring inside but they could hear muted voices. Angry voices.

Then a scream.

Bishop glanced at Gillette, hesitated a moment then tried the door. It was unlocked. He pushed inside, his hand on his pistol. Gillette entered after him.

The house was a mess. Dirty dishes and magazines littered the living room. There was a sour smell of unwashed clothing and liquor. They couldn't see anyone but the men heard a crash and a woman's slurred voice from a back room.

'Leave me alone. You don't understand anything. You're never here. How could you understand?'

'I'm not—' Bob Shelton's voice said. But his words were lost in another crash. 'Oh, hell,' he shouted. 'Now look what you've done.'

The hacker and the detective stood helplessly in the living room, not sure what to do now that they'd intruded on this difficult domestic situation.

Gillette happened to glance into the open doorway of a room nearby.

'Look at that.' What had caught his attention was a square metal box.

'What is it?' Bishop asked.

Gillette examined it. He gave a surprised laugh. 'It's an old Winchester hard drive. Nobody uses them any more but a few years ago they were state of the art. I thought Bob didn't know much about computers.'

The question as to why Bob Shelton had a server drive never got answered, though, because just then the detective stepped into the hallway and blinked in shock at the presence of Bishop and Gillette.

'We rang the bell,' Bishop said.

Shelton remained frozen, as if trying to decide how much the two intruders had heard. 'Emma has the flu,' he said quickly. He looked coldly at Gillette. 'What's *he* doing here?'

'We came by to pick you up, Bob. We have a lead to Phate in Fremont.' Bishop explained about the assault which was now preparing for the Bay View Motel.

'OK,' the cop said, with a glance towards where his wife now seemed to be crying softly. 'I'll be out in a minute. Can you wait in the car?'

'Sure, Bob.'

He hesitated, as if working up his courage, then walked through the doorway into the bedroom beyond.

THEY ARRIVED at the Bay View Motel. Bob Shelton braked hard and skidded into the parking lot next door.

There were a dozen state police and highway patrol cars in the lot and a number of uniformed, plain-clothes and armour-suited tactical officers.

The SWAT commander, Alonso Johnson, noticed Bishop and Shelton and ran up to the car. Bent down to the window. 'Guy fitting Holloway's description checked in two hours ago under the name Fred Lawson,' he said. 'Paid cash. He's in room one-eighteen. The blinds're down but he's still on the phone.'

Bishop glanced at Gillette. 'He still online?'

Gillette looked at his laptop screen. 'Yep.'

Bishop, Shelton and Gillette climbed from the car. Sanchez and Mott joined them.

The commander opened a diagram of the motel. 'We've got troopers here, here, here.' He tapped various places around the grounds and in the ground-floor corridor. 'We don't have much leeway. We'll secure the rooms on either side, then go in through the front door and take him.'

Bishop glanced up and saw Tony Mott pick up a short black automatic shotgun and study it lovingly. With his wraparound sunglasses and biker shorts he looked like a character in a bad science-fiction film. Bishop motioned the young man over. 'What're you doing with that?' Gesturing at the gun.

'I just thought I ought to have some better firepower.'

'Put it back.'

'But—'

'And, Officer?' Alonso Johnson muttered. 'Lose the sunglasses.'

Johnson cocked his head as he received a transmission. He nodded slightly and then looked up. 'We're ready.'

Bishop said, 'Go ahead,' as casually as if he were politely letting someone precede him into an elevator.

The commander spoke into the tiny microphone. Motioning half a dozen tactical officers to follow him, he ran through a line of bushes towards the motel. Tony Mott followed them, keeping to the rear as he'd been ordered.

Bishop walked back to the car and tuned the radio to the tactical operations frequency. From the radio headset he heard Johnson suddenly call, 'Go, go, go!'

Was Phate waiting for them with a gun? Bishop wondered. What would happen?

But the answer was: nothing.

A staticky transmission cut through the air on his radio. Alonso Johnson said, 'Frank, the room's empty. He's not here.'

'Not there?' Bishop turned to Wyatt Gillette, who glanced at the computer in the car. Phate was still online.

The detective radioed to Johnson, 'We can see him transmitting from the motel. He *has* to be there.'

'Negative, Frank,' was Johnson's response. 'Room's empty, except for a computer and a couple of empty cans of Mountain Dew.'

Bishop said, 'OK, Al, we're coming in to take a look.'

INSIDE THE HOT, close motel room half a dozen troopers opened drawers and checked out closets. Bishop motioned Gillette towards the computer, which sat on the cheap desk.

On the screen he saw the decryption program. He typed a few commands then frowned. 'Hell, it's fake. The software's decrypting the same paragraph over and over again.'

'What the hell was the point of *that?*' Shelton snapped. 'Is this part of his bloody games? Messing with our minds?'

Tony Mott said, 'All right. Phate must have set this thing up to get us out of the office, to keep us busy . . . Why?'

'Oh, Christ,' Gillette snapped. 'I know why!'

Frank Bishop did too. He looked quickly at Gillette and said, 'He's trying to crack ISLEnet!'

'Right!' Gillette confirmed. He grabbed the phone and called CCU.

'Computer Crimes. Sergeant Miller here.'

'It's Wyatt. Listen—'

'Did you find him?'

'No. Listen to me. Call the sysadmin at ISLEnet and have him suspend the entire network. Right now.'

A pause. 'They won't do that,' Miller said. 'The whole state relies on—'

'You have to do it now! Phate's trying to crack it.'

Bishop grabbed the phone. 'That's an order, Miller. Now!'

'OK, OK, I'll call. They aren't going to like it. But I'll call.'

Gillette sighed. 'This whole thing was a set-up—posting the picture of Lara Gibson, going through CCU's computer, sending us here. Man, I thought *we* were one step ahead of *him*.'

Bob Shelton barked at him, 'You said you were making sure he couldn't get inside ISLEnet.'

'I *did* make sure,' Gillette said to him. 'I took the system offline and then shredded every reference to usernames and passwords. He probably cracked ISLEnet because *you* went back online from CCU to check me out.'

'Impossible. I erased everything.'

'Did you *wipe* the free space on the drives? Did you overwrite the temp and slack files? Did you encrypt the logs and overwrite them?'

Shelton was silent.

Gillette said, 'No, you didn't. *That's* how Phate got online. He ran an undelete program and got everything he needed to crack into

ISLEnet.' He turned angrily to Bishop. 'If he got into ISLEnet you know what he'd have access to, don't you?' he asked.

'Everything,' Bishop said. 'He'd have access to everything.'

WYATT LEAPT from the car before Bishop had brought it to a complete stop in the CCU headquarters parking lot. He sprinted inside.

'Damage assessment?' he asked. Patricia Nolan was at a work station.

'I'm just going through the log files now.'

Log files retain information on which users have been connected to a system, for how long, what they do online.

Gillette took over and began keying furiously. He absently picked up his coffee cup from that morning, took a sip and shuddered at the cold, bitter liquid. He put the cup down and returned to the screen, pounding keys hard as he roamed through the ISLEnet log files.

A moment later he was aware of Patricia Nolan sitting beside him. She put a fresh cup of coffee next to him. He glanced her way. 'Thanks.'

He turned back to the screen and continued to key. His fingers slammed down angrily. He kept thinking about Bob Shelton. How could somebody who knew enough about computers to own a Winchester server drive be so careless?

Finally, he sat back and announced, 'It's not as bad as it could be. Phate *was* in ISLEnet but only for about forty seconds before Stephen suspended it.'

Bishop asked, 'Forty seconds. Is that enough time to get anything useful?'

'No way,' the hacker said. 'To get to anything classified he'd have to run a cracking program for the passcodes. That'd take a half-hour.'

Bishop nodded. 'At least we got *one* break.'

BUT WHAT THE COMPUTER Crimes Unit didn't know was that as soon as Phate had entered the system one of Trapdoor's clever demons had taken over the internal clock and rewritten all download logs. In reality Phate had spent a leisurely fifty-two minutes inside ISLEnet, downloading gigabytes of information.

Some of this intelligence was so classified that only a handful of law enforcers were allowed to see it: access numbers and passcodes to top-secret government computers; information about the FBI, the Secret Service and most other law enforcement agencies.

Now, as soft rain streaked the windows of his house, Phate was scrolling through the human resource files of the state police. There were many subfolders but Phate was interested only in one. It was labelled DETECTIVE DIVISION and it contained some very useful data.

0000100 / FOUR: ACCESS

LATE INTO evening the CCU team pored over the reports from the Bay View Motel, continuing to search for any leads to Phate. No witnesses had seen what kind of car he'd been driving. The computer left in the room was loaded with just enough software for the break-in. There was nothing to give any indication where Phate might be.

Linda Sanchez continued to be preoccupied with her daughter, calling her every few hours to see how she was doing. Bishop sent her home. Then he dismissed the rest of the troops too.

Gillette leaned back wearily at his station, cracked his knuckles and stretched. Bishop noted that the hacker's fingers kept typing— no, *keying*—in the air as he stared at the ceiling. He realised that he, too, had been pulled deep under the spell of the Blue Nowhere. Maybe it had skewed his thoughts. He now walked to the whiteboard and stared at the terrible picture of Lara Gibson.

Beneath her body the floor was poorly laid greenish tile. There was a square galvanised metal duct running from a beige air conditioner or furnace. The wall was the back side of unpainted Sheetrock. The FBI might be able to figure out if there was a particular builder who made residential properties with those brands of materials. It was a long shot, but Bishop called a friend of his in the FBI and told him about the picture. Bishop then glanced down at a nearby desk and noticed a large envelope addressed to him. The routing slip indicated it had come from California Juvenile. He opened it and read through the contents. It was the file on Gillette he'd requested when the hacker had escaped last night. He dropped it on the desk then glanced up at the dusty wall clock. It was half past ten at night. 'I think we all need some rest,' he said to Gillette. 'I don't feel like spending the night here again. I'm going home. And you're coming with me.'

Patricia Nolan gathered up a pile of floppy disks and her laptop, and left for the hotel suite that Horizon Online was paying for.

As Bishop and Gillette walked out the door the hacker asked, 'You mind if we make a stop on the way?'

'A stop?'

'There's something I want to pick up,' Gillette said. 'Oh, and speaking of which—can I borrow a couple of dollars?'

THE RANCH HOUSE was small but situated in a verdant yard that looked to be about half an acre, a huge plot for this part of Silicon Valley. They walked along a winding sidewalk, which was badly cracked and buckled. Bishop said, 'Watch your step there. I've been meaning to fix that. We have the San Andreas Fault to thank.' He unlocked the door and ushered the hacker inside.

Frank Bishop's wife, Jennie, was a petite woman in her late thirties. While Bishop—with his sideburns and short-sleeved white shirts—was a time traveller from the 1950s, his wife was very much an up-to-date housewife. Long hair in a French braid, jeans, a designer shirt. She didn't appear the least put out—or even surprised—that her husband had brought a felon home to spend the night. 'Have you eaten?' she asked.

'No,' Bishop said.

But Gillette held up a paper grocery bag. 'We stopped at a 7-Eleven,' he said.

Jennie unabashedly took the bag from him, looked inside. She laughed. 'You're not having Pop-Tarts for dinner. You need real food.'

'No, really—' With a smile on his face and sorrow in his heart Gillette watched the pastry disappear into the kitchen. *So near, yet so far . . .*

The place reminded Gillette of his own childhood homes. White wall-to-wall carpet in need of replacing. Furniture from Sears. An expensive TV and a cheap stereo. Gillette looked over some of the many framed pictures on the mantelpiece.

'That's quite a family.'

Bishop laughed. 'I'm the eighth of nine. Five boys and four girls.'

'I've got twenty-nine nieces and nephews,' the detective said proudly.

There was movement nearby. They turned.

A boy of about eight, wearing pyjamas decorated with tiny dinosaurs, walked into the living room.

'Say hi to Mr Gillette, son. This is Brandon.'

'Hello.'

'Hi, Brandon,' Gillette said.

'Mr Gillette writes software for computers.'

'You write script?' the boy asked enthusiastically.

'That's right,' Gillette said, laughing at the way the programmer's shorthand for 'software' tripped easily off his tongue.

The boy said, 'We write programs at our computer lab in school, but it's totally boring. We have to use QBasic. I'm gonna learn object-oriented programming.'

'So you want to go into computers when you grow up?'

'Naw, I'm going to play pro baseball.'

'Why don't you go show Mr Gillette your computer.'

'You play Tomb Raider?' the boy asked. 'Or Earthworm Jim?'

'I don't play games much.'

'I'll show you. Come on.'

Gillette followed the boy into a room cluttered with books, toys, sports equipment, clothes.

In the centre of the room was an IBM-clone computer and dozens of software manuals. Brandon sat down and, with lightning-fast keystrokes, booted up the machine and loaded Tomb Raider.

'You want to play?'

But this brought to mind the terrible game of Access and Phate's digital picture of the murdered Lara Gibson. He wanted nothing to do with violence, even two-dimensional, at the moment.

'Maybe later.'

He watched the boy's fascinated eyes dance around the screen. A while later the detective stuck his head in the door. 'Lights out, son.'

'Aw, Dad, I'm at level four! Five minutes.'

'Nope. It's bedtime.'

'Dad . . .'

Bishop made sure the boy's teeth were brushed and his homework was in his book bag. He kissed him good night, powered down his computer and switched off the overhead light.

Jennie Bishop summoned them to eat. 'I'm going to bed,' she said. 'I've got a busy day tomorrow. Nice meeting you, Wyatt.' She shook his hand firmly.

'Thanks for letting me stay. I appreciate it.'

To her husband she said, 'My appointment's at eleven o'clock tomorrow.'

'You want me to go with you? Bob can take over for a few hours.'

'No, I'll be fine. If Dr Williston sees anything funny I'll call you from the hospital. But that's not going to happen.'

He kissed her. 'Night, love.' Jennie disappeared into the dim hallway.

Bishop rose and walked to the refrigerator. 'I guess I can't get into any more trouble than I'm already in if I offer a prisoner a beer.'

Gillette shook his head. 'Thanks but I don't drink. That's one thing about hackers: we never drink anything that'll make us sleepy.'

Bishop poured himself a Budweiser and gave Gillette a can of cola. Gillette glanced round to make sure Jennie was gone, then walked to the counter where she'd left the Pop-Tarts. He opened them up and took four of the pastries, offering one to Bishop.

'Not for me, thanks.'

'I'll eat the roast beef too,' Gillette said, nodding at Jennie's sandwiches. 'It's just, I dream about these in prison. They're the best kind of hacker food—full of sugar, you can buy 'em by the case and they don't go bad.' He wolfed down two at once. 'This'd be my staple diet when I was hacking: Pop-Tarts, Mountain Dew and cola.' After a moment Gillette asked in a low voice, 'Is your wife all right? That appointment she mentioned?'

He saw a faint hesitation in the detective's hand as he lifted his beer and took a sip. 'Nothing serious . . . A few tests.' Then, as if to deflect the course of this conversation, he asked, 'Did you and your wife have children?'

'No. I didn't want to at first, and by the time I *did*, well, I'd been busted. And then we were divorced.'

'So you'd like kids?'

'Oh, yeah. My brother's got two. We have a lot of fun together.'

Bishop's eyes dipped to the tabletop. 'I read your file.'

'My file?' Gillette asked.

'Your juvenile file. The one you forgot to have shredded.'

The hacker slowly rolled up his napkin then unrolled it.

'When you escaped from CCU I ordered a copy, because I thought we might get some information that'd help track you down. The social worker's report was included. About your family life. Or *lack* of family life . . . So, tell me—why'd you lie to everybody?'

Gillette said nothing for a long moment.

Why'd you lie? he thought.

You lie because you *can*. When you're in the Blue Nowhere you can tell the world that you live in a big beautiful house in Menlo

Park and that even though your mother died of a tragic and unexpected heart attack you're still real close to your dad. He travels all over the world as a petroleum engineer but he always visits you and your brother for the holidays.

And guess what?

The world believes you. The world never knows you're the only child of a divorced mother and that it wasn't her heart that killed her but her liver. The world never knows that your homes were a series of caravans in the shabbiest parts of Silicon Valley, that your only treasure was a cheap computer and that the only bill that ever got paid on time was the phone bill—because you paid it yourself out of paper-delivery money so that you'd be able to stay connected to the Blue Nowhere, the one thing that kept you from going mad.

When Gillette finally looked up, he did what he'd never done before—not even to his wife. He told his entire story to another human being.

'I was eight when he left,' Gillette said, hands round a cola can, callused fingertips pressing the cold metal as if he were keying the words. 'My mother was out somewhere and he came into my room and said he had some shopping to do, why didn't I come along. That was pretty weird because we never did *anything* together. He drove to this diner next to the railroad station. I was too nervous to eat. He didn't notice. All of a sudden he put his fork down and looked at me and told me how unhappy he was with my mother and how he had to leave. I remember how he put it. He said it was a tough decision, but it was the right thing to do and asked if I felt happy for him.'

'He asked you *that*?'

Gillette nodded. 'When we left the restaurant, maybe he noticed I was upset. He saw this store and said, "Tell you what, son, you go in there and buy anything you want."'

'A consolation prize.'

Gillette laughed and nodded. 'I guess that's what it was. The store was a Radio Shack. I just walked in and I picked the first thing I saw. A Trash-80.'

'A what?'

'A TRS-80. One of the first personal computers.' Gillette smiled briefly. 'Did you see that article I wrote called "The Blue Nowhere"?'

'I did,' Bishop said. 'It means cyberspace.'

'It also means something else,' Gillette said slowly. 'My father was ex-air force, and when he got drunk he'd sing the air force song, "The Wild Blue Yonder". After he left I kept hearing that song in my head, only I changed "yonder" to "nowhere", because he was gone. He was nowhere.' Gillette swallowed hard. 'Pretty stupid, huh?'

But Frank Bishop didn't seem to think there was anything stupid about this at all. 'You ever hear from him?'

'Nope. All those letters supposedly from my father to the judge . . . I wrote them all myself.'

'I'm sorry,' Bishop said.

Gillette shrugged. 'Hey, I survived. It doesn't matter.'

'It probably does,' Bishop said softly.

They sat in silence for a few minutes. Bishop finished his beer. Then he rose and started to wash the dishes.

Gillette asked, 'You going to handcuff me somewhere?'

'Escaping twice in two days'd be bad form, even for a hacker. I think we'll forgo the bracelet. Guest room's in there. You'll find towels and a fresh toothbrush in the bathroom.'

'Thanks.'

When he was alone, surrounded by the particularly thick silence of someone else's house late at night, Gillette's fingers absently keyed a dozen messages on an invisible machine.

IT WAS JUST AFTER FIVE when his host woke him.

'We got a present,' the detective said. 'Triple-X called me on my cellphone five minutes ago. He's got Phate's real email address. It's *deathknell@mol.com*.'

'MOL? Never heard of that provider.' Gillette rolled from bed.

Bishop continued, 'I called everybody on the team. They're on their way to the office now.'

'Which means us too?' the hacker muttered sleepily.

'Which means us too.'

Jennie had coffee ready in the kitchen but they passed on food; they wanted to get to the CCU office as soon as possible. Bishop kissed his wife. 'About that appointment . . . say the word and I'll be at the hospital in fifteen minutes.'

She kissed his forehead. 'I'm having a few tests done, honey. That's all.'

As Gillette climbed into the car he turned to Bishop. 'Any chance we could stop at that 7-Eleven again? As long as it's on the way.'

PHATE—IN HIS NEW incarnation as Deathknell—continued to remain out of reach. It turned out that there *was* no MOL.com.

'Oh, that's smart,' a groggy Patricia Nolan muttered, sipping a Starbucks coffee. She was as dishevelled as ever in her floppy sweater dress—green today. Obviously not an early riser, she wasn't even bothering to brush her hair out of her face.

'I don't get it,' Shelton said. 'What's smart? What's it all mean?'

Nolan said, 'Phate created his own Internet provider. And he's the only customer. Well, probably Shawn is too. There's no way we can trace back to their machines.'

'But,' Gillette added, 'the address is still important.'

'Why?' Bishop asked.

'Because it means we can send him a love letter.' He asked Bishop, 'Can you get me a crime-scene photo?'

'I suppose,' the detective replied.

'I'm going to impersonate a hacker in Bulgaria that Phate used to trade pictures with, Vlast. I'll upload a picture for him.'

Nolan laughed and nodded. 'And he'll get a virus along with it. You'll take over *his* machine.'

'I'm going to try to.'

Bishop called headquarters and had a trooper fax a copy of a crime-scene photo in a recent murder case to CCU.

Gillette glanced at the picture—a young woman bludgeoned to death—but looked away. Stephen Miller scanned it into digital form.

Gillette went online to get his tool kit from his cache at the air force lab in Los Alamos. From it he downloaded and modified what he needed: the viruses and his own anonymising email program. He wasn't trusting Stephen Miller any more.

PHATE WAS CURIOUS about what Vlast, his Bulgarian friend, had sent, but he'd have to wait until later to find out. At the moment he was too excited about his latest hunt with Trapdoor. After an hour of serious passcode cracking on borrowed supercomputer time Phate had finally seized root in a computer system not far away from his house in Los Altos. He now scrolled through the main menu.

Stanford-Packard Medical Center Palo Alto, California

1. Administration
2. Personnel
3. Patient Admissions

4. Patient Records
5. Departments by Speciality
6. CMS
7. Facilities management

He chose number 6.

Computerised Medical Services

1. Surgical Scheduling
2. Medicine Dosage and Administration Scheduling
3. Oxygen Replenishment
4. Oncological Chemo/Radiation Scheduling
5. Patient Dietary Menus and Scheduling

He typed 2 and hit ENTER.

THE CHIME ON THE CCU computer sounded an hour later—to the team it rang out like a siren.

Gillette ran to the work station. 'Yes!' he whispered. 'Phate's looked at the picture. The virus is in his machine.'

He sat down and lifted his hands to the keyboard. Feeling the unparalleled excitement he always did just before he started a journey into an uncharted part—an *illicit* part—of the Blue Nowhere, Wyatt Gillette began keying.

THE FIRST THING he saw was a folder named Trapdoor.

Gillette's heart began to pound. Here was a chance to learn about this miraculous software, maybe even glimpse the source code itself.

But he had a dilemma: although he could slip into the Trapdoor folder and look at the program, he would be very vulnerable to detection because he had root control. The same way that Gillette had been able to see Phate when the killer had invaded the CCU computer. If that happened Phate would immediately shut down his machine and create a new Internet service provider and email address. They'd never find him.

No, despite his curiosity, he'd have to forgo a look at Trapdoor and search for clues that might find Phate or Shawn or the next victim's identity.

With painful reluctance Gillette turned away from Trapdoor and began to prowl stealthily through Phate's computer.

Like a living creature, each machine contains thousands of places to visit and myriad different paths by which to get to each destination. And each machine is unique from every other, a palace filled with hidden passages and secret chambers.

The virtual passageways of Phate's computer led finally to a folder labelled Correspondence, and Gillette went after it like a shark.

He opened the first of the subfolders, OUTGOING.

This contained mostly emails to *Shawn@MOL.com*.

The emails were highly technical—software patches and copies of engineering data and specifications downloaded from the Net. It was as if they had agreed never to refer to their personal lives.

There wasn't a shred of evidence as to who Shawn might be.

But then Gillette found a somewhat different email. It had been sent from Phate to Shawn several weeks ago—at 3.00am. 'Check this one out.' He began reading: '"Last night I'd finished working on the patch and lay in bed. Sleep was far, far away, and all I could do was think about you, the comfort you give me."'

Gillette looked up. 'Looks like they're a little more than friends.'

'Is there anything in it that'll help track him down?' Bishop asked.

The hacker skimmed the rest of the email quickly. 'No.'

Gillette backed out of OUTGOING and examined the INCOMING file. There were some old emails from Vlast and some from Triple-X—technical information about software. All the others were from Shawn but they were even more technical.

He opened another.

From: Shawn
To: Phate
Re: FWD: Cellular Phone Companies

Shawn had found an article on the Net describing which mobile phone companies were the most efficient and forwarded it to Phate.

The hacker hit the print-screen—also called the screen-dump—button, which sent the text on the monitor to the printer.

'Download it,' Miller said. 'Might be something in there about which phones they're using.'

'I don't think we want to do that.' The hacker explained that a download might also trigger an alarm in Phate's computer.

He continued searching through the killer's machine. More files scrolled past, opening, closing. A fast scan, then on to another file. Gillette couldn't help but feel exhilarated—and overwhelmed—by the sheer amount, and brilliance of the technical material.

'Can you tell anything about Shawn from his emails?' Mott asked.

Gillette gave his opinion that Shawn was brilliant, matter-of-fact, cold. Shawn's answers were abrupt, which suggested that Shawn was arrogant and would have no patience for people who couldn't keep up with him. He probably had at least one college degree from a good school—even though he rarely bothered to write in complete sentences, his grammar was excellent.

Keying softly now, as if Phate could hear him, Gillette returned to the main directory—a tree diagram of folders and subfolders.

```
C:/
—Operating System
—Correspondence
—Trapdoor
—Games
—Tools
—Viruses
—Pictures
```

'Games!' Gillette and Bishop shouted simultaneously, and the hacker entered this directory.

```
—Games
    —ENIAC week
    —IBM PC week
    —Univac week
    —Apple week
    —Altair week
    —Next year's projects
```

'The bastard's got it all laid out there,' Bob Shelton said.

'And more killings lined up.' Gillette touched the screen. 'The date the first Apple was released. The old Altair computer.'

'Check out this week—Univac,' Bishop said.

Gillette expanded the directory tree.

```
—Univac week
    —Completed games
    —Lara Gibson
    —St Francis Academy
    —Next projects
```

'There!' Tony Mott called. '"Next Projects".'

Gillette clicked on it.

The folder contained dozens of files—page after page of dense notes, graphics, diagrams, pictures, schematics, newspaper clippings. There was too much to read quickly so Gillette started at the beginning file, hitting the screen-dump button every time he jumped to the next page. He moved as quickly as he could but it took about ten seconds to print out each page.

'It's taking too much time,' he said.

'I think we should download it,' Patricia Nolan said.

'That's a risk,' Gillette said. 'I told you.'

'But remember Phate's ego,' Nolan countered. 'He thinks there's nobody good enough to get inside his machine, so he might not've put a download alarm on it.'

'It's your call,' Gillette said to Bishop. The detective leaned forward, staring at the screen, while the hacker's hands hung in the empty space in front of him, furiously pounding on a keyboard that didn't exist.

PHATE WAS SITTING comfortably at his laptop in the immaculate dining room of his house.

Though he wasn't really here at all.

He was lost in the Machine World.

Suddenly an urgent beeping sounded from his machine's speakers. A red box appeared in the upper-right corner of his screen.

ACCESS

He gasped in shock. Someone was trying to download files from his machine! This had *never* happened.

He knew instantly: the picture supposedly sent by Vlast had in fact been emailed to him by Wyatt Gillette to implant a back-door virus in his computer.

The Judas Valleyman was prowling through his system right now!

Instinctively, Phate reached for the power switch, but then he smiled coldly and let his machine keep running at full speed.

His hands returned to the keyboard and he held down the SHIFT and CONTROL keys on his computer while simultaneously pressing the E key.

ON THE MONITOR in front of Wyatt Gillette the words flashed in hot type:

BEGIN BATCH ENCRYPTION

A moment later another message:

ENCRYPTING—DEPARTMENT OF DEFENSE
STANDARD 12

'No!' Gillette cried, as the contents of the Next Projects file turned to digital oatmeal.

'What happened?' Bishop asked.

'Phate *did* have a download alarm,' Nolan muttered. 'I was wrong.'

Gillette scanned the screen hopelessly. 'He aborted the download and he's encrypting everything that's on his machine.'

Bishop asked in a troubled voice, 'Why didn't he just go offline? Why did he encrypt? That doesn't make sense.'

'Damn,' Gillette said. He knew the answer to that question. He swivelled round and pointed to a grey box on the wall; a red button rose prominently from the middle of it. 'Hit the scram switch! Now!' he cried to Stephen Miller, who was closest to it.

Miller glanced at the switch then back to Gillette. 'Why?'

The hacker made a dive for the switch. But it was too late. There was a grinding sound from the main box of the CCU computer and the monitors of every machine in the room turned solid blue as the system failed—the notorious 'blue screen of death'.

Sparks shot from the box and choking smoke and fumes began to fill the room.

The hacker slapped the scram switch with his palm and the power went off; halon gas shot into the computer housing and extinguished the flames.

'What the hell happened?' Shelton asked.

Gillette muttered angrily, 'That's why Phate encrypted his data but stayed online—so he could send *our* system a bomb.'

'What'd he do?' Bishop asked.

The hacker shook his head. 'He sent a command that shut down the cooling fan and then jammed the drive motor and it overheated.'

Bishop surveyed the smouldering box. He said to Miller, 'I want to be up and running again in a half-hour.'

Miller said doubtfully, 'Last time it took a couple of days to get a replacement drive, let alone a machine. The thing is—'

'No,' Bishop said, furious. 'A half hour.'

Miller's eyes scanned the floor. 'We could probably do a mini-network with some PCs and reload the back-up files. Then—'

'Just do it,' Bishop said and lifted the sheets of paper out of the printer—what they'd managed to steal from Phate's computer before he encrypted the data. To the rest of the team he said, 'Let's see if we've caught anything.'

UNDER THE GAZE of his imaginary family, watching him from the pictures in the living room, Phate paced round the room, nearly breathless with anger.

Valleyman had entered *his* machine . . .

And, worse, he'd done this with a simpleminded backdoor program, the kind that a high-school geek could hack together.

He'd immediately changed his machine's identity and his Internet address, of course. There was no way Gillette could break in again. And nothing in the machine would lead them to his house in Los Altos. But had Valleyman seen the Next Projects folder? Had he seen what Phate was about to do in a few hours?

All the plans were made for the next assault . . . Hell, it was already underway.

Should he pick a new victim?

More galling than the wasted effort was the thought that if he abandoned his plans it would be because of a man who'd betrayed him, who'd in effect murdered Jon Patrick Holloway, forcing Phate underground for ever.

He closed his eyes and, like any hacker trying to figure out how to debug some flawed script, he let his mind wander where it wished.

JENNIE WAS WEARING one of those terrible, open-up-the-back robes they give you in hospitals.

What exactly, she thought, is the point of those tiny blue dots on the cloth? She looked absently around the yellow room. Dr Williston was late.

She was thinking about Frank and how vastly relieved she was that her husband wasn't here. He was *such* a contradiction. Unfazed as he arrested killers twice his size, and chatted with prostitutes and drug dealers. And then last week a medical checkup had shown that Jennie's white blood cell count was out of whack. As she told him the news Frank Bishop had paled. She'd thought he was going to cry.

'So what does it all mean?' Frank had asked in a shaky voice.

'Might be some kind of weird infection,' she told him, looking him right in the eye, 'or it might be cancer.'

Might be cancer . . .

Well, she'd know soon enough what it was. She looked at the clock. Where was Dr Williston?

A squat nurse wheeled a drugs trolley into the room. 'Morning,' the woman said in a thick Latino accent. 'You Jennifer Bishop?'

'That's right.'

She looked at Jennie's plastic wristband and nodded.

Jennie smiled. 'Didn't believe me?'

The nurse said, 'Always double-check. My father, he was carpenter, you know. He always say, "Measure twice, cut once".'

Jennie struggled to keep from laughing, thinking that this probably wasn't the best expression to share with patients in a hospital.

She watched the nurse draw some clear liquid into a hypodermic syringe and asked, 'Dr Williston ordered an injection?'

'That's right.'

The nurse cleaned Jennie's arm with an alcohol wipe and injected the drug. After she withdrew the needle Jennie felt an odd tingle spread through her arm near the site of the injection—a burning coldness. She left before Jennie could ask her what the injection was. You had to be careful with medicines in her condition, but she told herself not to worry. The fact that she was pregnant was clearly shown in the records, and no one here would do anything to jeopardise the baby.

'ALL I NEED is the numbers of the cellphone he's using and I can walk right up this fellow's backside.'

This reassurance came from Garvy Hobbes, a blond man of indeterminate age, who was the head of security for the main cellular phone service provider in Northern California, Mobile America.

Shawn's email on cellular phone companies, which Gillette had found in Phate's computer, listed Mobile America as the best service for people wishing to use their mobile phones to go online. The team assumed that Phate would follow Shawn's recommendation. Tony Mott had called Hobbes, with whom the Computer Crimes Unit had often worked in the past.

Hobbes went on to add that, if he knew both the ESN (the electronic serial number, which was secret) and the MIN (the mobile identification number—the area code and seven-digit number of the phone itself), he could use radio direction finding equipment to track down the caller to within a few feet. Or, as Hobbes repeated, 'Right up his backside.'

'How do we find out the numbers of his phone?' Bishop asked.

'Ah, that's the hard part. Mostly we know the numbers because a customer reports his phone's been stolen. We need those numbers though—otherwise we can't do a thing for you.'

'How fast can you move if we do get them?'

'Me? Lickety-split. Even faster if I get to ride in one of those cars with the flashing lights on top of it,' he joked. He handed them a business card and left.

Miller announced that CCU's improvised network was up and running. Gillette had just finished running the final diagnostic check when the machine started to beep.

Gillette looked at the screen, wondering if his bot had found something else. But, no, the sound was announcing an incoming email. It was from Triple-X.

Reading the message out loud, Gillette said, '"Here's a file with some good stuff on our friend".'

Bishop mused. 'I thought Triple-X was paranoid—and was only going to use the phone.'

'He didn't mention Phate's name and the file itself's encrypted. But I'll bet I can crack it.' He slipped the disk containing his hacker tools into one of the PCs and loaded a decryption cracker he'd hacked together a few years ago.

Linda Sanchez, Tony Mott and Bob Shelton had been looking over the few pages of material that Gillette had managed to print out of Phate's Next Projects folder before the killer stopped the download and encrypted the data.

Bishop noted, 'There're a lot of references to facilities management—food services, personnel, payroll. It sounds like the target is a big place.' Bishop pointed to a block of type on one of the print-outs.

CSGEI CLAIMS ID NUMBERS—UNIT 44

'Something about that looks familiar.'

Suddenly Linda Sanchez said, 'Oh, sure, I know: it's our insurer—the California State Government Employees Insurance Company. And those must be the social security numbers of patients. But that information's confidential . . . How did Phate get it?'

Gillette muttered, 'Are the records on ISLEnet.'

Bishop nodded. 'They sure are.'

'Damn,' Gillette spat out. 'When he broke into ISLEnet Phate wasn't online for only forty seconds—shit, he changed the log files just to make us think that. He must've downloaded gigabytes of data. We should—'

'Oh, no,' a man's voice gasped, filled with wrenching alarm.

The team turned to see Frank Bishop, mouth open, stricken, pointing at the list of numbers.

'What's wrong, Frank?' Gillette asked.

'He's going to hit Stanford-Packard Medical Center,' the detective whispered.

'How do you know?'

'The second line from the bottom, that social security number? It's my wife's. She's in the hospital right now.'

A MAN WALKED into the doorway of Jennie Bishop's room.

She looked away from the silent TV set, where she had been absently watching a melodramatic soap opera. She was expecting Dr Williston but the visitor was somebody else—a man in a dark blue uniform. He was young and had a black moustache. 'Mrs Bishop?'

'That's right.'

'My name's Dick Hellman. I'm with the hospital security staff. Your husband called and asked me to stay in your room.'

'Why?'

'He didn't tell us. He just said to make sure nobody comes into your room except him or your doctor.'

'Why didn't Frank call me?'

Hellman toyed with the can of Mace on his belt. 'The phones at the hospital went down about a half-hour ago. Your husband got through on the radio we use for talking to ambulances.'

Just then, Dr Williston, a round, balding man in his late fifties, walked into the room.

'Hello, Jennie, how're you this morning?'

'OK,' she said uncertainly.

Then the doctor noticed the security guard and glanced at him with raised eyebrows.

The man said, 'Detective Bishop asked me to stay with his wife.'

Jennie said, 'Sometimes we run into a little trouble with the cases Frank's working on. He likes to be cautious.'

The doctor nodded and then put on his reassuring face. 'Right, Jennie, these tests won't take too long today.' He nodded at the bandage on her arm from the injection. 'They've already taken blood, I see, and—'

'No. That was from the injection.'

'There was no injection scheduled,' he said, frowning.

'But . . .' She felt the ice of fear run through her—as cold and stinging as the medicine spreading up her arm from the shot. 'The nurse who did it said you'd ordered an injection!'

'What was the medication? Do you know?'

Breathing fast now, in panic, she whispered, 'I don't know! Doctor, the baby . . .'

'Don't worry,' he said. 'I'll find out.'

The doctor's face scared the absolute hell out of her—he too was panicked. He leaned forward and pulled a flashlight from his pocket. He shone it into her eyes and took her blood pressure. He then looked up at the Hewlett-Packard monitor. 'Pulse and pressure are high. But let's not worry yet. I'll go find out what happened.'

He hurried out of the room.

The security guard rose and shut the door.

'No,' she said. 'Leave it open.'

'Sorry,' he responded calmly. 'Your husband's orders.'

FRANK BISHOP SKIDDED the police car into the parking lot of the Stanford-Packard Medical Center and leapt from the car, forgetting to shut the engine off or close the door.

Halfway to the front entrance, he realised what he'd done and turned back. But he heard a woman's voice call, 'Go ahead, boss. I got it.' It was Linda Sanchez. She, Bob Shelton and Tony Mott were in the unmarked car right behind Bishop's—he'd been in such a hurry to get to his wife he'd left CCU without waiting for the rest of the team. Patricia Nolan and Stephen Miller were in a third car.

In the main reception area three nurses were huddled round the receptionist, staring at a computer screen. Something was wrong. They were all frowning, taking turns at the keyboard.

'Excuse me, this is police business,' Frank Bishop said, flashing his shield. 'I need to know which room Jennie Bishop is in.'

A nurse looked up. 'Sorry, Officer. The system's haywire. We don't know what's going on but there's no patient information available.'

'I have to find her. Now.'

'Is she an inpatient?' the nurse asked.

'No. She's just having some tests. She's Dr Williston's patient.'

'Oncology outpatient.' The nurse understood. 'OK, that'd be the third floor, west wing. That way.' Bishop was already sprinting down the hall. His shirt was completely untucked. He shoved it back into his slacks, never breaking stride.

Up the stairs, along a corridor.

He found a nurse and she directed him to a room. The young blonde had an alarmed expression on her face, but whether that was because of something she knew about Jennie, or because of his concerned expression, Bishop didn't know.

He ran down the hall and burst through the doorway, nearly knocking into the young security guard who was sitting beside the bed. The man stood up fast, reaching for his pistol.

'Honey!' Jennie cried.

'It's OK,' Bishop said to the guard. 'I'm her husband.'

His wife was crying softly. He ran to her and gently enfolded her in his arms.

'A nurse gave me a shot,' she whispered. 'Dr Williston didn't order it. They don't know what it is. What's going on, Frank?'

He glanced at the security guard, whose name badge read 'R. Hellman'. The man said, 'Happened before I got here, sir. They're looking for that nurse now.'

'What is it, Frank?' Jennie repeated.

'That fellow we're after? He found out you were in the hospital. We think he might be here someplace.'

'Frank, what about the baby?' She was sobbing now. 'What if the nurse gave me something that hurts the baby?'

'It's going to be all right, honey. If anybody did anything he shouldn't've they can fix you up just fine in no time. There're more doctors per square inch here than anywhere in the Valley. Right?'

Jennie wiped her eyes and nodded. She seemed to relax a bit.

Bishop did too. But that bit of relief sat right beside another thought: that if his wife or the baby were harmed in any way neither Shawn nor Phate would make it into custody alive.

Tony Mott jogged through the door, not the least winded from his sprint to the room, unlike Bob Shelton and Linda Sanchez, who both staggered in through the doorway, gasping for breath. Bishop said, 'Phate might've done something with Jennie's medicine. They're checking on it now. I want you to—'

Suddenly the vital signs monitor on the wall began to buzz with a loud sound. The diagram showing Jennie's heart-rate was jumping frantically up and down.

Then a message popped up on the screen in glowing red type.

WARNING: Fibrillation

Jennie screamed.

The lines on the screen suddenly went flat. The warning tone changed to a piercing squeal and a new message burned on to the monitor.

WARNING: Cardiac Arrest

Mott rushed to the door and cried, 'We need a doctor in here now!'

A moment later Dr Williston ran into the room. He glanced at the monitor and then at his patient. 'She's fine,' he said.

'Fine?' Linda Sanchez questioned.

'There's nothing wrong with her,' he told the policewoman.

'But the monitor . . .' Bishop stammered.

'Malfunction,' the doctor explained. 'Something happened in the main computer system. Every monitor on this floor's been doing the same thing.'

Jennie closed her eyes and pressed her head back on the pillow. Bishop held her tightly.

'And that injection?' the doctor continued. 'I tracked it down. Somehow central pharmaceutical got an order for you to receive a vitamin shot. That's all it was.'

'A vitamin?'

Bishop, trembling with relief, fought down the tears.

The doctor said, 'It won't hurt you or the foetus in any way.' He shook his head. 'It was strange—the order went out under my name and whoever did it got my passcode to authorise it. I keep that in a private file in my computer. I can't imagine how anybody got it.'

'Can't imagine,' Tony Mott said with a sardonic glance at Bishop.

A man in his fifties with a military bearing walked into the room and introduced himself as Les Allen. He was head of security at the hospital.

Bishop told him about the killer's invasion of the hospital.

'You think this guy's here someplace?'

'Oh, yeah, he's here.' Bishop waved at the dark monitor above Jennie's head. 'He did this as a diversion, to get us to focus on Jennie and this wing. He's targeting a different patient.'

Mott added, 'Or somebody on the staff.'

Bishop said, 'This suspect likes challenges. What would be the hardest place in the hospital to break into?'

Dr Williston and Les Allen considered this. 'What do you think, Doctor? The operating suites? They all have controlled-access doors.'

'And a lot of doctors there would be masked, right?' Bishop asked. 'Yes.'

So Phate could roam his killing grounds freely. 'Let's go hunting,' Bishop said. He hugged Jennie again. As he left, the young security guard pulled his chair closer to the bedside. Once they were in the corridor the guard swung the door shut. Bishop heard it latch.

They walked down the hall quickly. Mott keeping his hand near his automatic, looking around, as if he were about to draw and shoot anybody who bore the least resemblance to Phate.

Bishop too felt unnerved, recalling that the killer was a chameleon and, with his disguises, could be walking past them right now and they might never know it.

They were at the elevator when something occurred to Bishop. Alarmed, he looked back towards the closed door of Jennie's room. He said to Allen, 'I didn't pay much attention to that guard in my wife's room. He's about the perp's age and build. You're sure he works for your department?'

'Who? Dick Hellman back there?' Allen answered, nodding slowly. 'Well, what I can tell you for sure is that he's my daughter's husband and I've known him for eight years. As far as the "work" part of your question goes—if putting in a four-hour day during an eight-hour shift is work then I guess the answer's yes.'

WHO DO YOU WANT TO BE?

Phate walked slowly down the main corridor of the state police's Computer Crimes Unit offices. He was wearing a worn, stained Pacific Gas and Electric uniform and a hard hat. Hidden just inside the coveralls was his KA-BAR knife and a large automatic pistol—a Glock—with three clips of ammunition. He carried another weapon as well but it was one that might not be recognised as such, not in the hands of a repairman: a large monkey wrench.

Who do you want to be?

Someone the cops here would trust, someone they wouldn't think twice about seeing in their midst. *That's* who.

Phate looked around, surprised that the CCU was empty. He'd expected at least three or four people here—hence the large pistol and the extra ammunition—but everyone was apparently at the hospital, where Mrs Frank Bishop was probably suffering quite a bit of trauma as a result of the nutrient-rich vitamin B shot he'd ordered for her that morning.

Phate had considered actually killing the woman—he could've done so easily by ordering a large dose of insulin, say—but that wouldn't've been the best tactic for this segment of the game. If she died the police might've concluded that she was his intended target and returned here to headquarters immediately. Now they were scurrying through the hospital trying to find the real victim.

In fact, this victim was right here, at CCU.

And his name was Wyatt Gillette.

Who was now only twenty feet away.

Phate listened to the astonishing staccato of Valleyman's fast and powerful keyboarding coming from a dingy cubicle in front of him.

There had been a chance, of course, that Gillette would go with the police to the hospital, so he'd sent the message that appeared to come from Triple-X, to make sure he'd remain here and try to decrypt it.

This was, he decided, a perfect round. Not only would it be a real challenge for Phate to get into CCU—worth a solid twenty-five points in the Access game—but, if he was successful, it would finally give him the chance to destroy the man he'd been after for years.

He looked around again, listened. Not a soul in the huge room other than Judas Valleyman, a man whose painful death Phate had idled away so very many hours imagining.

But, unlike the traditional game of Access, where you pierce the beating heart of your victim, Phate had something else in mind for Gillette.

He'd taken the idea from the young hacker at St Francis Academy, Jamie Turner. As the young man had once written in an email to his brother:

JamieTT: Man, can you think of anything scarier than going blind if you're a hacker?

No, Jamie, I sure can't, Phate now answered him silently. He crouched, listening to the steady clatter of the keys.

DRAWING BACK THE WRENCH for good leverage, Phate stepped into the centre of an empty cubicle.

'No!' he whispered.

The sounds of keyboarding were coming from a speaker connected to the work station's computer.

As Phate dropped the wrench, Gillette stepped out from the cubicle next to this one and pulled the killer's pistol from his hand.

'Don't move, Jon,' Gillette told him and pressed the gun into Phate's neck.

Gillette went through the killer's pockets. He lifted out a portable CD player and a set of car keys. Then he found the knife. He placed everything on the desk.

'That was good,' Phate said, nodding at the computer. 'You recorded yourself so I'd think you were in here.'

'That's right.'

Gillette stepped back and the wizards surveyed each other. This was their first face-to-face meeting. They'd shared hundreds of secrets and plans—and millions of words—but those communications had never been in person.

'Nice tailor,' Gillette said, nodding at the Pacific Gas and Electric uniform.

Phate smiled bitterly. He asked, 'How'd you know I was coming?'

'I figured you really *were* going to kill somebody at the hospital— but then you'd start to worry that I might've seen some of your notes when I got inside your machine, so you'd change your plans. You'd come after me.'

'That's pretty much it.'

'You made sure I'd stay here by sending us that encrypted email— supposedly from Triple-X. That's what tipped me off that you were coming. He wouldn't've sent an email. He would've called.'

'He's dead, you know. Triple-X.'

'*What?*'

'His name's Peter Grodsky. Lived alone in Sunnyvale. Worked as a code cruncher for a credit bureau during the day, hacked at night. He died next to his machine.'

'You son of a bitch.' Gillette thrust the gun forward and waited for Phate to cringe. He didn't. He simply looked back, unsmiling, into Gillette's eyes and continued, 'Triple-X *had* to die. He was the betraying character.'

'The what?'

'Triple-X was the turncoat. They all *have* to die. But you knew that.' Phate gave a bitter laugh. 'You were the quiet one in Knights of Access, the poet. But, damn, you played a good game.'

He stared at Gillette for a long moment. Then: 'Let me ask you a question—why'd you go over to the other side?'

'I'm working for them because I *am* a hacker,' Gillette snapped. 'You're not. You're just a goddamn loser who happens to use machines to kill people. That's not what hacking's about.'

'*Access* is what hacking's about. Getting as deep as you can into someone's system.'

'But you don't stop with somebody's C: drive, Jon. You're *killing* people. They're human beings, not bytes.'

'I don't see any difference between software code and a human being. They're both created, serve a purpose, then people die and code's replaced by a later version. Cells or electrons, there's no difference.'

'There's a difference, Jon.'

'Is there?' he asked, apparently perplexed by Gillette's comment. 'Think about it. How did life start? Lightning striking the primordial soup of carbon, hydrogen, nitrogen, oxygen, phosphate and sulphate. Every living creature is made up of those elements. Well, every one of those elements, you'll find in a machine. Which functions because of electrical impulses.'

'Save the bogus philosophy for the kids in the chat rooms, Jon. Machines're not alive. They don't reason.'

Phate laughed. 'Half the people on earth can't reason any better than trained dogs.'

'For Christ's sake, what happened to you? Did you get so lost in the Machine World that you can't tell the difference?'

Phate's eyes grew wide with anger. 'Lost in the Machine World? I don't *have* any other world! Jon Patrick Holloway, he had a life in the Real World. He lived in Cambridge, he worked at Harvard, he had friends, he was going to meet somebody, he was going to have a family!' The killer's voice broke. 'But what happened? *You* turned him in and destroyed him. And the only place left for him to go was the Machine World.'

Gillette said evenly. 'Jon Holloway's life was totally fake.'

'It was the closest I ever came to having a life!'

They fell silent for a moment. Finally Phate said, 'Oh, man, you were better than me . . . you just got derailed. You married that Greek girl. What was her name? Ellie Papandolos, right? You had no business being with a woman. When machines're your life you don't need a lover.'

Gillette countered, 'What about Shawn?'

A darkness crossed Phate's face. 'Shawn's none of your business.' Then a moment later he smiled. 'Come on, Wyatt, let's work together. Wouldn't you give *anything* to know how Trapdoor works?'

'I *do* know how it works. You use a packet-sniffer to divert messages. You embed a demon in the packet and it self-activates as soon as it's inside the target machine. It hides in the Solitaire program and self-destructs when somebody comes looking for it.'

Phate laughed. 'But don't you wonder what the source code looks like? Wouldn't you *love* to see that code? It'd be like getting a look at God, Wyatt. You know you want to.'

Gillette felt the terrible lust of curiosity consuming him. Oh, yes, he *did* want to see the source code. So very badly.

But he said, 'No.'

Phate glanced at the clock on the wall. 'Remember what I used to say about revenge when we were hacking?'

'"Hacker's revenge is patient revenge." What about it?'

'I just want to leave you with that thought.'

A second later the clock hit exactly twelve thirty and the virus Phate must have loaded in the electric company's computer shut off the power to the CCU office.

The room was plunged into blackness.

Phate's powerful fist slammed into Gillette's neck and the gun fell from his hand.

He heard a jangling as Phate grabbed his keys. Gillette reached for the desk, but all he could save was the CD player. He felt another stunning pain as the monkey wrench slammed into his shin and, as he went down onto the floor, a foot smashed into his jaw.

0000101 / FIVE: THE EXPERT LEVEL

'Are you all right?' Patricia Nolan asked, looking at the blood on Gillette's face, neck and trousers.

'I'm fine,' he said.

But she didn't believe him and played nurse anyway, disappearing into the kitchenette for damp paper towels. She bathed his cheek where he'd been cut in the fight with Phate. He smelt fresh nail conditioner on her fingers and wondered when she'd found time for cosmetics.

The team had returned to CCU from the medical centre and Gillette briefed them about Phate's attack on CCU.

'All I ended up with was that.' He nodded at the CD player. Then the hacker delivered the news that Triple-X was dead. He walked to the evidence board and wrote the name 'Peter Grodsky' next to Andy Anderson, Lara Gibson and Willem Boethe. 'That's his real name,' he said. 'He was a programmer who lived in Sunnyvale.'

Feeling heartsick at the death of a civilian who'd taken a risk to help them, Bishop called headquarters. He told them to find Grodsky's address and check the crime scene.

Gillette noticed a pink phone message slip. He said to Bishop, 'I took a message for you just before you got back from the hospital. Your wife called.' He read the note. 'Something about the test results coming back and it's good news. Uhm, I'm not sure I got this right— I thought she said she's got a serious infection. I'm not sure why that's *good* news.'

The look of immense joy in Bishop's face—a rare, beaming smile—told him that, yes, the message was right.

He was happy for the detective but felt his own disappointment that Elana hadn't called him yet. Probably she never would.

Bishop took a phone call. He glanced at Shelton. 'It's getting hot and heavy with the Marinkill case. The perps were spotted in our back yard. Santa Clara, just off the 101.'

Bob Shelton gave an uncharacteristic laugh. 'Doesn't matter whether you wanted a piece of that case or not, Frank. Looks like it's dogging you.'

Bishop shook his head. 'Maybe, but I sure don't want it around here, not for the time being. It's going to pull off resources and we need all the help we can get.' He looked at Patricia Nolan. 'What'd you find at the hospital?'

She explained how she and Miller had looked through the medical centre's network, but couldn't find any indication of where Phate had been hacking in from. Bishop looked around the dinosaur pen and frowned. 'Say, where's Miller?'

Nolan said, 'He left the hospital before us. He said he was coming straight back here.'

'He might've gone over to the computer centre at Stanford,' Mott said. 'He books supercomputer time there a lot. Maybe he was going to check out a lead.'

'What do we do now, Bishop?' Shelton asked.

Bishop smiled and said, 'Some old-fashioned police work.' He picked up Phate's CD player. The detective opened it up. Inside was a recording of *Othello*. He turned the machine over and jotted down the serial number. 'Maybe Phate bought this in the area. I'll call the company and see where this unit was shipped to.'

Bishop started making phone calls to the Akisha Electronic Products Company's various distribution centres. He was put on hold for an interminable period of time, then transferred. As he argued with someone on the other end of the line Wyatt Gillette spun round in a swivel chair to a nearby computer terminal and began keyboarding. A moment later he stood and pulled a piece of paper from the printer.

As Bishop's irritated voice was saying into the phone, 'We *can't* wait two days for that information,' Gillette handed the sheet to the detective:

Akisha Electronic Products Shipped—First Quarter
Model: HB Heavy Bass Portable Compact Disc Player

Unit Serial Shipping Numbers	Date	Recipient
HB40032 HB40068	1/12	Mountain View Music & Electronics 9456 Rio Verde, #4 Mountain View, CA

The phone sagged in the detective's hand and he said into the receiver, 'Never mind,' and hung up.

'How'd you get this?' Bishop asked Gillette. Then held up a hand. 'On second thoughts, I'd rather not know.' He chuckled. 'Old-fashioned police work, like I said.'

Bishop called headquarters again and told them to get over to Mountain View Music with a picture of Phate.

A trooper from the state police headquarters in San Jose dropped off an envelope for Bishop.

He opened it and summarised for the team, 'FBI report on the details from the computer-enhanced picture of Lara Gibson that Phate posted. They said it's a Tru-Heat gas furnace, model GST3000. The model's popular in new developments. The techs also found a manufacturing date on the Sheetrock: January of last year.'

'New house in a recently developed tract,' Mott said, and wrote these details on the evidence board.

Shelton called the planning and zoning commission. He asked about permits for tract developments built after January of last year around Mountain View. The list was discouragingly long.

He hung up and muttered, 'There's over forty of 'em,' he said. 'They can't build 'em fast enough to supply the demand. Dot-com, you know.'

Bishop took the list of developments and walked to the map of Silicon Valley. He circled the locations Shelton had written down, as well as the location of the music store. He tapped this, then the circle around Ollie's Theatrical Supply on El Camino Real, where Phate had bought the theatrical glue. The locations suggested that Phate was in the central or western part of Silicon Valley; still there were twenty-two new housing developments. 'Way too big for a door-to-door search.'

They stared at the map and the evidence board for ten minutes or so, offering largely useless suggestions about narrowing down the search. Officers called from the apartment of Peter Grodsky in Sunnyvale. The young man had died from a stab wound to the heart—like the other victims in this real-life game of Access. The cops were checking the scene but had not found any helpful leads.

'Hell,' said Bob Shelton, as he kicked a chair aside, expressing the frustration they all felt.

There was silence for a long moment as the team stared at the map—silence that was interrupted unexpectedly by a timid voice behind them. 'Excuse me.'

A chubby teenage boy, wearing thick glasses, stood in the doorway. It was Jamie Turner, Gillette recalled, the student from St Francis Academy.

'Hello, young man,' Frank Bishop said, smiling at the boy. 'How you doing?'

'OK, I guess,' he said, swallowing uneasily. 'I found something that might help you catch him—the man who killed Mr Boethe, I mean.'

'I KEEP THIS NOTEBOOK when I'm online,' Jamie Turner told Wyatt Gillette.

Everyone on the CCU team was feeling relentless desperation—that Phate might be making his move against his next victim at any moment. Still, Gillette let the boy talk at his own pace.

Jamie continued, 'I was looking through what I'd written before Mr Boethe . . . before what happened to him, you know.'

'Go on.' Gillette encouraged.

'OK, see, the machine I was using at school was fine until about two or three weeks ago. And then something *really* weird started happening. I'd get these fatal conflict errors. And my machine'd, like, freeze.'

'Fatal errors?' asked Bishop.

Nolan explained, 'Usually you get errors like that when your machine tries to do a couple of different tasks at once and can't handle it. The new operating systems let you run multiple programs, so you hardly ever see fatal error crashes any more.'

'That's why I thought it was so weird,' the boy said. 'And then I couldn't, you know, duplicate the errors on a different machine.'

Tony Mott said, 'Well, well . . . Trapdoor has a bug.'

Gillette nodded at the boy. 'Jamie, I think this is the break we've been looking for.'

'Why?' Bishop asked. 'I don't get it.'

'We needed the serial and phone numbers of Phate's Mobile America phone—in order to trace him.'

'I remember.'

'If we're lucky this is how we're going to get them.' Gillette said to the boy, 'You know the times and dates when some of the conflicts shut you down?'

The boy showed his notebook to Gillette. The crashes were carefully noted. 'Good.' Gillette nodded and said to Tony Mott, 'Get Garvy Hobbes on the speakerphone.'

Mott did this and a moment later the security chief from Mobile America was connected.

'Howdy,' Garvy Hobbes said. 'You got a lead to our bad boy?'

Gillette looked at Bishop, who waved his hand and said, 'This is *new*-fashioned police work. It's all yours.'

'Try this on, Garvy. If I give you four specific times and dates that one of your cellphones went down for about sixty seconds then went back on, calling the same number, could you identify that phone?'

'Hm. That's a new one but I'll give it a shot. Gimme the times and dates.'

Gillette did and Hobbes said, 'Stay on the line. I'll be back.'

The hacker explained to the team what he was doing: when Jamie's computer froze, it meant that Phate's cell phone call was interrupted for the same period of time while the killer also restarted his machine and reconnected. By cross-checking the exact times Jamie's computer froze and then went back online against the times a particular Mobile America cell phone disconnected and reconnected they'd know that cell phone was Phate's.

Five minutes later the security specialist came back on the line. 'This is fun,' Hobbes said cheerfully. 'I got it.' Then he added with some troubled reverence in his voice, 'But what's weird is the numbers of his phone are unassigned. The phone hasn't been used since yesterday.'

Gillette explained, 'Phate stole the numbers, and now he's changed them. No serious phreak uses stolen numbers for more than eight hours. But we can still narrow down where he was calling from in the past couple of weeks. Right, Garvy?'

'You betcha. Down to about one square kilometre.'

He laughed and asked warily, 'Mr Gillette, how is it you know as much about our system as we do?'

'I read a lot,' Gillette said wryly. Then he asked, 'Give me the co-ordinates of the location, can you?'

'Sure thing.' Hobbes rattled off four intersections and Gillette connected the dots on the map. Within the perimeter were six new housing developments.

'Six?' asked a dismayed Linda Sanchez. 'Must be three thousand people living there. Can we narrow it down any more?'

'We can try,' Bishop said. 'Because we know where he shops.' On the map Bishop tapped the development that fell halfway between Ollie's Theatrical Supply and Mountain View Music and Electronics. Its name was Stonecrest.

THE PARKING LOT of the First Baptist Church of Los Altos was hidden from the development by a high stockade fence. This was why Bishop had chosen it as a staging area. Sixteen police cars and two California State Tactical Services vans waited.

Wyatt Gillette was in the passenger seat of the police car, beside Bishop. Shelton sat silently in the back, staring at a palm tree waving in the wet breeze. In the car beside theirs were Linda Sanchez and Tony Mott. Now, Mott hurried from the car to join a cluster of tactical and uniformed police who were suiting up in body armour. Captain Alonso Johnson stood by himself, head down, nodding as he listened to his radio.

Nearby, Stonecrest was being scoured by a number of troopers.

They were disguised as fundraisers soliciting money for some children's cause, and were brandishing yellow buckets and flashing pictures of Jon Holloway.

The moments passed, however, and no one reported any success. Maybe Phate was in a different development. Maybe Mobile America's analysis of the phone numbers was wrong.

Then Bishop's cellphone buzzed and he answered. He nodded and smiled. 'Positive ID. A neighbour recognised him. He's at 34004 Alta Vista Drive.'

'Yes!' Shelton said, making a joyous fist with his hand. He climbed out of the car. 'I'll tell Alonso.'

Bishop called Garvy Hobbes and gave him the address. A moment later Hobbes called Bishop back and reported, 'He's inside on a cellphone. It's a data transmission, not voice.'

'He's online,' Gillette said.

Bishop, Gillette and Sanchez climbed out of the cars, found Shelton and Alonso Johnson and gave them this news.

Johnson sent a surveillance van to the street in front of Phate's house. The officer reported that the blinds were down and there were no interior lights visible.

Johnson opened a detailed map of the streets in Stonecrest. He circled Phate's house with a wax pencil and then examined a catalogue of model homes in the development. 'Team Alpha goes through the front, Bravo in the back, Charlie through the garage.' He looked up. 'All right. Let's go.'

Gillette, Shelton, Bishop and Sanchez jogged back to one of the police cars and drove into the development itself, parking just out of sight of Phate's house, next to the tactical vans.

Bishop turned to Gillette and surprised the hacker by reaching forwards formally and shaking his hand. 'Whatever happens, Wyatt, we couldn't've gotten this far without you. Not many people would've taken the risks you have and worked as hard as this.'

'Yeah,' Linda Sanchez said. 'Hey, you want a job when you get out maybe you oughta apply to CCU.'

Gillette was unable to think of anything to say by way of acknowledging this. He nodded in embarrassment.

Officers turned back several cars driving along Alta Vista. They flagged down one of Phate's neighbours, a white-haired woman pulling out of her garage, and directed her Ford Explorer down the street, away from the killer's house. Three young boys were ignoring the rain and happily doing acrobatics on noisy skateboards. Two troopers disguised in shorts and casual shirts walked up to them nonchalantly and ushered them out of sight.

The pleasant suburban street was clear.

'Looks good,' Johnson said, then ran in a crouch towards the house.

Bob Shelton returned and dropped heavily into the seat of the police car.

Gillette didn't hear any commands given but all at once the SWAT troopers emerged from hiding and raced towards the house.

Suddenly there were three loud bangs. Gillette jumped.

Bishop explained, 'They're shooting the locks out of the doors.'

Gillette, his palms sweating, found himself holding his breath, waiting for gunshots, explosions, screaming, sirens . . .

'Come on, come on,' Linda Sanchez muttered. 'What's happening?'

Long, long moments of silence.

When the car's radio crackled to life the sound was so abrupt that everyone jumped.

'Alpha team leader to Bishop. You there?'

Bishop grabbed the microphone. 'Go ahead, Alonso.'

'Frank,' the voice reported. 'He's not here.'

'What?'

'There's a can of Mountain Dew that's still cold. And the body-heat detector shows he was in the chair in front of the computer five minutes ago.'

In a desperate voice Bishop said, 'Al, he's *got* to be. Check in the *closets*. Check under the *bed*.'

'Frank, the infrareds aren't picking up anything.'

Despair eased into Bishop's hawklike face.

INSIDE, THE HOUSE was immaculate.

Completely different from what Gillette had expected. Most hacker lairs were filthy, impacted with computer parts, wires, books, tech manuals, tools, floppy disks, encrusted food containers, dirty glasses, books and just plain junk.

They walked into the dining room, where Phate's laptop was set up. Gillette glanced at the screen, shook his head in disgust. 'Look.'

Bishop and Shelton read the words:

INSTANT MESSAGE FROM: SHAWN CODE 10-87 ISSUED
FOR 34004 ALTA VISTA DRIVE

'That's the tactical assault code—a ten eighty-seven. If he hadn't gotten that message we would've collared him,' Bishop said. 'We were *that* close.'

'Shawn,' Shelton snapped.

A trooper called from the basement, 'I've got the escape route. It's down here.'

Gillette went downstairs with the others. But on the last step he paused, recognising the scene from the picture of Lara Gibson. The clumsy tiling job, the unpainted Sheetrock. The sight was wrenching.

He joined Alonso Johnson, Frank Bishop and the other troopers who were examining a small door in the side wall. It opened into a three-foot-wide pipe, like a large storm drain. One of the troopers shone his flashlight into the pipe. 'It leads to the house next door.'

Gillette and Bishop stared at each other. The detective said, 'No! The woman in the Ford Explorer! The one who pulled out of the garage. It was him.'

Johnson grabbed his radio and ordered troopers into the house.

It was completely empty. No furniture. Nothing. Holloway had owned both houses.

BACK AT CCU headquarters, Gillette broke the news to Patricia Nolan.

'Shawn tipped him off again?' she asked angrily.

Sanchez had removed Phate's laptop from the house in Stonecrest. She handed it to Gillette and Nolan and then took a phone call.

'How did he know we were assaulting the house?' Tony Mott asked. 'I don't get it.'

'I only want to know one thing,' Shelton said. 'Who the hell *is* Shawn?' Though he undoubtedly didn't expect an answer just then, one was forthcoming.

'I know who,' Linda Sanchez said in a horrified, choked voice. She stared at the team then hung up the receiver dangling in her hand. 'That was sysadmin in San Jose. Ten minutes ago he found someone cracking into ISLEnet and using it to get into the State Department database. He was instructing the State Department to issue two predated passports in fake names. The sysadmin recognised the pictures. One was Holloway's'—she took a deep breath—'the other was Stephen's.'

'Stephen who?' Tony Mott asked, not understanding.

'Stephen Miller,' Sanchez said. '*That's* who Shawn is.'

PATRICIA NOLAN SAID, 'But Shawn's brilliant—Stephen was an amateur next to him.'

'Social engineering,' Bishop said.

Gillette agreed. 'He had to look stupid so we wouldn't suspect him. Meanwhile, he was feeding information to Phate.'

Mott snapped, 'He's why Andy Anderson's dead. He set him up.'

Shelton muttered, 'Every single time we got close to Phate, Miller'd warn him.'

'Get Miller's picture out on the wire,' Bishop said.

Gillette sat down in front of Phate's laptop.

Scrolling over the monitor was the motto of the Knights of Access:

Access is God . . .

However, this machine contained only the operating system, Trapdoor and some files of downloaded newspaper clippings Shawn had sent to Phate. Most of them were about Seattle, which would have been the location of Phate's next game. But now that he knew they had this machine, of course, he'd go elsewhere.

Bishop dropped into one of the armchairs and, hands together, stared at the floor, discouraged. 'Not a thing.'

Nolan sat down next to Gillette then scrolled through the directory. 'He might've erased some files. Did you try to recover anything?'

'No, I didn't,' Gillette said. 'I figured he'd shred everything.'

She ran a recovery program and, in a moment, data that Phate had erased over the past few weeks appeared on the screen. She read through it. 'Nothing about any attacks. All I can find are bits of receipts for some of the computer parts he sold. Most of the data're corrupted. But here's one you can kind of make out.'

```
Ma%%%ch 27***200!!!++
55eerrx3^^shipped to:
San Jose Com434312 Produuu234aawe%%
2335 Winch4ster 00u46lke^
San Jo^^44^^^^9^^^$$###
Attn: 97J**seph McGona%%gle
```

Bishop and Gillette read the screen.

The hacker said, 'But that doesn't do us any good. That's a company that *bought* some of his parts. We need Phate's address, where they were shipped *from.*'

Bishop shook his head. 'Wait a minute.' He tapped the screen. 'This company—San Jose Computer Products—they'd have to have some record of where the parts were shipped from. Let's go over there and have a talk with this McGonagle.'

Gillette joined the detective. Nolan, though, said, 'You go on. I'll keep looking through his machine for any other leads.'

Pausing at the door, Wyatt Gillette glanced back and saw her sit down at the keyboard. She gave him a slightly wistful smile, perhaps the inevitable recognition that there was little hope of a relationship blossoming between them.

But then her smile vanished and Nolan turned back to the monitor, began to key furiously and slipped out of the Real World and into the Blue Nowhere.

THE GAME WAS NO longer fun.

This was a particularly painful admission because he considered this week—Univac Week—a very special version of his game. Silicon Valley was the new holy land and Phate had wanted to win big on every level.

But the police—and Valleyman—had proved to be a lot better than he'd expected.

So: no options. He now had yet another identity and would leave, taking Shawn with him to a new city.

There was, however, one more thing to do. He was so angry and agitated that he wanted to grab a machine gun and murder a dozen people to keep the police occupied. But that wasn't the weapon closest to his soul and so he now simply sat forward at his computer terminal and began placidly keyboarding a familiar incantation.

THE MAROON VOLVO went through an intersection on Stevens Creek Boulevard and began a howling skid straight towards Bishop's police car.

'Oh, man, look out!' Gillette cried, throwing up his arm instinctively for protection.

Maybe it was instinct or maybe it was his police tactical driving instruction but the detective chose not to brake. He jammed the accelerator to the floor and skidded the Crown Victoria *towards* the oncoming car. The manoeuvre worked. The vehicles missed by inches and the Volvo slammed into the Porsche behind the police car with a huge bang. Bishop controlled his skid and braked to a stop.

'Idiot ran the light,' Bishop muttered, pulling his radio off the dash to report the accident.

'No, he didn't,' Gillette said, looking back. 'Look, both lights're green.'

A block ahead, two more cars sat in the middle of the intersection, sideways, smoke pouring from their hoods.

The radio crackled, jammed with reports of accidents and traffic-light malfunctions. They listened for a moment.

'The lights're *all* green,' the detective said. 'All over the county. It's Phate, right?'

Gillette gave a sour laugh. 'He cracked public works. It's a smoke-screen so he and Miller can get away.'

Bishop started forward again but a quarter-mile from their destination traffic was at a complete standstill. They leapt out of the vehicle and began jogging, prodded forward by a sense of desperate urgency. Phate wouldn't have created the traffic jam until just before he was ready for his next kill.

They came to the building that housed the company and paused, leaning against a chain-link fence, gasping for breath.

The air was filled with a cacophony of horns and the whump, whump, whump of a helicopter that hovered nearby, a local news station recording the evidence of Phate's prowess—and Santa Clara County's vulnerability—for the rest of the country to witness.

The men hurried towards an open doorway next to the company's loading dock. A chubby, grey-haired worker stacking cartons glanced up.

'Excuse me, sir. Police,' Bishop said, and showed his badge. 'We're looking for Joe McGonagle.'

'That's me,' he said. 'Is this about an accident or something? What's with all the horns?'

'Traffic lights're out.'

'That's a mess. Near rush hour too.'

Bishop said, 'We have reason to believe that somebody may've sold you some stolen parts.'

'Stolen?'

'You're not under investigation, but it's important that we find the man who sold them to you. We need the address of the company the parts were shipped from.'

'All the shipping files're in here.' McGonagle started down the hall-way. 'What's his name?' he asked.

'We don't know. He has a lot of aliases.'

McGonagle stepped into a small office and walked to a filing cabinet, pulled it open. 'You know the date this shipment came in?'

Bishop consulted his notebook. 'We think it was March 27th.'

Wyatt Gillette couldn't help but smile to himself. It was pretty ironic that a computer supply company kept records in filing cabinets. Dead tree stuff. Then he happened to glance at McGonagle's left hand, which rested on the handle of the filing-cabinet drawer.

The fingertips, very muscular, were blunt and tipped with thick yellow calluses.

A hacker's manicure . . .

Gillette's smile vanished and he stiffened. Bishop noticed and he pointed at his own fingers and looked again at McGonagle's hand. Bishop, too, saw.

McGonagle looked up, into Bishop's revealing eyes.

Only his name wasn't McGonagle, of course. Beneath dyed grey hair, fake wrinkles, glasses, and body padding, was Jon Patrick Holloway. Joe McGonagle was just another of his identities. This company was one of his fronts. The receipt they'd found was for a computer part Phate had *bought,* not sold.

None of them moved.

Then, Phate pulled a gun from the filing-cabinet drawer. Bishop had no time to draw his own gun; he simply leapt forwards and slammed into the killer, who dropped his weapon. Bishop kicked it aside as Phate grabbed the cop's shooting arm and seized a hammer, which rested on top of a wooden crate. He swung the tool hard into Bishop's head. It connected with a sickening thud.

The detective gasped and collapsed. Phate hit him again, in the back of the head, then dropped the hammer and made a grab for his pistol on the floor.

Gillette charged forwards, seizing Phate by the collar and arm before the man could grab the pistol.

Together they tumbled through a door, out of the office and into an open area—another dinosaur pen, just like CCU headquarters.

Like grappling wrestlers they stumbled over the raised floor. Gillette glanced around him, looking for a weapon. He was astonished at the collection of old computers and parts here. The entire history of computing was represented.

For five minutes the hackers traded blows. Then Phate broke free. He managed to get to a crowbar and snatched it up. He started towards Gillette, who looked desperately for a weapon. He ripped off the lid of an old wooden box and pulled out the contents.

Phate froze.

Gillette held what looked like an antique glass lightbulb in his hand—it was an original audion tube, the precursor to the vacuum tube and, ultimately, the silicon chip itself.

'No!' Phate cried, holding up his hand. 'Be careful with it. Please!' He came forward slowly, the crowbar held like a baseball bat.

To him, the machines themselves're more important than people.

'Drop it!' Gillette snapped, gesturing at the crowbar.

The killer started to swing but at the last minute the thought of hurting the fragile glass bulb stopped him. Gillette paused, then tossed the audion tube at Phate, who cried out in horror and tried to catch the antique. But the tube hit the floor and shattered.

With a hollow cry, Phate dropped to his knees.

Gillette stepped into the office where Frank Bishop lay—breathing shallowly and very bloody—and grabbed his pistol. He pointed it at Phate, who was looking over the remains of the tube the way a father would stare at the grave of a child.

Phate picked up the crowbar and started forward, howling madly.

Gillette cringed, lifted the gun and started to pull the trigger.

'No!' a woman's voice cried.

Startled, Gillette jumped at the sound. He looked behind him to see Patricia Nolan hurrying into the dinosaur pen, her laptop case over her shoulder and what looked like a black flashlight in her right hand. Phate too paused at her commanding entrance.

Gillette started to ask how she'd got here, when she touched his tattooed arm with the dark cylinder she held. The rod, it turned out, wasn't a flashlight. Gillette heard a crackle of electricity, saw a flash of yellow-grey light as astonishing pain swept from his jaw to his chest. Gasping, he dropped to his knees and the pistol fell to the floor.

Thinking: Shit, wrong again! Stephen Miller wasn't Shawn at all.

He groped for the pistol but Nolan touched the wand to his neck and pushed the trigger once more.

UNABLE TO MOVE more than his head and fingers, Gillette returned to painful consciousness. He had no idea how long he'd been out.

He could see Bishop, still in the office, his breathing very laboured. Phate and Shawn would be gone by now, of course, and probably killing the final victim in this level of the game. But why was *he* still alive? They—

The man's scream came from behind him, very close. Gillette gasped in shock at the sound and managed to turn his head.

Patricia Nolan was crouching over Phate, who was cringing in agony as he sat against a metal column that rose to the murky ceiling. Gillette supposed she'd zapped him too with the stun wand, but in fact she'd exchanged the high-tech weaponry for the hammer Phate had struck Bishop with.

So, she *wasn't* Shawn. Then who was she?

'You understand I'm serious now,' she said to the killer, levelling the hammer at him like a professor holding a pointer. 'I have no problem hurting you.'

Phate nodded. Sweat poured down his face.

'I want the source code to Trapdoor. Where is it?'

Phate nodded towards a laptop computer on the table behind her.

'You wouldn't carry around the source code on a laptop, Jon.' She leaned closer to him. Calmly, she gripped his wrist and slowly pulled his arm outwards, resting his hand on the concrete.

'I want the source code. I know you don't have it here. You've uploaded it into a passcode-protected hiding place. Right?'

Phate hesitated.

Nolan said soothingly, 'Look at these fingers . . .' She caressed the blunt digits. After a moment she whispered, 'Where is the code?'

He shook his head.

The hammer flashed downwards towards Phate's little finger. Gillette didn't even hear it strike. He heard only Phate's ragged scream.

'I can do this all day,' she said evenly.

She lifted the hammer again.

'No, no!' Phate cried. He took a deep breath. 'All right . . .' He gave her the numbers of an Internet address, the username and the passcode.

Nolan pulled out a cellphone and hit one button. It seemed that the call connected immediately. She gave the details on Phate's site to the person on the other end of the phone then said, 'I'll hold on. Check it out.'

Phate's chest rose and fell. He squinted the tears of pain from his eyes. Then he looked towards Gillette. 'Here we are, Valleyman, act three of our play.' He sat up slightly and his bloody hand moved an inch or two. He winced. 'Didn't quite work out the way I thought. Looks like we've got ourselves a surprise ending.'

'Quiet,' Nolan muttered.

But Phate ignored her and continued, speaking to Gillette in a gasping voice, 'I've got something I want to tell you. Are you listening? "To thine own self be true, and it must follow, as the night the day, thou canst not then be false to any man."' He coughed for a moment. Then: 'I love plays. That's from *Hamlet,* one of my favourites. Remember that line, Valleyman. That's advice from a wizard. "To thine own self be true."'

Nolan's face curled into a frown as she listened to her phone. Her shoulders sagged and she said into the mouthpiece, 'Stand by.' She set the phone aside and gripped the hammer again, glaring at Phate, who—though consumed by the pain—was laughing faintly.

'They checked out the site you gave me,' she said, 'and it turned out to be an email account. When they opened the files the communications program sent something to a university in Asia. Was it Trapdoor?'

'I don't know what it was,' he whispered, staring at his bloody, shattered hand. A brief frown on his face gave way to a cold smile. 'Maybe I gave you the wrong address.'

'Well, give me the right one.'

'What's the hurry?' he asked cruelly. 'Got an important date with your cat at home? A TV show? A bottle of wine you'll share with . . . yourself?'

Again her anger broke through momentarily and she slammed the hammer down on his hand.

Phate screamed again.

Tell her, Gillette thought. For God's sake, tell her!

But he kept silent for an interminable five minutes of this torture, the hammer rising and falling, the fingers snapping under the impact. Finally Phate could stand it no more. 'All right, all right.' He gave her another address, name and passcode.

Nolan picked up the phone and relayed this information to her colleague on the other end. Waited a few minutes, said, 'Go through it line by line, make sure it's real.'

Who was she speaking to? Gillette wondered.

Five minutes later she nodded. 'OK. Burn the site and everything it's connected to. Use Infekt IV . . . No, I mean the whole network. I don't care if it's linked to Norad and air traffic control. Burn it.'

The Infekt IV virus was like an uncontrollable brushfire. It would methodically destroy the contents of every file in the site where Phate had stored the source code. It would turn the data on thousands of machines into unrecognisable chains of random symbols so that it would be impossible to find even the slightest reference to Trapdoor, let alone the working source code.

Phate closed his eyes and leaned his head back against the column.

Nolan stood and, still holding the hammer, walked towards Gillette. He tried to crawl away, but his body still wouldn't work after the electric jolts. Patricia leaned close. Looking beneath her blotchy make-up, he could see lean features. She was wearing body padding to add thirty pounds to what was undoubtedly a muscular body.

Then he noticed her hands.

Her fingers . . . the pads glistened slightly and seemed opaque. And he understood: all that time she'd been putting on fingernail conditioner she was adding it to the pads as well to obscure her fingerprints. *She's social engineered us too.*

Gillette whispered, 'You've been after him for a while, haven't you?'

Nolan nodded. 'A year. Ever since we heard about Trapdoor.'

'Who's "we"?'

She didn't answer but she didn't need to. Gillette supposed that she'd been hired not by Horizon Online—or by Horizon alone—but by a consortium of Internet service providers to find the source code for Trapdoor. Nolan's bosses wouldn't *use* Trapdoor. They would destroy the program, which was a huge threat to the trillion-dollar online industry, because subscribers would cancel if hackers could roam freely through their computers and learn every detail about their lives.

And she'd used Andy Anderson, Bishop and the rest of the CCU. Just as she'd used Gillette himself.

Suddenly he understood clearly what she had to do next.

He pleaded urgently, 'Don't.'

'I have to.'

'No, you don't. He'll be in prison for the rest of his life.'

'You think prison would keep him offline? It didn't stop you.'

'You can't do it!'

'Trapdoor's too dangerous,' she explained. 'And he's got the code in his head.'

'No,' Gillette whispered desperately. But his protest was futile.

From her laptop bag she took a small leather case, extracted a hypodermic syringe and filled it from a bottle of clear liquid. Without hesitating, she leaned down and injected it into Phate's neck. He didn't struggle. Gillette had the impression that he was embracing his death. '"To . . ."' His words vanished into a whisper.

He coughed and continued in a feeble voice, '"To thine own self be true . . ."' Then his head dipped forward and his breathing stopped.

Gillette couldn't help but feel a sense of loss. Jon Patrick Holloway deserved his death. He *was* evil, but within the young man was another person: someone who wrote code as *elegant* as a symphony, in whose keystrokes could be seen the brilliance of an unbound mind, which—had it been directed on a slightly different course . . .

Patricia Nolan stood and looked at Gillette.

He thought, I'm dead.

She drew some more liquid into the needle. She crouched beside him, pulled his collar down and massaged his neck to find the artery.

'No,' Gillette whispered. He closed his eyes, his thoughts on Ellie.

Then a man's voice yelled, 'Hey, hold up there!'

Without a second's pause Nolan dropped the hypodermic, pulled a pistol from her laptop case and fired towards Tony Mott, who stood in the doorway.

'Jesus,' the young cop cried, flinching. 'What the hell're you doing?' He dropped to the floor.

Nolan lifted her gun once more but before she could fire, several huge explosions shook the air and she fell backwards. Mott was firing at her with his glitzy silver automatic.

None of the bullets had struck her and Nolan rose fast, again firing her own pistol at Mott.

'Gillette,' he shouted. 'What the hell's going on? What's she doing?'

'She killed Holloway. I was next.'

Nolan fired again then eased towards the front of the warehouse.

Mott grabbed Gillette by his trouser legs and dragged him to cover then emptied the clip of the automatic in the woman's direction. He was a really bad shot. As he reloaded, Nolan disappeared behind some cartons.

'Are you hit?' Mott's hands were shaking and he was breathless.

'No, she got me with a stun gun or something. I can't move. But how'd you get through all the traffic?'

'On my mountain-bike, remember?' Nolan rose and fired six shots in their direction. She fled out of the front door.

Mott reluctantly started after her.

Gillette called, 'Be careful. *She* can't get away through the traffic either. She'll be outside, waiting . . .'

But his voice faded as he heard the distinctive sound of a helicopter, undoubtedly the one disguised as a press chopper that had delivered Patricia Nolan.

In less than thirty seconds the craft had picked her up and was in the air again, speeding away, the chunky sound of its rotors replaced by the curiously harmonic orchestra of car horns filling the late-afternoon sky.

GILLETTE AND BISHOP were back at the Computer Crimes Unit.

The detective was out of Accident and Emergency. A concussion, a fierce headache and eight stitches were the only evidence of his ordeal.

To no one's surprise Horizon Online claimed they'd never heard of a Patricia Nolan. Not a soul at CCU believed their denial, of course.

The whereabouts of Shawn—Stephen Miller—had been discovered. He'd shot himself with his service revolver after he learned that they'd caught on to his identity. His remorseful suicide note had, naturally, been in the form of an email.

At the moment, though, the attention of all the law enforcers had turned from Phate and Stephen Miller to the Marinkill case. Recent bulletins reported that the killers had been spotted again—this time right next door, in San Jose—apparently staking out several banks. Bishop and Shelton were in the task force. They'd spend a few hours with their families for dinner and then report to the bureau's San Jose office later tonight.

Bob Shelton was already at home. Bishop, however, had delayed his own departure home and was sharing a Pop-Tart and coffee with Gillette while they waited for the troopers to arrive to transport him back to San Ho.

The phone rang. Bishop answered, 'Computer Crimes.'

He listened for a moment. 'Hold on.' He looked at Gillette. 'It's for you.'

He took it. 'Hello?'

'Wyatt.'

Elana's voice. He could tell from her greeting that she'd called reluctantly. On the other hand, she *had* called.

'I heard that he's dead. Jon Holloway. I heard it on the news.'

'That's right.'

'Are you all right?'

'Fine.'

A long pause. 'I'm still going to New York.'

'With Ed.'

'That's right.'

He closed his eyes and sighed. 'So why'd you call?'

'I guess just to say that if you wanted to stop by, you could.'

Gillette wondered, Why bother? What was the point?

He said, 'I'll be there in ten minutes.'

They hung up. He turned to find Bishop looking at him cautiously. Gillette said, 'Give me an hour. Please.'

'I can't take you,' the detective said.

'Let me borrow a car.'

The detective considered, then tossed the keys to Gillette, pulled out his phone and called the troopers who'd be transporting Gillette back to San Ho. He gave them Elana's address and said he'd OK'd the prisoner's being there. The prisoner would be returning to CCU in one hour. He hung up.

'I'll come back.'

'I know you will.'

The men faced each other for a moment. They shook hands. Gillette nodded and started for the door.

'Wait.' Frowning, Bishop asked, 'You have a driver's licence?'

Gillette laughed. 'No, I don't have a driver's licence.'

Bishop shrugged and said, 'Well, just don't get stopped.'

The hacker nodded and said gravely, 'Right. They might send me to jail.'

THE HOUSE SMELT of lemons, as it always had.

Irene Papandolos, Ellie's mother, greeted Gillette with a cool, unsmiling nod and gestured him inside.

He sat on a couch. Gillette saw a picture of Elana in her wedding dress. He didn't recognise it and wondered if it had originally shown the two of them and had been cropped to remove him.

Elana entered the room. 'You're here by yourself?' she asked, not smiling. No other greeting.

'How do you mean?'

'No police babysitters?'

'Honour system.'

She sat and picked uneasily at the cuff of the Stanford sweatshirt she wore.

'I'm not going to say goodbye,' he said. She frowned and he continued, 'Because I want to talk you out of leaving. I want to keep seeing you.'

'Seeing me? You're in *prison*, Wyatt.'

'I'll be out in a year.'

She laughed at his effrontery. 'You chose machines over me. You got what you wanted.'

'That's in the past.'

'My life's different now. I'm happy.'

'Because of Ed.'

'He's part of it . . .'

'Come on, Ellie . . . I saw your emails. When you talk about Ed it doesn't exactly sound like he's perfect husband material.'

She stiffened and he saw he'd touched a nerve here. 'Leave Ed out of this.'

He pressed forward. 'Wait a month. Just one month. I get two visits a week.'

Her eyes swept the floor and he sensed that she was debating. She began to say something but her mother stepped into the doorway. Her dark face was even darker than before. 'There's a call for you.'

'Me?' Gillette asked.

'It's somebody named Bishop. He says it's important.'

'FRANK, WHAT'S—'

The detective's voice was raw with urgency. 'Listen to me carefully, Wyatt. We could lose the line any minute. Shawn isn't dead.'

'What? But Miller—'

'No, we were wrong. Stephen Miller isn't Shawn. It's somebody *else*. I'm at CCU. Linda Sanchez found a message for me on the main CCU voicemail. Before he died Miller called and left it. Remember when Phate broke into CCU and went after you?'

'Right.'

'Miller was just coming back from the hospital then. He saw Phate run out of the building and jump in a car. He followed him. He said he'd screwed up so many times that he wanted to prove that he could do something right.'

'Then he didn't kill himself?'

'Nope. Phate must've seen Miller following and then killed him.

Then he pretended to be Miller and intentionally got caught cracking into the State Department.'

'Well, then, who *is* Shawn?'

'I don't have a clue. All I know is we've got a real problem. Tony Mott's here. Shawn hacked the FBI's tactical command computers and he got through to ISLEnet—and he's got root access.' In a low voice Bishop continued. 'Now listen carefully. Shawn's issued arrest warrants and rules of engagement for the suspects in the Marinkill case. We're looking at the screen right now.'

'I don't understand,' Gillette said.

'The warrants say that the suspects are at 3245 Abrego Avenue in Sunnyvale.'

'But that's here! Elana's house.'

'I know. He's ordered the tactical troops to attack the house in twenty-five minutes.'

0000110 / SIX: IT'S ALL IN THE SPELLING

Elana stepped forward, seeing Gillette's alarmed expression. 'What is it? What's going on?'

He ignored her and said to Bishop, 'Call the FBI. Tell them what's happening. Call Washington.'

'We tried,' Bishop responded. 'The agents hung up on us. The rules of engagement that Shawn issued say that the perps will probably try to impersonate state cops and try to countermand the attack order. Only computer codes are authorised. Nothing verbal.'

'Jesus, Frank . . .'

How had Shawn found out he was here? Then he realised that Bishop had called the troopers to say that Gillette would be at Elana's place. Shawn must have been monitoring phone transmissions and heard Bishop's conversation.

Bishop said, 'They're near the house now, at a staging area.'

Gillette looked out of the window, thought that he saw some movement.

Bishop continued. 'Shawn's issued Level 4 rules of engagement— that means that the SWAT teams go in assuming they'll be met with suicidal resistance.'

'So kick the doors in,' Gillette muttered, 'and anybody who moves is going to get killed.'

Bishop paused. 'It could go like that.'

'Wyatt?' Elana asked. 'What's going on? Tell me!'

He turned, shouted, 'Tell your mother to get down on the living-room floor! You too! Now!'

Her black eyes burned with anger and fear. 'What've you done?'

'I'm sorry, I'm sorry . . . Just do it now. Get down!'

He turned back, looked out the window. He could see two large black vans easing through an alley fifty feet away. In the distance a helicopter fluttered a hundred feet in the air.

'Listen, Frank, are you in the FBI system?'

'Yeah, we can see the screen. Shawn's imping that he's the Tactical Operations Center in Washington, issuing codes.'

Outside, the sound of heavy trucks. The helicopter was closer. From the living room they heard the hysterical sobbing of Elana's mother.

What've I done?

Gillette said, 'Frank, maybe Shawn's in the San Jose Computer Products building? Maybe he got back inside.'

'I'll go over now and check their warehouse. Brother, I wish we knew who Shawn was.'

Something occurred to Gillette. 'Where's Bob Shelton?'

'At home. Why're you asking?'

'Call and find out if he's really there.'

A few minutes later Frank Bishop called back as he sped towards the warehouse.

'Bob *should* be home,' Bishop said, 'but there's no answer. You're wrong if you're thinking Bob's Shawn, though.'

Gillette said, 'No, Frank, listen: Shelton claimed he hated computers, but remember, he had that hard drive in his house.'

'The what?'

'That disk we saw—it's the kind of hardware only people who do serious hacking would use.'

'But I've known him for three years.'

'Social engineering.'

Gillette peeked through the curtain. He could see what looked like a military troop carrier parked not far away. There was activity in the bushes across the street.

Bishop came back on the line. 'Wyatt, I'm almost there. I'll call you when I'm inside.'

DESPITE THE TERRIBLE pain in his temple and the back of his skull, Bishop made his way to the warehouse. He didn't believe Gillette's conclusion about Bob Shelton. And yet he couldn't help but consider it. Of all the partners Bishop had had, he knew the least about Shelton.

But it didn't matter at the moment. Whether Shawn was Bob Shelton or someone else, Bishop had only about fifteen minutes before the federal tactical team began their attack. Drawing his pistol, he flattened himself against the wall beside the loading dock and paused, listening. He could hear nothing inside.

OK . . . Go!

Ripping the door open, Bishop ran into the dank warehouse itself. It was dark and unoccupied. He ran outside again to look for another building that Shawn might be using. But there were no other structures connected to the warehouse. As he was about to turn back, though, he noticed that the warehouse looked considerably larger from the outside than it had on the inside.

Hurrying back into the building he saw that a wall appeared to have been added at one end of the warehouse; it was a more recent construction than the original building. Yes, Phate must've added a secret room. *That's* where Shawn would be . . .

He found a knobless panel on hinges and tested it quietly. It was unlocked. He inhaled deeply, and pushed inside, gun up.

Empty.

Wyatt Gillette, his ex-wife and her family were doomed.

Reluctantly he called Gillette. 'Wyatt, I'm at the warehouse . . . But Shawn's not here. It's just a phone relay or something.' He described a large black metal box console on the floor of the room.

'It's not a phone relay,' Gillette muttered, his voice hollow with despair. 'It's an Internet router. But it won't do us any good.'

Bishop glanced at the box. 'There're no switches on it and the wiring's under the floor—this is one of those dinosaur pens like at CCU. So I can't unplug it.'

'Won't do any good anyway. Even if you shut that one down, Shawn's transmissions'll automatically find a new route to the FBI.'

'Maybe there's something else here that'll tell us where he is.' Desperately Bishop began searching through the desk and packing boxes. 'There're lots of papers and books.'

'What are they?' the hacker asked, but his voice was a monotone, filled with helplessness.

'Manuals, print-outs, worksheets, computer disks. Mostly technical stuff. From Sun Microsystems, Apple, Harvard, Western Electric—all the places where Phate worked.'

Then he heard Gillette shout, 'Wait!'

'What is it?'

'Those manuals. What were the companies again?'

Bishop looked over the documents. 'The places Phate worked. Harvard, Sun, Apple, Western Electric. And—'

'NEC!' Gillette shouted.

'Right.'

'It's an acronym!'

'What do you mean?' Bishop asked.

'The initials of those places he worked—Sun. Harvard. Apple, Western Electric, NEC . . . S, H, A, W, N . . . The machine in the room with you . . . It's not a router at all. The box—*that's* Shawn . . . *it's* generating the signals. Before he died Phate must've programmed it to crack the bureau system and arrange the assault. And Phate knew about Ellie—he mentioned her by name when he broke into CCU. He seemed to think I betrayed him because of her.'

Bishop, shivering fiercely from the raw cold, turned towards the black box. 'There's no way a computer could've done all this—'

But Gillette interrupted, 'No, no, no . . . A machine is the *only* way he could've done it. A supercomputer's the only thing that could monitor *all* of the phone calls and radio transmissions in and out of CCU. And it heard the assault code when we were about to nail Phate in Los Altos and sent the message to Phate to warn him.'

S-H-A-W-N.

It's all in the spelling . . .

'What can we do?' the detective asked.

'There's only one thing. You've got to—'

The line went dead.

'WE TOOK THEIR PHONE OUT,' a communications tech said to Special Agent Mark Little, the tactical commander for the FBI's Marinkill operation. 'And the cell's down. Nobody's mobiles'll work for a mile around.'

'Good.'

Taking the phones down was standard procedure. Five or ten minutes before an assault you had the subject's phone service suspended. That way nobody could be warned of the impending attack.

'Everybody locked and loaded?' Commander Little asked.

'Yeah. Three teams and snipers ready. Streets're secure.'

He hesitated, hearing the voice of that guy claiming to be Frank Bishop over and over in his head. He thought of the children killed at Waco. Little wondered if he should call San Francisco, where the bureau had a topnotch siege negotiator—

'Agent Little,' the communications officer interrupted, nodding at his computer screen. 'Message for you.'

Little leaned forward and read.

URGENT URGENT URGENT
FROM: DOJ TAC OP CENTER, WASHINGTON, DC
TO: TAC COMMANDER, DOJ NORTHERN DISTRICT CA

RE: DOJ NORTHERN DISTRICT CA OP 139-01
US ARMY REPORTS MARINKILL SUSPECTS BROKE INTO
SAN PEDRO MILITARY RESERVE AT 1540 HOURS TODAY
AND STOLE LARGE CACHE OF AUTOMATIC WEAPONS,
HAND GRENADES AND BODY ARMOUR.

Man alive, Little thought, his pulse skyrocketing. The message knocked any suggestion of a negotiator right out of his thoughts. He glanced at Special Agent George Steadman, his second in command and said calmly, nodding at the screen, 'Pass the word on this, George. Then get everybody in position. We go in six minutes.'

FRANK BISHOP WALKED around Shawn.

The housing was about four-feet square and made of thick metal sheets. On the back was a series of ventilation slats from which hot air poured, the white wisps visible, like breath on a winter day. The front panel consisted of nothing except three green eyes—glowing indicator lights that flickered occasionally, revealing that Shawn was hard at work carrying out Phate's posthumous instructions.

The detective had tried to call Wyatt Gillette back but the phone was out of service. He called Tony Mott at CCU and told him about the machine. 'I'm going to shut it down,' he said.

He looked at his watch.

Two minutes until the assault.

And so, just as he'd done six months ago in an alley in Oakland when a gang leader lifted a Remington twelve-gauge to his shoulder and aimed it at Bishop and two city cops, the detective calmly drew his service weapon and fired three well-grouped bullets into his adversary's torso.

But unlike the slugs that sent the gang leader to his death, these copper-jacketed rounds flattened into tiny pancakes and bounced to the floor; Shawn's skin was hardly dented.

Bishop walked closer, stood at an angle to avoid ricochets and emptied the clip at the indicator lights. One green light shattered but steam continued to pour from the vents into the cold air.

Bishop grabbed his cellphone and shouted to Mott at CCU. 'I just emptied a clip at the machine. Is it still online?'

He had to cram the phone against his ear, half-deafened from the gunshots, to hear the young cop tell him that Shawn was still operational.

Damn . . .

He reloaded and poked the gun into one of the back vents and emptied this clip as well. This time a ricochet—a bit of hot lead—struck the back of his hand and left a ragged stigmata in his skin. He wiped the blood on his slacks and grabbed the phone again.

'Sorry, Frank,' Mott replied hopelessly. 'It's still up and running.'

The cop looked in frustration at the box.

Sixty seconds. Shawn would be sending the confirmation signal at any moment.

Was there *anything* he could do to stop Shawn?

Maybe burn the damn thing?

Start a fire next to the vents? He ran to the desk and threw the contents of the drawers onto the floor, looking for matches or a cigarette lighter.

Nothing.

Then something clicked in his mind.

What?

He couldn't remember exactly, a thought from what seemed like ages ago—something Gillette had said when he'd walked into CCU for the first time.

He'd mentioned fire.

Fire.

Yes! Bishop suddenly turned from Shawn and looked frantically around the room. There it was! He ran to a small grey box with a red button in the middle—the dinosaur pen's scram switch.

He slammed his palm against the button.

A braying alarm sounded from the ceiling and with a piercing hiss, streams of halon gas shot from pipes above and below the machine, enveloping the room's occupants—one human, one not—in a ghostly white fog.

SPECIAL AGENT LITTLE looked at the screen of the computer in the command van.

RED CODE: <MAPLELEAF>

This was the go-ahead code for the assault.

'Print it out,' Little said to the tech agent. Then, 'We're going in. Any targets presenting through the windows?'

The snipers reported that there were none.

'All right. If anyone comes through the door armed, take them out. Drop 'em with a head shot.'

'Five by five,' the snipers confirmed that they understood.

Little listened as the search and surveillance team reported in. 'Infrared shows body heat in the living room.'

'Roger.' Then Little announced into his radio, 'I'm taking Alpha up the operation-side right of the house. We'll saturate with stun grenades—three in the parlour, three in the living room, thrown at five-second intervals. On the third bang Bravo goes in the front, Charlie in the back.'

The team leaders confirmed they had heard and understood.

Little pulled on his gloves, hood and helmet.

He gave a hand signal to three of his agents from whose belts dangled the powerful stun grenades. They ran into position beneath the parlour, living room and kitchen windows then pulled the pins of the grenades. Three others joined them and gripped billy clubs, with which they'd shatter the glass so their partners could pitch the grenades inside.

The men looked back at Little, awaiting the go-ahead hand signal.

Then: a crackle in Little's headset.

'Alpha team leader one, we have an emergency patch from a land-line. It's the SAC from San Francisco.'

Special Agent in Charge Jaeger? What was *he* calling for?

'Go ahead,' he whispered into the stalk mike.

There was a click.

'Agent Little,' came the unfamiliar voice. 'It's Frank Bishop. State police.'

'Bishop?' It was that cop who'd called before. 'Put Henry Jaeger on.'

'He's not here, sir. I lied. I had to get through to you.'

'Bishop . . . Do you know what kind of trouble you're going to be in for impersonating an FBI agent? I'm hanging up.'

'No! Don't! Ask for reconfirmation.'

'I don't want to hear any of this hacker crap.'

Little examined the house. Everything was still. Moments like this summoned a curious sensation—exhilarating and frightening and numbing all at the same time. You also had the queasy sense that one of the killers had his sights on you, picking out a target of flesh two inches off the vest.

The cop said, 'I just nailed the perp who did the hacking and shut his computer down. I guarantee you won't get a reconfirmation. Send the request.'

'That's not procedure.'

'Do it anyway. You'll regret it for the rest of your life if you go in there under Level 4 rules of engagement.'

Little paused. How had Bishop known they were operating at Level 4? Only someone on the team or with access to the bureau computer could have known that.

The agent noticed his second in command tap his watch impatiently then nod towards the house.

Bishop's voice was pure desperation. 'Please. I'll stake my job on it.'

The agent hesitated then muttered, 'You sure as hell just did, Bishop.' He slung his machine gun over his shoulder and switched back to the tactical frequency. 'All teams, stay in position. Repeat, stay in position.'

He ran back to the command post. 'Confirm the red code again.'

'Why? We don't need to reconfirm—'

'Now,' Little snapped.

The man typed.

FROM: TACTICAL COMMANDER, DOJ NORTHERN DIS-
TRICT CALIFORNIA
TO: DOJ TAC OP CENTER, WASHINGTON, DC
RE: DOJ NORTHERN DISTRICT CALIFORNIA OPERATION
139-01:
RED CODE CONFIRM?

A message popped up on the screen.

<PLEASE WAIT>

These few minutes could give the killers inside a chance to prepare for an assault or to rig the house with explosives for a group suicide that would take the lives of a dozen of his men. He said to the communications officer, 'Forget it. We're going in.' He started for the door.

'Hey, wait,' the officer said. 'Something's weird.' He nodded at the screen. 'Take a look.'

The man said, 'It's the right number. I checked.'

<No information. Please verify operation number>

Little: 'Send it again.'

Once more the agent typed and hit ENTER.

<No information. Please verify operation number>

Little pulled his black hood off and wiped his face. Christ, what *was* this?

Suddenly a voice in the radio: 'Alpha team leader one, this is sniper three. One of the suspects is on the front steps. White male, late twenties. Hands in the air. I have a shot-to-kill. Should I take it?'

'Any weapons? Explosives?'

'None visible.'

'What's he doing?'

'Walking forwards slowly. He's turned around to show us his back. Still no weapons. But he could have something rigged under his shirt. I'll lose the shot to foliage in ten seconds. Sniper three, pick up target when he's past that bush.'

Bravo team leader said, 'He's got a device on him, Mark. All the bulletins've said that's what they're going to do—take out as many of us as they can. This guy'll set off the charge and the rest'll come out the back door, shooting.'

<No information. Please verify operation number>

Mark Little said into his mike, 'Bravo team leader two, order suspect onto the ground. Sniper two if he's not face down in five seconds, take your shot.'

'Yessir.'

They heard the loudspeaker a moment later: 'This is the FBI. Lie down face forwards and extend your arms. Now, now, now!'

<No information>

The agent then called in, 'He's down, sir.'

LYING ON THE GRASS, smelling dirt, rain, and the faint scent of lilac, Wyatt Gillette blinked as the searing spotlights focused on him. He watched an edgy young agent move cautiously towards him, pointing a very large gun at his head.

The agent cuffed him and frisked him thoroughly, relaxing only when Gillette asked him to call a state trooper named Bishop, who could confirm that the FBI's computer system had been hacked and that the people in the house weren't the Marinkill suspects.

The agent then ordered Elana and her mother out onto the lawn, arms raised. It was clear from their grim faces that they were suffering nearly as much from indignity and terror as if they'd been physically injured.

The FBI agents huddled and made a number of phone calls and then huddled some more. They concluded that the assault had indeed been illegally ordered. They released everyone—except Gillette, of course, though they helped him stand up and loosened the cuffs a bit.

Elana strode up to her ex. He stood motionless in front of her, making not a sound as he took the full force of the powerful slap against his cheek. The woman, sensuous and beautiful even in her anger, turned away without a word and helped her mother up the stairs into the house.

As the agents packed up, Bishop arrived and found Gillette being guarded by a large agent. He walked up to the hacker and said, 'The scram switch.'

'A halon dump.' Gillette nodded. 'That's what I was going to tell you to do when they cut the phone line.'

Bishop nodded. 'I remembered you mentioned it at CCU. When you first saw the dinosaur pen.'

'Any other damage?' Gillette asked. 'To Shawn?'

He hoped not. He was keenly curious about the machine—how it worked, what it could do, what operating system made up its heart and mind.

It wasn't badly hurt, Bishop explained. 'I emptied two full clips at the box but it didn't do much damage.' He smiled. 'Just a flesh wound.'

A stocky man walked towards them through the blinding spotlights. When he got closer Gillette could see it was Bob Shelton. The pock-faced cop greeted his partner and glanced at Gillette with his typical disdain.

Bishop told him what had happened and the cop shook his head with a bitter laugh. 'Shawn was a computer? Somebody oughta throw every damn one of 'em into the ocean.'

'Why do you keep saying that?' Gillette snapped. 'You've been dumping on me and machines every chance you get. But it's a little hard to believe coming from somebody with a thousand-dollar Winchester drive sitting in his house.'

'A what?'

'When we were over at your place I saw that server drive sitting in your living room.'

The cop's eyes flared. 'That was my son's,' he growled. 'I was throwing it out. I was finally cleaning out his room, getting rid of all that computer shit he had.'

'He was into computers, your son?' Gillette asked, recalling that the boy had died several years ago.

Another bitter laugh. 'Oh, yeah, he was *into* computers. All he wanted to do was hack. He spent hours online. Only some cyber-gang found out he was a cop's kid and thought he was trying to snitch 'em out. They went after him. Posted lies about him on the Internet—that he was gay, that he had a record, that he molested little kids . . . They broke into his school's computer and made it look like he changed his own grades. That got him suspended. Then they sent some girl he'd been dating this filthy email in his name. She broke up with him because of it. The day that happened he got drunk and drove into a freeway abutment. Maybe it was an accident—maybe he killed himself. Either way it was computers that caused his death.'

'I'm sorry,' Gillette said softly.

'You're as bad as any of them, making my boy believe that those goddamn plastic boxes're the whole world. Well, that's bullshit. That's not where life is.' He grabbed Gillette's jacket. 'Life is *here!* Flesh and blood . . . human beings . . . Your family, your children . . .' His voice choked, tears filled his eyes. '*That's* what's real.'

Shelton shoved the hacker back, wiped his eyes with his hands. Bishop stepped forwards and touched his arm. But Shelton pulled away and disappeared into the crowd of police and agents.

Gillette's heart went out to the poor man but he couldn't help but think, Machines're real too, Shelton. They're becoming more and more a part of that flesh-and-blood life every day and that's never going to change. The question we have to ask ourselves isn't whether this transformation is in itself good or bad but simply this. Who do we become when we step through the monitor into the Blue Nowhere?

A WEEK AFTER WYATT GILLETTE returned to prison Frank Bishop made good on Andy Anderson's promise and, over the warden's renewed objections, delivered to Wyatt Gillette a battered, second-hand Toshiba laptop computer.

When he booted it up the first thing he saw was a digitised picture of a fat baby, a few days old. The caption beneath it read 'Greetings—from Linda Sanchez and her new granddaughter, Maria Andie Harmon.' Gillette made a mental note to send her a letter of congratulations; a baby present would have to wait, federal prisons not having gift shops as such.

There was no modem included with the computer of course, which isn't to say that Gillette was completely quarantined from the Net. He'd been allowed onto the library's dog-slow IBM PC to help with the analysis of Shawn, and what he had found within astonished him. To give himself access to as many computers as possible, via Trapdoor, Phate had endowed his creation with its own operating system. It was unique, incorporating all existing operating systems: Windows, MS-DOS, Apple, Unix, Linux, VMS and a number of obscure systems for scientific and engineering applications. It would also modify itself to incorporate any new operating systems Phate loaded into it. His system, which he called Protean 1.1, reminded Gillette of the elusive unified theory that explains the behaviour of all matter and energy in the universe.

Only Phate, unlike Einstein and his progeny, had apparently succeeded in his quest.

ON A TUESDAY in late April Gillette was sitting at his laptop in his cell, analysing some of Shawn's operating system, when the guard came to the door.

'Visitor, Gillette.'

It would be Bishop, he guessed. The detective, who was still working the Marinkill case, stopped by San Ho occasionally when he was in the area. Last time he'd brought some Pop-Tarts.

The visitor, however, wasn't Frank Bishop.

He sat down in the cubicle and watched Elana Papandolos walk into the room. She was wearing a navy-blue dress. Her dark, wiry hair was so thick that the hair-slide holding it together seemed about to burst apart. Noticing her short nails, perfectly filed and coloured lavender, he thought of something that'd never occurred to him. That Ellie, a piano teacher, made her way in the world with her hands too—just as he had done—yet her fingers were beautiful and unblemished by even a hint of callus.

She sat down, scooted the chair forwards.

'You're still here,' he said, lowering his head slightly to speak through the holes in the Plexiglas. 'I never heard from you. I assumed you'd left a couple of weeks ago.'

'I postponed my plans. To go to New York.'

'What about Ed?'

She glanced behind her. 'He's outside.'

This stung Gillette's heart. Nice of him to chauffeur her to see her ex, the hacker thought bitterly, inflamed by jealousy. 'So why'd you come?' he asked.

'I've been thinking about you. About what you said to me the other day. Before the police showed up.'

He nodded for her to continue.

'Would you give up machines for me?' she asked.

Gillette took a breath. He exhaled and then answered evenly, 'No. I'd never do that. Machines are what I'm meant to do in life.'

He expected her to stand up and walk out. It would have killed a portion of him, but he'd vowed that if he had a chance to talk to her again he'd never lie.

He added, 'I can promise you that they'll never come between us the way they did. Never again.'

Elana nodded slowly. 'I don't know, Wyatt. I don't know if I can trust you. I'll be in town for a while at least,' she said slowly.

'What about Ed? What's he going to say?'

'Why don't you ask him?'

'Me?' Gillette asked, alarmed.

Elana rose and walked to the door.

What on earth was he going to say? Gillette wondered in panic. He was about to come face-to-face with the man who'd stolen his wife's heart.

She opened the door and gestured.

A moment later Elana's staunch, unsmiling mother walked into the room. She was leading a small boy, about eighteen months old, by the hand.

Elana and Ed had a baby!

His ex-wife sat down in the chair once again and hauled the youngster up on her lap. 'This is Ed.'

'But . . .'

'*You* assumed Ed was my boyfriend. But he's my son . . . Actually, I should say he's *our* son.'

'Ours?' he whispered.

She nodded.

Gillette thought back to the last few nights they'd been together before he'd surrendered to the prison authorities to start his sentence, lying in bed with her, pulling her close.

He closed his eyes. Lord, Lord, Lord . . .

I saw your emails. When you talk about Ed it doesn't exactly sound like he's perfect husband material . . .

He gazed at the boy's thick, curly black hair. That was his mother's. He had her beautiful dark eyes and face too. 'Hold him up, would you?'

She helped her son stand on her lap. His quick eyes studied Gillette carefully. He reached forwards with his fat baby fingers and touched the Plexiglas, smiling, fascinated, trying to understand how he could see through it but not touch something on the other side.

He's curious, Gillette thought. *That*'s what he got from me.

Elana and Gillette faced each other across the Plexiglas divide.

'We'll see how it goes,' she said. 'How's that?'

'That's all I'm asking.'

She nodded.

Then they turned in separate directions and, as Elana disappeared out of the visitors' door, the guard led Wyatt Gillette back into the dim corridor towards his cell, where his machine awaited.

JEFFERY DEAVER

For as long as he can remember, Jeffery Deaver has wanted to be a writer. As a boy growing up in a small town near Chicago, he used to write stories and songs, and he edited his school's literary magazine. In the 1970s, however, after studying journalism at the University of Missouri, Deaver went to law school. His idea was to acquire legal expertise for his journalistic career, but in fact he became a lawyer, and practised civil law for several years.

The dream of becoming a writer did not fade, however, and when Deaver's first novel, *Voodoo*, was published in 1988, it marked the start of a career that has grown steadily over the years as each successive book has attracted new readers. His hallmark is a story filled with surprising plot twists which carry the reader along from the first page to the last. 'Ideally, I would like a reader to read my books in one sitting,' says Deaver.

He knows his books are scary—they're meant to be. Deaver works hard to frighten his readers, zeroing in on close-to-home fears for maximum impact. For *The Blue Nowhere*, that was what attracted the author to the computer—a familiar feature in offices and homes. On one level it's just a machine that processes binary code (an example of binary code appears in the chapter headings in this condensation of *The Blue Nowhere*). But what if it is also a Trojan Horse—a means to penetrate innocent lives?

'The next time you're on your computer,' says Deaver, 'and it seems that the keyboard doesn't feel quite right, or the screen looks a little fuzzy, or the hard drive makes a slightly unusual sound . . . well, it's nothing to worry about. Just a hardware glitch or a software bug. That's all. I'm sure you're not in any danger.'

And then he adds the all-important rider: 'Probably.'

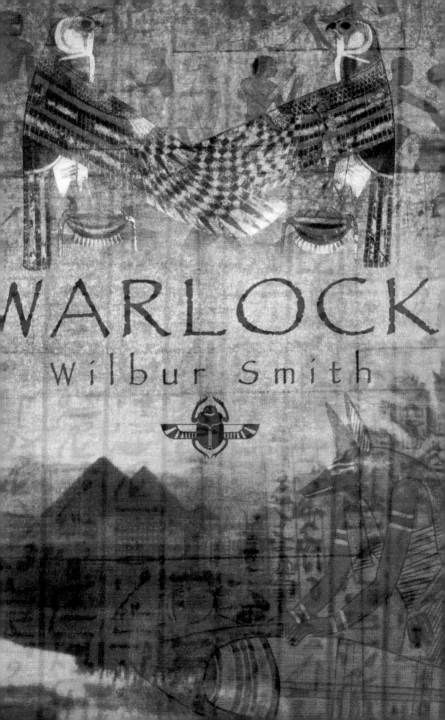

WARLOCK
Wilbur Smith

In the ancient lands that border the River Nile, fourteen-year-old Prince Nefer is being groomed by his wise friend Taita, in preparation for his eventual succession to the throne of Lower Egypt.

But behind the loyal faces at court, a traitor lurks. As cunning and as patient as a cobra.

Can the aged Taita, with his wisdom and wondrous magical powers, avert the danger that threatens to destroy his country's hopes of a peaceful future?

 CHAPTER ONE

Like an uncoiling serpent, a line of fighting chariots wound swiftly down the gut of the valley. From where he clung to the dashboard of the leading chariot, the boy looked up at the cliffs that hemmed them in. Openings to the tombs of the ancients honeycombed the rock, staring down at him like the implacable eyes of a legion of djinn. Prince Nefer Memnon shuddered and looked away, furtively making the sign to avert evil with his left hand.

Over his shoulder he glanced back down the column and saw that from the following chariot Taita was watching him through the swirling clouds of dust. The dust had coated the old man and his vehicle with a pale film, and a single shaft of sunlight that penetrated to the depths of this deep valley glittered on the mica particles so that he seemed to glow like the incarnation of one of the gods. Even at that distance his ancient eyes seemed to bore into the core of Nefer's being. Seeing all, understanding all. Nefer ducked his head guiltily, ashamed that the old man had witnessed his superstitious dread. No royal prince of the House of Tamose should show such weakness, not now when he stood at the gateway to manhood. But then, Taita knew him as no other did, for he had been Nefer's tutor since infancy, closer to him than his own parents or siblings.

Nefer turned back and drew himself up to his full height beside his father, who flipped the reins and urged the horses on with a crack of the long whip. Ahead of them the valley opened abruptly into the great amphitheatre that contained the ruins of the city of Gallala.

Nefer thrilled to his first sight of this famous battlefield. As a young man Taita himself had fought on this site when Nefer's grandfather, Tanus Lord Harrab, had destroyed the dark forces that were threatening Egypt. Taita had related to Nefer every detail of the fight.

Nefer's father, the god and Pharaoh Tamose, wheeled the chariot up to the tumbled stones of the ruined gateway and reined in the horses. Behind them a hundred chariots neatly executed the same manoeuvre. Stripped naked in the heat, the charioteers swarmed down from the footplates to begin watering the horses.

'My lord!' Pharaoh hailed Lord Naja, his army commander and beloved companion. 'We must be away again before the sun touches the hilltops. I wish to make a night run through the dunes to El Galsar.' He glanced down at Nefer. 'This is where I leave you to go on with Taita.'

Nefer opened his mouth to protest. Pharaoh forestalled him. 'What is the first duty of a warrior?' he demanded.

Nefer dropped his eyes. 'It is obedience, Majesty,' he replied softly.

'Never forget it.' His father nodded and turned away.

Pharaoh Tamose's battle plan was bold and brilliant. If it succeeded, it would bring to a close, at one stroke, the war with the Hyksos that had already raged through two lifetimes. Nefer had been taught that battle and glory were the reasons for his existence on this earth. But even at the advanced age of fourteen, they had so far eluded him. He longed with all his soul to ride to victory and immortality at his father's side. Now he felt himself spurned and discarded. His eyes smarted and his upper lip quivered, but Taita's gaze stiffened him. He blinked to clear his tears and took a pull from the water-skin that hung on the side rail of the chariot before turning to the old Magus with a jaunty toss of his thick, dust-caked curls. 'Show me the monument, Tata,' he commanded.

The pair made their way through the chariots, men and horses that choked the narrow streets of the ruined city, past temples and palaces now inhabited only by the lizard and the scorpion, until they reached the deserted central square. In its centre stood the monument to Lord Tanus and his triumph over the armies of bandits who had almost choked the life out of the richest and most powerful nation on earth.

Taita watched the prince as he walked round the monument, a bizarre pyramid of human skulls cemented together and protected by a shrine made of red rock slabs.

'Tata, show me where it was that you captured the leader of the robber barons.' Nefer's voice cracked with excitement and the onset of puberty. 'Was it here?' He ran to the broken-down wall at the south side of the square.

'No, it was here. This side,' Taita told him, and he strode on those long, stork-thin legs to the eastern wall. He looked up to the crumbling summit. 'The ruffian's name was Shufti, and he was one-eyed and as ugly as the god Seth. He was trying to escape by climbing over the wall here. I brought him down with a single throw.'

Even though Nefer knew, at first hand, the old man's strength, he was astonished when Taita suddenly stooped and picked up half a baked-mud brick and hurled it upwards. It sailed over the top of the high wall.

He is as old as the mountains, older than my grandmother, Nefer marvelled. Men say he has witnessed two hundred inundations of the Nile and that he built the pyramids with his own hands.

'You know the story well enough, for I have told it to you a hundred times.' Taita feigned modest reluctance to extol his own deeds.

'Tell me again!' Nefer ordered.

Taita sat down on a stone block while Nefer settled at his feet in happy anticipation and listened avidly until the ram's horns of the squadron sounded the recall.

There was a great bustle and scurry outside the walls of the ruined city as the squadron made ready to go on into the dune lands. The water-skins were bulging again, and the troopers checked and tightened the harnesses of their teams before mounting up.

Pharaoh Tamose looked over the heads of his staff as Taita and Nefer came through the gateway. He summoned Taita to his side with an inclination of his head. Together they walked out of earshot of the squadron officers. Lord Naja made to join them. Taita whispered a word to Pharaoh, then Tamose turned and sent Naja back with a curt word. Flushed with mortification, Naja shot a look at Taita that was sharp as a war arrow.

'You have offended Naja. Some day I might not be at hand to protect you,' Pharaoh warned.

'We dare trust no man,' Taita insisted. 'Treachery tightens its coils around your palace. Until you return from this campaign in the north only the two of us must know where I am taking the prince.'

'But Naja!' Pharaoh laughed dismissively. Naja was like a brother.

'Even Naja.' Taita said no more. His suspicions were hardening into certainty, but he had not yet gathered all the evidence he would need to convince Pharaoh.

'Does the prince know why you are taking him into the desert?' Pharaoh asked.

'He knows only that we are going to further his instruction in the mysteries, and to capture his godbird.'

'Good, Taita.' Pharaoh nodded. 'You were ever secretive but true. There is nothing more to say, for we have said it all. Now go, and may Horus spread his wings over you and Nefer.'

'Look to your own back, Majesty, for in these days enemies stand behind you as well as to your front.'

Pharaoh grasped the Magus's upper arm and squeezed. Then he went back to where Nefer waited beside the wheel of the royal chariot.

'It is my command that you go with Taita into the desert to capture your godbird, to prove your royal blood and your right one day to wear the double crown.'

NEFER AND THE OLD MAN stood together beside the shattered walls of Gallala and watched the column fly past. Pharaoh led it, leaning back against the pull of the horses, his chest bare, linen skirts whipping around his muscular legs, the blue war crown on his head.

Next came Lord Naja, haughty and proud, the great recurved bow slung over his shoulder. Naja was one of Egypt's mightiest warriors, and his name had been given to him as a title of honour. Naja was the sacred cobra in the royal crown.

The two were silent long after the last chariot had disappeared and the dust had settled. Then Taita turned without a word and went to where their horses were tethered. He hiked up his kilts and swung up with the limber movement of a much younger man.

Nefer, as he vaulted up onto the back of his favourite colt, cast a last, longing glance at the feather of distant dust left on the northern horizon by the squadron, then firmly turned his back upon it. 'Where are we going, Tata?' he demanded. 'You promised to tell me once we were on the road.'

Taita was always reticent and secretive, but seldom to this degree. 'We are going to Gebel Nagara,' he told him.

Nefer had never heard the name before, but he repeated it softly. It had a romantic ring. Excitement and anticipation made the back of his neck prickle, and he looked ahead into the desert where jagged hills stretched away to a horizon blue with heat haze and distance.

Taita looked on this terrible place with a sense of nostalgia and homecoming. It was into this wilderness that he had retired after the death of his beloved Queen Lostris, Nefer's grandmother. He was a physician and a surgeon, a master of the known sciences, and alone in the desert he had discovered the key to doorways of the mind beyond which few men ever journey. He had gone in a man but had emerged as a familiar of the great god Horus, adept at strange and arcane mysteries.

Taita had only returned to the world of men when his Queen Lostris had visited him in a dream as he slept in his hermit's cave at Gebel Nagara. 'Darling Taita,' she had whispered, as she touched his cheek, 'you were one of the only two men I have ever loved. My husband Tanus is with me now, but before you can come to me also there is one more charge that I lay upon you.'

'I am yours to command, mistress.'

'In Thebes, my city of a hundred gates, this night is born a child, the son of my son. They will name this child Nefer, which means pure and perfect. My longing is that he may carry my blood and the blood of Tanus to the throne of Upper Egypt. But great perils already gather around him. He cannot succeed without your help. Go to Nefer. Go swiftly and stay with him until your task is completed. Do not fail me, Taita.'

Taita awoke, his face wet with tears, gathered up his possessions, then strode away into the western desert, back towards the city of Thebes. That had been over fourteen years ago, and now he knew that the dark powers of which she had warned were gathering.

'Come!' he said to the boy. 'Let us go down and take your godbird.'

ON THE THIRD NIGHT after leaving Gallala, Pharaoh Tamose halted the squadron to water the horses and to eat a hasty meal of sun-dried meat, dates and millet cakes. Then he ordered the mount-up. There was no sounding of the ram's horn trumpet now, for they were into Hyksosian territory.

The column started forward again at the trot. As they went on, the landscape changed dramatically. Below them lay the strip of dense vegetation that marked the course of the Nile. They had completed a wide circuit and were in the rear of the main Hyksosian army on the river. Although they were a tiny force against such an enemy, they were the best charioteers in the armies of Tamose, which made them the finest in the world. Moreover, they held the element of surprise.

It was almost two centuries since Egypt had been split apart. Since then either an Egyptian usurper or a foreign invader had ruled in the northern kingdom. It was Tamose's destiny to drive out the Hyksos and unite the two lands once more. Only then could he wear the double crown with the approval of the ancient gods.

The night air blew cool in his face, and his lance-bearer crouched low behind the dashboard to shield himself. The only sound was the crunch of the chariot wheels over the coarse gravel, the lances rattling softly in their scabbards.

Suddenly a wide wadi opened ahead of him and Pharaoh Tamose reined down the team. The wadi was the smooth roadway that would lead them down to the river. Pharaoh tossed the reins to his lance-bearer and vaulted down. He stretched his stiff, aching limbs as Naja's chariot came up behind him.

'From here the danger of discovery will be greater,' Naja said. 'Look down there.' He pointed to where the dry riverbed debouched onto the plain below. 'That is the village of El Wadun, where our spies will be waiting to lead us through the Hyksosian pickets. I will go ahead to the rendezvous to make safe the way. Wait here, Majesty, and I will return directly.'

'I will go with you.'

'I beg you. There may be treachery. You are Egypt. You are too precious to risk.'

Pharaoh turned to look into the beloved lean and handsome face, and touched Naja's shoulder with trust and affection. 'Go swiftly, and return as swiftly,' he acceded.

Naja ran back to his chariot. He saluted as he wheeled past where the king stood, and whipped up his speeding horses, down towards the village of El Wadun. When he had gone, Pharaoh walked back down the waiting column, speaking quietly to the troopers, calling many by name, encouraging and cheering them. Small wonder they loved him, and followed him so gladly wherever he led them.

WHEN LATER PHARAOH TAMOSE saw the chariot returning, he knew by the impetuous manner in which Naja drove that something was afoot. He ordered the squadron to mount and stand with drawn weapons, ready to meet any eventuality.

The moment the chariot drew level with Pharaoh, Naja sprang down.

'What's amiss?' Tamose demanded.

'A blessing from the gods,' Naja told him. 'They have delivered Apepi defenceless into our power.'

'How is that possible?'

'My spies have led me to where the enemy king is encamped. His tents are set up just beyond the first line of hills.' He pointed back with his sword.

'What is his strength?' Tamose could barely control his excitement.

'With his usual arrogance he has a bodyguard of fewer than fifty, and half of them are asleep. He suspects nothing. A swift charge out of the darkness and we will have him in our grasp.'

'Take me to where Apepi lies,' Pharaoh commanded.

Naja led them, and the soft, silvery sands of the wadi muffled the sounds of the wheels. The squadron swept around the last bend and Naja raised his clenched fist high to order the halt. Pharaoh drew up alongside him.

Naja pointed up a pathway towards the crest of the hills. 'On the far side is an oasis. His tents are set among the trees.'

'We will take a small patrol with us to scout the camp. Only then can we plan our attack.'

Naja had anticipated the order. He selected a scouting party of five troopers. 'Muffle your scabbards,' he ordered. 'Make not a sound.' Then, with his bow in his left hand, he stepped onto the pathway. Pharaoh came close behind him. They went upwards swiftly, until Naja saw the crossed branches of a thorn tree silhouetted against the dawn sky. He stopped abruptly.

It was here, not half an hour before, that he had met secretly with his cousin Trok, a Hyksosian general. Not even Pharaoh knew that Naja's mother had been Hyksosian. In the decades of their occupation, with a dearth of their own women to choose from, many Hyksos had taken Egyptian wives, and over the generations the bloodlines had become blurred.

Naja held up his right hand for silence.

'What is it?' Pharaoh whispered close behind him.

I thought I heard voices on the crest,' Naja answered, 'speaking the Hyksosian tongue. Wait here, Majesty, while I clear the path ahead.' Pharaoh and the five troopers squatted beside the path, while Naja went on stealthily and disappeared from view. The minutes passed slowly and Pharaoh began to fret. As a soft whistle came down to him he sprang to his feet and hefted his fabled blue sword.

'The way is clear,' Pharaoh murmured. 'Come, follow me.'

Pharaoh went on upwards and reached a tall rock that blocked the pathway. He stepped round it then stopped abruptly. Lord Naja faced him at a distance of twenty paces. They were alone, hidden from the men who followed. Naja's bow was at full draw, a Hyksosian arrow aimed at Pharaoh's chest. This, then, was the foul thing that Taita, with his clairvoyant powers, had smelt in the air.

'May you live for ever!' Silently Naja mouthed the words as though they were a curse, and he loosed the arrow, which took Pharaoh high in the centre of his chest, throwing him against the red rock of the boulder. For a moment he clung to the rough surface but the flint arrowhead had pierced him through, and he began to slide down, his legs buckling under him. Naja sprang forward with a wild cry, 'Ambush! Beware!' and he slipped one arm around Pharaoh's chest below the protruding arrow.

Supporting the dying king he bellowed again, 'On me, the guards!' and two stout troopers appeared round the rock wall, responding to his cry. They saw at a glance how Pharaoh was struck and the unmistakable bright fletching feathers on the base of the Hyksosian arrow.

'Carry Pharaoh back to his chariot while I hold off the enemy,' Naja ordered, and whirled around, pulling an arrow from his quiver and loosing it up the path towards the deserted summit, bellowing a challenge, then answering himself with a muffled counter-challenge in the Hyksosian language. He snatched up the blue sword from where Tamose had dropped it, then bounded back down the path and caught up with the small party of charioteers who were carrying the king away.

'It was a trap,' Naja told them urgently. 'The hilltop is alive with the enemy. Hurry! The king must not fall into their hands.'

The troops below had heard the wild cries in the dawn, and the regimental surgeon was waiting for them beside Pharaoh's chariot. He had been trained by Taita, and, though lacking the old man's special magic, might be capable of staunching Pharaoh's terrible wound. Lord Naja would not risk that, so he ordered the surgeon away brusquely. 'The enemy is hard upon us. There is no time for your quackery now. We must get him back to the safety of our own lines before we are overrun.'

Tenderly he lifted the king onto the footplate of his own chariot. He snapped off the shaft of the Hyksosian arrow that protruded from the king's chest and held it aloft so that all his men could see it clearly. 'This bloody instrument has struck down our Pharaoh. Our god and our king. He wrapped the arrow in a linen cloth, and placed it in the chariot. He would need to deliver it to the council in Thebes to substantiate his report on Pharaoh's death.

'A good man here to hold Pharaoh,' Naja ordered.

While the king's own lance-bearer came forward, Naja unbuckled the sword-belt from around Pharaoh's waist and carefully stowed it in his own weapons bin.

The lance-bearer jumped onto the footplate and cradled Tamose's head, as the chariot wheeled in a circle then sped back up the wadi with the rest of the squadron. Facing forward so that none could see his expression, Naja laughed softly, the sound covered by the grinding wheels. Leaving the wadi, they raced on towards the dunes.

IT WAS MIDMORNING, and the blinding white sun was halfway up the sky before Naja allowed the column to halt and the surgeon to come forward again to examine the king. It did not need his special skills to tell that Pharaoh's spirit had long before left his body and started its journey to the underworld.

'Pharaoh is dead,' the surgeon said quietly. A terrible cry of mourning ran through the column.

'The state is without a head,' Naja told his captains. 'Egypt is in dire peril. Ten of the fastest chariots must take Pharaoh's body back to Thebes with all haste. I shall lead them, for the council may wish me to take up the duties of regent to Prince Nefer, who must be found and informed of his own succession.'

He unrolled a papyrus scroll, a map of the territory from Thebes down to Memphis. 'You must split up into your troops and scour the countryside for the prince. I believe that Pharaoh sent him into the desert with the ancient eunuch to undertake the rituals of manhood, so we will concentrate our search there, around Gallala, where we last saw him.'

Naja held them with a final command: 'When you find Prince Nefer, bring him to me. Give him into no other hand but mine.'

He ran back to his chariot and seized the reins, 'Onwards!' he cried with a clenched fist. 'Onwards to Thebes!'

FOLLOWING NAJA'S SECRET ORDERS, a full legion of the Phat Guards, his own special regiment that was oath-bound to him, were waiting for him at the oasis of Boss, only two leagues from Thebes.

The guards' pickets saw the dust of the approaching chariots and stood to arms. The colonel, Asmor, and his officers turned out in full armour to meet Lord Naja.

'Lord Asmor!' Naja hailed him from the chariot. 'I have dreadful news to take to Thebes. Pharaoh is killed by a Hyksosian arrow. Egypt is without a father.' He raised his voice so that it carried clearly to the rear ranks. 'Prince Nefer is a child still and not ready to rule. Egypt stands in desperate need of a regent to lead her.' He paused and stared meaningfully at Colonel Asmor. Asmor lifted his chin in acknowledgment of the trust that Naja had placed in him.

Naja raised his voice to bellow: 'If Pharaoh falls in battle, the army has the right by acclamation to appoint a regent in the field.'

Asmor took a pace forward and turned to face the ranks of heavily armed guards. He removed his helmet. His face was dark and hard. He pointed his drawn sword to the sky and shouted, 'Lord Naja! Hail to Lord Naja!'

There was a stunned silence before the legion erupted in a roar, 'Hail to Lord Naja, Regent of Egypt!'

THE JOURNEY FROM GALLALA took three days of hard riding. Naja was exhausted, yet he allowed himself only an hour to rest, bathe away the dust of the journey and change his apparel. He now wore a white linen skirt, with a pectoral plate of gold and semiprecious stones covering his bare, muscled chest. On his hip he carried the fabulous blue sword that he had taken from Pharaoh's dead body.

His bodyguard formed up around him, and with five thousand men at his back the new Regent of Egypt began his march on Thebes.

Colonel Asmor rode as Naja's lance-bearer. He was young for the command of a full legion, but he had proved himself in battle and he was Naja's close companion. He, too, had Hyksosian blood in his veins, and there was nothing he would not do to hasten his patron Lord Naja's ascension to the throne of Egypt.

'What stands before us now, my old comrade?' Lord Naja asked him as they rode.

'The Yellow Flowers have cleared all but one of the princes of the House of Tamose from your path,' Asmor answered, pointing with his lance to the hills across the grey, silt-laden Nile. 'They lie in their tombs in the Valley of the Nobles.'

Three years previously a plague had swept through the two kingdoms. The disease was named for the dreadful yellow lesions that covered the bodies of the stricken. Eight princesses and six princes of the House of Tamose had died. Of all Pharaoh's children, only one girl and Prince Nefer Memnon had survived. There were those who believed that they would have died also, had not the ancient Magus Taita cut their left upper arms and placed in their blood his magical charm against the Yellow Flowers.

Naja frowned. Even in this moment of his triumph he could still give thought to the strange powers possessed by the Magus. He had already lived so long that no one knew his age; some said a hundred years and others two hundred. Yet he still walked and ran and drove a chariot like a man in his prime. Surely the gods loved him, and had bestowed upon him the secret of life eternal.

Once he was Pharaoh, that secret would be the only thing that Naja lacked. Could he wring it out of Taita the Warlock? First, he must be captured and brought in along with Prince Nefer. The chariots Naja had sent to scout the eastern deserts would bring them back.

The gates of Thebes were thrown open as soon as the sentries recognised the blue standard, and the citizens ran out to meet them. But the welcoming cries soon gave way to wild ululations of mourning when they heard the shouts of the leading charioteers: 'Pharaoh is dead! He has been slain by the Hyksos.'

The wailing crowds followed the chariot that carried the royal corpse to the funerary temple. The rest of the usually swarming city was almost deserted, and Naja galloped his chariot team swiftly through the narrow, crooked streets to the river palace. He knew that every member of the council would hurry to the assembly chamber as soon as they heard the dreadful news. At the entrance to the palace gardens, Asmor and fifty men of the bodyguard formed up around Naja. They marched in close order through the inner courtyard, past the ponds of the water garden filled with hyacinth.

The arrival of the armed men took the council unawares. The doors to the chamber were unguarded, and only a few members were assembled. Naja paused in the doorway and looked them over. Menset and Talla were old and past their once formidable powers; Cinka had always been weak and vacillating.

'Noble lords!' Naja greeted them as he strode into the chamber. 'Pharaoh is dead. He was cut down by a Hyksosian arrow while storming the enemy stronghold above El Wadun.'

The council members gawked at him in silence. Instantly Naja realised his opportunity. 'I am the regent of the royal Prince Nefer.' he thundered. 'I was acclaimed by my legions in the field. My noble lords, is there any man among you who would question this?' He looked at each in turn and they dropped their eyes: there was no man to give them direction and the Phat Guards stood shoulder to shoulder around the wall of the chamber.

'My lord Menset'—Naja singled out the president of the council—'does the council ratify the appointment of Lord Naja as the Regent of Egypt?'

Menset raised his eyes and looked around at his fellow members, but not one would catch his eye. 'The president and all the councillors of this assembly acknowledge the new Regent of Egypt,' he whispered at last.

'I accept the duty and heavy responsibility you have placed upon me.' Naja mounted the dais to the throne. 'As my first official pronouncement in my capacity of Regent in Council I wish to describe to you the gallant death of the divine Pharaoh Tamose.' He paused significantly, then for the next hour he related in detail his version of the fatal campaign. 'His last words to me as I carried him down the hill were, "Care for my only remaining son. Guard my son Nefer until he is man enough to wear the double crown. Take my small daughter under your wings, and see that no harm befalls her."'

It took Lord Naja some moments to bring his grief under control. Then he went on firmly, 'I will not fail the god who was my friend and my pharaoh. Already I have sent my chariots into the wilderness to search for Prince Nefer and bring him back to Thebes. As soon as he arrives we will set him on the throne, and place the scourge and the sceptre in his hands.'

There was the first murmur of approval among the councillors, and Naja continued, 'Now, send for the princess.'

When she came hesitantly through the main doors, Heseret smiled shyly around this formidable gathering. She had inherited in full measure the celebrated beauty of her grandmother, Queen Lostris. Her skin was milky, her limbs were smooth and shapely, and there were intriguing lights in her huge dark green eyes.

'Come forward, my pretty darling.' Naja rose from the throne, and went down to meet her. His voice and his expression were tragic. 'You must be brave now, and remember that you are a princess of the royal house, because I have bitter news for you. Pharaoh, your father, is dead.' For a minute Heseret did not seem to understand, then she let out the high keening wail of mourning.

Gently Naja put his arms around her and led her to sit at the foot of the throne. 'The distress of the royal princess is plain for all to see,' he told the assembly. 'The trust and the duty that Pharaoh placed upon me is equally plain. As I have taken Prince Nefer Memnon into my care, now I take Princess Heseret under my protection.'

CHAPTER TWO

Nefer sat in the shadow of the cliff that towered above Gebel Nagara. He had not moved since the sun had first shown its upper rim above the mountains across the valley. At first the effort of remaining still had made his skin itch as though insects were crawling upon it. But he knew Taita was watching him, so he had forced his wayward body into a state of exalted awareness, his every sense tuned to the wilderness about him. He could smell the water that rose from its secret spring in the cleft in the cliff. It came up a slow drop at a time and dripped into a basin in the rock. Much life was supported by this trickle of water: butterfly and beetle, serpent and lizard, the speckled pigeons that nested on high ledges, all drank here. It was because of this precious pool that Taita had brought him to this place to wait for his godbird.

They had begun to make a net on the day of their arrival at Gebel Nagara. Taita had bought the silk in Thebes. It was stronger than thongs of leather but almost invisible to the eye.

When the net was ready Taita had insisted that the boy catch the decoys himself. So, in the baking daylight out on the valley floor, Nefer and Taita had studied the route up the cliff to the ledge where the pigeons roosted. When darkness fell Taita had sat beside a small fire by the entrance to a cave at the base of the cliff, and Nefer had started the precarious climb. He seized two birds while they were still disorientated by the darkness, and brought them down in the leather saddlebag slung on his back.

They selected a spot close to the base of the cliff, but exposed enough to make the birds clearly visible from the sky, and tethered the pigeons by the leg with horsehair thread and a wooden peg driven into the hard earth. Then they spread the gossamer net above them, supported on stalks of dried elephant grass, which would snap under the stoop of the godbird.

When all was set up to Taita's satisfaction, they began the long wait. Soon the pigeons became accustomed to captivity, and pecked greedily at the millet that Nefer scattered for them. Then they sunned and dusted themselves contentedly under the silken net. One hot, sun-riven day succeeded the next, and still they waited.

In the cool of the evening they brought the pigeons into the cave, and then they hunted for food. They grilled gazelle steaks over the fire. The cave had been Taita's retreat during all the years after the death of Queen Lostris when he had lived here as a hermit. It was his place of power.

They had been at Gebel Nagara for many days before Nefer began to understand that they had not come here to find the godbird alone. Taita was teaching him control over his body and being, teaching him to look inward, to listen to the silence and hear whispers to which others were deaf. Even the long hours of waiting beside the decoys were a lesson.

On the twentieth morning of their stay, Nefer took up his position over the decoys. As always, he was deeply aware of the presence of Taita, whose eyes were closed and who seemed to be dozing in the sunlight. His skin was crisscrossed with innumerable fine wrinkles and dappled with age spots. It looked as delicate as the finest papyrus parchment. His face was hairless, no trace of beard or eyebrows; only fine lashes, colourless as glass, surrounded his eyes. Nefer reached out to touch the old man's arm as he slept. Nefer had heard his father say that it was because Taita was a eunuch, gelded after puberty, that his face was beardless and little marked by the passage of time, but he was certain that there were more reasons for the persistence of his strength and life force.

Suddenly Taita's eyes opened, focused and aware. Nefer knew that he had not been asleep at all, but that all his powers had been concentrated on bringing in the godbird to the decoys.

Chastened, he composed himself, and brought his mind and body under control again as Taita had taught him. It was like passing through a secret doorway. Suddenly Nefer was blessed with a marvellous sense that he, too, hung above the world and saw everything happening below him. He saw Taita and himself sitting beside the well of Gebel Nagara, and the desert stretching away around them. He saw cities and kingdoms, the machinations of evil men, and the striving of the just and good. In that moment he was aware of his destiny with an intensity that almost overwhelmed his courage.

In that same moment he knew that his godbird would come on this day, for he was ready to receive it, aware with every fibre of his being.

The royal falcon was such a rare creature that few men had ever seen it in the wild. Possession of the bird was proof that Pharaoh had the divine approval of the god Horus to reign in Egypt.

And now the bird was here. He heard its cry, a faint lament, almost lost in the immensity of sky and desert. Seconds later the falcon called again, directly overhead, its voice shriller and more savage.

Now the pigeons were wild with terror, leaping against the threads that secured them to the pegs, while high overhead Nefer heard the falcon begin its stoop on them, the wind singing over its wings in a rising note. He looked up and saw the bird drop against the aching blue of the desert sky. It was a thing of divine beauty. Its wings were folded back, and its head was thrust forward. The strength and power of the creature made Nefer gasp aloud. He wanted to possess it with a longing he had never imagined possible.

He braced himself for the moment of impact. Beside him he felt Taita do the same. The falcon dropped like a thrown javelin, and tore into the pigeons with both sets of talons.

Then Nefer heard an explosive hiss of air. Something huge and glittering black whipped out from behind the net and slammed into the falcon. He saw the thick, glittering coils of a gigantic black cobra. The snake's head was raised, its hood marked with a bold pattern of black and white. Its fathomless black eyes held Nefer in a mesmeric stare. He tried to scream, but no sound came from his throat. Each scale was polished like a jewel, each coil, wrapped around the falcon, was as thick as Nefer's arm, and slowly they revolved upon themselves.

Without thought, Nefer hurled his leather bag away from him. The cobra's fangs hooked into the leather and the bag and the snake fell away together, the sinuous body still coiling and whipping furiously. It bounced away over the rocks until Nefer lost sight of it among the grey boulders.

'Oh, Taita. It was horrible. It killed my godbird.'

'Gently, lad. Drink.' He offered the water-skin. 'Thanks be to the great god who protected you,' Taita murmured. 'With this cobra apparition, Horus has sent you a portent of terrible dangers. That was no natural serpent.' He turned and walked back to the entrance of the cave. Nefer followed him slowly, his heart leaden with disappointment. In the gloom of the cave Taita seated himself on the stone ledge below the back wall, and leaned forward to build up the smoky fire of thorn branches until it burst into flames. Then he sighed, and said softly, almost sadly, 'I must work the Mazes of Ammon Ra.'

Nefer watched in awe as Taita went through the ritual of preparing the Mazes. First he crushed herbs and poured boiling water over them. The steam that rose was so pungent it made Nefer's eyes water.

While the mixture cooled, Taita brought the tanned leather bag that contained the Mazes from its hiding place at the back of the cave. The Mazes comprised ten ivory discs, each carved with one of the ten symbols of power. Taita rubbed the discs gently between his fingers as he began to chant the incantation to Ammon Ra, and between each verse he blew on them to endow them with his life force. When they had taken on the warmth of his own body he passed them to Nefer.

'Hold them and breathe upon them,' he urged, and while Nefer obeyed these instructions, Taita began to sway as he retreated into the secret places in his mind. He was already in the trance when Nefer stacked the Mazes in front of him, then offered up the infusion to him. Taita drank it to the last drop, and in the firelight his face turned white as chalk. He subsided onto the floor of the cave, and started to twitch and groan, and the sweat streamed down his face. His eyes opened and rolled back in their sockets until only the whites glared blindly into the dark shadows of the cave.

Nefer knew there was nothing he could do for the old man now. Taita had journeyed far into the shadowy places where Nefer could not reach him. Hardly able to bear the terrible suffering that the Mazes inflicted upon the Magus, Nefer lay down beside him, and after a while he fell into a sleep that was haunted by nightmares.

When he awoke, dawn was glimmering at the entrance to the cave. Taita was sitting at the fire, still looking pale and sick. 'What did you see, Tata,' the boy asked.

'It was obscured,' Taita told him, and Nefer knew that the omen had been unpropitious.

'Explain it to me, Tata,' Nefer insisted.

There was deep anguish in his voice, so Taita softened his answer. 'There are mysteries here. I saw their shadows in my vision. This is a thing beyond the natural order.'

Taita paused and looked to the sky, as if in deep thought. 'First we must fly from the great dangers that beset us. The cobra has returned from the shadows from which it sprang.'

Nefer shivered with superstitious awe, then scrambled up onto the back of his colt.

Taita led the way. By the time the sun was above the horizon they had left Gebel Nagara far behind them.

Nefer knew well that when Taita was in this mood it was wasted effort to speak to him, but he urged his horse alongside and pointed out respectfully, 'Tata, this is not the way to Thebes.'

'We are not going back there.'

Nefer was puzzled. 'Why not?'

Taita turned his head and looked at the boy with such pity that he was silenced. 'I will explain when we are in a safe place.'

Avoiding the crests of hills, where they might be silhouetted on the skyline, Taita wove a path through the gorges and valleys. Always he headed east, away from Egypt and the Nile, towards the sea.

The sun was setting before he reined in his mare and spoke. 'The main caravan road lies just beyond the next line of hills. We must cross it, but enemies may be watching for us there.'

They left the horses tethered in a hidden wadi, then climbed cautiously to the crest of the hills and found a vantage point behind a bank of purple shale from which they could look down onto the caravan road below.

'We will lie here until dark,' Taita explained. He swept another look along the road below them, and immediately ducked his head. 'Someone coming!' he warned.

Nefer flattened himself behind the shale bank and they watched the column of dust coming swiftly down the caravan road from the west. By this time the valley was in deep shadow and the sky was filled with all the glorious shades of the sunset.

'They are moving fast. Those are not merchants, they are fighting chariots,' Nefer said. 'Yes, I can see them now.' His bright young eyes picked out the shape of the leading chariot. 'They are not Hyksos,' he went on. 'They are ours. A cohort of the Phat Guards! We are safe, Tata!'

Taita reached up a bony hand and hauled him down violently. 'Those are the minions of the cobra. Hurry! They must not catch us.'

He dragged the boy off the ridge and started down the slope, jumping from rock to rock. He reached the horses first, and was on the mare's back in a single leap.

'What is happening, Tata?' Nefer panted.

'Mount! No time to talk.'

As they galloped out of the wadi, Nefer shot a longing look back over his shoulder, and saw the leading charioteer. 'That is Hilto, Tata. I know his face so well. He is a good man.'

Hilto was a famous warrior, who wore the Gold of Valour, but Taita told Nefer sternly, 'Don't be deceived. Trust nobody.'

Obediently Nefer rode on into the wilderness of broken rock. The faint sounds behind them dwindled and were snuffed out by the eternal silence of the desert. Before they had gone much further darkness forced them to dismount and walk through the difficult places where the twisting path narrowed.

At last they had to stop to water and rest the horses. They sat close together and, with his dagger, Taita sliced a loaf of millet bread, and they munched it as they talked softly.

'Tell me of your vision, Tata. What did you truly see when you worked the Mazes of Ammon Ra?'

'I told you. They were obscured.'

'I know that is not true.' Nefer shook his head. 'You said that to protect me.' He shivered from the chill of the night and a sense of dread. 'You saw something of terrible portent. That is why we are fleeing now. You must tell me all your vision. I must understand what is happening to us.'

'Yes, you are right,' Taita agreed at last. 'It is time for you to know.'

He put out one thin arm and drew Nefer close under his shawl. He seemed to be collecting his thoughts, and then at last he spoke.

'In my vision I saw a great tree growing on the banks of Mother Nile. It was a mighty tree and its blooms were blue as hyacinth and over it hung the double crown of the Upper and Lower Kingdoms. In its shade were all the multitudes of Egypt. The tree gave them all protection, and they prospered mightily and were content.'

'That was a good vision.' Eagerly Nefer translated it. 'The tree must have been Pharaoh, my father. The colour of the House of Tamose is blue, and my father wears the double crown. But then what did you see, Tata?'

'I saw a serpent in the muddy waters of the river, swimming towards where the tree stood. It was a great cobra. And it crawled from the waters of the Nile and climbed into the tree, twisting itself around the tree, supporting it and giving it strength.'

'That I do not understand,' Nefer whispered.

'Then the cobra reared up above the uppermost branches of the tree, struck down and buried its fangs in the trunk.'

'Sweet Horus.' Nefer shuddered. 'What did you see then, Tata?'

'I saw the tree wither. I saw the cobra still reared triumphantly on high, but now it wore on its evil brow the double crown. The tree began to throw out green shoots. As they appeared the serpent struck at them, and they, too, were poisoned. But one grew in secret beneath the surface of the earth, until it was strong. Then it burst out like a mighty vine and locked itself in conflict with the cobra. Although the cobra attacked it with all its strength and venom, still it survived.'

'What was the end of the conflict, Tata? Which of them triumphed? Which one wore the double crown at the end?'

'I did not see the conflict's end. It was obscured in the dust of war.'

Nefer was silent. Then he began to shake and Taita realised he was weeping. At last Nefer spoke, with a dreadful certainty. 'Pharaoh is dead. My father is dead. The poisoned tree was Pharaoh. It was the same message at the cave. The dead falcon was Pharaoh. My father is dead, killed by the cobra.'

Taita could not answer. All he could do was tighten his grip around Nefer's shoulders, and try to comfort him.

'And I am the green shoot of the tree,' Nefer went on. 'You saw this. You know that the cobra is waiting to destroy me as he did my father. That is why you would not let the soldiers take me back to Thebes. You know that the cobra waits for me there.'

'You are right, Nefer. We cannot return to Thebes until you are strong enough to defend yourself. We must fly from Egypt. There are lands and mighty kings to the east. It is my purpose to go to them.'

'But who is the cobra? Did you not see his face in the vision?'

'We know that he stands close to your father's throne, for in the vision he was entwined with the tree and gave it support.' He paused, and then went on, 'Naja is the name of the cobra.'

Nefer stared at him. 'Naja!' he whispered. 'Naja! Now I understand why we cannot return to Thebes.'

Despite his grief for his father, Nefer slept at last, but Taita roused him in the darkness before dawn. They mounted again and rode eastwards until the ground fell away behind them and Nefer smelt the salt of the sea on the wind.

'At the port of Seged we will find a ship to take us across to the land of the Hurrians,' Taita told him. 'King Sargon of Babylon is bound in treaty to your father against the Hyksos.'

Ahead of them the sun came up in a furnace glow, and when they topped the next rise they saw the sea below them. Taita turned to look back and stiffened as he made out not one but four separate plumes of yellow dust rising on the plain behind them.

'Hilto, again,' he exclaimed. 'Now he has thrown out a ring of chariots in an extended line to sweep for our tracks. He did not need a necromancer to tell him we would be heading east for the coast.'

Swiftly he looked in every direction for cover. Across the open plain he picked out an insignificant fold of ground that might offer concealment. 'Dismount!' he ordered Nefer. 'We must keep as low as possible and raise no dust.'

When they reached the hidden ground, Taita coaxed the horses to lie flat on their sides. Then he and Nefer lay beside them and watched the encircling columns of dust sweep across the plain.

'They won't be able to pick out our tracks on the stony ground, will they?' Nefer asked.

Taita grunted. He was watching the approach of the nearest chariot. In the dancing mirage it seemed insubstantial, wavering and distorted as an image seen through water. But it came on until they could make out the men on the footplate more clearly. Suddenly Taita muttered unhappily. 'They have a Nubian scout with them.' It was said that these scouts could follow the track left by a swallow flying through the air.

The tall black man was made even taller by the headdress of herons' feathers he wore. Five hundred cubits from where they lay concealed, the Nubian brought the chariot to a peremptory halt and jumped down. He had lost the tracks where they turned onto stony ground. Bent almost double, he circled out over the bare earth. After a few moments, the Nubian straightened with a fresh air of purpose, and gazed straight in their direction.

'He has found the twist in our tracks,' Nefer said, and they watched the chariot pull in behind the Nubian as he started towards them over the rocky ground.

The boy watched in trepidation as the chariot and its outrider came on steadily. The charioteer was standing high on the footplate and Nefer recognised him as Hilto.

When he finally saw Taita and Nefer, Hilto leapt out of the chariot and went down on one knee.

'Prince Nefer! We have searched for you these thirty days. Thank great Horus and Osiris, we have found you at last.' He cried out, in a voice pitched to giving commands on the battlefield, 'Pharaoh Tamose is dead! Hail, Pharaoh Nefer Seti. May you live for ever.'

Seti was the prince's divine name, given to him at birth but not used until this moment.

'Pharaoh! We have come to bear you to the Holy City.'

'What if I should choose not to go with you, Colonel Hilto?' Nefer asked.

Hilto looked distressed. 'With all love and loyalty, Pharaoh, it is the strictest order of the Regent of Egypt that you be brought to Thebes. I must obey that order, even at the risk of your displeasure.'

Nefer glanced sideways at Taita. 'What must I do?'

'We must go with them.'

THEY BEGAN THE RETURN to Thebes with an escort of fifty fighting chariots led by Hilto. Under strict orders the column rode first to the oasis of Boss. Fast horsemen had been sent ahead to Thebes and Lord Naja, the Regent of Egypt, had come out from the city to the oasis to meet the young Pharaoh Nefer Seti.

On the fifth day the squadron of chariots, dusty and battered from months in the wilderness, trotted into the oasis. Nefer stood between Hilto and Taita on the footplate of the leading chariot. His clothing was ragged and his thick locks were matted.

Hilto drove the chariot down the long alley formed by a full regiment of Phat Guards, who cheered Nefer spontaneously. They had loved his father, and now they loved him.

In the centre of the oasis there was an assembly of multicoloured tents. In front of the royal tent Lord Naja, surrounded by courtiers, nobles and priests, waited to receive the king. He was mighty in the power and grace of regency, glistening and beautiful in gold and precious stones, redolent of sweet unguents and fragrant lotions.

On his left hand stood Heseret, the princess of the royal House of Tamose. Her face was pearly white with make-up, eyes huge and dark with kohl, and her skirts were so heavy with pearls and gold thread that she stood as stiffly as a carved doll.

As Hilto brought the chariot to a halt in front of him, Lord Naja stepped forward and led Nefer by the hand to the dais of the council, carved from precious black woods and inlaid with mother-of-pearl. He placed him upon it, then went down on his knees and kissed Nefer's feet. 'As your regent I salute you, Pharaoh.'

He stood up and lifted Nefer to his feet, stripped away the torn kilt to reveal the pharaonic cartouche on the smooth skin of his inner thigh. Taita had tattooed the design, and it was a miniature masterpiece that would for ever endorse Nefer's claim to the double crown. Naja turned the boy slowly so that everyone in the audience could see it clearly.

'Hail, Pharaoh Seti, god and son of the gods. Behold thy sign. Look upon this mark, all the nations of the earth, and tremble. Bow down before the might of Pharaoh.'

A great shout went up from the soldiers and courtiers packed around the dais. 'Hail, Pharaoh! May he live for ever.'

Naja led the princess forward, and she knelt before her brother to take her oath of allegiance. Then, one by one, the mighty lords of Egypt came forward to take the loyal oath. The ceremony ended when Lord Naja clapped his hands. 'Pharaoh has come on a long journey. He must rest before leading the procession into the city.'

He took Nefer's hand and led him into the spacious royal tent where the master of the wardrobe, the perfumers and hairdressers, the keeper of the royal jewels, the valets, manicurists, masseurs and the maids of the bath were waiting to receive him.

Taita had determined to stay at the boy's side where he could protect him. He tried unobtrusively to include himself among this entourage, but almost immediately a sergeant-at-arms confronted him. 'Greetings, Lord Taita. The Regent of Egypt has sent for you.'

Lord Naja's tent was even larger and more luxuriously appointed than Pharaoh's. He sat on a throne decorated in gold and silver and the sandy floor was covered with woollen rugs, woven in wonderful colours. Incense burned in silver pots suspended on chains from the ridgepole of the tent, and there were open glass vases filled with perfume on the low table in front of the throne.

At the entrance to the tent, Taita knelt to make obeisance. There was a hum of speculation as he rose to his feet. The foreign ambassadors stared at him curiously, and the warriors and priests nodded and leaned close together as they told each other, 'It is the Magus, the holy Taita, adept of the Mazes.'

Lord Naja looked up from the papyrus he was scanning and smiled. He was truly a handsome man, with sculpted features and sensitive lips. His nose was straight and narrow, and his eyes were the colour of golden agate, lively and intelligent.

Swiftly Taita surveyed the ranks of men who now sat closest to the throne. Many familiar faces were missing, and many others had emerged from obscurity into the sunshine of the regent's goodwill. Not least of these was Asmor of the Phat Guards.

'Come forward, Lord Taita.' Naja's voice was pleasant and low. Taita moved towards the throne and the ranks of courtiers opened to let him pass. The regent smiled down at him. 'Know you that you stand high in our favour. You have given Prince Nefer invaluable instruction and training. 'Now that the prince has become Pharaoh Seti, he will stand in even greater need of your guiding hand.'

'May he live for ever,' Taita responded.

Lord Naja gestured. 'Take your seat here, in the shadow of my throne. Even I will have much need of your experience and wisdom when it comes to ordering the affairs of Pharaoh.'

'The royal regent does me more honour than I deserve.' Taita turned a gentle face to Lord Naja. It was prudent never to let your hidden enemy recognise your animosity. He took the seat that was offered him and listened as the business of the regency proceeded.

'We move on now to an important royal matter,' Lord Naja said. 'I come to the consideration of the well-being and status of Princess Heseret. I have consulted with the members of the council. All are agreed that, for her own good, I should take Princess Heseret in marriage. As my wife, she will come under my protection. The ceremony will take place on the day of the next full moon after the burial of Pharaoh Tamose, and the coronation of his heir, Prince Nefer Seti.'

Taita remained unmoving, his face blank, but he felt chilled to his bones. He knew that Lord Naja was intent on making himself a member of the royal House of Tamose, and thus the next in line of succession. There remained only twelve days of the required seventy for the royal embalming of the dead pharaoh. Immediately after the interment of Tamose, the coronation of his successor and the wedding of his surviving daughter would take place. Then the cobra would strike again. Taita felt the certainty of it. He was roused from his preoccupation when the regent declared the levee closed, and retired through the tent flap behind the throne. Taita rose with the others to leave the tent.

Colonel Asmor stepped forward to stop him with a smile and a courteous bow. 'Lord Naja asks you not to leave. He invites you to a private audience.'

There was no point refusing the summons, and so Taita allowed Asmor to lead him to the back of the tent and through to a smaller, single-roomed tent, a place of secret council. At a command from Asmor, the guards posted at the entrance stood aside and the colonel ushered Taita into the shaded interior.

Naja looked up from the bronze bowl in which he was washing his hands. 'You are welcome, Magus.' He waved to the pile of cushions in the centre of the rug-covered floor. While Taita seated himself, Naja nodded to Asmor, who went to take up position at the tent opening, his sickle sword drawn. There were only the three of them in the tent, and their conversation would not be overheard.

Naja had discarded his jewellery and insignia of office. He was affable and friendly, and indicated the tray of sweetmeats that stood between them. 'Please refresh yourself.'

Taita's instinct was to decline, but he knew that to refuse would advertise his hostility, and alert Naja to his deadly opposition. Instead, he inclined his head in thanks.

'You are a person of inestimable value,' Naja told him. 'You have faithfully served three pharaohs and all have relied on your advice without question.'

'You overestimate my worth, my lord Regent. I am an old man and feeble.'

Naja smiled. 'Old? Yes, you are old. I have heard it said that you are more than two hundred years old.' Taita inclined his head, neither confirming nor denying it. 'But feeble, no! All men know that your wisdom is boundless. Even the secrets of eternal life are yours.'

The flattery was blatant and Taita searched behind it for the hidden reason, tuned his mind to catch the other man's thoughts. They were fleeting but he captured one entire, and suddenly understood what Naja wanted from him. The secret of eternal life. The knowledge gave him power, and the way ahead opened before him like the gates of a captured city.

'My lord, two hundred years is not life eternal.' Taita spread his hands deprecatingly, and dropped his eyes.

'We will speak of these deep matters another time.' There was a triumphant light in Naja's yellow eyes. 'But now there is something else I would ask of you. It would be a way for you to prove that my good opinion of you is fully justified. Taita, beloved of kings and gods, I wish you to work the Mazes of Ammon Ra for me.'

He twists and turns like an eel, Taita thought. And I once believed him to be a dull clod of a soldier. He has been able to hide his ambition from all of us. Not only the double crown of Egypt and eternal life! He wishes also to have the future revealed to him, Taita marvelled. He nodded humbly and replied, 'My lord Naja, I have never worked the Mazes for anyone who was not a queen or a pharaoh, or one who was not destined to sit upon the throne of Egypt.'

'It may well be that one such person asks you now,' said Lord Naja, with deep significance in his tone.

Great Horus has delivered him to me. I have him in my hands, Taita thought, and said, 'I bow to the wishes of Pharaoh's regent.'

'Will you work the Mazes for me this very day?'

'No man should enter the Mazes lightly,' Taita demurred. 'It will take time to prepare for the journey into the future.'

'How long?' Naja's disappointment was evident.

Taita clasped his forehead in a pantomime of deep thought. Let him sniff the bait for a while, he thought. It will make him more eager to swallow the hook. At last he looked up. 'On the first day of the festival of the Bull of Apis.'

THE NEXT MORNING, when he emerged from the great tent for his ceremonial journey to Thebes, Pharaoh Seti was transformed. His dark curls had been shampooed and combed until they shone with russet highlights. On top of them he wore a circlet of gold depicting Nekhbet, the vulture goddess, and Naja, the cobra. On his chin was the false beard of kingship. His false fingernails were of beaten gold, and there were gold sandals on his feet. On his chest was one of the most precious of the crown jewels of Egypt: the pectoral medallion of Tamose, a jewelled portrait of the god Horus the falcon. He walked with a stately tread for one so young, carrying the scourge and the sceptre crossed over his heart, and Lord Naja walked a pace behind him, splendid with jewels and awesome with authority.

Next came the princess, with the golden feathers of the goddess Isis on her head, and from throat to ankles she was encased in a long dress, the linen so fine and transparent that the sunlight struck through it. Heseret's body was moulded into voluptuous curves, her breasts rosy-tipped through the diaphanous folds.

Pharaoh mounted the processional carriage and took his seat on the elevated throne. Lord Naja stood at his right hand, and the princess sat at his feet.

Companies of priests from the fifty temples of Thebes fell in ahead, strumming the lyre, beating the drum, sounding the horn, chanting praises and supplications to the gods.

Then Asmor's bodyguard took up their positions in the procession, and after them came Hilto's squadron of chariots, all freshly burnished and decked with pennants and flowers. The horses were curried until their hides glowed, and ribbons were plaited into their manes. The bullocks that followed in the traces of the royal carriage were all of unblemished white. Their widespread horns and even their hoofs were covered with gold leaf.

A thousand warriors of the Phat Guards fell in behind them and burst into the anthem of praise. The populace of Thebes had opened the main gates of the city in welcome and were lining the tops of the walls. From a mile outside it they had covered the dusty surface of the road with palm fronds, straw and flowers.

The procession passed through the gates, with the crowds dancing with joy, filling the narrow streets so that the pace of the royal carriage was that of a giant tortoise. It was late afternoon before they reached the docks at the riverside where the royal barge waited to ferry Pharaoh's party across to the Palace of Memnon. Once they had gone on board, two hundred rowers in massed ranks plied their paddles. When they reached the west bank another royal carriage bore Nefer through the crowds to the funerary temple of his father, Pharaoh Tamose. He rode up the causeway, lit on both sides by bonfires, and the uproar was deafening as Pharaoh dismounted and climbed the stairway into the Hall of Sorrow, that holy place where Tamose's mummy lay on its embalming slab of black diorite.

Lord Naja took up his position on the far side of the diorite slab, facing Nefer, and the high priest stood at the head of the dead king. When all was in readiness two priests drew aside the linen sheet that covered the corpse, and Nefer recoiled involuntarily as he looked down on his father.

For all the weeks after his death, while Nefer and Taita had been in the desert, the embalmers had been at work on the king's body. Now as desiccated as firewood, it had been bound up. The linen bandages were laid on it in an intricate design, as incantations to the gods were chanted by choirs of priests. Under them were placed precious talismans and amulets, and each layer was painted with resins that dried to a metallic hardness. Only the head was left uncovered, upon which four of the most skilful artists of the guild of embalmers, using wax and cosmetics, had restored the king's features to lifelike beauty.

They had replaced the eyes with perfect replicas of rock crystal and obsidian that seemed endowed with life and intelligence, so that now Nefer gazed into them with awe, expecting to see his father's pupils widen in recognition. The lips were shaped and rouged so that at any moment they might smile, and his painted skin looked silken and warm, as though bright blood still ran beneath it. His hair had been washed and set in the familiar dark ringlets that Nefer remembered so well.

The high priest came to Nefer's side and placed a golden spoon in his hand. Nefer had been coached in the ritual, but his hand trembled as he placed the spoon on his father's lips and recited, 'I open thy lips that thou might have the power of speech once more.' He touched his father's nose with the spoon. 'I open thy nostrils that thou might breathe once more.' He touched each eye. 'I open thine eyes that thou might behold the glory of the world to come.'

When at last it was done, the embalmers wrapped the head and painted it with aromatic resins. Then they laid a golden mask over the blind face, and once more it glowed with splendid life.

For the rest of that night Nefer stayed beside the golden sarcophagus, praying and burning incense, entreating the gods to take his father and seat him in the midst of the pantheon.

THAT NIGHT TAITA went out and prayed to Horus for guidance. At dawn he returned to the palace, and had barely time to bathe and change his raiment before he hurried to the royal bedchamber. At the door his way was barred by the two guards, who crossed their spears across the entrance.

Taita was astonished. This had never happened before. He glared at the sergeant of the guard, who dropped his eyes. 'I mean no offence, mighty Magus. It is on the specific orders of the commander of the bodyguard, Colonel Asmor. No person not approved by the regent is allowed in the royal presence.'

Taita strode down the terrace to where Naja was at breakfast with his particular favourites and toadies. 'My lord Naja, you are fully aware that I was appointed by Pharaoh's own father as his tutor and mentor. I was given the right of access at any time.'

'That was many years ago, good Magus,' Naja replied smoothly, as he accepted a peeled grape from a slave. 'Pharaoh Seti is a child no more. In future he looks to me, his regent, for guidance.' Naja stood up from the breakfast board. His bodyguard closed in around him so that Taita was forced to fall back.

The old man watched as Naja's entourage set off towards the council chamber, then turned aside and sat down on the coping of one of the fish pools to ponder this development.

Naja had isolated Nefer. He was a prisoner in his own palace.

Once again Taita considered the idea of flight from Egypt, to spirit Nefer away across the desert to the protection of a foreign power until he had grown strong enough to return to claim his birthright. However, he was certain that Naja not only barred the door to the royal quarters but that every escape route from Thebes and Egypt would have already been closed.

There seemed no easy solution, and, after an hour of deep thought, Taita rose to his feet. The guards at the door to the council chamber stood aside for him, and Taita went down the aisle and took his accustomed seat on the front bench.

Wearing the light crown of Upper Egypt, Nefer was seated on the dais beside his regent. The council was considering the latest reports from the northern front, where the Hyksosian King Apepi had recaptured Abnub after a siege that had lasted the previous three years. Taita found the council was bitterly divided in every consideration of the crisis, and he felt more strongly than ever that this war was a running abscess in Egypt's body. Exasperated, he rose quietly and left the council chamber. There was nothing further he could accomplish here, for they were still wrangling over who should be given command of the northern armies to replace the dead Pharaoh.

Next he went to the women's quarters of the palace. Because he was a eunuch he could pass through the gates, which were barred to other men. It was three days since the princess had learned that she was so soon to become a bride, and Taita knew he should have visited her before. She would be confused, sorely in need of his comfort and advice.

When he entered the courtyard, Heseret, who had been strumming her lyre, looked up at him with a sad little smile. 'Darling Taita, I am so glad you have come.'

'I am sorry to have kept you waiting, moon of all my nights.' She smiled faintly at the pet name. 'What service do you wish of me?'

'You must go to Lord Naja, and present him with my sincere apologies, but I cannot marry him.'

She was so much like her grandmother had been at the same age. Lostris, too, had saddled him with an impossible task. Heseret now turned her enormous green eyes on him. 'You see, I have already promised Meren that I will be his wife.'

Meren was a boon companion of Prince Nefer. Taita had noticed him looking at Heseret with calf's eyes, but had never suspected that she returned his feelings.

'Heseret, I have explained to you many times that you are not like other girls. You are a princess royal. Your marriage cannot be undertaken in the light fancy of youth. It is of political consequence.'

'You don't understand, Taita,' Heseret said softly. 'I love Meren, I have loved him since I was little. I want to marry *him*, not Lord Naja.'

'I cannot overrule the decree of the Regent of Egypt,' he tried to explain, but she shook her head and smiled at him.

'You are so wise, Taita. You will think of something. You always do,' she told him, and he felt as though his heart would break.

'LORD TAITA, I REFUSE to discuss your access to Pharaoh or my impending marriage to the royal princess. In both these matters my mind is set.' To emphasise that he had closed the subject, Naja returned his full attention to the scroll spread on the writing table in front of him. Enough time passed for a flock of wild geese to rise from the swampland on the east bank and pass over the palace gardens where they sat. At last Taita brought his eyes down from the sky, and rose to leave. As he bowed to the regent and began to back away, Naja looked up at him. 'I have not given you leave to go.'

'My lord, I thought you had no further need of me.'

'On the contrary, I have the most urgent need.' He glared at Taita and gestured for him to sit again. 'You are testing my good temper and favour. I know that you were wont to work the Mazes for Pharaoh Tamose whenever he called upon you to do so. Why do you procrastinate with me? As regent I will brook no further delay. I command you to work the Mazes of Ammon Ra on my behalf.'

Taita bowed his head. For weeks past he had been prepared for this ultimatum, and had delayed only because he was convinced that Lord Naja would make no move against Nefer until he had been given the sanction of the Mazes.

'The full of the moon is the most propitious period for the Mazes,' Taita told him. 'I have already made preparations with the priests at the temple of Osiris at Busiris. I will conduct the mystery in the inner sanctum of the temple. This holy place will magnify the force of our deliberations.' Taita's voice was heavy with arcane meaning. 'Only you and I will be present in the sanctuary. No other mortal must overhear what the gods have to tell you.'

Naja was an Osiris man, and Taita had known that he would be impressed by the place he had chosen.

'So let it be,' Naja agreed.

THE JOURNEY TO BUSIRIS in the royal barge took two days. They landed on the yellow beach under the walls of the temple, and the priests were waiting to welcome the regent with psalms and offerings of gum arabic and myrrh. Afterwards, at Taita's suggestion, they withdrew and left him to make his preparations for the evening. He would put on an impressive show for Lord Naja, but had no intention of subjecting himself to the harrowing ordeal of the authentic ritual.

After sunset the high priest entertained the regent at a banquet and Lord Naja consumed a flagon of rich and heady wine. Then, to the beat of gong and drum, the priests chanted an epic poem of the struggle between good and evil. Finally, as the silver beam of the full moon moved across the flags of the nave towards the closed door of the sanctuary, the high priest gave a signal and the other priests rose and moved out in procession, leaving Lord Naja and Taita alone.

When the chanting of the departing priests had dwindled into a heavy silence, Taita took the regent by the hand and led him down the nave to the sanctuary, which was lit by four braziers, one in each corner. There was a low stool in the centre of the tiled floor. Taita gestured for him to be seated, and placed a hand on his shoulder. 'No matter what you see and what you hear, do not move. Do not speak. As you value your life, do nothing. Say nothing.'

Taita left him sitting and, with stately tread, approached the gigantic statue of the god. He raised a golden chalice high and called on Osiris to bless the contents, then brought it back to Naja and urged him to drink. The honey-viscous liquid tasted of crushed almonds, rose petals and mushrooms. Taita made a mystical pass before Naja's face, and in the blink of an eye the Mazes of Ammon Ra filled his cupped hands. He invited Naja to cover them with his own hands, while he recited an invocation. 'Greatness in light and fire, furious in divine majesty, approach and harken to our pleas.'

Naja squirmed on his stool as the Mazes grew hot to the touch, and it was with relief that he passed them back to Taita. The old man carried them across the sanctuary and placed them at the feet of the statue of Osiris. The Magus knelt there, bowed over them. For a while there was no sound within the chamber. Then, abruptly, a terrible shriek rang out. Naja moaned and covered his head with his shawl. Suddenly the flames of the braziers flared as high as the roof, and turned from yellow to fierce shades of green and violet. Clouds of smoke boiled from them and filled the chamber. Naja choked and coughed. He felt as though he were suffocating, and his senses reeled.

Taita turned slowly to face him, and Naja shuddered in horror, for the Magus was transformed. His face glowed with green light and his eyes were blind orbs that flashed silver rays in the light of the braziers. He glided towards where Naja sat, and from his gaping mouth issued a terrible chorus of screams and moans, hisses and grunts, retching and insane laughter.

Lord Naja tried to rise, but the sounds and the smoke seemed to fill his skull, and blackness overwhelmed him. His legs gave way and he slumped forward off the stool onto the tiles in a dead faint.

WHEN THE REGENT of Egypt regained consciousness, the sun was high, sparkling on the waters of the river. He found himself lying on a silken mattress on the deck of the royal barge under its yellow awning. He looked around him blearily, and saw the sails of the escort galleys. The sunlight was dazzling, and he closed his eyes again. He had a consuming thirst, and there was a pounding in his skull as though all the demons of his vision were trapped within it.

Taita came to his side, raised his head and gave him a cool draught of some miraculous brew that soon eased the pounding in his head. When he had recovered enough to speak again, he whispered, 'Tell it all to me, Taita. I remember nothing. What did the Mazes reveal?' Clearly the effects of the essence of the magical mushroom, which Taita had administered to him the night before, had not yet worn off.

Before he would reply Taita sent all the crew and slaves out of earshot. Then he knelt beside the mattress. 'We have almost reached Sebennytos, my lord . We will be back at Thebes before nightfall.'

'What happened, Taita?' He shook Taita's arm. 'Tell it to me! Tell it all to me!'

'Do you not remember how the roof of the temple opened like the petals of the lotus, and we were borne upwards on the backs of two winged lions?'

Naja shook his head, and then nodded uncertainly. 'Yes, I remember the lions, but after that it is all shadowy and vague.'

'These mysteries numb the mind and dim eyes unaccustomed to them. Even I, an adept of the seventh and final degree, was amazed by what we endured,' Taita explained kindly. 'But do not despair, for the gods have commanded me to explain them to you.'

'Speak, good Magus, and spare no detail.'

'On the backs of the flying lions we crossed high above the dark ocean and over all the kingdoms of earth and heaven. We came at last to the citadel in which the gods dwell, and there it was that great Osiris rose up in all his terrible glory, lifted you off the winged lion and placed you beside him on the throne of fire and gold.'

'Was he not deifying me, Taita? Surely there can be no other meaning?'

'If there had been any doubt it was immediately dispelled, for Osiris took up the double crown of Upper and Lower Egypt, placed it upon your head and spoke "Hail, Brother Divine! Hail, Pharaoh who shall be."' Naja stared at Taita with glittering eyes as the old man went on, 'With the crown upon your brow, your holiness was manifest. I knelt before you and worshipped you.'

Naja's made no effort to hide his emotions. He was in transport. Taita seized the moment. 'Then Osiris spoke again: "In these wondrous things, your guide shall be the Magus Taita, for he is the Master of the Mazes. Follow his instruction faithfully."'

He watched Naja's reaction, but the regent seemed to accept this without resistance.

'What else, Taita? What more did the great god have to say to me?'

'Nothing more to you, my lord, but now he spoke directly to me. These are his exact words, each one branded in fire upon my heart. "Taita, Master of the Mazes, henceforth you have no other love, loyalty or duty. You are the servant of my divine brother, Naja. Your only concern is to help him fulfil his destiny. You will not cease until you see the double crown of Upper and Lower Egypt placed upon his head."'

'"No other loyalty or love",' Naja repeated softly. 'And did you then accept the charge that great Osiris placed upon you, Magus? Say fair and true, are you my man now, or would you deny the word of the great father?'

'How could I deny the great god?' Taita asked simply. He lowered his head and pressed his forehead to the planking of the deck. 'I accept the charge that the gods have placed upon me. I am your man, Divine Majesty. I belong to you.'

Naja raised him up and stared into his eyes, searching for any trace of deceit or guile. Taita looked back at him serenely. The wish is father to the deed, Taita thought. He will allow himself to believe, because he longs for it to be so.

He watched the doubts clear in those yellow eyes and Naja embraced him. 'I believe you. When I wear the double crown you will have rewards beyond your imagination.'

CHAPTER THREE

Over the days that followed, Naja kept Taita close to his side, and the old man used this new position of trust to change some of the regent's intentions. He slaughtered a sheep and examined its entrails. From these he determined that the god would sanction no marriage of Naja to the princess until at least the next inundation of the Nile waters or the flooding would certainly fail. The life of Egypt depended upon the inundations of the great river, so with this prophecy Taita delayed the danger to Nefer, and the agony of the princess.

Naja protested, but he found it impossible to resist Taita's predictions. He was made more amenable by the news from the northern war front. On Naja's orders, and against Taita's counsel, the Egyptians had launched a desperate counterattack to try to retake Abnub. They had failed, losing three hundred chariots and almost a regiment of foot in the fighting around the city. Now Apepi seemed poised to come storming on to Thebes. It was no time for a wedding.

'The only way in which you can stave off an annihilating defeat at the hands of Apepi is to negotiate a truce,' Taita advised the regent.

'This I believe also, Magus,' Naja agreed eagerly, excited by this unexpected support. He had tried without success to convince the individual members of the council to agree to a truce with the Hyksos, but none had supported him. Even the loyal Asmor had risked his wrath by vowing to fall on his own sword rather than surrender to Apepi.

Peace with the Hyksos was the cornerstone of Naja's vision of the two kingdoms reunited and a single pharaoh ruling both. Only a pharaoh who was part Egyptian and part Hyksosian could hope to achieve that, and he knew that this was what the gods had promised him through the Mazes.

He went on earnestly, 'I should have known that you, Taita, were the one person who would not let yourself be blinded by prejudice. After sixty years in the Nile valley, the Hyksos are becoming more Egyptian than Asian. Their savage blood has been softened and sweetened by ours. I know there are many among them who agree with these sentiments. It would take little for them to join us. Then we can bring peace and unity to the two kingdoms.'

The regent's response to his tentative suggestion was so enthusiastic that Taita was taken aback. Then the veils began to part, and he was reminded of a suspicion he had once heard expressed but had rejected.

'Who are these Hyksos sympathisers?' he asked. 'Are they highly placed? Close to Apepi?'

'Noblemen, indeed. One sits on Apepi's war council.'

It was enough for Taita. That faint rumour of Hyksosian connections in Naja's background must have had substance, and if it was true the rest fell neatly into place. 'Would it be possible to meet these noblemen and speak to them?' Taita asked carefully.

'Yes,' Naja confirmed. 'We could reach them within days.'

For Taita the implications of that simple statement were enormous. The Regent of Egypt had covert allies in the ranks of the traditional enemy. This was the loving friend who was at Pharaoh's side when he was struck down, the only witness to Pharaoh's death. This creature of boundless ambition and cruel purpose admitted to being an intimate of Hyksosian noblemen, and it was a Hyksosian arrow that killed Pharaoh. How deep did the plot run?

He let nothing of this show on his face, but nodded thoughtfully. 'First we must determine if this treaty is feasible. Apepi might believe his military position is unassailable and might decide to prosecute this war to the bitter end.'

'I do not think that will happen. One of our allies on the other side is a man called Trok, paramount chief of the Clan of the Leopards. You must go to him secretly, Taita. I will give you a talisman that will prove you come from me. You are the best emissary for our cause.'

Taita sat a while longer in thought. He tried to see if he could wring any further advantage to Nefer and the princess from the situation, but at this stage he could find none. Whatever happened, Nefer would still be in mortal danger.

'It is my duty, a duty placed upon me by the gods, to help you in every way. I will undertake this mission,' Taita said. 'What is the safest way for me to pass through the Hyksosian lines?'

Naja had foreseen this query. 'You must use the old chariot road through the dunes and down the wadi at El Wadun. My friends on the other side keep the road under surveillance. I will send my own lance-bearer and a squadron of the Blues to take you through,' he promised. 'But the road is long and hard. You must leave at once. Every day, every hour might make the difference.'

TAITA HAD DRIVEN the chariot all the way from the ruined city of Gallala with only four halts. The troopers in the nine vehicles that followed him were in awe of the Magus's reputation. They knew him as the first Egyptian ever to build a chariot and harness a team to it. The old man's stamina was amazing, and his concentration never wavered. His gentle but firm hands on the reins never tired, as hour after hour he coaxed the horses into giving their best. He had impressed every man in the squadron, not least the one riding beside him in the cockpit.

Gil was Naja's lance-bearer. He had a rugged, sun-darkened face and was lightly built, which was desirable for a charioteer, but he possessed also a wiry strength and cheerful disposition.

With the moon waxing and the weather at its hottest they had driven through the cool of the night. Now, in the dawn, they halted to rest. When he had watered the horses, Gil came to where Taita sat on a boulder overlooking Hyksosian territory and handed him a ceramic water jug. Taita took a long swig. It was the first drink he had taken since their last stop at midnight.

The old devil-rouser is tough as a Bedouin raider, Gil thought, and squatted at a respectful distance to await any order.

'Where is the place at which Pharaoh was struck down?' Taita asked at last.

The two men had spoken briefly once or twice since leaving Thebes, but until now there had not been the opportunity for any long conversation.

Gil shaded his eyes against the glare of the rising sun and pointed down the wadi. 'There, my lord, near that distant line of hills.'

'Are any other men here who were with you on that day?'

'Only Samos, but he was waiting with the chariots in the wadi when we were attacked,' Gil replied.

'I want you to take me over the battleground,' Taita told him.

Gil shrugged. 'It was no battle, just a skirmish. First Pharaoh dismounted and we went forward with Lord Naja to scout the camp of Apepi. Then I and the rest of the men were ordered to wait, while Lord Naja went forward beyond an outcrop of boulders.'

'Where was Pharaoh? Did he go forward with Naja?'

'No. Not at first. The king waited with us. Lord Naja heard something up ahead, went to scout and disappeared from our view.'

'I do not understand. At what point were you attacked?'

'We waited. I could see that Pharaoh was becoming impatient.

After a while Lord Naja whistled from beyond the rocks. Pharaoh sprang up. "Come on, lads!" he told us, and went up the path.'

'Did you see what happened next?'

'Pharaoh disappeared behind the boulders. Then there was shouting and the sound of fighting. I ran forward but Lord Naja was shouting that Pharaoh had been struck down, and they dragged the king back to where I was standing. I think he was dead even then.'

'How close were the Hyksos? How many? Were they cavalry or infantry? Did you recognise their regiments?' Taita demanded.

For the first time Gil looked uncertain 'My lord, I did not actually set eyes on the enemy. You see, they were behind the rocks.'

Taita frowned at him. 'Did any of the others, apart from Naja, see the enemy?'

'I do not know, honourable Magus. You see, Lord Naja ordered us back down to the chariots. We could see that the king was mortally wounded, probably already dead. We had all lost heart.'

'You must have discussed it later with your companions. Did any of them tell you he had engaged an enemy? That he had hit one of the Hyksos with arrow or lance?'

Gil shook his head. 'I don't remember. No, I don't think so.'

'Apart from the king, were any others wounded?'

'None.'

'Why did you not tell this to the council? Why did you not tell them that you had not seen an enemy?' Taita was angry now.

'Lord Naja told us to answer the questions simply and not to waste the council's time with idle boasting.' Gil hunched his shoulders with embarrassment. 'I suppose none of us wanted to admit that we ran without a fight.'

'Do not feel ashamed, Gil. You carried out your orders,' Taita told him, in a kinder tone. Gil's evidence had been coherent and credible, and he had spoken out like the honest, simple soldier he was. When the Hyksosian arrow taken from the Pharaoh's body by the surgeons was shown to him, he had recognised it as the one that had struck down Pharaoh Tamose. The shaft had been snapped in two. Lord Naja had broken it off to ease the pain of the wound.

Taita, too, had examined the broken, blood-caked arrow, fletched in green and red, that had killed Pharaoh, and had peered closely at the signet etched into the painted shaft. It was a stylised head of a leopard, holding the hieratic letter T in its jaws. Now Taita was on his way to see one of Naja's Hyksos allies, a man named Trok.

THEY WAITED HIDDEN in the wadi until after nightfall. Then, the wheel hubs freshly greased with mutton fat to stop them squealing, the horses' hoofs covered with leather boots, they went on deep into Hyksosian territory, with Gil guiding them.

By now they were down on the alluvial plain of the Nile. Twice they had to turn off the road and wait while parties of armed men, anonymous in the darkness, rode past their hiding place. After midnight they came to an abandoned temple of some forgotten god that had been hollowed out of the side of a low clay hill. The cave was large enough to shelter the entire squadron, vehicles, horses and men. It was immediately apparent that it had been used before for this purpose. Lamps and an oil amphora were hidden behind the ruined altar, and bales of horse fodder were stacked in the sanctum.

As soon as they had removed the horses' harnesses and fed them, the troopers ate their own meal and then settled down on mattresses of dried straw. In the meantime Gil had changed his uniform for the nondescript attire of a peasant. 'I cannot use a horse,' he explained to Taita. 'It would attract too much interest. On foot it will take me half a day to reach the camp at Bubasti. Do not expect me back before tomorrow evening.' He slipped out of the cave and disappeared into the night.

Honest Gil is not such a simple, bluff soldier as he seems, Taita thought, as he settled down to wait for Lord Naja's allies to answer the message that Gil was taking to them.

They came in the short summer dusk, twenty armed men riding hard, Gil leading them on a borrowed steed. They swept up to the entrance of the temple, where they dismounted with a clatter of weapons. The leader was a tall man, wide across the shoulders with a heavy beetling brow and a fleshy hooked nose.

'You are the warlock. Yes?' he said, in a thick accent.

Taita did not think it opportune to let them know he spoke Hyksos, so he replied modestly in Egyptian. 'My name is Taita, a servant of the great god Horus. I call his blessing down upon you. I see you are a man of might, but I do not know your name.'

'My name is Trok, commander of the north in the army of King Apepi. You have a token for me, Warlock?'

Taita showed him a broken shard of blue glazed porcelain, the upper half of a tiny votive statue of the god Seueth.

Trok examined it briefly, then took another fragment of porcelain from the pouch on his sword-belt and fitted the two pieces together.

The broken edges matched perfectly, and he grunted with satisfaction. 'Come with me, Warlock.'

Trok strode out into the gathering night with Taita beside him. They climbed the hill and squatted down facing each other. Trok kept his scabbard between his knees and his hand on the hilt of his heavy sickle sword. From habit more than distrust, Taita thought.

'You bring me news of the south,' Trok said.

'My lord, you have heard of the death of Pharaoh Tamose?'

'We know of the death of the Theban pretender.' Trok was careful not to acknowledge the authority of the Egyptian Pharaoh. To the Hyksos, the only ruler of the two kingdoms was Apepi. 'We heard also that a child now pretends to the throne of Upper Egypt.'

'Pharaoh Nefer Seti is only fourteen years of age,' Taita confirmed, equally careful to insist on the title of Pharaoh when he spoke of him. 'Until he attains his majority, Lord Naja acts as his regent.'

Trok leaned forward. 'So, then, you come to us with the authority of the Regent of the South. What message do you bring from Naja?'

'Lord Naja wants me to carry his proposal directly to Apepi.'

Trok took immediate umbrage at this. 'Naja is my cousin,' he said coldly. 'He would wish me to hear every word he has sent.'

Taita showed no surprise, although it was a grave indiscretion on Trok's part. His suspicions as to the regent's connections were confirmed. 'Yes, my lord, this much I know. However, I can tell you nothing more.'

'As you wish, Warlock.' Trok stood up angrily. 'King Apepi is at Bubasti. We will go there immediately.'

In silence they returned to the subterranean temple, where Taita called Gil and the sergeant of the bodyguard to him. 'You have done your work well,' he told them, 'but now you must return to Thebes as secretly as you have come. I will remain here. When you report to the regent tell him that I am on my way to meet Apepi.'

By the dim light of the oil lamps the horses were harnessed to the chariots, and within a short time they were ready to leave. Gil saluted respectfully. 'It has been a great honour to ride with you, my lord.'

Taita embraced him. 'Go well, young Gil. I cast your horoscope last night. You will have a long life, and attain much distinction.'

By this time Lord Trok's troop was also mounted and ready to leave. They gave Taita the horse on which Gil had returned to the temple, then clattered out of the cave and turned west, in the opposite direction to that taken by Gil's column of chariots.

With Taita in the centre of the party, they rode on through the night, heading west towards the main enemy base. As they came closer to the river, Taita saw the fires of the Hyksosian troops encamped around Bubasti. It was a field of flickering light that stretched many miles in both directions along the river bank, a huge agglomeration of men and animals.

There was nothing on earth like the smell of an army encamped. It was a mixture of odours: manure and smoke, leather and mouldy grain, unwashed men, cooking food and fermenting beer, unburied rubbish, and the ammoniacal reek of the latrine pits.

Underlying this stifling blend Taita picked out another sickly taint. He thought he recognised it, but it was only when one of the sufferers staggered in front of his horse, forcing him to rein in sharply, that he saw the rose-coloured blotches on the pale face and he was certain. He knew now why Apepi had failed so far to follow up his victory at Abnub, why he had not yet sent his chariots tearing southwards towards Thebes where the Egyptian army was at his mercy. The plague had struck his troops.

They passed the first of the burial carts, laden with corpses, and the men around Taita used their cloaks to cover their mouths and noses against the stink and the evil humours.

Closer to Bubasti the encampments became more numerous, tents, huts and hovels crowding right up to the walls that surrounded the garrison town. The more fortunate among the plague victims lay under tattered roofs of palm fronds, scant protection from the hot morning sunlight. Others lay out in the trampled mud of the fields, abandoned to thirst and the elements, the dead mixed with the dying.

Although his instincts were those of a healer, Taita would do nothing to succour them. They were condemned by their own multitudes, for what could one man do to help so many?

They entered the fortress and found that conditions were not much better within its walls. Plague victims lay where they had been struck down, and rats and pariah dogs gnawed at their corpses.

Apepi's headquarters was the principal building in Bubasti, a massive mud-brick and thatch palace in the centre of the town. Grooms took their horses at the gates, and Lord Trok led Taita through courtyards and dark shuttered halls to Apepi's private quarters. The walls were hung with magnificent carpets and the furniture was of precious wood, ivory and mother-of-pearl, much of it plundered from the palaces and temples of Egypt.

Trok ushered Taita into a luxuriously furnished antechamber, and left him there. It was a long wait. A sunbeam through the single high window moved sedately along the wall. At intervals Taita heard the distant sound of weeping. Finally there came the tramp of heavy foot-steps down the passage outside, and the curtains over the doorway were thrown open. A burly man stood in the doorway. He wore a crimson linen kilt belted with a gold chain, there were heavy sandals on his feet and greaves of polished leather covered his shins. His beard and hair were in disarray. His dark eyes were wild and distracted.

'You are Taita, the physician,' he said.

Taita knew him well: to him Apepi was the invader, the bloody barbarian, mortal enemy of his country. It took all his self-control to keep his voice calm as he replied, 'I am Taita.'

'I have heard of your skills,' said Apepi. 'I have need of them now. Come with me.'

Taita slung his saddlebag over his shoulder and followed him out into the cloister. Ahead the sound of weeping became louder, until Apepi threw aside the heavy curtains that covered another doorway and took Taita's arm to push him through.

Dominating the crowded chamber was a large contingent of priests from the temple of Isis in Avaris, chanting over the brazier in one corner and shaking sistrums—percussion instruments of rods that rattled in metal frames. Twenty others, most of them women, were kneeling on the floor, wailing and keening. Only one was making any attempt to nurse the boy who lay on the couch. She seemed not much older than her patient, probably thirteen or fourteen, a strik-ing-looking girl with a determined, intelligent face, and she was sponging him down with perfumed water from a copper bowl.

Taita switched his attention to the boy. His naked body was also well formed, but wasted by disease. His skin was blotched with the plague and dewed with perspiration. On his chest were the wounds where he had been bled by the priests of Isis. Taita saw that he was in an advanced stage of the disease.

'This is Khyan, my youngest son,' Apepi said. 'The plague will take him, unless you can save him, Magus.'

Khyan groaned and rolled onto his side. At once the healers renewed their chants, and the high priest took up a knife and came towards the bed.

Taita stepped forward, barring the man's way. 'Get out!' he said softly. 'You and your butchers have done enough damage here.'

'I must bleed the fever out of his body,' the man protested.

'Out!' Taita repeated grimly, then to the others who crossed the chamber, 'Out, all of you.'

Eventually the chamber was deserted except for Apepi and the girl at the sickbed. 'Who are you?' he demanded.

'I am Mintaka. This is my brother.' She laid her hand protectively on the boy's sweat-damp curls. 'I will not leave him.'

'Good,' said Taita briskly, 'Then you can be of use to me. When did the boy last drink?'

'Not since this morning.'

'Can't those quacks see that he is dying of thirst as much as of the disease? He has sweated and voided most of the water from his body.' Taita picked up a copper jug from beside the bed. 'Go to the kitchens and fetch water. Make sure it is clean. Fill it from the well, not with river water. Hurry, girl.'

She fled, and returned almost immediately with a brimming jug of clean water. Taita opened his bag, prepared a potion of herbs, and heated it on the brazier. When it had brewed, he showed her how to position her brother's head and to stroke his throat as he dribbled the water into his mouth. Soon Khyan was swallowing freely.

'What can I do to help you?' the king asked.

'My lord, there is nothing for you here. You are better at destroying than at healing.' Taita dismissed him without looking up from his patient. There was a long silence, then the tramp of Apepi's bronze-studded sandals as he left the chamber.

Mintaka was quick and willing. She forced her brother to drink while Taita brewed up another cup of medicine on the brazier. Between them they were able to get this down his throat without losing a drop. She helped smear a soothing ointment on his chest. Then they wrapped Khyan in linen sheets and soaked them with well water to cool his burning body. By next morning the fever had broken and Khyan was resting more comfortably.

'Look, my lord,' Mintaka exclaimed, stroking her brother's cheek, 'the blotches are fading, and his skin feels cooler.'

'You have the healing touch of a nymph of paradise,' Taita told her, 'but do not forget the water jug. It is empty.'

She raced away to the kitchens, and came back with a brimming jug. While she gave it to him, Taita studied her face. In the Hyksosian way, it was a little too broad, and her cheekbones too prominent. Her mouth was large, her lips full, her nose strongly bridged. Not one of these features was perfect in itself, but each was finely balanced with, and matched to, all the others. Hers was a different kind of beauty, he thought, but beauty nonetheless.

By that evening Khyan was able to sit up with a little help from his sister, and to drink from the soup bowl she held to his lips. Two days later his rash had disappeared.

Three or four times a day Apepi visited the chamber. On the fifth day Khyan tottered from the couch and tried to prostrate himself before the king, but Apepi stopped him and lifted him back onto the pillows. Even though his feelings for the boy were clear, the king had little to say and left again almost immediately, but in the doorway he looked back at Taita and ordered him to follow with a curt inclination of his head.

THEY STOOD ALONE on the summit of the highest tower of the palace. From here they had a view upriver over the captured citadel of Abnub, which lay ten miles upstream. Thebes was less than a hundred miles beyond that.

Apepi had ordered the sentries to go down and leave them alone in this lofty place, so that they would not be spied upon or overheard. He stood staring out over the great grey river towards the south.

'At least something they say of you is true, Magus.' Apepi broke the long silence. 'You are a physician of great skill.' He looked down over the encampments of his army.

'My lord,' Taita said softly, 'Pharaoh will have reinforced and regrouped his forces before the plague burns itself out and your men are ready to fight again.'

Apepi shook himself with annoyance, like a lion shaking off flies. 'Nefer Seti is a child. I have defeated him once, I will do it again.'

'What is more crucial to you, there is no plague in his army. Your spies will have told you that Pharaoh has five more legions at Aswan, and another two at Asyut. They are already on the river coming north with the current. They will be here before the new moon.'

Apepi growled softly, but made no response.

Taita went on relentlessly. 'Sixty years of war have bled both kingdoms white. Would you pass on the legacy of bloodshed? Is that what your sons will inherit from you?'

Apepi rounded on him, scowling, 'Do not press me too hard, old man.' After an interval long enough to express his disapproval, Apepi spoke again. 'How long will it take you to arrange a parley with this so-called Regent of the Upper Kingdom, this Naja?'

'If you give me safe conduct through your lines, and a fast galley to carry me, I can be in Thebes in three days. The return with the current will be even swifter.'

'I will send Trok with you to see you safely through. Tell Naja I will meet him at the temple of Hathor on the west bank at Perra beyond Abnub. But tell him not to expect many concessions. I am the victor, and he the vanquished. Go now.'

Taita stood his ground. 'Pharaoh Nefer Seti is almost of an age with your daughter, Mintaka,' he said stubbornly. 'You might wish to bring her with you to Perra.'

'To what purpose?' Apepi stared at him suspiciously.

'An alliance between your dynasty and that of the Tamosian pharaohs might seal a lasting peace in the two kingdoms.'

Apepi stroked his beard to hide his smile. 'You intrigue as cunningly as you mix a potion, Warlock. Now, get you gone before you irk me past forbearance.'

THE TEMPLE OF HATHOR had been excavated out of the rocky hillside above the river hundreds of years previously. The priestesses were a rich, influential sisterhood who had survived and even prospered during the long civil wars between the kingdoms.

Dressed in their yellow robes they were gathered in the courtyard of the temple, between the two massive statues of the goddess. They chanted and rattled the sistrum as the suite of Pharaoh Nefer Seti filed into the courtyard from the eastern wing, while King Apepi's courtiers entered through the western colonnade. Both parties had agreed to eschew the double crown. Apepi wore the red crown of Lower Egypt, while Nefer Seti confined himself to the white crown of Upper Egypt.

The entourages of both rulers packed the spacious courtyard, their ranks facing each other, unsmiling and grim. Only a few paces separated them physically, but the bitterness of sixty years' strife formed a mighty barrier between them.

The hostile silence was shattered by a rolling fanfare of rams' horns and the thunder of bronze gongs. This was the signal for the royal parties to emerge from the two wings of the temple.

Lord Naja and Pharaoh Nefer Seti paced out solemnly and took their places on the high-backed thrones, while the Hyksosian royal family emerged from the opposing wing of the temple. Apepi led them, an impressive, warlike figure in full battle armour. He glared across the courtyard at the boy pharaoh. Eight of his sons followed him—all save Khyan, who had not recovered sufficiently from the plague to make the journey upriver—and his daughter.

None of the Egyptians had laid eyes on Mintaka before, and there was a subdued rustle and murmur through their ranks. They had been unprepared for her beauty. The myth was that all Hyksosian women were as ugly as their menfolk.

Pharaoh Nefer Seti leaned forward slightly, and Taita was so familiar with the boy, so attuned to his mind, that he could read his thoughts with ease. He sensed that Nefer was in a ferment of elation and excitement, and he felt smug at what he had achieved with so little effort. It would have complicated all his plans if Nefer had taken a dislike to the Hyksosian girl.

Lord Naja, the Regent of Upper Egypt, greeted Apepi in measured tones, diplomatically referring to him as King of the Hyksos but avoiding any reference to his claims to Egyptian territory. Mintaka stared at him with fascination. He was such a splendid sight, so different from her own father. He shone with gold and precious stones, and his linen was dazzling in its purity. She could smell his perfume across the distance that separated them. His face was a mask of make-up, his skin almost luminous and his eyes outlined and enhanced with kohl. Yet she thought that his was the beauty of a snake or a poisonous insect. She shivered and turned to the figure on the throne beside the regent.

Pharaoh Nefer Seti was staring at her with such intensity that she caught her breath. His eyes were so green—that was the first thing that struck her. She wanted to look away but could not. Instead she started to blush. Then, suddenly, Pharaoh gave her a warm and conspiratorial smile. Instantly, his face was boyish and appealing, and unaccountably her breath came faster. She dropped her eyes and looked at her hands in her lap, twisting her fingers together until she realised that she was fidgeting and stopped herself.

In the ranks opposite, Taita missed not a single nuance of the surreptitious exchanges between Nefer and Mintaka. He saw more than that. Lord Trok, Naja's cousin, was standing close behind Apepi's throne, his arms folded over his chest. Over one shoulder was slung a heavy bow, over the other an arrow quiver covered with gold leaf. Trok was watching the Hyksosian princess with a dark, brooding gaze. Taita could sense his anger and jealousy. He had not foreseen this. Is Trok's interest in Mintaka romantic or political? he wondered. Does he lust for her, or see her merely as a staircase to power? In either case it is dangerous.

The speeches of greeting were coming to an end and nothing of significance had been said; negotiation of the truce would begin in secret session the next day. Both sides were rising from their thrones and exchanging salutations, and the gongs began to beat and the rams' horns to sound again as they withdrew.

Lord Trok was the last of the Hyksosians to march out between the granite pillars of the gateway. As he did so, the arrows in his quiver rattled softly, and their coloured fletchings caught Taita's eye. The feathers were red and green, and, as he gazed after Trok, something evil stirred in Taita's memory.

Taita returned to the stone cell in the temple annexe that had been allocated to him for the duration of the peace conference. His pleasure at what had transpired between Mintaka and Nefer was forgotten as he considered Trok's relationship to the Hyksosian princess, and the complications that might ensue.

Even during their long ride together, Trok had kept his war quiver firmly stoppered and it had not been possible for Taita to compare one of the arrows it contained to the one found in Pharaoh's body. How many other Hyksosian officers had red and green fletchings he could only guess, but it was probably a great number, though each would have its owner's unique signet. The only way to connect Trok to the death of Pharaoh Tamose, and through him to implicate his cousin Naja, was to study one of his arrows. But how to do this without arousing Trok's suspicions?

His train of thought was interrupted. There were voices in the passage outside the door of his cell. One was young and clear, and he recognised it at once. The others were gruff.

'Lord Asmor has given specific orders—'

'Am I not Pharaoh? Are you not bound to obey me? I wish to visit the Magus. Stand aside.' Nefer's voice was strong and commanding. The uncertain timbre of puberty was gone.

The young falcon is spreading his wings, Taita thought.

Nefer jerked aside the curtain that covered the doorway, and stepped through. Two armed bodyguards followed him helplessly. Nefer ignored them and faced Taita with his hands on his hips.

'Taita, I am much displeased with you,' Nefer said. 'You have been avoiding me. Whenever I send for you they tell me that you are gone on a secret mission to the Hyksos. Then suddenly you pop up from nowhere, but still you ignore me. You did not even look in my direction during the ceremony. Where have you been?'

'Majesty, there are long ears about.' Taita glanced at the guards.

Immediately Nefer turned upon them wrathfully. 'I have ordered you more than once to be gone. Go this instant.'

They withdrew unhappily. Nefer soon forgot his anger and was grinning delightedly.

'Where have you been, Tata? I have missed you so.'

'I will tell you everything,' Taita assured him, and rapidly, in simple outline, he told Nefer what had happened to him since their last meeting. He explained the relationship between Naja and Trok, and described what he had learned from the lance-bearer, Gil. 'Now you can appreciate the danger you are in,' Taita told Nefer. 'I am certain that Naja had much to do with Pharaoh's murder, and the closer we come to the proof of it, the greater that danger becomes.'

'One day I will avenge my father.' Nefer vowed.

'And I will help you do it,' Taita promised, 'but now we must protect you from Naja's malice.'

'How do you plan to do that, Tata? Can we escape from Egypt as we planned before?'

'No.' Taita shook his head. 'Naja has us too securely imprisoned here. If we tried to run for the frontier again we would have a thousand chariots hot behind us.'

'What can we do, then? You are in danger also.'

'No. I have convinced Naja that he cannot succeed without my help.' He described the false divination ceremony and how Naja believed that Taita could share with him the secret of eternal life.

Nefer grinned at the Magus's cunning. 'So what do you plan?'

'Naja sent me to Apepi to arrange this peace conference.'

'Yes, they told me that when I demanded to see you.'

'Well, once Apepi had agreed to the meeting with Naja, I was able to convince him that they should seal the treaty by a marriage between you and Apepi's daughter. Once you are under the protection of the Hyksosian king, Naja's knife will be blunted.'

'Apepi is going to give me his daughter as a wife?' Nefer stared at him in wonder. 'The one I saw at the ceremony this morning?'

'Yes.' Taita agreed. 'Mintaka is her name.'

'I know her name,' Nefer assured him vehemently. 'She is the most beautiful . . .' Seeing the expression on Taita's face, he subsided. 'I mean, she is quite pleasing.' He grinned ruefully. 'When may I speak to her? She does speak Egyptian, doesn't she?'

'She speaks it as well as you do,' Taita assured him.

'Then when can I meet her? You can arrange it for me.'

Taita had anticipated this request. 'You could invite the princess and her suite to a hunt here in the swamps tomorrow at dawn, and perhaps a picnic afterwards.'

'I will send Asmor to invite her this very afternoon,' Nefer decided, but Taita shook his head.

'He would go to the regent first, and Naja would immediately see the danger. Once he was alerted he would do everything in his power to prevent you coming together.'

'What shall we do, then?' Nefer looked agitated.

'I will go to her myself,' Taita promised, and he did, that same day.

THE DAWN SKY the next morning was the glowing shade of a sword blade fresh from the coals of the forge. In this time before the sunrise there was no breath of air, no sound to break the stillness.

Two hunting skiffs were moored in a small lagoon, hard against the reeds that surrounded the open water. Less than fifty cubits separated them. The royal huntsmen had bent tall papyrus stems to form a screening roof over the hunters.

The surface of the lagoon was still and unruffled. It was just light enough for Nefer to make out the graceful form of Mintaka in the other boat. She had her bow across her lap, and sat as motionless as a statue. Any other girl he could think of, particularly his own sister Heseret, would have been hopping around like a canary on a perch.

Out in the swamp a heron boomed. As though this was a signal, the air was filled suddenly with the sound of wings. Nefer tore his eyes off the dainty figure in the boat across the water, and reached for his throwing sticks, determined to impress Mintaka with his hunting skills.

The first flight of glossy black and white ducks came sweeping in low out of the dawn. They turned in a wide circle then started to drop and line up on the open water. They set their wings and streamed in, losing height swiftly, passing directly over Nefer's skiff. Pharaoh judged his moment neatly, with the stick cocked and ready to throw. He waited for the lead bird to flare out and then let fly. The duck saw the missile coming and dropped a wing to avoid it.

Lost bird, Nefer thought bitterly, and before he could throw the second stick, the flight of ducks had angled across the lagoon, directly towards Mintaka's boat. They were still keeping low, going very fast, their blade-shaped wings whistling through the air.

Nefer had almost discounted the hunter in the other boat—at that height and speed the targets were too difficult for all but the most expert archer—but in quick succession two arrows rose to meet the straggle of birds. The sound of the double impact carried clearly across the lagoon. Then two ducks were falling, killed cleanly in the air at the same time. They plopped onto the water and floated there, motionless. The slave-boy retrievers picked them up easily and swam back to Mintaka's skiff, carrying the carcasses gripped in their teeth.

'Two lucky arrows,' Nefer said.

In the bows of the skiff, Taita added, 'Two unlucky ducks.'

Now the sky was filled with birds, which rose in dark clouds as the first rays of the sun struck the waters. They squawked and honked and quacked and bleated and wailed. Mintaka's light bow was well suited to the task. It was quick to align and draw without taxing her strength unduly. She was firing sharp metal heads especially forged for her by Grippa, the famous armourer. The needle-points drove through the dense plumage and went straight to the bone. She had realised, without a word being exchanged, that Nefer intended to make a contest of the hunt, and she was proving that her competitive instincts were every bit as fierce as his.

Nefer had been badly rattled by his first failure and by Mintaka's unexpected skill. Many of the birds he brought down were only stunned, and eluded his slave boys by diving under the surface and swimming into the thick papyrus beds. The number of dead birds piled on the floorboards of the skiff grew pitifully slowly. In desperation Nefer discarded his sticks and snatched up his heavy bow, but it was too late. His right arm was exhausted by his efforts with the sticks, and his draw was laboured.

Taita watched Nefer flounder ever deeper into the trap he had set for himself. A little humiliation will do him no real harm, he told himself. For once his sympathy was not with the boy, and he smiled secretly as he watched Nefer miss again and Mintaka take down two birds from the same flight as they passed over her head.

However, he felt pity for his king when one of Mintaka's slaves swam across the lagoon, and hung onto the side of Nefer's skiff. 'Her Royal Highness Princess Mintaka's boat begins to sink under the weight of her bag. Now she is hungry for her breakfast.'

An untimely sally! Taita thought, as Nefer scowled furiously at this impertinence. It was time for him to intervene. 'Pharaoh apologises for his thoughtlessness, but he was enjoying the sport so much that he forgot the passage of time. Please tell your mistress that we shall all go in to breakfast immediately.'

Nefer glowered at him, but put up his bow and made no effort to revoke Taita's decision. The two boats paddled back towards the island in close formation. Not a word was said by the crew of either skiff, but everyone was conscious of the results of the morning's hunt.

'Your majesty,' Mintaka called across to Nefer, 'I must thank you for a truly diverting morning. I cannot remember when last I enjoyed myself so much.'

'You are too kind.' Nefer made a regal gesture of dismissal, turned half away from her, and stared broodingly out at the horizon. First love is such unmitigated joy, Taita thought with sympathetic irony.

They came in to the landing on the island. The boatmen jumped over the side into the knee-deep ooze and held the first skiff steady while the slaves handed the princess and her maids across the gap onto the firm, dry ground at the top of the bank.

As soon as they were safely ashore the royal skiff came in and the slaves handed Nefer across to join Mintaka on the high bank. He led her to a giant kigelia tree under whose spreading branches a breakfast feast was laid out in the shade. At first Nefer was restrained and cool, but soon his natural high spirits reasserted themselves, and he joined in the banter and the chatter.

Mintaka loved to riddle and she challenged him to an exchange. She made it more difficult for Nefer by couching her clues in the Hyksosian language. 'I have one eye and a sharp nose. I run my victim through and through, but I draw no blood. What am I?'

'That's easy!' Nefer laughed triumphantly. 'You are a sewing needle.' And Mintaka threw up her hands in surrender.

Of course Nefer had brought his bao board and stones. Taita had taught him to love the game, and he had become expert. When he tired of the riddles he inveigled Mintaka into a game. Bao was an Egyptian game, and this time he expected confidently to outmatch her.

Taita smiled because he and Mintaka had whiled away a few hours at bao in the palace of Bubasti when they were nursing her little brother. Within eighteen moves her red stones dominated the west castle and were menacing Nefer's centre.

'Have I done the right thing?' she asked sweetly.

Nefer was saved by a hail from the river and looked up to see a galley flying the regent's pennant coming swiftly down the channel. 'What a pity. Just when the game was getting interesting.'

He had been expecting this visitation all morning. Sooner or later the regent must hear about this outing and send Asmor to bring in his errant charge.

The galley nosed into the bank below, where they sat, and Asmor sprang ashore. He strode up to the picnic party. 'The regent is much displeased by your absence. He bids you return at once to the temple, where matters of state await your attention.'

'And I, Lord Asmor, am much displeased by your ill manners,' Nefer told him. 'I am not a house servant to be addressed in that manner, and neither have you shown respect for the Princess Mintaka.' But there was no escaping that he was being treated like a truant from the classroom.

Still, he put a good face on it and invited Mintaka to sail back with him in the skiff while her maids followed in the second vessel. Taita kept tactfully to the bows as this was their first opportunity to hold a private conversation.

The journey was far too short for Nefer's liking, and as they came into the landing he took her hand. 'I should like to see you again.'

'I should like that well enough,' she replied.

'Soon,' he insisted.

'Soon enough.' She smiled and gently took back her hand. He felt strangely bereft as he watched her walk away towards the temple.

'MY LORD, you were present at the divination of the Mazes. You know of the charge placed upon me by the gods. You know that I am committed to your interest. I had good reason to assist the boy in what was only, after all, a harmless escapade.'

Naja was not so easily placated. He was furious that Nefer had given Asmor the slip and managed to spend the morning out in the swamps with the Hyksosian princess. But Taita diplomatically turned aside each of the regent's accusations, until he was no longer ranting but merely grumbling bitterly. 'However, it must not happen again. Of course I trust your loyalty, Magus.'

'My lord, how goes the negotiation with King Apepi? Is there aught that I can do to help you ensure a successful outcome in this matter?' Adroitly Taita set the hounds on a different scent, and Naja followed them.

'I have that old rogue Apepi at the brink,' he gloated. 'This morning he is about to make more concessions than he realises.' He started towards the door, then looked back over his shoulder. 'Come with me,' he ordered. 'I might have use of your powers before I am done with Apepi.'

Binding Apepi to the treaty was not the easy task that Naja had suggested it would be. The Hyksosian leader was still ranting, shouting and banging his fist on the table long after the watchman on the temple walls had called the midnight hour. At last Naja adjourned the conference and staggered off to bed.

The next day, when they met again at noon, Apepi was no more amenable to reason. Taita used his influences to calm him, but Apepi allowed himself to be wooed only very slowly. So it was only on the fifth day that the scribes began to write down the terms of the treaty.

Up to this time Naja had excluded Pharaoh Nefer Seti from the conclave. But by the morning of the sixth day, when the scribes had completed their work and the fifty tablets of the treaty were ready to be ratified, Naja sent for Pharaoh to take part in the proceedings. Likewise, all Apepi's offspring, including Mintaka, were to be present at the ceremony.

Once again the courtyard of the temple was filled with a glittering congregation as, in stentorian tones, the herald royal began to read out the text of the treaty. Immediately Nefer was absorbed by what it contained, certain that he detected Taita's shadowy influence in many areas of the long document.

At last it was time to affix the seals. To a series of blasts on the rams' horns Nefer pressed his cartouche to the damp clay and Apepi did the same. Then, while Naja watched with an enigmatic expression, the new co-rulers of the two kingdoms embraced. Apepi folded Nefer in his bearlike embrace and men rattled their weapons against their shields, or hammered the butts of their lances on the stone flags. Finally Apepi turned to face the crowded courtyard.

'Citizens of this mighty land, which is once again united, I pledge you my duty and my love. In token of these, I offer the hand of my daughter, Princess Mintaka, in marriage to the Pharaoh Nefer Seti, who shares with me the double crown of the Upper and Lower Kingdoms, and who shall be my son.'

There was a long moment of utter stillness in the courtyard. Then the assembly burst out in enthusiastic cries of approval while the drumming of weapons became deafening.

Pharaoh Nefer Seti had an expression on his face that in any lesser mortal would have been described as an idiotic grin. He was gazing across the courtyard at Mintaka. She was frozen, with one hand covering her mouth, and her eyes were wide with astonishment as she gazed at her father. Slowly a dark blush suffused her face and she turned her eyes to meet Nefer's. The two gazed at each other as if no other person was in the crowded courtyard.

Taita watched from the foot of Pharaoh's throne. He realised that Apepi's timing of the announcement had been masterly. Now there was no possible way in which anybody—Naja, Trok or any other— could stand in the way of the marriage.

Standing close to Naja's throne, Taita was keenly aware of the regent's deep consternation. Naja must have sensed Taita's eyes on him, for he glanced in his direction. For a moment only, Taita looked into his soul, and saw the cobra of his vision, the cobra for which the regent was named. Then Naja veiled his fierce yellow eyes, smiled coolly and nodded in approval, but Taita knew that he was thinking furiously.

The Magus turned his head and sought out the burly figure of Lord Trok in the Hyksosian ranks opposite. Unlike the regent, Trok was making no attempt to disguise his feelings. He was in a black rage. He opened his mouth as if to protest, then closed it. With a huge effort he regained control of himself, smoothed down his beard, then turned abruptly and pushed his way out of the courtyard.

As Trok disappeared between the tall granite pillars, Naja rose and stepped in front of Apepi. 'On this auspicious and joyous day, we rejoice not only in the joining of the two kingdoms, but also in the betrothal of Pharaoh Nefer Seti and the Princess Mintaka. Therefore, be it known that the marriage will take place in this temple on the day that Pharaoh Nefer Seti celebrates his majority, or fulfils one of the conditions to ratify his claim to the crown and rules in his own right without a regent to protect and advise him.'

Apepi frowned and Nefer made a small gesture of dismay, but it was too late. It had been announced in full session so, as regent, Naja spoke with the authority of both crowned heads. Unless Nefer captured his own godbird, thereby ratifying his claim to the throne, Naja had prevented the marriage taking place for a number of years.

That was a masterly stroke, Taita thought bitterly. Naja had averted disaster for himself by his quick thinking. Now, he went even further. 'On an equally happy note, I invite Pharaoh Apepi and

Pharaoh Nefer Seti to celebrate my own marriage to Princess Heseret. This joyous ceremony will take place ten days from now, at the temple of Isis in the city of Thebes.'

So, Taita thought grimly, in ten days' time Lord Naja will be a member of the Tamosian royal family, and will stand next in succession to Pharaoh Nefer Seti.

BY THE TERMS of the Treaty of Hathor, Apepi's capital would remain at Avaris and Nefer Seti's at Thebes. Each would govern his former kingdom, but in the name of the duumvirate. Twice every year, at the beginning and the end of the inundation of the Nile, the two kings would hold a combined royal assize at Memphis, where all matters concerning the two kingdoms would be dealt with.

However, before the two pharaohs parted, Apepi and his train would sail upriver in company with Nefer Seti's fleet to Thebes. There they would attend Lord Naja's wedding.

The embarkation of both trains from the wharf below the temple was a chaotic affair that took up most of the morning. Taita mingled with the throng of boatmen and dockers, slaves and important passengers. Occasionally a man would look up from what he was doing, recognise him and ask for his blessing, or a woman would bring him a sick child to tend. However, he was able to work his way gradually along the beach, casually looking out for the chariots and equipment of Lord Trok's regiment. He recognised them by their green and red pennants, and as he approached he made out the unmistakable figure of Trok among his men. Taita edged closer and watched him pause to talk to his lance-bearer, then take the path up to the temple.

As soon as Trok had disappeared, Taita approached the lance-bearer. The trooper was stripped to breech-clout and sandals, and as he stooped over one of the chests of Trok's equipment Taita saw the distinctive circular rash of the ringworm on his naked back. 'Come here, soldier,' Taita called him across. 'How long have you had the itch on your back?'

Instinctively the fellow twisted up one arm between his shoulder blades, and scratched himself vigorously. 'Cursed thing has been bothering me ever since we captured Abnub. I think it's a gift from one of those dirty Egyptian whores—' He broke off guiltily. 'Forgive me, Warlock, we are allies and fellow countrymen now.'

'That is why I will attend to your affliction, soldier. Go up to the temple, ask at the kitchens for a jar of lard and bring it to me. I will

351

mix an ointment for you.' Taita sat down on the pile of Trok's luggage, and the lance-bearer hurried away down the beach.

Taita's seat was a stack of wooden chests. The top one bore the seal of Grippa, the Avaris fletcher who made arrows for all the high-ranking Hyksosian officers. Taita untied the cord that secured the lid. A layer of dry straw protected the arrows. He picked one out and turned it in his fingers.

The carved signet leapt out at him, the stylised head of the leopard with the hieratic letter T held in its snarling jaws. The arrow was identical to the one found in Pharaoh's body. It was the last thread in the fabric of treason. Naja and Trok were linked in the bloody plot.

Taita slipped the incriminating arrow under the folds of his kilt and closed the lid of the chest. Deftly he retied the cord, and waited for the lance-bearer to return.

The old soldier was grateful for Taita's ministrations, then pleaded for a further favour: 'A friend of mine has the pox, Magus. What should he do?' It always amused Taita that no man ever contracted the pox himself but always had a friend suffering from it.

THE FEAST TO CELEBRATE the marriage of Lord Naja to Princess Heseret was the most lavish ever recorded. To the common citizens of Thebes, Lord Naja gave five hundred head of prime oxen, and to each of the four thousand invited guests a commemorative carved jewel with the guest's own name engraved upon it between the names of the regent and his bride.

The bride came to meet her groom on one of the state carriages drawn by sacred white oxen. The road was strewn with palm fronds and flowers, and a chariot drove ahead of the wedding coach throwing rings of silver and copper to the crowds that lined the way.

When she reached the temple she was met by her brother. Heseret was as lovely as a nymph of paradise in her snowy robes and glittering jewellery. Months ago she had come to terms with the fate the gods had apportioned her and her girlish interest in Meren had begun to fade. She came to realise that he was an impecunious boy, a common soldier without favour or prospects. Lord Naja's social rank almost matched hers, and his fortune far exceeded her own. He was also a magnificent-looking man.

Now she kept a chaste demeanour as Nefer led her down the temple to the sanctuary where Lord Naja was waiting. He wore a plumed headdress of ostrich feathers and his perfume was a blend of essences from a land beyond the Indus. The aroma stirred her, and she took the hand the Naja offered her without hesitation.

Watching from the roof of the western enclosure, Taita shuddered with a sense of foreboding. Now Naja is of the blood royal, I am the only shield Nefer has, and I am one man and old. Will my powers be enough to turn away the cobra?

LORD NAJA AND HIS NEW WIFE rode back in splendour to the palace gates. There they dismounted and went in procession through the gardens to the banquet hall. Most of the guests had arrived ahead of them, and the commotion as the wedding party entered was deafening. The pair moved through the throng and inspected the gifts stacked in the centre of the banquet hall. Apepi had sent a chariot covered in gold leaf, so brilliant that even in the dimly lit hall it was difficult to look at directly. From Babylon King Sargon had sent a hundred sandalwood chests, filled with jewellery, precious stones or golden vessels. Pharaoh Nefer Seti, at the suggestion of Lord Naja, had deeded to his new brother-in-law three lakhs of pure gold. The regent had become almost as rich as his pharaoh.

When the connubial pair took their seats at the head of the wedding board, the palace cooks laid a feast before them, and to entertain them there were musicians and jugglers, acrobats and huge brown bears.

By nightfall most of the guests were so drunk that few could stand when Lord Naja and his bride retired. Naja led Heseret by the hand to his sumptuous bedroom, which overlooked the river. There Heseret's handmaidens took her behind a screen of bamboo to remove her wedding dress and jewellery.

Lord Naja went out onto the terrace and inhaled deeply the cool river air. A slave brought him a bowl of spiced wine, and he sipped appreciatively. It was the first wine he had allowed himself all evening. He returned to the chamber as two more slaves staggered in, bearing between them a cauldron of hot water, in which floated lotus petals. Naja set aside the wine bowl and went to bathe. One of the slaves dried and braided his hair, while the other brought him a clean white robe. He dismissed them and lay upon the marriage bed, stretching out his long, elegant limbs.

From the far end of the chamber came the rustle of clothing and feminine whispers. He propped himself up on one elbow and looked across at the bamboo screen. The gaps in it were just large enough to afford him tantalising glimpses of pale, smooth skin. Power and political aspiration were the main reasons for this marriage, but Naja had a voluptuous nature. For years he had watched Heseret surreptitiously, and his interest had increased at each stage in her journey towards womanhood. Now, at last, two of the handmaidens led her out from behind the screen, then slipped away quietly, leaving her standing alone in the middle of the floor.

Her silken night-robe fell to her ankles. It was creamy in colour and so fine that it seemed to float around her like river mist, stirring with every breath she took. There was an oil lamp on a tripod in the corner behind her, and the soft yellow light shone through the silk, highlighting the curves of her hips and shoulders. Her skin was flawless and her green eyes hinted at a sly, lascivious streak in her.

'You are beautiful.' His voice caught.

Now a hint of a smile lifted the corners of her lips. 'I am glad that my lord regent finds me so.'

He rose from the bed and went to her. Slowly he lifted her face.

'You also are beautiful,' she whispered, and it was true. In this moment she realised that he was the most beautiful creature she had ever known.

He kissed her and his mouth startled her. His tongue was as flickeringly quick as a snake's, but it did not revolt her. She closed her eyes and touched it with her own. She was so lost in his kiss that when his hand closed over her breast she was unprepared. Her eyes flew open and she gasped. She tried to pull away but he held her, and now he caressed her with a skilful touch that stilled her fears.

With a single movement he swept off her silken robe and let it fall to the floor. She had not the slightest inclination to resist.

Twice during that enchanted night she cried out in a frenzy of pleasure, and when the dawn suffused the chamber with its rose and silver light she lay still in his arms. She felt as though the life force had been drawn out of her, and there was a soft ache deep in her belly that she savoured.

When she opened her eyes he was watching her, and he smiled gently. 'What a splendid queen you would make,' he said softly. This he meant sincerely, sensing that he had found in her someone whose desires and instincts were in perfect harmony with his own.

'And what a splendid pharaoh you would make.' She smiled back, reached up and touched his cheek. 'But that could never happen.' She stopped smiling abruptly and asked softly, seriously, 'Could it?'

CHAPTER FOUR

King Apepi's entourage remained in Thebes for almost a month after the wedding. They were the guests of Pharaoh Nefer Seti and of his regent, and were entertained in royal fashion. Taita encouraged this delay. He felt certain that Naja would take no action against Nefer while Apepi and his daughter were in Thebes.

The royal visitors spent their days hunting, and during these days Mintaka was often at Nefer's side. She rode in his chariot and handed him the lance when they drove up alongside a galloping oryx. She carried her own falcon on her arm as they quartered the reed beds for heron. At the hunting picnics in the desert, she sat beside him and prepared little treats for him.

Every evening there were banquets in the palace and there also she sat at his side. She made him laugh with her wry wit and she was a marvellous mimic: she imitated Heseret to perfection, simpering and rolling her eyes, and speaking of 'My husband, the Regent of Egypt' in the portentous tones Heseret now employed.

As Nefer's chariot sped through the streets of Thebes with Mintaka on the footplate as his lance-bearer, men paused from their labours to shout greetings and good wishes. Their love was so apparent that it cast a glow upon all those around them. Even Naja smiled benignly upon them, although he fiercely resented the attention of the populace being diverted from his own nuptials, and he saw to it that Nefer and Mintaka could never be completely alone.

Their chance came, however, when a royal huntsman came in from the hills above the village of Dabba one day to report that a lion had raided the cattle pens during the night. It had killed eight of the terrified beasts. In the dawn a horde of villagers, brandishing torches, blowing horns, beating drums and screaming wildly, had driven it off.

'When did this happen?' asked Naja.

'Three nights ago, Your Grace.' The man was prostrate before the throne. 'I came upriver as soon as I could, but the current runs strongly and the winds were fluky.'

'What has happened to the beast?' King Apepi interrupted eagerly.

'It has gone back into the hills, but I have sent two of my best Nubian trackers to follow it.'

'I will have the chariots loaded onto the boats at once,' Apepi decided. 'With the state of the river we can be at Dabba early tomorrow morning.'

Naja hesitated. He was not so addicted to the hunt that he wished to neglect the numerous affairs of state that awaited his attention. He had looked forward to the departure of Apepi, whose boisterous, uncouth presence in Thebes had long since palled. And he had other plans afoot. 'Majesty, you are expected to sail back to Avaris tomorrow.'

'You are right, Regent. However, most of our baggage is already loaded and the fleet lies ready to depart. Moreover, Dabba lies on my way homewards. I can afford a day or two in the hunt.'

'Your Majesty,' Nefer intervened, 'we will join in the hunt with the greatest of pleasure.' He saw an opportunity for magnificent sport, and before Naja could prevent him he turned to the huntsman, who still lay with his forehead pressed to the floor. 'Well done, my good fellow. The chamberlain will give you a gold ring for your trouble. Return to Dabba at once in the fastest felucca in our fleet. Make ready for our arrival.'

Nefer's only cause for regret was that Taita would not be with him during his first lion hunt. The old man had disappeared into the wilderness on another of his periodic and mysterious forays.

IN THE EARLY MORNING of the next day the hunting party disembarked on the river bank below the village of Dabba. All the horses and chariots were off-loaded and the lance-bearers sharpened the spear blades, restrung the hunting bows and checked the arrows. While the horses were watered, the hunters ate a hearty breakfast that the villagers had provided. The mood was ebullient.

'Sound the mount up,' Nefer ordered, and the rams' horns blared as the hunters scattered to the waiting chariots. Mintaka walked at Nefer's side. In these informal circumstances all royal dignity was forgotten, and they were simply boy and girl on an exciting outing.

Led by the royal huntsman, who rode bareback astride a tough little pony, the column climbed into the bare, stony hills. They went at the trot, saving the horses, letting them blow after every steep gradient. Within the hour they found one of the Nubian trackers waiting for them on a hilltop, and the huntsman trotted back to report to the royal party, 'The Nubians have cast the hills but without finding the spoor again. From where we last saw him, he may have gone to the small oasis at the head of the valley, but there are

Bedouin encamped there. They might have scared off the beast. There is also a water seep below those hills.' He pointed at a low line of purple peaks on the horizon.

'You have not the least idea where he is, have you?' Lord Naja complained. 'We should call off the hunt.'

'No!' Nefer cut in. 'How can we give up?'

'We must go on,' Apepi agreed, 'but there is much ground to cover.' He paused, then reached a decision. 'We must split up and search each area separately.' He looked at Naja. 'My Lord Regent, take your squadron to the Bedouin encampment. I will ride to the seep below the hills.' He turned to Trok. 'Take three chariots down the valley.' Then he looked at Nefer. 'Pharaoh, you cast in the opposite direction, north towards Achmim.'

Nefer realised he was being given the least promising ground to cover, but he had no complaint. This new plan meant that for the first time he and Mintaka would be away from the direct surveillance of his guardians. He waited for someone to point this out, but they were all so wrapped up in the hunt that no one seemed to realise the significance of this move. Except Naja.

He looked hard at Nefer, weighing the advisability of countermanding Apepi's orders, but in the end he concluded that Nefer was guarded by the desert as effectively as he would have been by Asmor: there was no place to run to. If he took Mintaka on some wild adventure he would soon have the armies of both kingdoms upon him.

Apepi went on to nominate an assembly point, and to give his final orders. At last the rams' horns sounded the advance, and the columns drove out of the valley. On the level ground they split into their separate squadrons and headed out in diverging directions.

There were two other chariots in Nefer's squadron, commanded by Colonel Hilto, the old soldier who had discovered him and Taita when they had tried to escape from Egypt. He had served under Nefer's father and Nefer knew he could trust him.

Nefer led them fast, and within an hour the vast green vista of the river plain opened beneath them. He reined in to admire it. 'Colonel Hilto, if the lion is here it will probably be lying up somewhere on the slope of the hills down below us.' He indicated the area with a sweep of his arm. 'I want to extend in line abreast. The left flank must be on the edge of the plain and our right up here on the crest of the hills. We will sweep northwards.' He made a wide gesture, but Hilto looked dubious.

'That is a broad front, Your Majesty. It's almost half a league to the valley bottom. At times we will be out of sight of each other.'

Nefer cut in with a sharp tone and cold expression: 'Do you presume to argue with your pharaoh?'

'Never, Majesty!' Hilto was shocked at the accusation.

'Then do your duty, fellow.'

Hilto saluted and hurried back to his own chariot, shouting orders to his men. As the squadron wheeled out down the slope, Mintaka nudged Nefer and smiled. 'Do your duty, fellow!' She mimicked his haughty tone then laughed. 'Please never look at me like that or use that tone to me, Your Majesty. I am sure I would die of fright.'

She lifted her face to him and her lips were parted slightly. He could smell her sweet breath, and the temptation to reach down for those lips was almost irresistible. 'We have only a little time,' he replied instead. 'We must make the most of it, and find a place where we can be alone.'

He swung the chariot down towards a small grove of thorn trees, almost hidden by a fold in the ground, where a narrow ravine had been cut into the hillside by wind and weather. There must have been subterranean water, for the thorn trees were robust. Their thick foliage provided shade and privacy in this hot midday. Nefer drove down the bank and into the shade. He jumped down and went to fill the bucket from the water-skin to water the horses. Mintaka, aware of a fullness in her bladder, picked her way deeper into the grove of thorn trees.

THE LION WATCHED HER with yellow eyes, flattening its ears against its skull and pressing its body closer to the stony earth. The previous night it had missed an oryx, and hunger was a dull, insistent pain in its gut. It lifted its head, and slashed its tail back and forth, the prelude to the charge.

As Mintaka stood and started back towards Nefer, she heard the rhythmic swish and thud of the tail, stopped and looked up, puzzled. She looked straight into the yellow gaze of the beast. She screamed, a high-pitched sound that struck Nefer to the heart. He whirled round and in an instant took in the situation: the girl, the crouching beast facing her, and his bow and quiver ten paces away, in the rack on the chariot's dashboard.

At that moment the lion growled. It was a terrible sound that seemed to vibrate in Mintaka's bones and make the ground tremble.

Then its mane rose like a dark aura around its head and it launched itself into its charge, coming straight at her.

'Come! Here I am! Come to me!' Nefer yelled wildly, and it swung its huge head towards him. His arm was shaking as he reached down and drew his dagger from the sheath on his belt.

It was a flimsy weapon against this furious beast. The thin bronze blade was not long enough to stab through to the heart, but he had heard the royal huntsman tell tales of miraculous escapes from just such a deadly predicament. The lion hurled itself towards him and, as it launched into the death spring, Nefer fell backwards, not even attempting to resist the beast's weight and impetus. He lay between its forepaws, and the lion opened its jaws to full stretch and thrust its head down to crush Nefer's skull with its terrible fangs. He steeled himself and thrust his hand, holding the dagger with the blade aligned upright, deep into the open jaws. The lion bit down instinctively, driving the bronze point up through the roof of its mouth. Nefer snatched away his hand before the fangs could crush the bones of his wrist, but the lion's jaws were fixed open by the dagger held between them, and it could not bite down. It ripped at him with both its forepaws, claws fully extended. He writhed beneath the heavy body, evading some of the claw strokes, but felt the bony hooks tearing into his flesh.

Mintaka's own fear was now forgotten. She raced towards the chariot, the screams and roars behind her goading her on. Ahead of her the terrified horses reared and threw their heads. They would have bolted long ago had not Nefer secured the locking brake on one wheel so they could only turn in a tight right-handed circle. Mintaka ran in under their flying hoofs, jumped up onto the footplate and brought them under control. She knocked off the brake and drove them straight at the lion and its victim. She then snatched the long lance from its rack and, guiding the horses with the reins in her left hand, leaned far out over the side panel and raised the lance high. As they ran past the crouched lion, the back of its neck was exposed. The exact juncture of spine and skull was covered by the dense black bush of its mane, but she guessed at the spot and thrust down with all the strength of her fear and her love for Nefer.

Her lance hand had the impetus of the flying chariot behind it. To her amazement the blade slid in readily, full length through the taut hide, deep into the back of the animal's neck to sever the spinal column. As the chariot raced past, the lance was plucked from her grip. But the lion collapsed in a loose, inert heap on top of Nefer. It did not twitch again, killed on the instant.

She wheeled the crazed horses back to where Nefer lay beneath the huge carcass, and jumped down from the footplate. It was obvious how badly Nefer was hurt. She could see that the enormous weight of the dead beast was crushing the wind from his lungs. Seizing the long tufted tail she heaved with all her strength. Slowly the hindquarters began to swing, then the whole carcass flopped over and he was free.

Mintaka knelt beside him and helped him into a sitting position, but he swayed drunkenly and reached out to her for support.

'You are desperately wounded,' she cried. 'There is so much blood.'

'Not all of it is mine,' he blurted, but from his right thigh rose a crimson fountain where the claws had ripped open a blood vessel. Taita had instructed him long and earnestly in the treatment of wounds, and he thrust his thumb down into the torn flesh and pressed until the jet of blood shrivelled.

'Get the water-skin,' he said, and Mintaka did so and held it for him while he drank thirstily. Then she washed the blood and filth from his face, relieved to find it unmarked. However, when she inspected his other injuries she saw how grievous they were.

'My bedroll is in the chariot.' His voice was weaker. When she brought it to him he asked her to undo the bundle, where she found a needle and silk thread. He showed her how to tie off the spurting blood vessel. Her hands were bloody to the wrists, as with nimble fingers she pulled a thread round the open artery then closed the deeper rents in his flesh. She used strips torn from his tattered kilt to bind up the wounds. It was rough, rudimentary surgery, but sufficient to stem the worst of the bleeding.

'That is all we can do now. I must help you into the chariot and get you to where a surgeon can do the rest. Oh, if only Taita were here.'

Nefer was staring longingly at the carcass of the lion. 'My first lion,' he whispered ruefully. 'Unless we skin it, the trophy will spoil. The hair will slip and slough off.'

In the heat of her terrible concern for him, she lost her temper. 'That is the most stupid piece of man's nonsense I have ever heard. Would you risk your life for a stinking bit of fur?' Angrily she helped him to his feet. He leaned on her with all his weight as he hobbled to the chariot and collapsed weakly onto the footplate. Mintaka used the sheepskin from the bedroll to make him as comfortable as she could, then climbed up and stood over him with the reins in her hands.

'Which way?' she asked.

'The rest of the squadron will be far up the valley by now,' he told her. 'The other hunters are scattered across the desert. We could search for them all day without finding them.'

'We must return to where the fleet is lying at Dabba. There is a surgeon with the ships.' She had reached the only feasible conclusion, and he nodded. She urged the horses into a walk, and they left the grove and climbed to the high ground, heading south once again.

Even though Mintaka kept the horses down to a trot, the collision with every stone or hump was transmitted through the rigid chassis into Nefer's torn body. He winced and sweated, trying to hide his pain from her, but as the hours wore on it became unbearable. He groaned aloud at a particularly nasty impact, and she reined the pair to a halt.

'You are going to be all right, my darling,' she told him, with a confidence she did not feel. She sponged his face, kissed the top of his dusty, blood-caked head, and took up the reins again.

An hour later she gave the last of the water to Nefer and the horses, not drinking herself. Then she stood as high as she could on the dashboard of the chariot and looked about her. At her feet Nefer stirred and moaned, and she looked down with a brave face and smiled. 'Not much further now, my heart. We should see the river over the next crest.'

She rearranged the sheepskin under his head, then stood up and gathered the reins. Suddenly she realised how exhausted she was: every muscle in her body ached and her eyes were sore from the sun's glare and the dust. She forced herself and the team onwards.

Soon the horses were showing signs of distress. They had stopped sweating and the salt rime had dried white across their backs. She tried to urge them into a trot but they could not respond, and at last despair overtook her. She sank down, helpless and lost, and whispered to Nefer as he lay, now unconscious, 'I am sorry, my darling. I have failed you.' She stroked the matted hair from his face. Then she looked up at the low hilltop to the east and blinked. She shook her head to clear her vision, then looked again, but still she could not be sure that what she was seeing was illusion or reality.

On the crest of the hills above them, a gaunt figure stood on the skyline, leaning on his long staff. His silver hair shone like a cloud and the hot, light breeze of the desert flapped his skirts against his heron-thin legs. He was staring down at them.

Beside her, Nefer opened his eyes. 'Taita is near,' he murmured. 'I feel him close.'

'Yes. Taita is here.' Her voice was faint. 'But how did he know where to find us?'

'He knows. Taita knows,' Nefer replied, closed his eyes and slumped back into unconsciousness.

TAITA DROVE DOWN the escarpment towards the river. The horses responded to his touch, moving with an easy motion that cosseted the wounded boy on the footplate. Taita seemed to have known with some deep instinct just what medicines and dressings Nefer would need, and he had carried these with him. After he had re-dressed the wounds, he led the horses to a hidden water seep nearby to revive them. Then he took Mintaka up on the footplate and turned the horses' heads unerringly in the direction of Dabba.

A red and angry sunset was fading over the Nile like a dying bush fire as they approached the spot where the fleet was still anchored in the stream. Apepi and Naja rode out to meet them. Lord Naja was agitated, and Apepi bellowed at his daughter as soon as they were in range, 'Where have you been, you stupid child? Half the army is out looking for you.'

Lord Naja's agitation abated when he saw Nefer bandaged and unconscious in the chariot cockpit. Barely conscious, the boy was carried gently aboard one of the galleys.

'I want Pharaoh taken up to Thebes with all possible speed,' Taita told Naja, 'even if it means a night journey.'

'You can order the galley to sail at once,' Naja said, in front of the company, but then took Taita's arm and led him a short way along the river bank to where they could not be overheard. 'Bear in mind, Magus, the charge laid on you by the gods. If Pharaoh were to die from his wounds no person in either kingdom would take it as unnatural.' He said no more but gazed into Taita's face.

'The will of the gods will prevail against all else,' Taita agreed.

Naja read in his reply what he wanted to hear. 'We are in accord, Taita. I place my trust in you. Go in peace. I will follow you to Thebes after Apepi has been taken care of.' This last remark struck Taita as odd, but he was too distracted to ponder it.

When he hurried back on board the galley, Taita found Mintaka kneeling beside the litter in tears.

She looked up at him piteously. 'My father is taking me back to

Avaris in the morning, but I should be with Nefer. I am his betrothed. He needs me.' She seized his hand. 'Oh, Magus! Will you not go to my father and ask him to let me go back to Thebes to help you to take care of Nefer? My father will listen to you.'

But when Taita attempted to persuade Apepi to let her go back to Thebes with Nefer, the king snorted with laughter, 'Place my lamb in Naja's pen?' He shook his head with amusement. 'I trust Naja as I would a scorpion. Who knows what tricks he would try if I gave him that coin to bargain with? No, Warlock, Mintaka comes back under my wing to Avaris until her wedding day.'

Sadly Mintaka went to take her leave of Nefer. He was on the edge of consciousness, weak from loss of blood, but when she kissed him he opened his eyes. She took the golden locket that hung at her throat. 'This contains a lock of my hair. It is my soul, and I give it to you.' She placed it in his hand and he folded his fingers tightly round it.

So Mintaka stood alone on the bank of the Nile, watching forlornly as the galley bearing Nefer and Taita breasted the current, heading upstream towards Thebes.

THE NEXT MORNING there was a final meeting between Apepi and the regent, Lord Naja, on board the Hyksosian royal barge. All Apepi's nine sons were present, and Mintaka was seated beside her father. Then, with protestations of mutual trust and devotion to the peace, the two fleets diverged, one to return to Thebes, the other to Avaris, and garlands and wreaths of palm fronds were tossed from one vessel towards the other, bestrewing the surface of the wide river.

That evening King Apepi's fleet anchored at Balasfura, opposite the temple of Hapi, where Trok and the officers under his command arranged a banquet and entertainment. On the river bank pavilions were hung with vivid red, yellow and green curtains to receive the royal family. Whole oxen were grilled over pits of glowing ash, and amphorae of the choicest wines cooled in the river waters. Slaves staggered up the bank under the weight of them as one after the other they were drained and Apepi bellowed for fresh jars to be brought.

The king's mood lightened with each bowl he lowered, and soon he encouraged his sons to join him in singing the ribald marching songs of his army. Some were so scurrilous that Mintaka pleaded exhaustion and retired with her maids to the barge.

Mintaka lay on her mattress and listened to the sounds of revelry. She tried to compose herself to sleep, but Nefer was in the forefront of her mind. The sense of loss that she had held at bay all day, and her concern for Nefer's injuries, flooded back, and though she tried to prevent them, her tears welled up.

At last she sank into a black, dreamless sleep, from which she woke with difficulty, roused by drunken laughter and heavy footfalls from the deck over her head. It seemed that her father and her brothers were being carried on board. She had sipped only a little of the wine, but she felt herself drugged and her head ached. Almost immediately she succumbed to sleep again.

The next time she woke she believed that she was in a nightmare, for she could hear screams and she was choking on clouds of thick smoke. Before she was fully conscious she found herself bundled out of her bed, swaddled in a blanket and carried on deck. She struggled, but she was as helpless as an infant in a powerful grip.

On deck the moonless night was lit by leaping flames. They were roaring out of the forward hatch of the royal barge, climbing the masts and rigging in a hellish torrent. She had never seen a wooden hull burn before and the ferocity of the flames appalled her.

She could not stare at them for long, for she found herself carried swiftly across the deck and down the side into a waiting felucca. As it pushed off into the stream she fought to free herself, but the arms that pinioned her were remorseless. She managed to twist her head and see the face of the man who held her.

'Trok!' She was angered by his presumption, at the way he was ignoring her cries. 'Let me go! I command you!'

He did not respond. He held her easily but he was watching the burning galley with a calm, detached expression.

'Go back!' she shrieked. 'My family! Go back and fetch them!'

His only response was to snap an order to the oarsmen. 'Hold the stroke!' They shipped their paddles and the felucca rocked on the current. The crew watched the burning hulk with fascination. There were agonising screams from those trapped below the decks.

Suddenly the main hatch on the burning deck was thrown open, and a figure emerged. Lord Trok's arms tightened around Mintaka. 'It cannot be!' he grated.

Through the smoke and flames, Apepi staggered towards the side of the barge. He carried his youngest son, Khyan, in his arms, and his mouth was wide open, gasping for air.

'The monster is hard to kill.' Trok's anger was tinged with fear.

Even in her own distress Mintaka read the meaning of his words.

'You, Trok!' she whispered. 'You have done this to them!'

Trok ignored the accusation.

Apepi was no longer moving forward, but he stood with legs astraddle and lifted Khyan high above his head. Perhaps he was attempting to throw the boy over the ship's side into the river to escape the flames, but suddenly the deck under Apepi's feet burst open. He and his son dropped through, and in a tall fountain of flame, sparks and smoke were gone.

'It's over.' Trok's voice was dispassionate. He released Mintaka so suddenly that she fell into the bilges of the felucca. He looked at his horrified crew. 'Row to my galley,' he ordered.

'You did this to my family,' Mintaka repeated, as she lay at his feet. 'You will pay for it. I swear to you. I will make you pay.'

But she felt numbed. Her father was gone, that monumental figure in her life whom she had hated a little and loved a great deal. Her family was gone, all of her brothers, even Khyan. She had watched him burn and she knew that the horror of it would stay with her all her days.

The felucca drew alongside Lord Trok's galley and she made no protest as he carried her on board, then down to the main cabin. 'Your slave girls are safe. I will send them to you,' he said, and went out. She heard the locking bar placed across the door, then the sound of him climbing the companion ladder.

She hid her face in pillows that smelt of Trok's stale sweat and wept until her tears were exhausted. Then she slept.

THE BURNING HULL of Apepi's royal barge drifted up onto the river bank opposite the temple of Hapi. In the dawn the smoke rose high into the still air, tainted by the stench of burnt flesh. When Mintaka awoke the smell sickened her. The smoke seemed to act like a beacon, for the sun had hardly risen above the eastern hills before the fleet of Lord Naja came sweeping round the bend of the river.

The slave girls brought the news to Mintaka. 'Lord Naja has come in full array,' they told her excitedly. 'Yesterday he left us to return to Thebes. Is it not strange that he could reach here so soon when he should be twenty leagues upriver?'

'Surpassing strange,' Mintaka agreed grimly.

Her baggage had all gone up in flames in the royal barge, but her maids borrowed clothing from the other noble ladies in the fleet, and they dressed her in a simple linen shift, gold girdle and sandals.

Before noon an armed escort came aboard the galley, and she followed them on deck. Her eyes went to the blackened timbers of the royal barge that lay on the far bank, burnt down to the water line. It was her family's funeral pyre. With an effort she held back further tears, went down into the waiting felucca, and was taken to the bank where Lord Naja was waiting with all his company assembled.

She remained aloof and pale when he embraced her. 'This is a bitter time for all of us, Princess,' he said. 'Your father was a mighty warrior and statesman. In view of the recent treaty between the two kingdoms, he leaves a dangerous gap. For the good of all, this must be filled immediately.'

He took her hand and led her to the pavilion that had last evening been the scene of feasting and festivity, but where now were assembled in solemn conclave most of the nobility of both kingdoms.

She saw Trok in the forefront of this throng, and behind him in packed ranks all his officers, grim, cold-eyed and menacing. They stared at her, unsmiling, and she was bitterly aware that she was the last of the Apepi line, abandoned and unprotected.

She wondered to whom she could appeal, and whose loyalty she still commanded. She searched for friendly, familiar faces in the multitude. They were all there, her father's councillors and advisers, his generals and comrades of the battlefield. But their eyes slid away from her face. None smiled at her. She had never felt so alone.

Naja led her to a cushioned stool at one side of the pavilion. When she sat down, Naja and his staff formed a screen round her, hiding her from view. She was certain that this had been deliberately arranged.

Lord Naja opened the conclave with a lamentation for the death of King Apepi and his sons. Then he continued, 'In the tragic circumstances of his death, King Apepi leaves no male heir to the Crown.' Smoothly he passed over any mention of Mintaka. 'As a matter of urgency I have consulted the senior councillors of both kingdoms. Their choice for the new pharaoh has been unanimous. With one voice they have asked Lord Trok of Memphis to pick up the reins of power, to take the double crown upon himself and steer the nation forward.'

In the uproar that followed, strong hands took Mintaka and spirited her away through the cheering press. She struggled ineffectually, her voice unheard in the storm of cheering. On the river bank she twisted in the arms of her captors and glanced back. Over the heads of the crowd she glimpsed Lord Naja raising the double crown over the head of the new Pharaoh.

Then she was hustled down the bank to the waiting felucca, and back to her locked and guarded cabin on board Lord Trok's galley.

DURING THE THE VOYAGE downriver from Balasfura, Mintaka had the freedom of the deck while they were under way, but at anchor or at moorings she was locked in her cabin.

One morning Trok insisted that she join him for a lavish breakfast on the foredeck. There were twenty other guests, and Trok seated himself next to Mintaka. She pointedly ignored him and directed all her charm and wit to the officers of his army.

At the end of the meal Trok clapped his hands for attention, and was rewarded with an obsequious silence. 'Your Royal Highness,' he addressed her gravely, 'your divine father of illustrious memory must have had some premonition of the fate that awaited him. Before his tragic death he spoke to me. He placed you under my protection. I accepted this as a sacred charge. You need never appeal to any other for protection.' He placed his right hand upon her bowed head, and in the other hand he raised a scroll of parchment.

'This is my royal proclamation setting aside the betrothal of the Princess Mintaka of the House of Apepi to Pharaoh Nefer Seti of the House of Tamose. Furthermore, it contains a proclamation of the marriage of the Princess Mintaka to Pharaoh Trok Uruk. The proclamation has been ratified by the cartouche of Lord Naja, accepting and confirming it in the name of Pharaoh Nefer Seti.' He handed the scroll to his chamberlain with a terse instruction. 'Have one hundred copies made of this proclamation and cause them to be publicly displayed in every city in Egypt.'

Then, with both hands, he lifted Mintaka to her feet. 'You and I will be husband and wife before the rise of the Moon of Osiris.'

THREE DAYS LATER Pharaoh Trok Uruk arrived at Avaris, his military capital in the Lower Kingdom. The populace was delirious with joy at the news of the Treaty of Hathor, and at the promise of peace and prosperity in the years ahead. However, there was some dismay when one of the first acts of the new pharaoh was to put in hand another massive draft of men for the army. It soon became clear that he was intent on doubling the size of his infantry regiments and building two thousand more fighting chariots.

The question was asked, but not to Trok's face, where he expected to find an enemy now that Egypt was united and at peace. The loss of working men from fields and pastures to the army resulted in a shortage of food, and the expenditure on chariots and equipment necessitated an increase in taxation. There were mutters now that Apepi had not been as bad a ruler as they had believed him to be.

The muttering grew louder when Trok ordered work to commence on the extensive enlargements and refurbishment of the palace in Avaris into which he intended to move with his bride. The architects estimated these works would cost over two lakhs of gold.

A revolt started in the delta, where a regiment of foot, unpaid for over a year, murdered their officers and marched on Avaris. Trok met them with three hundred chariots near the village of Manashi and cut them to pieces with his first charge. He then impaled five hundred mutineers on stakes. Like a macabre forest, they decorated both sides of the road for half a league beyond the village.

A few hundred mutineers escaped the massacre and disappeared into the desert. Trok did not bother to pursue them, for this petty matter had delayed his wedding. He hurried back to Avaris, using up three pairs of horses in his furious impatience.

There his wedding with Princess Mintaka Apepi was carried out in the ancient Hyksosian tradition. First the high priest bound Mintaka to him with a halter rope, and then, at the culmination of the ceremony, Trok cut the throat of his favourite warhorse, a beautiful chestnut stallion, as a sign that he placed a higher value on his bride than on this other precious possession. As the animal fell, the company shouted their acclamation and lifted the couple into the flower-bedecked chariot.

Trok drove back to the palace with one arm firmly round his bride. The army lined the way, showering gifts of amulets and good-luck charms into the cockpit. Others held up bowls of wine to Trok as he drove past, and he gulped them down.

By the time they reached the palace, Trok was sweating and dusty from the ride, reckless with wine, and wild-eyed with lust.

He carried Mintaka through the crowd into their new apartments, and the guards at the door turned back the wedding guests with drawn swords. However, they did not disperse but surrounded the palace, chanting encouragement to the bridegroom and ribald advice to the bride.

In the bedchamber Trok threw Mintaka onto the white sheepskin that covered the mattress, and used both hands to struggle with his sword-belt, trying to loosen the clasp. Mintaka leapt up and raced to the terrace door but locking bars on the outside had been put in place. Desperately she tried to beat open the panels, but the doors were thick and did not even tremble to her onslaught.

Behind her, Trok had at last rid himself of the sword-belt and came lumbering unsteadily after her. 'Fight as much as you wish,' he slurred. 'It sets me on fire when you kick and scream.'

He placed one arm round her waist, and threw her down again, this time pinning her with one huge muscular arm across her chest. His face was inches from hers. His beard prickled her cheeks, and his breath smelt of sour wine. She twisted her face away. He laughed and hooked one finger in the neck of her shift and ripped the silk to below her waist.

He straddled her, sitting across her lower body with all his weight so that she could not struggle, and tore off his tunic. Under it he was naked, and although her vision was distorted by terror, she had an impression of wide shoulders and bulging muscle, limbs thick and thewy as the branches of a cedar of Lebanon.

Still pinning her under him, he twisted round until his belly pressed against hers. He tried to force a knee between her thighs, but she kept them locked together, hooking one of her legs over the other. She fought not only for her modesty, but as if for her very life. Every muscle in her lower body was frozen in a rigor of fear and revulsion, hard and as impenetrable as a granite statue.

Suddenly he swung a heavy blow, flat-handed, across her face. It jarred her clenched jaws, crushing her lips. She felt blood flood into her mouth and darkness fill her head and knew she could not last out much longer.

'Hathor, help me!' She closed her eyes and prayed. 'Sweet goddess, do not let it happen!'

She heard him groan above her, and her eyes flew open. She saw him arch his back and he moaned as though in pain. Mintaka did not understand what was happening. For a moment she thought the goddess must have heard her plea and struck him through the heart with a divine dart. Then she felt hot liquid spray onto her stomach. She tried to twist away to avoid it, but he was too heavy and strong.

At last, he groaned and collapsed on top of her. Then he roused himself and looked down at her. 'You have shamed me, you little slut. You have made me spill my seed in vain.'

Before she knew what he was about, he had grabbed her by the back of her neck and forced her face into the white sheepskin.

'Never fear, I shall use the blood from your nose if I can't have it from your honeypot.' He rolled her aside and inspected the crimson stain from her bleeding face on the pure white wool with grim satisfaction. Then he jumped to his feet, strode to the shutters and kicked them open with a crash. He disappeared out into the bright daylight.

His sword-belt lay where he had dropped it. Quietly Mintaka slipped from the bed and drew the burnished bronze blade from its scabbard. She crept to the door that led onto the terrace and flattened herself against the jamb.

Out on the balcony, Trok was acknowledging the applause of the crowd and flapping the stained sheepskin for all to see. Mintaka tightened her grip on the haft of the sword and gathered herself.

'Farewell, my friends,' Trok shouted. 'I am going back for another bite at that sweet fig.'

She heard his bare feet swish on the tiles as he returned and then his shadow fell across the entrance. She drew back the heavy sword with both hands, and held the point at belly height.

As he stepped into the chamber she braced herself and then with all her strength thrust at him. But Trok possessed a feral instinct for danger and twisted away from the sharp bronze point. It flew the width of a finger past his hairy stomach, without drawing a drop of blood. Then he clamped both her wrists in one of his huge paws and squeezed until she had to let the weapon drop.

He was laughing as he dragged her across the room, but it was an ugly sound. He threw her face down onto the rumpled, sweat-sour bed, and picked up the sword scabbard from where it lay. 'This lesson in obedience is for your own good. A little pain now will save us both a great deal of unhappiness later.'

The scabbard was of polished leather, bound with gold and studded with metal rosettes. He swung it down across the back of her naked legs. It left a welt with the pattern of rosettes in brighter scarlet.

He lifted the scabbard again. She tried to roll away from him but the next blow caught her across her raised right arm, and the next across her shoulder. Then he knocked her off the bed and when she rolled herself into a ball he lashed her across her back. He spoke to her while he kept the blows falling. 'You will never lift a hand to me again! Next time I come to you, you will behave as a loving wife, or I will have four of my men hold you down while I mount you!'

She clenched her jaws as the blows rained down upon her until mercifully he stepped away, breathing heavily, and pulled on his dust-streaked tunic. He stalked to the door of the chamber. There he paused and looked back at her.

'Remember one thing, wife. Either I break my mares,' he said, 'or, by Seueth, they die under me.' He turned and was gone.

IT WAS LONG after the waning of the Moon of Isis before Mintaka's bruises faded to greenish-yellow stains on her smooth, creamy skin.

Since their calamitous wedding day Trok had left her alone. Most of that time he was campaigning in the south. Even when he returned for brief periods to Avaris he avoided her. Perhaps he was repelled by her unsightly injuries or shamed by his failure to consummate their marriage. Mintaka did not ponder the reason too deeply, but she rejoiced in being free of his brutish attentions.

There had been further serious rebellion in the south of the kingdom, and Mintaka knew that Trok had returned triumphantly to Avaris three days ago, but she had still not seen him. She thanked the goddess for that, but it was premature. The summons came from him on the fourth day. Mintaka was to attend an extraordinary session of the state council. His message warned her that should she choose to ignore his summons he would send his bodyguards to drag her to the conclave. She had no option.

This was the first occasion on which Mintaka had appeared in public since her wedding. With her make-up carefully applied she was as lovely as ever as she took her seat on the queen's throne, below that of Pharaoh, in the lavishly redecorated assembly hall of the palace.

Trok acknowledged the herald, then called upon him to rise and state his news to the council. When he rose to his feet Mintaka saw that he was in the grip of deep emotion. 'Sacred Majesty, I bring tragic tidings from Thebes.' He paused and spread his arms in a gesture of despair. 'Last month, on the eve of the festival of Hapi, the young Pharaoh Nefer Seti, whom we all loved, and in whom we placed so much trust and hope, died of the grievous wounds that he received while hunting.' There was a concerted sigh of despair.

The herald spoke again: 'The Regent of the Upper Kingdom, Lord Naja, who is next in succession, has been raised to the throne in the place of the departed Pharaoh. He purifies the land in his name, he endures unto eternity in his name of Naja, the fear of him through all the world is great in his name of Pharaoh Naja Kiafan.'

The cries of mourning for the dead Pharaoh and the clamour of acclamation for his successor filled the hall.

In the uproar, Mintaka stared at the herald. Trok was watching her and she knew he was revelling in her pain. She listened to the rest of the proceedings, but her thoughts were with Nefer. In her mind a picture of him appeared as though he still lived. She wondered what point he had reached on his dread journey through the netherworld, and she prayed for his safety. She prayed for him to reach the green hills of paradise, and that she should soon be reunited with him there. I shall follow you soon, my heart, she promised him.

TAITA HAD BROUGHT Nefer back to Thebes from Dabba still in a deep sleep. As soon as the galley carrying them moored at the stone jetty below the palace, Taita had him carried ashore on a curtained litter. It would have been unwise to allow Pharaoh's critical condition to become widely known.

Once Nefer was safe in his royal quarters at the palace, Taita was able to work on him in seclusion. His first concern was to examine again the boy's terrible lacerations and assess if there had been any morbid changes.

He unwrapped the bandages, probed the openings gently, and was greatly relieved to find no taint of contamination. He syringed the deepest wounds with a mixture of vinegar and oriental spices. Then he stitched them closed with catgut and bandaged them.

He was rewarded when at last Nefer recovered consciousness and smiled at him. 'Taita, I knew you were with me.'

The following day he sat up and ate a meal of millet bread and chickpea soup. Then he looked around him. 'Where is Mintaka?'

When Taita explained her absence, Nefer's disappointment was almost palpable. Taita tried to console him by telling him that he would soon be well enough to visit Avaris.

The next day the terrible news of the tragedy at Balasfura reached Thebes from the Lower Kingdom. Nefer tried to convince Taita that he was strong enough to make the long journey to be with Mintaka in her bereavement. Gently Taita dissuaded him, but promised that as soon as Nefer was strong enough he would use all his influence to convince Lord Naja to allow him to go. With this goal to strive towards, Nefer rallied strongly. Taita could see him subduing the evil humours in his blood by sheer strength of will.

Lord Naja returned from the north, and within hours Heseret came to visit Nefer for the first time since his mauling by the lion. She brought him gifts of sweetmeats and a pot of wild honey in the comb, excusing herself for having neglected him.

'My dear husband, the Regent of the Upper Kingdom, has been away all these weeks,' she explained, 'and I have pined so much for his return that I was afraid that my unhappiness might affect you badly, my poor darling.' She stayed an hour, sang to him, and related some of the scandalous doings of the court. At last she excused herself: 'My husband does not like me to leave his side for long. We are so much in love, Nefer. He is a wonderful man. You must learn to trust him completely, as I do.' She rose to her feet and then, as though in an afterthought, she remarked lightly, 'You must have been relieved to hear that Pharaoh Trok Uruk and my dear husband, the Regent of Upper Egypt, have agreed to cancel your betrothal to that little Hyksosian barbarian, Mintaka. I was so sorry for you when I heard that such a disgraceful marriage had been thrust upon you. My husband was against it from the beginning, as I was.'

After she had gone Nefer sank back weakly on the pillow and closed his eyes. When Taita came to him a little later he was puzzled by the way in which he had relapsed. He stayed with him through that night, exerting all his powers to ward off the shadows of evil that surrounded the young Pharaoh.

At dawn he was startled to hear Lord Naja's commanding voice ordering the guards at the door to stand aside. The regent strode into the chamber and, without greeting Taita, stooped over Nefer's still form and peered into his face. After a long moment he straightened up and signed to Taita to follow him onto the terrace.

'You wished to speak to me, my lord?' Taita asked.

Naja turned to him. His expression was grim. 'You have disappointed me, old man,' he said, and Taita bowed his head but made no reply. 'I had hoped that my way forwards would be cleared by now of impediment.' He stared hard at Taita. 'Yet it seems that, far from allowing this, you have done all in your power to prevent it.'

'This has been pretence. I have merely made a show of caring for my patient. As you can see for yourself, Pharaoh hangs over the great abyss.' Taita made a gesture towards the sick chamber where Nefer lay. 'Surely you can sense the shades drawing in around him. My lord, we have almost obtained our object. Within days the way ahead will be cleared for you.'

Naja was not convinced. 'I am reaching the limit of my patience,' he warned, and strode from the terrace. He passed through the chamber without another glance at the still form upon the bed.

During that day Nefer's condition fluctuated. Taita sat for a while collecting his thoughts, reviewing the plans he had laid so carefully over the past weeks. He could not do it alone, and would have to rely on others, but he had chosen the best. They were ready to act, and they had been waiting for his word. He could delay no longer.

AT HIS BIDDING the slaves brought kettles of hot water and Taita washed Nefer from head to foot. When he had finished, he warned the guards not to let anybody pass, and barred all the entrances to the chamber. He prayed for a while and then threw incense on the brazier, and in the blue and aromatic smoke made an ancient, potent incantation to Anubis, the god of death and cemeteries.

Only then did he prepare the elixir of Anubis in a new and unused vessel. He warmed the mixture on the brazier until it was the temperature of blood, and took it to the bed where Nefer was sleeping quietly. Gently he turned his head to one side and poured the elixir into the eardrum a drop at a time. Carefully he wiped away the excess, taking care that it should not touch his own skin. Then he plugged Nefer's ear with a small ball of wool, pushed deeply into the passage.

He watched Nefer's chest rise and fall to his breathing. Each breath was slower and the intervals between them longer. At last they ceased altogether. He placed two fingers on Nefer's throat beneath his ear, and felt the slow deliberate pulsing of the life force within him. Gradually that also faded away until it was only an occasional flutter that took all his skill and experience to detect. Gently he closed the boy's eyes and placed an amulet upon the lids in the traditional preparation of the corpse. Next he bound a strip of linen over them, and another under his jaw to keep his mouth from gaping open. At last he went to the door and removed the locking bar.

'Send word to the Regent of the Upper Kingdom. He should come immediately to hear terrible tidings of Pharaoh.'

Lord Naja arrived with surprising alacrity. Princess Heseret was with him, and they were followed by the Assyrian doctor, Noom, and most of the members of the council.

Heseret was weeping ostentatiously and covering her eyes with an embroidered linen shawl. Naja glanced at the bandaged body laid out on the couch, then glanced at Taita with a question in his eyes. In reply Taita nodded slightly. Naja masked the gleam of triumph in his eyes, then clapped his hands.

'Let the good doctor Noom come forward,' Naja ordered. 'Let him confirm the Magus's pronouncement of Pharaoh's death.'

The Assyrian's long locks had been curled with hot tongs and dangled to his shoulders. His beard had also been curled in the fashion of Babylon. His robe swept the floor and was decorated with embroidered magical symbols. He knelt beside the deathbed and began an examination of the corpse. He sniffed at Nefer's lips, then placed his ear against Nefer's chest and listened. Taita had placed much store in the Assyrian's ineptitude.

Then Noom took a long silver pin from the hem of his robe and opened Nefer's limp hand. He pricked the point deeply up under the fingernail and watched for a muscular reaction. At last he stood up slowly, and shook his head. 'Pharaoh is dead,' he announced.

Lord Naja threw back his head and gave the first cry of lamentation, and Heseret, standing behind him, took up the wailing cry.

Taita waited for the mourners to file past the couch, and one by one to leave the chamber. When only Naja and Heseret remained, Taita stepped forward. 'Lord Naja, I beg your indulgence. You are aware that I have been Pharaoh Nefer Seti's tutor and servant since his birth. I owe him respect and duty, even now in death. I beg you to allow me to be the one to convey his corpse to the Hall of Sorrow, and there to make the incision to remove his heart and viscera. I would take that as the greatest honour you could bestow on me.'

Lord Naja thought for a while, then nodded. 'You have earned that honour. I charge you with the duty of conveying Pharaoh's sacred body to the funeral temple for embalming.'

THE OLD WARRIOR, Hilto, came swiftly to Taita's summons. He had been waiting in the guardroom at the palace gates. With him he brought four of his most trusted men. One of these was Meren, the friend and companion of Nefer's childhood. He was now a handsome ensign of the guards, and Taita had asked for him particularly.

Between them they carried the long woven basket that the embalmers used to transport their cadavers to the funerary temple. It was heavier than one might have expected.

Taita let them into the death chamber and whispered to Hilto, 'Swiftly now! Every second is precious.'

He had already wrapped Nefer in a long white winding sheet, with a loose fold of linen covering his face. The pallbearers laid the basket beside the couch and lifted Nefer into it. Taita closed the lid, and nodded. 'To the temple,' he said. 'All is in readiness.'

Taita trusted his leather instrument bag to Meren, and they moved quickly through the passages and courtyards of the palace. The sounds of mourning and lamentation followed them. The guards lowered the points of their weapons and knelt as the dead Pharaoh passed. The women covered their faces and wailed.

In the entrance courtyard a squadron of Hilto's chariots was drawn up with the horses in the traces. The bearers laid the basket on the footplate of the leading chariot and secured it. Taita mounted and took the reins. The rams' horns of the regiment sounded a dirge, and the column moved out through the gates at a walk.

The news of Pharaoh's death had spread throughout the city. Crowds lined the route along the river. Women ran forward and threw sacred lotus blossoms onto the basket.

Taita pushed the horses into a trot, then into a canter, desperate to get the basket into the sanctuary of the funerary temple.

The tall, rose-coloured granite walls and portico of the temple were set upon a low prominence overlooking the river. The priests, hastily assembled, were waiting to greet the column. Their heads were freshly shaven and anointed with oil. Taita drove up the wide causeway and halted the chariot at the foot of the staircase that mounted to the Hall of Sorrow.

Hilto and his warriors lifted the basket and climbed the staircase with it balanced on their shoulders. The priests fell in behind them, singing mournfully. Before the open wooden doors of the Hall of Sorrow the pallbearers paused, and Taita looked back at the priests.

'By the grace and authority of the Regent of Egypt, I, Taita, have been charged with lifting Pharaoh's viscera.' He fixed the high priest with a mesmeric gaze. 'All others will wait without while I perform this sacred charge.'

Taita led the bearers through the doorway and they solemnly laid the basket on the floor beside the black diorite slab in the centre of the Hall of Sorrow. Hilto closed the doors with great dignity in the faces of the assembled priests, then hurried back to Taita's side. Between them they opened the basket and lifted Nefer's body. They laid it on the black slab.

Taita folded back the cloth that covered Nefer's face, gently turned his head to one side and nodded at Meren, who placed the leather bag close to his right hand and opened it. Taita selected the ivory forceps, slipped the points into Nefer's ear and drew out the woollen plug. Through a gold tube he carefully sluiced the dregs of the elixir of Anubis from Nefer's eardrum. He had the antidote ready in another phial. When he opened the stopper it released a sharp odour of camphor and sulphur. Hilto helped them to lift Nefer into a sitting position and Taita administered the entire contents of the phial.

Suddenly Nefer coughed harshly. Taita massaged Nefer's bare back and he coughed again, vomiting yellow bile. While Taita kept working steadily at reviving him, Hilto ordered his men to their knees and made them swear a dreadful oath of secrecy as to all that they were witnessing.

Satisfied at last, Taita rewrapped Nefer in the linen sheet, turned back to the basket, and lifted out the false bottom to reveal another corpse laid in the compartment beneath, also wrapped in a white linen winding sheet.

Under Taita's sharp eye they changed the two bodies. They laid Nefer in the hidden compartment in the bottom of the basket, and Meren squatted beside it to watch him and check his condition. The others laid the strange corpse on the diorite slab.

Taita swept away the winding sheet and revealed the body of a youth of about the same age and bodily shape of Nefer. He had the same thick dark hair. The young thief had been put to death by strangulation that very morning and his body was not yet cold.

The Canopic jars were arranged in the small shrine at the end of the hall. Taita ordered Meren to fetch them and open the stoppers ready for filling. While he was doing this, Taita rolled the corpse over and made a sweeping incision down his left side. There was little time for surgical finesse. He thrust his hand into the opening and drew forth the viscera. Then he cut through the diaphragm to gain access to the chest cavity, reaching deep until he could sever the windpipe above its juncture with the lungs. When all the contents of the interior of the chest and abdomen were unanchored, he brought them out onto the diorite slab in a single mass. Meren blanched, fled to the stone basin in the corner and puked noisily into it.

Bloodied to the elbows, Taita flushed out the contents of the stomach and entrails and packed them into their jars. He filled every jar with the pickling natron salts, and sealed the stoppers. Then he washed his hands and arms in the bronze basins filled with water expressly for that purpose.

Working with controlled haste, Taita stitched the abdominal incision closed. Then he bandaged the head until its features were hidden. When that was done, he and Hilto carried the corpse to the large natron bath and lowered it into the harsh alkali mixture, which would leach the fats out of the body and peel the skin away. It would remain in the bath, with the head covered, for the next sixty days. At the end of that time the priests would remove the bandage and discover the substitution. By then, however, Taita and Nefer would be far away.

It took only a little longer to sluice down the slab and pack Taita's instruments before they were ready to leave. Taita knelt beside the basket in which Nefer lay, and laid a hand on his chest to feel its warmth and check his breathing. It was slow and even. Satisfied, he stood up and gestured for Hilto to cover the hidden compartment. When this was done the bearers lifted the basket and Taita led them to the doors. As they approached Hilto threw them open, and the assembly of priests craned forward. They gave the empty basket only a cursory glance as it was carried out, then rushed into the Hall of Sorrow with almost indecent haste.

Ignored by the crowds that had gathered outside the temple, Taita's men loaded the basket onto the leading chariot and drove it to the guard's barracks near the east gate. There the basket was carried through the back entrance of Hilto's private quarters. Here, everything was in readiness. They lifted Nefer out and Taita went to work to revive him fully. Within hours he was well enough to eat a little millet bread and drink a bowl of warm milk and honey.

At last Taita judged it safe to leave him for a while, and drove through the narrow streets. Ahead of him he heard the sudden din of wild cheering. At the palace he found himself enveloped in a dense crowd of citizens celebrating the ascension of the new pharaoh. 'Eternal life to His Sacred Majesty Pharaoh Naja Kiafan!' they cried with loyal fervour, and passed the wine jugs from hand to hand.

The palace guards recognised Taita, and used the butts of their spears to clear the way for him to pass. Once he was in the grounds he hurried to the great hall, and there he found another press of obsequious humanity, waiting to swear fealty.

Pharaoh Naja Kiafan and his queen were in the private cabinet beyond the doors at the end of the hall, but Taita had to wait only a short while before he was granted access to the royal presence.

Naja was already wearing the double crown, and holding the flail and the crook crossed over his chest. Beside him Queen Heseret was as lovely as Taita had ever known her. When Taita entered, Naja dismissed those around him and soon the three were alone. Then Naja laid aside the scourge and the sceptre and came to embrace Taita.

'Magus, I should never have doubted you,' he said. 'You have earned my gratitude.' He took from his right hand a magnificent ring of gold and ruby, and placed it on Taita's right index finger. 'This is but a small token of my favour.'

Heseret came forward and kissed him. 'Dearest Taita, you have always been faithful to my family. You shall have gold, land and influence beyond anything you have ever coveted.'

After all these years she knew so little of him. 'Your generosity is exceeded only by your beauty,' he said. Then he turned back to Naja. 'I have done what the gods required of me, Your Grace, but it has cost me dear. You know that I loved Nefer. Now I owe you that same love. But I must mourn Nefer, and make my peace with his shade.'

'It would be strange indeed if you did not feel for the dead Pharaoh,' Naja agreed. 'What do you wish of me, Magus? You have only to speak.'

'Your Grace, I ask to go into the desert to be alone for a time.'

'How long?' Naja asked, and Taita could see he was alarmed by the thought of losing the key to eternal life, which he truly believed Taita held in his hands.

'Not too long, Majesty,' Taita assured him.

Naja thought about it for a while. He was never a man for hasty decisions. At last he sighed. 'You may absent yourself until the next inundation of the Nile begins, but then you must return to me.' Swiftly he wrote out a safe pass and sealed it with his cartouche. 'This will allow you to travel at large and avail yourself of whatever food and equipment you may need from my royal storehouses.'

Taita prostrated himself in gratitude, but Naja lifted him to his feet in another act of condescension. 'Go, Magus! But return to us on the appointed day to receive the rewards you so richly deserve.'

Clutching the roll of papyrus Taita backed towards the door making the signs of blessing and benediction.

THEY LEFT THEBES early the next morning while most of the city still slept and the guards at the east gate were yawning and heavy-eyed.

Nefer was laid in the back of the wagon, which was drawn by a team of four horses and loaded with essential supplies and the equipment they might need once they had left the river valley. Hilto was dressed as a wealthy farmer and Meren as his son.

Nefer was laid on a straw mattress in the bed of the wagon, under a screen of tanned leather. He was now fully conscious and able to understand all that Taita had to tell him. When the sergeant of the guard climbed into the wagon to inspect the contents, Nefer peered out at him with his gaunt features spotted with the unmistakable stigmata of the plague that Taita had applied. The sergeant swore with horror and leapt down.

'Get you gone!' he shouted. 'Take that poxy wretch out of the city.'

It took them several days to cross the littoral plain of the river and reach the hills that marked the frontiers of the desert, following the old trade route eastwards towards the Red Sea. Now Nefer was able to climb down from the wagon, and for short periods limp along beside it. Soon he was walking more easily and for longer periods.

They rested for three days at the ancient ruined city of Gallala. They refilled the water-skins at the well and let the horses recover from the rigours of the hard, stony road. When they were fit to resume the journey, they travelled in the cool of the night, and took the path known only to Taita that led to Gebel Nagara. Hilto swept their back-trail and covered all signs of their passage.

They arrived in the cave in the middle of a night lit by bright stars. There was not enough water in the tiny seep to supply so many men and horses, so once the wagon was unloaded Hilto started back, leaving Meren to serve Taita and Nefer. Hilto had resigned from his regiment on the pretext of ill health, so he was free to return with every full moon to bring supplies, medicine and news from Thebes.

The first month at Gebel Nagara passed swiftly. In the clean, dry desert air Nefer's wounds healed fully, and soon he was limping out into the desert to hunt with Meren.

At the end of that month Hilto returned from Thebes with the news that Taita's subterfuge had not yet been discovered. He also brought news of insurrections in the Lower Kingdom, and unrest in the Upper Kingdom also, where Naja, like Trok, had increased taxation and ordered an enlistment of men into the army.

'What other news have you from the Lower Kingdom?' Nefer asked eagerly. 'What news is there of Princess Mintaka?'

Hilto looked puzzled. 'None that I know of. I should think she is in Avaris, but I cannot be certain.'

The following evening, Hilto left Gebel Nagara at the setting of the sun, and struck out into the wilderness.

THE NEXT MOON passed more swiftly than the last, as Nefer grew stronger and more restless. Each day his limp became less noticeable. On his latest visit, Hilto had brought with him a full-weight war-bow. Under Taita's instruction Nefer now practised with it every day, building up the muscles in his back and shoulders. Hilto had also brought them a rack of heavy sickle swords, and Taita would bring them out and lead Nefer and Meren through the entire repertoire of cuts, thrusts and parries.

On other evenings Nefer and Meren stripped naked, oiled their bodies and wrestled, while Taita umpired their bouts and called advice and instruction. Then, late into the night, Taita and Nefer sat by the fire and debated every subject from medicine and politics to war and religion. Often Taita placed hidden traps and illogicalities in these lessons, and more often now, and with greater alacrity, Nefer would uncover and question them.

The month passed so swiftly that it was with a small shock of surprise that Nefer, while running through the desert in pursuit of a gazelle, suddenly noticed on the horizon the distant shape of the wagon returning from the river valley. On the instant, he forgot the gazelle he was chasing and raced to meet Hilto.

'Hilto!' Nefer yelled, still at a distance. 'What news? What news?'

Hilto pretended to misunderstand the question, and as Nefer walked at his side he began a long-winded recital of political events in the kingdoms. 'There has been another rebellion in the north. This time Trok found it harder to put down. He lost four hundred men and half the rebels escaped his wrath.'

Later, around the campfire in the cave, it was agony for Nefer to have to listen to Hilto making a long, detailed report to Taita, the most important part of which was that the substitution of bodies had been discovered when the priests of Anubis had unwrapped the head of the corpse in the Hall of Sorrow. Pharaoh Naja Kiafan had done his best to prevent the news becoming public knowledge, for the foundations of his throne would be undermined if the populace suspected that Nefer was still alive. However, it was impossible to keep such an extraordinary event secret, and rumours were rife in Thebes and the outlying towns and villages.

Added to this, trouble was brewing in the east. The Egyptian pharaohs had sent word to King Sargon of Babylon, that mighty kingdom between the Tigris and Euphrates, demanding that Sargon's annual tribute be increased to twenty lakhs of gold. It was a crippling amount to which Sargon could never agree.

'So, this accounts for the build-up of the armies in both kingdoms,' Taita said, as Hilto paused in his report. 'It is clear at last that the two pharaohs are greedy for the riches of Babylon. They are intent on conquest. They know too that war is a uniting factor. If they march on Mesopotamia the populace will rally behind them in a patriotic frenzy. It is a marvellous way to take the minds of the people off their grievances.'

'Yes.' Hilto nodded. 'You are right.'

'Of course, this is to our advantage,' Taita mused. 'I have been seeking a haven for us. If he is at war with Trok and Naja, then Sargon will welcome us to his side.'

'We are leaving Egypt?' Hilto interjected.

Taita explained, 'Now that Naja and Trok know that Nefer still lives, they will come after us. The road to the east is the only one open to us. It will not be for long, just until we have built up our strength and support throughout the two kingdoms and have made ourselves powerful allies. Then we will return to reclaim Pharaoh Nefer's birthright.'

They stared at him. It was Nefer who broke the silence. 'We can't do that,' he said. 'I cannot leave Egypt. I took an oath on my life and eternal spirit that I would not desert Mintaka.' He turned to Hilto. 'You have been evading my questions, Hilto. What news do you have of the princess?'

Hilto opened and closed his mouth, trying to find the courage to tell him the dire news.

'Speak!' Nefer ordered. 'Have you forgotten your duty?'

'Gracious Majesty, the news will not please you. Six weeks ago the Princess Mintaka was married in Avaris to Pharaoh Trok Uruk.'

Nefer stood as still as if he had been turned into a granite statue. For a long time the only sound in the cave was the crackle of the acacia logs in the fire. Then without another word, Nefer stood up and walked out into the desert night.

When he returned the dawn was a faint red promise in the eastern sky. Hilto and Meren were wrapped in their sheepskins at the back of the cave, but Taita sat in exactly the same position as Nefer had left him. For a moment he thought that the old man was asleep also. Then Taita raised his head and looked at him.

'I need you now, more than ever, old friend,' said Nefer. 'You will not desert me?'

'You need not ask,' Taita said softly.

'I cannot leave her with Trok,' Nefer said.

'No.'

Nefer came back to his seat opposite Taita. He picked up a charred stump of firewood and pushed it deeper into the flames. Then he looked up at Taita again. 'You have tried to teach me to overlook at a distance,' he said. 'I have never acquired the gift. Not until this night. Out there in the darkness, I tried to overlook Mintaka. This time I saw something, Taita, but only dimly.'

'Your love for her has made you sensitive to her aura,' Taita explained. 'What did you see?'

'I saw only shadows, but sensed sorrow and grief and despair so insupportable that it made me wish for death. I knew that these were Mintaka's emotions and not my own.'

Taita stared expressionlessly into the fire, and Nefer went on, 'You must overlook her for me. There is something terribly wrong. Only you can help her now, Taita.'

'Do you have anything of Mintaka's?' the old man asked. 'Any gift or token that she gave you?'

Nefer's hand went to the necklace at his throat. He touched the tiny golden locket that hung in its centre. 'It is my most precious possession. It contains a lock of her hair.'

'Then it is highly potent. It contains her essence. Give it to me, if you wish me to help her.'

Nefer opened the clasp and passed him the amulet.

'Wait here,' Taita said, and stood up. He went out into the dawn and climbed to the crest of the dunes, then squatted in the sand, facing the rising sun. He pressed Mintaka's amulet to his forehead and closed his eyes. It seemed to take on some strange life of its own, pulsing softly in rhythm with his own heartbeats. Taita opened his mind and let the currents of existence enter freely, swirling round him like a great river. His own spirit broke free of his body and he soared aloft. In his mind he called for her, Mintaka! And felt the amulet grow warm then burning hot in his hand.

Slowly the images cleared away, and he heard her sweet voice reply, 'I am here. Who is it that calls?'

'Mintaka, it is Taita,' he replied, but he was aware that something evil had intervened and broken the stream between them. He focused all his powers upon it, trying to disperse the dark clouds. They seemed to coalesce, and took the shape of a rearing cobra. Suddenly he knew this was a direct and mortal threat against Mintaka. He redoubled his efforts to reach her, but so much pain and grief interposed between them that it was an impenetrable barrier.

Then he saw a hand, slim and graceful, reach out towards the sinister scaly head. It was Mintaka's hand and Taita understood. Mintaka, overwhelmed with grief, was about to take the way of the goddess and find peace in her bosom.

He held the serpent in check with all his life force, and prevented it from striking Mintaka's hand as she stroked the back of its hood. 'Mintaka!' He exerted himself to reach her, and was rewarded.

'Taita?' she whispered, and because Mintaka was at last aware of him, Taita's view expanded so that he could see it all clearly.

Mintaka was in a stone-walled bedchamber. She was kneeling in front of a large basket woven from palm fronds. Out of it reared the deadly snake.

'You must not take this road,' Taita ordered her. 'It is not for you. The gods have prepared a different destiny for you. Do you hear me?'

'Yes!' Mintaka turned her head, as though she could see his face.

'Nefer is alive. Nefer lives. Do you hear me?'

'Yes! Oh, yes.'

'Be strong, Mintaka. Nefer and I will come for you.'

So fierce was his concentration that he dug his fingernails deeply into the palms of his hands until the blood welled, but he could hold her no longer. She began to slip away from him, but before she was gone he saw her smile, full of love and renewed hope.

'Be strong!' he urged her. 'Be strong, Mintaka!' The echo of his voice came back to him as though from a great distance.

NEFER WAS WAITING for him at the foot of the dunes. When Taita was only halfway down the boy realised that something momentous had taken place. 'You saw her!' he shouted, and ran forward. 'What has happened to her?'

'She needs us,' Taita said, and laid a hand on Nefer's shoulder. He could never tell him of the despair in which he had found Mintaka, nor of the fate she had prepared for herself. It might drive him to some wild endeavour. 'You were right,' Taita went on. 'All my plans to leave this land and find sanctuary in the east must be set aside. We have to go to Mintaka. I have promised her that.'

'Yes!' Nefer agreed. 'When can we leave for Avaris?'

Taita replied, 'There is great urgency. We will leave at once.'

IT TOOK THEM FIFTEEN DAYS of hard travel to reach the tiny garrison station of Thane, a day's travel south of Avaris. En route, they discussed their plans endlessly, knowing that they were pitted against the might of Pharaoh Trok Uruk. The officers they spoke to at the garrisons and camps they passed estimated that Trok now had twenty-seven fully trained and equipped regiments at his disposal and almost three thousand chariots. To oppose this multitude they had a wagon showing the effects of long, hard service, with a back wheel that had a propensity to fall off at the most inappropriate times. There were only the four of them: Nefer and Meren, Hilto and Taita.

Hilto knew the captain in charge of the encampment at Thane, a grizzled old warrior named Socco. Long ago they had fought, roistered and whored together. After they had reminisced for an hour and shared a pot of sour beer, Hilto handed him the requisition scroll that Naja had given to Taita. Socco held it upside down at arm's length and looked wise.

'See the cartouche of Pharaoh.' Hilto touched the seal.

'If I know you at all, Hilto, you probably drew that pretty picture yourself.' Socco handed back the scroll. 'What do you need, you old rogue?'

They selected fresh horses, then Taita went over the ranks of parked chariots in the garrison pool that had just been sent out from the makers in Avaris. He chose three vehicles, and they harnessed the fresh horses.

When they left Thane, Taita was driving the old wagon, while Meren, Hilto and Nefer each drove a chariot. They did not head directly for Avaris but made a detour to a small oasis on the edge of the desert to the east of the city.

While the others unloaded the wagon, Taita went to barter with the Assyrian master of a caravan that was encamped nearby. He bought an armful of tattered clothing and twenty woollen rugs for an extortionate price. 'That Assyrian ape is a robber,' he muttered, as they loaded the carpets onto the wagon.

That night Taita dyed his silver hair with an extract of mimosa bark, which altered his appearance dramatically. In the darkness of early morning they left Meren in charge of the horses and chariots, got into the dilapidated wagon and, sitting on the pile of carpets, headed west towards Avaris. They were dressed in the castoffs that Taita had procured. Taita wore a long robe and sash, the lower half of his face veiled in the fashion of a citizen of Ur of the Chaldeans.

With his dyed dark hair he was unrecognisable as the Magus.

When they reached the royal city of the north, Hilto went to tour the taverns of the old quarter where he hoped to gather news from former comrades-in-arms. Taita and Nefer made their way to the palace gates, and spent the morning listening to the chatter of those around them, and gossiping with other idlers.

At last Taita struck up a conversation with a merchant from Babylon, who introduced himself as Nintura. The two shared a pot of coffee and Taita exerted all his wiles to charm Nintura, who had been loitering outside the palace for the last ten days, waiting for his turn to display his wares to Trok's new bride.

'They say that Trok has been cruelly treated by his young wife. She will not allow him into her bed.' Nintura chuckled. 'He is wild for her, and is trying to win her favours with expensive gifts. They say he will refuse her nothing.'

'Where is Trok now?' Taita asked

'He is campaigning in the south,' Nintura replied. 'He is stamping out the flames of rebellion, but no sooner does he turn his back than they flare up again behind him.'

'Whom should I approach to enter the presence of his queen?'

'The palace vizier. Soleth is his name, the fat, gelded freak.' Nintura had not realised Taita's own condition.

Taita knew Soleth only by reputation and that he was one of the secret brotherhood of eunuchs. 'Where can I find him?' Taita asked.

'It will cost you a gold ring just to enter his presence,' Nintura warned him.

Soleth was sitting beside the lotus pond in his own walled garden when Taita was brought to him. Taita made a dignified salutation as he introduced himself under an assumed name. He followed that with the recognition sign of the brotherhood. Soleth waved to Taita to seat himself on the cushions opposite him, and they swiftly established Taita's credentials and common acquaintances within the brotherhood. Without seeming to do so, Soleth was studying Taita's features. At last he asked softly, 'In your travels you might have met the famous Magus, known through both kingdoms as Taita?'

'I know Taita well,' Taita agreed.

'Perhaps as well as you know yourself?' Soleth asked.

'At least as well as I know myself,' Taita affirmed.

Soleth's chubby face creased in a smile. 'Say no more. What service can I perform for you? You need only ask.'

THAT EVENING NEFER and Hilto were on the carpet load when Taita drove the creaking wagon up to one of the side gates of the palace.

Soleth had sent one of his underlings, an old black slave, to act as a guide. He hobbled ahead of them, ushering them past the guards and guiding them through narrow passages to an elaborately carved sandalwood door guarded by two huge eunuchs. There was a whispered exchange then the sentries stood aside and the slave went through into a large airy room, 'Your Majesty,' he quavered, 'There is a merchant with fine silk carpets from Samarkand to wait upon Your Grace.'

'I have seen enough rubbish for one day,' a woman replied, and Nefer thrilled to her familiar, well-beloved tones. 'Send them away.'

The guide looked back at Taita and spread his hands helplessly. Nefer dropped the carpet off his shoulder and strode onto the terrace. Mintaka was sitting on the parapet wall with two of her slave girls at her feet.

'Forgive me, Majesty,' he murmured softly. 'I am but a poor fool from Dabba.'

Mintaka screamed, then covered her mouth with both hands. The black slave drew his dagger, but Mintaka recovered herself at once. 'No, leave him.' She raised her right hand to reinforce the command. 'Leave us. I will speak with the stupid fellow.'

Confused, the slave sheathed his blade and backed away. The curtains over the entrance fell back into place as he withdrew. Mintaka was still staring at Nefer. Her girls knew that something strange was afoot. Then suddenly she flew to Nefer and he ran to meet her, enfolding her in his embrace. They clung to each other, both talking at the same time. The slave girls recovered from their astonishment and clapped their hands with joy. Taita silenced them with a few prods of his staff, then turned back to Hilto. At his direction the man spread the largest carpet out on the tile.

'Mintaka, listen to me! There will be time for that later. We are going to hide you in the carpet to get you out of the palace. Hurry!'

'Do I have time to fetch my—'

'No,' Taita said. 'You have time for nothing other than to obey me.'

She kissed Nefer once more, then threw herself full length on the carpet. She looked up at her girls, who stood amazed in the doorway. 'Do whatever Taita tells you.'

Nefer helped Hilto roll Mintaka in the patterned red carpet, while Taita instructed the slave girls: 'Stay here in the vestibule. You must not open the door to any demands. Tell anyone who asks that your mistress is laid low by her moon sickness and can see no one. Delay them as long as you are able, but when you are discovered, tell them what they want to know. Do not try to hold out under torture. Now, bar the door behind us when we leave.'

The old slave was waiting in the passage when they carried out the rolled carpet on their shoulders.

'I am sorry. I did my best for you,' he told them, 'but since her marriage Queen Mintaka has become curiously sad and angry.' He beckoned them to follow and led them back through the warren until at last they reached the small side gate.

The wagon stood where they had left it. Gently they loaded the carpet and Nefer scrambled up behind Taita on the wagon box as he urged the horses forward.

Taita whipped up the horse. 'The city gates will soon be closed for the night. When Mintaka's escape is discovered the first thing they will do is seal off the city.'

They galloped down the wide avenue leading to the eastern gate but the way was blocked by other wagons and their progress was tantalisingly slow. The sun had already sunk behind the walls and the light was fading, but there were still two vehicles ahead of them when the captain of the guard yelled at his men, 'That is enough! The sun has set. Close the gates!'

There were yells of protest from all the travellers still trying to pass out. One of the wagons drove forward and tried to block the efforts of the guards to force the gates shut. A small riot broke out, with shouting guards swinging clubs, outraged citizens screaming back at them and frightened horses rearing and whinnying.

'Help me!' Nefer shouted to his companions. Lifting the rolled carpet off the wagon and carrying it between them, they squeezed through the narrow gap between the closing gates, then ran into the encampment below the city walls. There, among the leather tents and shacks, they lowered their burden to the ground and unrolled it. Dishevelled and hot, Mintaka sat up and smiled to see Nefer kneeling in front of her. They reached for each other and embraced.

Taita brought them back to reality. He pulled Mintaka to her feet. 'We have lost the wagon. Ahead of us we have a long journey on foot. Unless we set out now it will be after daylight tomorrow before we reach the oasis where we left Meren with the chariots.'

Mintaka sobered immediately. 'I am ready,' she said.

TROK DROVE THROUGH THE PALACE GATES and reined in his dusty, lathered horses in the courtyard before his own magnificent quarters. Two colonels of his cavalry, both members of the leopard clan and his particular cronies, stumped after him into the banquet hall with weapons and bucklers clattering. The house slaves had laid out a feast to welcome Pharaoh home, but Trok was aware that the manner in which his new wife treated him was weakening his reputation, and he was determined to change that this very night.

'There is more food than even you two oxen can eat,' he told his companions, waving at the groaning board. 'Do your worst, but don't expect me to join you before morning. I have a field to plough and an incorrigible filly to break to my will.'

He strode from the hall and two slaves with burning torches ran ahead of him to light his way. In front of the doors to Mintaka's quarters the eunuch sentries had heard him coming. They crossed their weapons over their fat chests in salute.

'Open up!' Trok ordered.

'Your Majesty.' One of the sentries saluted again nervously. 'The doors are barred by order of Her Majesty Queen Mintaka.'

'By Seueth, I'll have none of that!' Trok kicked open the door and marched into the room beyond. The slave girls were against the far wall in a terrified huddle. 'Where is your mistress?'

'She cannot see you. Her moon has come,' they gabbled.

Trok laughed. 'She has used that excuse too often.' He hammered on the door. 'Open up, you little witch!'

At his next blow the door flew open, torn off its leather hinges, and Trok swaggered through. 'Have you missed me, my little lily?' he called. 'Where are you?' He rampaged through the room and kicked in the doors of her closet. It took him only a minute to make sure that Mintaka was not hiding. He strode to the door and seized one of the slave girls. 'Where is she?'

'She has gone,' cried the girl. 'Men came and took her away in a carpet.'

Trok gave her a brutal kick and shouted at the sentries, 'Find Soleth. Bring the fat slug here immediately.'

Soleth came cringing and wringing his plump hands. 'Divine Pharaoh! Greatest of the gods!' He threw himself at Trok's feet.

Trok kicked him with a full swing of his armoured sandal. 'Who were these men you allowed to enter the *zenana*?'

'On your own orders, gracious Pharaoh, I allowed any vendor of fine merchandise to display it before the Queen.'

'Who was the carpet seller, the last one to enter these quarters?' Trok kicked him again. 'What was his name?'

'I remember now. The carpet merchant from Ur. I forget his name.'

'I will help your memory.' Trok picked up his discarded sword-belt and drew the weapon. 'Now, tell me. Who was the carpet merchant?'

'It was Taita!' Soleth screamed, 'Taita took her away.'

'Taita!' Trok exclaimed with astonishment. 'Taita, the Magus.' There was superstitious dread in his tone. 'Where has he taken her?'

'He did not tell me.'

Trok touched the point of the sword to the eunuch's breast.

Soleth whimpered, 'He did not tell me, but we spoke of the land between the two rivers, the Tigris and the Euphrates. Maybe that is where he intends taking the Queen.'

Trok thought about it. By now Taita would know of the strained relationships between Egypt and the eastern kingdoms. He would know that he might find protection there, if he could run that far. But what was his reason for abducting Mintaka? Had she appealed to him to help her escape from Avaris and her marriage? Certainly, she must have gone with him willingly. The manner in which her slave girls had tried to cover her escape proved that.

He put aside those considerations for the moment. The main concern now was to get the pursuit in hand and recapture her and the warlock before they crossed into territories loyal to Sargon of Babylon. He smiled at Soleth. 'I will deal with you when I return. There are hungry hyenas and vultures to be fed.'

The two colonels, Tolma and Zander, were still in the banquet hall, hogging the food and wine.

'How many chariots can we have manned and running eastward before midnight?' Trok demanded.

Colonel Tolma spat out the wine he was about to swallow and leapt to his feet. 'I can have fifty on the road within two hours,' he blurted.

'I want that to be a hundred,' Trok demanded. 'And another hundred running east before dawn.'

TAITA LED THEM through the night, the tip of his staff clicking on the stony path, and his shadow flitted ahead of him like a monstrous black bat. The others had to stretch their legs to keep him in sight.

After midnight Mintaka began to fail. Nefer shortened his stride to stay with her. 'It is not far now,' he told her, and took her hand to lead her faster. 'Meren will have the horses ready for us. We will ride the rest of the way to Babylon in royal style.'

She laughed but it was a strained, painful sound.

'What is it that ails you?' he demanded.

'Nothing,' she said.

He forced her to sit on a rock beside the path, and unlaced the straps of her sandals. He pulled one off and slabs of skin and flesh came with it, the blood shining in the moonlight. He gently eased off the other sandal. 'You should have warned me of this earlier.' He turned his back to her and braced himself to receive her weight. 'Put your arms around my neck and jump up!' Then he set off after the others who, by this time, were merely a dark shadow on the moonlit desert ahead.

Before long, however, Taita and Hilto came back to search for them. Taita bound up Mintaka's feet and they took turns at carrying her. They went on faster, but the stars were fading and the dawn light was growing stronger when they finally reached the oasis where Meren waited for them with the horses.

All of them were exhausted, but Taita would not allow them to rest. They watered the horses for the last time and refilled the water-skins. While they were doing this Taita half filled a bucket with water from the well and washed the dye from his hair.

'Why does he wash his hair at a time like this?' Meren wondered.

'Perhaps it restores some of his force that he lost when he dyed it,' Mintaka suggested, and no one questioned this.

When they were ready to leave, Taita took Meren in the leading chariot as his lance-bearer. Nefer followed with Mintaka clinging to the dashboard to take the weight off her feet. Hilto brought up the rearguard in the last chariot.

The Assyrian merchant who had sold them the carpets turned to watch them as they passed, and he called a farewell to Taita. But his interest quickened as he saw the girl in the second chariot. Not even her dusty clothing and dishevelled hair could hide her striking looks. He was still staring after them as they topped the last rise and disappeared into the wilderness, heading east.

THE SUN WAS HOT and halfway up the sky when Trok topped the hills above the oasis at the threshold of the wilderness. Following him were two hundred chariots, and five miles behind came Colonel Zander with another two hundred. Each vehicle carried two armed troopers, and was loaded with water-skins and sheaths of spare arrows.

Below them they saw an Assyrian trader coming up the slope from the well at the head of his caravan. Trok rode forward and reined in his chariot in front of him. When he turned from the trader a few short minutes later, Trok began issuing orders to Colonel Tolma, who followed him closely in the second chariot of the column. 'They are only hours ahead of us,' he exulted. 'Top up the water-skins at the well, and let the horses drink their fill. But swiftly, Tolma. Be ready to leave again before noon. In the meantime send your wizards to me.'

Trok found a patch of shade under a gnarled tamarind near the well. The wizards came in response to his summons and squatted around him, two priests of Seueth in their black robes, and a sorcerer from the east known as Ishtar the Mede. Ishtar had one wall eye and his face was tattooed with whorls and circles.

'The man we are pursuing is an adept of the occult arts,' Trok warned them. 'He will exert all his powers to frustrate us. His name is Taita.'

'I know Taita only by reputation,' said Ishtar, 'but I have long looked for an opportunity to match him.'

'Weave your magic,' Trok ordered them.

The priests of Seueth went aside a short distance, laid out their accoutrements and began to chant softly. Ishtar built a small fire near the well and squatted over it, muttering incantations to Marduk, the must powerful of all the gods of Mesopotamia.

Watching him at work, Trok grunted sceptically, but secretly he was impressed. He walked a short way along the road and glared at the line of eastern hills. He was hot for the pursuit. On the other hand he was enough of a general to realise the need to rest and water the horse after the long night ride.

TAITA SIGNALLED the two vehicles that followed him to halt. They stopped in the shade thrown across the sands by a tall dune shaped like an elegant seashell. The horses were already showing signs of distress. They hung their heads and their chests heaved as they breathed. Carefully he measured out a water ration from the water-skins into the leather buckets and the horses drank eagerly.

When he had finished he led Hilto out of earshot of the others.

'We are being overlooked,' he said flatly. 'There is a baleful influence slowly enveloping us. Do you know who Trok has with him who can work such a potent spell?'

'He has sorcerers with all his regiments, but the most powerful of them is Ishtar the Mede.'

'I know of him.' Taita nodded. 'He works in fire and blood. I shall try to turn his influence back on him.'

They went back to where the chariots waited. Before they mounted again Taita spoke to the others. 'We are entering the most dangerous area of the dune-lands. I know you are all tired and thirsty, drained by the rigours of the journey, but it could be fatal for any of you to become careless. Watch the horses and the ground ahead. Do not allow yourselves to be distracted by any strange sound or sight.'

They went forward again, following the valleys between the high dunes, and the heat seemed to increase with every turn of the chariot wheels. The quality of light changed: distances were rendered confusing and distorted. Nefer slitted his eyes against the shimmering glare of the brazen sky. It seemed close enough to touch with the end of his whip.

As they went on Taita looked to the sky more frequently. His expression was sober.

'I have never seen a sky like this,' Hilto said, when they stopped to water the horses. 'The gods are angry.'

It was Hilto, with his warrior's eyes, who picked out the dust cloud behind them. 'Magus!' he shouted. 'Those are chariots behind us, and many of them.'

Trok was there. Even at distance they could make out his bearlike form at the head of his moving column.

'One last fight!' Hilto loosened his blade in its scabbard.

Taita looked up at the bile-coloured sky as another sultry gust rippled his hair. He did not raise his voice but it carried to all of them, 'This way. Mark well my wheel tracks and follow them faithfully.'

To their astonishment Taita turned his horses off into the sand, heading at a right angle from the track. He went on at a steady trot and they followed him closely.

Looking back, Nefer could see there was not the least chance that, when Trok reached it, he would not find the place where the three chariots had left the track. Unless, of course, Taita could weave a spell of concealment.

They kept on for almost another league until abruptly the land ahead changed character. From the soft sand waves rose a dark island of rock, its peak as sharp as the fang of some fabulous monster.

When Nefer and Mintaka saw the rock pile looming ahead they were astonished.

'Did Taita know it was here?' Mintaka asked.

'How could he have known?' Nefer replied.

'You told me once that he knows everything.'

Nefer was silenced. He looked back and saw the dust of the pursuit close behind. 'It matters not at all. We might be able to defend those rocks for a while, but there are hundreds of Trok's men.'

'We must trust Taita,' Mintaka said.

He laughed bitterly. 'It seems the gods have deserted us. Who else is there to trust but Taita.'

They went forward. Behind them they heard the faint cries of the captains urging their troopers, the jingle of loose equipment and the groan and whine of dry wheel hubs.

At last they came up under the hill of black and ochre-coloured rock. The accumulated heat radiated from it like a bonfire.

'Drive the chariots close in against the cliff,' Taita ordered, and they obeyed. 'Now free the horses and bring them this way.' Taita led his own team round the angle of the rock face. Here there was a deep fissure cutting into the rock pile.

'This way.' He led them as far as they could go along the sandy floor of the deep, vertical crack. 'Now make the horses lie down.'

At the urging of their handlers, the horses, trained to perform this trick, lowered themselves to their knees and then, grunting and blowing, they went flat on their sides on the floor of the fissure.

Taita had brought a bedding roll from the chariot. With strips torn from it he blindfolded the horses to keep them quiet and submissive. Then he drove a javelin deep into the loose earth and used it as an anchor to tie down the horses' swathed heads and prevent them from rising again. The others followed his example.

Almost as if he knew of its existence, Taita led them to a shallow overhang in the cliff. The headroom under it was so low that anyone trying to enter would have to go down on hands and knees.

'Use the loose scree from the cliff to wall this in.'

Nefer looked puzzled. 'We cannot defend this place. Once we are inside we could not even stand, let alone swing a sword.'

'There is no time to argue.' Taita glared at him. 'Do as I tell you.'

Nefer glared back at Taita. The others watched with interest: the young bull challenging the older one. Abruptly Nefer capitulated. Only one person could save them now. He stooped and picked up a large rock from the scree pile and staggered with it to the shallow cave. The others joined in the work.

Meanwhile Taita climbed until he reached the peak of the hillock. He stood there gazing back in the direction from which Trok would come, and when their work was finished the little party in the gully at the foot of the hillock watched him, outlined against that dreadful sulphur sky. Nobody spoke, nobody moved, until they heard the faint squeal of chariot wheels.

Slowly Taita raised both arms and pointed them to the sky.

'What is he doing now?' Hilto asked, in an awed tone.

Taita stood as still as if he had been chiselled out of the living rock. His head was thrown back, his hair fluffed out silver on his shoulders. The heavens swirled. The light was transient, fading as the sun was covered more heavily, flaring as the clouds thinned.

Still Taita did not move, his staff aimed at the heavens. The sound of the approaching column became clearer still, and suddenly there was a distant blare of a ram's horn trumpet.

'That is Trok's battle call,' Mintaka said quietly.

TROK SHOUTED AT HIS TRUMPETER, 'Sound the advance!'

'Wait!' said Ishtar the Mede. He was watching Taita's tiny figure on the peak of the rock hill. 'Wait!'

'What is it!' Trok demanded.

'As yet I cannot fathom it,' Ishtar said, without taking his gaze off the warlock, 'but it is pervasive and powerful.'

The column remained halted, every man in it staring at the figure on the peak with awe. Only the sky moved. It formed a whirlpool over the head of the Magus, a great turning wheel of smouldering cloud. Then slowly the centre of the whirlpool opened like the single eye of an awakening monster. From the heavenly eye a shaft of dazzling sunlight burst forth.

'The eye of Horus!' Ishtar breathed. 'He has called up the god.' He made a sign of protection, and at his side Trok was silent and rigid with superstitious dread.

The brilliant shaft of light struck the peak, and lit the figure of the warlock. Around his head it spun a nimbus of silver radiance.

He made a slow circular pass with his long staff, and the Hyksosian charioteers cringed like curs under the whip. The clouds opened wider, and the sky was clear. The sunlight danced on the dunes, and they lifted their hands to protect their eyes.

On the peak, Taita described another circle with his staff, and there was a sound, soft at first, like a lover's sigh, then becoming a soughing, a gentle whistling. It came from the east, and slowly all their heads turned towards it.

Out of that strange, cloudless brilliance, they saw it coming: a solid dun wall of sand that reached from the surface of the earth to the highest heavens.

'Khamsin!' Trok whispered the dread word.

The wall of sand undulated and pulsed like a demon, and its voice became a rising howl.

'Khamsin!' The word was yelled from chariot to chariot. They were no longer warriors hot for war, but terrified creatures in the face of this destroyer of men, cities and civilisations, this eater of worlds.

The column of chariots lost its formation as the drivers wheeled their teams and tried to run from it. Instinctively the horses sensed the menace and reared and screamed, trying to escape by kicking themselves free of the traces.

The khamsin bore down upon them inexorably. They looked back and saw the great storm rolling and roiling upon itself, twisting curtains of sand, brazen where the sunlight struck them, dun and sombre where their own mountainous heights shaded them.

Taita lowered his staff and, without haste, started down the hillock to where Nefer and Mintaka were standing. They welcomed him with bemused expressions. Mintaka's tone was subdued as she asked, 'You called up the storm?'

'It has long been brewing,' Taita said. 'You have all remarked the heat and the yellow mists.'

'No,' said Nefer. 'It was not in nature. It was you.'

'Go into the shelter now,' said Taita. 'It is almost upon us.'

Mintaka led the way, crawling into the low narrow cave through the opening in the rude wall. The others followed her, crowding into the tiny space. Before he entered, Hilto handed in the water-skins. Then, as the storm hurled down on them in all its terrible majesty, Taita stooped through the opening and sat with his back to the inner wall.

'Close it up,' he said, and Meren and Hilto blocked the entrance with the rocks they had placed at hand.

'Cover your heads,' said Taita, and wound his headcloth over his face. 'Keep your eyes closed, or you will lose your sight. Breathe carefully or you will drown in sand.'

THE STORM WAS OVERWHELMING. Trok and Ishtar were gone with magical swiftness, they and all their men, chariots and horses, gone in the rolling billows of the khamsin. The first front picked up Trok's chariot and rolled it over with the horses screaming.

Trok was thrown free. He fought his way to his feet, but the storm struck him down again. He managed to pull himself up. When he tried to open his eyes he was blinded by sand.

As the khamsin ripped at his face, Trok screamed, 'Save me, Ishtar!'

It seemed impossible that anyone could have heard his cry. Then he felt Ishtar seize his hand and together they stumbled on. It seemed endless, their tormented journey to nowhere. Then abruptly Trok felt the force of the wind diminish. For a minute he thought that the storm had already passed them by, but then a sudden gust almost lifted him off his feet and he crashed into a wall of rock.

He clung to the rock like a child to its mother. How Ishtar had brought them to it he neither knew nor cared. All that mattered was that the cliff above them was breaking the full force of the storm.

FOR TWO DAYS and three nights the wind never relented. During this time Nefer managed to keep back the sand just enough to move his head and his arms, but his lower body was encased solidly. At times he felt Mintaka sobbing quietly beside him and tried to comfort her. She laid her head on his shoulder and they clung to each other. They were entombed in the roaring darkness, dumb and blinded, half suffocated. Each hot breath they drew had to be strained through cloth and taken only a sip at a time to prevent a rush of talcum-fine sand passing between their lips.

They drank the water that remained in their water-skin. Then the thirst came. Even though they were unable to move their bodies to use up moisture, the hot dry sand and air sucked it out of them. Nefer felt his tongue slowly cleave to the roof of his mouth.

He felt himself drifting into haunted dreams of water. He forced himself up from the darkness, and listened. He heard nothing. There was no sound. The roaring clamour of the khamsin had given way to a profound silence. The silence of a sealed tomb, he thought.

He began to struggle, to try to work his way out of the sand, but the effort soon exhausted him and his throat ached with thirst. He closed his eyes wearily, giving up. Then, even through the folds of his headcloth, he was aware of fresh air and a glimmer of light. He pulled the cloth from his face. When his vision had adjusted he saw that there was a hole to the outside.

It was the middle of the morning. Nefer did not know what morning or for how many days they had been buried. There was still a haze of fine sand like gold dust in the air.

He shook his head in wonder, and looked at Taita. He could see that he also was dried out and suffering the same agonies as they were.

'Water,' Nefer whispered, touching his swollen mouth.

'Come,' said Taita.

Nefer took Mintaka's hand and slowly they followed the Magus out into the sands. Thirst and exposure had taken their toll on Taita, and he seemed to be wandering aimlessly with Hilto and Meren through the new valleys of fine sand. Once or twice he lowered himself to his knees and touched the earth with his forehead.

'What is he doing?' Mintaka whispered. 'Is he praying?'

Nefer shook his head as once again Taita knelt and placed his face close to the earth. This time Nefer watched him with more attention, and saw that he was sniffing the air close to the surface of the sand. Then he knew what Taita was doing. 'He is searching for the buried chariots of Trok's division,' he whispered to Mintaka. 'He is sniffing for the scent of putrescence below the sand.'

Taita stood up painfully and nodded at Hilto. 'Dig here,' he ordered.

They all crowded forward and began to scrape away the sand with cupped hands. An arm's span deep they struck something hard. Soon they exposed the wheel rim of a chariot that was lying on its side.

Suddenly Nefer reached deeper into the hole and they all heard the gurgle and slosh of water. He swept away more of the loose sand and between them they lifted out bulging water-skin. The water was the temperature of blood, but when Taita held the skin to Mintaka's lips she closed her eyes and drank in a quiet ecstasy.

'Not too much at first,' Taita warned her, and passed it to Nefer. They drank in turn, then Mintaka drank again.

The next time they dug they were lucky: not only was the chariot under less sand, but there were three water-skins.

'Our horses now,' Taita told them, and they looked at each other guiltily. In their desperate preoccupation they had forgotten them. Carrying the water-skins they trudged back through the sand to the base of the cliff.

The narrow gully in which they had pegged down the horses was well aligned to avoid the full force of the khamsin. They found the first horse almost at once. The beast was alive, but barely. The men lifted it between them. It stood weak and shivering, but drank greedily from the bucket Mintaka held and seemed at once to improve.

In the meantime the men were digging for the other horses. They found three dead of thirst or suffocation, but another two still alive. They also responded immediately they were given water.

The men left Mintaka to care for the three pathetic beasts and went back to search for fodder and more water-skins under the sand.

Suddenly they heard Mintaka screaming.

Nefer raced back to her, a sword in his hand, the others following. Mintaka had been hiding behind a ledge in the cliff.

'What is it?' Nefer demanded, as she slid down the cliff into his arms.

'Trok!' she sobbed. 'Trok is alive. Look!'

Taita stayed with Mintaka while the other three men followed a set of footprints in the sand as if they were tracking a wounded lion. They moved along the base of the cliff until they reached a second rocky fissure. Nefer examined the disturbed sand within it and interpreted the signs.

'Two of them,' he said. 'They were buried by the storm, as we were. They dug themselves out. One waited here.' He picked up a thread of wool that had adhered to the rock, and held it to the light. 'Black.' It was a colour seldom worn by Egyptians. 'Almost certainly the Mede.'

Hilto nodded agreement. 'Ishtar would have the witchcraft to survive the storm. 'It is certain he saved Trok, just as Taita saved us.'

'Here.' Nefer stood and pointed out the sign. 'They went this way.'

They followed the footprints a short way out into the desert. 'They have gone west. Back towards the Nile. Will they ever reach it?'

'Not if I catch up with him,' Nefer said grimly, and hefted the javelin he was carrying.

'Majesty.' Hilto was respectful but firm. 'They have a long start. They will be well away from here by now. You dare not follow without water.'

Nefer hesitated. Though he saw the sense in what Hilto said, it galled him sorely to let Trok escape. In the end he turned aside and ran to the top of the nearest dune. Shading his eyes he looked westward, along the string of footsteps on the pristine, windswept sands, until in the distance he made out two tiny figures moving steadily towards the west. They disappeared in the wavering heat mirage.

'There will be another time,' Nefer whispered. 'I will come for you. I swear it.'

THEY FOUND AND UNCOVERED another sixteen of the buried chariots. With such an abundant supply of water and food, horses and men recovered swiftly, and by nightfall on the tenth day they were ready to move. The khamsin had altered the landscape so greatly that Taita had to navigate by the stars. They kept going steadily through the whole of that night, and the one that followed. Before dawn on the second day they reached an old caravan road.

Here, Nefer had a difficult decision to make. 'If we are to make the long journey to the east, we will need supplies and gold. When we go to King Sargon we must arrive in some state to show him the support we still command in Egypt.'

Taita nodded.

'Hilto and Meren must go back to Thebes,' Nefer went on. 'I would go myself but all the world will be searching for Mintaka and me.' He removed one of his rings and handed it to Hilto. 'This will be your token of recognition. Show it to our friends. You must return bringing us men and gold, chariots and horses. Also you must gather news. We must be informed of every action of the false pharaohs.'

'I will do as you command, Majesty,' Hilto agreed.

'We will wait for you at Gallala,' were Nefer's last words to Hilto. Then they watched him and Meren take the high road and disappear.

Twelve days later, with only a few drops remaining in the water-skins, Taita, Mintaka and Nefer reached the deserted ruins.

CHAPTER FIVE

The weeks became months, and still they waited at Gallala.

Mintaka set up quarters for them among the ruins. As a Hyksosian princess, she had never been called upon to cook a meal, so her efforts were disastrous. As he chewed a charred mouthful Taita remarked, 'If we want to destroy Trok's army the most effective way would be to send you to them as a cook.'

'If you are so skilled, then perhaps you might honour us with your great culinary skills.'

'It is either that or starve,' Taita agreed, and took her place at the hearth.

Nefer resumed his old role of hunter, and after his first day out in the desert returned with a plump young gazelle and four marvellously patterned giant bustard eggs that were only slightly addled.

Mintaka sniffed her share of Taita's omelette and pushed it away. 'Is this the same man who complained of my cooking?' She looked across the fire at Nefer. 'You are as guilty as he is. Next time I will go with you to make sure that what you bring back is edible.'

Several more hunting trips followed. Then, one evening when they came into the room in the ancient building that they had restored and made habitable, Mintaka shyly stood in the open doorway with the last light of the day behind her. 'I am sorry we are late back, Taita,' she said. 'We followed the gazelle out into the desert.' Taita was at the hearth stirring the contents of the pot upon the coals. He looked up at her. She had never apologised for their late return before, and Nefer was hovering over her with a soft, dazed expression. The emanation of their love was so strong that it seemed to form a shimmering aura around them.

So what was inevitable has happened at last, he mused. The only wonder is that it took so long. He grunted. 'It is evident that you did not catch up with them. Did they run too fast or were you distracted?' They stood awkwardly, knowing that to him they were transparent.

Taita turned back to the cooking pot. 'At least there is one provider among us. I have been able to snare a brace of wild pigeon. We need not go hungry to bed.'

The days that followed passed for the two of them in a golden haze. The lovers spent their time in talking, making love and forming plans for the future, deciding how they might marry and how many sons and daughters she would bear him.

They were so lost in each other that they forgot the world that lay beyond the lonely desert spaces, until one morning when they left the ruined city before dawn and sat down to watch the magnificent spectacle of the dawn breaking over the blue, secret hills.

'Look!' cried Mintaka suddenly, pointing back towards the west along the old trade route. A strange caravan was coming towards them. There were five ramshackle vehicles leading, followed by a straggling column of humanity.

'There must be a hundred men, at least,' Mintaka exclaimed. 'Who can they be?'

'I don't know,' Nefer admitted grimly, 'but I want you to run back and warn Taita of their approach while I go and spy on them.'

She did not argue, but set off immediately for Gallala, racing down the back slope of the hills, while Nefer restrung his bow and checked the arrows in his quiver.

Suddenly he stood up from behind the rock that had hidden him, and shouted with excitement. 'Meren!' He had at last recognised the tall figure who held the reins of the first chariot. Meren pulled up the horses, then he, too, shouted and waved as he saw Nefer on the sky-line. Nefer ran down the slope, and he and Meren embraced, laughing and both speaking at once.

'Where have you been?'

'Where are Mintaka and Taita?'

Then Hilto was hurrying to Nefer, and making loyal salutations. Behind him crowded a host of exhausted and wounded men. Even the men in the wagons and on the litters, who were too far gone to stand, lifted themselves to stare in awe at Nefer.

After Hilto had greeted Nefer he turned back to them, and shouted, 'It is even as I promised you! Here before you stands your true pharaoh, Nefer Seti. Pharaoh is not dead! Pharaoh lives!'

They were silent. They stared at him uncertainly. Most had never laid eyes on their king before. Even the few who had seen him in formal palace processions had done so from a distance. They could not reconcile that remote figure with this strapping young man, his face tanned by the sun and his expression alive and alert.

While they still stared without comprehension, or exchanged dubious glances, another figure seemed to materialise beside Nefer. This one they knew well, both by repute and by sight.

'It is Taita the Warlock,' they breathed with awe.

'I know what you have suffered,' Taita told them, in a voice that carried clearly to every ear. 'I know what price you have paid to resist the tyranny of the assassins and usurpers. I know that you have come here to find if your true king still lives.'

Suddenly Nefer knew who they were: survivors from the rebellion against Naja and Trok. Where Hilto had found them was a mystery, but these had once been fighting troopers and elite charioteers.

'This is where it begins,' Taita said softly at his side. 'Hilto has brought you the seed of your future legions. Speak to them.'

Nefer picked out a man in the ranks who was older than the others. His expression was intelligent and he had an air of authority. 'Who are you, soldier? What is your rank and your regiment?'

The man lifted his head and squared his gaunt shoulders, 'I am Shabako, Commander of the Mut Regiment.'

A lion of a man! Nefer thought, but said only, 'I greet you, Shabako.' He lifted his kilt and exposed the cartouche tattooed upon his thigh. 'I, Nefer Seti, the true Pharaoh of Upper and Lower Egypt, greet you.'

A sigh went through the scarecrow ranks. As one man they threw themselves to the earth in obeisance.

Mintaka had come with Taita and now Nefer reached out and took her hand. 'I give you the Princess Royal, Mintaka of the House of Apepi. Mintaka, who will be my queen and your sovereign lady.'

They greeted her with a shout of acclamation.

'Hilto and Shabako will command you,' Nefer decreed. 'For the time being Gallala will be our base, until we return victoriously to Thebes.'

They rose to their feet and cheered him, their voices thin in the silence of the desert, but the sound filled Nefer with pride. He climbed up into the leading chariot, took the reins from Meren and led his raggle-taggle army down into his ruined capital city.

LATE INTO THAT FIRST NIGHT, and for many nights that followed, Nefer sat with Shabako and the other officers and listened to their accounts of the rebellion, their defeat by the combined forces of the two pharaohs, and the terrible retribution that they had visited on those rebels who had fallen into their clutches. They also detailed the order of battle of the new Egyptian army, and the total of men, chariots and horses that Naja and Trok had at their disposal.

In the meantime Taita, with Mintaka assisting him, set up an infirmary where they worked during all the daylight hours, setting broken bones, drawing out barbed arrowheads, stitching sword cuts and in one case even trepanning a skull that had received a blow from a hardwood war club.

When the light faded and he could no longer work with the sick, Taita joined Nefer and his commanders as they pored over maps drawn on tanned lambskins, planning and scheming by the light of the oil lamps. Although Nefer was nominally their supreme commander, in reality he was a student of the art of war and these experienced old soldiers were his instructors.

In total there were fewer than a hundred and fifty souls and fifty horses in Gallala, but within the first few days it became evident that the wells of the city could not support even these meagre numbers. Each day they emptied them and each night it took longer for them to refill, and the water became more bitter and brackish.

At last, after they were forced to ration the water, Taita took Nefer and Mintaka and a party of fifty-six men, all carrying shovels and metal-tipped digging staves, up the valley to the foot of the hill.

For two days they dug into the rock, prising out each lump, digging out the earth that lay behind it. When they struck a solid stratum of blue, crystalline rock, they stacked firewood against it, let it burn until the rock glowed, and quenched it with water from the failing wells. In clouds of hissing steam, the rock crackled and burst. They let it cool, prised out great blackened chunks of it, then repeated the arduous process until they had driven a shaft of twenty cubits into the hillside.

On the third morning, the teams of weary, disgruntled men assembled round the mouth of the tunnel to await the Magus. With his usual sense of the dramatic, Taita came up the slope with the first rays of the rising sun behind him, suffusing his silver hair with light. He stood in the entrance to the excavation and began to chant the invocation to Horus. Then he strode down the shaft until he stood before the blue-grey wall of newly exposed rock at the end. Tiny crystals of feldspar were embedded in it and sparkled in the sun.

'*Kydash!*' Taita cried, and struck the wall with his staff. '*Mensaar!*' He struck again '*Ncube!*' He struck for the third and last time, then stepped back.

Nothing happened, and Taita stood unmoving as the sun climbed higher. Then the men stirred and whispered as a dark, damp spot appeared in the centre of the rock face. It spread gradually and a single drop of moisture oozed out and trickled slowly down the wall.

Taita turned and walked out of the shaft. Behind him there was a sharp sound, and a fine crack split the rock from top to bottom. Water dripped to the floor. Then with a roar the entire rock face collapsed, there was a rush of mud and a gushing fountain of crystal-bright water. Knee-deep, it swept the length of the shaft, burst from the mouth and spilled down the hillside, rippling over the rocks.

There were shouts of amazement, praise and disbelief from the dusty ranks. Men threw off their clothing and rushed naked into the stream. Nefer could not long resist the temptation before he, too, shed all dignity and jumped in.

Taita stood on the bank of the stream and looked down on the mayhem with a benign expression. Then he turned to Mintaka. 'Put the thought out of your mind,' he said. 'It would be an outrage to have a princess of Egypt cavorting with a rabble of rough, naked soldiers.' He took her hand and led her away down the hill, but she looked back wistfully at the revels.

'How did you do it, Taita?' she asked. 'How did you make the fountain appear? What kind of magic was it?'

'The magic of common sense and observation. The water has been there for centuries, just waiting for us to dig down to it.'

'But what about the words of power?'

Taita smiled and touched the side of his nose. 'Sometimes a little magic is a tonic for flagging spirits.'

FOR MONTHS THEREAFTER every man was employed in the digging of a channel to lead the sweet flood of water down the hillside into the old wells. When they brimmed over, Taita surveyed the old fields at the lower end of the valley that were now a stony desolation. The outlines of ancient irrigation ditches were still visible, however, and it took small effort to clean out the contour lines and divert the overflowing waters into them, so that within months they had reaped their first millet harvest.

Almost every day more fugitives drifted into the city, having braved the desert crossing to escape the tyranny of the false pharaohs. They came singly or in small parties, weary and almost dying of thirst. The guards posted along the hills intercepted them, and sent them in to Hilto. He made them swear the oath of fealty to Pharaoh Nefer Seti, then issued them with rations and sent them to the training regiments or put them to work in the fields or restoring the city. These waifs were not the only recruits, however. A cohort of deserters from the armies of the false pharaohs marched in smartly with their javelins, shouting the praises of Nefer Seti as soon as they were in sight of the walls. Then a squadron of twenty chariots brought plundered treasure and the momentous news that Naja and Trok were at last marching against King Sargon of Babylon.

The two pharaohs had crossed the desert that linked Egypt with the eastern lands in the full of the moon, using its light and the cool nights to sweep past Ismailiya and on up to Beersheba, gathering the forces of their vassal satraps as they went.

Nefer and Taita had been preparing the defences of Gallala against an imminent attack by the false pharaohs. Their presence in the ancient city should by now have been common knowledge throughout the two kingdoms, and they had expected Naja and Trok to move against them first, before starting on the Mesopotamian adventure. They were amazed to have this reprieve.

'Can we be certain that this is not a diversion?' Nefer asked thoughtfully. 'Is the eastern expedition a pretence? Perhaps their true offensive will be directed against us after they have lulled us into a false sense of security.'

'There is always that possibility. Trok is a bull, but Naja is cunning and devious. It is the type of bluff he might try.'

'We must keep the expeditionary army under observation,' Nefer decided.

The following day Shabako and his most trusted men were sent as scouts and spies to the towns and villages of the Nile valley. They drank in the taverns and questioned the travellers they met on the road. They scouted each fort and garrison, and counted the troops they saw entering, leaving and drilling. When they returned weeks later, the intelligence they brought back was detailed and accurate.

They reported that the false pharaohs had left at least half of their army to counter any threat to their rear. All the border forts were fully manned, and the garrisons seemed alert and vigilant.

'What of the remount divisions?' Nefer asked, when Shabako had come to the end of his long report.

'Trok has taken most of his chariots with him to Mesopotamia. He has left less than two regiments in reserve in Egypt. However, all the army workshops are hard at work building more chariots.'

'Horses?' Nefer demanded.

'They have commandeered every animal in both kingdoms that they could lay their thieving hands on. They have even sent army dealers to Libya to buy what they could find. It seems that the remount depots at Thane and Manashi are at full strength. However, most of these animals appear young and untrained. The battle-hardened animals have been taken with the main army to the east.'

'Thane,' Nefer decided. 'It's much closer to the edge of the desert than Manashi.' He recalled that Thane was where Hilto had used his requisition order to obtain fresh horses and chariots from Socco, his old comrade-in-arms, while they were on their way to rescue Mintaka from Avaris.

'Tell me all you can about Thane. Is Socco still in command there?'

'We drank beer in the local brothel with a sergeant of the garrison. He told me that Socco has done such a good job there that Trok has promoted him to the rank of Best of Ten Thousand.'

TEN DAYS LATER, Nefer and Taita sat in the thick green grass and pretended to watch over the herd of goats that grazed around them. Although the land around the garrison of Thane was rich in grazing, it was also flat and featureless. There were no hills from which they could overlook the camp.

The two of them were disguised in the ragged dusty black robes of the Bedouin and were able to blend into the landscape. At intervals they herded the goats a little closer to the garrison, then squatted down again in the characteristic attitude of the Bedouin herdsman.

Not far from where they sat, the herds of remounts were grazing.

'I would think there are upward of two thousand animals here,' Nefer guessed.

'Perhaps not as many as that.' Taita shook his head. 'Closer to fifteen hundred, but still more than we can handle.'

They watched and waited through the long, lazy afternoon. In the stockades alongside the cavalry lines the handlers were breaking the young animals to the chariot harness. Their shouted commands and the crack of the whips carried faintly to where Nefer and Taita sat.

In the late afternoon the herds of horses were driven in from the fields and stockades to the long horse lines beyond the fort. From a distance they watched them tethered and bedded down for the night.

As the sun was setting Nefer and Taita rounded up their goats and drove them slowly back towards the desert. In the dusk a small detachment of four chariots came bowling down the road from Avaris. At the reins of the leading vehicle stood a burly officer wearing the silver pectoral plate of the Best of Ten Thousand. As he came closer they both recognised him.

'The curse of Seth on it,' Nefer murmured. 'It is Socco, Hilto's old comrade-in-arms. Will he recognise us?'

They bowed their heads, slumped their shoulders, and shuffled along after the goats. Socco swerved off the road and drove directly at them. 'You stinking scum!' he shouted. 'How often must I warn you to keep your filthy, disease-ridden beasts off my grass and away from my horses?' He leaned out and struck Nefer across the shoulders. The whiplash hummed and cracked against his flesh, and red rage blinded Nefer. Before he could drag Socco out of the chariot, though, Taita made a restraining gesture that riveted him where he stood. It seemed to affect Socco, too, for suddenly the bellicose light in his eyes faded. He stammered wordlessly. He was gawking at the cartouche on Nefer's thigh.

'Majesty,' he gasped. 'Forgive me! Strike! Take my worthless life as forfeit for those stupid words of mine. I heard the rumours that you still lived, but I had wept at your funeral and could not believe in such a miracle.'

Nefer smiled with relief. He had not wanted to kill him—he was an attractive old rogue, and Hilto said that he was one of the finest horse-handlers in all the armies of Egypt. Hilto should know. 'Will you swear the loyal oath to me as Pharaoh?' he demanded sternly.

'Gladly, for all the earth fears you in your name of Nefer Seti, beloved of all the gods, and light of this very Egypt. My heart beats only for you and my soul will sing my duty to you until the hour of my death.'

'Then, Socco, I promote you to Master of a Thousand Chariots, for you turn a pretty phrase.'

'Let me kiss your foot, Pharaoh,' Socco pleaded.

'Give me your hand, rather,' Nefer said, seizing his horny fist.

Three days later, when they rode into Gallala, they were driving nigh on four hundred horses, and Socco rode proudly at the right hand of his new pharaoh.

As QUARTERMASTER GENERAL of the armies of the false pharaohs, Socco had been able to bring with him much of the depot's treasure store. He was also able to give Nefer and his council the exact tally of all the enemy fighting chariots and transport wagons, and where they were deployed. From memory he drew up a list of the numbers of horses and bullocks in depots of the delta, and the latest inventory of weapons stored in the armouries.

'Trok and Naja have taken almost the last serviceable fighting chariot with them on the expedition to the east. There are fewer than fifty left in Egypt, in either the Upper or Lower Kingdom. The military workshops at Avaris, Thebes and Aswan are working day and night, but every chariot they turn out is sent immediately along the road to Beersheba and Mesopotamia.'

'Horses we now have, thanks to you, even though most are young and unbroken, but we cannot fight a campaign without chariots,' said Hilto gloomily. 'Soon Trok must hear of our successes. He will realise that we have become a real threat. As soon as he has captured Babylon, he will divert part of his army to attack us here. If he sent only a hundred chariots, we could not stand against them in our present state.'

When all the others had had their say, Nefer stood to address the council. He did not speak long. 'Socco, you train the horses for me,' he said. 'Taita and I will find the chariots.'

FAR OUT IN THE DESERT, Taita stood on a black rock outcrop. Around him the sand dunes stretched away to the limit of the eye. From the base of the rock a hundred men watched him, puzzled but intrigued. All of them were warriors who had come to Gallala of their own accord, forsaking the false pharaohs to offer their allegiance to Nefer Seti. That allegiance would wear a little thin if they found themselves without chariots, for daily there were fresh rumours that Trok was on the march to seek vengeance for their desertion.

Pharaoh Nefer Seti stood beside the warlock. They were in deep discussion. Occasionally one or the other would point towards the west, where there was nothing to see but sand. They talked through the heat of the day and came down from the pinnacle and walked out into the dunes. Without any apparent purpose the warlock wandered along one of the dune faces. He stopped at intervals and made strange, esoteric gestures with his long staff, then went on again.

At last, in the gathering dusk, the Magus planted his staff in the soft sand and spoke quietly to Pharaoh Nefer Seti. Now, suddenly, orders were shouted and twenty men ran forward carrying the digging tools with which they had been issued. Under the direction of Hilto and Meren, and under the daunting eyes of their king and the Magus, they began to dig. When the hole was shoulder deep the loose sand ran back into it almost as fast as they shovelled it out, and they were forced to redouble their efforts. Finally there came an excited shout from the bottom of the excavation. Nefer strode forward and stood on the lip.

'There is something here, Divine Majesty.' A man was kneeling in the bottom of the hole.

'Let me see.' Nefer jumped down and pushed the man out of the way. A patch of hide was exposed, still covered with hair.

Nefer looked up at Taita. 'It is the body of a horse!' he called.

'What colour?' Taita asked. 'Is it black?'

'How did you know?' Nefer was not really surprised.

Taita answered his question with another. 'Does the halter carry the golden cartouche of Pharaoh Trok Uruk?'

'Dig it open!' Nefer ordered the sweating men around him. 'But gently now. Do no damage.'

They worked with great care, using their bare hands to sweep away the sand. Gradually they exposed the complete head of a black horse that wore on its forehead the cartouche of Trok, embossed on a gold disc, just as Taita had foreseen.

Then they went on to uncover the rest of the carcass, wonderfully preserved by the hot dry sand. The embalmers in Thebes would have difficulty in matching what the desert had achieved. Beside it lay its harness mate. Nefer had last seen these magnificent animals as they drew Trok's chariot forward under the dust clouds of the khamsin.

By this time night had fallen and the workmen lit the oil lamps and went on with the work through the night. The dead horses were unbuckled from the traces and lifted out, and the harness was recovered in a perfect state of preservation. Nefer set his grooms to work oiling the leather and polishing the gold and bronze parts.

Now they worked on the chariot itself, and a gasp went up from the diggers as the dashboard was cleared of sand: it was covered with gold leaf, and gleamed in the lamplight. The javelins and lances were still in their bins on either side of the cockpit, ready to the hand of the charioteer. Trok's great war-bow, too, was still in its rack, and only the bowstring needed to be replaced.

When the entire chariot had been uncovered they passed ropes under the chassis and lifted it out of the excavation.

Now it was morning, and the sun was climbing above the horizon. Nefer and Taita circled the chariot as it gleamed in the light. It was so sleek and graceful that it seemed already in motion.

Nefer stroked the lovely gold work. 'It seems to be a living creature,' he breathed. 'Surely there was never a more magnificent weapon of war ever conceived. Now I need only the blue sword that Naja stole from my father to complete my armoury.'

Over the weeks that followed Taita pinpointed the other buried vehicles and their accoutrements. Teams of workmen dug them out and sent them to the chariot-makers and armourers, who sharpened swords and lances, rebound the shafts and checked each vehicle, balancing and lubricating the wheels to run true and sweetly. Then they sent them on to Gallala, to equip the army that Hilto, Shabako and Socco were training.

Many of the vehicles were so deeply buried under the burning yellow dunes that they were lost for ever, or until the next great storm uncovered them, but in the end they salvaged a hundred and five. Enough to equip five squadrons.

BY THIS TIME a thriving smuggling route existed between Gallala and Egypt, and other caravans came in regularly from the port of Safaga on the eastern sea. Nowadays there were few luxuries that could not be obtained in the city's souks, so Mintaka was able to procure a wagonload of the finest red wine for the welcome banquet she had arranged for the evening that the charioteers returned.

At her orders, the butchers spitted and roasted ten oxen, and fast relays of the new chariots brought up fresh fish and baskets of lobsters from the coast. The banquet was a joyous celebration, and the wine had flowed to great effect when Nefer rose to welcome the guests.

'With the weapons and chariots we now have, we are well able to defend ourselves against Trok and Naja. As you are aware, every day sees fresh recruits to the blue banner. Soon it will be a case not merely of defending ourselves but of avenging the terrible deeds that those two monsters have perpetrated. They are the murderers of King Apepi, who was the father of the noble lady at my side, and they slew my own father, Pharaoh Tamose.'

The guests were silent now and puzzled.

Then Hilto rose to his feet. Nefer had primed him, and placed the question on his lips. 'Divine Majesty, forgive my ignorance but I do not understand. King Apepi died in an accident when his barge caught fire while anchored at Balasfura. Now you lay the guilt for his death on the pretenders. How can that be?'

'There is one among us who was a witness to the true events of that tragic night.' Nefer reached down and drew Mintaka to her feet. The company listened to her with all their attention as she related the story of the murder of her father and brothers. She used simple words and spoke to them as friends and comrades, yet she was able to share with them her own horror and grief.

Now Shabako rose and asked his prepared question: 'But, Divine Pharaoh, you spoke also of the death of your own father, King Tamose of blessed memory. How was he murdered—and by whom?'

'For the answer to this question I must call upon the Magus, Lord Taita, from whom no secret, however grisly, can be hidden.'

Taita faced them and spoke in a whisper that riveted their attention. His every word carried to the ears of even those on the outskirts of the gathering. At the end he held up a broken arrow with crimson and green feathers. 'This is the instrument of Pharaoh Tamose's death. The arrow that bears the signet of Trok and which was loosed by Naja, the man whom Pharaoh trusted as a brother.'

They howled their outrage and their craving for justice to the star-lit skies above Gallala. Taita hurled the arrow onto the nearest fire over which one of the oxen was roasting. It would not have borne closer inspection, for it was not the arrow that had killed Pharaoh but one of those he had taken from the buried chariot. He sat down and closed his eyes, as if composing himself to sleep.

CHAPTER SIX

Between the two great rivers the city lay before him like a lotus flower, ready for plucking. Its walls were of burned brick. They were twenty-seven cubits thick and taller than the tallest palm trees of this fertile and well-watered land.

'How far is it to ride around this city?' Trok asked Ishtar the Mede. He knew that Ishtar had lived in Babylon for fifteen years, and had learned much of his magic here in the temple of Marduk.

'Ten leagues, Majesty,' Ishtar told him. 'Half a day's ride.'

Trok stood on the footplate of his chariot and cast a general's eye along the wall. There were watchtowers at every two hundred paces, and at regular intervals the massive walls were heavily buttressed.

Ishtar knew what he was thinking. 'There is a road along the top of the wall, wide enough for two chariots to ride abreast. Within an hour Sargon can move five thousand men along it to any point threatened by a besieging army.'

Trok grunted. 'Any wall can be undermined and sapped. We need only one breach.'

'There is an inner wall, Divine Pharaoh,' Ishtar murmured in a silky tone. 'It is almost as impregnable as the first.'

'If we cannot go through, we will find a way round.' Trok shrugged. 'Are those the gardens of Sargon's palace?' He indicated the terraces that rose in tiers into the sky. They were so skilfully raised upon each other that they seemed to float, free of the bounds of the earth.

Ishtar pointed with one sinewy, blue-tattooed arm. 'There are six terraces built round a vast courtyard. The *zenana* alone has five thousand rooms, one for each of Sargon's wives. His treasure is buried deep below the palace, Majesty, and I tell you straight that in all your army you do not have sufficient wagons to carry away such a treasure.'

'And I tell you straight, Ishtar, that I can always build new wagons.'
Trok threw back his head and laughed with animal high spirits.

Once Ishtar had dissuaded him from leading an army into the
eastern desert to attack Nefer Seti and to capture Mintaka, his run-
away woman, the march to Babylon had been one long triumph, an
unbroken string of victories.

They had met Ran, Sargon's eldest son, on the banks of the Bahr
al Milh: between the chariots of Trok and Naja they had ground his
army to fragments, and had sent Ran's severed head to his father,
skewered on a spear. Maddened with grief, Sargon had charged into
the trap they had prepared for him. While Naja retreated before him
to lure him on, Trok had circled out to the south then come at him
from the rear with a thousand chariots. When Sargon turned back to
defend his baggage train, they had him in a glittering ring of bronze.

Sargon had managed to break out with fifty chariots, but in his
headlong retreat he had left two thousand chariots and eleven thousand men behind him. Now Babylon lay before Trok, little more
than a year since he and Naja had marched from Avaris.

'You know the defences, Ishtar. You helped design some of them.
How long before the city falls?' Trok demanded impatiently.

'A year,' Ishtar murmured thoughtfully. 'Or two, maybe three.' But
there was a sly look on his tattooed face, and his eyes were shifty.

Trok laughed and pushed him away so hard that he almost fell
from the footplate of the chariot. 'A year, you say? Two? Three? I
have not that amount of time to sit here. I am in a hurry, Ishtar the
Mede, and you know what that means, don't you?'

'I know, god without peer. And I am but a man, fallible and poor.'

'Poor?' Trok shouted in his face. 'By Seueth, you slimy charlatan,
you have milked me of a lakh of gold already, and what do I have to
show for it?'

'You have a city and an empire. After Egypt itself, the richest in the
world. I have laid it at your feet.'

'I need the key to that city.' Trok watched his face, happy with
what he saw there. He knew Ishtar well. 'Give me the city, Ishtar.
Give it to me within three full moons and you shall have two more
lakhs of gold from the treasure of Sargon,' he promised.

'If I give it to you before the next full moon?' Ishtar rubbed his
hands together like a carpet trader.

Trok's grin left his face at the prospect. He said seriously, 'Then you
shall have three lakhs, and a convoy of wagons to carry them away.'

THE ARMY OF THE TWO PHARAOHS went into camp before the legendary Blue Gate, and Trok sent an emissary to Sargon to demand the surrender of the city. Sargon, defiant behind his walls, sent the messenger's decapitated head back to Trok. The preliminaries having been dealt with, Trok and Naja made a circuit of the walls to allow the Babylonians to view their full might and splendour.

They drove golden chariots, Trok's drawn by six black stallions, Naja's by six white. Heseret rode beside Naja, glittering with jewels. They were preceded by a vanguard of five hundred chariots and followed by a rearguard of another five hundred. The slow, stately circuit of the city took all that day, and at sunset Heseret retired to her tent with all her slave girls, leaving her husband and Trok to pore over a map of the city by lamplight with Ishtar. The map was a work of art, drawn in coloured detail on finely tanned sheepskin.

'How came this map into your possession?' Naja demanded.

'Twelve years ago, by the command of King Sargon, I surveyed the city and drew this map with my own hands,' Ishtar replied. 'No other could have achieved such accuracy and beauty.'

'If he commissioned it, why did you not deliver it to Sargon?'

'I did.' Ishtar nodded. 'I delivered the inferior draft to him, while secretly I kept the fair copy you see before you. I knew that one day someone would pay me more handsomely than Sargon ever did.'

For another hour they studied the map, silent and absorbed. As fighting generals with a professional eye for the salient features of a battlefield, they were able to admire the depth and strength of the walls, the towers and redoubts.

At last Trok stood back from the table. 'There is no weakness that I can divine, magician. You were right the first time. It will take three years of hard work to break through those walls. You will have to do better than this to earn your three lakhs.'

'The water,' whispered Ishtar. 'Look to the water.'

'I have looked to the water.' Naja smiled at him, thin-lipped. 'There are canals supplying every quarter of the city, enough water to grow Sargon's six terraces of gardens for a hundred years.'

'Pharaoh is all-seeing, all-wise.' Ishtar bowed to him. 'But where does the water come from?'

'From two mighty rivers that have not failed in this millennium.'

'But where does the water enter the city? How does it pass through, under or over those walls?' Ishtar insisted, and Naja and Trok exchanged looks of dawning comprehension.

HALF A MILE NORTH of Babylon, outside the city walls, on the east bank of the Euphrates, at a point where the river broadened and ran sluggishly, stood the temple of Ninurta, the lion-headed winged god of the Euphrates. It was built on stone piers that extended out into the river, with multiple images of the god engraved on a frieze on the outer walls.

Trok, with twenty troopers at his back, strode through into the temple courtyard where the purple-robed priests of Ninurta were gathered. He killed the high priest with a single thrust through the old man's throat. Wailing at such sacrilege, the other priests prostrated themselves before him.

Trok sheathed his sword and nodded to the captain, who commanded the guard. 'Kill them all. Make certain no one escapes.'

Then he turned to watch Ishtar, who had entered the courtyard to work a charm to counteract the baleful influence of Ninurta. At four corners he burned bundles of herbs, which emitted thick, greasy smoke. Once Ishtar had completed the purification, he took a bunch of heavy keys from the body of the high priest, then led Trok and his troopers into the holy places of the temple.

Their cleated sandals rang hollowly in the high cavernous hall, and even Trok felt a religious chill as they approached the image of the god on his plinth. The lion's head snarled silently and the wings of stone were spread wide. Ishtar led Trok into the narrow space between the rear wall and the idol's back. Built into the body of Nintura was a grilled gate. Trok tried two of the keys in the lock, and the second turned the ancient mechanism. The gate swung open on creaking hinges.

Trok peered down a descending spiral staircase into darkness, and he heard the sound of running water far below.

'Bring torches!' he ordered, and the captain sent four of his troopers to take down the burning torches from their brackets. With a torch held above his head, Trok started down the narrow steps. He went gingerly, for the stone treads were slippery. The sound of running water grew louder as he went down.

Ishtar followed him closely. 'This temple and the tunnels beneath it were built almost five hundred years ago,' he told Trok.

Now there was the gleam of water below them, and the sound of the torrent running swiftly in the darkness. At last Trok reached the bottom, and by the wavering torchlight he saw that they stood in a wide tunnel with a curved roof, an aqueduct of impressive dimensions.

The roof and walls were lined with ceramic tiles, laid in geometric patterns. Both ends of the tunnel shaded off into deep darkness.

'This footpath on which we stand runs the full length of the aqueduct,' Ishtar explained. 'The priests who repair and maintain the tunnel use it to gain access.'

'Where does it start and where does it end?' Trok demanded.

'The far end of the aqueduct emerges in the other temple of Ninurta within the walls of Babylon. Only the priests know of the existence of this tunnel. All others believe that the water is a benevolent gift from the god. After it gushes from the fountain in the temple precinct, the water is lifted by water wheels to the gardens of the palace, or sent by canals to every quarter of the city.'

'I do believe, Ishtar the Mede, that you are close to earning your three lakhs.' Trok laughed with delight. 'It remains only for you to lead us down this rabbit hole, and into the city.'

TROK CHOSE two hundred of his best and most reliable men, all members of his own leopard tribe. He divided them into two groups. Once they had fought their way through the aqueduct into the city, the first group was to secure the Blue Gate and keep it open until Pharaoh Naja Kiafan could lead the main force through it. The second, smaller group was to make its way into the palace and seize Sargon's treasury.

The chosen two hundred were dressed in the uniforms of Sargon's army, taken from the prisoners and the dead men left on the battlefield. They wore only a red sash to distinguish them from the foe. Rough copies of the city map were hastily drawn by army scribes and issued to the captains of both divisions so that they knew the layout of streets and buildings. By evening every man knew exactly what was expected of him once he entered the city.

As soon as it was dark, Naja quietly moved his assault force up into position outside the Blue Gate, ready to dash through into the city as soon as Trok's men threw it open.

In the courtyard of the river temple of Ninurta, Trok mustered his division. While it was still daylight, he and Ishtar led them in single file down the spiral staircase. They marched in silence, every tenth man carrying a torch, giving just sufficient light for the men who followed to make out their footing on the slimy stones. At their left hand the never-ending flow of water rustled darkly by.

Abruptly Ishtar stopped and pointed ahead. The faint glimmer of light was reflected off the shiny ceramic walls. Trok signalled the men following him to halt, then went forward with Ishtar. Over their own garments they wore headdresses and purple robes taken from the bodies of the slaughtered priests.

As they went towards the source of the light, they saw another gate across the tunnel, and the distorted shadows of men thrown on the walls by the light of a torch set in a bracket. On the other side of the grille two robed priests were seated on stools, with a bao board between them, absorbed in their game. They looked up when Ishtar called softly to them.

The fat one stood up. 'Are you from Sinna?' he called.

'Yes!' Ishtar assured him.

'You are late. We have been waiting since nightfall.'

'I am sorry,' Ishtar sounded contrite, 'but you know Sinna.'

The fat priest chuckled, 'Yes, I know Sinna. He taught me my responses thirty years ago.'

His key jangled in the lock of the gate, and then he swung it open. 'You must hurry,' he said. Trok trotted forward with the hood over his face, holding his sword in the fold of his robe. The priest stood back against the wall to let him pass. Trok stopped in front of him, whispered, 'Ninurta will reward you, brother,' and killed him.

With a shout of alarm, the priest's companion leapt to his feet, knocking over the bao board and scattering the stones across the pier. With two long strides Trok reached him and chopped his head half off. Without another sound, the priest fell backwards.

Trok gave a soft whistle and his men moved up into the torchlight with drawn swords. Ishtar led them forward until they reached the foot of another steep stone stairway. They went up it quickly until they came to a heavy curtain blocking their way. Ishtar peeped around its edge and nodded. 'The temple is empty.'

Trok stepped through and looked about him. Below them the image of the god crouched over the mouth of the aqueduct from which the water spurted into a deep pond, then spilled over into the canal that carried it to the city. Although the smell of incense was thick in the air, the great hall of the temple was deserted.

Trok signalled his men to come forward. Ishtar led the smaller band through a side door of the hall into a corridor that connected with the palace of Sargon. Trok led his men out into the narrow lane behind the temple and, working only from his memory of the map, turned at the second lane into the wide avenue that he knew led to the Blue Gate. It was still dark in the sleeping city.

They met a number of cloaked figures on the way, one or two staggering drunk, but the others scurried out of their way and let the column of dark armed warriors pass. They reached the end of the avenue without being challenged, but as the gateway loomed ahead a voice sang out at them from the door of the guardhouse.

'Stand ho!' The centurion of the gate, with five men at his back, stepped out into the torchlight. But they were ill-prepared, without helmets and body armour, their faces still crumpled with sleep.

Trok gave the hand signal for his troops to charge. 'Open the gate and stand aside!' he ran straight at the centurion.

For a moment longer the man stood uncertainly. Then Trok was on him, and dropped him with a single blow. His men swarmed over the other guards before they could defend themselves, but the noise had alerted the sentinels on the parapets above the gate. They sounded the alarm with braying rams' horns, and hurled their javelins down into the attackers.

'Winkle them out of there!' Trok ordered, and half of his men rushed up the ramps on either side of the gateway to reach the parapet. They were at once locked in close and desperate fighting with the guards on the wall. Trok kept half of his men with him.

Ishtar had described the gate room that housed the heavy winches and pulleys that operated the massive gates. After only a few minutes of furious fighting Trok's men had killed or wounded most of the defenders within. The survivors fled out of the postern gate, and Trok led his men to the massive winches. With two men on each spoke of the capstans they began to open the gates.

Outside the walls Naja's men had swarmed forward with crowbars and levers. They forced the heavy gates wider and wider, until at last a squadron of chariots could pass through. Then they stood aside, and Naja led a phalanx of fighting chariots in a brutal charge through the gateway, and swept the avenue from side to side. The army of Egypt poured through behind them. Trok took command of them and led them rampaging through the city towards the palace.

The sack of Babylon had begun.

THE DEFENCE OF THE PALACE was stubborn, led by Sargon himself. However, by that evening Trok had opened a breach in the outer walls of the first terrace. He led a strong contingent through and the defence collapsed. When they burst into Sargon's bedchamber he was kneeling before the image of Marduk, the devouring god of Mesopotamia, with a bloody sword through his breast. Beside him lay the body of his favourite wife, a grey-haired woman who had been with him for thirty years. Before falling on his sword he had given her a merciful death, compared to what she might have expected from Trok's men.

The women from the zenana were herded out of the palace. Trok selected twenty, the youngest and prettiest, for his personal entertainment, and the rest were given to his senior officers.

It took another two days to break into the treasury buried deep in the earth below the palace, for many ingenious constructions and devices guarded it. Without the expertise and first-hand knowledge of Ishtar the Mede, it might have taken even longer to penetrate to the chamber.

When the way was clear, Trok and Naja, Heseret following them, descended the stairway and entered the chamber. Ishtar had lit the interior with a hundred oil lamps, and even the two pharaohs were stunned into silence by the splendour of the treasure. Heseret had to shade her eyes against the dazzle of the masses of precious metal. Naja walked forward slowly between the stacks, which were higher than his head, stopping every few paces to stroke the ingots.

Trok picked up a heavy bar in each hand and laughed with delight. 'How much?' he demanded of Ishtar.

'Splendid and Divine Majesty, the scrolls of Sargon's scribes record the total weight of silver at fifty-five lakhs, the gold at thirty-three.' He spread his tattooed hands deprecatingly. 'But who would trust the count of a Babylonian?'

'Sargon is a greater robber than I gave him credit for.' Trok made it sound like a compliment.

'At least there is enough here to pay me the pittance you promised?' Ishtar suggested smoothly.

'I think we should discuss that further.' Trok smiled at him genially. 'I am a kindly and generous man, Ishtar, as you know full well. However, stupid I am not.'

There was much else to see and marvel at within the city. Trok and Naja toured the palace, climbing to the top terrace with its fountains and gardens. From this height they could look down on both the great rivers and the vista of fields, marshes and papyrus beds outside the city walls.

Next they visited all the temples, for these magnificent buildings were also stuffed with bullion, beautiful furniture, statuary, mosaics and other works of art. The greatest of these temples was that of Marduk the Devourer. Trok found this to be not only a mine of precious metal and jewellery but a place of endless fascination.

He knelt on a pile of leopardskins spread on the stone floor in the inner sanctum of the temple before the altar. The golden image of the god was of a comely youth, three or four times life-sized.

'You told me that Marduk was a terrible god, crueller than any other in the pantheon, more ferocious even than Seueth,' Trok challenged Ishtar, 'yet this is a pretty boy.'

'Divine Pharaoh, be not deceived!' Ishtar warned him. 'This is the face that Marduk shows the world. His true aspect is so hideous that any man who looks upon it is instantly rendered blind and mad.'

Sobered by that thought, Trok remained silent while the priests brought in two kids and offered them to the god. Ishtar slit their throats so skilfully that they made hardly a sound as they bled into the golden divination bowl that he held beneath them and then placed before the altar into the incense braziers. Chanting and mumbling, he threw handfuls of herbs on the flames until the vault filled with fragrant blue smoke. After a while Trok found it difficult to think clearly and his vision became distorted. He closed his eyes and pressed his fingers into the lids. When he opened them again he saw that the sweet smile on the face of the god had become a leer. He tried to look away but found he could not.

'The great god Marduk is pleased,' Ishtar announced, reading the auguries reflected in the surface of the blood-filled bowl. After a long silence he began to rock gently back and forth with the bowl in his lap. He looked up at last. 'Behold Marduk, the great god of Babylon! Speak to us, dreadful one, we entreat you!'

He opened his arms to the golden statue, and the god spoke in the voice of a child, lisping and mellifluous.

'I greet you, my brother Trok,' said this strange voice. 'You wish to know about the fledgling falcon that spreads its wings and sharpens its talons in the desert places.'

Trok was startled not only by the disembodied voice but also by the accuracy of this statement. Indeed, he had intended asking for counsel on his plans to attack and destroy Nefer Seti. He recalled bitterly how Ishtar had dissuaded him from leading another army into the eastern desert to attack Nefer Seti, with predictions of dire consequences, with warnings of disaster and death. Now he spoke as much to himself as to the golden god. 'I must have Nefer Seti. The double crown will sit uneasily on my head until I kill him and throw his body on the flames so that he will never know resurrection.'

In his anger and hatred he sprang to his feet. 'I demand that you deliver the person and the soul of Nefer Seti to me, in justice and retribution. I will not accept another refusal from you and your minion here.' In his fury Trok aimed a kick at Ishtar. His sandal caught the divining bowl and the blood of the kids splattered down the altar.

A hush had fallen over the sanctum. Then there was the sound of breathing, like that of a sleeping child to begin with but then growing harsher and stronger. Now it was the breathing of a wild beast, then of some monster that echoed through the temple.

Then a terrible voice spoke, harsh and unearthly. 'Hear me! Trok Uruk, you mortal man who claims to be Pharaoh, part of the godhead!' The thunder rolled around the dark recess of the sanctum. 'Hear me, blasphemer! If you march against Gallala in defiance of me and my prophet, Ishtar the Mede, I shall destroy you and your army just as I buried your other army in the sands of the desert. This time you shall not escape my wrath.'

Even though he was fearful of the rage of Marduk, Trok still sensed some false note in the force of his fury.

He tried to identify exactly what had given him pause. He realised that the thunderous voice issued from the belly of the statue. He stared and saw that the navel of the god was a dark slit. He took a step towards it and Ishtar cried, 'Beware, Pharaoh! Do not approach him.'

Trok ignored him and took another step forward, seeing a faint gleam in the depths of the aperture, a shadowy movement. Often in battle he had sensed the exact moment when the fates had swung in his favour and he felt it now. He steeled himself and shouted, above the awful sound of the god's breathing, 'I defy you, Marduk the Devourer! Strike me down if you are able.'

Suspicion became certainty as that glimmer showed again in the slit in the god's belly. Trok drew his sword and, with the flat of the blade, knocked Ishtar out of his way. Then he ran forward, ducked down, and peered into the slit. A human eye looked back at him. The pupil widened with astonishment, and Trok gave a mighty shout: 'Come out of there you slime!' He placed his shoulder against the idol and heaved with all his strength. The statue wobbled on its stone base, and Trok heaved again. Slowly the image went down with a crash onto the stone flags.

Ishtar screamed and leapt out of the way. In the silence after the shattering impact there was a scrabbling sound from the interior of the fallen idol. A trap door at the back of the idol flew open and a girl crawled out. Trok seized her by a thick head of curls. 'Mercy, great King Trok,' the girl pleaded, in a honey-sweet voice. 'I was doing the bidding of others.' She was such a lovely child that, for a moment, Trok felt his rage subside. Then he snatched her up by the ankles and dangled her upside-down in one fist, writhing in his grip.

'Who ordered you to this?' Trok demanded.

'Ishtar the Mede,' she wept.

Trok dashed the child against a temple column then let her corpse drop. He turned back to the golden idol and thrust his sword into the opening, rummaging around in the belly of the god. There was another squeal and a grotesque creature shot out, a hunch-backed dwarf, the ugliest man Trok had ever laid eyes upon.

'Forgive me that I tried to deceive you, mighty god and King of Egypt!' Trok slashed at him with the sword, but the creature ducked and dodged roaring with terror. Trok found himself laughing at his antics. The dwarf shot behind the curtains at the back of the chamber and disappeared through a secret doorway.

Trok let him go and turned back to Ishtar, just in time to seize a handful of his hair as he tried to flee from the chamber. He flung him full length on the stone floor.

'You have lied to me.' Trok was no longer laughing. 'You have deliberately misled me and diverted me from my purpose.'

'Please, master,' Ishtar wailed. 'It was for your good alone. How could we go against a warlock who commands the storm to his will?'

'You are afraid of Taita.' Trok stood back to regain his breath. 'The warlock?' he demanded incredulously.

'He overlooks us. He can turn my own spells back upon me! I cannot prevail against him. I sought only to save you from him, great Pharaoh.'

'You sought only to save your own blue-tattooed skin,' Trok snarled, and rushed in to slam kicks into Ishtar's doubled-up body.

'I beg of you, first of all the gods,' Ishtar cried, covering his head with both arms, 'give me my reward and let me go. Taita has dissipated my powers. I cannot confront him again. I can be of no further use to you.'

Trok stood with one foot drawn back, frozen in the act of delivering another kick. 'Your reward?' he demanded in astonishment.

'Surely you do not believe that I will reward your disloyalty? If you wish to live another day then you will lead me to Gallala, and take your chances in a trial of magical strength with the warlock.'

IT SEEMED THAT ALL EGYPT had heard that Nefer Seti had an army in Gallala. Each day visitors from all over the country arrived. Some were colonels of the regiments that Trok and Naja had left to guard Egypt in their absence. Others were emissaries from the great cities along the Nile—Avaris and Memphis, Thebes and Aswan—and the high priests from the temples in those cities. Sickened by the excesses of Naja and Trok, and emboldened by their absence in Babylon so far to the east, all had come to swear allegiance to Nefer Seti.

'Egypt is ready to welcome you,' the emissaries told him.

'Our regiments will declare for you as soon as they see your face, and know that the rumours of your survival are true,' the colonels assured him.

Nefer and Taita questioned them keenly. It soon became apparent that Trok and Naja had skimmed the cream of the regiments for their Mesopotamian adventure, and left only the reserve battalions, made up mostly of new recruits, the very young and untried, or the elderly nearing the end of their military lives.

'What of the chariots and horses?' Nefer asked the crucial question. They shook their grey heads and looked grave. 'Trok and Naja stripped the regiments bare. Almost every vehicle went with them. They left hardly enough to patrol the eastern borders to discourage the Bedouin raiders from the desert.'

Taita assessed this information. 'The false pharaohs are fully aware of the threat we pose to their rear. They want to ensure that if the regiments they have left in Egypt rebel against them and declare for the true Pharaoh, Nefer Seti, they will lack cavalry and chariots to be an effective force.'

'You must return to your regiments,' Nefer ordered the officers. 'We are too many in Gallala already, and we are near the limits of our food and water. Do not allow any more vehicles or horses to leave Egypt. Keep your men in training, and equip them with new chariots as they become available. I will come to you very soon, to lead you against the tyrants.'

They left, with renewed assurances of their loyalty, and the little army of Gallala redoubled its efforts to build itself into a force to challenge the might of the false pharaohs. They were inspired by their young commander, for Nefer worked harder than any of them. He rode out with the first squadrons long before dawn, and gradually forged his divisions into a cohesive body. When he rode back into the city, weary and dusty in the evening, he would go to the workshops where he cajoled and argued with the armourers and chariot builders. Then, after he had eaten, he would sit up in the lamplight with Taita, going over the battle plans and the dispositions of their forces. Usually it was after midnight when he stumbled to his bedchamber, where Mintaka took his head onto her bosom and held him until he woke to dawn's first promise.

NEFER LOOKED BACK along the column of chariots. They were at full gallop, four abreast. The platoon commanders were watching for his signal. He looked ahead and saw the line of enemy foot soldiers out in the plain, distorted by the heat mirage so that they seemed to be swimming in a lake of shimmering water where there was no water. He steered for their centre.

As they raced in he saw the enemy formation change. Like a giant hedgehog, it rolled itself into a ball, a tight circle two ranks deep, facing outwards, the outer rank with their long lances levelled, and the second rank with their lances thrust through the gaps, so that they offered a glittering wall of bronze spearheads. Nefer raced straight at the centre of the double row of lances, and then, when they were only two hundred paces away, he gave a hand signal and the formation of chariots opened, wheeling alternately right and left, spreading like wings to envelope the crouching infantrymen. The chariots whirled around them and the arrows from the short recurved cavalry bows flew into them.

Nefer gave the signal to break off the attack and withdraw. As he swept past the infantry circle, he raised his right fist in a salute, and shouted, 'Well done! That was much better.'

He slowed the horses and turned them, trotting back to halt his squadron in front of the ranks of infantry. Taita stepped out of the defensive circle to greet him.

'Any injuries?' Nefer asked. The tips of the arrows they shot into the hedgehog were padded, but they could still inflict damage.

'A few bruises.' Taita shrugged.

'They have done well,' Nefer said, then shouted to the centurion commanding the infantry, 'Let your lads fall out. I want to speak to them. Then we will practise the false retreat.'

There was an outcrop of rock that formed a natural podium, and Nefer climbed to the top of it while all the men—infantry and charioteers—gathered below him.

Taita squatted at the base of the rock and watched and listened. Nefer reminded him strongly of Pharaoh Tamose, his father, at the same age. He had the easy manner, and spoke simply, in language that his men understood.

Nefer reviewed the morning's exercises, giving them the credit they deserved, but ruthlessly picking out every deficiency. 'I think you are almost ready to give Trok and Naja the surprise of their lives,' he ended. 'Now, get something to eat. We have not finished for the day.' They began to disperse.

Nefer jumped down from the rock, and as he did so Taita sprang to his feet and said quietly but urgently, 'Stop, Nefer! Do not move!'

The cobra must have had its nest in the rock pile, but the noise and the trampling of feet and hoofs had disturbed it. Its hood was flared open, and its feathery black tongue flickered between the thin, grinning lips. Its eyes were beads of polished onyx, with sparks of light in the black centres, and they were fastened on Nefer's long bare legs, which were within easy striking distance.

The nearest men had heard Taita's warning. They turned back but none dared move. They stared in horror at the mortal predicament of their pharaoh.

The cobra gaped wide, the preliminary to the attack, and the bony fangs came erect in the pale roof of its mouth. Drops of venom sparkled on the needle points.

Suddenly there was a shrill cry from the sky above. They had all been so intent on the cobra that no one had seen the falcon hovering high in the blue above them. Now it stooped towards the earth, and in full flight sank its talons into the flared hood, an inch behind the head. Then it rose on heavily flogging wings, carrying the cobra dangling and twisting below it.

Taita watched the bird as it bore away the snake. It dwindled in size in the distance and at last disappeared into the blue-grey heat-haze that shrouded the horizon. Taita stood a long time staring after it. When he turned his expression was grave.

'It was an omen,' Nefer said, and glanced at him. He saw by Taita's face that this was so.

'Yes,' said Taita. 'It was a warning and a promise.'

'What does it mean?'

'The cobra threatened you. That means great danger. The royal bird flew towards the east with the snake in its talons. It means great danger in the east. But in the end the falcon triumphed.'

They both looked towards the east. 'We will take out a scouting expedition tomorrow at the first light of dawn,' Nefer decided.

IN THE CHILL DARKNESS before the dawn Nefer and Taita waited on the mountaintop. The rest of the scouting party were encamped on the back slope. All told they were twenty men.

Hilto, Shabako and Meren had taken other scouting parties to cover the terrain to the south; between them they could sweep all the eastern approaches to Gallala.

Nefer had brought his party down along the western shores of the Red Sea, looking in on every port and fishing village along the way. Apart from a few trading caravans and wandering bands of Bedouin they had found nothing, no sign of the danger foreshadowed by the omen. Now they were camped above the port of Safaga.

Taita and Nefer had woken in the darkness and left the camp to climb to the lookout peak. They sat close together in companionable silence. Taita looked to the eastern sky, where the morning star hung low on the horizon. He stood up suddenly and leaned on his staff. Nefer never failed to be amazed by the acuity of those pale old eyes. He knew Taita had seen something.

'What is it, Old Father?'

'The omen was not false,' Taita said simply. 'The danger is here.'

The sea was grey, but as the light strengthened, the surface was speckled with white. Like a vast flock of egrets returning to the roost, a fleet of dhows was heading into the port of Safaga.

'If this is the army of Trok and Naja, why would they come by sea?' Nefer asked quietly.

'It is the shortest route from Mesopotamia. The crossing will save the horses and men for the road through the desert. Without the warning of the snake and the falcon, we would not have expected danger from this direction.' Taita nodded approval. 'It is a cunning move.'

They scrambled back down the mountain to the camp below. Nefer called in the sentries and gave them their orders. Two would ride back with all speed to Gallala, carrying his orders to Socco, whom he had left in command. Most of the other men he split into pairs and sent south to find the scouting parties and bring them in.

Nefer and Taita watched the men Nefer had dispatched ride away, then they mounted and rode down through the hills to an abandoned watchtower overlooking Safaga.

'The first boats are entering the bay.' Nefer pointed out the largest of them all. At the peak of her stubby mast she flew the snarling leopard-head gonfalon of the House of Trok Uruk. 'There he is.' He pointed to the unmistakable figure in the bows.

'And that is Ishtar beside Trok: the dog and its master.' Taita had a fierce gleam in his eyes as watched the strange pair wade ashore.

'Do you see Naja's standard on any of the ships?' Nefer asked.

Taita shook his head. 'Trok alone leads the expedition. He must have left Naja to hold Babylon and Mesopotamia. He has come to take care of personal business.'

'How do you know that?' Nefer demanded.

'There is an aura around him. It is like a dark red cloud. I can sense it even from here,' Taita said softly. 'All that hatred is focused on one person alone. He comes for Mintaka.'

THE MORNING AFTER HIS LANDING at Safaga, Trok captured two Bedouin leading a string of donkeys down the road to Safaga. His reputation had penetrated even into these desert fastnesses, so the Bedouin were desperate to please. They told Trok of the lush pastures that surrounded Gallala. They also gave him an estimate of the numbers of chariots that Nefer Seti commanded, and Trok realised that he outnumbered his enemies five to one. Most important of all, they told him the route from Safaga to the ancient city and assured him he could reach Gallala in two days and a night of hard riding.

It took him two more days to disembark all his squadrons. On the second evening he was ready to begin the forced march on Gallala. Each of the chariots had two spare teams behind it on lead reins. They would not stop during the night to rest the horses, but would change them as they tired. Any exhausted animals would be turned loose and left behind for the remount herds to bring up.

Trok led the vanguard, and set a killing pace. Once the water-skins were empty there would be no turning back. By midmorning the following day the heat had become fierce, and they had used up most of the spare horses. The Bedouin guides kept assuring Trok that Gallala was not far ahead, but each time they topped a rise the same daunting vista of rock and baked earth shimmered in the heat mirage ahead. Fifty or sixty chariots burned out their last horses, and Trok left them scattered back along the road.

The sun came up on the second day, warm as a kiss, but soon it stung and dazzled their bloodshot eyes. For the first time Trok faced the possibility of dying here on this dreadful road to nowhere.

'One more hill,' he called to his last team of horses, and tried to whip them into a trot, but they stumbled up the easy incline with their heads hanging, and the sweat long ago dried to white salt on their flanks. Just below the crest Trok looked back down the straggling column of his army. Even without counting them he saw that he had lost half of his chariots. Hundreds of dismounted troopers were staggering along behind the column, and there were vultures in the sky following them, dark specks turning in high circles against the blue.

'There is only one way,' he told Ishtar, 'and that is forward.' He cracked the whip over the backs of his team. They went on painfully.

They reached the top of the hill, and Trok gawked in astonishment at the scene in the valley below him. The ruins of the ancient city of Gallala lay before him, ghostly but eternal. As he had been promised, the city was surrounded by fields of cool green, and a network of canals. His horses smelt the water and strained against the reins with renewed strength.

Even in his desperate haste, Trok took time to assess the tactical situation. He saw at once that the city was helpless and undefended. The gates stood wide open and from them poured the panic-stricken populace. Carrying their children and bundles of possessions they streamed away up the narrow valley to the west. There was no sign of cavalry or of fighting chariots. They were a flock of sheep before the wolf pack, but the wolves were parched and weak with thirst.

'Seueth has delivered them into our hands,' Trok shouted with triumph. 'Before the sun sets this day you will have more women and gold than you can use!'

The men who had followed him over the ridge rode down to the first irrigation ditch and spread out along the length of it, the horses sucking up the blessed liquid. The men threw themselves full length along the bank, plunging their faces under, or filling their helmets and pouring it over their heads and down their throats.

'YOU SHOULD HAVE LET ME POISON the canals,' Nefer said flatly, as they watched from the other side of the valley.

'You know better than that.' Taita shook his head. 'That would have been an offence against nature that the gods would never forgive.'

428

He and Nefer gave their full attention to the unfolding scene in the valley below. Trok's men and horses had drunk until their bellies bulged and now they were mounting. Even though he had lost many chariots on the approach march, Trok still outnumbered Nefer's forces at least three to one.

'We dare not meet him on open ground,' Nefer mused, and looked down upon the mass of refugees escaping up the valley below them. Mintaka, together with all the women and children, the sick and wounded, had been evacuated from Gallala two days before. Nefer had sent them all to Gebel Nagara, where Trok would never find them.

Now Gallala was stripped of everything of value. Nefer gazed down on the refugees with satisfaction. Even from this close it was difficult to tell that they were not women and civilians but disguised foot soldiers, stumbling in their long skirts and shawls. The bundles they carried were not swaddled infants, but their bows and swords. Their lances had been cached among the rocks higher up the valley where the main force was concealed.

The enemy's chariots were coming on across the pastures in tight formations. The water had revived them, and before them lay the promise of plunder. They were close enough now for Nefer to be able to pick out Trok's chariot at the front of the moving mass of vehicles, as it wheeled into a position across the mouth of the valley.

'Come, Trok Uruk!' Nefer whispered. 'Order the charge! Ride into history!'

ISHTAR THE MEDE crouched beside Trok in the leading chariot. He was so agitated that he reached up to tug at Trok's beard.

'The smell of the warlock hangs in the air.' His voice was shrill, and saliva frothed on his lips. 'He waits for you, I can feel his presence. Look up, mighty Pharaoh!'

Trok was distracted enough to glance up at the sky. The vultures had dropped lower.

'Yes! Yes!' Ishtar pressed the small advantage. 'They are Taita's chickens. They wait for him to feed them with your flesh.'

Trok looked back at the prize that lay before him, but the shadows of the vultures flitted over the earth between them and he turned his head to look down at the skinny figure of Ishtar beside him.

The Mede tugged at his armour. 'It is a snare laid for you by the warlock. If you never trust me again, you must trust me now. There is death in the air.'

Trok scratched his beard, and glanced over his shoulder at the ranks of chariots parked wheel to wheel and his troopers leaning forward in cruel anticipation of his order.

'Turn aside, mighty Trok. Seize the city and the water. Nefer Seti and the warlock will perish out there in the desert. That way is certain. The other way is madness.'

ON THE HILLSIDE Nefer narrowed his eyes as he watched his disguised troopers scurrying away up the valley, and he knew that the moment was passing. 'What is holding Trok? Will he not commit to the charge?'

'Look to the head of the valley.' Taita had not opened his eyes.

Nefer glanced up the valley, and stiffened with alarm. His fist tightened on the hilt of his sword. 'It is not possible!' he growled.

Near the top end of the valley, but fully visible from where Trok's chariots were drawn up, was a slab of rock. On top of this, above the stream of fleeing refugees, had appeared a woman, young and slim, with long, dark hair that hung to her waist.

'Mintaka!' Nefer breathed. 'I ordered her to go to Gebel Nagara.'

'We know that she would never have disobeyed you.' Taita smiled ironically. 'Therefore, it seems that she must have misheard you.'

'This is your doing,' Nefer said bitterly. 'You are using her as bait for Trok. You have placed her in mortal danger.'

'Perhaps I can control the khamsin,' Taita said, 'but not even I can control Mintaka. What she does, she does of her own free will.'

BELOW THEM, TROK had turned round and was staring up the long rising valley. He saw the tiny figure standing high on the yellow rock platform, and recognised in an instant the object of all his hatred.

'Mintaka Apepi,' he snarled, 'I have come for you, you adulterous little bitch. I will make you plead for death.'

'It is an illusion, Pharaoh,' Ishtar howled. 'Don't let the warlock deceive you. There is death all around us.'

He tried to leap down from the footplate and run, but Trok seized him and hauled him back. He raised his clenched fist high above his head and shouted, 'Forward! March!'

The chariots on either hand rolled forward together, and the ranks behind followed Trok into the valley. The tail of the fleeing refugees was three hundred paces ahead when Trok gave his next order.

'Forward at the gallop! Charge!'

The horses leapt away, and in a rising thunder of hoofs and wheels they swept up the narrow valley.

'Trok has committed,' Nefer said softly. 'But at what cost? If he takes Mintaka . . .' He could not bring himself to go on.

As the phalanx of chariots swept by below where Nefer stood on the side of the valley, he stepped out from behind the rock that had concealed him. The complete attention of Trok and his troopers was fixed on the victims ahead of their racing chariots, but all Nefer's men could see him clearly. They were hidden among the boulders down both slopes of the valley. Nefer raised his sword above his head, and as the last chariot sped past he brought it down sharply.

The wagons were poised on the steep gradient, screened from view with dried grass and so heavily laden with rocks that the axles sagged. At Nefer's signal his wagoners pulled out the wooden chocks that held them, and from both sides of the valley the wagons rolled forward, gathering speed, bounding down to the massed chariots below.

When Ishtar screamed at his side, Trok tore his eyes from Mintaka's figure at the far end of the valley, and he saw the huge vehicles tearing down upon his squadrons. 'Back!' he shouted. 'Break away!' But there was no space to manoeuvre.

The first wagons crashed into the head of the charge. There was the rending of wood, the screams of crushed men and horses, the thunder of wagons overturning and shedding their loads of rock. In an instant the magnificent charge was transformed into a shambles of shattered vehicles and crippled horses.

The wagons had sealed off the valley at both ends. Even the chariots that had not been smashed and capsized were now bottled up, held by walls of stone, and Nefer's archers were on the slopes above them. The first volleys decimated the unprotected charioteers. Within minutes the valley was transformed into a slaughterhouse.

Trok looked around him wildly, seeking some way out of the trap, but behind him the other vehicles were so crowded that there was no room for him to turn or back up. Arrows and javelins were singing around him, clattering against the sides of the chariot, clanging off his helmet and breastplate.

Before Trok could restrain him, Ishtar took advantage of the confusion to spring down from the footplate and scuttle away between the plunging horses. Then Trok looked ahead again, and saw Mintaka still standing on the rock pile just ahead of him, a cold look of revulsion on her lovely face.

He drew his sword, sprang down to the ground and ran forward under the hoofs of his rearing horses. Two of Nefer's men jumped out from behind the rocks to oppose him but he hacked them down, his eyes fastened hungrily on the girl.

Nefer saw Trok break out of the trap, and he ran down the slope and sprang out onto the level ground in front of him.

Trok went on guard as Nefer confronted him and his face twisted into a ferocious grin. 'Come, puppy,' he said. 'Let us test your claim to the double crown.'

Nefer's men had seen him charge down the hillside. They followed his example, left the cover of the rocks and within seconds the valley was choked with struggling, hacking, thrusting men.

Nefer feinted at Trok's hip, aiming at the joint of his armour. When Trok covered, he swung backhanded at his face. Trok was surprised by the change of direction and by the speed of the stroke. Though he jerked his head back the point of Nefer's blade split his cheek open. The wound galvanised him, and Trok rushed at Nefer, his sword seeming to form an impenetrable wall of shining bronze around him. Nefer fell back before the attack until he felt the stone slab on which Mintaka stood pressing into his back.

He could no longer retreat or manoeuvre, and he was forced to pit himself against all Trok's strength, and trade him blow for blow. In a contest of this nature, there were few men who could stand against Trok, who never seemed to flag. As much as the years of battle training had hardened Nefer they had not prepared him for this. He felt his right arm tiring. He knew that his only chance of surviving was to break away.

He caught the next cut high on his blade and deflected it just sufficiently to make an opening through which he could escape, but as he leapt into it he exposed his left flank. Trok recovered and drove in a low thrust that laid open his thigh. The blood ran down into his sandal and squelched at every pace he took. The last of Nefer's strength was ebbing away, and Trok swept up his blade and locked it with his own, forcing his guard higher. Nefer knew that if he attempted to break away he would expose his chest for the killing thrust.

Gradually Trok forced aside his blade and towered over him, so they came chest to chest, then suddenly he shifted his weight to the left, towards Nefer's wounded leg. Nefer tried to counter, but his leg gave way under him. Trok hooked his foot behind Nefer's heel and threw him over backwards.

The sword flew from Nefer's grip, and as he sprawled on the sun-baked earth, Trok lifted his blade above his head with both hands for the killing stroke. Suddenly his expression changed. He opened his mouth to say something, but a double stream of bright blood trickled from the corners of his mouth and he turned slowly away from Nefer. Trok stared up at Mintaka, who stood on the rock above him. With a detached feeling of disbelief, Nefer saw the shaft of her javelin sticking out of the back of Trok's neck.

Trok toppled forward on his face, and Nefer turned to Mintaka. She flew to him, and clung to him with all her strength. Now that the danger was past, she had lost all her icy control and was sobbing, barely coherent. 'I thought he was going to kill you, my love.'

'He almost did, but for you,' Nefer gasped. 'I owe you my life.'

He became aware that the sounds of battle from further down the valley had changed. With his arm still around her, he turned to look back. Trok's men had seen him cut down, and the fight had gone out of them. They were throwing down their weapons.

With the realisation of victory, Nefer felt the last strength flow out of his body. He had just enough left to raise his voice, and shout, 'Give them quarter. They are our brother Egyptians. Give them quarter!'

As Nefer slumped down, Taita materialised at his side and helped Mintaka lower him to the ground. While the two of them staunched the bleeding from the deep cut in his thigh, his officers came to report to Nefer. And with joy, he saw that his trusted captains, Hilto and Meren, Shabako and Socco, were among the men who crowded around him, exulting in the victory.

They made a litter of lances and carried him back down the valley to Gallala. Three times before they reached the gates of the city, Nefer signalled for his litter to be lowered and allowed captured centurions and captains to come forward. 'I spare you from the traitor's death you so richly deserve,' he told them sternly, 'but you must prove once more your duty and loyalty to the House of Tamose.'

They praised him for his mercy, and his own men joined their voices to those of the defeated.

Nefer issued his orders with a frowning mien. 'The corpse of Trok Uruk, the false claimant to the double crown of Egypt, shall be burned without ceremony, here upon the battlefield, so that his soul shall wander through all eternity. The name of Trok Uruk shall be erased from every monument and building in the land.'

They shouted their approbation at this decree, and Nefer went on.

'All the possessions of Trok Uruk, all his treasure and estates and slaves, shall be forfeited to the state. Send water wagons back along the road to Safaga, and bring in all the horses, chariots and men that Trok Uruk left along the way during his march on Gallala. If they repudiate the false pharaohs and swear allegiance to the House of Tamose, the prisoners shall be pardoned and recruited into our armies.'

By the time Nefer had issued his last decree for that day, his voice was hoarse, he was pale and almost exhausted. As they carried him through the city gates he asked Mintaka quietly, 'Where is Taita? Has anybody seen the Magus?' But Taita had disappeared.

ON THE HILLSIDE above the battlefield, Taita had picked up the tracks that Ishtar had left as he escaped out of the valley. He followed them until they were impossible to discern in the earth on the top of the hills, which was baked hard as mosaic tiles by the sun. Then he stopped and crouched down. He opened his mind and reached out to detect the Mede's aura, the trace he had left as he passed.

The aura was dark and tainted. Taita stood up and went on again after it, striding out on his long legs. Every so often he saw physical confirmation that he was on the right track, a smudged footprint in softer earth or a recently dislodged pebble.

Ishtar had circled round to the south then come back towards Gallala. Taita was alarmed and lengthened his stride. If Ishtar was trying to get close to Nefer again to work some mischief, Taita must intercept him. However, the pursuit led him to one of the chariots Trok had abandoned on his march up from the coast. From the wreck Ishtar had salvaged a water-skin, and had then gone back to the ridge above the city, where he had crept down to the bank of the closest irrigation canal. The imprint of his knees was clear in the wet clay where he had knelt to drink and then to fill the skin he carried. Taita drank himself. Then he rose and followed the traces Ishtar had left as he started back eastwards along the road towards Safaga and the coast.

Night fell and Taita kept on. Sometimes the aura of the Mede faded away completely, but Taita followed the road. At other times it grew stronger, until Taita smelt it, a faint, musty, unpleasant odour. When it was this strong he could fathom the essence of the Mede. He could detect his vengeful nature. He divined that Ishtar was demoralised by the turn that the fates had taken against him, but his powers were still formidable. He constituted a great and real danger. Taita himself was not immune to his baleful spirit.

A LEAGUE AHEAD Ishtar the Mede was hurrying along the track. He was by now fully aware of the pursuit. I must turn aside and conceal my path, he decided. He ran on along the road and found the place where it crossed an intrusion of grey schist, so hard that even the passing of Trok's legions had left no mark upon it.

With his left forefinger he traced out lightly the sacred symbol of Marduk on the rock, spat on it and uttered the three hidden names of the god that would summon him.

'Hide me from my enemies, mighty Marduk. Bring me back safely to your temple in Babylon.' Then he turned sharply off the road and set out at right angles to it, heading into the northern wilderness. He went swiftly, trying to open the distance between him and the man who pursued him.

TAITA REACHED THE POINT where the ridge of grey schist crossed the road and stopped abruptly. The aura that had been so strong only moments before had disappeared like mist in the warmth of the rising sun. Quickly he retraced his steps until he reached the point where he had lost the trail.

He looked up at the sky, from the starry firmament picked out the single red star low on the horizon, the star of the goddess Lostris, and began to chant the Praise to the Goddess. He had barely completed the first stanza when he felt an angry, alien presence. Another god had been invoked on this spot, and knowing Ishtar he could guess well enough who that was. He started on the second stanza of praise and on the bare rock ahead of him appeared a glow, like that of a furnace.

Marduk is affronted, and shows his anger, he thought. He intoned, 'You are far from your own land, Marduk of the furnace. Few worship you in Egypt. Your powers are dissipated. I invoke the name of the goddess Lostris, and you cannot stand against it.'

He lifted his kilt. 'I quench your fire, Marduk,' he said, and urinated on the rock. It sizzled like a bar of metal from the forge, drenched in the trough. 'In the name of the goddess Lostris, Marduk the Devourer, stand aside and let me pass.'

The rock cooled quickly, and as the steam dispersed the veil that Ishtar had laid was pierced and torn. Taita stepped through it and set off again after him.

The horizon paled and the light increased to a golden radiance. Taita knew that he was gaining steadily, and he strained his eyes ahead for the first glimpse of his quarry. Instead he came to an abrupt halt. At his feet gaped a terrible abyss, whose sheer sides dropped into darkness far below.

Taita looked across at the far side. It was a thousand paces across, and there were vultures soaring over the bottomless gulf. Taita shook his head with admiration. 'Wonderful, Ishtar!' he murmured. 'Even the vultures. That was a masterful touch. I could not have improved upon it. But such an effort called for a great expenditure of strength. It must have cost you dearly.'

Taita stepped out over the edge of the cliff. Instead of airy space there was firm ground under his feet. The vista of cliffs and vultures wavered and broke up as a mirage does when you walk towards it.

The abyss was gone and in its place was a gentle plain of stony ground. In the middle of this plain, not five hundred paces away, stood Ishtar the Mede. Seeing Taita striding towards him he turned and broke into a shambling run, his black robes swirling around his legs. Taita followed him with his long, indefatigable strides, and Ishtar was only a few hundred paces ahead when he reached the low hills and disappeared into one of the gullies.

When Taita reached the mouth of the gully he saw Ishtar's footprints strung along the sandy floor ahead of him, but they disappeared round the corner where the gully turned sharply to the right. Taita followed him, but as he reached the corner of pale limestone pillars, he heard the thunderous roaring of a wild beast. Standing foursquare in the way, its tail lashing from side to side, was a huge male lion. Its eyes were golden, the pupils implacable black slits.

Taita didn't break his stride. As he walked straight at the slavering animal, the roaring became muted, the outline of its head turned transparent and then, like river mist, the lion faded and was gone.

Taita walked through the space where it had stood and rounded the corner. Ahead of him the gully became narrower and the sides were steeper. It ended abruptly against a wall of rock.

Ishtar stood with his back against the rock, staring at Taita with mad eyes. He raised his right hand and pointed a long bony finger at Taita. 'Back, Warlock!' he screamed. 'I warn you!'

Taita walked towards him and he screamed again, this time in a guttural language. Then he turned and bolted into a narrow opening in the rock wall behind him, which had been screened from Taita by his body. Taita paused before the entrance, and tapped the stony portals with his staff. The rock rang true. This was no illusion, but the rear entrance to a cavern in the limestone cliff.

Taita stepped through after him, and could hear the echoes of Ishtar's footsteps distorted in the tunnel ahead. Taita counted his paces as he went forward into darkness. After a hundred and twenty the tunnel took a sharp bend, and as he stepped round it Taita found himself in a large, high-roofed cavern. From the floor rose sharp-pointed stalagmites, the crystals glimmering. From the high roof hung down matching stalactites, some shaped like spearheads and other like the shining wings of the gods. In the centre of the roof was an aperture through which a beam of bright sunlight fell to the floor.

Across the cavern Ishtar crouched against the far wall. There was no escape that way. When he saw Taita appear in the mouth of the tunnel he began to blubber, 'Mercy, mighty Magus! There is a bond between us. We are brothers. Spare me.'

So abject were his entreaties that, despite himself, Taita felt his resolve waver. Ishtar picked up the tiny chink in his armour, and exploited it instantly. He flung out one hand with the thumb and forefinger forming a circle, the sign of Marduk, and shouted something in that strange guttural tongue.

From behind him Taita felt an insupportable physical weight bear down upon his body, trapping his arms to his sides, wrapping around his throat in a strangler's grip. He smelt scorching human flesh, the aura of the Devourer, suffocating him. He could not move.

On the far side of the cavern Ishtar danced and capered, his tattooed face contorted in a grotesque mask. 'Your goddess cannot protect you here deep in the earth, Taita. You can no longer prevail against Marduk the Devourer and Ishtar, his minion,' he shrieked, 'Our contest is over. I have defeated you and all your wiles, Warlock! Now you will die.'

Taita turned his eyes up towards the high, dim roof of the cavern and fixed all his attention on one of the long, gleaming stalactites that hung down from it like a great shimmering dagger. He gathered all his reserves, lifted the staff in his right hand and pointed it upwards. With the last breath in his lungs he shouted, '*Kydash!*' the word of power.

There was a crack like the ice shattering in the depths of a glacier, the stalactite broke from the roof and plunged downwards. Driven by its own immense weight, the point struck Ishtar on the top of his shoulder, transfixed him through chest and belly and pegged him down on the cavern floor.

As Ishtar twitched convulsively in his death throes, Taita felt the weight lifted from his shoulders and the pressure on his throat relax. Marduk retreated and the smell of burnt flesh was gone.

He picked up his staff, turned and walked back along the tunnel into the open air. At the entrance he turned back and with his staff struck the limestone portals of the tunnel, once, twice, three times.

Deep in the earth there was a rumble of collapsing rock, and a gust of air blew from the tunnel mouth as the cavern roof caved in.

'With the stone spike driven through your heart, not even your foul god can free you from your tomb. Lie in it through all eternity, Ishtar the Mede,' Taita said, and he turned and struck out along the road back to Gallala.

WHEN THE MESSENGERS reached Babylon, Pharaoh Naja Kiafan gave them audience on the uppermost terrace garden of the palace of Babylon. Queen Heseret sat beside his throne, wearing the most magnificent jewels that the treasury of King Sargon had yielded.

The messengers were all high officers from the army that Pharaoh Trok had taken westward four months before. They threw themselves at the foot of the throne on which Naja sat in glory and splendour. 'All hail to you, Pharaoh Naja, mightiest of the gods of Egypt,' they greeted him. 'We are bearers of terrible tidings.'

'Speak!' Naja commanded sternly.

'In the desert that surrounds the ancient city of Gallala there took place a mighty battle between the armies of Pharaoh Trok Uruk and those of the usurper Nefer Seti,' said one of the officers. 'By the means of cowardly deceit the army of Pharaoh Trok Uruk was lured to destruction. He is slain. Those of his men who survived have gone over to the enemy, and have rallied to the standard of the false pharaoh Nefer Seti.'

Naja sank back on his throne and stared at him in astonishment. At his side Heseret touched Naja's arm with a bejewelled finger, and when he leaned towards her she whispered in his ear, 'Praise to the gods, and all hail to the one and only Pharaoh of the Upper and Lower Kingdoms, the mighty Naja Kiafan!'

Naja tried to remain expressionless but a tiny smile played for an instant over his features. It took him a moment to suppress it then he rose. His voice was soft but menacing. 'Pharaoh Trok Uruk is dead. We commend his soul to the gods. I declare before you all that there is now only one ruler over both kingdoms, and over all the territories and all the conquered lands and possessions of Egypt. I declare further that ruler to be myself, Pharaoh Naja Kiafan.'

The courtiers and captains who stood around his throne drew their swords and beat them on their shields. 'Exalted be the king-god Naja Kiafan!'

'Send word to all my commanders and the generals of all my armies. We will meet in war council at the noon hour this same day to prepare all our forces for the campaign against Nefer Seti.'

He looked down at Heseret. 'Do you feel no pity for your brother?'

'None!' She shook her head 'You are my pharaoh and my husband. Whosoever rises against you deserves death.'

'Death he shall have, and the treacherous warlock will share his funeral pyre,' Naja promised her grimly.

THEY SMELT THE RIVER from afar, the perfume of the sweet cool waters on the desert air. The horses lifted their heads and whickered. The infantry quickened their step and gazed ahead, eager for the first glimpse of the Nile's waters.

Nefer and Mintaka rode together in his chariot at the head of the long cavalcade that wound down the caravan road from Gallala. Meren rode at his right hand in the second chariot of the column.

The leading chariots topped the escarpment, and below them stretched the green valley of the Nile. Coming to meet them was the army Trok Uruk had left in Avaris, armed charioteers, generals and captains leading their regiments, legions of foot soldiers following. Behind them came the elders, the priests and the governors of every nome, all dressed in their robes, chains and decorations of office, and after them the dense masses of citizenry, laughing and dancing.

The two cavalcades came together and mingled, and elders and generals prostrated themselves before Pharaoh's chariot. Then Nefer led the vast concourse back along the river bank towards the city of Avaris. For a league outside the city the road was lined with the welcoming crowds.

When they reached the city the gates stood wide open and the populace lined the walls. They sang anthems of loyalty, praise and welcome as Nefer, with Mintaka beside him, drove under the arch of the gateway.

Beautiful as a young god and goddess, they drove first to the magnificent temple on the river bank to give thanks to the god and to sacrifice a pair of perfect black bulls before the stone altar. After the religious service Nefer declared a week of holiday, festivity and feasting.

'You are a sly one,' Mintaka told him. 'They loved you before; now they will adore you.'

For how long? Nefer wondered. As soon as the news of our arrival reaches Naja in Babylon, he will be on the march, if he is not already. The common people will love me until he knocks upon the gates.

PHARAOH NAJA KIAFAN left five hundred chariots, two thousand archers and infantry to hold and secure Babylon. Then, with the bulk of his army, he began the march on Egypt. As he went, vassal kings flocked to his standard, so that by the time he stood on the heights of the Khatmia Pass his army had almost trebled in size.

Ahead of him lay a great expanse of desert, with no spring or oasis to sustain his army until he reached Ismailiya. Once again he was reduced to laying down water points along the route ahead, and for months had been at work building up dumps in the desert, burying the filled pots in the sand, then leaving detachments of infantry to guard them while they returned for the next load.

It would take his army ten days and nights to make the crossing. During that time they would be strictly rationed, allowed just enough water to sustain the long night marches, and to eke out the burning days when they lay up to rest, enduring the heat in any scrap of shade afforded by tents or shelters made from branches and grass.

'I will ride with you in the vanguard.' Heseret spoke at his elbow, breaking into his train of thought.

He glanced at her. 'We have discussed this before.' He frowned. 'You will come up with the other women in the baggage train, under the wing of Prenn, the centurion of the rearguard.'

Heseret pouted. Once, that had been appealing but now it was merely irritating.

'You become tiresome, wife.' Naja lifted his upper lip in a smile that was more a snarl.

She gave him a furious glare, then called for her litter to take her back down the column, to where Prenn was bringing up the rearguard.

ON TAITA'S ADVICE, Nefer had established a screen of scouts along the edge of the Great Sand Desert. Taita was certain that Naja's main invasion force must come this way. Naja knew the route well, and his army was too large to bring across the Red Sea in boats as Trok had done with his much smaller force.

Very soon it became apparent that Taita had assessed the situation correctly, and Naja was indeed intent on a frontal assault through the Great Sand Desert. A squadron of scouts commanded by Meren watched Naja's water carts carrying their loads of clay jars forward and building up dumps in the arid land. Meren asked to be allowed to attack them but Nefer sent orders to him merely to keep them under observation and note carefully where they placed the water stores.

Then Nefer ordered the last reserves that he had been holding on the river to be brought up. When these were encamped around Ismailiya, he called a war council of all their commanders. Mintaka sat on the council. Her contributions were invaluable: she was Hyksos born, and knew well those officers on Naja's staff who had once been on her own father's staff. As a child she had listened to her father's assessment of each of them, and she had a formidable memory.

'Now, there is one, Centurion Prenn, who commands Naja's rear-guard, who is related to me, for he was one of my father's cousins. I know him well. He taught me to ride. I used to call him Uncle Bear.' She smiled at the memory. 'My father said of him that he was loyal as a hound, and once he had sunk his teeth into the throat of an enemy he would hang on to the death.'

All that night they sat in council while Nefer laid out his battle plan. They were to let Naja advance unopposed for the first five days. Then, once he was deeply committed, they would raid and destroy his water stores, both in front and to the rear of his advance. This would trap him in the midst of the sands.

'Taita and I have devised a plan to lead his vehicles into a trap in which we can exploit the small advantage that we have. In front of the town we will throw up a series of low stone walls behind which our archers and infantry can conceal themselves. These works will be just high enough to block the advance of a chariot.' With a charcoal stick Nefer sketched out a design on the sheet of papyrus spread in front of him. 'The walls will be laid out in the design of a fish trap.' He drew an inverted funnel with the apex aimed back towards the fort of Ismailiya.

'How will you lead him into the funnel?' Shabako asked.

'With a charge of our own chariots and the mock retreat you have practised so often,' Nefer explained. 'Our archers and slingers will remain concealed behind the walls until Naja follows us into the funnel. The deeper they penetrate, the more tightly his squadrons will be compressed between the walls. I intend to shut them up in a stockade like cattle, just as we did with Trok.'

They discussed the plan with enthusiasm, offering suggestions and refinements. In the end Nefer put Shabako in charge of building the walls, work that must begin as soon as it was light the next day.

The council broke up at last, the officers hurried away, and only three remained in the room: Nefer, Taita and Mintaka.

Mintaka spoke up again. 'We have already discussed Centurion Prenn,' she said. 'If I could meet him, I am sure I could convince him to throw in his lot with us.'

'What do you mean?' Nefer's voice was harsh. 'Meet him?'

'Dressed as a boy, with a small detachment of good men and fast horses, I could circle around Naja's main army and get through to Prenn in the rear. There would be little risk.'

Nefer's face blanched with anger. 'Madness!' he said quietly. 'Stark raving madness of the kind you exhibited at Gallala when you showed yourself as bait to Trok. I will not hear of it. Can you imagine what Naja would do to you if you fell into his hands?'

'Can you imagine what Naja would do if, in the critical moment of the battle, Prenn and his legions fell upon him from his own rear?' she flashed back at Nefer.

'We will not speak of it again.' Nefer came to his feet and slammed his fists down on the tabletop.

Taita looked on, expressionless. He waited with interest to see how this would be resolved.

'You deliberately disobeyed my orders at Gallala. I cannot trust you not to do the same now. You leave me no alternative.' Nefer shouted to the sentry outside the door to send for Zugga, the head eunuch of the royal harem. Then he turned back to Mintaka. 'I am sending you back to the zenana in the Avaris palace. You are to remain there in the care of Zugga.' And Zugga led Mintaka away. At the door she looked back over her shoulder at Nefer, and Taita smiled as he read her expression. Nefer had taken on a more stubborn adversary than both the false pharaohs combined.

TAITA AND NEFER rode out and inspected the stone walls that Shabako had hastily thrown up along the eastern approaches to the oasis of Ismailiya.

'Shabako's efforts will not rank among the great architectural achievements of the age,' Taita gave his opinion, 'but that is all to the good. From the direction in which Naja will come, they appear to be natural features and will excite no suspicion until he enters the funnel and finds his front progressively narrowed.'

Nefer nodded. 'Your plan has the towering virtue of allowing us to choose our own battleground. With the help of Horus, we will turn it into a slaughter-ground.' Then he laid his hand upon Taita's skinny arm. 'Once again I find myself deeply in your debt, Old Father. This is all your work.'

'No.' Taita shook his head. 'It was a gentle nudge I gave to you. The rest of it is yours. You have inherited the military instincts of your father, Pharaoh Tamose. You will achieve the greatness that might have been his, had he not died so cruelly.'

'It is time for me to avenge that death,' Nefer said. 'Let us ensure that we do not let the cobra slither away again.'

MINTAKA SPENT MUCH of the journey back to Avaris huddled in the screened litter. Her first endeavour was to make herself agreeable to Zugga, her guardian and jailer, and impress him with her submissive resignation to his authority. By the time they reached the palace in Avaris four days later, she had him completely gulled. There, in the most convincing manner, she appealed to him to allow her to visit the temple of Hathor to pray for Nefer and his victory in the looming battle. With some misgivings Zugga acquiesced, and she was able to spend almost an hour alone with the high priestess in the sanctuary of the temple. Great was Zugga's relief when she re-emerged.

A few days later when she asked to be allowed to pray again in the temple, and to make sacrifice to the goddess, Zugga was amenable to the request. Once again the high priestess led Mintaka into the sanctum and without misgivings Zugga settled down to await her return.

Two hours later a priestess came to him with a message: 'The princess has pleaded for sanctuary within the temple. The holy mother has granted her plea, and taken her under her protection.'

Zugga was thrown into turmoil. The sanctuary of the temple was inviolate. He could not demand the return of his charge. The only course open to him was to return to Ismailiya and confess his failure, but that was risky. The young pharaoh had not yet revealed his true nature, and his rage might well be fatal.

THE MOMENT THE TEMPLE DOORS closed behind her, Mintaka dropped her pretence of resigned innocence. 'Have you made the arrangements, Holy Mother?' she demanded eagerly.

'Have no fear, daughter. All is in readiness.' The priestess's old eyes sparkled with amusement. Clearly she was enjoying this escapade, a break from the tranquil routine of temple life. She led the way to a cell where the items Mintaka had requested were laid out. Mintaka dressed hastily in rough peasant garments and covered her head with a woollen shawl. Then she followed the high priestess out through a low doorway into the sunshine and onto the jetty where a large dhow was moored. 'The captain has been paid,' the priestess told her.

'You know what to tell Zugga,' Mintaka said.

The old woman smiled again. 'I am sure that Hathor will forgive me such an insignificant falsehood. It is in such a good cause.'

As Mintaka jumped down onto the deck of the dhow, the captain steered out into the mid-flow of the current and turned the bows downstream, heading for the delta. In the late afternoon the dhow moored briefly against the east bank and two armed men came aboard. Immediately the dhow captain hoisted sail again and they pressed on with all speed downriver. The two men came to the cabin and prostrated themselves before Mintaka.

'May all the gods love you, Majesty,' said the bigger of the two, a bearded Hyksos with large nose and strong features. 'We are your servants. We came as soon as we received your summons.'

'Lok!' Mintaka smiled with pleasure to see his well-remembered face, and then turned to the other man. 'And surely this is your son, Lokka.' He seemed as doughty as his father. 'You are both well met. You, Lok, served my father well. Will you and your son do the same for me?'

'With our lives, mistress!' they told her.

'I will have hard employment for you once we go ashore, but until then rest and prepare your weapons.'

The dhow captain selected one of the many mouths of the delta where the current meandered through swamps and lagoons, and steered his craft unerringly until at last the miasma of the swamps was blown away on the clean salt airs of the Mediterranean.

During the rest of that day and the following night they sailed eastwards along the coast. Next morning the dhow edged in towards the beach at El Arish, and as soon as the water was waist-deep the two bodyguards, Lok and Lokka, carried Mintaka ashore then waded back to the boat to fetch the baggage. The small party stood and watched the crew of the dhow set the sail and head back out to sea for the return to Egypt.

It was not quite as easy to find transport as Mintaka had imagined. The quartermasters of Naja's army had been ahead of them seizing wagons and horses, and in the end they had to settle for a string of five decrepit donkeys. On the third day after landing they reached the tail of the army of Pharaoh Naja, this great host filling the main east-to-west road in both directions as far as the eye could see, and fell in with the baggage train.

In her dusty, bedraggled clothing Mintaka excited little notice. Lok and Lokka chaperoned her closely, and discouraged the attentions of any other travellers. The rate of march was of the slowest, so even on the poor donkeys they were moving a little faster than the rest of the cavalcade and drifted forward towards the head.

That evening they kept on travelling after the main army had encamped, and after sunset they came upon a large zareba of poles and thorn bushes just off the road. This had been set up in an easily defended defile of low hills. The entrance was heavily guarded, and there was much marching and countermarching of the sentries around it. Above the gate of the stockade flew a gonfalon that Mintaka recognised at once: the head of a wild boar.

'This is the man we are looking for,' Mintaka whispered to Lok.

'But how do you get in to see him?' he asked doubtfully, eyeing the sentries.

They made their open camp a little further down the road, but within sight of the gates of the regimental headquarters of General Prenn, the commander of the rearguard of the pharaonic army.

From one of the leather saddlebags Mintaka brought out the precious oil lamp that had so far survived the journey, and by its light she wrote a short message on a scrap of papyrus parchment. It was addressed to 'Uncle Bear' and signed 'from your little cricket'.

She washed her face, dressed her hair, and shook out her tunic. Then she approached the gate of the stockade.

'You look like a kind and good man,' Mintaka told the sergeant of the guard. 'Will you deliver a message for me to Centurion Prenn?' She proffered the rolled parchment.

The sergeant took it, and gawked at her. She spoke the Hyksos language in the cultured tones of the aristocracy. Despite her clothes she was clearly a young woman of high rank.

'Forgive me, my lady,' he mumbled. 'I am sorry but I will have to ask you to wait here until I have an instruction from him.'

He came hurrying back within a very short time. 'My lady! I am desolated to have kept you waiting. Please follow me.'

He led her to a pavilion of coloured linen in the centre of the stockade, and there was another short delay as he whispered to the junior officer in charge of the entrance. Then she was led through into the tent, its floor covered by animal skins, oryx, zebra and leopard. On these a man was sitting cross-legged with maps and scrolls spread about him. His face was gaunt, his cheeks sunken, and a leather patch covered one eye.

'Uncle Bear!' Mintaka stepped into the lamplight and threw back her head shawl. The man came to his feet slowly, then suddenly he grinned. 'I did not think it possible!' He embraced her and lifted her off her feet. 'I heard you had deserted us and gone over to the enemy.'

When he put her down again she gasped, 'That's what I have come to speak to you about.'

He heard her out silently, but his expression changed as she described to him in detail the events of that terrible night when her father and all her brothers had died in the burning galley on the river at Balasfura.

When at last she finished speaking Prenn said simply, 'I loved your father, almost as much as I love you, little cricket, but what you are proposing is treason.' He sighed. 'All this I will have to think on. But in the meantime, you can't return whence you came. It is much too risky. You must stay under my care until this affair is resolved.'

When she protested, he overrode her brusquely. 'It is not a request. It is an order.'

'Can I at least send a message to Nefer Seti?' Mintaka pleaded.

'That also is too great a risk. Have patience. It will not be for long. Naja is poised on the heights of the Khatmia. Within days he will begin the march on Ismailiya.' His voice dropped to a growl. 'And I will be forced to a decision.'

CHAPTER SEVEN

From a distance Meren watched the great host of Pharaoh Naja come down the escarpment from the Khatmia Pass into the arid lands. He shadowed the stately progress of the enemy legions across the desert, and when Naja's full army was committed to the crossing, and the leading elements had passed the halfway mark between Khatmia and Ismailiya, Meren circled out in front of the heavily encumbered, slowly moving host, back to where he had left the bulk of his force concealed. They were fifty chariots manned by crack troops and drawn by some of the finest horses in all Nefer's army. He paused only to water, and to change the pennants his chariots flew from the blue to the red of Naja's army. He consoled himself that this was a legitimate ruse of war. Then he drove his squadron furiously ahead of Naja's intended line of march.

The men who had been left to guard the water dumps saw the approaching chariots coming from where they expected their comrades to arrive. When they recognised the colours flying above them they were lulled. Meren gave them no time for second thoughts, but raced in upon them, and cut down any who tried to resist. The survivors were given a choice: death or defection. Most came over to Nefer Seti. A single mallet blow was sufficient for each of the disinterred clay jars, and the precious fluid poured out into the sand. Meren's squadron mounted again and went on to the next dump.

PHARAOH NAJA REINED in his chariot and gazed out over the remains of his water dump. Although the scouts had warned him, he was still appalled by the extent of the destruction.

'Will you give the order to turn back?' asked one of his captains.

Naja turned on him coldly. 'The next coward who suggests such a thing I will have tied behind my chariot and I will drag him into battle.' He wiped the sweat from his forehead and gave new orders. 'Collect all the water-skins from the entire army. From now on the water supply is under my direct control. There is no turning back, no retreat. All the fighting chariots will move to the front of the column. I will take the cavalry ahead and seize the wells at Ismailiya . . .'

HESERET THRUST HER HEAD out of the opening of her tent, and called to the captain of her bodyguard, 'What is the trouble, fellow? This is a royal and sacred enclosure, so what are those rogues doing in my stockade?' She pointed at the men who were taking the water-skins from one of her personal baggage carts parked alongside her tent. 'What do they think they are up to? How dare they remove our water! I have not yet bathed.'

'It is your divine husband Pharaoh's order, Majesty,' the captain explained. 'All the water is needed for the forward squadrons.'

'Such orders cannot apply to the Queen of Egypt,' Heseret screamed. 'I shall go at once to Prenn. I shall have new orders for you when I return.' Then she turned to the officer of her bodyguard. 'Ready my chariot and an escort of ten men.'

Across the flat and open plain, Prenn's headquarters camp was in clear view of Heseret's tent. It took only minutes for her chariot to carry her there, but the guard at the gate of the stockade barred her way. 'Your Divine Majesty, General Prenn is not here,' he told her. 'He left an hour ago with all his cavalry. He had orders from Pharaoh to join the vanguard.'

'I do not believe that. I know he would not have left without informing me. Stand aside!' He jumped hurriedly out of her way, and she went straight to the yellow and green striped command tent, stooped through the doorway, and stopped dead in the threshold.

A young woman was sitting on the piles of animal skins in the centre of the floor. She looked up at her startled.

'Who are you?' Heseret demanded. 'Where is the general?' Suddenly Heseret's eyes narrowed. 'You!' she screamed. 'You treacherous, poisonous bitch!' She pointed a quivering finger at the girl. 'Guards!' Heseret shrieked at the top of her voice. 'Guards, here, at once!'

Mintaka came to her senses. She darted across the tent and out through the rear opening.

'Guards!' Heseret yelled again. 'This way!' Her bodyguard burst in through the doorway behind her.

'Stop her!' Heseret shouted. 'Don't let her escape. She is a spy and a traitor.'

Her bodyguard charged after Mintaka, shouting to the guards at the gate, and the sentries drew their swords and ran to cut her off. She fought desperately, kicking, scratching and biting, but the soldiers overwhelmed her at last and dragged her back to the command tent to face Heseret.

The Queen was smiling vindictively. 'Bind her securely. I am sure that my husband, the sole ruler of Egypt, will devise a suitable punishment for her crimes when he returns. Until then she is to be caged and kept at the door of my tent where I can keep her under my eye.'

One of the carts of Heseret's baggage train carried her stock of livestock in cages, chickens, pigs and young goats for her kitchen. The cage that had contained the suckling pigs was now empty—they had been slaughtered and eaten—and the guards shoved Mintaka in through the narrow door.

'There will be guards standing over you day and night,' Heseret warned her. 'Should you try to escape I will have one of your feet cut off, to discourage further attempts.'

FROM THE WATCHTOWER above the fort at Ismailiya the sentry shouted the warning, 'Pharaoh! The pickets are coming in!'

Nefer sprang up from the table under the awning in the courtyard where he and Taita were eating the midday meal. He climbed swiftly up the ladder to the platform and shaded his eyes. Through the yellow glare he made out the chariots of his forward pickets. As they drove down the bank of the wadi, the guards threw open the gates and allowed them to enter the fort.

'The enemy comes on apace!' the sergeant of the pickets shouted up.

'Well done, sergeant,' Nefer called back to him, and then to the trumpeter on the wall above the gate, 'Sound the call to arms!'

The ram's horn blared out across the plain, and the entire army encamped down the length of the broad wadi began to stir. Soon lines of marching men and columns of chariots were moving forward to their prepared positions.

Taita clambered up onto the high platform, and Nefer smiled at him. 'So, even deprived of his water, Naja has not turned back.'

'We never though he would,' Taita said softly.

In the east the horizon started to darken, as the dust cloud of the advancing enemy army boiled like a brewing thunderstorm.

'Will you ride out to meet him with me, Old Father?' Nefer asked, as he strapped on the sword-belt that his orderly handed to him.

'No, I will overlook the battle from here. Perhaps in my own feeble way I might be of more help to you than if I wielded a javelin or drew a bow.'

Nefer smiled. 'Your weapons are sharper and fly more truly than any I have ever held in my hand. Horus love and protect you, Old Father.'

They watched as the battalions of archers and slingers marched out of the wadi to take up their positions behind the breastworks. Every man among them knew what was expected of him, and had rehearsed this manoeuvre many times. As the last of them disappeared into the ambuscade, the field seemed deserted.

The dust cloud of Naja's advance was less than a league off when at last Nefer embraced Taita and climbed down the ladder. Meren handed him the reins as he leapt up onto his chariot's footplate. Nefer lifted his right fist high and gave the command: 'March! Forward!'

The ram's horn sounded the advance and he led the van out, rank upon rank, down between the low breastworks from behind which not a single archer showed himself, out onto the open plain. On the markers he had laid out weeks before, Nefer halted his leading squadron, and let the horses rest while he studied the enemy advance.

Meren murmured, 'Sweet Horus be praised. It seems he has committed all his vehicles. He holds no depth of chariots in reserve.'

'They must be desperate for water,' Nefer answered. 'His only chance of survival is to break our ranks with a frontal charge and win through to the wells.'

Closer and closer came the enemy, until two hundred paces away the mighty host rolled to a halt. A vast silence settled over the brooding landscape, broken only by the fretting susurration of the wind.

From the enemy centre a single chariot pulled forward. Even though dust coated the coachwork the gold leaf gleamed through, and the royal pennant flew above the driver's head. Naja halted less than a hundred paces to the front, so that Nefer recognised the cold, handsome face under the blue war crown.

'Hail, Nefer Seti, puppy of the dog I slew with my own hand!' Naja called and Nefer stiffened to hear him confess so openly to regicide. 'Upon my head I wear the crown I took from Tamose as he was dying. Will you claim it from me, puppy?'

With a huge effort Nefer kept his face expressionless, but his voice rang like metal on stone. 'Make ready!'

Naja laughed, wheeled his own chariot and drove back to his place in the centre of the opposing line.

'March! Forward!' Naja raised the blue sword. His front ranks gathered momentum, rolling towards Nefer's line. 'At the gallop! Charge!' They surged forward in a solid mass.

Nefer stood his ground and let them come on. Then he lifted his sword again and described three flashing arcs with the blade above his head. His legions responded instantly, turning as though possessed of a single controlling mind, and racing away over the plain, back the way they had come, drawing together from extended order into a column of four.

Naja tore after them, but within three hundred paces his flanks came upon a low stone breastwork that slanted across their front. They could not stop now, so they veered left and right towards their own centre. Like the current of a wide river forced suddenly into the mouth of a narrow rocky gorge, they were squeezed together. Wheel snagged wheel, and horse teams were forced to give way to each other. The charge wavered and slowed as chariots and horses jammed into a solid mass.

At that fatal moment, the rams' horns brayed across the field, and the heads and shoulders of the archers and slingers rose from behind the breastworks on either hand. The slingers whirled their weapons on high, and the archers held their aim a moment, choosing their targets with care. The first volley was always the most telling.

The slingers loosed their missiles and the archers their arrows in a single concerted volley. They had been ordered to aim for the horses, and to pick out the enemy captains. The first rank of Naja's charge was shot down, and as the horses fell the chariots piled up over their carcasses, swerving out of control into the stone walls on either hand, or capsizing and rolling.

The vehicles that followed were unable to stop the charge, and crashed into the wreckage of those in front. Wheels shattered and were torn from their axles. Men were hurled from their cockpits and trampled under the frantic hoofs of the rearing, milling horses.

At the head of his squadron, Nefer gave the signal that the men following him were expecting, and foot soldiers leapt out of hiding and dragged away the thorn bushes that concealed the openings that had been left in the walls on either hand. In quick succession Nefer's chariots swerved through them and into the open ground beyond the walls. No longer constricted, they doubled back, circling in behind Naja's trapped squadrons, and falling on their rear echelons.

Now both armies were locked together. Not all of Naja's vehicles had been lured into the trap between the walls. These chariots now came rushing forward to engage Nefer, and a traditional chariot battle swiftly developed. The squadrons broke up into smaller units, and across the plain single vehicles viciously engaged each other, wheel to wheel, and man to man.

Despite the frightful losses he had inflicted on the enemy in the opening phase, Nefer was still heavily outnumbered. As the advantage swung back and forth, Nefer was forced to call in more and more of the reserves he had been holding concealed in the wadi behind the fort. Now he signalled in the last of them. He was fully committed. But they were not enough. Slowly his horses and his men were being ground down by the sheer numbers of his enemy.

In the dust and clamour and turmoil, Nefer knew that his army would soon be in rout, and he shouted encouragement to the charioteers close enough to hear him, to rally them. Then beside him Meren shouted, 'Look, Pharaoh!' and he pointed to the east out into the desert. With the back of his hand Nefer wiped his sweat and splashes of enemy blood from his face, and stared out into the glare.

He knew then beyond all doubt that it was over, and that they had lost the battle. A fresh mass of enemy chariots was tearing in towards them. He had thought that Naja had committed all his vehicles. That did not matter now, for the battle was lost.

'How many?' Nefer wondered, black desolation filling his soul.

'Two hundred,' Meren guessed. 'Maybe more.' His voice was resigned. 'It is all over, Pharaoh. We will die fighting.' As the enemy closed he saw that the leading enemy chariot flew the pennant of a general, a centurion. 'By Horus, I know him,' Meren cried. 'It's Prenn—and he flies the blue!' Prenn's pennant was streaming back, directly away from them, which was why Nefer had not noticed it until this moment, but Meren was right: Prenn was flying the blue of the House of Tamose, and all his chariots with him.

Now Prenn slowed, held his right arm across his chest in salute to Nefer, and shouted in a great voice, 'What are your orders, Pharaoh?'

'What strange business is this, General Prenn? Why do you call on me for orders?' Nefer called back.

'The Princess Mintaka delivered to me your message, and I have come to place myself under your command.'

'Mintaka?' Nefer was confused, for surely she was still in Avaris. But his warrior instincts took over and he thrust aside those thoughts. 'Well met, General Prenn. You arrive none too soon. Lay your chariot alongside mine and we will sweep this field from end to end.'

They charged side by side, and Nefer's broken and scattered legions saw the blue pennant coming and took new heart. The red squadrons of Naja Kiafan were in hardly better case and could offer only scant resistance as Prenn's fresh troops charged into them. They fought on for a while, but the heart was torn out of them.

Nefer quartered across the field with Meren, searching for Naja. He reached the stone breastworks and looked over the low wall into the narrow defile where he had trapped the forward legions of Naja's army. Around each smashed chariot lay the dead and the wounded. Some were still moving and weeping, calling to the gods and to their mothers. Others sat dazed with the agony of their wounds. Nefer looked for Naja's body among the dead, but all was confusion. Then he picked out a flash of gold leaf, and the royal standard of Naja Kiafan lying in the dust.

'I must find him,' Nefer told Meren. 'I must know he is dead.' He jumped down from the chariot.

'I will help you search.' Meren tethered the horses to the walls.

Nefer vaulted over the breastworks and scrambled over the other wreckage until he reached the golden chariot. It lay on its side, but the cockpit was empty. Suddenly Meren shouted and stooped to pick up something from among the debris. He lifted his trophy high, and Nefer saw that he had found Naja's blue war crown.

'His body must be close,' Nefer called to him. 'He would not have discarded that. It means too much to him.'

At that moment Nefer caught a flash of movement from the corner of his eye. He ducked and whirled about. Naja had risen from where he had been crouching behind the dashboard of the chariot. He still carried the blue sword of Tamose and he launched a double-handed blow at Nefer's head, but Nefer ducked under the hissing blade and drew his own sword.

Naja stepped back and looked about him. He saw Meren coming to Nefer's aid and he saw the empty chariot hitched to the wall. He drove Nefer back with another thrust of the blue blade, then whirled and sprinted away. As he jumped over the wall he cut the horses free and leapt up onto the footplate. Startled, the pair lunged forward together and within half a dozen strides were both at full gallop.

Behind them Nefer jumped to the top of the wall and saw Naja being carried away across the plain. He drew a long breath and whistled, the high piercing blast his horses knew so well. He saw their heads go up, their ears prick and swivel towards him. Then they changed gait and swung into a tight turn, and came pounding back towards where Nefer stood poised on the wall. As they swept by below him, Nefer leapt lightly onto one horse's back, and with his knees steered it onto the open plain. He glanced back and saw Naja climbing out of the cockpit, then edging along the shaft to get at Nefer.

Nefer leaned down and with his own blade sliced the leather rope that hitched the horses to the shaft. Running free, the chariot veered off to one side. The shaft dug into the soft earth, flicking the vehicle over, and Naja was thrown clear. He struck the ground with his shoulder and even above the sound of hoofs Nefer heard the bone break.

Nefer charged at him. Naja had climbed painfully to his feet and stood swaying, clutching his damaged right arm across his chest. In his fall he had lost his grip on the hilt of the blue sword. It had spun out of his hand, and ten paces away from where he stood the point had pegged into the earth. The blade still quivered from the impact. The wondrous blue metal threw slivers of blue light, and the jewelled hilt whipped from side to side.

Naja staggered towards the weapon, but then he saw Nefer bearing down on him, and an expression of utter terror turned his face the colour of cold ashes. When Nefer leaned down and plucked the sword from the sand, Naja knew then that he could not escape his terrible vengeance. He fell to his knees and lifted both hands in supplication, as Nefer jumped down and stood over him.

'Mercy!' Naja sobbed. 'I yield to you the double crown and all the kingdom.' He crawled pitifully to Nefer's feet.

'I already have that. I lack only one thing. Vengeance!'

'Mercy, Nefer Seti, in the name of the gods and for the sake of your sister, the goddess Heseret, and the infant in her womb.' Suddenly there was a dagger in his right hand, and he stabbed up viciously at Nefer's groin. Nefer twisted away just in time, and struck the weapon out of Naja's grasp with a flick of his blade.

'I admire your consistency. To the very end you are true to your base nature.' Nefer smiled down on him coldly. 'You I grant the same mercy that you showed my father, Pharaoh Tamose.' He drove the point of the blue sword into the centre of Naja's chest, and it came out between his shoulder blades.

Naja toppled face first into the dust, and drew one more ragged breath, but the air from his lungs bubbled out of the wound between his shoulder blades and he shuddered and died.

Nefer hitched Naja's body by its heels to the traces that dangled from the horse's harness, then mounted and dragged it back across the field. Cheering followed him as he rode up to the gates of the fort. He cut the rope and left Naja's bloody corpse lying in the dust.

Then he looked up to the figure who stood high upon the watchtower of the fort, and raised the blue blade to him in salute. Taita lifted his hand in acknowledgment.

He was on the tower through the whole day. What part did the Magus play in the battle? Nefer asked himself. There was no answer, and he put the thought aside. He mounted the ladder to the top of the tower and stood beside Taita. From there he spoke to his men.

He thanked them for their duty and their bravery. He promised them their rewards, a share of the plunder to all, and the honours of valour to the captains and centurions.

By the time he had named them all the sun was sinking through a low bank of purple thunderclouds towards the horizon. He ended his speech with a call to prayer: 'I dedicate this victory to the golden Horus, the falcon of the gods,' he cried, and as he prayed there was a wild cry from above. Every head lifted and every eye turned towards the sky. A great murmur went up from the multitude. A royal falcon hovered in the air above the head of Pharaoh, and as they stared in wonder it uttered that strange, haunting sound again, then circled three times, and at last shot away in a straight line on rapid, incisive wingbeats into the eastern sky.

'A blessing from the god,' the soldiers chanted. 'Hail, Pharaoh! The gods salute you.'

But beside him Taita spoke softly. 'The falcon brought a warning, not a blessing.'

'What is the warning?' Nefer demanded.

'When the bird called, I heard Mintaka cry out,' Taita whispered.

'Mintaka!' Nefer had forgotten her in the exigencies of the battle. 'What did Prenn tell me about her?' He turned to the ladder and shouted down to the guards. 'Prenn! Where is the centurion Prenn?'

Prenn came at once, and knelt before Pharaoh. 'You have earned our deepest gratitude,' Nefer told him. 'Without you we could not have prevailed.'

'Pharaoh is gracious,'

'At the start of the battle, you spoke of the Princess Mintaka. I thought that she was safe in Avaris.'

'Pharaoh, you are mistaken. Princess Mintaka is not in the temple. She came to me with your message. I could not bring her into battle with me, so I left her two days ago in my camp in the desert.'

A foreboding seized Nefer. 'Who else is in the encampment?'

'Some of the other royal women. Her Majesty Queen Heseret—'

'Heseret!' Nefer wrung his hands. 'Heseret! If Mintaka is in her power, what will she do to her when she hears that I have slain her husband? We must ride at once.'

HESERET AWOKE IN THE DARKNESS and chill of that dread time before the dawn when the human spirit at its lowest ebb. At first she was uncertain of what had interrupted her sleep, but then she became aware of the sound of many voices, faint but growing stronger. She sat up and tried to make sense of the distant hubbub. She was able to make out words now: 'defeated' and 'slain' and 'flee at once'. She called for her maids and two stumbled in.

'What is going on?' Heseret demanded.

The eldest maid was breathless. 'They say there has been a great battle at a place called Ismailiya, Majesty.'

Heseret felt a great surge of joy. Naja had triumphed: in her heart she was certain of it. 'What was the outcome of the battle?'

'We don't know, mistress. We did not ask.'

Heseret seized the girl nearest to her by the hair, and shook her violently. 'Have you not a speck of brain in your thick skull?' She slapped her across the face, and left her lying on the floor of the tent. She grabbed a lamp and hurried to the door.

The guards were gone, and she felt the first pangs of fear. She ran to the cage outside and held up the lamp, peering into the pig cage. Part of her anxiety was allayed as she saw that Mintaka was still pinioned and tied to the struts at the back of the cage.

Heseret left her and ran to the gate of the stockade. In the starlight she made out a dark cavalcade streaming past. She saw the loom of carts and wagons being drawn by teams of oxen. Some were piled high with bales and boxes, others were crowded with women clutching their children. Hundreds of soldiers hurried past on foot and Heseret saw that most had thrown away their weapons.

She picked out a soldier in the passing throng, who wore the collar of a sergeant. 'What news of the battle? Tell me. Oh, please tell me,' she begged.

He peered into her face. 'The most dire news, Majesty.' His voice was gruff. 'There has been a terrible battle and our army has been defeated. The enemy will be upon us soon. You must flee at once.'

'What of Pharaoh? What has happened to my husband'

'Pharaoh Naja Kiafan is slain, cut down in single combat by Nefer Seti himself.'

Heseret let out a keening wail. She gathered up a double handful of dust and poured it over her head. Still wailing she clawed her face with her fingernails.

Her handmaidens came out of the stockade to fetch her in, but she screamed incoherent obscenities at them. She ran to the pig cage on the cart, and screeched at Mintaka through the bars: 'My husband is dead. Slain by my own monstrous brother.'

'Praise be to Hathor and all the gods,' Mintaka cried.

'You blaspheme!' Heseret raved. 'Naja Kiafan was a god.' She turned to the captain of her guards. 'Drag the sow from her cage.'

The captain hesitated. Nefer and his captains would be here soon.

Heseret grabbed a spear out of the hand of the nearest soldier and struck him across the back. 'I order you, Captain, to obey me.'

The man backed away. 'You are mad. What punishment would Nefer Seti heap upon my head?' He turned suddenly and bolted from the stockade to join the flood of fleeing refugees in the roadway. His men hesitated only a moment longer, then rushed to the gate hard after him.

Heseret ran after them. 'Come back! I order you!' But they mingled with the crowds and were gone. Dazed as a sleepwalker she went to her tent. She picked a robe at random from the pile in the corner, and pulled sandals onto her feet. 'I am going to find Naja,' she said. Then with new determination she headed for the door.

As she stepped out into the early sunlight, Mintaka called to her from the cage. 'Please release me, Heseret. In all charity, let me go.'

'You don't understand.' Heseret shook her head wildly. 'I have to go to my husband, the Pharaoh of all Egypt. He needs me.'

She did not glance at Mintaka again but hurried out of the stockade, shaking her head and muttering incoherently to herself. She turned towards the west, in the opposite direction from the flood of terrified humanity, and started to run back towards Egypt.

MINTAKA STRUGGLED against her bonds, bracing her bare feet against the struts of the cage to give herself better purchase. She felt the skin smearing from her wrists, and blood dripping down her hands, but the leather thongs were tight and strong and she could neither stretch nor snap them.

Once Mintaka heard a stealthy scuffle at the entrance to the tent and saw Heseret's two maids creeping out, each carrying a large bag. Mintaka called to them, but they glanced at her with startled, guilty expressions and scurried from the stockade.

Then she heard something else, hoofbeats and the sound of men's voices growing stronger, and stronger still, until she could recognise one. 'Nefer!' She tried to scream his name, but her voice was a draughty whisper. 'Nefer!'

She twisted her head and saw Nefer storm through the gateway, Meren and Taita close behind him.

Nefer ran to the cage. He tore the gate off its hinges with his bare hand and pulled his dagger from its sheath to slash loose the leather thongs from her wrists. Gently he drew her out of the stinking cage and held her to his chest. Mintaka shut her eyes and slumped into unconsciousness. Nefer was weeping as he carried her into the tent.

MINTAKA CAME AWAKE slowly as though she were rising up from the depths of a pit. When she opened her eyes she saw with immense relief the two most beloved faces in her world. Taita sat at one side of her couch and Nefer at the other.

'How long?' she asked. 'How long was I gone?'

'A day and a night,' Nefer answered her.

'You are not angry with me for disobeying you?'

'You have given me a crown and a land.' He shook his head and one of his tears fell upon her face. 'Above that you have given me your love. How could I ever be angry with you?'

Taita rose softly and left the tent, and they stayed together all the rest of that day, speaking softly together.

In the evening Nefer sent for two priestesses from the temple of Hathor. 'You have come to see justice done,' he told them, then turned to the guards at the door.

'Bring in the woman named Heseret,' he ordered.

Mintaka started and tried to sit up, but he pushed her gently back upon the bolster.

'Where? How did you find her?'

'Our pickets found her wandering in the desert on the road back to Ismailiya,' Nefer explained. 'At first they did not recognise her or believe her claims to be a queen. They thought her a madwoman.'

Heseret came into the tent. Nefer had allowed her to bathe and provided her with fresh raiment, and Taita had treated the grazes on her face and body. Now she shrugged off the hands of her guards and looked around her. 'Prostrate yourselves before me,' she ordered. 'I am a queen.'

No one moved, and Nefer said, 'You are a queen no longer.' He stared at her so coldly that Heseret started to weep.

'I am your own sister. You would not harm me.'

'You are right, Heseret. I will not harm you.'

He sighed and turned to the two priestesses. 'I give into your keeping the body and the life of Heseret Tamose, who was a princess of the royal House of Egypt.'

Heseret began to scream but no one took notice of her cries as gently they dragged her blubbering and wailing from the tent.

They sat in silence, and through the linen walls listened as Heseret's wailing, entreaties and blandishments faded into the distance. Then Mintaka covered her face with both hands and Nefer made the sign against evil with his right hand.

WHEN MINTAKA HAD RECOVERED sufficiently to begin the long journey back to Avaris, Nefer insisted that she be carried in a litter to ease the jolting over the rough road that lay ahead. They travelled slowly, and it was fifteen days later that they reached the escarpment and looked down upon the wide green valley of the Nile.

Nefer helped Mintaka from the litter, and together they walked a short way from the road, so that they could be alone and savour this joyous moment of homecoming. They had not been there long when Nefer stood up and shaded his eyes.

'What is it, my heart?' Mintaka asked.

'We have a visitor,' he said, but when she exclaimed with annoyance at the intrusion he went on, 'This visitor is always welcome.'

She smiled then as she recognised the figure approaching them. 'Taita. But what strange attire is this?'

He was dressed in a simple robe and sandals, and slung on his back he carried the leather satchel of a holy man on a pilgrimage.

'I have come to take my leave of you,' Taita explained.

'You will not leave me now.' Nefer was dismayed. 'Will you not attend my coronation?'

'You were crowned on the field of Ismailiya,' Taita told him gently.

'Our wedding!' Mintaka cried. 'You must stay for our wedding.'

'You were married long since,' Taita smiled, 'perhaps on the day of your birth, for the gods intended you for each other.'

Nefer knew that there was nothing further to say, that more words would degrade this moment. He did not even ask where Taita was going. Perhaps he did not know.

He embraced Taita, then he and Mintaka stood and watched him walk away, and his distant shape slowly dwindle in the shimmering wastes of the desert wilderness, and they shared the same deep ache of regret and bereavement.

'He has not really gone,' Mintaka whispered, when at last he had disappeared from view.

'No,' Nefer agreed. 'He will always be with us.'

WITH THE HIGH PRIESTESS and fifty acolytes from the temple of Hathor preceding her, the Princess Mintaka Apepi came for her marriage to Pharaoh Nefer Seti.

They stood together on the terrace of the palace of Thebes that overlooked the broad brown floor of the Nile in flood, in the season most propitious to all living things in the land of this very Egypt.

It seemed that all of Egypt had come to bear witness to the nuptials. The crowds stretched back along both banks of the river as far as the eye could see. The couple embraced and broke the jars of Nile water, and then Nefer Seti led his new queen out by the hand and showed her beauty to the populace, who fell to their knees and wept.

Suddenly a silence fell over this vast congregation. Slowly every eye turned upwards to the tiny speck in the vaulted sky above the palace.

In the silence there was the wild, lonely cry of a royal falcon, and the bird began its stoop out of the high blue. Just as it seemed it must come into violent collision, the falcon flared its wings wide and hovered over the tall figure of Pharaoh. Nefer lifted his right arm, and softly as a feather the magnificent bird alighted upon his fist.

A sound like the sea on a stormy day rose from ten thousand throats as they greeted the miracle. But Nefer's eyes fell on the loop of gold that was fastened about the bird's right foot. Engraved into the precious metal was a symbol that made Nefer's heart race.

'The royal cartouche!' he whispered. 'This was never a wild bird. This is Nefertem, my father's falcon. That is why it came to me so often in times of greatest danger, to warn and guide me. It was my father's spirit.'

'And now Nefertem has come to affirm before all the world that you are king indeed.' Mintaka stood closer to him and gazed into his face with eyes that glowed with pride and love.

WILBUR SMITH

Since breaking into print with his hugely successful first book, *When the Lion Feeds*, an epic of 19th-century South Africa, Wilbur Smith has written a string of best-selling novels, most of them about the continent where he was born and brought up, the continent that has always inspired him. He was born at Broken Hill, Zambia (in those days Northern Rhodesia) and educated in South Africa, where he still lives today. As well as his house in Capetown he has a large ranch where he indulges his love of African wildlife—a passion that comes across in his books.

In the wake of *Sunbird*, a novel set in ancient Africa and published in 1973, fans badgered Wilbur Smith for another story with an ancient setting. Eventually, in 1993, they were rewarded with a stunning Egyptian saga, *River God*, and then in 1995 with its sequel, *The Seventh Scroll*. *Warlock*, the author's latest blockbuster, builds on the stories told in those two books, and many readers will enjoy reacquainting themselves with the extraordinary character of Taita.

Much of the history of Ancient Egypt is known from the research of archaeologists, but Wilbur Smith was drawn to a particularly troubled period—that of the Hyksos invasions—precisely because the history of that time is very confused and obscure. His books are always an inspired mixture of fact and imagination and he wanted to have the freedom to write creatively and to be able to say to any Egyptologists who tried to attack his writings for historical inaccuracy: 'You don't know for certain either.'

Between them, *River God*, *The Seventh Scroll* and *Warlock* form a memorable and dramatic trio of novels that succeed in transporting readers back to a fascinating time and place.

James Patterson

Suzanne's for

Dear Nicky,

I hope when you grow up that everything you want comes your way, but especially love. When it's right, love can give you the kind of joy that you can't get from any other experience . . .

Daddy and I laugh about all the good things that wait for you. But what we want most for you is love. It is a gift. Because to be without love is to be without grace, what matters most in life. We is so much better than I.

If you need proof, just look at us . . .

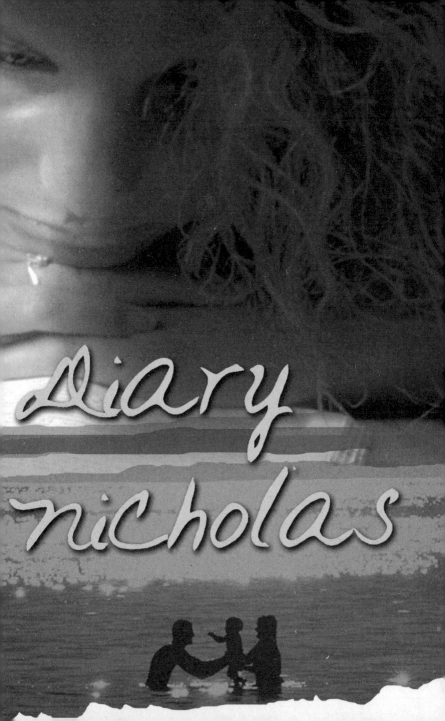

Katie

Katie Wilkinson sat in warm bath water in the weird but wonderful old-fashioned porcelain tub in her New York apartment. The apartment exuded 'old' and 'worn' in ways that practitioners of shabby chic couldn't begin to imagine. Katie's Persian cat, Guinevere, looking like a favourite grey woollen sweater, was perched on the washbasin. Her black labrador, Merlin, sat in the doorway leading to the bedroom. They watched Katie as if they were afraid for her.

She lowered her head when she stopped reading the diary and set the leather-bound book on the wooden stool beside the tub. Her body shivered.

Then Katie started to sob, and she saw that her hands were shaking. She was losing it, and she didn't lose it often. She was a strong person, and always had been. Katie whispered words she'd once heard in her father's church in Asheboro, North Carolina. 'Oh Lord, oh Lord, are you *anywhere*, my Lord?'

She could never have imagined that this small volume would have such a disturbing effect on her. Of course, it wasn't just the diary that had forced her into this state of confusion and duress.

No, it wasn't just Suzanne's diary for Nicholas.

She visualised Suzanne in her mind. Katie *saw* her at her cottage on Beach Road on the island of Martha's Vineyard.

Then little Nicholas. Twelve months old, with the most brilliant blue eyes.

And finally, Matt.

Nicholas's daddy. Suzanne's husband. And Katie's former lover.

What did she think of Matt now? Could she forgive him? She wasn't sure. But at least she finally understood some of what had happened. The diary had told her pieces of what she needed to know, as well as deep, painful secrets that maybe she didn't need to know.

Katie slipped down further into the water, and found herself thinking back to the day she had received the diary—July 19.

Remembering the day started her crying again.

ON THE MORNING of the 19th, Katie had felt drawn to the Hudson River, and to the Circle Line, the boat ride round Manhattan Island that she and Matt had first taken as a total goof, but had enjoyed so much that they kept coming back.

She boarded the first boat of the day. She was feeling sad, but also angry. Oh God, she didn't know what she was feeling. She took a seat on the upper deck and watched New York from the unique vantage point of the waterways surrounding it.

A few people noticed her sitting there alone—especially the men.

Katie stood out in a crowd. She was tall—almost six foot, with warm, friendly blue eyes. She had always thought of herself as gawky and felt that people were staring at her for all the wrong reasons. Her friends begged to differ; they said she was breathtaking. Katie didn't see herself that way. She was an ordinary, regular person, a North Carolina farm girl at heart.

She often wore her brunette hair in a long braid, and had since she was eight years old. The only make-up she ever wore was a little mascara and sometimes lipstick. Today she wore neither. She definitely didn't look breathtaking.

She had been crying for hours, and her eyes were puffy. The night before, the man she loved had suddenly and inexplicably ended their relationship. She hadn't seen it coming. It almost didn't seem possible that Matt had left her.

Damn him! How could he? Had he been lying to her for all these months? Of course he had! The bastard. The total creep.

She wanted to think about Matt, about what had happened to separate them, but she wound up thinking of times they'd shared, mostly good times.

Begrudgingly, she had to admit that she had always been able to talk to him about anything. Even her girlfriends, who could be catty, liked Matt. *So what happened between us?*

He was thoughtful—at least he *had* been. Her birthday was in June, and he had sent her a single rose every day of what he called 'your birthday month'.

He liked a lot of the same things Katie did, or so he said. *Ally McBeal, Memories of a Geisha.* Foreign movies at the Lincoln Plaza Cinema. Vintage black and white photos, oil paintings that they found at flea markets.

He went to church with her on Sundays, where she taught a Bible class of preschoolers. They both treasured Sunday afternoons at her apartment—with Katie reading the *New York Times* from cover to cover, and Matt revising his poems, which he spread out on her bed, on the floor, and even on the butcher-block kitchen table.

He made her feel at peace with herself. Completely, blissfully at peace. *What could beat being in love with Matt?* Nothing that Katie knew of.

One night they had stopped at a little juke bar on Avenue A. They danced, and Matt sang 'All Shook Up' in her ear, doing a funny but improbably good Elvis impersonation.

She had wanted to be with him all the time. Corny, but true.

When he was away on Martha's Vineyard, where he lived and worked, they would talk every night on the phone—or send each other funny email. They called it their 'long-distance love affair'. He had always stopped Katie from visiting him on the Vineyard, though. Maybe that should have been her early-warning signal.

Somehow, it had worked—for eleven glorious months that seemed to go by in an instant. Katie had expected him to propose soon. She was sure of it. She had even told her mother. But, of course, she had been so wrong that it was pathetic. It wasn't like her to be this out of touch with her instincts. They were usually good; she was smart; she didn't do really dumb things.

Until now. And, boy, had she made a mistake this time.

Katie suddenly realised that she was sobbing and that everyone around her on the boat was staring at her.

'I'm sorry,' she said, and motioned for them to look away. She blushed. She felt like such an idiot. 'I'm OK.'

But she wasn't OK. Katie had never been so hurt in her life. She had lost the only man she had ever loved; God, how she loved Matt.

She couldn't bear to go into work that day. She'd had enough curious looks on the boat to last a lifetime.

When she got back to her apartment after her boat trip, a package was propped up against the front door.

She thought it was a manuscript from the office and cursed under her breath. Couldn't they leave her alone for a single day? She worked so hard for them. They knew how passionate she was about her books.

She was a senior editor at a highly-thought-of New York publishing house that specialised in literary novels and poetry. She loved her job. It was where she had met Matt. She had enthusiastically bought his first volume of poetry from a small literary agency in Boston about a year before.

The two of them had hit it off right away. Just weeks later they had fallen in love—or so she had believed with her heart, soul, body, mind.

As she reached for the package, she recognised the handwriting. It was Matt's. There was no doubt about it. She took a deep breath and tore away the brown paper wrapping.

What she found inside was a small antique-looking diary. Katie didn't understand. Then she felt her stomach knot.

Suzanne's Diary for Nicholas was handwritten on its front cover—but it wasn't Matt's handwriting.

Suzanne's?

Suddenly Katie's head was reeling and she could barely catch a breath. Matt had always been secretive about his past. One of the things she had found out, one night after they had drunk two bottles of wine, was that his wife's name was Suzanne. But Matt hadn't wanted to talk about Suzanne.

Katie had insisted on knowing more, which only made Matt quieter. It was so unlike him. After they had a fight about it, he'd told her that he wasn't married to Suzanne any more; he swore it, but that was all he was going to say.

Who was Nicholas? And why had Matt sent her this diary? Why now? She was completely puzzled.

Her fingers were trembling as she opened the diary at its first page. A note from Matt was affixed. Her eyes began to well up and she angrily wiped the tears away. She read what he'd written.

Dear Katie,
 No words could begin to tell you what I'm feeling now. I'm so sorry about what I allowed to happen between us. It was all my

fault, of course. I take all the blame. You are perfect, wonderful, beautiful. It's not you. It's me.

Maybe this diary will explain things better than I ever could. If you have the heart, read it.

It's about my wife and son, and me.

I will warn you, though, there will be parts that may be hard for you to read.

I never expected to fall in love with you, but I did.

Matt

Katie turned the page.

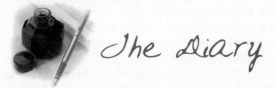

The Diary

Dear Nicholas, my little prince—

There were years and years when I wondered if I would ever be a mother. But during this time I had a recurring daydream that it would be so wonderful to make a videotape every year for my children, to tell them what I thought about, how much I loved them.

So, I am going to make a videotape for you every year—but there's something else I want to do for you, sweet boy. I want to keep a diary, this diary, and I promise to be faithful about writing in it.

As I write this very first entry, you are two weeks old. But I want to start by telling you about some things that happened before you were born. I want to start *before* the beginning, so to speak.

This is for your eyes only, Nick.

This is what happened to Nicholas, Suzanne and Matt.

LET ME START the story on a warm and fragrant spring night in Boston.

I was working at Massachusetts General Hospital. I had been a physician for eight years. There were moments that I absolutely loved: seeing patients get well, and even being with some when it was clear they wouldn't recover. Then there were the bureaucracy and hopeless inadequacy of our country's health-care programme.

I had just come off a twenty-four-hour rotation and I was tired beyond anything you can imagine. I was walking my faithful golden retriever, Gustavus, a.k.a. Gus.

I suppose I should give you a little snapshot of myself back then. I had long blonde hair, stood about five foot five, not exactly beautiful but nice enough to look at, a friendly smile most of the time, for most of the human race. Not *too* caught up in appearances.

It was a late Friday afternoon, and I remember that the air was as clear as crystal. We were in the Boston Public Garden, by the swan boats. This was our usual walk, especially if Michael, my boyfriend, was working, as he was that night.

Gus had broken from his lead to chase a duck, and I ran after him. I was suddenly struck by the worst pain I have ever felt. It was so intense that I fell to my hands and knees.

Then it got worse. Razor-sharp knives were shooting up and down my arm, across my back, and into my jaw. I gasped. I couldn't be sure of what was happening to me, but something told me *heart*.

The tree-laden garden was spinning like a whirligig. Concerned people began crowding around. I was flat on my back, holding my chest. *Heart? My God. I am only thirty-five years old.*

'Get an ambulance,' someone cried. 'She's in trouble. I think she's dying.'

I am not! I wanted to shout. *I can't be dying.*

My breathing was becoming shallower and I was fading into black nothingness. *Oh God*, I thought. *Stay alive, breathe, keep conscious, Suzanne.*

I must have passed out for several minutes. When I came to, I was being lifted into an ambulance. Tears streamed down my face. My body was soaked with sweat.

The woman paramedic kept saying, 'You're gonna be fine. You're all right, ma'am.' But I knew I wasn't.

The last thing I recall is an oxygen mask being slipped over my face, a deathly weakness spreading through my body.

The following day I had a coronary bypass at Massachusetts General. It put me out of action for almost two months, and it was during my recuperation that I had time to think, really think, maybe for the first time in my life.

I thoroughly examined my life, just how hectic it had become with rounds, overtime and double shifts. I thought about how I'd been feeling just before this awful thing happened. I also dealt with my own denial. My family had a history of heart disease. And still I hadn't been as careful as I should have been.

It was while I was recuperating that a doctor friend told me the story of the five balls. You should never forget this one, Nicky. This is terribly important. It goes like this.

Imagine life is a game in which you are juggling five balls. The balls are called work, family, health, friends and integrity. And you're keeping all of them in the air. But one day you finally come to understand that work is a rubber ball. If you drop it, it will bounce back. The other four balls—family, health, friends, integrity—are made of glass. If you drop one of these, it will be irrevocably scuffed, nicked, perhaps even shattered. And once you truly understand the lesson of the five balls, you will have the beginnings of balance in your life.

Nicky, I finally understood.

NICK—

As you can probably tell, this is all pre-Daddy, pre-Matt.

Let me tell you about Dr Michael Bernstein.

I met Michael in 1996 at the wedding of John Kennedy and Carolyn Bessette on Cumberland Island, Georgia. Both of us had led pretty charmed lives up until then. My parents had died when I was two, but I was fortunate enough to have been raised with great love by my grandparents in the town of Cornwall, New York. I went to Lawrenceville Academy, then Duke, and finally Harvard Medical School. I couldn't have had a better education—except that nowhere did I learn the lesson of the five balls.

Michael also went to Harvard Medical School, but he had graduated four years before I got there. We didn't get together until the Kennedy wedding. I was a guest of Carolyn's; Michael was a guest of John's. The wedding itself was magical, full of hope and promise. Maybe that was part of what drew Michael and me together.

What kept us together for the next four years was a little more complicated. Part of it was physical attraction; Michael was—is—tall and dashing, with a radiant smile. We also had a lot of mutual interests. And we were both workaholics.

But none of these things is what love is really about, Nicholas. Trust me on that.

About four weeks after my heart attack, I woke up one morning at eight o'clock. The apartment where we lived was quiet, and I luxuriated in the peacefulness for a few moments. Finally I got up and went to the kitchen to make myself breakfast before I went off to rehab.

I jumped back when I heard a noise, the scratch of a chair leg against the floor. It was Michael. I was surprised to see him still at home, as he was almost always out of the house by seven. He was sitting at the small pine table in the breakfast nook.

'You almost gave me a heart attack,' I said, making what I thought was a pretty decent joke.

Michael didn't laugh. He patted the chair next to him.

Then, with the calmness and self-reverence I was used to from him, he told me the three main reasons why he was leaving me: he said he couldn't talk or relate to me the way he could to his male friends; he didn't think that I could have a baby now, because of my heart attack; he had fallen for somebody else already.

I ran out of the kitchen, and then out of the house. That morning the pain I felt was even worse than the heart attack. Nothing was right with my life; I had got it all wrong so far. Everything!

I did love being a doctor, but I was trying to do it in a large, bureaucratic, big-city hospital, which just wasn't right for me.

I was working so hard—because there was nothing else of value in my life. I earned over $100,000 a year, but I was spending it on dinners in town, getaway weekends, clothes that I didn't need.

I had wanted children all my life, yet here I was without a significant other, without a child, without a plan.

Here's what I did, little boy.

I began to live the lesson of the five balls.

I left my job at Massachusetts General. I left Boston. I left my murderous schedule. I moved to the one place in the world where I had always been happy. I went there, truly, to mend a broken heart.

NICKY,

I arrived on the island of Martha's Vineyard like an awkward tourist, lugging the baggage of my past, not knowing what to do with it yet. I would spend the first couple of months filling cupboards with farm-fresh foods, throwing out magazines that had followed me to my new home, and I would settle into a new job.

From the time I was five until I was seventeen, I had spent summers with my grandparents on Martha's Vineyard. My grandfather was an architect, as my father had been, and he could work from home. My grandmother, Isabelle, was a gifted homemaker.

I loved being back on the Vineyard, loved everything about it. Gus and I often went to the beach in the early evening, and we huddled together on a blanket until the sun went down.

I had negotiated for the practice of a general practitioner who was moving to Illinois. My office was one of five in a white clapboard house in Vineyard Haven. The house was more than a hundred years old and had four beautiful antique rockers on the front porch. I even had a rocker at the desk where I worked.

'Country doctor' resonated with a wonderful sound for me, like recess bells of an old country school. I was inspired to hang out a sign that said as much: SUZANNE BEDFORD—COUNTRY DOCTOR—IN.

This was for me. I was experiencing a fantasy that had seemed a million miles away when I lived in Boston. In fact, it was just down Route 6 and across the water.

I felt I had come home.

NICHOLAS,

I had no idea that the love of my life was here—waiting for me. If I had, I would have run straight into Daddy's arms. In a heartbeat.

When I first arrived on Martha's Vineyard, I was unsure where to settle. I drove around looking for something that said 'home', 'you'll be OK here', 'look no further'.

There are so many parts of our island that are beautiful. Up-Island was always special to me, because this is where I had spent so many glorious summers. It lay like a child's picture book of farms and fences, dirt roads and cliffs. Down-Island was a whirl of widow's walks, gazebos, lighthouses and harbours.

It was a turn-of-the-century boathouse between Vineyard Haven and Oak Bluffs that finally stole my heart. And still does. This truly was home.

It needed to be fixed up, but I loved it at first sight, first smell, first touch. Old beams, which had once supported stored boats, criss-crossed the ceiling. The walls *had* to be painted robin's egg blue because the downstairs opened to a view of the sea. Big barnlike doors slid port and starboard to bring inside everything that was once outside.

Can you imagine, Nicky, living practically right on the beach, like that? Every part of me, body and soul, knew I'd made the right decision. Sometimes I'd be working out of my home or making house calls; the rest of the time I'd be at Martha's Vineyard Hospital.

I was alone, except for Gus, but I was content.

Maybe it was because I had no idea what I was missing at the time: your daddy and you.

WHO THE HECK was sitting on my porch? As I returned one afternoon from Martha's Vineyard Hospital, I couldn't really tell.

It couldn't be the electric guy, or the phone guy, or the cable guy—I'd seen all of them the day before.

Nope, it was the painting guy, the one who was going to help me with everything around the cottage that needed a ladder or an outlet or a finish.

We walked around the cottage as I pointed out windows that wouldn't close, floors that buckled, a leak in the bathroom, a cracked gutter, a whole cottage that needed scraping and painting.

What this house had in cute, it lacked in practical.

But this guy took notes, asked pertinent questions, and told me he could fix everything. We struck a deal on the spot. Suddenly, life was looking a lot better to me. I had a new practice that I loved and a house-painter with a good reputation.

When I was finally alone in my little cottage by the sea, I threw up both arms and shouted hooray.

DEAR NICKY,

The house-painter was over here this morning. I know this because he left me a bouquet of beautiful wild flowers—pinks, reds, yellows and purples, sitting pretty in a mason jar by the front door.

There was also a note.

Dear Suzanne,

The lights are still out in your kitchen, but I hope these will brighten your day. Maybe we can get together sometime and do whatever you want to do, whenever you want to.

At the end of the note, he signed himself: *Picasso—more readily known as your house-painter.*

I was blown away. I hadn't wanted to date since Michael left me.

Anyway, I heard the handyman hammering, and I went outside. There he was, perched like a gull on the steep slanted roof.

'Picasso,' I yelled, 'thank you so much for the beautiful flowers. What a nice thought.'

'Oh, you're welcome. They reminded me of you.'

'Well, they're all my favourites.'

'What do you think, Suzanne? Maybe we could grab a bite, go for a ride, catch a movie, play Scrabble. Did I leave anything out?'

I smiled in spite of myself. 'It's kind of a crazy time for me right now, with patients and all. I just have to make that a priority for the time being. But it was really nice of you to ask.'

He smiled down at me. But then he ran his hand through his hair and said, 'I understand. Of course you realise if you don't go out with me just once, I'll have no choice but to raise your rates. It's despicable, a totally unfair business practice. But what can you do? It's the way of the world.'

I laughed, and told him I'd give that serious consideration. 'Hey, by the way, what do I owe you for the extra work you've already done over the garage?' I asked.

'That? That's nothing . . . nothing at all. No charge.'

I smiled. What he'd said was nice to hear—maybe because it *wasn't* the way of the world.

'Hey, thanks, Picasso.'

'Hey, no problem, Suzanne.'

And he resumed his task of putting a roof over my head.

DEAR NICHOLAS,

I am watching over you as I write this, and you are absolutely gorgeous. Sometimes I look at you and just can't believe you're mine. You have your father's chin, but you definitely have my smile.

There's a little toy that hangs over your crib and, when you pull on it, it plays 'Whistle a Happy Tune'. This makes you laugh immediately. I think Daddy and I love to hear that song as much as you do.

Sometimes at night, if I'm driving home late, I'll hear that little melody in my head, and I'll feel such a longing for you.

Right now I just want to pick you up out of your sleep and hold you as close as I can.

The other thing that always makes you laugh is 'One Potato, Two Potato'. I don't know why. Maybe it's the silly lyrical bounce of the words. All I know is, the word *potato* can send you into fits and wiggles of happiness.

Sometimes I can't imagine your being any other age than the one you are this second. But I think all mothers tend to hold their children frozen in time, pressed like flowers, forever perfect. Sometimes, when I rock you, I feel as if I were holding a little bit of heaven in my arms. I have a sense that there are protective angels all around you, all around us.

I believe in angels now. Just looking at you, sweet baby boy, I would have to.

I loved you the moment we met. Seeing you for the first time, you looked right at Daddy and me. The look in your eyes said, 'Hey, I'm here. Hi!'

Finally, Daddy and I could see you after nine months of imagining what you would be like. I took your head and pulled it gently to my chest. You were six pounds three ounces of sheer happiness.

Daddy held you next. He couldn't believe how a baby, just minutes old, could be looking back at him.

Matt's little boy.

Our beautiful little Nicholas.

Katie

Matt's little boy. Our beautiful little Nicholas.

Katie Wilkinson put down the diary, sighed and took a deep breath. Her throat felt raw and sore. She ran her fingers through Guinevere's soft grey fur, and the cat purred gently. She blew her nose into a tissue. She hadn't been ready for this. She definitely hadn't been ready for Suzanne. Or Nicholas.

And especially not Nicholas, Suzanne and Matt.

'This is so crazy and so bad, Guiny,' she said to the cat. 'I've got myself into such a mess. What a disaster!'

Katie got up and wandered around her apartment. She had always been so proud of it. She had done much of the work herself, and liked nothing better than to build and hang her own cabinets and bookcases. Her place was filled with antique pine, old hook rugs, small watercolours.

Her grandmother's jelly cabinet was in her study and the interior planks still held the aroma of homemade molasses and jellies. Several hand-sewn books were displayed in the jelly cabinet. Katie had learned bookbinding and made them herself at the Penland School of Crafts in North Carolina.

She had so many questions right now, but no one to answer them. No, that wasn't completely true. She had the diary.

Suzanne. She liked her, damn it. Under different circumstances they might have been friends. Suzanne had been gutsy to move to Martha's Vineyard. She had chased her dream to be the kind of woman she needed to be. She had learned from her near-fatal heart attack: she'd learned to treasure every moment.

And what about Matt? What had Katie meant to him? Was she just another woman in a doomed affair? Suddenly, she was ashamed. Her father used to ask her a question all the time when she was growing up: 'Are you right with God, Katie?' She wasn't sure now.

'Jerk,' she whispered. 'You creep. Not *you,* Guinevere. I'm talking about Matt! Damn him!'

Why didn't he just tell her the truth. Had he been cheating on his perfect wife? Why hadn't he talked about Suzanne? How could she have allowed Matt to seal off his perfect past from her? She hadn't pushed as much as she could have. Why? Because it wasn't her style to be pushy.

But the most compelling reason had been the look in Matt's eyes whenever they started to talk about his past. There was such sadness. And Matt had *sworn* to her that he was no longer married.

Katie kept remembering the horrible night Matt left her, the night of July 18. She had prepared a special dinner, set the wrought-iron table on her small terrace with her Royal Crown Derby china. She'd bought a dozen roses, a mixture of red and white. She had Eric Clapton on the CD player.

When Matt arrived, she had the most wonderful surprise waiting for him: the first copy of the book of poems he'd written, which she had edited. She also gave him the news that the printing was 11,000 copies—very large for a collection of poems.

Less than an hour later, Katie found herself in tears. Matt had barely come in the door when she knew something was wrong. She could see it in his eyes. Matt had finally told her, 'Katie, I can't see you again. I won't be coming to New York any more. I know how awful that sounds, how unexpected. I'm sorry. I had to tell you in person. That's why I came here tonight.'

No, he had no idea how awful it sounded, or was. She had trusted him. She'd left herself completely open to hurt. She'd never done that before. And she had wanted to talk to him that night—she'd had important things to tell him.

After he left her apartment, she opened a drawer in the antique dresser near the door leading to the terrace.

There was another present for Matt hidden inside.

Katie held it in her hand, and she began to shake. Her lips quivered. She couldn't help herself. She pulled away the wrapping paper and then opened the small oblong box.

Katie started to cry as she peered inside. The hurt she felt almost wasn't bearable.

She'd had something so wonderful to share with Matt that night.

Inside the box was a beautiful silver baby rattle.

She was pregnant.

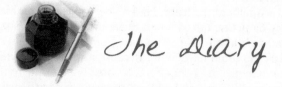

The Diary

Nicholas:

This is the rhythm of my life, and it is as regular and comforting as the Atlantic tides I see from the house.

I get up at six and take Gus for a long romp down past the Rowe farm. We eventually come out to a stretch of beach rimmed with ten-foot-high dunes and waving sea grass. Sometimes I wave back. I can be such a kook that it's embarrassing.

What I especially like about the walks is the peaceful, easy feeling I have inside. I think a lot of it is due to the fact that I've taken back my life, reclaimed myself.

Remember the five balls, Nicky—always remember the five balls.

That is my thought as I head home.

Just before I turn in to my driveway, I pass the Bone house next door. Melanie Bone was amazingly generous when I first moved in, supplying me with everything from helpful phone numbers to cold, tangy lemonade. In fact, Melanie recommended Picasso to me.

She is my age and already has four kids. I'm always in awe of anybody who can do that. Melanie is small, just a little over five foot, with jet-black hair, and the loveliest smile.

Did I mention that the Bone kids are all girls, ages one through four? I've always been bad with names, so I keep them organised by calling them by their ages. 'Is Two sleeping?' 'Is that Four outside on the swings?'

The Bones all giggle when I do this, and they think it's so silly they've inducted Gus as honorary number Five. Lord, if anyone ever overheard my system, they'd never come to see Dr Bedford.

But they do come, Nicky, and I am healing myself.

MY LITTLE MAN—listen, watch closely now, this next part is magic. There is such a thing. Believe me.

One night after a very long day at my office, the intrepid country doctor decided to grab a bite to eat on her way home.

I guess it was a little past eight when I strolled inside Harry's Hamburger. I didn't notice him at first. He was sitting by the window, eating his dinner and reading a book.

In fact, I was halfway through my burger when I saw him. Picasso, my house-painter.

I'd had very little contact with him since he left me those beautiful wild flowers. Occasionally I'd hear him fixing something on the roof as I was leaving for work, but we seldom spoke more than a few words. I got up to pay the bill. I could have walked out without saying hello because his back was turned towards me, but that seemed ungracious.

I stopped at his booth and asked him how he was. He was surprised to see me and asked if I'd join him for a cup of coffee.

I gave him a lame excuse, saying I had to get home to Gus, but he was already clearing a spot for me and I sat down. I liked his voice— I hadn't noticed it before. I liked his eyes, too.

'What are you reading?' I asked, feeling awkward, maybe a little scared.

'Two things: Melville'—he held up *Moby-Dick*—'and *Trout Fishing in America.* Just in case I don't catch the big one, I have a back-up.'

I laughed. Picasso was pretty smart, and funny. We talked for more than an hour that night, and the time just flew. Suddenly, I noticed how dark it was outside.

I looked back at him. 'I have to go. I start work early in the morning.'

'Me, too,' he said, and smiled. 'My current boss is an absolute slave driver.'

I laughed. 'So I've heard.'

I stood up at the table and for some goony reason I shook his hand.

'Picasso,' I said, 'I don't even know your real name.'

'It's Matthew,' he said. 'Matthew Harrison.'

Your father.

THE NEXT TIME I saw Matt Harrison, he was on my roof, hammering shingles like a madman. It was a few days after we had talked at Harry's Hamburger.

'Hey, Picasso!' I yelled, this time feeling relaxed and even happy to see him. 'You want a cold drink?'

'I'd love something cold.'

Five minutes later he entered the cottage as brown as a burnished copper coin.

'How's it going up there?' I asked.

'Good and hot! Believe it or not, I'm almost done with your roof.'

Damn. Just as I was starting to like having him around.

'How's it going down here?' Matt asked me, sliding into my porch rocker in his cut-off jeans and open denim shirt. The rocker went back and bumped the trellis.

'Pretty good,' I said. 'No tragic headlines in the trenches today.'

Suddenly, behind Matt, the trellis broke away and began to tumble towards us. We both leapt up, and managed to press the white wooden frame back into place, our heads covered with rose petals and clematis.

I began laughing as I looked over at my handyman. He looked like a bridesmaid gone wrong. He responded by saying, 'Oh, and you don't look like Carmen Miranda yourself?'

Matt got a hammer and nails and resecured the trellis. My only job was to hold it steady.

I felt his strong leg brush against mine, then I could feel his chest press against my back as he hovered over me, banging in the last nail.

I shivered. *Had he done that on purpose? What was going on here?*

Our eyes met and there was a flash of something significant between us. Whatever it was, I liked it.

Impulsively, I asked him to stay for dinner. 'Nothing fancy. I'll throw some steaks and corn on the grill . . .'

He hesitated, and I wondered whether there was someone else. But my insecurity evaporated when he said, 'I'm kind of grubby, Suzanne. Would you mind if I took a shower? I'd love to stay for dinner.'

'There are clean towels under the basin,' I told him.

And so he went to wash and I went to make dinner. That's when I realised I didn't have any steak or corn. Fortunately, Matt never knew that I ran over to Melanie's for food . . . and that she threw in wine, candles, even half a cherry pie. She also told me that she adored Matt, that everyone did, and 'Good for you.'

After dinner the two of us sat talking on the front porch. The time flew again, and when I looked at my watch I saw that it was almost eleven. I couldn't believe it.

'Tomorrow's a hospital day for me,' I said.

'I'd like to reciprocate,' Matt said. 'Take you to dinner tomorrow? May I, Suzanne?'

I couldn't take my eyes away from his. Matt's eyes were this incredibly gentle brown. 'Yes, you may take me to dinner. I can't wait,' I said. It just came out.

He laughed. 'You don't have to wait. I'm still here, Suzanne.'

'I know, and I like it, but I still can't wait for tomorrow. Good night, Matt.'

He leaned forward, lightly kissed my lips, and then went home.

As IT ALWAYS HAS in my life—so far, anyway—tomorrow finally arrived. It came with Gus. Every morning he goes out to the porch and fetches the *Boston Globe*. What a retriever; what a pal!

Picasso took me around the island in his beat-up Chevy that afternoon, and we ended up at the lovely, multicoloured Gay Head Cliffs. Matt reminded me that Tashtego in *Moby-Dick* was a native harpooner and a Gay Head Indian. I guess I'd forgotten.

Two days later we went for another ride, out to Chappaquiddick. There was a tiny sign on the beach: PLEASE DON'T DISTURB THE CLAMS OR SCALLOPS. Nice. We didn't disturb anything.

I know this might sound silly, or worse, but I liked just being in the car with Matt. I looked at him and thought, Hey, I'm with this guy and he's very nice. We're out looking for an adventure. I hadn't felt like that in a long time. I missed it.

It was at that very moment Matt turned and asked me what I was thinking about.

'Nothing. Just catching the sights,' I said.

He persisted. 'If I guess right, will you tell me?'

'Sure.'

'If I guess right,' he said, and grinned, 'then we get to have another date. Maybe even tomorrow night.'

'And if you guess wrong, then we never see each other again. Big stakes riding on this.'

He laughed. 'Remember, I'm still painting your house, Suzanne.'

He paused then nailed his guess. 'You were thinking about us.'

I couldn't even bluff, though I did blush. 'Maybe I was.'

'Yes!' he shouted, and raised both arms in triumph. 'And so?'

'So keep your hands on the steering wheel.'

'So what would you like to do tomorrow?'

I started to laugh, and realised I did that a lot around him. 'Boy, I have no idea. I was going to give Gus a badly needed bath, do some food shopping, maybe rent a movie.'

'If you want some company I'd love to tag along.'

I had to admit, it was great fun being with Matt. He was the polar opposite of my former boyfriend, Michael, who never seemed to do anything without logical reason, never turned down a pretty winding road just because it was there.

Matt couldn't have been more different. He seemed to take an interest in just about everything: he was a gardener, bird-watcher, avid reader, pretty good cook, and, of course, he was very handy round the house.

I felt so damn happy that day. Just taking a ride with him, going absolutely nowhere. I breathed in everything around me: the sea grass, the minty blue sky, the beach, the roaring ocean. But mostly I breathed in Matthew Harrison. His freshly laundered plaid flannel shirt, his glistening rose-brown skin, his longish brown hair.

I breathed Matt in, held him there, and never wanted to exhale.

NICKY,

I saw Matt Harrison every day for the next two weeks. I almost couldn't believe it. I pinched myself a lot. I smiled when no one was around.

'Have you ever ridden a horse, Suzanne?' Matt asked me on Saturday morning. 'This is a serious question.'

'I reckon. When I was a kid,' I said with a cowgirl drawl.

'A perfect answer—because you're about to be a kid again. By the way, have you ever ridden a sky-blue horse that has red stripes and gold hooves?'

I shook my head. 'I'd remember if I had.'

'I know where there's a horse like that,' he said. 'In fact, I know where there are lots of them.'

We drove to Oak Bluffs, and there they were. Dozens of brightly painted stallions stood in a circle beneath the most dazzling ceiling I'd ever seen. Hand-carved horses with flared red nostrils and black glass eyes galloped in their tireless tracks in a circle of joy.

Matthew had brought me to the Flying Horses, the oldest carousel in the country.

We climbed aboard as the platform tilted and rotated beneath us, and we found perfect steeds.

As the music began, I clenched the silver horse rod, rising and falling, rising and falling. I fell under the carousel's spinning spell. Matt reached out to hold my hand and even tried to catch a kiss, which he succeeded at admirably. What a horseman!

'Where did you learn to ride like that, cowboy?' I asked.

'Oh, I've ridden for years,' Matt said. 'Took lessons here when I was three. You see that blue stallion up ahead? Blue the colour of the sky? Wild-blue-yonder blue?'

'Reckon I do.'

'He threw me a couple of times. That's why I wanted to make sure you got National Velvet first time out. She's got an even temper, lovely coat of shellac.'

'She's beautiful, Matt. You know, when I was a kid I used to go riding with my grandfather. Funny I should remember that now.'

Good memories are like charms, Nicky. You collect them, one by one, until one day you look back and discover they make a long, colourful bracelet.

Katie

Katie would never forget the very first time she saw Matt Harrison. It was in her small, comfortable office at the publishing house, and she had been looking forward to the meeting for days.

She had loved *Songs of a House-painter*, which seemed to her like magical short stories condensed into powerful, moving poems. He wrote about everyday life—tending a garden, painting a house, burying a beloved dog—but his choice of words distilled life so perfectly.

She was still amazed that she had discovered his work.

And then he walked through the door of her office, and she was even more amazed. No, make that entranced. The most primitive parts of her brain locked onto the image before her—the man. Katie felt her heart skip a beat, and she thought, *Careful, careful.*

He was taller than she was—she guessed about six foot two. He had a good nose and strong-looking chin, and everything about his face held together extremely well, like one of his poems. His hair was longish, sandy brown and lustrous. He had a working man's tan. He smiled at something, hopefully not her height or the goofy look on her face—but she liked him, anyway. What was there not to like?

They had dinner that night. Then they went to a jazz club, on a 'school night', as Katie called her work nights. He dropped her off at her apartment at three in the morning, apologised profusely, gave her the sweetest kiss on the cheek, and then off he went in a cab.

Katie stood on the front steps and was finally able to catch her breath. She tried to remember . . . Was Matthew Harrison married?

He was back in her office the following morning—to work—but the two of them skedaddled off to lunch at noon and didn't return for the rest of the day. They went museum hopping, and he certainly knew his art. She kept thinking, *Who is this guy? And why am I allowing myself to feel the way I'm feeling?*

And then, *Why am I not trying to feel like this all the time?*

He came up to her place that night, and she continued to be astonished that any of this was happening. Katie was infamous with her friends for not sleeping around, for being too romantic and way too old-fashioned about sex; but here she was with this good-looking, sexy house-painter–poet from Martha's Vineyard, and she couldn't *not* be with him.

They went to bed for the first time on that rainy night, and he made her notice the music of the raindrops as they fell on her street and the trees outside her apartment. It was beautiful, but soon they had forgotten the patter of the rain, and everything else, except for the urgent touch of each other.

He was so natural and easy that it scared Katie a little. It was as if he had known her for a long time. He knew how to hold her, how and where to touch her, how to wait, and then when to let everything explode. She loved the gentle way he kissed her lips, her cheeks, the hollow of her throat, her back—well, everywhere.

'You're absolutely ravishing, and you don't know it, do you?' he whispered to her, then smiled. 'You have the most delicate body. Your eyes are gorgeous. And I *love* your braid.'

'You and my mother,' Katie said. She loosened the braid and let her long hair cascade over her shoulders.

When he finally left her apartment the next morning, Katie had the feeling that she had never before experienced such intimacy.

She kind of missed Matt already. It was insane, completely ridiculous, not her; but she did miss him.

When she got to her office that morning, he was already there, waiting for her. Her heart nearly stopped.

'We'd better do some work,' she said. 'Seriously.'

He didn't say a word, just shut her office door, and kissed her until Katie felt as if she were melting into the floor.

He finally pulled away, looked into her eyes again, and said, 'As soon as I left your place, I missed you.'

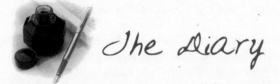

The Diary

Nicholas,

I remember all of this as if it happened yesterday. Matt and I were riding on the Edgartown–Vineyard Haven road in my old, blue Jeep.

'Can't you drive any faster?' Matt asked. 'I walk faster than this.'

'Hey, I got the safety-first award in my driver's ed class in Cornwall-on-Hudson. I hung the diploma under my medical degree.'

Matt laughed. He got all of my dumb little jokes.

We were driving to his mother's house. Matt thought it would be interesting for me to meet her.

'Oops, there's my mom!' Matt said when we got there.

She was up on the roof of the house, fixing an ancient TV antenna. We got out of my Jeep, and Matt called up to her.

'Mom, this is Suzanne. Suzanne . . . my mother, Jean. She taught me how to fix things around the house.'

His mother was tall, lanky, silver-haired. She called down to us. 'Very nice to meet you, Suzanne. You two go have a seat on the porch. I'll only be a minute.'

Matt and I took our seats at a wrought-iron table on the porch. The house was an old saltbox with a northern view of the harbour. To the south lay cornfields, and then deep woods.

'It's gorgeous here. Is this where you grew up?' I asked.

'No, I was born in Edgartown. This house was bought a few years after my father died.'

'I'm sorry, Matt.'

He shrugged. 'It's another thing we have in common, I guess.'

'So why didn't you tell me?' I asked him.

He smiled. 'You know, I guess I just don't like to talk about sad things.'

Jean suddenly appeared with iced tea and a plate heaped with chocolate-chip cookies.

'Well, I promise I won't give you the once-over, Suzanne. We're too mature for that sort of thing,' she said with a wink. 'I'd love to hear about your practice, though. Matthew's father was a doctor, you know.'

I looked over at him. Matt hadn't told me that, either.

'My dad died when I was eight years old,' he said. 'I don't remember too much.'

'He's private about some things, Suzanne. Matthew was hurt badly when his dad died. I think he believes it might make other people uncomfortable to hear about how much he hurts.'

She winked at Matt; he winked back at her. I could tell they were close. It was nice to see.

It turned out that Jean was a local artist—a painter. She showed me some of her work. It was good. She had a sense of humour about her work, too. About anything, really. I saw a lot of her in Matt.

The afternoon turned into evening, and Matt and I ended up staying for dinner. There was even time to see a priceless album of Matt's baby pictures.

He was a cutie, Nick. He had your blond hair and that spunky look you have sometimes.

'No naked bottoms on bear rugs?' I asked Jean as I went through the pictures.

She laughed. 'Look hard enough, and I'm sure you'll find one. He has a nice butt. If you haven't seen it, you should ask for a look.'

I laughed. Jean was a hoot.

It was about eleven when we finally got up to leave. Jean grabbed me in a hug and whispered against my cheek, 'He never ever brings anybody home. So whatever you think of him, he must like you a lot.

Please don't hurt him. He *is* sensitive, Suzanne. And he's a pretty good guy.'

'Hey!' Matt finally called from the car. 'Knock it off, you two.'

'Too late,' his mother said. 'The damage is already done. I had to spill the beans. Suzanne knows enough to drop you like a bad habit.'

THE DAMAGE was probably already done—to me. I was falling for Matthew Harrison. I couldn't quite believe it, but it was happening.

The Hot Tin Roof is a fun nightclub in Edgartown. Matt and I went there to eat oysters and listen to the blues on Friday night. At that point, I would have gone anywhere with him.

'Want to slow dance?' Matt asked me after we'd had our fill of oysters and cold beer.

'Dance? No one is dancing, Matt.'

'This is my favourite song, and I'd love to dance with you. Will you dance with me, Suzanne?'

I blushed.

'Come on,' Matt whispered against my cheek.

'All right. One dance.'

We began to slow dance in our little corner of the bar. Eyes started to turn our way.

'Is this OK?' Matt checked.

'You know, actually, it's great. What is this song, anyway? You said it was your favourite.'

'Oh, I have no idea, Suzanne. I just wanted an excuse to hold you close.'

With that, Matt held me a little tighter. I loved being in his arms. I felt a little dizzy as we spun round with the music.

'I have a question to ask you,' he whispered in my ear.

'OK,' I whispered back.

'How do you feel about us? So far?'

I kissed him. 'Like that.'

He smiled. 'That's how I feel, too.'

'Good.'

Matt leaned in and lightly kissed me on the lips. 'Would you come home with me tonight, Suzanne?' he asked. 'I want to do some more dancing.'

I told him I would love to.

I have this wink that Matt calls 'Suzanne's famous wink'. I did it for the first time to Matt that night. He loved it.

MATT'S HOUSE was a small Victorian covered in gingerbread lace that draped itself over the eaves. The trellises and overhangs looked as if they'd been lifted off some elaborately trimmed wedding cake.

It was the first time I had been invited, and I was suddenly nervous. We went inside and I immediately noticed a library. There were thousands of books in there. My eyes travelled up and down the bookshelves: Scott Fitzgerald, John Cheever, Virginia Woolf. An entire wall was devoted to collections of poetry. W. H. Auden, Wallace Stevens, Sylvia Plath. There was an antique globe; an old English pond boat, its sails stained and listing; a big pine table covered in writing pads and papers.

'I love this room. Can I look around?' I asked.

'I love it, too. Of course you can look.'

I was totally surprised by the cover page on top of a stack of pages. It read, *Songs of a House-painter*, *Poems by Matthew Harrison.*

Matt was a poet? He hadn't told me about it. He really didn't like to talk about himself, did he? What other secrets did he have?

'OK, yes,' he admitted. 'I do some scribbling. That's all it is. I've had the bug since I was sixteen, and I've been trying to work it out since I left Brown. I majored in English and House-painting. Just kidding. You ever write, Suzanne?'

'No, not really,' I said. 'But I've been thinking about starting a diary.'

Then Matt said, 'Let's take a walk to the beach. I have an idea.'

'I've noticed that you have a lot of ideas.'

'Maybe it's the poet in me.'

He grabbed an old blanket, his CD player, and a bottle of champagne. We walked on a winding path through high sea grass, finally finding a patch of sand where we could spread the blanket.

Matt popped open the champagne, and it sparkled in the midnight air. Then he pushed PLAY and the strains of Debussy whirled up into the starry night sky.

In the South of France there is supposedly a special time known as the Night of the Falling Stars, when everything is perfect and magical and the stars seem to pour out of the sky like cream from a pitcher. It was like that for us.

Matt and I danced again. Around and around we went, in sync with the rhythm of the sea, turning up fountains of sand, leaving footprint patterns in our wake. I let my fingers play on his back, his neck. I let my hands comb through his hair.

'I didn't know you could waltz,' I said.

He laughed. 'I didn't know, either.'

It was late when we made our way back up from the beach, but I was more awake than ever. I hadn't expected any of this to happen. Not now, maybe not ever. It seemed a thousand years from my heart attack in the Public Garden in Boston.

Nicky, I felt so lucky—so blessed.

Matt gently took my hand and led me up the stairs to his room. I wanted to go with him, but still I was afraid. I hadn't done this in a while.

Neither of us spoke, but suddenly my mouth opened wide. He had converted the top floor to one big, beautiful space, complete with skylights that seemed to absorb the evening sky.

Matt told me that he could count falling stars from his bed. 'One night I counted sixteen. A personal record.'

He came to me slowly, drawing me towards him like a magnet. I could feel the buttons in the back of my blouse coming undone. His fingers travelled down to the base of my spine, playing so very gently. He slipped off my blouse, and I watched it float to the floor, milkweed in a breeze.

I stood so close to Matt, barely breathing, feeling light, dizzy, magical and very special.

He slipped his hands down onto my hips. Matt then gently laid me on his bed. I watched him in the moon shadows. I found him to be beautiful. How had this happened? Why was I suddenly so lucky?

He stretched over me like a quilt on a cold night. That's all I will say of it, all I will write.

DEAR NICKY,

I hope when you grow up that everything you want comes your way, but especially love. When it's right, love can give you the kind of joy that you can't get from any other experience. I have been in love; I *am* in love, so I speak from experience. I have also lived long periods without love in my life, and there is no way to describe the difference between the two.

We is always so much better than *I*.

Please don't listen to anyone who tells you otherwise. And don't ever become a cynic, Nicky. Anything but that!

I look at your little hands and feet. I count your toes over and over, moving them gently as if they were beads on an abacus. I kiss your belly till you laugh. You are so innocent. Stay that way when it comes to love.

Just look at you. Your nose and mouth are just right. Your eyes and your smile are your very best features. Already I see your personality blossoming. What are you thinking about right now? The mobile over your head? Your music box? Daddy says you're probably thinking about girls and tools and flashy cars. 'He's a real boy, Suzanne.'

Daddy and I laugh about all the good things that wait for you. But what we want most for you is love and that it should always surround you. It is a gift. If I can, I will try to teach you how to receive such a gift. Because to be without love is to be without grace, what matters most in life.

We is so much better than *I*.

If you need proof, just look at us.

'OK. WHAT'S GOING ON? Spill the beans, Suzanne,' said my friend Melanie Bone. 'I know there's something going on with you. I feel it in my bones.'

We were walking along the beach near our houses, the kids and Gus romping in front of us.

'You're smart,' I told her. 'And nosy.'

'I know that already. So tell me what I don't know. Spill!'

I couldn't resist any longer. It had to come out sooner or later. 'I'm in love, Mel. I'm head over heels in love with Matt Harrison. I have no idea what's to become of us!'

Melanie screeched. Then she jumped up and down a few times in the sand. 'That is so perfect, Suzanne. I knew he was a good painter, but I had no idea about his other talents.'

'Did you know he's a poet? A very good poet.'

'No, you're kidding,' she said.

'A beautiful dancer?'

'That doesn't surprise me. He moves pretty well on rooftops. So, how did it go from adding a touch of Cape Cod white to your house to this?'

I started to giggle and felt like a schoolgirl. 'I talked to him one night at the hamburger place. I can talk to Matt about anything, Melanie. I've never had that happen with any man before. He even writes poems the way he talks. He's passionate, exciting. He's humble, too. Maybe more than he should be.'

Melanie suddenly gave me hug. 'God, Suzanne, this is it! As IT as it can get. Congratulations!'

We laughed like a couple of giddy fifteen-year-olds, and headed back with her kids and Gus. That morning at her house, we talked about everything from first dates to first pregnancies. Melanie confessed that she was thinking of having a fifth baby, which blew me away. For her it was as easy as organising a cabinet. She had her life as under control as a well-stocked grocery shelf lined neatly with canned goods.

I also fantasised about having kids that morning, Nicholas. I knew I would have a high-risk pregnancy because of my heart condition, but I didn't care. Maybe there was something in me that knew you'd be here one day. A flutter of hope. A deep desire. Or just the sheer inevitability of what love between two people can bring.

You—it brought you.

BAD STUFF HAPPENS, Nicholas. Sometimes it makes no sense at all.

Gus was crossing the street, heading towards the beach, where he likes to race the surf and bark at seagulls. Bad timing.

I saw the whole thing. I opened my mouth to stop him, but it was already too late.

The red pick-up swung round the blind curve like a blur. I could almost smell the rubber of the tyres as it skid, then I watched as the left front fender caught Gus. It was over, done, and he lay like a rag discarded by the side of the road.

'No!' I yelled. The truck had stopped, and two stubble-faced men in their twenties got out.

'Gee, I'm sorry, I didn't see him,' the driver stammered.

I didn't have time to argue. I threw the driver my keys. 'Open the back of my Jeep,' I snapped as I gently lifted Gus up into my arms. He was limp and heavy, but still breathing, still Gus.

I laid him in the back of the Jeep. His sweet, familiar eyes were as far away as the clouds. Then he whimpered pitifully, and my heart broke.

'Hold on, boy,' I said as I pulled out of my driveway. 'Please don't leave me.'

I called Matt on my cellphone, and he met me at the vet's. Dr Pugatch took Gus in at once.

'The truck was going way too fast, Matt,' I told him.

Matt was even angrier than me. 'It's that damn curve. I need to lay you a new driveway on the other side of the house. That way you'll be able to see the road.'

'This is so horrible. Gus was right there when I—' I stopped myself. I still hadn't told Matt about my heart attack. I had to tell him soon.

'Shhhh, it's OK, Suzanne. It's going to be OK.' Matt held me. I burrowed into his chest and stayed there. Then I could feel Matt shaking. He and Gus had become close, too.

Two hours later the vet came out. It seemed like an eternity before she spoke. 'Suzanne, Matt,' Dr Pugatch finally said. 'I'm sorry. I'm so, so sorry. Gus didn't make it.'

I began to cry, and my whole body shook uncontrollably. Gus had always been there with me, for me. He was my good buddy, my room-mate, my jogging partner. We had been together for fourteen years.

Bad stuff does happen sometimes, Nicholas. Always remember that, but remember that you have to move on, somehow.

You just pick your head up and stare at something beautiful like the sky, or the ocean, and you move the hell on.

NICHOLAS,

An unexpected letter arrived in the mail for me the next day.

I stood at the end of the driveway in front of the weather-beaten mailbox. I opened the letter carefully and held it tight so it wouldn't be blown away by the ocean wind.

Rather than try to paraphrase what the letter said, Nicky, I'm enclosing it in the diary.

> *Dear Suzanne,*
> *You are the explosion of carnations*
> *in a dark room.*
> *Or the unexpected scent of pine*
> *miles from Maine.*
> *You are a full moon*
> *that gives midnight its meaning.*
> *And the explanation of water*
> *for all living things.*
> *You are a valentine*
> *tattered and loved and reread a hundred times.*
> *You are a medal found in the drawer*
> *of a once sung hero.*

You are honey
and cinnamon
and West Indies spices,
lost from the boat
that was once Marco Polo's.
You are a pressed rose,
a pearl ring,
and a red perfume bottle found near the Nile.
You are an old soul from an ancient place
a thousand years, and centuries and millenniums ago.
And you have travelled all this way
just so I could love you.
I do.
Matt

What can I say, Nicholas, that your good, sweet father cannot say better? He is a stunningly good writer, and I'm not even sure he knows it.

I love him so much.

Who wouldn't?

NICKY,

I called Matt very early the next morning, as soon as I dared. about seven. I had been up since a little past four, rehearsing what I should say and how I should say it.

This was hard.

This was impossible.

'Matt, hi. It's Suzanne. Hope I'm not calling too early. Can you come by tonight?' was all I could manage.

'Of course I can. In fact, I was going to call you.'

Matt arrived at the house a little past seven that night. He was wearing a yellow plaid shirt and navy-blue trousers—kind of formal for him.

'You want to take a walk on the beach, Suzanne? Take in the sunset with me?'

It was exactly what I wanted to do. He'd read my mind.

As soon as we crossed the beach road and had our bare feet in the still-warm sand, I said, 'Can I talk? There's something I have to tell you.'

He smiled. 'Sure. I always like the sound of your voice.'

Poor Matt. I doubted that he was going to like the sound of what was coming next.

'There's something I've wanted to tell you for a while. I keep putting it off. I'm not even sure how to broach the subject now.'

He took my hand, swung it gently in rhythm with our strides. 'Consider it broached. Go ahead, Suzanne.'

I squeezed his hand a little. 'OK, here goes.'

Matt finally said, 'You are scaring me a little now.'

'Sorry,' I whispered. 'Sorry. Matt, right before I came to the Vineyard—'

'You had a heart attack,' he said. 'You almost died in the Public Garden, but you didn't, thank God. And now, here we are, two of the luckiest people. I know that *I* am. I'm here holding your hand, looking into your beautiful blue eyes.'

I stopped walking and stared at Matt in disbelief. The setting sun was just over his shoulder.

'How did you know?' I stammered.

'I heard before I came to work for you. This is a small island, Suzanne.'

'So you knew, but you never told me you knew.'

'I knew that you'd tell me when you were ready. I've been thinking about what happened to you a lot in the past few weeks. I even arrived at a point of view. Would you like to hear it?'

I held on to Matt's arm. 'Of course I would.'

'Well, I think: isn't it lucky that Suzanne didn't die in Boston and we have today together. Now we get to watch this sunset. Or isn't it lucky Suzanne didn't die and we're sitting out on her front porch playing cards. Or listening to Mozart. I keep thinking, *Isn't this moment incredibly special, because you're here, Suzanne.*'

I started to cry, and that's when Matt took me into his arms. We cuddled on the beach for a long time, and I never wanted him to let me go. I kept thinking, *Aren't I the lucky one?*

'Suzanne?' I heard him whisper, and I felt Matt's warm breath on my cheek.

'I'm here. I'm not going anywhere.'

'That's good. I want you to always be there. I love having you in my arms. Now there's something I have to say. Suzanne, I love you so much. I treasure everything about you. I miss you when we're apart for just a couple of hours. I've been looking for you for a long time, I just didn't know it. Suzanne, will you marry me?'

I pulled back and looked into the eyes of this precious man I had found, or maybe he had found me. I couldn't stop smiling, and the warm glow spreading inside me was the most incredible feeling.

'I love you, Matt. I've been looking for you for a long time, too. Yes, I'll marry you.'

Katie

Katie closed the diary again. She slammed it shut this time. It hurt her so much to read these pages. She could take them only in small doses. Matt had warned her in his letter: *there will be parts that may be hard for you to read.* What an incredible understatement that was.

The diary was making her jealous of Suzanne. She felt like a jerk, a petty person. Not herself. Maybe it was hormones. Or maybe it was just a normal reaction to everything abnormal that had happened to her recently.

She shut her eyes tight, and felt incredibly alone. She needed to talk to someone besides Guinevere the cat and Merlin the labrador. Ironically, the person she wanted to reach out to was on Martha's Vineyard. As much as she wanted to, she wouldn't call him.

Her eyes moved over to the bookshelves she had built. Her apartment was like a small bookstore. *Orlando, The Age of Innocence, Bella Tuscany, Harry Potter and the Goblet of Fire.* She'd been reading voraciously ever since she was seven or eight.

She was feeling queasy again. Cold, too. She wrapped herself in a blanket and lay on her living-room couch. She couldn't stop thinking about the baby inside her. 'It's all right, little baby,' she whispered.

Katie remembered the night when she had got pregnant. She'd had a fantasy in bed that night, but she dismissed it, thinking, I've never got pregnant before. She hadn't ever missed a period.

That last night with Matt, Katie had felt that something had changed between them. She could feel it in the way he held her and looked at her with his luminous brown eyes. She felt some of his walls come down, felt *This is it.* He was ready to tell her things that he hadn't been able to talk about.

Had that scared Matt? Was that what had happened?

It had started so simply: all he had done was wrap his fingers around hers. He slid his free arm beneath her, and stared into her eyes. Next their legs touched, then their bodies reached towards each other. His eyes said, I love you, Katie. She couldn't have been wrong about that.

She had always wanted it to be like this, just like this. She'd had this dream a thousand times before. His strong arms were around her back, and her long legs were wrapped around his. She knew she could never forget any of those images.

He was athletic, graceful, giving, dominating. He whispered her name over and over: *Katie, sweet Katie, my Katie.*

This was it, she knew—he was completely aware and attuned to her, and she had never experienced such love with anyone before. She loved it, loved Matt, and she pulled him deep inside, where they made a baby.

KATIE KNEW what she had to do the next morning. She called home—Asheboro, nestled between the Blue Ridge and Great Smoky Mountains in North Carolina—where life had always been simpler.

'Hey, Katie,' her mother answered on the third ring. 'You're up with the city birds this morning. How are you doing, sweetie?'

They had Caller ID in Asheboro now. Everything was changing, wasn't it?

'Hey, Mom. What's the latest?'

'You doing better today?' her mother asked. She knew all about Matt and had loved it when Katie called to talk about him, especially when she said they would probably be getting married. Now he had left her, and Katie was suffering. She didn't deserve that.

'Some. Yeah, sure. Well, actually, no. I'm still a mess. I'm pitiful. I'm hopeless. I swore I'd never let a man get me into a state like this—and here I am.'

Katie began to tell her mother about the diary and what she had read so far. The lesson of the five balls. Suzanne's daily routine on Martha's Vineyard. How she met Matt.

'You know what's so strange, Mom? I actually like Suzanne. Damn it. I'm such a sap. I ought to hate her, but I can't.'

'Of course you can't. Well, at least this dumb bunny Matt has good taste in women,' her mother said.

Tell her, Katie thought. *Tell her everything. She'll understand.*

But Katie couldn't tell her mother she was pregnant. The words just wouldn't come out. She choked on them and felt bile rising from her stomach.

Katie and her mother talked for almost an hour, and then she spoke to her father. She was almost as close to him as she was to her mom. He was a minister, much beloved in the area. The only time he'd ever been mad at Katie was when she had packed up and moved to New York. But he got over it.

Her mother and father were like that. Good people. And so was she, Katie thought, and knew it was true.

So why had Matt left her? And what was the diary supposed to tell her that would somehow make her understand? That Matt had a wonderful wife and a darling child and that he had slipped up with her? Had strayed for the first time in his picture-perfect marriage? *Damn him!*

When she had finished talking to her dad, Katie curled up on the couch with Guinevere and Merlin and looked out of the window at the Hudson. She loved the river, the way it changed every day.

'What should I do?' she whispered to Guinevere and Merlin. Tears welled up in her eyes, then spilled down her cheeks.

Katie picked up the phone again. It took all the courage that she had, but she finally dialled the number.

She almost hung up—but she waited through ring after ring. Finally, she got the answering machine.

She choked up when she actually heard a voice. 'This is Matt. Your message is important to me. Please leave it at the beep. Thanks.'

Katie left a message. She hoped it was important to Matt. 'I'm reading the diary,' she said. That was all.

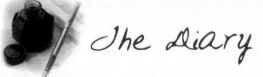

The Diary

Come to our wedding, Nicky. This is your invitation. I want you to know exactly what it was like on the day your mother and father pledged their love.

Snow was falling gently on the island. The bells were ringing in the clear, crisp December air as dozens of frosty well-wishers crossed the threshold into the Gay Head Community Church, the oldest Indian Baptist church in the country. It's also one of the loveliest.

There is only one word that can describe our wedding day . . . *joy.* Matt and I were both giddy. I was just about flying among the angels carved in the four corners of the chapel ceiling.

I really did feel like an angel in an antique white dress strung with a hundred luminescent pearls. My grandfather came to Martha's Vineyard for the first time in fifteen years, just to walk me down the aisle. All my doctor friends from Boston made the trip in the dead of winter. Some of my patients came, too. The church was standing room only for the ecumenical service. As you might have guessed, just about everybody on the island is a friend of Matt's.

He was incredibly handsome in a jazzy black tux, with his hair trimmed for the occasion, but not too short, his eyes shining, his smile more radiant than it had ever been.

Can you see it, Nicky—with the snow lightly blowing in from the ocean? It was glorious.

'Are you as happy as I am?' Matt whispered as we stood before the altar. 'You look incredibly beautiful.'

I felt myself blush. A feeling of vulnerability washed over me as I looked into Matt's eyes. This was so right.

'I've never been happier, never surer of anything in my life,' I said.

We made our pledge on December 31, just before the New Year arrived. There was something almost magical about becoming husband and wife on New Year's Eve. It felt as if the whole world were celebrating with us.

Seconds after Matt and I pledged our vows, everyone in the church stood and yelled, 'Happy New Year, Matt and Suzanne!'

Silvery white feathers were released from dozens of satin pouches that had been strung from the ceiling. Matt and I were in a blizzard of angels, clouds and doves. We kissed and held each other tightly.

'How do you like the first moment of marriage, Mrs Harrison?' he asked me. I think he liked saying 'Mrs Harrison', and I liked hearing it for the first time.

'If I had known how wonderful it was going to be, I'd have insisted we marry twenty years ago,' I said.

Matt grinned and went along with me. 'How could we? We didn't know each other.'

'Oh, Matt,' I said, 'we've known each other all our lives. We must have.'

I couldn't help remembering what Matt had said the night he proposed on the beach. 'Isn't it lucky,' he'd said, 'Suzanne didn't die in Boston and we have today to be together?' I was incredibly lucky, and it gave me a chill as I stood there with Matt on our wedding night.

That's what it felt like—that was the exact feeling—and I'm so happy that now you were there.

MATT AND I went on a whirlwind, three-week honeymoon that started on New Year's Day.

The first week we were on Lanai in Hawaii. It is a glorious spot, with only two hotels on the entire island.

The second week we went to Maui, and it was almost as special as Lanai. We had our mantra: *Isn't it lucky?* We must have said it a hundred times.

Matt and I spent the third week back home on the Vineyard, but we didn't see much of anyone. We were luxuriating in the newness of being together for the rest of our lives.

Nick, here's something your father did that I will always hold close to my heart. Every single day of our honeymoon, Matt woke me in bed—with a honeymoon present. Some of them were small, some were funny jokes, and some were extravagant, but every present came straight from Matt's heart.

Isn't it lucky?

I'LL NEVER FORGET this. It hit me like a wave of seasickness on February 7. Unfortunately, Matt had already gone to work. I sat down on the edge of the tub, feeling as if my life were draining away.

A cold sweat broke out on the back of my neck, and for the first time in over a year I wanted to call a doctor. Instead, I threw cold water on my face and told myself it was probably a touch of the flu.

I took something to settle my stomach, dressed, and went to work. By noon I was feeling much better, and by dinner I had forgotten about it.

It wasn't until the next morning that I found myself sitting on the edge of the tub once more—spent, tired, and feeling nauseated.

That's when I knew.

I called Matt on the cellphone. He was surprised to hear from me.

'Are you OK? Is everything all right?'

'I think . . . that everything just got perfect,' I told him. 'If you can, I'd like you to come home right now. On your way, could you pick up an EPT kit? I want to be absolutely sure but, Matt, we're pregnant.'

Nicholas. You were growing inside me, a speck no larger than a grain of cereal. What can I tell you—happiness flooded our hearts and every room of the beach cottage. It came like high tide on a full moon.

After the wedding, Matt had moved into my house. It was his idea. He said it was best to rent his place out since I was so established with my patients, and my proximity to the hospital was ideal. It was considerate and sweet of him, which is his way. For a big, tough guy he's awfully nice. Your daddy *is* the best.

We decided to make the sunroom of the house yours. We thought you'd love the way the morning light comes pouring over the sills. Daddy and I began converting it into a perfect nursery, gathering things that we thought you might love.

We hung wallpaper that danced with Mother Goose stories. There were your first books, and colourful wall quilts that hung over your crib, the same crib Daddy had when he was a baby. Grandma Jean had saved it all these years. Just for you, pumpkin.

We jammed the shelves with far too many variously coloured stuffed animals, and every variety of ball. Daddy made an oak rocking horse that boasted a beautiful crimson and gold mane. He also made you delicately balanced mobiles filled with moons and stars. And a music box to hang in your crib.

Every time you pull the cord, it plays 'Whistle a Happy Tune'. Whenever I hear that song, I think of you.

We can't wait to meet you.

NICK,

Matt is at it again. A present was on the kitchen table when I got home from work. Gold paper covered in hearts and tied blue ribbon concealed the contents.

I shook the small package, and a tiny note dropped out from under the bow. It read: *Working late tonight, Suze, but thinking about you as always. Open this when you get in and get relaxed. I'll be back by ten. Matt.*

I unwrapped the box carefully and lifted the tiny lid. Inside was a locket in the shape of a heart, hung from a silver chain. I pressed the clasp, and the heart opened to reveal a message that had been engraved inside.

Nicholas, Suzanne and Matt—Forever One.

NICK,

A few years back there was a book called *The Bridges of Madison County*. An underlying premise of the novel was that romance can last for only a short time; in this particular book, only a couple of days for the main characters, Robert and Francesca.

Nicky, please don't believe it. Love between two people can last a long time if the people love themselves and are ready to give love to another person.

I was ready, and so was Matt.

Your father is too good to me and makes me so happy. Like today. He did it to me again.

The house was filled with friends and family when I came downstairs this morning, in floppy pink pyjamas no less, with a sleepy expression on my face.

I had almost forgotten that today was my birthday. My thirty-sixth birthday.

Matt hadn't. He had made a surprise breakfast . . . and I was surprised, all right.

'Matt?' I said, laughing, embarrassed, 'I'm going to murder you.'

He weaved through the people crowded into the kitchen, holding a glass of orange juice for me and wearing a silly grin. 'You're all witnesses. You heard my wife,' he said. 'She looks kind of harmless and sweet, but she's a killer. Happy birthday, Suzanne.'

Grandma Jean handed me her present, and she insisted I open it then and there. It was a beautiful blue silk robe, which I put on to hide my pyjamas. I gave Jean a big hug for bringing the perfect gift.

'The grub is hot, pretty good, and it's ready!' Matt yelled.

After everyone had their fill of the sumptuous breakfast—and, yes, birthday cake—they filed from the house and left us alone. Matt and I collapsed onto the big, comfy couch in the living room.

'So, how does it feel, Suzie? Another birthday?'

I couldn't help smiling. 'You know how most people dread a birthday. They think, *Oh God, people will start looking at me like I'm old*. Well, I feel the exact opposite. I feel that every day is an extraordinary gift. Just to be here, and especially to be with you. Thanks for the birthday party. I love you.'

Then Matt knew just the right thing to do. First, he leaned in and gave me the sweetest kiss on the lips. Then he carried me upstairs to our room, where we spent the rest of my birthday morning and, I must admit, most of my birthday afternoon.

DEAR NICKY,

I am still a little shaky as I write about what happened a few weeks ago at the hospital.

A local construction worker was rushed into the emergency room about eleven in the morning. Matt knew him and his family. The worker had fallen eighteen feet from a ladder and had suffered trauma to his head.

The man's name was John Macdowell, thirty years old, married with four kids. The MRI showed an epidermal haematoma. The pressure on his brain had to be alleviated immediately. *Here is a young man, so close to dying*, I thought. *I don't want to lose this young father.*

I worked as hard as I have since I was in Boston.

It took nearly three hours to stabilise his condition. We almost lost him. He went into cardiac arrest. Finally, I knew we had him back. I wanted to kiss John Macdowell, just for being alive.

His wife came in with their children. Her name was Meg, and she was carrying an infant boy. The poor young woman looked as if she were carrying the weight of the world on her shoulders.

I ordered a mild sedative for Mrs Macdowell and sat with her until she could gather herself. The kids were obviously scared, too.

I took the second smallest, two years old, into my lap and gently stroked her hair. 'Daddy is going to be OK,' I said.

The mother looked on, letting my words seep in. This was meant for her even more than for the children.

'He just fell down. Like you do sometimes. So we gave him medicine and a big bandage. He's going to be fine now. I'm his doctor and I promise.'

The little girl—all the Macdowell kids—fastened on to every word I had to say. So did their mother.

'Thank you, Doctor,' she said. 'We love John so much. He's one of the good guys.'

'I know he is. I could tell by the concern everybody showed. His entire crew came to the ER. We're going to keep John here for a few days. When it's time for him to leave, I'll tell you exactly what you'll need to do at home. He's stable now. Why don't I watch the kids. You can go in and see him.'

The little girl climbed down from my lap. Mrs Macdowell unravelled the baby from her arms and lowered him into mine. He was so tiny, probably only two or three months old.

'Are you sure, Dr Bedford? You can spare the time?' she asked me.

'I have all the time in the world for you.'

I sat there, holding the baby boy, and I couldn't help thinking about the little boy growing inside me. And also about mortality, and how we face it every day of our lives.

I already knew I was a pretty good doctor. But it was only at that moment, when I held the little Macdowell baby, that I knew I was going to be a good mother.

No, Nick, I knew I was going to be a *great* mom.

'WHAT WAS THAT?' I said. 'Matt? Honey?' I spoke with difficulty. 'Matt . . . something's going on. I'm in . . . pain. Whew! More than a little pain, actually.'

I dropped my fork on the floor of the Black Dog Tavern, where we were having dinner. *This couldn't be happening.* Not yet. I was still a good month away from my delivery date. There was no way I could be having a contraction.

Matt jumped into action. He was more prepared for the moment than I was. He tossed cash onto the table and escorted me out of the Black Dog.

Part of me knew what was happening. Or so I believed. Braxton Hicks. Contractions that don't represent true labour. Women sometimes have these pains, occasionally even in the first three months of pregnancy, but when they come in the last three they can be mistaken for labour.

However, my pain seemed to be *above* my uterus, spreading up and under my left lung. It came like a sharp knife. Literally took my breath away.

We got into the Jeep and headed directly to the hospital.

'I'm sure it's nothing,' I said. 'Nicky's just giving a heads-up, letting us know he's physically fit.'

'Good,' Matt said, but he kept driving.

I had been getting weekly monitoring because this was considered a high-risk pregnancy. But everything had been fine, until now. If I was in trouble, I would have known it. Wouldn't I? I was always on the lookout for the least little problem. The fact that I'm a doctor made me even more prepared.

I was wrong. I was in trouble. The kind of trouble you're not quite sure you want to know about before it happens.

This is the story of how we both almost died.

MY NICHOLAS,

We had the best doctor on Martha's Vineyard, and one of the best in all of New England. Dr Constance Cotter arrived at the hospital about ten minutes after I got there with Matt.

I felt fine by then, but Connie monitored me herself for the next two hours. I could see her urgency; I could read it in the tightness of her jaw. She was worrying about my heart. Was it strong enough? She was worrying about you, Nicky.

'This is potentially dangerous,' Connie said, allowing me no illusions. 'Suzanne, your pressure is so high that part of me wants to start labour right now. I know it's not time, but you've got me worried. What I *am* going to do is keep you here tonight. And as many nights as I feel are warranted. No, you have no say in this.'

I looked at Connie as if to say, *You must be kidding!* I was a doctor. I lived right down the road from the hospital. I would come in immediately if necessary.

'Don't even think about it. You're staying. Check in, and I'll be up to see you before I go. This isn't negotiable, Suzanne.'

It was strange to be checking into the hospital where I worked. An hour or so later, Matt and I sat in my room waiting for Connie to return. I was telling him what I knew about a condition called pre-eclampsia. He wanted every detail explained in clear layman's terms. So I told him, and he shifted uncomfortably in his chair.

'You wanted to know,' I said.

Connie finally came in. She took my blood pressure again and then monitored the baby's heartbeat. I studied her face, looking for any kind of sign of trouble. She stared at me oddly, and I couldn't quite figure it out.

Then she said, 'Suzanne, I'm not getting a strong reading from the baby's heart. The baby has to come out *now*.' Connie grasped my hand tightly in both of hers. 'Suzanne,' she whispered, 'I wanted to bring this baby into the world the way you expected it would happen. But I'm not going to put either you or this baby at risk. We have to do a C-section.'

I nodded. 'I know, Connie. I trust you.'

Everything began to move too fast after that.

Connie inserted an IV in my arm and administered magnesium sulphate. I immediately felt sicker than ever. A blinding headache overcame me.

Matt was right there as they prepped me for the Caesarean section.

He was told by a new doctor that this was an emergency. He couldn't stay with me.

Thank God, Connie came back in just then and overrode the decision. She then told me what was happening.

My liver was swollen. The blood platelet count was alarming, and my blood pressure was 190/130.

Worse, Nicky, *your* heartbeat was weakening.

'You're going to be OK, Suzanne,' I kept hearing Connie say. Her voice was like an echo from a distant canyon.

'What about Nicky?' I whispered through parched lips.

I waited for her to say, 'And Nicky will be fine, too.' But Connie didn't say it, and tears came to my eyes.

I was rolled into the operating room, where they were ready not only to deliver a baby but also to transfuse me with eight units of blood. I knew what was going on here. If I started bleeding internally, I would die.

As I was being given the epidural anaesthesia, I saw Dr Leon, my cardiologist, standing right by the anaesthetist. Why was Leon here? Oh God, no. Please don't do this. Oh please, please. I beg you. An oxygen mask was placed over my face. I tried to resist.

Connie raised her voice. 'No, Suzanne. Take the oxygen.'

The next few minutes were a blur. I saw a retractor come out. There were concerned looks from Connie.

I heard staccato orders and cold, unfeeling machine beeps and Matt chanting only positive things. I heard a loud sucking noise as amniotic fluid and blood were cleaned out of me.

There was numbness, some dizziness, and the oddest feeling of not being there, of not being anywhere, actually.

What brought me out of the surreal feeling of having entered another world was—a cry. A distinct and mighty cry. You had announced your arrival like a strong warrior.

I began to cry, and so did Matt and Connie. You were such a little thing, just over six pounds. But so strong. And alert. Especially considering the stress you had been through.

You looked right at Daddy and me. I'll never forget it. The first time ever I saw your face.

I got to hold you in my arms before you were whisked away to the neonatal unit. I got to look into the beautiful eyes that you struggled to keep open, and I got to whisper for the first time, 'I love you.'

Nicholas the Warrior!

Katie

Fear and confusion swept over Katie again. While she read a few more diary pages, she forced herself to eat pasta primavera and drink tea.

Everything was moving way too fast in her head, and especially inside her sore, bloated body.

A baby boy had been born. Nicholas the Warrior.

Another child was growing inside her.

Katie had to be logical about this. What *were* all the possibilities? What could really be happening now?

Matt had been cheating on Suzanne all these months?

Matt had been cheating, and Katie wasn't the first?

Matt had left Suzanne and Nicholas for some reason and they were divorced?

Suzanne had died—her heart had finally given out?

Suzanne was alive, but very ill?

Where was Suzanne right now? Maybe she should try to call her on Martha's Vineyard. Katie wasn't sure if that was a good idea.

She tried to work it through. What did she have to lose? A little pride, but not much else. But what about Suzanne? What if she had no idea about Matt? Was that possible? Of course it was. Wasn't that pretty much what had happened to Katie? Anything seemed possible to her now. Anything *was* possible.

This was so overwhelming. The man she had loved and trusted, and thought she completely understood, had left her.

She remembered a particular moment with Matt that kept her going. He had woken up beside her one night and was crying. She had held him in her arms for a long time. She stroked his cheek. Finally, Matt had whispered, 'I'm trying hard to get everything behind me. I will. I promise, Katie.'

God, this was crazy! Katie pounded her thigh with a closed fist. Her pulse was racing too fast. Her breasts really hurt.

She pushed herself out of her sofa, hurried into the bathroom, and threw up the pasta she'd just eaten.

A LITTLE WHILE LATER, Katie went into the kitchen and fixed herself more tea. She had hung the kitchen cabinets herself. She had her own toolbox and prided herself on never having to call on anyone to fix anything. *So fix what's wrong with your heart*, Katie thought. *Fix that!*

Finally, she reached for the phone, nervously punched some numbers and heard a pick-up on the other end of the line.

'Hi, Mom. It's me,' she said.

'I know, Katie. What's the matter, sweetheart? Couldn't you just come home for a couple of days? I think it would do us all a world of good.'

'Could you get Daddy to pick up, too?' she asked.

'I'm here, Katie,' her father said. 'I'm on in the den. I picked up when the phone rang. How are you?'

She sighed loudly. 'Well . . . I'm pregnant,' she said.

Then all three of them were crying over the phone—because that's the way they were. But Katie's mother and father were already comforting her, saying, 'It's all right, Katie, we love you, we're with you, we understand.'

Because that's the way they were, too.

The Diary

Nicholas,

Just for the record. You started sleeping through the night early on. Not every night, but most, starting when you were about two weeks old, to the envy of all the other moms!

When you go through your little growth spurts, you wake up hungry. And what a little eater you are! You will eat anything— whether you're breast-fed, or bottle-fed formula, or water, you chow down and aren't picky.

On your first visit to the paediatrician the doctor couldn't believe how you were already focusing on the toys she had laid out. She exclaimed, 'He's extraordinary—sensational, Suzanne.'

That's a great feat for a two-week-old. Nicholas the Warrior!

You were baptised at the Church of Mary Magdalene. It was a beautiful day. You wore my christening gown—a handmade heirloom. You looked so cute and were such a charmer.

Monsignor Dwyer was completely taken with you. During the baptism, you kept reaching for the service book and touching his hand. You were looking right at him, attentive as could be.

Towards the end of the service, after you hadn't missed a trick, Monsignor Dwyer said, 'I don't know *what* you're going to be when you grow up, Nicholas. On second thoughts—you *are* grown up!'

IT'S MY FIRST DAY back at work today. Not surprisingly, I miss you already. No, let me make that a little stronger: I'm bereft without you.

I wrote something as I sat thinking about you, between patients.

> *Nickels and dimes*
> *I love you in rhythms*
> *I love you in rhymes*
> *I love you in laughter*
> *Here and ever after*
> *Then I love you a million*
> *Gazillion more times!*

I think I could come up with dozens of Nicky nursery rhymes if I tried. They just come to me when you do something silly, or smile, or even when you sleep. What can I say? You inspire poetry.

Yikes, here comes one now!

> *You're my little Nicky Knack*
> *I love you so, you love me back.*
> *I love your toes, your knees, your nose,*
> *And everywhere a big kiss goes.*
> *I kiss you tons, and know what then?*
> *I have to kiss you once again.*

OK, little man, I have to go now. My next patient is here already. If she knew what I was doing behind closed doors in my office, the poor woman would flee to the free clinic in Edgartown.

I thought I'd ease into work with a half-day, just to get used to the routine again. But ever since I arrived this morning, all I wanted to do was look at your pictures and write silly poems.

Anyone peeking in at me would think I was in love.

I am.

NICKY, IT'S ME AGAIN—

I heard you crying tonight and got up to see what was the matter. You looked up at me with such sad little eyes.

I looked to see if you needed changing—but it wasn't that. Then I checked to see if you were hungry—but it wasn't that, either.

So I lifted you up and sat with you in the rocker next to your crib.

Back and forth we went, back and forth. Your eyes started closing, and your tears dissolved into sweet dreams. I placed you back in your crib and watched your little tummy rise and fall.

I think all you wanted was a little company. I'm here, sweetie. I'm right here, and I'm not going anywhere. I'll always be right here.

'What are you doing, Suzie?' Matt whispered. I hadn't heard him come into the nursery.

'Nick couldn't sleep.'

Matt looked into the crib and saw your tiny hand clenched to your mouth like a teething ring.

'He's beautiful,' Matt whispered.

I looked down at you. There wasn't an inch of you that didn't make my heart leap.

Matt put his arms around my waist. 'Want to dance, Mrs Harrison?' He hadn't called me that since our wedding day. My heart fluttered like a sparrow in a birdbath.

'I think they're playing our song.'

And to the notes that came out of your music box, Matt and I danced in your nursery. Past the stuffed animals, past your rocking horse, past the stars and the moon that float from your mobile. We danced slowly and lovingly in the low light of your tiny cocoon.

When the music finally wound down, Matt kissed me and said, 'Thank you for this night, this dance, and most of all for this little boy. My whole world is right here, in this room. If I never had another thing, I would have everything.'

And then strangely—magically—as if your music box had been merely taking a rest, it played one more sweet refrain.

NICK,

Melanie Bone came over to baby-sit while I went to work. Full day, full load. It feels strange to leave you for this long, and I can't stop thinking about what you're doing.

Something happened at the hospital today that made me think of your delivery.

A forty-one-year-old woman who was on vacation from New York was brought in. She was in her seventh month, and not doing well. Then all hell broke loose in the emergency room. She began to haemorrhage. The woman ended up losing her baby, and I had to try to console her. Just seeing that poor woman today made me realise more than ever how lucky we were.

Oh, Nicky, sometimes I wish I could hide you like a precious heirloom. But what is life if you don't live it? I think I know that as well as anyone.

There's a saying I remember from my grandmother: One today is worth two tomorrows.

DEAR SHOW-OFF,

You are starting to hold your own bottle. No one can believe it. This little guy feeding himself at two months. Every new experience that you have, I take as a gift.

Sometimes I can be such a goofball, reduced to gauzy visions of station wagons, suburbia and bronzed baby shoes. So I had to do it. I had to have your picture professionally taken.

Every mother has to do it once. Right?

Today is the perfect day. Daddy is off on a trip to New York, where someone has taken a liking to his poems. He's very low-key about it, but it's the greatest news. So the two of us are home alone.

I got you dressed in washed-out blue overalls (so cool), your little work boots (just like Daddy's), and a Red Sox baseball cap (with the peak bent just so).

When we got to the photography studio, you looked at me as if to say, *Surely you have made a grotesque mistake.*

Maybe I had.

The photographer was a fifty-year-old man with no kidside manner at all. I got the idea that his real speciality might be still life, because he tried to warm you up with a variety of fruits and vegetables.

Well, we now have a unique set of pictures. You begin with the surprised look, which quickly dissolves into a more annoyed attitude. After that you enter the cantankerous phase, which disintegrates into the angry portion of our programme. And last, but not least, irreconcilable meltdown.

Forgive me this one. I promise I will never show these pictures to new girlfriends, old fraternity brothers, or Grandma Jean. She'd have them in every shop window on the Vineyard before dusk.

NICKY,

It was a little cool out, but I bundled you up and we took a picnic basket down to Bend in the Road Beach—to celebrate Daddy's thirty-seventh birthday.

We made castles and sand angels and wrote your name in big bold letters until the surf came and washed it away. It was a blast to watch you and Daddy play together. You are very much a chip off the old block. You are both joyful, graceful and athletic, beautiful to watch.

So there you were, just back to our blanket from fighting sand monsters, when Matt reached into his pocket and pulled out a letter. He handed it to me.

'The publisher in New York didn't want my collection—yet—but here's a consolation prize.'

He had sent a poem off to a magazine called the *Atlantic Monthly*. They had accepted it. He didn't even tell me he was doing it.

I asked if I could read it, and Matt unfolded a separate sheet of paper. It was the poem. Tears welled up in my eyes when I saw the title, 'Nicholas and Suzanne'.

Matt told me that he had been writing down all the things I say and sing to you, my little poems and rock-a-bye rhymes. He said that this wasn't just his poem but mine, too. He told me that it was my voice he heard in these lines; so we had created it together.

Daddy read part of it out loud, above the crashing surf and screeching gulls.

> '*Who makes the treetops wave their hands?*
> *And draws home ships from foreign lands,*
> *And spins plain straw back into gold*
> *And has a love too large to hold . . .*
> *Who chases the rain from the sky?*
> *And sings the moon a lullaby,*
> *And grants the wishes from a well*
> *And hears whole songs sung from a shell . . .*
> *Who has the gift of making much?*
> *From everything they hold or touch,*
> *Who turns pure joy back into life?*
> *For this I thank my son, my wife.*'

What could be better than this?
Absolutely nothing.
Daddy said it was his best birthday ever.

NICHOLAS,

Something unexpected has happened, and I'm afraid it's not so good.

It was time again for your dreaded baby shots. Your paediatrician on the Vineyard was on vacation, so I decided to call a doctor friend in Boston. While I was there, I would get my own physical.

We took the ferry over to Woods Hole and hit Route 6 by nine in the morning. This was our first adventure off the island. Nicholas's Trip to the Big City!

Your appointment was first. Other babies were crying and fidgety, but you sat as quiet as a mouse, checking out your new surroundings.

'Nicholas Harrison,' the receptionist finally called. It was funny to hear your name announced so officially by a complete stranger.

It was good to see my old buddy Dan Anderson. 'You seem so happy, Suzanne,' he said as he measured, tapped and tuned you up. 'Leaving the city did you a world of good. And just look at this future quarterback you've got here.'

I beamed. 'He is the best little boy on earth.'

He handed you back over to me. 'It's wonderful seeing you again, Mother Bedford. And as far as this one goes, he's the poster child for good health.'

Of course, I already knew that.

NOW IT WAS MY TURN.

After the examination I sat on the edge of the examining room table, already dressed, waiting for Dr Phil Berman to come back in. Phil had been my doctor in Boston and had kept in touch with the specialist on Martha's Vineyard.

The physical had taken a little longer than usual. One of the nurses outside was watching over you, but I was anxious for a hug and also to hit the road back to the Vineyard. That's when Phil came in and asked me to step into his office.

We exchanged small talk for a minute or two. Then Phil got down to business. 'I noticed a few irregularities on your electrocardiogram. I took the liberty of calling downstairs to Dr Davis. I know Gail was your cardiologist when you were here as a patient. She's going to squeeze you in today.'

'Wait a minute, Phil,' I said. I was stunned. This had to be wrong. I was feeling fine—great, actually. 'That can't be right. Are you sure?'

'I know your history, and it would be remiss of me not to insist that Gail Davis take a look. It won't take long. We'll keep Nicholas here until you're done. Our pleasure.'

And then Phil continued, his tone changing slightly, 'Suzanne, it could be absolutely nothing, but I want a second opinion. You'd give the same advice to your own patients.'

It felt like déjà vu, walking through the halls, heading to Gail Davis's office. *Dear God, please don't let this happen again. Not now. Everything in my life is so good.*

I entered the waiting room as if I were in a bad dream. I couldn't focus or think.

A nurse walked right up to me. I knew her from the hospital visits after my heart attack. 'Suzanne, you can come with me now.'

I followed her like a prisoner about to be executed.

I WAS IN THERE for nearly two hours. I think I was given every cardiology test known. I was worried about you, even though I knew you were in good hands in Dr Berman's office.

When it was finally over, Gail Davis came in. She looked grave but Gail usually does, even at parties where I've seen her socially. I reminded myself of that, but it didn't really help.

'You have *not* had another heart attack, Suzanne. Let me put your mind at ease about that. But what I detect is some weakness in two of your valves. I suspect it was caused by the last cardiac infarction. Or possibly the pregnancy. Because the valves are damaged, your heart is having difficulty pumping blood. When you get back to Martha's Vineyard, there'll be more tests, then we can talk about your options. Valves may have to be replaced.'

Now I was having trouble catching my breath. I absolutely refused to cry in front of Gail. 'It's so strange,' I said. 'Everything can be going along just great, and then one day, *whack,* you're blindsided— a lousy, crummy blow you didn't see coming.'

Gail said nothing; she just put her hand gently on my back.

I WATCHED YOU in the rearview mirror on the way home, your little feet kicking up and down, your arms reaching towards me. The world swept past us on both sides.

I talked to you, Nicky, really talked.

'My life feels so connected to you. It seems impossible that something bad could happen now. But I guess that's the false sense of security that love gives.'

I thought about that for a second. Falling in love with Matt, and being so much in love with him now, *had* given me a feeling of security. How could anything harm us? How could I not see you grow up? That would be too cruel for God to let happen.

The tears I had held back in Dr Davis's office suddenly flooded my eyes. I quickly wiped them away. I concentrated on the road home, and kept our journey at my usual slow and steady pace.

I talked to you again in the rearview mirror. 'So let's make a plan. All right, baby boy? Every time I can make you smile means that we have one more year together. Magical thinking, Nicky, that's what this is. Already we have a dozen more years together, because you've smiled at least that many times on this car ride. At this rate, I'll be a hundred and thirty-six, you a spry eighty-two.'

Suddenly, you broke into the biggest smile I have ever seen you make. You made me laugh so hard, I just looked back at you and whispered, 'Nicholas, Suzanne and Matt—Forever One.'

That is my prayer.

NICHOLAS,

Four long, nervous weeks have passed since I received the troubling news in Boston. Matt is out with you riding in the Jeep, and I'm sitting in the kitchen with the sun falling through the window like yellow streamers in a parade. It is so beautiful.

The medical opinions are all in. I have heart-valve disease, but it is treatable. For the moment, we won't be replacing the valves.

I have been warned, though: *Life doesn't go on for ever. Enjoy every moment of it.*

I can smell the morning unfolding, carrying with it the salt and grassy perfume of the marshes. My eyes are closed, and the wind chimes are being tickled by the ocean breeze outside the window.

'Isn't it lucky?' I finally say out loud. 'That I'm sitting here, looking out on this beautiful day . . . That I live on Martha's Vineyard, so close to the ocean that I could throw a stone into the surf . . . That I am a doctor and love what I do . . . That somehow, however improbable, I found Matthew Harrison and we fell wildly in love . . . That we have a little boy, with the most wonderful smile, and the nicest disposition, and a baby smell I love. Isn't it lucky, Nicky? Isn't it just so lucky?'

That's what I think, anyway.

That's another of my prayers.

YOU ARE GROWING UP before our eyes, and it is such a glorious thing to watch. I savour each moment. I hope all the other mommies and daddies are remembering to savour these moments.

You love to ride bikes with Mommy. You have your own little Boston Bruins helmet and a seat that holds you safely on the back of my bike. I tie a water bottle with a ribbon and attach it to your seat for you to enjoy on the ride—and we're off.

You love singing, and looking at all the people and sights on the Vineyard. Fun for Mama, too.

You have a lot of the blondest of blond curls. I know that if I cut them, they'll be gone for ever. You'll be a little boy then, no longer a baby.

I love watching you grow, but at the same time I don't like seeing this time fly by so fast. I want to hold on to every moment, every smile, every hug and kiss. I suppose it has to do with loving to be needed and needing to give love.

I want to relive this all over again.

Every single moment since you were born.

I told you I would be a great mom.

EACH DAY LATELY has felt so complete for me.

Every morning, without fail, Matt turns to me before we get up. He kisses me, and then whispers in my ear, 'We have today, Suzanne. Let's get up and see our boy.'

But today feels a little different to me. I'm not exactly sure why, but my intuition tells me there's something going on. I don't know if I like it. I'm not quite sure yet.

After Daddy goes off to work and I have you fed and dressed, I still don't feel right. I am light-headed, and more tired than usual.

So tired, in fact, I have to lie down.

I must have fallen asleep after I tucked you into your crib, because when I opened my eyes again, the church bells from the town were striking. It was noon already. Half the day was gone.

That's when I decided to find out what was going on.

And now, I know.

NICHOLAS,

After Daddy put you to bed tonight, the two of us sat out on the porch and watched the sun set on the ocean in a blaze of streaking oranges and reds. He was stroking my arms and legs, which I love more than almost anything on the planet. I could let him do this for hours, and sometimes I do.

He is very excited about his poetry lately. His great dream is to have a collection published, and suddenly people are interested. I love the excitement in his voice, and I let him talk.

'Matthew, something happened today,' I finally said once he had told me all his news.

He turned on the couch and sat up straight. His eyes were full of worry, his brow creased.

'I'm sorry, I'm sorry.' I soothed him. 'Something good happened today.'

I could feel Matt relax in my arms. 'So what happened, Suzanne? Tell me all about your day.'

The nice thing is that your daddy listens, and even asks questions. Some men don't.

'Well, on Wednesdays I don't go to work unless there's an emergency. There wasn't any today so I stayed home with Nick.'

Matt put his head in my lap and let me stroke his thick, sandy brown hair. 'That sounds pretty nice. Maybe I'll start taking Wednesdays off, too,' he teased.

'Isn't it lucky?' I said, 'that I get to spend Wednesdays with Nicky?'

Matt pulled my face to his and we kissed. I don't know how long this incredible honeymoon of ours is going to last, but I love it. Matthew is the best friend I could have ever wished for. Any woman would be lucky to have him. And if it ever came to that—another mommy for you—I'm sure Matt would choose wisely.

'Is that what happened? You and Nick had a great day together?' he asked.

I looked deeply into Matt's eyes. 'I'm pregnant,' I told him.

And then Matt did just the right thing. He kissed me gently. 'I love you,' he whispered. 'Let's be careful, Suzanne.'

'OK,' I whispered back. 'I'll be very careful.'

NICHOLAS,

I don't know why, but life is usually more complicated than the plans that we make. I visited my cardiologist on the Vineyard, told him about the pregnancy, had a few tests. Then, on his recommendation, I went to Boston to see Dr Davis again.

I hadn't mentioned the checkup to Matt, thinking it might worry him. So I went to work for a few hours, then I drove to Boston in the afternoon. I promised myself that I would talk to Matt as soon as I got home.

The porch light of the house was on when I pulled into the driveway at about seven that night. Matt was already home. He had relieved Grandma Jean of her baby-sitting duties.

I could smell the delicious aroma of home cooking: chicken, pan potatoes and gravy warming the whole house. He's made dinner, I thought.

'Where's Nicky?' I asked as I entered the kitchen.

'I put him to bed. He was exhausted. Long day for you, sweets. You're being careful?'

'Yeah,' I said, kissing him on the cheek. 'I actually only saw a couple of patients this morning. I had to go to Boston and see Dr Davis.'

Matt stopped stirring the gravy. He looked hurt.

'I should have told you, Matthew. I didn't want to worry you. I knew you'd want to come with me.'

It was a nervous, run-on thought, my attempt to explain what I had done.

'Well?' he said. 'What did Dr Davis have to say?'

'I told her about the baby.'

'Right.'

'And she was . . . she was very concerned.' The next few words locked in my throat. I almost couldn't speak. Tears flooded my eyes. 'She said it was too risky for me to be pregnant. She said I shouldn't have this baby.'

Matt's eyes filled with tears now, too. He took a breath. Then he spoke. 'Suzanne, I agree with her. I couldn't bear to risk losing you.'

I was crying, sobbing terribly. 'Don't give up on this baby, Matt.'

I looked at him, waiting for some comforting words. But he was quiet. He finally shook his head slowly. 'I'm sorry, Suzanne.'

Suddenly I needed to breathe some fresh air. I left the house in a spin. I ran through the sea grass until I reached the beach, lay down in the sand and wept. I felt so sad for the baby inside me. I thought about Matt and you waiting for me back at the house. Was I being selfish, headstrong, foolish? I was a doctor. I knew the risks.

I held myself and rocked for what seemed like hours. I talked to the little baby growing inside me. Then I looked up at the full moon, and I knew it was time to go back to the house.

Matt was waiting for me in the kitchen as I trudged up from the beach. I did a strange thing, then, and I'm not exactly sure why. I knocked on the door, then knelt on the first step. Maybe I was drained from the stressful day. Maybe it was something else, something more important, something I still can't explain.

Maybe I was remembering the English king who had knelt in the snow hoping not to be excommunicated, and to be forgiven by Pope Gregory.

I had been hurting badly out on the beach, but I also knew I had acted selfishly. I shouldn't have run away and left you and Matt alone at the house.

'Forgive me for running off like that,' I said as Matt opened the screen door. 'For running away from you. I should have stayed and talked it out.'

'You know better,' he whispered. 'There's nothing to forgive, Suzanne.' Matt pulled me to my feet and into his arms. I let his warmth seep into me.

'It's just that I want to keep this baby. Is that so terrible?'

'No, Suzanne. That isn't terrible. It's losing you that I couldn't bear. If I lost you, I don't think I could live. I love you so much. I love you and Nicky.'

OH, NICKY,

Life can be unforgiving sometimes. Learn that lesson, sweet boy. I had just got home from a couple of hours at the office. Routine, really. Nothing unusual, nothing stressful. Actually, I was feeling pretty chipper.

I had driven back to the cottage to take a cat nap before seeing one more patient in the afternoon. You were at Grandma's house for the day. Matt had a job over in East Chop.

I fell onto the day bed, feeling dizzy suddenly. My heart began to pound a little. Strange.

Easy, Suzanne, I told myself. *Lie down and close your eyes and tell every part of your body to relax.*

All you need is an hour, a break, and when you wake up, it will all feel better. Just fall asleep, fall asleep now, fall . . .

'SUZANNE, what's the matter?'

I turned over on the day bed at the sound of Matt's gentle whisper. He looked concerned. 'Suzanne? Can you talk, sweetheart?'

'Seeing Connie tomorrow,' I said. It took all my strength just to get those few words out.

'You're seeing Connie right now,' Matt said.

When we arrived at Connie's office, she took one look at me and said, 'No offence, but you look less than stellar, Suzanne.'

Following my examination, she sat down with Matt and me. She didn't look happy. 'Your blood pressure is up, but it will be a day or so before we get your blood work back. I'll put a rush on it. In some ways things are steady, but I don't like how you were feeling today. Or how you *look*. I'm inches away from admitting you. I agree with Dr Davis about the abortion. It's your decision, but you're putting yourself at risk.'

'Connie,' I said, 'short of stopping my practice I'm doing everything right. I'm being so careful.'

'Then stop working,' she said without missing a beat. 'I'm not kidding, Suzanne. If you go home and rest, then we have a chance. Otherwise, I'm checking you in.'

'I'm going home now,' I mumbled. 'I can't give up on this baby.'

DEAR NICHOLAS,

I am so sorry, sweetie. A month has passed and you have kept me busy. I am also tired, and I haven't had a chance to write. I'll try to make it up to you.

At eleven months, your favourite words are Dada, Mama, wow, boat, ball, water (wa), car, and your very favourite is LIGHT. You are crazy about lights. You say, 'Yight.'

You are like a wind-up toy these days. You just keep going and going and going.

I was in the middle of giving you my 'be a good boy' rap when the phone rang. It was Connie Cotter's nurse, who put me on hold for the doctor.

'Suzanne?'

'Yeah, I'm here, Connie. Taking it easy at home.'

'Listen, we got your recent blood test back . . .'

Oh, that awful doctor's pause. I know it only too well.

'And . . . I'm not happy. I want to check you in right away. Start you on fluids. How soon can you get here?'

The words roared through my head. I had to sit down immediately. 'I don't know, Connie. I'm here with Nicky. Matt's at work.'

'Unacceptable, Suzanne. You could be in trouble, sweetie. I'll call Jean if you won't.'

'No, no. I'll call her. I'll do it right now.'

I hung up, and you held on to my hand like a strong little soldier—you must have learned it from your daddy.

I remember tucking you into your crib and pulling the cord on your music box. 'Whistle a Happy Tune' began to play. I remember turning on your nightlight and closing the curtains. I remember that I was on my way downstairs to call Grandma Jean, then Matt.

That's all I remember.

MATT FOUND ME lying as limp as a rag doll at the bottom of the stairs. I had a deep gash alongside my nose. He called Grandma Jean and rushed me to the ER.

From there, I was transferred to the critical care unit. I awoke to a whir of activity around my bed. I cried out for Matt, and both he and Connie were at my side in seconds.

Matt was the first to speak. 'You passed out at the house.'

'Is the baby OK? Connie, my baby?'

'We have an OK heart rate, Suzanne, but *your* pressure is off the charts, your proteins are skyrocketing and . . .'

'And what?' I asked.

'And you have toxaemia. That could be why you passed out.'

I knew what this meant, of course. My blood was poisoning both the baby and me. I thought I could actually feel the toxic blood swelling up inside me as if I were a dam about to break.

Then I heard Matt being ordered out of the room, and an emergency team rushing in. I could feel the oxygen mask covering my nose and mouth.

I knew what was happening to me. I knew I was shutting down. I knew so much more than I wanted to. I was scared. I was falling into a dark tunnel. The passing black walls were narrowing and squeezing the breath out of me.

I was dying.

MATT SITS VIGIL by my bedside, day and night. He is the best husband, the best friend, a girl ever had.

Connie visits three or four times a day. I never knew what a great doctor she is, and a great friend.

I hear her, and I hear Daddy. I just can't respond to either of them. I'm not sure why. From what I can tell listening to them, I know that I've lost the baby. If I could cry, I would weep for all eternity. If I could scream, I would. I can do neither.

Grandma Jean comes and sits with me. So do friends of mine from around the Vineyard.

'If it's OK, I'm going to bring Nicky in this afternoon,' I hear Daddy say to Connie. 'He misses his mother. I think it's important he sees her.' And then Matt says, 'Even if it's for the last time. I think I should call Monsignor Dwyer.'

Matt brings you to my hospital room, Nicholas. And then you and Daddy sit by my bedside, telling me stories, saying goodbye. I hear Matt's voice cracking, and I'm worried about him.

I just hold on. I think I'm still here. What other explanation can there be? How could I possibly hear your laughter, Nicky? Or you calling out 'Mama' to me, in the black hole of my sleep?

But I do.

Your sweet little voice reaches down into this dark place where I'm trapped. It is as if you and Daddy were calling me out of a strange dream, your voices guiding me.

I struggle upward, reaching towards the sound of your voices.

I need to see you and Daddy one more time . . .

I need to talk to you one more time . . .

I feel a dark tunnel closing behind me, and I think that maybe I've found my way out of this lonely place. Everything is getting brighter. There is no more darkness surrounding me, just rays of warmth, and the welcoming light of Martha's Vineyard.

That's when the unexpected happens.

I open my eyes.

'Hello, Suzanne,' Matt whispers. 'Thank God, you came back to us.'

Katie

There was only so much of the diary that Katie could take at any given time. Matt had warned her in his note: *there will be parts that may be hard for you to read.* Not just hard, Katie knew now, but overwhelming.

It was difficult for her to imagine right now, but there *were* happy endings in life.

There were normal, sane couples like Lynn and Phil Brown, who lived in Westport, Connecticut, on a farm with their four kids, two dogs and a rabbit and who were still in love, as far as she could tell.

The next day Katie called Lynn Brown and volunteered to sit for the kids that night. She needed the comfort of a family around her.

Lynn was immediately suspicious. 'Katie, what's this all about? What's going on?'

'Nothing, I just miss you guys.'

She took the train to Westport and was at Lynn and Phil's by seven.

The Brown kids—Ashby, Tory, Kelsey and Roscoe—were eight, five, three and one. They loved Katie, loved her long braid, loved that she was so tall.

So off went Lynn and Phil on their hot 'date', and Katie took the kids. What a great Friday night it turned out to be. The Browns had a small guest house where Katie always went to hang out with the kids. She took their pictures with her Canon camera. They washed Lynn's car. Went on a group bike ride. Watched the movie *Chicken Run*. Ate an 'everything' pizza.

When Lynn and Phil got home about eleven, they found Katie and the kids asleep on pillows and quilts thrown all over the guest-house floor.

She was actually awake and heard Lynn whisper to Phil, 'She's so cool. She'll be a great mom.' It brought tears to Katie's eyes, and she had to choke back a sob as she pretended to be asleep.

She finally took the train back to New York on Saturday afternoon. Before she left, she told Lynn that she was pregnant. She was exhausted, but she also felt alive again. She had hope. She knew there were some happy endings in life. She believed in families.

About halfway into the trip, Katie reached down into her bag and pulled out the diary.

SHE GOT OFF the train from Westport at the gorgeously renovated and restored Grand Central Station, and she needed to walk. It was a little past seven thirty and Manhattan was filled with traffic, most of it honking taxis or cars returning from weekend and vacation homes, the drivers already on edge.

She was on edge, too. The diary was doing that to her more and more.

Immersing herself in someone else's reality had made Katie re-examine things that she had been doing on autopilot for the past nine years. She'd got her job at twenty-two, fresh out of the honour programme at the University of North Carolina. She had been lucky enough to intern for two summers at Algonquin Press in Chapel Hill, which had opened doors for her in Manhattan. She had settled into New York City with the best of intentions, yet she never felt that she truly fitted.

Now she thought that she knew why. Her life had been out of balance for such a long time. She had spent so many late nights at work editing manuscripts, trying to make them as good as they could be. Rewarding work, but work was a rubber ball, right?

Family, health, friends and integrity were the precious glass ones.

The baby she was carrying was a glass ball for sure.

THE FOLLOWING MORNING she was in a yellow cab with two of her best friends, Susan Kingsolver and Laurie Raleigh. She was going to see her gynaecologist, Dr Albert K. Sassoon, in the East Seventies.

Susan and Laurie knew about the pregnancy and had insisted on coming along. Each of them held one of Katie's hands.

'You feel OK, sweetie?' Susan asked. She was a grade-school teacher on the Lower East Side. They had all met one summer in the Hamptons, and had been best buddies ever since.

'I'm OK. Sure. I just can't believe what's happened, that I'm going to see Sassoon right now.'

As she got out of the taxi, Katie found that she was blankly staring at familiar storefronts. Everything was a blur, even though Susan and Laurie were chatting amiably, keeping her up.

'Whatever you decide,' Laurie whispered as Katie was called into Dr Sassoon's examination room, 'it will work out great.'

Whatever she decided.

She just couldn't believe this was happening.

Albert Sassoon was smiling, and that made Katie think of Suzanne and her kindly way with patients.

'So,' Dr Sassoon said as Katie lay down.

'So. I was so much in love I stopped using my birth control. I guess I got knocked up,' Katie said, and laughed. Then she was crying, and Albert tenderly held her hand.

'I think I know what I'm going to do,' Katie sobbed. 'I think . . . I'm going . . . to keep . . . my baby.'

'That's great, Katie,' Dr Sassoon said, and patted her back gently. 'You'll be a wonderful mother.'

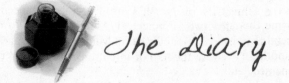

The Diary

Nicholas,

Today I came home from the hospital, and it's a thrill to be here again. To be anywhere, actually.

Life is such a miracle, a series of small miracles. It really is, if you learn how to look at it with the right perspective.

I love our little cottage on Beach Road. More than ever, Nicky. I appreciate it more, every crevice and crease.

Matt laid out a picnic in the sunroom on a red and white chequered blanket. A salad niçoise, fresh twelve-grain bread. Fabulous. After lunch he held my hand and I held yours.

Nicholas, Suzanne and Matt.

Happiness is this simple.

NICK, YOU LITTLE SCAMP,

Every moment with you fills me with incredible such wonder and happiness.

I took you into the Atlantic Ocean for the first time yesterday. It was the first day of July. The water was beautiful, with very small waves. Just your size. Even better was the sand, your own private sandbox.

Big smiles from you. And from me, of course. Mommy see, Mommy do!

When we got home, I showed you a picture of two-year-old Bailey Mae Bone, our neighbour. You started to smile, and then you puckered your lips. You're going to be a killer with the ladies.

You have good taste—for a guy. You love to look at pretty things—trees, the ocean, light sources, of course.

You also like to tickle the ivories on our piano, which is so cute.

And you love to *clean*. You push around a toy vacuum cleaner and wipe up messes with paper towels. Maybe I can take advantage of that when you're a little older.

You are such a joy. I treasure and hold close to my heart every giggle, every laugh, every needy cry.

'WAKE UP, BEAUTIFUL. I love you even more today than I did yesterday.'

Matt wakes me this same way every morning since I got home from the hospital. Even if I'm still half asleep, I don't mind being woken by his soothing voice and those words.

The weeks passed, and I was getting my strength back. I began taking long walks on the beach in front of the cottage. I even saw a few patients.

Matt was hovering over my bed again one morning. He was holding you, and smiling down on me. You both were grinning. I smelt a conspiracy.

'It's official! The three-day-long Harrison family weekend has begun. Wake up, beautiful. I love you! We're already late for today, though!'

'What?' I said.

'Down, pup,' Matt said, putting you on my bed, beside me. 'Pack your bags. I booked us into the Hob Knob Inn in Edgartown. King-size beds, full country breakfast and afternoon tea. You won't have to lift a finger. Sound good?'

It sounded wonderful, exactly what I needed.

THIS IS A LOVE STORY, Nicholas. Mine, yours, Daddy's! It's about how good it can be if you find the right person. It's about treasuring every moment with that special one. Every single millisecond.

Our three-day adventure began at the Flying Horses Carousel, where we mounted the enchanted horses and circled the high hills of Oak Bluffs, just like old times. What a rush!

We visited the beaches that we had been away from for as long. Lobsterville Beach, Quansoo, Hancock—and my very favourite, Bend in the Road Beach.

We took a carriage ride at Scrubby Neck Farm, and you fed carrots to the horses and laughed so hard that I was afraid you might get sick.

We ate at all the nicest restaurants, too. The Red Cat, the Sweet Life Café, L'Etoile. You looked like such a big boy in your high chair, sitting with us, so grown up, smiling in the candlelight.

Not far from where we were staying, there was a craft store called Splatter. We made our own cups and saucers. You painted your plate, Nickels, drawing little splotches we took to be me and Daddy, and yourself, in bright blues and yellows.

And then it was time to go home.

Nicky, do you remember any of this?

I noticed cars parked helter-skelter all along Beach Road as we turned the last curve to our house. Several more cars and trucks were leading up to the driveway, but the driveway was no longer there.

Instead, a new addition was in its place, and a new driveway lay on the far side of the addition.

'What,' I asked Matt, shocked, 'is all this?'

'A little extension, Suzanne. It's your new home office. Now you can make fewer house calls, or *no* house calls.'

Dozens of our friends and Matt's pals were on the lawn, applauding as we climbed out of the car. I was speechless.

'This is too much,' I finally said as I hugged him tight.

'No,' he whispered back, 'it isn't nearly enough, Suzanne. I'm just so happy to have you home.'

NICHOLAS, SWEET NICHOLAS,

Time is really flying. Tomorrow, you will be one! Isn't that just something?

What can I say, except that it is a godsend to watch you grow up, to see your first tooth, watch you take your first step, make a half sentence, develop your personality day by day.

This morning you were playing with Daddy's big, bad work boots that he keeps at the bottom of the closet; when you came out, you were standing in them. You started to laugh. Then I was laughing, and Daddy came in, and he started laughing, too.

Nicholas, Suzanne and Matt! What a trio.

We're going to celebrate your first twelve months tomorrow. I have your gifts all picked out. One of them is the pictures from our vacation. I'm having them framed. I won't tell you which picture I like best; that'll be a surprise. But I will tell you that it will be in a silver frame with carved moons, stars and angels. Just your style.

NICHOLAS,

It's late, and Daddy and I are being silly geese. It's a little past midnight, so it's officially your birthday. Hooray! Congratulations, you!

We couldn't resist, so we sneaked into your room. Daddy brought along one of your birthday presents, a bright red Corvette convertible. He placed it carefully at the foot of your crib.

Matthew and I hugged each other as we watched you sleep, which is one of the greatest pleasures in the world—don't miss watching your child sleep.

Then I got a little playful, and I pulled the cord on your music box. It played 'Whistle a Happy Tune'.

Matt and I held each other and swayed to the music. I think we could have stayed there all night. Holding each other, watching you sleep, dancing to your music-box tune.

'Isn't it lucky?' I whispered to Matt. 'Isn't this the best thing that could ever happen to anyone?'

'It is, Suzanne. It's so simple, but it's so right.'

Finally, Daddy and I went to bed, and experienced the second best thing. Matt eventually fell asleep in my arms—guys do that if they really like you—and I got up to write this little note to you.

Love you, sweetie. See you in the morning. I can't wait.

Hello, my sweet Nicholas, it's Dada.

Have I told you how much I love you? Have I told you how precious you are to me? There—now I have. You are the best little boy, the best anyone could ever hope for. I love you so much.

Yesterday morning something happened. And that's why *I'm* writing to you today instead of Mommy.

I am compelled to write this. I don't know anything for sure right now, except that I have to get this out. I have to talk to you.

Fathers and sons need to talk more than they do. I always want to be able to tell you what I'm feeling.

Like right now.

But this is so hard, Nicky.

It's the hardest thing I have ever had to say to anybody.

Mommy was going to the store to pick up your birthday present, your beautiful framed pictures. She was incredibly happy. She was dressed in a yellow jumper and white blouse. Her blonde hair was full of curls and swung with her body as she walked. She was humming your song, 'Whistle a Happy Tune'.

I should have kissed Suzanne goodbye, should have hugged her. But I just called, 'Love you,' and, since her hands were full, she blew me a kiss.

I keep seeing Suzanne blowing me that kiss. I see her looking back, giving me her famous wink.

Oh, Nicky, Nicky. How can I write these words?

Mommy had a heart attack on the way into town, sweet baby. Her heart, which was so big, so special in so many ways, could no longer hold out.

I can't imagine that it really happened; I can't get it into my head. I was told that Suzanne was unconscious before she crashed into the guardrail on Old Pond Bridge Road. Her Jeep dropped into the water, landing on its side.

Dr Cotter says that Suzanne died instantly after the massive coronary, but who really knows about those final seconds? I hope she didn't feel any pain. I hate to think that she did. It would be too cruel.

She was unimaginably happy the last time I saw her. She looked so pretty, Nick. Oh God, I just want to see Suzanne one more time. Is that too much to ask? It doesn't seem so to me.

I loved Suzanne so much. She was the most generous-hearted person I have ever known, the most caring and compassionate. Maybe what I loved best about her was that she was a great listener. And she was funny. She would make a joke, right now. I know she would. And maybe she is. Are you smiling now, Suzanne? I'd like to think that you are.

I went today to the cemetery on Abel's Hill, to choose Mommy's special place. She was just thirty-seven when she died. What a shame; what a waste. Sometimes, it makes me so angry—and I get this irrational urge to break glass.

Tonight, I sit in your nursery and watch your clown lamp throw happy shadows against the walls. The oak rocking horse I made for you reminds me of the Flying Horses Carousel. Remember when we all went there and rode the colourful horses?

I held you in front of me, and you loved to stroke the real horse-hair mane. I can see Mommy riding ahead of us. She turns—and there's that wink of hers.

Oh, Nick, I wish I could turn back time to last week, or last month, or last year. I can't bear to face tomorrow.

I wish this had a happy ending.

I wish I could say just one more time: *Isn't it lucky?*

Dear, sweet Nick,

There is one image that keeps coming back to me about Suzanne. It captures who she was, and what was so special and unique about her.

She is kneeling on our front porch. She wants my forgiveness, even though there is nothing to forgive. If anything, I should have been seeking *her* forgiveness. She had been given some sad news that day but could only think about how she might have hurt *me*. Suzanne always thought about other people first, but especially about the two of us. God, did she spoil us, Nicholas.

I was startled out of my thoughts and reveries this afternoon by an unexpected phone call.

It was for Mommy.

Obviously someone had no idea what had happened, and, for the first time, those strange and awful words passed through my lips like heavy weights: 'Suzanne has passed away.'

There was a long silence on the other end, followed by quiet apologies, then nervous condolences. It was the man from the frame shop on the other side of the island. Mommy had never made it there, and the pictures she had framed for you were still at the store.

I told the shop owner that I would come around for the photos. Somehow I would manage to do it. I feel so out of it all the time. I have a hollow feeling inside me, and it seems I could crumble like old tissue paper and blow away. At other times, there is a stone column inside my chest.

I never used to be able to cry, but now I cry all the time. I keep thinking that I'll run out of tears, but I don't. I used to think it wasn't manly to cry, but now I know that isn't so.

I walk aimlessly from room to room, trying desperately to find a place where I can feel at peace. I always end up back in your room, sitting in the same rocker Mommy so often did when she talked and read to you.

And so I sit here now, looking at the pictures of us I finally picked up this afternoon.

We are all sitting in front of the Flying Horses Carousel on a perfect, blue-skied afternoon.

You are wedged between us, Nick. Mommy has her arm around you and her legs crossed on mine. You're kissing Mommy, and I'm tickling you, and everyone is laughing.

Nicholas, Suzanne and Matt—Forever One.

IT'S TIME TO TELL you a story, Nick. Actually, it is the saddest story that I've ever heard, certainly the saddest one I've told.

I'm finding it hard to breathe right now. I'm shaking like a leaf.

Years ago, when I was just eight, my father died very suddenly while he was at work. We didn't expect it, so we never got to say goodbye. For years my father's death has haunted me. I've been so afraid of losing someone like that again. I think it's why I didn't get married earlier, before I met Suzanne. I was afraid, Nicky. Big, strong Daddy was so terribly afraid he might lose someone he loved. That's a secret I never told anyone before I met your mother. And now I've told it to you.

I pull the cord on your music box in your crib, and it begins to play 'Whistle a Happy Tune'. I love this song, Nicky. It makes me cry, but I don't care. I love your music and I want to hear it again.

I reach into the crib and touch your sweet cheek.

I tussle your golden hair, always so soft and fragrant.

I do a nose to nose, gently touching my nose to yours, and you smile gloriously.

I place an index finger in each of your small hands and let you squeeze. You're strong, buddy.

'Whistle a Happy Tune' continues to play.

Oh my dear little boy, my darling baby.

The music plays, but you aren't in your crib.

I remember Mommy leaving on her errand that morning. I called out, 'I love you,' and she blew me a kiss. Her arms were full, because she was carrying *you*. She wanted you to be the first to see the framed photographs on your birthday morning.

Suzanne carried you outside and carefully strapped you in your car seat. You were in the Jeep with Mommy when she crashed on Old Pond Bridge Road.

I should have been there, Nicholas. I should have been there with you and Mommy! Maybe I could have saved you somehow. At least I could have tried.

Oh, my dear little boy, my innocent little sweetheart, my baby son for ever. I miss you so much, and it destroys me that you will never hear how much your daddy loves you.

But isn't it lucky that I held you and loved you for the twelve months before God took you away?

Isn't it lucky that I got to know you, sweet little boy, my darling, darling son?

Katie

Katie slowly raised her face towards the bathroom ceiling and shut her eyes as tight as she could. A soft moan rose from her throat. Tears squeezed from under her eyelids and rolled down both cheeks. Her chest was heaving. She wrapped both arms around herself.

Merlin was in the doorway, whining, and Katie whispered, 'It's OK, boy.'

A column of pain rose inside her like a hot poker cutting into her lungs. *Oh God, why would you let something like that happen?*

Finally, she opened her eyes again. She could barely see through her tears. There was an envelope taped inside the diary on the very last page.

It said, simply, *Katie.*

She wiped away her tears with both hands. She took a deep, calming breath. And another. She opened the plain envelope that was addressed to her. The letter inside was in Matt's handwriting. Her fingers trembled as she unfolded it. The tears started again as she began to read.

Katie, dear Katie,

Now you know what I haven't been able to tell you all these months. You know my secrets. I wanted to tell you, almost since the day that we met. I have been grieving for such a long time, and I couldn't be comforted. So I kept my past from you. You, of all people. There are words from a poem about the local fishing boats and their crews that have been carved into the bar of Docks Tavern on the Vineyard. 'The longed-for ships / Come empty home or founder on the deep / And eyes first lose their tears and then their sleep.' I saw the words one night at Docks, when I couldn't cry any more, and couldn't sleep, and I was almost crushed by the awful truth in them.

Matt

That was all that he wrote, but Katie needed more.
She had to find Matt.

SHE'D ALWAYS BEEN a fighter. She'd always had the courage to do what she had to do.

Katie took the shuttle to Boston first thing in the morning. At Logan Airport, she was met by a car service that took her to the Steamship Authority terminal in Woods Hole. She bought her ticket and got on a two-decker ferry to Martha's Vineyard.

She had to talk to Matt. He needed to know about the baby.

During the forty-five-minute ride, she thought of Suzanne, and *her* arrival on the Vineyard. She remembered the last words Suzanne had written to Nicholas: *See you in the morning. I can't wait.*

Katie realised she hadn't brought a manuscript to read on the trip. Work is a rubber ball, she thought. Look what she would have missed if she had brought along paperwork: the rhythmic chop of the waves against the ferry's bow; the island getting closer and closer.

Matt was a glass ball. He had been scuffed, marked, damaged, but maybe he hadn't been shattered. Or maybe he had been.

The mystery would never be solved unless she found him.

As the ferry got closer and closer to the Vineyard, Katie could see the small town of Oak Bluffs. Her eyes searched the town—looking for Matt. She didn't see him anywhere. Of course Matt wasn't waiting there. He didn't know she was coming, and even if he had, he might not have come.

Katie spotted Docks Tavern as she started towards a taxi stand. Her heart skipped a beat. She walked towards the bar instead of searching for a cab.

Was Matt in there? Probably not, but Docks was where Matt had read the lines that he had included in his note in the diary.

It was dark inside, a little smoky, pleasant enough though. About a dozen patrons were at the bar, and several more were seated in the weathered wooden booths on either side. Most of them looked up at her as she entered.

'I come in peace,' Katie said, and smiled nervously.

Her eyes roamed slowly over the faces. She didn't see Matt.

She went looking for the poem carved into the bar. It took her a few minutes to find it at the far end, near a dartboard and a public phone. She read the words again:

> *The longed-for ships.*
> *Come empty home or founder on the deep.*
> *And eyes first lose their tears and then their sleep.*

'Help you with something? Or is your interest wholly literary?'

She looked up at the sound of the male voice. She saw a bartender, mid-thirties, red-bearded, ruggedly good-looking. Maybe a sailor himself.

'I'm just looking for someone. A friend. I think he comes in here,' she said.

'He has good taste in taverns, anyway. Does he have a name?'

She took a deep breath and tried to keep the tremor out of her voice. 'Matt Harrison,' she said.

The bartender nodded, but his dark brown eyes narrowed. 'Matt comes in here for dinner sometimes. He paints houses on the island. You say you're a friend of his?'

'He also writes poetry,' Katie said, feeling a little defensive now.

The red-bearded man shrugged. 'Not that I know of. At any rate, Matt's not here today. As you can see for yourself.' He finally smiled at her. 'So what will it be? You look like a Diet Coke to me.'

'No, nothing, thanks. Could you tell me how to get to his place? I'm a friend of his. I'm his editor. I have the address.'

The bartender thought about it, and then he tore off a sheet of his order pad. 'You driving?' he asked, as he began to write directions.

'I'll probably take a cab.'

'They'll know the place,' the man said, but didn't elaborate. 'Everybody knows Matt Harrison.'

KATIE SLOWLY CLIMBED into a rusted, sky-blue cab at the ferry terminal. Suddenly she was feeling tired. She said to the driver, 'I'd like to go to the Abel's Hill Cemetery. Do you know it?'

By way of an answer, the cab driver pulled away from the kerb. She guessed he knew where everything was on the island. She hadn't meant to offend him.

Abel's Hill was a good twenty minutes away, a small, picturesque place that looked at least as old as any of the houses they had passed on the way.

'I won't be too long,' she said to the driver as she struggled out of the back seat. 'Please wait for me.'

'I'll wait, but I have to keep the meter running.'

'That's fine. I understand,' she told him. 'I'm from New York City. I'm used to it.'

The cab waited while she slowly walked from row to row in Abel's Hill, checking all the headstones, but especially the newer ones.

Her chest felt tight and there was a lump in her throat as she searched for the grave. She felt as if she were intruding.

Finally, she found it. She saw the carved lettering on a stone set on a hill: SUZANNE BEDFORD HARRISON.

Her heart clutched and she felt dizzy. She bent and went down on one knee.

'I had to come, Suzanne,' she whispered. 'I feel as if I know you so well by now. I'm Katie Wilkinson.'

Her eyes travelled across the inscription. COUNTRY DOCTOR, MUCH LOVED WIFE OF MATTHEW, PERFECT MOTHER OF NICHOLAS.

Katie offered up a prayer, one that her father had taught her when she was only three or four. Then she turned to the smaller stone right beside Suzanne's. She sucked in a breath.

NICHOLAS HARRISON, A REAL BOY, CHERISHED SON OF SUZANNE AND MATTHEW.

'Hello, sweet baby. Hello, Nicholas. My name is Katie.'

She began to sob uncontrollably then. Her whole body shook like a weeping willow in a storm. She mourned for poor baby Nicholas. She couldn't begin to understand how Matt had survived this.

There were daisies and gladioli at both of the graves. Someone had been there recently. And then Katie noticed something else, the date that was carved into the two headstones: JULY 18, 1999.

She felt a shiver vibrate through her, and her knees were weak again. July 18 was two years to the day before the party she'd had planned for Matt on her terrace in New York, the night she'd given him the copy of his book of poems. No wonder he ran away. And now, where *was* Matt?

Katie had to see him—one more time.

IT TOOK another twenty minutes for the creaky island cab to bump its way from the cemetery to the old boathouse that she immediately recognised as Suzanne's.

It was painted white now. The barnlike doors and the trim were grey. There was a flower garden perched right on the sea.

She could see why Suzanne had loved it so much. Katie did, too. It was a real home.

She slowly got out of the cab. She paid the driver, and he sped off. Her heart was stuck in her throat as she walked up the gravel path to the house. She glanced over the property. She saw no sign of Matt. No car. Maybe it was at the back.

She knocked on the front door, waited, fidgeted, then used the old wooden knocker.

No one answered.

God, it was so weird to be here.

Her heart just wouldn't stop pounding.

She didn't see a sign of anyone, but she was determined to wait for Matt. It was her turn to talk. She had secrets to share.

So she waited and waited. Then Katie sat on the front lawn for a while, massaging her stomach, listening to the waves. Eventually, she crossed Beach Road . . . where Gus had been struck by a truck.

She sat on the beach where Matt and Suzanne had danced. She could *see* them. And then she imagined dancing with Matt again. She had loved being in his strong arms. She didn't like admitting it now, but it was the truth. It would always be the truth.

She thought that she probably had most of the mystery solved: Matt couldn't stop grieving. He probably didn't think that he ever could. Maybe he couldn't bear the thought of losing someone again.

She couldn't blame him. Not since she'd read the diary. If anything, she loved Matt more now than she ever had.

Katie picked her head up and saw a small, dark-haired woman walking towards her across Beach Road. When the woman was close, Katie said, 'You're Melanie Bone, aren't you?'

Melanie had the friendliest smile, just what she would have imagined. 'And you're Katie, Matthew's editor from New York. He told me about you. He said you were willowy and pretty, and that you usually wore your hair in a braid.'

'Do you know where he is?' Katie asked.

Melanie shook her head. 'I'm sorry, Katie. I don't know where Matt is. We're all worried about him, actually. I was hoping that he was with you in New York.'

'He's not,' Katie said. 'I haven't seen him, either.'

Late in the afternoon Melanie gave Katie a ride back to the ferry terminal in Oak Bluffs. The kids rode in the back of the station wagon. They were just about as good-natured as their mother.

'Don't give up on him,' Melanie said as Katie was about to board the ferry. 'He's worth it. Matt's had the worst experience of anyone I know. But I think he'll recover. He's a really good person. And Katie, I know he loves you.'

Katie nodded, and she waved goodbye to the Bone family. Then she left Martha's Vineyard the way she had come, alone.

ANOTHER LONG, BAD WEEK passed for her. Katie fell deeper into her work, but she thought a lot about going home to North Carolina. She would have the baby there, among the people she loved and who loved her.

Katie hadn't been in the office very long that Monday morning when she heard her name being called. She had just transferred her tea from its paper cup to the antique china one she kept on her desk.

'Katie? Come over here right now. Katie! Now.'

She was slightly annoyed. 'What? *What?* I'm coming.'

Her assistant, Mary Jordan, was poised beside a floor-to-ceiling window that looked down on East 53rd Street. She motioned for Katie to come to the window. 'Come here!'

Curious, she walked to the window and looked down. She spilt hot tea on herself, nearly dropping her antique cup. Mary deftly snatched it from her.

Katie then walked past Mary, down a short hallway to the single elevator. Her knees were weak, her head spinning. She was self-consciously brushing strands of hair away from her face. She didn't know what to do with her hands.

She passed the publisher, who was getting out of the elevator. 'Katie, I need to talk—' he started to say, but she cut him off with a raised hand. 'I'll be right back, Larry,' she said, the rushed into the elevator. The publishing-house offices were on the top floor.

Time to compose yourself, she thought.

No, not enough time. Not even close. The elevator descended to the first floor without making any stops.

Katie stood in the lobby and forced herself to be very still inside. Her thoughts were amazingly concise. Suddenly, everything seemed so clear and simple.

She thought about Suzanne, about Nicholas, and about Matt.

She thought about the lesson of the five balls.

Then Katie walked outside the building and onto the streets of New York. She took a deep breath as the warmth of the sunshine struck her face. *Dear God, make me strong enough for whatever is going to happen now.*

She saw Matthew on 53rd Street.

HE WAS KNEELING on the sidewalk, less than a dozen feet away from where Katie stood. His head was bowed slightly.

She couldn't take her eyes off him.

He looked good: tan, trim, his hair a little longer than usual; jeans, a clean but frayed chambray shirt, dusty work boots. He looked like the Matt she knew, the Matt she had loved, and still did.

Kneeling in front of her building. Right there in front of her.

Just as Suzanne had knelt that one night on their porch—to ask forgiveness.

Katie knew what she had to do. She followed her instincts on this, followed her heart.

She took a breath, then she got down on one knee beside Matt, facing him, as close as she could get. Her heart was thumping.

Pedestrians were starting to clog up the sidewalk. A few of them made unkind remarks, complaining about the loss of a few precious seconds on their journeys to work.

Matt reached out his hand. Katie hesitated, but then she let him take her long, thin hands in his.

She had missed his touch. She had missed a lot about him, but especially the way she felt at peace when he was with her.

Strangely, she was starting to feel calm now. What did that mean? What was supposed to happen next?

Finally, Matt raised his head and looked at her. She had missed those soft brown eyes. She'd missed his strong cheekbones, the furrowed brow, his perfect lips.

Matt spoke, and, God, she had missed the sound of his voice. 'I love looking into your eyes, Katie, the honesty I see there. I love being with you. I never tire of it. Not for one minute since I've known you. You are a great editor. You're a great carpenter, too. You are tall, but you are ravishing.'

Katie found that she was smiling. She couldn't help it. Here they were, the two of them, on their knees in midtown.

'Hello, stranger,' she said. 'I went looking for you, Matt. I travelled to the Vineyard. I finally got up there.'

Matt smiled now. 'So I heard. From Melanie. She thought you were ravishing, too.'

'What else?' Katie asked. She needed to learn more, anything that he would tell her.

'What else? Well, the reason I'm here, on my knees, I want to give myself over to you, Katie. I'm sure of it. I'm finally ready. I'm yours, if you'll have me. I want to be with you. I love you. I'll never leave you again. I promise, Katie. I promise with all my heart.'

And then, they finally kissed.

THAT OCTOBER on the gorgeous Outer Banks of North Carolina, Katie Wilkinson and Matt Harrison were married at the Kitty Hawk Chapel.

The Wilkinson and Harrison families hit it off right from the start. Katie's friends from New York came down, spent a few extra days at the beach, and got lobster pink, of course.

Only a few of the wedding guests knew that she was going to have a baby. When she had told Matt, he kissed her and said he was the happiest, luckiest person in the world.

'Me, too,' said Katie. 'Actually, me three.'

It was a simple but beautiful wedding and reception, held under cloudless blue skies with temperatures hovering in the low seventies. Katie looked like an angel. Tall. Ravishing. The wedding was completely unpretentious from beginning to end. The tables were decorated with family photographs. The bridesmaids carried pale pink hydrangeas.

While they were exchanging vows, Katie couldn't help thinking to herself, *Family, health, friends, integrity*—the precious glass balls.

She understood it now.

And that was how she would live the rest of her life, with Matt and their beautiful baby.

Isn't it lucky?

JAMES PATTERSON

Suzanne's Diary for Nicholas is a completely new departure for American author James Patterson, whose phenomenal worldwide fame has been achieved with a string of hard-hitting and suspenseful best sellers. Six of his books, including *Kiss the Girls*, which was made into a film in 1997, and *Along Came a Spider*, which is due for box-office release in Spring 2001, feature his hugely popular black homicide detective, Alex Cross.

This year, as well as a new Alex Cross thriller, *Roses are Red*, Patterson has produced two stories written from a female perspective. One is *Suzanne's Diary for Nicholas*, a moving love story that was partly inspired by a diary Patterson's wife is actually compiling for their young son; the other, *First to Die*, is the first in a new mystery series that will star four women—a homicide inspector, a medical examiner, an assistant DA and a reporter—who club together out of office hours to solve crimes in their own unique way. Patterson has said in interviews that because he grew up in a houseful of women—mother, grandmother and three sisters—he finds it easy to write from a woman's point of view. Indeed, he finds women 'more complex, thoughtful and emotionally open' than men.

Patterson joined J. Walter Thompson, the world's biggest advertising agency, in 1971 and rose through the ranks to become its youngest-ever chief executive officer, making his mark creating innovative campaigns for companies like Kodak, Burger King and Toys 'R Us. Now, in his mid fifties and recently married, this phenomenally successful author lives in Palm Beach, Florida, with his photographer wife and their three-year-old son.

THE ICE CHILD. Original full-length version © 2001 by Elizabeth McGregor. US condensed version © The Reader's Digest Association, Inc., 2001. British condensed version © The Reader's Digest Association Limited, 2001.

THE BLUE NOWHERE. Original full-length version © 2001 by Jeffery Deaver. US condensed version © The Reader's Digest Association, Inc., 2001. British condensed version © The Reader's Digest Association Limited, 2001.

WARLOCK. Original full-length version © 2001 by Wilbur Smith. British condensed version © The Reader's Digest Association Limited, 2001.

SUZANNE'S DIARY FOR NICHOLAS. Original full-length version © 2001 by James Patterson. US condensed version © The Reader's Digest Association, Inc., 2001. British condensed version © The Reader's Digest Association Limited, 2001.

The right to be identified as authors has been asserted by the following in accordance with sections 77 and 78 of the Copyright, Designs and Patents Act, 1988: Elizabeth McGregor, Jeffery Deaver, Wilbur Smith and James Patterson.

ACKNOWLEDGMENTS AND PICTURE CREDITS: *The Ice Child:* pages 6–8: polar bear and cub: Bruce Coleman Collection/Johnny Johnson; photomontage by Shark Attack. Page 149: © Jerry Bauer. *The Blue Nowhere:* pages 150–152: man at computer: Photodisc; photomontage by Shark Attack. Page 295 © Jerry Bauer. *Warlock:* pages 296–298: © Mark Preston; page 461 © Julian Calder. *Suzanne's Diary for Nicholas:* pages 462–464: girl: Images Colour Library; inkwell and sea scene: Photodisc; photomontage by DW Design Partnership; page 539: © Sue Solie Patterson. Volume design consultant: Shark Attack.

DUSTJACKET CREDITS: Spine from top: Bruce Coleman Collection/Johnny Johnson; photomontage by Shark Attack. Photodisk; photomontage by Shark Attack. © Mark Preston. Images Colour Library; photomontage by DW Design Partnership. Back cover: Wilbur Smith © Julian Calder.

Printed by Maury Imprimeur SA, Malesherbes, France
Bound by Reliures Brun SA, Malesherbes, France